FROM EVIL

DEVASTATE · TAKE · MANIPULATE

PAM GODWIN

NEW YORK TIMES BESTSELLING AUTHOR

DEVASTATE
PAM GODWIN

Book 4

Four years ago...

Tate Vades reclined in a shadowed booth, glaring at a high-top table of women across the grimy tavern. They'd been stealing glances at him all night, winking and licking their lips and abrading his nerves.

There had been a time when he would've invited them over with a crook of a finger. But his hands didn't twitch. Neither did his cock.

He hardened for only one woman. A fierce woman with eyes of molten brown and fire in her soul.

What a cruel thing love was, silent and desolate in its torture. How ironic that loving someone was the thing that hurt the most.

He knew how to suppress the physical, psychological, and emotional repercussions of violence. How to tune out the echoes of his weakened screams. The unholy pain of his bludgeoned flesh. The sharp, bitter scent of blood.

He was a survivor of captivity and sexual torture, and despite it all, he still considered himself a proud, dominant man. But when it came to love, he was a victim, powerless and unbearably alone in its apathetic clutches.

Two years ago, Camila Dias rescued him from his ruthless captors. She'd appeared out of nowhere, stunningly beautiful with guns blazing as she murdered the man who had paid Van Quiso a million dollars for Tate's body. A man who meant to own Tate and use him in depraved ways.

But Camila saved him from that fate. She freed him. Then she stole his heart.

"Can I get you another beer?" A server stopped at the table, his tattooed fingers deftly collecting the empty bottles in front of Tate.

"No, thanks." He lit a cigarette but didn't inhale.

He wasn't a smoker. Not anymore. He just needed to keep his hands busy while he came to terms with what he planned to do.

His long-suffering patience with Camila had finally reached its end.

He'd helped her bring down Van Quiso's sex trafficking operation in Texas. Her small vigilante group—the Freedom Fighters—was her therapy, her way of consoling the wounds she'd collected during her own captivity in Van's shackles.

She, Tate, and five others—Ricky, Tomas, Luke, Martin, and Kate—lived together, fought together, and slowly recovered from their shared experiences as Van's slaves-in-training. After they escaped, Tate bided his time, giving Camila space to heal, to focus on her revenge, and to open her heart.

Two years later, she still didn't belong to him.

Of all her roommates, he was her closest friend. When they were alone, she spoke of her darkest desires and forbidden fantasies, her seductive voice leaving him endlessly hard and desperate. But he hadn't fucked her, hadn't so much as kissed her.

He thought he was being chivalrous, providing her a safe place to put her trust and with time, her love.

He was a fool.

She didn't want chivalry or patience or love. At least, not with him. She was holding herself back for something. Or, if his intuition was correct, *someone*.

But who? *Who* did Camila dream about when she slept alone every night?

He snuffed out the cigarette and tossed a wad of cash on the table. He was done waiting. Done being friend-zoned. It was time to introduce her to the real Tate Vades. The man who would compel her to her knees with a look, grip her by her stubborn throat, and demand her secrets, her submission, and her love.

Rising to his feet, he turned and collided with a rock-hard body. "Excuse me—"

"Have a drink with me." Hazel eyes and dark hair, the ridiculously attractive stranger gestured at the booth, his accent hinting at south of the border. "I insist, Mr. Vades."

He knows my name? What the fuck?

"Who are you?" Tate held the stranger's intense stare with one of his own.

"We'll get to that. First..." The man waved over the server. "A glass of *aguardiente*. Neat. And another beer for my friend."

2

DEVASTATE

Camila drank *aguardiente*. Always neat. She said it was the way Colombians preferred their soft vodka.

This man, with his accent, Colombian features, and choice of drink… He was connected to her somehow. Tate was certain of it.

"I'm sorry." The server scraped a hand through his hair. "You said ah…gwar…dee…?"

"They don't serve *aguardiente* here." Tate slid back into the booth, eyes on the mysterious man. "You're a long way from Colombia, *ese*."

"It's Matias." He held out a large hand in greeting.

Never heard of him. Tate stared at the outstretched fingers in silent rejection.

With a sigh, Matias lowered his arm, ordered vodka, and sent the server away.

"You've been taking care of someone extremely important to me." He sat across from Tate and rested a muscled, tattooed forearm on the table. "Someone who belongs to me. For that, you have my deepest gratitude."

Camila belonged to no one. She never talked about her Colombian roots or her cartel connections, never mentioned any names from her past. Except her dead sister. She spoke of Lucia with a longing that trembled her pretty lips.

Tate blanked his expression. He didn't know this man, didn't trust the purpose of this visit.

"You have feelings for her. This, I know." Matias hardened his clean-shaved jaw, his accent thickening. "Have you fucked her?"

Tate had been on his way to do just that. Of all the nights for his relationship with Camila to be questioned, why tonight? Why now? He narrowed his eyes into slits of suspicion.

"Answer me," Matias said, his voice as black as his scowl.

"I fuck a lot of women."

A lie. Tate hadn't had sex since…

His nude body in shackles.

Van's grunts. Musky sweat. Dry thrusts.

Stretching, ripping, violating his dark opening.

Blinding pain.

Shame. A lifetime of maddening shame.

"That's a *no* then." Matias visibly relaxed, briefly closing his eyes before whispering, "We both know that if you were fucking Camila Dias, there would be no other lovers."

A protective jolt of anger spiked through Tate's veins. "How do you know her?"

"We grew up together."

"That's funny." Tate balled his hands on his lap. "She's never

3

mentioned you."

"I don't suppose she would." Regret clouded Matias' eyes. "I'm the one she calls to deal with the bodies."

Stunned by his candor, Tate flicked his attention around the quiet bar. It was late, nearing closing time, and most of the patrons had shuffled home. The small table of women remained, their glasses empty and eyes still drifting in his direction. They were out of hearing range.

Near the exit, two men occupied a booth, sipping... Water? Vodka? He hadn't noticed them before.

Black hair, dark complexions, and powerful physiques, they looked like they could be related to Matias. The way they subtly watched every movement in the bar left zero doubt they came here with him. Armed guards, most likely. Camila's cartel connections.

Tate removed the phone from his pocket. He didn't want to alarm her or involve her in whatever this was, but he needed confirmation—

"Set the phone on the table." Matias flashed his teeth, his grin devoid of amusement.

It wasn't the words that lowered Tate's gaze. It was the long blade of a knife pressing against his inner thigh, sharp enough to slash denim, skin, and muscle, with the pointy end a hairbreadth from his balls.

His pulse hammered. Would the bastard neuter him? Right here in the bar? The glint in those cold eyes said, *Yes.*

The server approached, dropping off the beer and vodka, oblivious to the tension coiling beneath the table. "Can I get you anything else?"

"We good?" Matias arched an inky brow at Tate.

"We're good." Tate placed the phone on the table.

When the server left, the knife retreated.

"Hear me out," Matias said, "and I won't kill you."

"Comforting."

"Two months ago, she called me to collect a body."

Van Quiso's body. Tate gritted his teeth through a torrent of conflicting emotions. Van was a sadist, a rapist, the very monster that inhabited Lucifer himself. But something had changed in him around the time he was shot and left to die. He'd withdrawn from sex trafficking, avenged the wrongdoings against his first slave, Liv Reed, and left her the money he'd earned through his vile operation.

Six million to be exact, which she split between Van's nine slaves. Tate received $666,666. A fitting number from the devil incarnate.

"As you know," Matias said, flaring his nostrils, "Van Quiso didn't die from that gunshot wound. I arrived to find him driving away from the house where he imprisoned and tortured my girl."

My girl. Tate's stomach hardened, every muscle in his body coiling

4

with denial.

"She's mine, Tate." Matias flexed his hand on the table. "I know he enslaved you in that house, as well. By my count, nine captives total over the past six years."

"And each of those captives had buyers," Tate said. "All of which are dead and the bodies never to be found, thanks to you." That was as much gratitude as he was willing to give the man.

"Van Quiso should be among them. I wanted to gut the sick fuck when I saw him drive away." Matias sipped from his glass. "But he was my only lead to discovering Camila's whereabouts. She trusts me to dispose of the dead, but she doesn't trust me with her location. So I followed Van. He led me to Liv Reed, who unwittingly took me right to Camila."

Camila doesn't know she's been found. She'd been so careful about remaining hidden, evading the law and keeping her cartel connections at a distance.

"I've been watching her for a couple of months. Learning her habits, where she goes, what she does, who her closest friends are." Matias met his eyes.

If that were true, he would know how committed Camila was in her pursuit to abolish human sex trafficking. She was so passionate about it she didn't consider the danger she put herself in. But Tate did. Constantly. He adored her tenacity, marveled at her fearlessness, but keeping her alive and out of prison was an endless worry.

"You grew up with her." Tate cocked his head. "You know where she lives. Yet you haven't approached her."

"Puzzling, isn't it? I'm the kind of man who takes what he wants. As much as I want to *take* her—restrained and at my mercy—I won't. She suffered enough in the hands of that despicable slave trader." Matias spat the words, his accent seething with venom. "I will not take what isn't given. When she comes to me, it will be of her own volition."

Yet he'd stalked her, invaded her privacy for months. Tate opened his mouth to argue the hypocrisy, but Matias raised a silencing hand.

"All bets are off when her safety's in question." Matias heaved a frustrated breath. "Now that Van's operation is dismantled, she intends to take down another slave ring in Austin."

Tate knew every detail of her plan and would protect her at all costs. "If you stop her, she'll never forgive you."

Against his expectations, Matias closed his eyes and said, "I won't stop her."

Then why is he here?

The thugs in the booth near the door surveyed the surroundings, not once making direct eye contact with Tate. Their dark jeans and bulky sweatshirts only partially obscured the sidearms they were clearly packing.

"What do you want?" Tate leaned back in the vinyl seat, watching with fascination as Matias struggled through whatever was darkening his expression.

After a long moment of silence, he spoke in a voice almost too low for Tate's ears. "I'm the capo of the Restrepo cartel. She doesn't know this. They" — he nodded at his companions near the exit — "don't know this. My enemies would bribe, torture, and butcher for that information."

"Why the fuck are you telling *me*?" Tate angrily whispered, jerking forward with forearms braced on the table. "You don't even know me."

"I know you love her." Matias raised the glass of vodka to his mouth, his gaze sharp. "I know you'd lay down your life to protect her. That works in my favor as long as you understand she's not yours."

"She's not yours, either."

"She will be, and you're going to help me."

Two hours later, Tate closed the front door of the five-bedroom house he shared with Camila and the others. He rubbed his eyes, his head pounding with the weight of Matias' crazy goddamn plan. A plan that would bolster Camila's pursuit while keeping her safe.

If Tate weren't so viciously jealous, he might've admired Matias' selfless devotion to her.

His heavy boots carried him into the kitchen — the only room still illuminated at three in the morning.

"Where've you been?" Camila looked up from a spread of maps and news articles on the kitchen table.

"The bar."

She leaned back in the chair, her seductive eyes stroking him from head to toe before returning to his face. "With a woman?"

It was an opening. An opportunity to tell her he hadn't been with anyone since she freed him from captivity. Because he loved her with a madness that choked his senses.

But the fact that she'd asked about another woman without a hint of jealousy or anger spoke volumes.

She doesn't care who I fuck.

Because I'm not the one she wants.

He stepped to the sink, filled a glass from the tap, and guzzled it. When the cool water failed to extinguish the fire in his chest, he refilled the glass and drank again.

"What's wrong?" The chair scuffed behind him, followed by the tread of her socked feet. "Tate?"

"Have you ever been in love?" He gripped the edge of the sink, keeping his back to her.

"What kind of question — ?"

"Yes or no." Turning, he sank into her dark gaze.

"Yes." Her throat bobbed.

"And now? Do you still love him?"

"Where is this coming from?"

"Do you still love him, Camila?"

"Doesn't matter." She looked away, shoulders hitching. "He no longer exists."

She denied him a view of her eyes, but the pain seeping into her posture confirmed what he already knew.

Her heart belonged to Matias.

Acknowledging it, however, didn't change his feelings for her. Love was love. It didn't just go away when it wasn't reciprocated. It endured, persisted, and waited like a pathetic, unwanted pussy.

He could tell her everything — Matias' surveillance of her, his plan to decimate the Austin slave ring, his desire to eventually lure her to Colombia where she could help him fight against the worst slavery in the world, and the biggest shocker of it all, his refusal to reunite with her until the unrest in his cartel was controlled.

Matias calculated every detail because he didn't want to endanger her.

Because he loved her.

Tate could tell her all of this. Declare his own love. Make her choose. But it would benefit no one. She would run headlong toward Matias, straight into the kind of danger Tate wouldn't be able to protect her from.

"I'm going to bed." He cupped the back of her head and pulled her into a hug, relishing the warm softness of her petite body.

The kitchen window felt like a spotlight on his back. Was Matias watching from the street? Were there cameras in the house? During the meeting at the bar, the cartel boss had described — in vivid, gory detail — all the ways he would remove limbs and organs if Tate touched Camila in a sexual way.

Tate didn't scare easily, but a man in love wasn't a force to be taken lightly. Especially when that man was the king of a cartel.

"Why don't you call it a night?" He released her and stepped back.

"I will…soon." She stared longingly at the scatter of papers on the table.

With an aching hunger, he left her with her outlined maps of revenge and climbed the stairs to his room.

He hadn't agreed to help Matias with his insane plan to win Camila, but they'd exchanged phone numbers before parting ways.

A month later, curiosity led him to Colombia at Matias' request.

He wanted to learn more about the dangerous capo and the anti-slavery raids he supposedly operated. It was on one of these raids, in a dilapidated barn, where Tate saw the horrifying goodness in Matias Restrepo.

He watched from the safety of a barn window as children—naked, beaten, and bloody—were auctioned off, one by one, for the wretched pleasures of men. Then he watched Matias save them all, leaving a bloodbath of wrath in his wake.

It was on that night that he knew he would do anything for the man who held Camila's heart.

After spending weeks with Matias in the slums of South America raiding slave operations, he gained a friend and lost all hope of requited love from Camila.

He might've been her closest friend, but Matias... He was the counterpart to her passion, the mate to her vengeful soul. They shared a spirit Tate couldn't begin to understand.

So he consented to Matias' plan. He would watch over her, protect her, and call Matias every day with every detail of her life.

But he wouldn't, *couldn't* stop loving her.

"You need to return to her." Matias eyed him from across the table at his Colombian estate. "Her safety is my number one priority."

"I'll head home tomorrow," Tate said, distracted.

He scanned the floor of Matias' veranda, every inch of it covered with piles of papers, maps, and photos of warehouses and slave traders.

When he left Camila in Texas three weeks ago, he told her he was going on a soul-searching journey across the States. Now he found himself in the luxury of Matias' home, poring over an unsolved mystery.

"There's nothing there." Matias rose from the table and stepped toward the interior door. "I searched for Camila's sister for two years. She's dead, Tate."

"She's *missing*."

"For *six* years."

"You don't know she's dead." Tate stared at a photo of Lucia Dias, hypnotized by the huge brown eyes of a girl who looked so much like her sister.

"I know she was inside a transport of trafficked slaves that crashed in Peru. No one survived. That's where the investigation ends."

"You gave up."

"I prioritized." Matias gripped the door jamb and straightened his spine. "My priority is—"

"Camila." Tate swiped a hand down his face. "Mine, too. But there's no harm in digging further, to see if there's something you missed."

"Camila can't know. If you get her hopes up, I'll cut your—"

"Yeah, yeah, I know. I won't tell her." Tate lifted a photo of Lucia and Camila embracing each other in an orange grove.

In their teens, their likeness was uncanny—long black hair, delicate bones, stubborn chins. Yet there were notable differences. Lucia was two years older, her features sharper with maturity, her smile more relaxed, carefree. She was even more beautiful than her sister, if that were possible.

"I'll make copies of the documents." Matias blew out a breath. "I can digitalize everything and send it to you."

Tate nodded, his gaze glued to the image of the lost girl.

He might not hold Camila's heart, but could find her sister—dead or alive. He could bring her closure. It would give him purpose, a distraction from the persistent ache inside him. He desperately wanted to do this for her.

Because he loved her.

ONE

Present day…

The electronic beats of Ke$ha's "Take It Off" followed Tate through the dimly lit halls of The Velvet Den. The worn wallpaper, creaking wood floors, and faint scent of perfume evoked a tantalizing nostalgia for his old stomping grounds. But beneath the swell of sentimentality lay a prickle of unease. Not all his memories of this place were pleasurable.

Stepping out of the final corridor, he lingered at the entrance of the main room. Settees and lounge chairs surrounded an empty stage. The rich textures and dark decor was designed to make club members feel relaxed and safe, and the exceptional service catered to their upscale tastes. Then, of course, there were the girls. Scantily dressed and easy on the eyes, they served drinks and sex with alluring smiles.

Nestled in a suburban border town in southern Texas, the invite-only establishment was older than his twenty-five years. It hadn't always been a swinger's club, but as laws cracked down on prostitution, The Velvet Den evolved. Money still exchanged hands after a sweaty fuckfest in a private room, but no one spoke of those transactions. A narc would lose more than his membership.

The club owner didn't just enforce the rules, authorize the contracts, and hire the well-vetted staff. She set the mood, simply through the elegance and grace of her presence.

As he scanned the room for her long blond hair and voluptuous body, her husky voice caressed his back.

"Your guest has arrived, darling."

"Lela," he breathed, turning to meet the sharp green eyes of his oldest friend. "It's good to see you."

"Is it?" Her plump, red-painted lips pouted her disapproval. "You never visit. I'm under the impression you don't miss me at all."

"You know that's not true." He wrapped his arms around her and smoothed a hand down the corset's lacing along her spine. "I've missed you more than you know."

Hard to believe she was in her forties. She didn't look a day older than thirty. He could still picture her towering over him and pommeling his ass for the mischief he'd stirred up as a boy.

She framed his face and caressed her lips against his. The lingering kiss, the exotic aroma of her shampoo, and the press of her fingers against his jaw—all of it filled him with warm memories.

The Velvet Den was his home, and while Madame Lela Pearl wasn't his mother, she was the closest thing he ever had to one.

"Thank you for letting me hold my meeting here." He glanced over his shoulder, searching the crowd. "Where's my guest?"

"I set him up in the Cognac Room." She trailed a blood-red fingernail down the placket of buttons on his shirt. "Unless you prefer a room with more *privacy*."

"It's not that kind of meeting."

"No?" Disappointment creased her pretty features. "I hoped you returned to work for me again."

"Lela—"

"You're even more handsome than you were as a boy. Stronger. More virile." She petted his bicep. "The ladies would empty their purses to experience your dominant nature."

His stomach buckled. The clientele tended to be older, with marriage, careers, and kids behind them. Too old for the downtown club scene, they came here with unique proclivities, looking to quench darker appetites.

It didn't matter. Young or old, male or female, locals or out-of-towners, no one would be paying him for sex. Never again.

"I don't need money." He caught her arm and gently set her away. "There's more to life than getting off."

Her eyes bugged. "Shut your mouth. I raised you better than that." She propped her fists on the flare of her hips. "Have you forgotten what it feels like to fuck without commitment or strings—?" She snapped her teeth together, eyes growing wider. "Oh shit. Are you in love?"

That was only part of it. She didn't know what happened to him when he disappeared from The Velvet Den's parking lot six years ago. He was nineteen when Van Quiso took him at gunpoint and raped him for ten weeks in a soundproof attic.

She assumed he ran away, and he let her hold onto that belief. The truth would wreck her.

"Yes, there is someone." He averted his gaze, unable to hide the resentment in his expression.

"But?"

"She's engaged."

"So? Win her away from her fiancé."

"They belong together, and I love her enough to let her have that. To let her go."

It'd been four years since Matias approached him in that Austin bar. Four of the most miserable years of his life. After going along with Matias' plan, watching Camila reunite with him, and losing her completely when she moved to Colombia, Tate no longer wanted to stay in the Austin house he'd shared with her.

Visiting her a few times in Colombia hadn't helped his miserable jealousy.

So he came here.

Home.

But it wasn't the same.

No, *he* wasn't the same.

"My guest is waiting." He kissed the top of Lela's head. "I'll stay a few days, maybe longer, okay? We'll catch up."

"Very well." She fussed with the collar of his shirt. "I'll have a room prepared for you. Stay as long as you want."

"Thank you."

He turned back down the hall, slipped into a stairwell, and exited one floor below. The same dark furnishings adorned the Cognac Room, but the pungent aroma of cigars deterred non-smokers from using this space.

A bald man reclined on a couch, his trousers unzipped beneath the bobbing head of a young woman. Nearby, several other couples engaged in various forms of fornication and sexual orientation. Across the room, a topless dancer writhed on a pole, grinding to the low volume of club music.

An attractive man sat alone at a table a few feet from her. He was the only man in the room who could've been Cole Hartman. Tate's guest.

Black leather jacket, short brown hair, early thirties, he watched the dancer with a strange expression. It wasn't curiosity. Definitely not desire. His furrowed brow and pinned lips hinted at displeasure.

Maybe it was shock. Especially if he'd never been in a place like this. And fair enough. Swingers were a peculiar breed. They paid outrageous fees for the convenience of ogling, sampling, or boning other people's partners. There weren't a lot of life experiences that prepared a person for a room full of naked, oversexed strangers.

DEVASTATE

Tate had deliberately withheld the nature of The Velvet Den when he suggested it as a location to meet. He wanted to hire Cole to help him find Camila's sister. But if the big, leather-clad guy couldn't handle an open display of sex, he wasn't up for the task.

Since Cole didn't appear to notice anyone but the dancer, Tate remained in the doorway, studying him, searching for anything that might've raised a red flag.

After four years and five private investigators, Tate had made zero progress on locating Lucia Dias. So he did the one thing he thought he'd never do.

He asked Van Quiso for help.

Liv and Camila had both been enslaved by Van, yet they'd found something redeemable in him. Something they trusted.

Van had connections with unsavory people—slavers, drug and weapon dealers, assassins, and bounty hunters. People with specialized skills in shady situations.

People like Cole Hartman.

Tate didn't know how Van was connected to Cole or if that was even his real name. All he had was Van's unwavering conviction: *If Cole Hartman can't locate Camila's sister, no one can.*

On the far side of the room, Cole shrugged off his jacket, tossed it in a nearby chair, and crooked a finger at Tate without removing his eyes from the dancer.

Evidently, he was more attuned to his surroundings than he let on. *Good.*

As Tate crossed the room, Cole lifted a beer from the table. Heavy ink tattooed his forearm, but the lighting was too low to make out the artwork.

He didn't move or meet his eyes until Tate reached the table.

"You're drinking Bud Light in the Cognac Room," Tate said in greeting.

"Am I breaking a rule?"

"No. But the cognac's free."

"So is the beer." Cole tipped the neck of the bottle in the direction of the dancer. "Tell her to leave."

"You have a problem with dancers?" Tate pointedly looked at Cole's tattoo.

From wrist to elbow was an inked silhouette of a woman swinging on a dance pole.

"I've seen better." Cole brought the beer to his lips for a hardy swallow. "Much better."

On the surface, Cole seemed relaxed. But with each rotation the dancer made on the pole, his jaw grew harder, the cords in his neck pulling tighter. For whatever reason, the dancing put him on edge, and it undoubtedly had something to do with the woman tattooed on his arm.

While Tate didn't know the dancer, all of Lela's employees knew him. His history at The Velvet Den gave him the authority to send her away, but how did Cole Hartman know that? Maybe he'd done his homework?

Approaching the dance pole, Tate touched the girl's shoulder, his voice low. "Take a break, sweetheart."

"Thank you, Mr. Vades." With a small smile, she sashayed toward the exit.

Christ, she had a great ass. Big and round, it jiggled in her thong, sending provocative messages to his cock.

With an inward groan, he returned to the table, lowered into a chair, and caught Cole's eyes. "How do you know Van Quiso?"

"Client confidentiality, pal. He's *your* friend. Why don't you ask him?"

Van wasn't his friend and had been annoyingly cryptic on the subject of Cole Hartman.

"I requested this meeting because I need you to find someone." Tate clasped his hands together on his lap. "A woman."

"How long has she been missing?"

The answer tried to stick in his throat, but he forced it out. "Eleven years."

Cole didn't grimace or flinch like the other investigators Tate had hired. He simply nodded and sipped the beer.

"Aren't you going to ask her name, age, last place she was seen, all the usual shit?"

"Nope." Cole leveled him with an incisive look. "We're going to discuss *you*, the reason you're looking for her, and the price you're willing to pay."

"Money isn't an issue."

"I'm not talking about money."

Tate rubbed his head, losing patience. "I don't understand your meaning."

"Why did you choose this place to meet?"

"If you were good at your job, you'd be able to tell me."

"All right." Cole leaned forward, keeping his voice soft. "Let's start with your childhood."

This should be interesting. Tate had never told anyone about his past, not even Camila. "Go on."

"Tate Anthony Vades. Son of a prostitute. Father unknown. After your mother died from a drug overdose, you became a ward of the state, all before your second birthday. But her friend, Lela Pearl, took you in, kept you hidden and out of the system." He took a swig of beer and lowered it without looking away. "You were raised by whores in a brothel, *this* brothel, until you were old enough to turn tricks and earn your keep."

Jesus. Tate didn't know whether to be pissed or freaked out that he'd dug up so many buried secrets. But Cole's ability to elicit a vulnerable reaction was a good thing. If he could arouse fear in people, taunt them with personal information and provoke them to talk, maybe he really could make headway on Lucia's case. Because somewhere, someone knew what happened to her.

"I'm impressed." Tate tilted his chin down, measuring his words. "So I was raised among whores and earned a living as one for a while. What of it? You going to turn me in?"

"Rumor is, generations of sheriffs, judges, and mayors have kept this place in operation in exchange for VIP treatment." He glanced around the room, watching topless women serve cigars and cognac. "To be honest, I'm waiting for the girls to break out in song, a la *The Best Little Whorehouse in Texas.*" A smirk stole across Cole's face. "I work outside of the law, Tate. Your secrets are safe with me."

"I appreciate that." He narrowed his eyes. "Not sure how any of this helps you find the woman I'm searching for."

"I'll find her, but it won't bring you any closer to the woman you want."

He stopped breathing, and his heart flew against his ribcage. He didn't care if Cole knew he lost his virginity to a man at age fourteen or that he'd sold his body to female clients for a few years. Hell, he didn't even care if Cole had gleaned what happened to him in Van's attic.

But Camila was off-limits. In her crusade against slavery, she committed the kind of felonies — kidnapping, torturing, and murdering criminals — that would earn her a death sentence if caught. He didn't want Cole near her, asking about her, or investigating her in any way.

"This was a mistake." Tate moved to stand.

"Camila Dias is safe." Cole gripped his wrist, holding him in the chair with a cutting glare.

"She's none of your concern." He yanked his arm away and sat back.

"True, but she's in your head, messing with your thoughts. Isolating you. That's why you're here. You came back to the beginning, to the one place that gave you a sense of belonging."

"What are you? A fucking psychologist?"

"No." Cole laughed, a hollow sound. "Nothing like that. I just know from experience that a broken heart is the worst kind of hell, a goddamn lonely path from which you can never recover."

He touched a thin chain that hung around his neck, lifting it from beneath the t-shirt and letting it drop in full view. A tiny silver ring dangled at the end. A woman's wedding band.

If he was married or engaged, he wasn't any longer. Not with her ring in his possession and no ring on his finger.

Tate removed a pack of smokes from his pocket, lit a cigarette, and inhaled deeply. "What happened to her?"

"I let her go." Sadness whispered through Cole's voice, but an admirable amount of fortitude sharpened his eyes.

"Let me guess. She's with someone else?" At Cole's nod, Tate repeated the same words he gave Lela upstairs. "They belong together?"

"Yeah."

The air around them agitated before settling into a quiet hush. Cole did a good job tucking away his feelings. But Tate knew how deep that well could go and how hot and relentless the turmoil could burn within it.

"We're in the same hell, then."

"I don't think we are." Cole rubbed his whiskered jaw. "I watched you check out that dancer. You'll have her on her back by the end of the night."

Her or one of the other girls who worked here. Tate wasn't picky, as long as she was restrained and trembling beneath him. "I'm a man, not a saint."

"I'm a man, but there isn't a woman out there who compares to the one I had."

Given the tattooed silhouette on his arm, his ex-fiancé…wife…whatever must've been a dancer. That explained his displeasure with the dancer earlier.

"What's your point?" Tate asked.

"If you truly loved her, you wouldn't be fucking every tight ass that crossed your path."

He wanted to deny the accusation, but after Matias walked into that bar with a claim on Camila, he'd reverted to some old vices, such as smoking cigarettes and fucking anything in a skirt.

But that was beside the point.

"You did your research." Tate tapped the cigarette in the ashtray. "Which means you knew my background and the reason I asked you here before you walked in the door."

Cole nodded. "You're looking for Lucia Dias, because you think you're in love with her sister."

He did love her, but the dickhead could believe whatever he wanted.

"What I haven't figured out…" Cole studied him for a moment. "What is the price you're willing to pay?"

Back to this again. "How about we start with your fee?"

"A hundred grand."

His pulse raced. "A hundred—?"

"She's been missing for eleven years. It'll take time, but I'll get you the location of her body—dead or alive. That's the *finder* fee. It doesn't include retrieval. If she lives and *wants* to be removed from her situation…" Cole folded his hands on the table and exhaled slowly. "You can't afford it."

"How much?"

"Depends on the level of risk, the location, and whether she's being held against her will. Extraction jobs can last months, man, and the expenses add up—surveillance technology, specialized weapons, informant bribes, recruitment of resources, hush money, travel costs… The bill would run higher than the six-hundred thousand sitting in your bank account."

Tate's stomach bottomed out, and it wasn't only from the outlandish price. Knowing Cole had hacked into his finances, the fucking pity etching his face—all of it made Tate want to slam a fist into the wall.

"Let's just…slow down." He took a drag on the cigarette and squashed it out. "We need to find her first. I doubt she's even alive."

"You believe that?"

Did he? With a deep inhale, he mentally probed his gut and found the hope he'd held onto for years. "I know she was abducted from her home. Her parents were tied in with cartel. Both were murdered after she disappeared. And justly so. They gave her up to spare their own lives."

When Matias had learned they'd sold their daughters—both Lucia *and Camila*—he'd killed them. Camila had eventually escaped Van Quiso, but Lucia's kidnapper died eleven years ago, taking her whereabouts to the grave.

"Her last known location," Tate said, "was in a sex trafficking transport in Peru. It crashed. No survivors, but her body was never identified. I traveled to the crash site myself a few months ago. Talked to the locals in the village. No one knows anything, or so they claim." He met Cole's eyes. "To answer your question, I believe she survived that crash and is being held somewhere against her will."

"What will you do when I confirm your suspicions? When I give you proof of her life? Since you can't afford my retrieval fee, will you ask Matias Restrepo for help? We both know he has the power and resources to assist."

Fucking hell. Since Cole was privy to Tate's relationship with Camila, it shouldn't have been a surprise that he knew about the man she lived with. While the cartel capo could fund his own operation to find and extract Lucia, he'd already looked for her. And failed. Because he'd given up.

Tate wouldn't be asking Matias for shit. He was doing this, in part, as a gift to Camila. He didn't want Matias involved.

"No?" Cole's gaze pressed against him, probing too close for comfort. "Okay, so what's your plan? Will you try to retrieve her on your own and get yourself killed in the process? Or maybe you'll ask your roommates to help you? Are you willing to risk their lives?"

What the hell was this guy's problem? Tate just needed to know if Lucia lived. If she did, he'd figure it out from there.

"I don't care what you do, man." Cole leaned back, drummed his fingers on the table. "But before you go down this rabbit hole, you need to really think hard on why you're doing it and the price you're willing to pay. Right now, you can assume she's dead and walk away. If you hire me, it'll be too late to turn back."

Cole was right. If he found her, if she was still alive, it didn't matter how dangerous the situation, Tate would do whatever it took to reunite her with her sister. He ached to see the relief on Camila's face. To know that he was the one who put it there. That he had given her something Matias couldn't.

That was the fucked-up part, wasn't it? His motivation was perverse, bordering on obsession, because dammit, he still wanted to win her heart. He wanted to be the one Camila belonged with.

So when Cole asked what price he was willing to pay, what he really wanted to know was how much Tate loved Camila. The answer was easy.

"I'll send you everything I have on Lucia Dias." Tate pushed away from the table. "Find her."

TWO

Five weeks later, Tate woke in an unfamiliar bed to the muffled chirp of his phone. Blinking away grogginess, he pushed a feminine arm off his chest and scanned the moonlit room for his pants. A trail of women's clothing led out the door and into the hall, where he spotted his shoes and shirt.

"Where's my — ?"

"Here." A naked woman sat up beside him and dragged his jeans from the floor, bringing the sound of his phone closer.

While searching the pockets, he slid off the bed and shuffled through the room. *1:13 AM* glowed from the clock on the nightstand amid a clutter of empty beer bottles and condom wrappers.

Fuck, he hadn't meant to fall asleep here — wherever *here* was.

The blonde he'd gone home with rolled to her stomach, her mascara-smudged eyes roaming his naked body. What was her name? Alicia? Allison? Did it matter?

Jesus, I'm an asshole.

His fingers bumped against the phone in the pocket, and he connected the call from an unknown number. "Hello?"

"It's Cole."

His pulse spiked. He hadn't heard from Cole Hartman since he wired the finder fee. After five weeks, he started to wonder if he'd been scammed.

"Hang on." He shoved on his jeans and slipped into the hall, shutting the door behind him. "Did you find her?"

"Yes. We'll talk in person when I get back to the States in about..." A pause. "Fifteen hours."

"Is she—?"

"I'll come to you."

"Is she alive?"

Dead air.

"Hello?" He glanced at the phone, and the call was disconnected. "Motherfucker!"

After spending a week at The Velvet Den, Tate had returned to Austin. Evidently, Cole didn't need to be told that. But Tate had a million questions, so he hit redial. When the call wouldn't connect, he tried the contact number he had for Cole.

No answer. No voicemail.

Frustration roiled through him as he grabbed the rest of his clothes and left the woman's apartment without a word.

Over the next twelve hours, he tried to sleep between attempts to contact Cole. If Lucia were dead, wouldn't Cole have just told him on the phone? They wouldn't need to meet in person. The same could be said if she were alive and happy and safe.

His insides twisted as he dug through the laundry on his bedroom floor, sniffing each shirt in his hunt for something clean to wear. If Cole was coming to him, he needed to get out of the house. Two of his roommates, Tomas and Martin, were home. He didn't want them volunteering for a dangerous retrieval operation. Their untrained vigilante group, the Freedom Fighters, wouldn't hesitate to help him. But this wasn't their fight.

An hour later, he pulled into Liv's driveway and parked beside Kate's car, knowing his timid little roommate would be there. When Camila moved to Colombia, Kate started spending more time with Liv. Not that he blamed her. She was the only girl living in a house with five overprotective men who monitored her every move.

As he knocked on the front door, he didn't have to worry about Liv or Kate risking their necks for his cause. Liv's husband would never allow it, and Kate... Well, she was still recovering from her time in Van's attic, which made her painfully guarded and cautious.

The door opened, and Josh's bulky frame filled the entrance.

Tate had been Liv and Van's sixth captive. Kate came next. Then Josh—the last one. The one Liv fell in love with. While Camila and the others had helped Liv free each slave, it was Josh who had been the nail in the slave operation's coffin. Somehow, he achieved the impossible and broke through Liv's cold mask.

"Hey, man." Josh's smile lit up his green eyes. "What are you doing here?"

"Is Liv around?"

"Yeah. Come in." Josh retreated, leading him through the house.

"She's back here with Kate. Everything okay?"

"I don't know yet. It's about Lucia Dias." As he passed the living room and kitchen, there were no signs of Liv's teenage daughter. "Where's Livana?"

"She's at a friend's house this weekend." A sheen of perspiration slicked Josh's nude back, his feet bare and hair mussed.

Christ, had he and Liv been fucking? With Kate here? Surely not. But they were into some kinky shit, and he was headed straight toward the master bedroom.

"Hey, uh..." Tate paused in the hallway, unwilling to be part of anything that involved Liv's whips. "If I'm interrupting something..."

"I wouldn't have been able to answer the door." With a wink, Josh disappeared into the bedroom.

Wouldn't have been able to because he would've been tied up. Literally.

Tate exhaled a sharp laugh. Of all the men Liv had captured and trained, Josh was the only true submissive.

Since Tate had spent ten weeks in her restraints, he was intimately familiar with her dominant nature. The whole Mistress thing was a total turnoff, but when she'd had him naked and chained to the wall, she found ways to arouse him, torturing his cock until he begged for release. Unlike Van, she never fucked him, but there had been times when she'd taken pity on him and relieved him with her hand.

He rubbed the back of his head and tried to clear the memories. Over the past six years, he and Liv had become good friends, and he rarely dwelled on those dark hours of his life. But he'd never been in her bedroom, and as he stepped into the room, his stomach cramped.

Josh knelt on the bed, messing with a chain that connected to the headboard. Liv stood behind him, directing the work. In the corner of the room, Kate was curled up in a chair, her gaze drifting to the doorway.

A toolbox sat open on the floor. A drill on the nightstand. A package of heavy-duty eyehooks on the bed. Hairline cracks splintered the frame of the headboard. If he looked closer, he'd find more hooks and bolts. Probably a hidden rig of chains. Maybe a ball gag and a cock ring. The usual.

That explained why Josh was shirtless and sweaty. He was fixing the bondage equipment he'd built into the frame, which clearly hadn't held his powerful physique.

"You're doing it wrong." Liv parked her hands on her hips. "Stop."

Goddamn, that commanding tone took Tate right back to the attic. His spine tingled with echoes of pain, the burning lashes of leather on his back, the skin-crawling feel of Van's touch, and the fucking rules. *Kneel.*

Eyes down. Bend. Suck.

The memories pissed him off, heating his face and clenching his fists.

Something moved in Tate's periphery, and a moment later, Kate's slender arms encircled his waist, her head tucking beneath his chin.

He pulled in a calming breath, ruffled her blond, baby-soft hair, and sent her back to the chair.

Liv smiled at him in greeting, and the scar that bisected her cheek pulled taut. The same scar that marred Van's face. The matching lacerations served as permanent reminders that Van and Liv had suffered as much as Tate and the others before they escaped.

"Josh said you were here about Lucia?" she asked.

As Josh packed up the tools, Tate updated them on his search. They all knew he was looking for Camila's sister. They just didn't know the extent in which he'd gone with the private investigators and Cole Hartman.

"Cole found her, but I don't know if she's dead or alive. He said he'd come to me..." Tate glanced at his watch. "Anytime now."

"He'll come here?" Josh sat on the edge of the bed and pulled Liv onto his lap.

"Is that okay? I can leave."

"Stay." Liv hooked an arm around Josh's shoulders. "If Van referred you to him, I trust him in my home."

At the mention of Van, the room fell quiet. They'd all been there during Van's reign of cruelty, but in the past few years, they'd watched him transform into something more human.

Still, there were things a person couldn't forget.

While Josh and Kate had been forced to participate in intimate acts with Van, their buyers had demanded virgins, saving them from the worst of Van's depravity. Tate and Liv hadn't been so lucky. Ricky, Tomas, and his other roommates had likely been raped by Van as well, but they didn't talk about it.

"Van seems hellbent on redeeming his transgressions," Josh said, breaking the silence.

"Transgressions?" The whisper came from the chair in the corner. Kate shifted to the edge of the seat, gripping the armrests, her voice soft. "He's a monster. There is no redemption for him."

"Kate." Liv's cold tone cut like a whip. "I was a monster, too."

"You saved us." She pulled her knees to her chest and angled her face away.

"In the end," Liv said, "he saved us in his own way. The money he gave—"

Tate shook his head at Liv. He knew Kate hadn't touched her

share of the six million. Despite his protests, she waited tables at a local diner in order to contribute to the household bills.

With a tug on Kate's hair, he guided her out of the chair and toward the living room. There, he continued the conversation with Liv and Josh, outlining his speculation on Camila's sister.

If Lucia had survived that crash, she would be thirty years old now. If she'd maintained a youthful appearance like Camila, she could still be valuable as a sex slave. She could still be alive.

Talking about it with his friends reignited the flame of hope he'd carried for so long. They didn't ask him why he was so gung-ho about finding her. Maybe they knew. Hell, Van's wife, Amber, had called him out for the way he looked at Camila. They all knew.

When a knock sounded on the door an hour later, he leapt to his feet, his heart hammering like a piston.

"I'll get it." Josh crossed the room and opened the door. "Can I help you?"

"Cole Hartman." A tall silhouette hovered on the dark porch. "Tate's expecting me."

Josh stepped to the side and let him in.

"Is she alive?" Tate asked the instant Cole entered.

"Yes."

Relief sang through his nerve endings and loosened his chest. Good fucking God, he didn't realize how badly he needed to hear that. "Is she safe?"

Dressed in black denim and a wrinkled t-shirt, Cole looked like he hadn't shaved or slept in days. As he slid a backpack off his shoulder, his expression was pensive. Solemn. "Take a seat."

Not good. Not fucking good at all. She'd been missing for eleven years. Was she enslaved all this time? Beaten? Raped?

He shut the door on those thoughts and gathered his composure to make introductions. "This is Liv and —"

"I know who they are." Cole gave the empty side of the couch a pointed look. "Sit down, Tate."

Dread held him in place until Kate gripped his hand and pulled him down beside her, holding tight to his fingers. Josh settled in the side chair with Liv on his lap.

"She's in Caracas." Cole sat on the other side of Tate, removed a laptop from his backpack, and woke the screen.

"Venezuela." Tate released a breath. "That isn't that far away."

Cole narrowed his eyes at him.

"What?" He straightened. "It could be worse, right? At least she's not chained in a dog kennel on the other side of the world." At Cole's silence, Tate set his jaw. "Tell me she's not in a dog kennel."

"She's not."

Returning to the laptop, Cole opened a photo of a dingy alley with overflowing dumpsters, laundry on clothes lines, and bars on the windows. Sagging balconies hung from the buildings, and graffiti covered the brick walls.

"I shot this from the second-floor apartment I rented." He pointed to a battered red door among a dozen others in the picture. "She lives in that one. Alone. In the largest slum in South America." He glanced at Tate. "In the most dangerous city on the planet."

"Why?" Tate had so many qualifiers for that question, he didn't know where to start.

Why was she alone? Why did she live there? Why didn't she come home? Why hadn't his other investigators been able to find her? Every cell in his body buzzed with urgency to go to her, to get her the fuck out of that hellhole.

"Why is it the most dangerous city?" Josh asked. "Drugs? Cartel?"

"It's the most weaponized city with the highest homicide rate. A gun for every two people, and a murder every twenty-one minutes. Street gangs and crime lords are in charge. There's political corruption and drug trafficking, but those aren't the only problems."

"It's the kidnap capital of the world," Tate said quietly, recalling a headline he'd read somewhere.

"That's right." Cole flipped to a new image—another view of the slum with a huge iron gate dominating one side of the road, surrounded by armed guards in street clothes. "This compound is the main hideout for Tiago Badell, the man Lucia works for."

"Works for?" His head pounded as every assumption he'd made about her over the years unraveled. *Armed guards. Iron gate. Main hideout.* "Who the fuck is Tiago Badell?"

"One of the wealthiest crime lords in Venezuela." Cole met his eyes. "His specialty is kidnapping."

THREE

A chill crept over Tate's scalp. Aside from Cole, every person in the room had endured their own personal hell at the hands of a kidnapper. As unease vibrated between his friends, he wanted to shelter them from it.

He turned to Liv. "I can take this conversation elsewhere."

"How does it work?" She asked Cole, ignoring Tate's concern. "Are they trafficking humans?"

"No. Badell leads a gang that targets tourists, missionaries, Venezuelan middle class, anyone who is too ignorant to avoid Kidnap Alley and not wealthy enough to travel in armored vehicles. He grabs people off the street and gives their families three days to cough up the ransom. If payment isn't received, the victim is murdered."

Lucia was part of this? It didn't make sense. How could she go from being abducted and sold into slavery to working for a man like Tiago Badell?

He was certain he wouldn't like the answer, but he asked anyway. "What does she do for him?"

"You won't believe me unless I show you." Cole clicked on a video file and hovered the mouse over the play button. After a moment of hesitation, he leaned around Tate to speak to Kate. "It's graphic."

Tate twisted at the waist to see her face. She'd watched Josh kill her buyer and had spent weeks, bloody and broken, beneath a whip. She didn't look it, but the girl was tough as hell.

She wrapped a tiny hand around Tate's bicep, shoulders squared. "I can handle it."

Cole pushed play.

On the screen, a naked man lay on his back on a concrete floor.

Eyes swollen, nose busted, and chest heaving, he jerked against the ropes that restrained him. He was skinny, pale, and *hard*, his engorged dick pointing heavenward, and he didn't look happy about it.

Whoever held the camera handed it off to someone else, changing the angle to show at least two other men in the windowless room. The footage stayed below the necks, capturing dust on black boots and blood stains on pants. Assault rifles hung across their torsos, their tattooed fingers resting on the trigger guards.

"Who are they?" Tate asked.

"Badell's men. And that" — Cole pointed at the screen as a woman walked into view — "is Lucia."

The camera lowered, keeping her head out of the frame. A tight miniskirt exposed the curves of her perfect figure, and a black bra bared her flat stomach. Her hair was either pulled up or cut short, putting all that satiny, bronze skin on display. Her shoulders, arms, chest...every inch of her was toned, smooth, flawless.

No, not flawless. He leaned closer to the image. "Is that — ?"

"A scar." Cole paused the video and zoomed in on her abdomen. "See how it zigzags like that?" He traced it on the screen, following the jagged white line from the bottom of her breastbone to her hip. "Blunt force trauma. It's pretty faded. Old."

"Eleven years old?" He inhaled sharply. "Is it from the crash in Peru?"

"Yes. She barely survived. Badell's men pulled her out, and his personal doctors saved her. I know there were multiple surgeries because I've heard Badell discuss it with her. But the details are unknown. It's strange, because his doctors keep meticulous medical records on every person they touch, yet there's no record of her."

Goosebumps blanketed Tate's arms. "Why did his men save her?"

"From what I've gathered, they happened to be in the area and pillaged the crash site for survivors. Easy targets for ransom. They found her and patched her up just enough to keep her alive, only to discover — "

"She has no living family." Tate's chest tightened. "No one to pay his ransom and compensate him for his trouble." His pulse sped up as everything clicked into place. "Instead of killing her, Badell made her work for him? Since he saved her life, does he think she owes him?"

"It's more complicated than that." Cole returned to the laptop. "Watch the video."

When he un-paused it, Lucia strolled across the screen and straddled the naked man's torso, facing his feet. The camera operator kept her face out of view, honing in on her hands as she wrapped them around the swollen erection.

A pained wailing sound came from the man, his body bucking

beneath her. "No, please. I'm married. I don't want this."

She preceded to stroke him. No hesitation. No apparent prodding or force by the others in the room. It was as if she was orchestrating it.

The video panned to a black painted wall, where words had been scratched with chalk.

200,000 bolivars
72 hours
No money, he dies

"Ransom," Tate breathed, his stomach filled with lead. "This is a kidnapping."

Cole nodded. "The video was sent to the victim's wife with a bank account linked to it."

Tate was about to ask why Lucia was molesting the poor guy, but the camera angle returned to her. She stood over the man now, a pistol in her hand, aimed at his legs.

"No! No!" His high-pitched shouting crackled the speaker. "We'll pay. Please—"

She squeezed the trigger, and his knee exploded in a splatter of red. The camera jostled, lowering the view to focus on the pooling blood and gruesome injury.

No faces. No voices. Just the man's yowling screams. Then the video cut off.

"Christ." Tate leaned back, sick to his stomach.

His friends didn't move, their faces pale as they stared at the black screen.

"His wife wasn't able to collect the money in time," Cole said. "His body was dumped in an alley a mile away from the compound."

"Did Lucia kill him?" Liv closed a hand around Josh's bouncing knee, stilling him.

"No. She doesn't do the kidnapping or the murdering. Her job is to inflict physical and emotional pain. Torture. Sometimes she rapes them. Sometimes she causes non-fatal injuries, like this." He gestured at the screen. "When the victim is female, Lucia operates the camera while one of the men puts on the grisly show."

"How did you get the footage?" Tate asked, his throat dry.

"I dropped a hack on her burner phone and—"

"Don't you have to have physical access to the device to do that?"

"Juice jacking." Cole's eyes lit up. "I tampered with her charging port, turned it into a data connection. When she charged her phone, I copied everything she had on it, including this video."

"Hang on." His neck went taut. "You were in her apartment? Why didn't you just take her?"

"Yes, I accessed her apartment." Cole scowled at him. "I didn't *just take her*, because I'm not in the business of kidnapping."

"It's not kidnapping if—"

"She's not being held against her will, Tate. She makes no attempt to flee, and there are plenty of opportunities. She knows the city, knows how to evade the gangs. In eleven years, she would've succeeded in an escape."

"Or died trying." He knew that denying the truth didn't make the facts go away, but maybe Cole had missed something. Something glaringly important. "The woman in the video… You're certain that's Lucia? There were dozens of women in that crash in Peru. What if you followed the wrong trail?"

Cole opened another photo on the laptop—a wide shot of a woman walking along an urban road in daylight. He maximized the view, bringing her face into beautiful clarity. Her hair hung like a shiny black curtain to her shoulders, emphasizing her delicate, ethereal features.

At first glance, she looked like Camila with short straight hair. Her huge brown eyes, warm complexion, stubborn chin—every familiar detail made his chest ache for the sister he'd spent the last six years with.

The woman in the photo had a narrower face and slimmer build. Too slim. Her bones jutted sharply, pressing against her skin. The smile he'd memorized from Lucia's childhood photos was missing, yet her beauty remained. A dangerous kind of beauty, like if he got too close, he would become hypnotized. Infatuated. Totally fucked.

"Still have doubts?" Cole asked.

"That's Lucia." Tate blinked, forcing himself to look away. "But the anonymous woman in the video—"

"Has the same scar." Cole re-centered the image, moving the focus from Lucia's face to the faded wound beneath the cropped shirt.

Identical scar. Same toned stomach and body shape. The evidence was there, undeniable. Lucia had aimed that gun and shot an innocent without flinching.

Ice filled his veins. He wasn't naive, and as much as he hated it, he could accept the fact she was a coldblooded criminal. The question was, what the fuck would he do about it?

"Can you still copy her phone?" he asked. "Wait. Do you have the number? I could call her."

What would he say to her? *Hey, you don't know me, but Camila escaped her kidnapper. She's alive and misses you. How about you come home, and we'll pretend you never tortured innocent people?*

"The phone was destroyed the day after the video was taken," Cole said. "As of yesterday, she still hadn't replaced it.

"The man she works for, this Badell guy... He must be blackmailing her. I mean, she's not working for money if she lives in a slum."

"They all live in the slum, outside of the law. It's their kingdom, where they make their own rules. She eats dinner with Badell every night. Goes in and out of his compound freely. She *is* watched and never leaves the city. I've seen his guards trailing her, but he puts guards on all his high-ranked officials."

She's a high-ranked official? For a street gang? Camila would be heartbroken if she knew this.

"What about the police?" Tate rose from the couch and paced through the room. "We could turn over the video and any evidence you have against him and shut down his entire operation."

"You're not getting it." Cole propped his elbows on his knees, pulling in a deep breath. "This is Caracas. The police are poorly trained, under-equipped, and aren't paid shit. They tip off the gangs when something isn't right, and the crime lords thank them for that service by giving them a cut of the profits."

Of fucking course. He dropped his head back and heaved a frustrated breath to the ceiling. He needed answers, and the only way he'd get them was to pay Lucia Dias a visit.

"Tate." Liv's melodic voice wove around him as she stood from Josh's lap and approached. "You need to call Camila."

"And say what? She breathes and bleeds a passionate crusade against people like Tiago Badell. If she saw that video of her sister, it would hurt her irreparably. She thinks Lucia is dead and... Fuck, Liv, that's better than the truth, don't you think? I can't tell her. Not until I talk to Lucia."

"If you go to Caracas," Cole said, "you'll be kidnapped and killed inside of a week. You're untrained and unprepared. At a minimum, you need someone with you, preferably a security guard. Someone to watch your back."

"I'm not a security guard, but I'm good with a gun." Liv touched Tate's jaw, drawing his gaze to hers. "I'll go with you."

"The hell you will!" Josh leapt from the chair, eyes blazing.

"Josh," she snapped. "I'll do whatever—"

"No. End of discussion."

Josh glared at her, and she glared right back. Tension shivered between them, a silent battle of wills. Tate was certain Liv would win, but it wasn't up to her.

"Josh is right," he said. "You're not going. No—" He held up a hand when she tried to interrupt. "I'm not budging on this."

She sniffed, turned on her heel, and strode down the hallway, shutting the bedroom door behind her.

"Shit, man." Tate scrubbed a hand through his hair. "I didn't mean to cause problems. I'm sorry."

"Don't be. I'll enjoy the punishment later tonight." Josh's eyes gleamed, his smile twitching with mischief. Then he sobered, nodding at Cole. "Why can't he do it? He knows where Lucia lives and seems to have the *training* to move around the city without getting killed."

"Yeah, well..." Tate blew out a breath. "I can't afford him."

"Even if I were to help you pro bono — which I won't." Cole gave him a hard look. "I don't extract people unless they're willing."

"I just want to talk to her." Tate studied him for a moment, an idea forming. "If I approached her, would she shoot me on the spot?"

"Her guards would." Cole shook his head. "You can't just walk in there, Tate. The gangs decide who enters the neighborhood."

"But you can. You rented an apartment across the street from hers. How'd you do it?"

"I know which palms to grease."

"Then get me in. I'll pay you to set me up in that apartment and tell me everything you know about Tiago Badell. I'll do the rest. Just name the price."

"It's a suicide mission. The price is your life."

"Train me." Tate paced through the room, fueled with determination. "Teach me whatever I need to know to make contact with her." He paused in front of Cole, hands flexing at his sides. "You know my account balance. Take it all."

Cole considered him for a nerve-wracking minute before lowering his head in his hands and exhaling. "Okay."

Hope surged. "Okay?"

"You're a stubborn asshole." Cole lifted his eyes. "If I don't help you, you'll go anyway, and I'll have your moronic death weighing on my conscience."

"Good man." Tate clapped him on the back and lowered onto the couch beside him. "For the record, I think she picked the wrong guy." He motioned toward the tattoo on Cole's arm.

Cole looked down, his eyes stark and unblinking as he traced the inked silhouette of the woman, his finger gliding with reverence and longing. He seemed to forget himself in that private moment, his gaze turning inward and the hard lines of his jaw softening.

Then, like a flip of a switch, he curled his hand into a fist and snapped his spine straight. "Do you think this thing with Lucia will give you what you need to finish *your* tattoo?"

Startled, Tate glanced at his own ink. How did Cole know it wasn't finished?

Roses of various sizes and blooms sleeved his arm in shades of black and gray. His mother's name had been Rose, but each flower on his skin represented the women who had helped raise him at The Velvet Den. They might've been whores, but they were also his friends. His only family.

The cluster of roses stretched above his elbow and faded away. The artwork was supposed to blur into another image across his bicep— the profile of a woman. He always imagined Camila's face would complete the design, but she didn't belong to him.

As he stared at the blank space on his bicep, he knew Josh and Kate were watching him, waiting for him to answer Cole's question. *Will I have what I need to finish it? Will I have someone to call my own?* He wanted Camila, and that dream was unattainable.

"No. The tattoo is finished."

Cole rubbed the stubble on his cheek, studying Tate with those perceptive eyes. Then he looked back at the laptop and sighed. "The apartment in Caracas is paid through the end of the month. I'll extend the lease for another month, get you into the neighborhood, train you on basic self-defense, and walk you through Lucia's patterns. After that, you're on your own."

"Thank you."

"I don't like this." Josh lowered into the chair, perching on the edge. "Can you hire a security guard to go with you?"

"Maybe." Tate didn't know how much money he'd have left after he paid Cole for the help, but he'd figure it out. He turned to Cole. "Do you have more photos of her?"

"Hundreds."

For the next hour, Tate scoured the images on Cole's laptop, memorizing every expression, gesture, and article of clothing that belonged to Lucia Dias. Cole showed him blueprints of Badell's compound, but other than the windowless concrete room in the video, there were no pictures of the interior. Cole hadn't tried to breach the iron gates because that level of intel hadn't been included in the finder fee.

As they ironed out an action plan, they decided to leave in a week. That would give Cole time to train Tate on basic weaponry and self-defense.

Liv eventually emerged from the bedroom, and about five minutes later, someone knocked on the door.

Tate pulled his attention from the laptop as Josh greeted whoever was on the porch.

"Hey." Confusion threaded through Josh's voice. "I didn't expect you guys tonight."

"I called him." Liv approached the door, opening it wider to reveal

Van Quiso and his wife, Amber.

Kate, who had her nose in her phone for the last hour, shot from the couch. Shoulders hunching, she fumbled with her purse on the coffee table. "I need to…" She made a beeline to the door. "I'm gonna go."

"Kate." Josh moved to chase her.

"Let her go." Tate cast a glare at Van. "She needs time."

"She's had four years." With a grip on Amber's hand, Van approached the couch with a casual gait, his gaze clapping onto Tate. "I don't think time is what she needs."

Probably not, but Van's dark baleful presence wasn't a cure for any of them.

Tate sent off a text to his roommates, letting them know Kate left Liv's house. They would find her if she didn't head home.

Cole stood from the couch and extended a hand to Van. "It's good to finally meet you in person."

"Same." Van shook his hand and introduced his wife.

Tate could guess why Liv called Van here, but before he asked, he had another question.

"How do you know each other?" He gestured between Van and Cole.

"Traquero." Van pulled a toothpick from his pocket and cut his eyes at Liv and Josh.

"What did you say?" Josh whispered, the blood draining from his face.

Traquero? The name was familiar, but Tate couldn't place it. "Is that…?"

"The misogynist prick who was supposed to buy Josh." Liv crossed the room, pausing in front of Van.

Right on her heels, Josh looped an arm around her waist, holding her against him as he spoke to Van. "Cole helped you find Traquero?"

With a nod, Van moved to the chair and settled Amber on his thigh. The room fell still as everyone focused on the cozy position of the odd couple.

Amber curled against Van's chest, arms around his neck, clinging to him compulsively. It was one of her many tics that became acutely transparent whenever she left the safety of their house. All toned limbs and long brown hair, she had once been a renowned beauty pageant queen and fitness model. Something tragic had happened to her, ending her career and forcing her into isolation. Severe isolation. She didn't leave her house for years. Van said she was recovering from agoraphobia and OCD, but the rapid heave of her breaths and the way her fingers dug into Van's neck suggested she was still as nutty as ever.

Contrarily, Van reclined in the chair with a toothpick rolling between his lips. The six-inch scar on his cheek radiated intimidation and ice-cold confidence, as if to say, *Stare all you want. I'm a mean son of a bitch, and I won't apologize for it.*

Mean was an understatement, but since his days of human trafficking, he'd taken steps to make amends, like slaughtering the man who sodomized Liv.

Traquero.

Heavy silence clotted the room. No doubt everyone was thinking about that atrocious meeting when Josh's buyer raped Liv while Josh was forced to watch. When Van found out, he went ballistic and dismantled the whole sex slave operation. Shortly after, Traquero was murdered. *Passionately.* They all knew Van was responsible for that gruesome death. They just didn't know he'd hired Cole Hartman to hunt down the slave buyer. Until now.

"I always wondered how you found Traquero," Liv said quietly and turned her attention to Cole. "I guess I owe you my gratitude."

"I didn't kill him," Cole said. "I'm not in the business of murdering—"

"Or kidnapping. We know." Tate caught Liv's steady gaze. "Why did you call Van here?"

"You're going to the kidnap capital of the world. Who better to take as backup than—"

"The man who kidnapped me?" *The man who chained me in an attic and raped me for ten weeks?* He released a humorless laugh. "Are you serious?"

"He's not that man anymore." Amber straightened on Van's lap, her eyes alight with fire. "I know he hurt you, all of you, but he's driving himself into the grave to make it up to you!"

"Amber." Van rubbed his hands along her upper arms, the affection at odds with the chill in his voice. "Calm down."

"No, I won't calm down." She climbed off his lap and stepped into Tate's space, glaring up at him. "When Liv called tonight and told him what you're planning, he didn't hesitate." She pivoted and strode through the room, stopping to straighten a frame on the wall. "He's here, willing to risk his life to help you." She whipped around and thrust at finger at Tate. "So don't you dare judge him."

This, coming from the agoraphobic woman Van had abducted and raped because hey, she was a shiny new toy to play with. Yet she was still with him four years later. Married him, even.

A shudder rippled through her, and she clutched her hand, cracking her knuckles. *Pop-pop-pop-pop.* Another tic.

Van reached for her, but she sidestepped him and scanned the room wildly until her attention locked on the kitchen doorway. "Did you know there are dishes in the sink? Can I...?"

"Sure." Josh said. "Have at it."

When Amber left the room to feed her OCD, Liv arched a brow at Van, her voice low. "Did she stop going to therapy?"

"*I* am her therapy." Van bit down on the toothpick, flashing her a grin.

"That makes me feel so much better," she said dryly.

Cole remained quiet as his gaze pinged between Van and Liv. Did he know about the history they shared? That they had a daughter together? Livana technically lived with her adopted mother, but she spent most of her time either in this house or at Van and Amber's two-hundred-acre property. Because of this shared custody, Van and Liv had grown into an amicable, trusting partnership.

Tate shifted toward Van, hands resting on his hips. "Are you actually considering this? Do you understand the stakes?"

"Yes."

"What about Amber? You're willing to leave your wife for weeks, if not months?"

A dish clanked in the kitchen, and Amber poked her head through the doorway. "I'm not a helpless ninny, Tate!"

Van cracked a smile, straining the scar on his cheek. "Come here, baby."

"One minute." She slipped back into the kitchen, and the sound of running water drifted from the sink.

Tate moved to the couch and took the seat closest to Van, keeping his voice soft. "What happens to Amber and your daughter if you're captured or killed?"

"Liv explained the risks." Van sat back, legs sprawled wide, taking up too much space. "I'm not going to Caracas to die, Tate."

Bullheaded dumbass. He pinched the bridge of his nose, warring with the emotions that always accompanied interactions with Van Quiso. Tate forgave his former captor years ago, but had he ever admitted that aloud? Part of him wanted to hang onto the grudge, because what kind of man would he be if he made allowances for the monster who raped him?

The other part of him recognized this as what it was. An opportunity to wipe the slate clean. He wouldn't forget those weeks in Van's attic. He couldn't. But he could hold out an olive branch to the man.

"I forgive you." Tate lowered his hand and met Van's eyes. "For all of it. I mean it. You. Are. Forgiven. So take your wife home and sleep easier knowing one less person in the world wants to castrate you."

"Yeah? Well, here's the thing." Van plucked the toothpick from his mouth and pointed it at him. "I'm not doing this for forgiveness or preservation or whatever rose-colored reason you concocted in your head.

I'm doing it because it's the right thing to do, and I have the *experience* to impact how this turns out." He turned his silver-bladed eyes to Cole. "When do we leave?"

FOUR

Deafening screams of agony chased Lucia out of the basement, sharpening the cramps that plagued her insides. She yanked off the balaclava face mask and dropped it in the hall.

Though she'd done nothing more than operate the camera this morning, she stayed long after the recording ended, ensuring she was the last one to leave the chamber. Tiago's stooges enjoyed forcing themselves on the female captives, but it was Lucia's ass on the line if the victim was too broken or lifeless to exchange for ransom.

The *click-click* of her heels along the spiral stone stairwell conjured power and confidence. She tried hard to exude that perception, even when she was alone, but she couldn't stop herself from gripping the handrail and using its support for the upward climb.

Fuck, it hurts.

It always started with a rush of saliva over her tongue. Nausea and excruciating stomach pain came next. Then the loss of coordination and the tingling sensation of impending paralysis, like now.

Her ankle twisted, and she righted it, dragging herself around the final bend on the stairs. The doorway to the main floor came into view, and standing just beyond it was Tiago.

She breathed a sigh of relief.

His authoritative stance, hard lines of his lean body, unflinching intensity of his gaze — all of it embodied strength. Strength she so badly needed to scale those last few steps.

Her pulse weakened, and her legs wobbled as she struggled to close the distance. Tiago didn't move, didn't stretch out a hand to help her. He simply watched her, his disarmingly handsome features void of emotion.

When she finally reached him, she handed over the burner phone with the video footage from this morning. He turned, passing it off to one of his lackeys.

The video would be sent to the victim's father, who would watch a faceless man rape and kick his daughter repeatedly with steel-toed boots. The woman was an American college student, whose vacation was cut short when she stumbled into the wrong alley. If her father didn't pay the demand, her pretty face would be blown away by a shotgun.

"You look pale." Tiago brushed the backs of his fingers across Lucia's cheek with aching tenderness.

If he didn't have an armed guard standing beside him, she would've drawn one of the Berettas from her waistband and shot him in the face.

"I feel worse than usual today."

"I thought you might." He offered her a bent elbow and stroked the hand she curled around the crook of his arm. "I'll take care of you. I always do, don't I?"

"Yes." She canted against him as her abdomen clenched through a wave of pain. "Thank you."

He wrapped an arm around her waist and led her through the dank halls toward his bedroom. Two armed guards flanked them. Others loitered in the doorways, lounge areas, and dining hall. All men.

Tiago kept women in the compound to entertain his gang, but the girls weren't free to wander. Only she had that luxury. Because he knew she wouldn't flee.

She leaned against his side and did her best to match his long-legged gait. Raised by Colombian parents, she could speak Spanish, but Tiago always reverted to English with her. He did so now as he told her about the new recruitments he hired, the shipment of high-velocity weapons he acquired —*stole*— and the recent intel he gathered. He knew most of the local private bodyguards, and when they felt they were underpaid, they gave him the information needed to kidnap their employers. In return, they received a cut of the ransom.

She stopped flinching at these conversations years ago. Violence and corruption was the way of life here. Embracing it was a means of survival.

Thankfully, her hard-earned position in his gang allowed her to live outside of the compound. Tiago gave her an apartment within walking distance. A room with four mildewed walls and intermittent electricity and running water. She couldn't afford to furnish it or make it pretty, but it was a thousand times better than this crumbling dump.

Tiago's hideout had once been a popular hotel in Caracas. Like the rest of the city, it was abandoned during the country's economic crisis, and the squatters moved in. She didn't know when Tiago had chased them out and made it his primary residence, didn't know the locations of his other homes, but over the past eleven years, this was where he spent most of his time. And he'd done nothing to fix it up.

It smelled like smoke and death. Bullet holes riddled the concrete walls. Sheet metal covered every window. It was dark. So fucking dark and musty and packed with rotten, sweaty men. She didn't trust any of them, and she didn't think Tiago trusted them, either.

"With the new recruits," she said as they rounded a turn in the corridor, "how many men do you have now?"

"Why do you ask?" He stared straight ahead, his expression empty, except for the twitch in his clean-shaved cheek.

Shit. She'd angered him. The man was suspicious of everyone and everything. Though he seemed to confide in her the most, she often wondered if he kept her the closest because he trusted her the least.

As for the size of his gang, it was a number he never confirmed. She estimated it exceeded two-hundred men, which was larger than the local police force. He was physically unstoppable. Not that anyone ever tried. As King of the City, he had lackeys and informants positioned in every nook and alley, including in the military and police.

They strolled down a long hall. Or rather, *he* strolled. She was lucky to line up one heeled shoe in front of the other without face-planting. By the time they reached his bedroom door, a sheen of perspiration blanketed her skin. Agony coiled her guts, and bile rose in her chest.

Two more guards waited on either side of the steel door. The old-fashioned dead bolt required an old-fashioned key, one that Tiago kept on his person at all times.

He didn't move to unlock the door. She knew the drill. Clothes first.

The heels came off. Then she removed the handguns from her waistband, shimmied out of the jeans, the shirt, and unclasped the bra, setting everything on the wooden bench that existed only for this purpose. For *her*. As far as she knew, she was the only visitor he allowed in his room.

Clad in nothing but black panties, she rose to her full height, shoulders back, and waited for their inspection.

The two guards who had escorted them here remained at the entrance of the hall. The other two swept clinical hands over her butt and groin, digging fingers against the satin between her cheeks in search for weapons. She held still, muscles loose, and breathed.

Tiago watched with detachment until they finished. Then he stepped forward and combed his fingers through her hair, massaging her scalp. It wasn't out of affection. He was searching for weapons.

Knowing that didn't thwart a deep ache from swelling inside her. An ache for companionship. Desire. Love.

Oh, the hopeless dreams of a silly girl. She didn't know that girl anymore, but sometimes she entertained thoughts of her, imagined what life would be like if she hadn't been abducted from her beloved home in the citrus grove.

Satisfied with his search, Tiago unlocked the bedroom door, guided her inside, and bolted them in.

His living space was as spartan and crude as the rest of the compound. Deteriorated sheetrock peeled away from old stone walls. A small unmade bed was shoved into the corner. Two mismatched chairs sat in front of a fireplace filled with ash and cobwebs. A bare bulb glowed in the ceiling — the room's only source of light.

It was a sad space. Humble. But Tiago Badell's presence made it feel enigmatic, ominous, cloaked in secrets. He was one of the wealthiest men in the country, yet here he slept on a tiny old mattress in an abandoned hotel. Alone.

She stood near the chairs, as expected, while he opened a medium-size safe in the closet. The depth of the alcove prevented her from seeing the combination lock. She'd followed him to that side of the room once, hoping for a peek at the safe. But the punishment for doing so had been so grave she never did it again.

"Have you vomited this morning?" He removed her precious lifeline from the safe and relocked it.

"No. Just nauseous." She remained as immobile as possible beside the chair, refusing to give him any reason to send her away.

"Coughing blood?" Rolling up his sleeves, he approached her slowly, like a lazy lion with all the power and strength in the world.

"No blood since last time." Her attention fixated on the syringe cradled in his fingers. *Please hurry.*

He took his time walking toward her, knowing full well he held her life in his hands.

When he finally lowered in the chair and patted his thigh, she didn't hesitate to sit on his lap and recline back against his hard chest.

Her leg moved on its own, hooking over the armrest and bringing her thigh within his reach. A tremble shook through her and her hands flexed, joints cracking and tendons straining — the anticipation all-consuming.

He cleaned the injection area with the supplies on the side table and plunged the needle into the middle of her thigh. It was just a prick, nothing compared to the aches that endlessly tormented her.

"Shhh." He caressed her quivering abs, tracing the serrated scar from her breastbone to her hip. "It'll feel better soon."

"Thank you." She relaxed against him and waited for the relief to come.

It would take fifteen, maybe twenty minutes to saturate her system. In the meantime, he would hold her in this position, as he did every morning, and use his hands to fuck with her head.

When he set the syringe aside, he trailed fingertips around her breasts, ribs, hips, and the crotch of her panties.

"You're beautiful, Lucia." He found the seam of her pussy and slid his touch along the slit, up and down, keeping that small scrap of satin between his finger and her flesh. "You love to fuck, even though you pretend otherwise."

For as long as she could remember, she'd been a highly-sexual person. She gave her virginity to a Texan boy when she was fifteen and explored her sexuality with countless guys in high-school.

Then she was abducted, and all her choices were taken from her.

With her back against his chest and his hands roaming her body with distracting affection, it was easy to forget how cruel he was. When they were alone, he coddled her, cared for her, and whispered seductive compliments in her ear. But when they left the privacy of his room, his ruthlessness took center stage.

A numbing sensation trickled through her abdomen, and she inhaled deeply, relishing the initial effects of the injection. "Why do you make me fuck other men?"

His cock swelled against her backside, and he nuzzled his nose in her neck, his breaths growing heavier, faster. "It pleases me."

So vague. So damn mysterious. She knew nothing of his background or the thoughts that churned his mind. He had no family to speak of. No close friends. No wife or mistress. Yet the artwork that covered his arms meant something. It told a story. His story.

She lifted a hand and stroked the raised welts on his wrist. Scarification, he called it. She assumed he'd cut the images into his skin himself, only because she'd seen him do it to others. It was his preferred method of torture and the most barbaric thing she'd ever witnessed.

Suppressing a shudder, she traced the scarred outlines of animals and landscapes that marred his forearm. "Is this tribal-inspired?"

"You must be feeling better." Lifting her off his lap, he set her on her feet. "Leave."

A bout of dizziness made her sway, but the cramps in her stomach had faded to a dull ache.

With the flick of a finger at the door, he propped a foot on his knee and stared at the unused fireplace.

She lingered for a moment, willing him to look at her, to reveal something of himself. A twitch. A word. An emotion. Anything that might clue her in on what he was thinking. If he was angry, she wanted him to lash out, hit her if he had to. Then she would know.

Knowing was better than walking out of his room, wondering if a gun was trained on her back. Because he had no moral code. When he killed, his victims rarely saw him coming.

As she stepped toward the door, the space between her shoulders blades tingled and chilled. She didn't breathe until she entered the hall, grabbed her guns and clothes, and heard him turn the lock behind her.

FIVE

Tate leaned against the window of the second-floor apartment Cole had leased, growing more impatient by the second.

Come on, Lucia. Where are you?

The rustling of Cole's papers sounded behind him, followed by the clink of Van's tequila against the coffee table.

"Do you miss your wife yet?" Tate stared down at the grungy alley through a pair of high-powered binoculars.

"I missed her the instant I left the driveway," Van said from the couch.

They'd only been in Caracas for three hours, and in that time, Tate had watched a man drag a woman out of the apartment next door to Lucia's, punch her in the face, and stroll away. She called the police, and the five uniformed officers who showed up two hours later decided to rob her instead of helping her. They left with their arms loaded with shit, including a TV, a laptop, and her tiny dog. She'd crumpled on the sidewalk as they drove away and was still sitting there, head down, smoking a cigarette.

In the distance, the report of gunfire sounded. One shot. Then three more in rapid succession.

It wasn't the first time he'd heard that unnerving noise since he'd been here. He was already getting used to it.

"You should've stayed home." He glanced back at Van, who stared blankly at his empty glass.

"I have an idea." Van lifted his eyes, his smile clenched with straight white teeth. "Shut the fuck up."

"I didn't ask you to come." Tate sure as shit didn't want him here.

Forgiveness was one thing. Trusting Van to watch his back was a level of camaraderie they hadn't reached.

Beside Van, Cole bent over a spread of maps and circled all the danger zones. There were a lot of fucking circles.

They'd left their IDs and personal phones in a locker at the airport. Didn't bring photos of family members. No wedding ring on Van's finger. No calling home to check in on loved ones. No connection whatsoever to their lives in Texas. These were Cole's rules. *In the event one of them was kidnapped.*

Cole would only stay with them for a week. If something happened to Tate or Van after that, they were to give the kidnappers Cole's number. He promised to handle any potential ransoms as painlessly as possible.

"Technically, every alley in Caracas is a kidnap alley. But this is *the* Kidnap Alley." Cole circled another area on the map and looked up at Tate. "Give the window a rest and come here."

"But—"

"She eats dinner with Badell every night and isn't due back for another twenty minutes."

With reluctance, Tate left his vigilance and crouched beside him.

"See how winding this road is?" Cole traced a snaking street on the map. "It's a prime target for kidnappers. Lots of places for them to hide and trap motorists. And its proximity to the main motorway makes an easy escape." He cast Tate a flinty glare. "Stay the fuck away from this road."

"Got it."

"I'm going to make this clearer, just in case you don't." He pulled a document out of his backpack and set it on the coffee table.

The letter header was stamped with a United States seal, and beneath it was a long list of first and last names. At least a hundred names. Maybe more.

"There's a fuckton of competition in the Venezuelan kidnapping business. A lot of cops do it, too." Cole tapped the paper. "These are just the kidnappers the U.S. government watches."

A quick glance confirmed Tiago Badell was at the top of the list.

"Am I on any of those government watch lists?" Van arched a brow.

"I wouldn't know." Cole returned the document to his backpack.

"Bullshit." Digging in his pocket, Van removed a toothpick and popped it between his teeth. "I looked you up. Know what I found? Nothing. Nada. You might be able to cover your electronic tracks, but no one is that good. Unless you work for an entity like the United States. So what is it? FBI? CIA? Some kind of secret government agency?"

Tate wanted to know those answers, too, but it was none of their business. "Van, don't be a dick."

"I work for myself." Cole straightened, meeting the challenge in Van's eyes.

"Guys in your line of work can't be married or committed. Gives your enemies a target. Makes you weak." Van lowered his gaze to the tattoo on Cole's arm. "Is that why you lost the girl?"

"You don't have to answer that." Tate shot Van a warning look.

Cole slowly rose from the couch and paced to the window. With his back to the room, he gripped the window ledge and said quietly, "I gave up that job for the girl."

And he lost her anyway. Tate felt bad for the guy and struggled for something to say to break up the thick silence. "I'm sorry, man."

"I'm not." Cole turned and rested his fingers in his front pockets. "She's happy. Happier than I've ever seen her. There isn't a single part of me that regrets that." He shrugged. "It's all I ever wanted for her."

Taking the high road. Good for him. But what about *his* happiness?

Tate wasn't in a position to preach. He'd walked into the innards of kidnapping hell to talk to a woman he'd never met. Why? Because he wanted to repay Camila for rescuing him? Wanted her to look at him the way she looked at Matias? Wanted to do something for her that Matias was unable to do? Yep. All those things. Fucked-up or not, his ego demanded it.

"I thought I loved Liv."

The monotone declaration swung Tate's head in Van's direction, his eyebrows lifting in stunned silence. Van's obsession with Liv hadn't exactly been a secret, but it was in the past. No one discussed it. Especially not Van.

"Don't look at me like that." Van stretched his arms along the back of the couch, smiling at Tate. "You were there."

"Yeah, I had a front row seat to that madness. Thanks for the reminder."

Sitting on the floor, Tate reclined against the wall and lit a cigarette. During his captivity, the dynamic between Van and Liv had been the mindfuck of all mindfucks. Van's temper was unpredictable, and more often than not, he'd unleashed it on Liv—hitting her without warning, fucking her despite her protests—while Tate watched from his chains.

He shuddered.

"I only brought it up to make a point." The toothpick jogged in Van's mouth, and his gaze turned inward. "The thing with Liv is I never put her before myself. Fuck her happiness. I wanted her, and that was that. Then I met Amber." He shook his head and laughed to himself. "Setting her free was the bravest thing I ever did."

Amber's agoraphobia had been unmanageable back then, and Van realized he wasn't helping. It shocked the hell out of everyone when he returned her to her isolated life.

Tate dropped the cigarette in an empty beer bottle. "But you got her back."

"At the time, I was certain I wouldn't. And here's my point. When I lost Amber, I had a goddamn eye-opening epiphany, like a lightning bolt to the chest. I fucking love that woman so much it redefines the meaning of happiness. It's not a matter of putting her happiness before mine. When she smiles, I feel a peace unlike anything I've felt in my life. And if letting her go is the only way for her to keep that smile, I would do it again in a heartbeat."

"Poetic." Cole stared at the floor, his mouth twisting in a sad grin. "I mean it. Because I feel the exact same way."

"I know why you're telling me this," Tate said, "and let me remind you Camila is with Matias. I let her go."

"No, you didn't." Van leaned forward with elbows braced on his spread knees. "She was never yours. When she moved to Colombia, you didn't have a choice in the matter."

Not exactly true. Tate could've told her how he felt, fought for her, made her choose. He certainly didn't have to go along with Matias' plan to reunite them.

Matias would crap a cartel brick if he knew Tate was on a meet-and-greet mission with the man who abducted Camila eleven years ago. If Matias had it his way, Van would be dead, because he didn't just grow up with Camila. He grew up with Lucia, too. Loved her like a sister. He wouldn't want Van anywhere near her.

"Why are we here?" Van sat back, eyes glinting like razors.

Tate didn't owe anyone an explanation, so he decided to throw Van's words back at him. "It's the right thing to do."

"Good answer." With a wolfish smile, Van turned to Cole. "So tell me, hot shot secret agent, what happens if we leave the neighborhood?"

"Don't call me that." Cole pushed off the window ledge and knelt beside the map, pointing at an intersection of streets. "We entered the neighborhood here. Remember the men who approached the taxi?"

Tate nodded. The armed thugs had shared words with Cole through the open window. Since Tate didn't speak Spanish, the short conversation had been abstruse. But when Cole slapped some bills in their palms, the gist was clear. Cole had paid an entrance fee.

"When I came here six weeks ago," Cole said, "I made a deal with the gang that patrols that corner. Had to work my way up to the boss to negotiate safe passage. Which means that as long as I pay a toll each time I enter, they won't throw a grenade in my car window. But that only works for me. The gang boss doesn't know you."

"So what you're saying is, if we leave the neighborhood…"

"You won't be able to return. And one more thing…" Cole scratched his stubbled cheek. "Matias Restrepo doesn't have any sway here. Badell has more resources, more men, more guns, more everything. I'm not saying not to call him if you need help. Just don't expect a fast and successful rescue. It would take him weeks to get his men into this neighborhood, and coming here would be at a huge risk to his cartel."

Fucking great. Not that Tate intended to call him, but it had lingered at the back of his mind like a security blanket.

Cole glanced at his watch. "Lucia should be home any minute."

They moved to the window, and Tate trained the binoculars on the entrance of the alley, his entire body wound tight with nerves.

He'd only seen her in photos. *And that vile video.* How would his first encounter with her go? What if there was nothing more to her story? No redeemable reason for her involvement with Badell?

No matter what happened, he would have to tell Camila when it was over. Christ, he wanted more than anything to be the bearer of *good* news.

Dusk began to move in, making the gloomy street all the more gloomier. The woman who was robbed earlier was still sitting on the curb, hugging her knees to her chest.

Five minutes later, a feminine silhouette emerged in the alley. He didn't need the binoculars to see her, but he used them anyway, dialing in on her face.

The pale illumination of the moon haloed her head, giving her glossy raven hair an earthshine effect. The graceful curve of her neck, thinly arched brows, deep smoky eyes, and cheekbones so sharp they could draw blood — it was like staring into the face of Queen Nefertiti, one of the hottest women who ever lived.

Fuck him, but she was compelling. A living work of art. It wasn't just her beauty that arrested him. It was the way she moved, as if cutting through water with finesse and purpose. Not a single motion wasted.

Her black pants and sleeveless top looked painted on, her lips full and parted as she breathed through each seductive stride. Then her chin lifted, and her gaze scanned the top floor apartments, pausing on the one he was in.

Breathless, he lowered the binoculars and stepped back.

"She can't see us," Cole said beside him.

Tate pressed a hand against the glass. During Cole's previous stay here, he'd installed one-way window film. Even with the interior lights on at night, it was supposed to make the apartment look dark and vacant.

Sure enough, her attention quickly moved on.

"Let me see those." Van grabbed the binoculars and trained them on Lucia. "Not bad. Objectively attractive, in a male model sort of way. Looks like she skipped a few too many meals. I prefer women with more meat on their bones."

"You're so full of shit." Tate snatched the binoculars. "Your wife weighs a hundred pounds soaking wet."

"Amber's a fucking knockout, and if you mention her again, I'll chloroform you while you sleep and hang you by an ankle from the ceiling with a thirteen-inch dildo shoved up your ass."

Tate stared at him and blinked.

"Too soon?" Van asked.

"Yeah, Van. *Fuck.*"

"You two are giving me a headache." Cole leaned a shoulder against the glass, staring down at Lucia. "We all know she's a solid ten. Eloquent yet cute. She's…"

"One of the billions of women who wouldn't touch you with a fifty-foot pole?" Van grinned.

"I was going to say…" Cole squinted at him and returned to the window. "She's beautiful in an innocent, unintentional way, and she knows how to use that to her advantage. Something to think about when you make contact."

Tate raised the binoculars as she breezed past the sobbing woman on the street. The woman leapt up and said a string of words while chasing Lucia to her apartment door.

As the woman continued to speak, her body language grew frantic in her efforts to get Lucia's attention. Without looking at her or acknowledging her in anyway, Lucia unlocked her apartment and shut the door in the woman's face.

"Cold," Tate muttered.

"Listen to me." Cole stabbed a finger at the window. "Out there, every single person is your enemy. Remember that."

"I get it, but that lady was just—"

"Trust. No one."

Tate touched his brow to the glass and exhaled. *Fuck this place.* What on earth would compel Lucia to live here?

The distraught neighbor finally went inside her apartment, and a few seconds later, Lucia's door opened. She stepped out and locked up again.

"Where's she going?" Tate asked.

"I don't know. She never deviates from her patterns." Cole took the binoculars from Tate and watched her stride down the alley in the direction she'd just come. "She changed her shoes."

"You sure?"

"Yeah. She always carries two compact 9mm Berettas in her waistband and *always* wears the same black heels. She had the heels on a second ago."

Tate hadn't noticed those details. *Because he'd been too enamored with the rest of her.*

"She's wearing flat-soled boots." Cole handed the binoculars to him. "The guns are still at her back, wedged in her waistband."

As Tate validated that, Van said, "Wherever she's going, it's too far to walk in heels."

"We need to follow her." Tate glanced at the door, calculating the logistics of tailing her.

The main entrance to their apartment building opened on a different street, a block over from Lucia's alley. It made coming and going without her detection easier, but circling the exterior of the huge complex to catch up with her would take a few minutes.

"We're not going anywhere." Cole paced away from the window, headed toward the open kitchen. "You can't see them from the window, but her guards are watching. They'll see *us* coming from a mile away."

Hard to argue. They didn't exactly blend in. At Cole's suggestion, they'd packed plain clothes — jeans and t-shirts — and hadn't shaved in over a week. But the whiskers didn't hide their Caucasian complexions and pale eyes. The three of them didn't just look American. They looked like Marines on an undercover mission.

Given the total absence of body fat on their muscled frames, Cole and Van clearly shared Tate's dedication to working out. If they strolled down the street together, the locals would notice.

But Cole had a plan for everything. A local woman would deliver groceries and necessities at a scheduled time every week. Vetted and paid handsomely, she would guard her job with the utmost discretion. In the meantime, they would be cooped up in the tiny one-bedroom apartment until Cole gave them the green light to venture out.

In the kitchen, he lifted a long duffel bag from the table. When they'd arrived at the apartment, the first thing Cole did was pull the bag from one of the tiles in the drop ceiling in the bedroom.

He set it on the coffee table and unzipped it, revealing an arsenal of firearms, knives, and high-tech gadgets. "I collected this stuff during my previous visit here."

Made sense. It wasn't like he could sneak an assault rifle into his carry-on.

"When we eventually go out there," Cole said, "you'll be fully armed and *armored*." He held up a black t-shirt from the bag. "This is bullet-resistant."

"What?" Tate reached out and touched what appeared to be high-quality cotton. "No way."

"I was shot in the chest wearing something similar." Cole lifted the hem of his shirt, baring flawless skin over washboard abs and sculpted pecs. "The bullet broke skin. Fractured ribs."

"No scar." Tate couldn't believe it.

"The bullet didn't enter my body." Cole pulled another shirt from the bag and tossed at Van.

"Badass." Van held it up to his chest. "Machine-washable?"

"Good luck finding a washing machine." Cole laughed and nodded at the view beyond the window, where laundry hung from sagging balconies from one end of the alley to the other.

Who cared about laundry? Those shirts, though… If they could really bounce bullets, they were worth their weight in gold.

No wonder Cole's fees were so outrageous. He didn't just know what he was doing. He had the gear to stay alive. Tate couldn't imagine what this arsenal cost on the black market or wherever he'd acquired it. And he'd left it all behind after his last trip?

"You have to build a new stockpile of weapons on every job?" Tate asked.

"Yeah." Cole motioned at the duffel bag. "This was included in your finder fee. Now you're going to learn how to use it."

Over the next hour, Cole instructed Van and Tate on the nuances of each firearm and how to conceal the pieces beneath their clothing. They couldn't hit the streets looking like avatars in a first-person shooter game. Discretion was paramount.

During the instruction, rain began to pelt the glass. By the time Tate made his way to the window, a tropical downpour was fully underway. The deluge of water fell from broken spouts and overfilled dumpsters, rushing a river of sewage through the alley.

Where was Lucia? Surely, she wasn't walking the steep, winding streets in this storm? After eleven years in this shanty town, she was probably used to it. But he didn't like it. Every instinct begged him to go out there, hunt her down, and drag her back to the States.

Instead, he stayed at the window, watching, waiting, and finally, she appeared.

"She's back," he said, drawing Cole and Van to his side.

Despite the torrential rain, her steps were unhurried, measured, as she navigated streams of rainwater. Her clothes stuck to her thin sodden body, her hair clinging to her face, and in her arms…

"What is she carrying?" He gave the binoculars to Cole, who shook his head and handed them back.

She strode toward her apartment, but before she got there, she stopped and knocked on the door next to hers.

"That's the apartment that was robbed earlier," Van said.

The woman poked her head out. Then she swung the door open and grabbed whatever Lucia was holding.

Amid the blur of motion, Tate spotted a furry head. "Holy shit, she has the dog. How did she—?"

"Badell owns this neighborhood," Cole said. "She must've tracked down the officers and demanded Badell's cut of the loot."

"She could've taken the laptop or demanded money, right?" His chest filled with hope. "But she took the dog. That's—"

"Don't read too much into it. The most corrupt explanation is usually the right one. Lucia knows what the woman values most, and now she's in Lucia's debt."

"Christ, you're jaded."

"I'm realistic." Cole paced to the couch and packed away the weapons. "Lucia will stay in her apartment for the rest of the night. At dawn, she heads back to the compound."

"Every morning?"

"Without fail," Cole said behind him.

Tate remained at the window as she left the woman without saying a word and vanished inside her own apartment.

What's going on in your head, Lucia? Why are you here?

"You know why I abducted Camila." Van stepped beside him and stared out into the rain. "Why she was even on my radar."

"Yeah."

Van's father, Mr. E, had given him Camila's information and ordered him to take her. Her disappearance had been part of a revenge plan led by Matias' own brother.

"Two months after I took Camila," Van said, "Lucia disappeared. It's related, isn't it? To Matias' cartel?"

"Yes, and Matias killed every person involved in the sisters' kidnappings."

Except Van. He had Tate to thank for that. Since Camila had made peace with her former captor, Tate had talked Matias out of retaliating.

"When Lucia was captured, Camila was presumed dead." Tate trained the binoculars on Lucia's apartment door, and an ache pinched his chest. "When Badell brought her here, he would've tried to collect a ransom from her parents, who were already dead." He met Van's eyes. "She believes she's alone."

He wanted so badly to storm into her apartment and tell her Camila was alive. But he couldn't. Not while she was being watched.

"I'm trying to be patient," he said, turning toward Cole, "but I need to know the plan."

"There's somewhere she goes twice a month." Cole lowered onto the couch. "Her guards don't follow her in."

"Twice a month?" His pulse raced. "When? Is it always the same days of the month?"

"Yes. Ten days from today, she'll be there."

Ten days? That's an eternity.

Tate paced the length of the room, agitated. "You're leaving in seven days."

"I have another job." Cole narrowed his eyes. "And I don't want to be a part of whatever you decide to do after you confront her."

"I'm not going to kidnap her."

Cole glanced between him and Van, eyebrows arched. "If you say so."

"Whatever. You already told us we'd be on our own." He continued to pace. "Where does she go twice a month?"

"A sex club. That's where you'll make contact with her."

"What?" Tate slammed to a stop.

"Don't look so offended. You should feel right at home there."

True, but... "What are you suggesting I do?"

"You'll go in there, and if she's willing, you'll fuck her until she loses all logic and paranoia. Then you'll put your mouth at her ear and say—"

"Thanks for the good time… Oh, and by the way, your sister's alive?"

"Exactly."

Tate closed his eyes and breathed, "That's a terrible idea."

SIX

It was the worst idea ever. But as Tate walked to the X ten days later, he was all in. Shoulders back, weapons concealed, bullet-resistant shirt straining across his chest, he was battle ready.

Except the shirt wouldn't protect his head. Or his dick.

Christ. There it was. The X.

The sex club didn't have a name, but a huge black X marked the otherwise nondescript door — the only indication he'd arrived at the right place.

The temptation to glance back and scan the shadows for Van prickled his scalp, but he knew Van had followed him as planned, staying far enough back to not raise suspicion.

Cole left Caracas three days ago with the promise that he was only a phone call away. But who knew what part of the world he'd traveled to or how long it would take him to return?

Deep breath. Follow the plan. Don't look sketchy.

Hell, every person he'd passed on the short walk here looked sketchy as fuck. Thankfully, no one approached him. *Yet.* The locals were probably taking their time scoping him out and gathering their buddies so they could gang rush him.

He slid his hands into his pockets and approached the door all casual like. Nothing to see here. Just going to a sex club to get laid.

To fuck Camila's sister.

That was going to be hard to explain to Camila, but first things first. He needed to get inside, and once he walked through that door, he would truly be on his own.

Van was a lot of things, but he wasn't a cheater. His refusal to step foot in the sex club was as inconvenient as it was admirable. He was here to help Tate, but his wife was and always would be his number one priority. Tate respected that.

He knocked on the black X and removed a wad of bolivars from his pocket.

The door swung open, revealing a rangy Hispanic man with a cigarette protruding from the toothy gap in a scraggly beard. "*Sí?*"

Tate put the bills in the man's hand.

"*Sin armas.*" The man motioned at Tate's waistband, where his untucked shirt concealed a handgun.

Cole had warned him about the no weapons policy. There was also a no clothing policy, but the disrobing would take place inside.

He handed over the gun and pushed through the doorway until bony fingers circled his arm, stopping him.

"*Sin armas.*" The bearded man pointed his cigarette at Tate's boot.

Fuck. He relinquished the knife from under his pant leg, certain he'd never see either of those weapons again.

Then he was free to go in.

The only doorway up ahead led him into a dim locker room. The tiled space was vacant, except for a lone woman sitting on the floor in the corner. As he stripped his clothes, she was more absorbed by the syringe in her arm than his nudity.

There were no locks on the lockers. He had no choice but to stuff his belongings into one, loathing the idea of leaving the protective shirt. The material looked plain enough, nothing to indicate its worth. If someone robbed him, his biggest concern would be the naked walk back to the apartment.

Moving toward the exit, he grabbed a haphazardly folded robe from a pile, pulled it on, and tied the front closed.

Two baskets sat on a table by the door. He grabbed a fistful of condoms from one, shoving them into the pocket of the robe. The other was filled with silicon bracelets.

Cole's intel had been right. There were four different colored bracelets. No labels, but Cole said black specified a *straight* orientation. White was *gay*, and gray was *bisexual*. The red ones… Well, he said not to worry about those.

Choosing a color wasn't difficult. When Tate had unwillingly lost his virginity to a man at fourteen, it had emotionally and physically scarred him enough to *never* put himself in a situation like that again. And he'd succeeded.

Until Van.

With a bitter taste in his throat, he grabbed a black bracelet. Wrestled it onto his wrist. Left the locker room.

And walked into a setting unlike anything he'd ever seen.

Sex.

Everywhere he looked.

Piles of naked, writhing, sweaty bodies.

By his estimation, there were forty or fifty people with an even ratio of men to women. All naked and moaning, sucking and fucking, moving from partner to partner, and taking turns.

Group sex seemed to be the theme here—threesomes, foursomes, too-many-to-count-somes, gang bangs, daisy chains, double penetration, and the random circle jerk in the corner.

Holy.

Fuck.

Few things shocked him, and orgies were commonplace at the Velvet Den. But the similarities ended there.

A sticky smell clung to the air—a sour brew of smoke and body odor—made worse by the sweet aroma of a Febreze-type spray.

Scuffed furniture, cigarette burns, patched upholstery, dark stains—it was a germaphobe's worst nightmare. Not that he was obsessed with cleanliness, but some of these folks had clearly thrown hygiene to the wayside. At least they were using condoms. Most of them, anyway.

The seedy club consisted of one room, vast and dimly lit, with a plethora of shadowed alcoves hidden by half walls and equipment rigged for impact play and other fetishes.

Fully aware that several heads had turned his way, he clasped his hands behind him and stepped through the room like he owned it. As his bare feet moved along the worn carpet, he tried not to think about the fluids that were transferring to his skin.

The mismatched couches and futons appeared to be surface-clean, but some of those stains should've been burned off. Like most clubs of this kind, the lights were kept low enough to hide stretch-marks and cellulite and just bright enough to ensure intended appendages were stuffing intended holes. Though there didn't seem to be a right or wrong hole here.

He checked his black bracelet and realized most of the club-goers wore gray or red ones.

The general male fantasy wasn't picky, but the majority of the men he knew preferred women.

Not the case here.

His aversion to having sex with men was deeply ingrained. Had his life taken a gentler path, maybe he wouldn't have so much damn dread building in his gut right now. But as he caught the interested stares of numerous men around the room, he couldn't stop a resentful scowl from thinning his lips.

One thing he hadn't counted on was his inability to get a hard-on.

He was always ready to fuck, but as it stood — or didn't stand — he wasn't sure he'd be able to perform.

Then he saw her.

On the far side of the room, Lucia bent over a table, eyes closed and mouth parted, as a burly naked man beat her ass with a cane.

Every muscle in Tate's body tensed to go to her, but he forced himself to remain in place, to watch and evaluate.

The man's erection was as impressive as his strikes. He was huge…everywhere, his swings powered by bricks of muscle. With each new stripe across her backside, she relaxed deeper onto the table. There were no creases of tension on her face. No restraints on her arms or legs. Nothing to hold her there but her own will.

She was enjoying the beating, and fuck if that didn't make Tate's dick swell with blood. He wasn't a sadist, but he loved it rough, loved the feel of a woman bending and sighing beneath the aggressive force of his unchecked desire.

He could approach her now, make his move, but that wasn't his style. When he wanted a woman's attention, he preferred a subtle approach.

He spotted an unoccupied couch and sat at the center of it, ensuring the robe protected his butt from whatever was breeding in the crusty cushion. The location put him in her direct line of sight. She only needed to open her eyes.

Goddamn, she was hot. Flirty shoulder-length hair. Creamy coffee skin. Thick dark eyelashes. A little on the thin side, but she had a great Latina ass.

He settled back on the couch. Then the piranhas closed in. He held his black bracelet in view, discouraging the men. But three women crept toward him with sex-induced oblivion written all over their faces.

One of them crawled on her knees from a nearby pile of men. Her Barbie-thin waist pinched in between an abundance of hips and tits. She was pretty enough, and as her hand slid up his leg and disappeared beneath his robe, he knew his concern about performance had been unwarranted.

He was as hard as a rock. It had nothing to do with the fingers curling around his length and everything to do with the woman who had just opened her eyes.

Lucia stared at him from twenty-feet away, her cheek pressed against the table and her focus unwavering. She didn't blink, and neither did he. The cocky part of him exclaimed triumph, knowing he'd irrevocably seized her interest. He only needed to wait for her to come to him, and she would. They always did.

The other two women joined him on the couch. One on each side, they untied the knot on his robe, spreading it open.

He was prepared for this, had made the decision before coming here that he would allow touching and blowjobs from women. What straight man wouldn't? But the only woman he would fuck tonight was the raven-haired beauty watching him from the table.

The man behind her set aside the cane and gripped his latex-wrapped erection, stepping closer to her to line himself up.

Tate's jaw tightened, and he shot her a look she couldn't misinterpret. *No.*

It was an irrational demand, considering the three women who were currently exploring every inch of his body with hands, lips, and teeth. He was tempted to stop the girl between his legs from rolling a condom down his shaft, but he decided to let this play out, to see what Lucia would do.

He captured her gaze as warm lips stretched around his girth. Ahhh, fuck, that felt good. His skin heated, and his balls tightened, and the ungodly pleasure only intensified in the prison of Lucia's watchful stare.

He didn't lift his hands, didn't touch or look at the women grinding against him. He couldn't ignore the intoxicating desire they spread through his body, didn't want to. He felt like putty beneath their ministrations and melted into the couch.

His breathing accelerated, and his cock pulsed in the hot wet cavity of the woman's mouth. But his eyes were narrowed on Lucia and her alone.

She reached behind her, gripped the burly man's dick, and stroked it a few times before nudging him away. The man didn't look too put off by it as he moved to the next girl in line for a beating.

Then she stood and turned to face him fully.

Smallish tits, light pink nipples, sharp collarbones—her delicate physique rounded into curvy hips and slender legs. The dark trimmed patch of hair between her thighs created a shadow over the part of her he so desperately wanted to see, to taste, to pound until they were both exhausted and sated.

Maybe she was a coldblooded bitch in a kidnapping gang, but unless she had a blade clenched between those tight ass cheeks, she didn't have the upper hand here.

He found her eyes and sharpened his in silent command. *Come here.*

Her chest hitched, an exquisite response. Then she slowly walked toward him.

SEVEN

Sweet mother of God, he was beautiful. Easily the sexiest man in the room. Hell, in Lucia's thirty years, she'd never seen a man that jaw-droppingly stunning.

And that was the most crucial part. She'd never seen him before. Not in this sex club. Not in Caracas.

She would've remembered the intensity in those crystal blue eyes, the way they honed in on her, tracked her every move, and took her breath away.

She floated toward him, propelled by curiosity, desire, stupidity. He could've been any number of deadly traps — an enemy of Tiago, a Fed for the United States, a kidnapper or serial killer.

Her insides might've been damaged, but her gut was trustworthy, and it told her he was none of those things. Besides, it wasn't like she would leave with him or tell him anything incriminating. If he were simply here to fuck, she'd gladly take him for a ride.

While this was the only place she could have sex on her own terms, the pursuit of pleasure wasn't the reason she came. She had a job to do, a mandate from Tiago to visit twice a month. He didn't care who she fucked while she was here, as long as she cataloged the words exchanged around her. Some of Tiago's competitors frequented the club, and their tongues tended to loosen after an orgasm or two.

This moonlighting gig also aided her own agenda. An agenda Tiago could never, ever find out about.

Sliding one foot in front of the other, she approached the gorgeous stranger with deliberate slowness so that she could savor every glorious inch of him. Dark brows hooded those captivating eyes. Pillowy lips parted with his aroused breaths. Stubble shadowed his cheeks and jaw. And what a jawline. Even with the scruff, she could make out the chiseled angles.

His nose was perfect, no bumps or bends to suggest it'd ever been broken. *Unlike most of the brutes she kept company with.* His brown-blond hair was cut short. Neither buzzed nor long enough to style. *Low maintenance.*

For a white guy, his complexion had a remarkable glow, as if soaked with sunlight and lathered with oil. It was probably just the low lighting. But good lord, all that flawless tanned skin, the way it stretched over defined pecs and abs… No wonder every woman in the room was watching him, waiting for a turn to choke on his dick.

The one between his legs blocked Lucia's view of his package. The two on the couch looked like they were seconds from humping his face.

Time for them to go.

Lucia picked up her pace, suddenly very aware of her nudity. What a novel feeling. She'd thought the first couple of years with Tiago had broken her of all modesty. But now, goosebumps rose on her arms. Her nipples hardened in the stuffy air, and she fought the urge to hug the scar on her abdomen.

The man didn't break eye contact, and as if held in hypnosis, she couldn't either. She paused within arm's reach, and without removing her gaze from his, she made a shooing motion.

At the edges of her periphery, the women skulked away, knowing better than to challenge Tiago Badell's favorite confidant.

Her eyes stayed on his as he lowered his hand and removed the condom. Then he sat back and rested his arms along the back of the couch, unabashedly nude with the robe open, as if inviting her to look.

She meant to take a leisurely stroll down the length of his body, but she only made it to the thick column of his neck before skipping straight to his cock.

Her breath caught, and heat flushed between her legs. God almighty, the man was blessed in both length and girth. So hard and thick. Beautifully shaped. A vein pulsed along the fat shaft. The wide, suckable crown and silky skin pulled taut—

Wait. He was circumcised? It'd been so long since she'd seen a cut penis. It wasn't a common practice in South America. Or Europe.

But it was prevalent in the United States.

Her gaze lifted to the blue of his, which hadn't moved from her face. "You're American."

He glanced at his erection, a frown piercing his forehead. Then he returned to her eyes. "So are you."

Her Colombian heritage made it easy to blend in here, but her

American accent always gave her away.

For the first time since she spotted him, he released her gaze, lowering his down her body, inspecting her mouth, throat, chest, and lower. He gave her ugly scar a cursory glance and paused on her pussy.

The brazen way he examined that part of her made her inner muscles spasm. Could he see the throbbing? The desire dripping onto her thighs?

She endured his predatory stare for long seconds before lowering to her knees and settling between his spread legs. Her hands itched to wrap around his swollen length, but she wouldn't. Not until he was feverish and ready to crawl out of his skin with need.

She started with his ankles, trailing feather-light caresses up the backs of his calves. The dusting of coarse hair tickled her fingers, and his muscles bounced against her touch. She gave the fronts of his legs the same attention and moved above his knees, inching her body closer and relishing the feel of his powerful thighs around her.

When she reached his heavy sac, she let her fingernails graze the skin but otherwise neglected the neediest part of him.

His arms lowered from the back of the couch to his sides, and his breathing deepened, his lips separating to accommodate the pull and release of air.

He looked ravenous, and she fed off it, her hands traveling over his torso, exploring every brawny bump and carved furrow. She kept the motion unhurried, rhythmic, seductive. Then she added her mouth, licking and nibbling his velvety skin.

God help her, he smelled heavenly. Clean and pure, without a hint of cologne or aftershave. He smelled natural, fresh, like a man who took care of himself. His pubic hair was trimmed. His teeth were white, and his physique was a powerhouse of sculpted muscle. The perfect example of a healthy male.

The sounds of slapping flesh and hoarse groans saturated the room, spurring her on. She worshiped his body with her hands and mouth, delighting in every twitch, every moan. His erection pressed like a hot iron against her belly, and his lashes fell half-mast over sexy bedroom eyes as he teasingly caught the edge of his bottom lip between his teeth.

Oh, how she wanted to taste the hunger on that sinful mouth. Which was crazy. She couldn't remember the last time she'd kissed someone, the last time she'd been kissed. It was before Venezuela. Before she was taken.

It wasn't like she avoided it. She just didn't have access to the kind of sex that invited intimacy. But as his tongue darted out to wet his lips, she knew she would kiss him. She just wished she remembered how to do it well.

Peering up through her lashes, she fell into his vivid stare and waited for him to get bossy. He would. She knew his type. She just had to be patient. Or maybe give him a little push.

Sliding her fingers over his hard nipple, she pinched it, twisted it hard.

He groaned and rocked his hips. Then he gripped the base of his cock and met her eyes. "Put your mouth on me."

"Hmm. I don't know." She fought a smile.

He held out a foil packet from the pocket of his robe. "I'm not asking."

There he is. Demanding. Coarse. So fucking sexy.

She plucked the condom from his fingers and rolled it on, fighting to stretch it into position. One-size-fits-all didn't quite cover the full length of him. *Poor guy.* A chuckle escaped her lips.

"Stop laughing at it," he said, gripping the hair at her nape, "and work it into your mouth."

Her thighs clenched, and she lowered her head, keeping her gaze locked with his. Then she stopped.

She never gave blowjobs without a condom protecting her mouth from disease. But she didn't want to taste the latex on him. She wanted his flavor on her tongue and the warmth of his skin sliding against her lips.

He looked and smelled like the kind of man who kept himself clean and safe.

Fuck it.

She unrolled the condom, tossed it aside, and brought her face close, inhaling the salty, masculine scent of his cock. Her mouth watered.

The first brush of the broad tip against her lips produced a tremble across his thighs and a rumbling groan in his chest.

He adjusted the fist in her hair, tightening the hold to guide her mouth, closer, deeper, forcing her to swallow him. And she did, as much of him as she could, flattening her tongue and measuring her breaths.

Jesus, he was long. And unbelievably hard and hot. If he kicked his hips, she'd feel the bruise in her throat for days.

But he didn't. He used his hand instead, guiding her head up and down at the pace and rhythm he wanted. She might've been the initiator, but she wasn't the one in control.

Dominance encapsulated every bone, muscle, and breath in his body, and he knew it. Owned it. It was right there—the glare of masculine confidence in those brilliant blue eyes. He stared her down as if to illustrate that very point, to make her squirm.

She wasn't the squirmy type, but he did affect her—the erratic pulse in her throat, the clenching heat between her legs, the impulse to submit to him on a fundamental level—if only for one night.

Her instincts said he wouldn't abuse the gift. He wasn't Tiago. Wasn't any of the other selfish, corrupt men she'd encountered over the past eleven years. He reminded her of Matias. Even as a young man, Camila's boyfriend had that persuasive *something* in his bearing, in his eye contact, and in the way he handled her sister.

Camila…

Her heart gave a heavy pang, and she quickly shoved those thoughts away.

Re-doubling her efforts, she tongued and sucked the beautiful cock in her mouth.

Blood pulsed along the length, beating strong and hot beneath his velvety skin. He was close, his breathing labored and muscles taut.

But she didn't want him to come. Not until he was impaled deep inside her pussy.

His cock slid from her mouth, and she crawled up his body, the welts on her ass pulsing deliciously with each movement. She kissed a path from his sternum to his neck and lingered on his whiskered jawline.

Then she felt it — the excess of saliva in her mouth, the flare of nausea in her gut, and the sudden sweep of vertigo.

No, please. Not now.

She held still, blanking her expression to hide the stabbing pain.

It'll pass. It'll pass.

"Hey."

His lips moved, his voice raspy. She focused on that, on his mouth and how badly she wanted to feel it against hers.

EIGHT

A strange look crossed Lucia's face. It was such a fleeting twitch Tate wondered if he'd imagined it.

"Are you okay?" He cupped her cheek, searching her beautiful brown eyes.

She stared at him, stared at his lips. Then she attacked his mouth in a bruising kiss.

Fuck, he was primed for it, had spent the last few minutes warring between blowing his load in her throat and pounding her into the filthy carpet.

Either way, the onset of orgasm pushed against the edges of his tenuous control. He needed to calm the fuck down and remember why he was here.

Hard to do with her sweet tongue working against his with diabolical skill. The tongue that had just ruined him for all other blowjobs.

Commanding her to suck him had been gratuitous and narcissistic. He only needed to get her alone to tell her about Camila. But he couldn't bring himself to regret the ungodly pleasure her mouth had given him.

Just like he couldn't stop his hands from learning every dip and curve of her shape. She was so damn small, all delicate bones and compact muscle. He could snap her in half. But it wasn't just her fragile size that turned him on. It was the compliant way she responded to him, the ease in which she knelt and bent to his will.

He let her lead the kiss as he stroked her from tits to ass and back again. Then he took over, chasing her tongue and setting the tempo. Her palms pressed against his chest, her fingers curling in as she met him bite for bite, opening as he deepened the kiss, and sighing as they unraveled into groping, rubbing, heedless hands and grinding hips.

Heat panted through him as he lowered his touch to her cunt and stroked the soft flesh, sliding through the wetness and pressing inside. The clasp of her body sucked him, clenching and pulsing and scrambling his brain.

Goddamn, she was tight. Swollen and slick and so fucking hot. He ached to be inside her. Felt rabid with the need to spear her with his cock. But he was too big. He'd hurt her if he didn't start slow and gentle.

When she reached between them and gripped his length, he nudged her arm away. She'd removed the condom, which he greatly appreciated during the blowjob, but he never had unprotected sex.

Quickly rolling on another rubber, he positioned himself. His other hand caught her waist, stilling her, making her wait for it.

The elegant column of her neck filled his view, the vein in her throat pulsing wildly. The tips of her stick-straight black hair brushed against the sharp lines of her shoulders. As her greedy hands prowled his body, her thick lashes lowered, partially concealing the lust in her eyes.

She was, without question, the sexiest, most striking woman he'd ever seen. But it changed nothing. She was still a gang member, and he still loved her sister.

This was just sex. An exchange of pleasure and, by the end of the night, information.

She squeezed her thighs around his hips, leaking honey all over his shaft.

"Your impatience only makes me hungrier, sweetheart." He licked the seam of her lips.

"Take what you need, American." She licked him back.

Christ, she couldn't say shit like that to him. As it was, he struggled to keep himself from tearing into her with unrestrained barbarity. And she would let him. Maybe she was masking her expressions, but her body's responses were honest and real. She'd let him use her savagely and selfishly, let him bite her nipples, bruise her skin, and welt her ass. It was incredibly erotic to know he could fuck this woman any way he desired, and she would allow it.

Because it pleased him.

Because she was submissive to her core.

She's also Camila's sister.

The inconvenient reminder gave him pause.

When the time came to talk to Camila, he wouldn't provide details of this encounter. Wouldn't tell her how fucking perfect her sister's pussy felt sliding against his dick, pulsing and dripping and begging to be stuffed.

Fingernails bit into his arms, narrowing his focus on the sexy woman on his lap. She'd waited long enough.

Clutching her waist with both hands, he sank her onto his cock with excruciating slowness. As the suction of her body stretched and clamped around him, he released a low, long groan.

His cock strained so hard and full inside her it was agonizing. He wasn't even buried yet. Could she take him to the hilt?

The question was answered as she slammed downward and ground her clit against his pelvis. He grunted, and she moaned, scratching her nails down his chest.

Then he fucked her, lifting her up and down, pushing into her, and riding the intoxicating waves of bliss. There were no traces of pain in her body's reactions, nothing to dissuade him from deepening his thrusts. His balls tightened, and his hips flexed as he devoured the view of her bouncing, perky tits.

He wasn't a fan of this position, preferred to be on top, but he allowed it for a moment because it gave him unrestricted access to her body. And he took advantage, gliding his hands from her waist to roam her feminine peaks and valleys, plucking at her nipples, and caressing the velvety smoothness of her neck.

The fissured scar across her midsection glowed white against her caramel skin. He traced it, just a steady slide of reverent fingers, but didn't linger. He would demand the full story from her…later.

It was remarkable how well they moved together—the synchronization of their rolling grinds, the give of her body with the force of his thrusts, and the stretch of her pussy as he pounded her inner muscles. It felt as though they'd been lovers for years, like there was a familiarity between them, a uniquely matched closeness he'd never experienced with another woman.

The reason was simple. She yielded to him in a way no one ever had, craved the freedom in relinquishing control. And it was in his nature to take the reins.

With his hands on her hips, he drove inside her, feeding her every ruthless inch and unleashing the last of his restraint. The tip of him hit her so deeply he felt the back of her narrow cunt, groaned, and hammered her again.

Driven by primal instinct and the urge to punish her for making him want her so goddamn badly, he fucked her viciously, mercilessly, gasping and plunging, his fingers digging into bone.

With a whimper, she fell against his chest, pressing her mouth into the bend of his neck, kissing, licking, and panting noisily. Then she leaned up and nibbled his earlobe.

"You feel incredible, American." She nipped and teased the sensitive skin beneath his ear before whispering again, "Are you a doctor?"

"What?" He slowed his thrusts and nudged her back to see her face. "No. Why?"

"Oh, I…" She returned to his neck, distracting him with those soft, hot lips. "I thought I saw you at the hospital."

She was lying. The hospital was miles away, outside of a neighborhood she never left.

"Why are you looking for a doctor?" *In a sex club of all places?* He clutched her shoulder and pushed her up, studying the vastness of her deep brown eyes.

"I'm not—"

He gripped her throat to silence another lie. But something else happened. She didn't struggle, didn't claw at the collar of his unyielding fist, didn't show any of the fight-or-flight responses expected from a woman being choked by a stranger.

Instead, she *melted* into the restraint. Lips parted, eyes dilated, she squeezed her pussy so tightly around him he saw stars. Shudders exploded through his body, and his dick throbbed and swelled so hard it was the only heartbeat he felt.

He couldn't hold back. The robe came off in a frenzy, tossed on the couch at the last second to protect her from the cushion, before he flipped her onto her back and plowed his way inside her.

Goddamn, he was stark raving mad with need and couldn't fuck her hard enough, deep enough. It was raw and beautiful, not just where they were joined or the urgency they shared, but the way she stared up at him, her eyes glazed with desire, awe, and *trust*. She stared at him like she wanted to give him everything, like she wanted him to take it, to liberate her.

He wrapped his fingers around her fragile throat, taking more care this time with her windpipe. Just the right amount of pressure, the illusion of strangulation, and…

There she goes.

Her mouth gaped in a silent scream as she detonated around the stabbing drives of his cock. He swooped in and feasted on the curves of her lips, the warm hidden caverns around her tongue, and the clean wet flavor of her frantic breaths.

She tasted like sin and paradise, a sweet combination that would never tire, never completely sate, because he would always want more. More of her mouth. More of her pussy. More of *this*.

But he'd reached the limit of his self-discipline, his entire body trembling and overdosed on pleasure chemicals. He needed to come.

He released her throat and braced his arms on the cushion to buffer the force of his thrusts. A few more deliriously brutal strokes and he fell still, staring into her dazed eyes as he filled the condom with his spent enthusiasm.

The eruption of orgasm throbbed for long seconds through his cock, attacking every nerve-ending with delicious sparks of electricity. Had he ever come that hard? No way. He felt like he was going to pass out.

But he couldn't. He had to finish this, say what he needed to say, and get this gorgeous, unexpectedly perfect woman reunited with her sister.

Piloting his movements with deliberate care, he peppered her neck with kisses as his fingers moved along her arms to hold her hands against the cushion above her head. Just a light hold, not enough pressure to cause alarm.

Then he leaned back and watched her face. "Listen carefully, Lucia Dias."

Her eyes widened at her name, and he tightened his hold on her wrists.

"Shh. I won't hurt you." He kissed her slack lips. "Ten years ago, your sister escaped her kidnapper. Camila's alive and well and living with Matias in Colombia." He pressed another kiss to her mouth. "She misses you."

She stopped breathing, didn't blink. He released her hands and gave her room. There was no emotion in her expression. Was she in shock?

He removed the condom and sat back on his heels, letting her see the honesty in his eyes as she processed his words.

She lay there for a moment, breathless, unmoving. Then she pushed off the cushion, limbs loose and face relaxed. Her hands slid up his chest, and her body followed. It was strangely sensual and totally not the reaction he expected.

Curling her fingers through his hair, she kissed a path from his mouth to his ear and whispered, "If you want to live, do *not* follow me."

With that, she rose from the couch and strode out of the room.

NINE

Lucia leaned over the toilet in her dark apartment and spit the last of the bile into the bowl. There were traces of blood in her vomit, but it wasn't uncommon. At least tonight's sick spell hadn't been debilitating. Now that her stomach was empty, she felt almost healthy. *Almost.* It would take a while before her heart slowed down. It'd been hammering uncontrollably since she sneaked out of the sex club two hours ago.

Camila's alive and well and living with Matias.

Was it possible? Yes. But not likely. If her sister lived, Tiago would've found her. Because above all, he loved collecting ransoms and had searched long and hard to find someone willing to cough up money for Lucia.

The fact that he hadn't killed Lucia was a mystery that tormented her daily. She was the only exception he'd ever made, which was why she didn't take risks, didn't do anything that would give him a reason to end her life.

Until tonight.

The first thing she did when she exited the club was slip past her guards. They didn't see her leave through the back door, didn't know she hid in a nearby building, waiting for the American.

When he'd finally emerged, she'd tracked him to his apartment. Not just him. Another man had trailed the American, keeping a block of distance between them. They were smart to not walk together — made it easier for them to protect each another. But they weren't smart enough to sense they had a tail.

Once she'd learned where they were staying, she returned to the club, sneaked back in, and walked out the front where her guards expected her.

Then she had no choice but to go home. Any diversion from her routine would've been reported to Tiago. Under no circumstances could he find out Camila might be alive. Even if her sister had the funds to pay a ransom, it would only end in devastation.

Camila's alive and well.

Why would the American lie about that? Was he in contact with Camila? Did her sister know she was alive? If not, she had to stop that man from telling her, whoever the hell he was.

Kissable, commanding, well-endowed, insanely, wildly attractive—he was all those things. Good God, she'd never been fucked like that. The power he'd wielded, the gravelly rumble in his voice, and the poise in which he'd seduced her had turned her into a carnal creature intent on wringing every last drop of seed from his body.

She wasn't even close to being done with him.

The next few minutes was a whirlwind of determination. She flushed the toilet. Brushed her teeth. Kicked off her heels. Pulled on the boots. The Berettas sat snugly between her tailbone and the waistband of her jeans. She would definitely need those.

There were no windows in her apartment. No other doors. Just a mattress, open bathroom and kitchenette, and a closet.

The closet. As quietly as possible, she removed her meager belongings from within it.

It'd been a couple years since she'd slipped her guards, and she was about to do it for the second time tonight.

God help me.

The closet now empty, she stepped inside and dragged her fingers down the back corner, prying at the hidden seam.

Years ago, she cut a narrow passage in the wall and used it to sneak out. She was more tenacious then. Braver. But that was before the gruesome incident with that poor doctor. Her chest tightened.

She wouldn't make the same mistakes. Wouldn't leave the neighborhood. Wouldn't try to make contact with the outside world. She was just going to pay the American a visit, threaten him at gunpoint, and would be home by dawn.

The wood paneling creaked as she slid it open. The worried whine of a dog sounded on the other side, and she hurried through, squeezing between the gap in the vertical wall supports and stepping into her neighbor's closet.

Franchesca didn't own much before she was robbed, but as Lucia crept into the dark one-room unit, the space looked cruelly bare.

A furry ball on short legs scurried toward her. She scooped up the dog before it started barking and patted its head.

"Franchesca?" she whispered, approaching the sleeping silhouette on the mattress.

When her neighbor popped her head up, Lucia handed over the dog and held a finger against her lips, demanding silence.

They had a long-standing agreement. Lucia would protect Franchesca when she could, and Franchesca wouldn't ask questions when Lucia came and went through the hidden passage.

Her neighbor was a passive woman and didn't have enemies — except for a dirtbag father, who came around every couple months to beat her. While Lucia did favors for her, like getting the dog back tonight, it didn't mean she trusted Franchesca. If the price was right, Franchesca would sell Lucia down the river.

With a steadying breath, she left the woman in bed and strode toward the rear of the room.

Lucia's apartment sat at the intersecting point of a T-shaped complex, surrounded by other units on three sides. But Franchesca's apartment didn't, and she had a back door. Lucky for Lucia, her guards didn't watch the rear alley.

She slipped out the back, and fifteen minutes later, stood in front of another apartment door in an unlit corridor. This was where her plan met its first obstacle.

The apartment building was a shit hole, much like the rest of the slum. She'd expected a flimsy lock, one she could pick without making a sound.

This lock had been upgraded with a heavy-duty, electronic-looking thing. *Goddammit!*

It'd been added recently, given the shiny steel casing. Definitely not the kind of hardware one would find in a shanty town.

Her pulse sped up. Who the fuck were these guys?

Deep breath.

She could shoot off the deadbolt, rush in, and take them by surprise. Gunshots rang out all night long, so the neighbors wouldn't bat an eye at the racket.

Or, since there wasn't a peep hole, she could knock and let one of them open it to the barrel of her 9mm.

Option two was less dramatic, so she drew one of the Berettas from her waistband and rapped on the door with her knuckles.

She expected to wait a while or maybe hear an apprehensive *Who's there?* on the other side. But the lock turned within seconds.

Were they stupid?

Then she saw it. Wedged in a crack high on the door frame was a tiny black disk.

A camera.

The door opened, and with a racing heart, she trained the gun on a chiseled bare chest. Shifting her gaze, she followed the stretch of tight boxer briefs to carved packs of muscle and inched upward to a dark trimmed beard, a toothpick lolling from smirking lips, a mean-looking facial scar, and finally, the sharpened slits of silver eyes.

So this was the American's companion. Despite the welted laceration across his cheek, his smile was arresting, and he ranked pretty high up there on the handsome scale. But there was an echo of something in his eyes, something chilling and fractured, like a frozen scream in a haunted basement.

"Don't make a sound." She locked her outstretched arm and rested a finger against the trigger of the gun. "Do exactly what I say."

"I appreciate the spirit in that," he drawled with an American accent. "But when it comes to orders, I'm a giver, not a taker."

He motioned for her to enter the unlit apartment. She didn't move.

"I can see how that's worked out for you." She flicked her gaze between his scars—a bullet wound on his shoulder and a knife wound across his cheek. "I won't hesitate to put another bullet in you."

"Suit yourself." With a shrug, he retreated into the apartment and flipped a light switch. "I'm Van, by the way."

The fluorescents flickered on, illuminating a sleeper sofa converted into a bed, an open kitchen, a bedroom door, and leaning against the frame of that door was the man who had fucked her so soundly she still felt him in her teeth and her legs and everywhere in between.

Head tipped down, he stared at her from beneath heavy brows. His arms folded across his chest, with one sleeved in tattoos. Like his friend, he was clad only in fitted boxer briefs, his short hair disheveled and eyes sleepy.

She must've woken them. Neither man was armed, and the weapons they carried earlier were out of reach on the kitchen table. There were probably more firearms, but hers was out and ready.

Drawing the second Beretta from her back, she trained a gun on each of them, stepped into the apartment, and kicked the door shut behind her.

The one with the toothpick— *Van*—tilted his head as he watched her approach. "I expected you to walk funny. With more of a limp." At her confused look, he said, "As small as you are, it wouldn't have been easy to take Tate's beast of a cock."

Tate. The name fit him, and his cock… Her inner muscles clenched in memory, reawakening the delicious soreness there.

"How was it?" Van asked. "Did he ram it inside you with all the ferocity and pain it deserves?"

"Boundaries," Tate growled. "Heed them."

"Did the ol' dog at least make you come?" Van asked conversationally, as if she weren't aiming a bullet at his chest.

"That's enough." Tate lifted his chin in her direction. "Lucia, lower the weapons."

"Who are you?" She steadied both guns, ticking her gaze between them.

Tate straightened from the doorframe and slowly closed the distance. His strides were slow but long, eating up the floor with muscled nonchalance. But there was nothing casual in the way he looked at her, those blue eyes seeking her most intimate places and setting her on fire from the inside out. He looked at her as though he were recalling the feel of being sheathed inside her, like he wanted to feel her again.

She took great pleasure in the knowledge that such a ridiculously handsome man was attracted to her. But the stupid, girly, instantaneous attachment she felt for him was an embarrassing sentiment, so very un-Lucia-like. What was her deal with this guy?

It had just been sex, really fucking good sex, with a beautiful stranger. She wasn't here for a repeat.

She was here to save her sister from more heartache.

"Who are you?" she asked again.

Two feet away, Tate pressed his chiseled chest against the barrel of the gun. "I'm Camila's best friend."

He could've been lying, but there wasn't a trace of deceit on his stunning face.

Everything inside her cried with joy. Not only was Camila alive, she had a strong, protective friend who cared for her enough to track down her only family.

It was more than Lucia could've ever wanted for Camila, and she felt the sudden need to sit down. Hard. But her arms and legs remained stubbornly locked.

"What about him?" She gestured at Van with the gun she trained on him.

"He's...uh..." Tate gripped his nape, stalling, holding something back.

"He's what?" Her stomach tightened.

Van lifted his chin, giving her the full force of his icy eyes. "I'm the one who kidnapped your sister."

TEN

Confusion spiked through Lucia, followed by furious understanding. This scary-looking, scarface motherfucker abducted her sweet, innocent, seventeen-year-old sister.

"What did you do to her?" She directed eleven years of pain into the scalding glare she aimed at Van.

A day hadn't passed without the loss, the torment, and the dire unknowns that surrounded Camila's disappearance. She hadn't saved Camila from being taken, but dammit, she could avenge her, right now, with the squeeze of a trigger.

"You won't shoot him," Tate said quietly, his chest pushing against the other gun barrel. "Think about it. He captured Camila and me with the intent to sell us into slavery. Yet I'm here. Camila's with Matias, and Van's still alive. There's a good reason for that."

"He captured *you*?"

Tate nodded, his eyes growing heavy and dark. "Six years ago."

"Put down the guns, little girl," Van said, "and I'll confess all my sins."

She held her ground, seething with venom. "How dare you?"

"The weapons, Lucia." Tate held out a palm. "Now."

The command in his deep voice was meant to subdue her, but it was the compassion softening his eyes that urged her rage to creep back into the darkness and go dormant once again.

It took longer to lower the guns, but after a few calming breaths, she placed them in his huge hand. "Don't make me regret this." *Please don't abuse my trust.*

He set the weapons aside and twined his fingers around hers.

Then he steered her toward the bedroom. "Give us a minute, Van."

In the bedroom, he left the door open and directed her to sit on the foot of the bed, out of view from the main room.

"We'll tell you everything you want to know. Every secret. Every crime." He pulled on a pair of jeans, zipped, and left the button undone. "But first, I want to make something clear."

She stared at him, mesmerized. How could she not be? It wasn't just his sculpted perfection. There was something extraordinary beneath the physical strength. Something in the tenderness of his touch, the vigilant way he watched her, the gentle inflections he wove into his commands. As if no matter how damaged or sick she was, he would still hold her hand, hold her close, and let her lean on him as hard and as long as she needed. He was that person.

She never had a person and didn't know what to do with the warm feelings it soaked into her bones.

He perched on the mattress beside her and touched her face, studying her eyes.

"Tonight was..." He rested his forehead against hers and inhaled deeply. "I'm not going to label it. Just know that I didn't fuck you as part of some scheme. I went to the club, willing to do exactly that to get you alone. To talk to you. But once I had you..."

He edged closer and dragged his nose along her neck, sniffing her. It was such a primal gesture, animalistic, and the reverberating groan in his throat produced a groan of her own.

Sliding her cheek against his, she indulged in the scratch of his whiskers. His proximity instilled her with an addictive sense of security— something she didn't even know she craved until now.

"When I was inside you," he breathed against her ear, "it was real and natural and just us. Understand?"

She nodded, her throat too tight for sound as she floated to an imaginary hinterland where *everythings* and *forevermores* glittered like stars in the sky.

"Sex between us... That was a straightforward thing. But everything else..." He leaned back and rubbed the crease between his eyebrows. "There are complications, histories."

"My sister?"

"Yes. And Tiago Badell, the work you do for him. We have a lot to discuss."

The mention of Tiago made her wonder how Tate found her, but more importantly... "Does Camila know I'm alive?"

"No. We need to talk about that, too." He clasped her hand and stood, leading her to the sitting room. "Did you run into trouble on your way back?"

"My way back...?" She stopped and released his hand, her mind spinning to understand his meaning. "Wait. You knew I followed you earlier?"

"Of course. And I knew you had to return to the club where your guards were waiting. How did you dodge them again to get back here?"

She could tell him. She could lay bare all her secrets and ugly truths and hope she was right about his compassion. But that required trust — something he had to earn.

She left the question adrift and stepped along the window in the main room. Below, two of Tiago's guards stood across the street from her apartment door, smoking cigarettes and shooting the shit.

Could they not see her up here? She flattened a hand against the window, studying the glass.

"There's a film on it." Tate stood so close to her back his breath stirred her hair. "It makes the apartment look dark from the outside."

No wonder she hadn't noticed movement in the window when she came and went in the alley. "How long have you been watching me?"

"Ten days. The man I hired to find you watched you for weeks."

"Tell me about that, about your relationship with Camila, all of it." Shifting away from his intoxicating presence, she sat on the unfolded sleeper sofa and settled in. "Start at the beginning."

"It started with me." Van, now dressed in athletic pants and a shirt, brought her a glass of tequila, which she refused. "My father was the Police Chief of Austin. But in the criminal underground, he was known as Mr. E." He swallowed the tequila and set the glass on the coffee table. "He trafficked sex slaves, and I was the kidnapper and trainer for the operation."

She sat motionless and silent as he outlined seven years of blackmail, kidnapping, submission training, and rape. He explained how Liv Reed shot him the same night she killed Mr. E, how the slaves escaped over the years, and the roles Camila, Tate, and Matias played in that.

It was agonizing to hear how her sister had been forced to kneel, beg beneath a whip, and suck his dick. But when he confirmed he never raped her, Lucia sagged with relief. Then he spoke about the ten weeks he imprisoned Tate.

"I'm attracted to submissives. Women *and* men." Van stood with his back to the window, moving only his lips around an ever-present toothpick. "As you already know, Tate is neither gay nor submissive. I preyed on that. Used it to humiliate him, hurt him, and yes, I fucked him countless times while he fought uselessly in his restraints."

As Van delivered his monotone confession, Tate smoked one cigarette after another without interjecting a word. She peeked at him, expecting to see fury in his eyes. There were remnants of that in the blue depths, but there were so many other emotions twisting and turning at the forefront. Unease, turmoil, distrust... But she might've glimpsed forgiveness there, too.

He'd had six years to come to terms with what Van had done to him. There must've been some level of resolution, because here they were, together. During Van's account of the events, he admitted he wanted to help Tate and Camila any way he could. Even so, the unfinished tension between him and Tate electrocuted the air.

Another thing she noticed... If Van was bisexual, why didn't he look at Tate with sexual interest? Tate was so damn eye-catching even a straight man would give him a second glance.

Though now that she thought about it, Van didn't look at her with desire, either. Maybe he had a partner or spouse he was faithful to? If so, he didn't mention it. Not that she blamed him, given her connection to Tiago.

At some point during the conversation, nausea and muscle aches crept in. Her earlier bout of vomiting had given her a momentary reprieve, but it didn't always keep the symptoms at bay.

Come what may, she hid the pain and turned to Tate. "If my sister helped rescue all the slaves, does that mean she saved you, too?"

"Yes." His eyes caught fire. "She's fucking fierce, Lucia. Brave and beautiful and determined. You would be so proud of her."

As he outlined the four years that followed Mr. E's death, his expression grew brighter and more alert. His entire existence seemed to be centered on Camila and her vigilante group, the Freedom Fighters. He'd lived with her, protected her, and even helped Matias reunite with her.

With restless strides, he paced through the room, expounding on Camila's fight against slavery and the sacrifices she made. After all these years, she and Lucia were still considered missing persons. But Camila had the impenetrable shield of a cartel in front of her, keeping her safe from enemies and invisible to the law.

That explained why Tiago never found her.

And holy shit, Matias was the capo of the Restrepo cartel? He was such a good-looking man in his teens. And one-hundred-percent, head-over-heels in love with Camila. Add to that his powerful position and Lucia couldn't be happier they were together.

Then Tate told her about her own abduction—how and why Matias' brother orchestrated it, her parents' involvement, and their ultimate death at Matias' hand.

She waited for the tears to come, but she'd cried enough for them when she was taken. They'd sold both of their daughters into slavery. She would mourn them no more.

"You okay?" Tate asked.

"Yeah. How did you find me?"

He detailed the efforts Matias had made to track her to the crash in Peru, the investigators he himself had hired, and finally Cole Hartman, the man who located her here.

When all the hard questions were answered, she asked him easy things—*Is Camila happy? Healthy? Still as ornery as ever?*—and he was all too eager to answer. The adoration he felt for Camila was as clear as his crystal blue eyes. He spoke of her as if he were eternally bound to her and wouldn't want it any other way. They shared a connection that had nothing to do with Lucia. He was here, doing what he thought was right, not for Lucia, but for Camila.

Realization gut-punched her. "You love her."

"I do."

It stung. Like a thousand angry bees stung. Even though she'd only just met him and her jealousy didn't make a lick of sense, she felt what she felt and there wasn't a damn thing she could do about it.

Still, she couldn't stop herself from pointing out, "She loves Matias. Always has." She gentled her voice. "That's not going to change, Tate."

"I know." His tone matched hers despite the flare of persistence in his eyes.

Her stomach chose that moment to cramp painfully, but she didn't let the illness reveal itself, didn't show a hint of discomfort on her face. "Do you intend to win her heart with news of my survival?"

"No. And let's talk about that—*your survival*. I know Tiago's men pulled you from the crash and brought you here. You're not locked up, and you've already demonstrated your ability to evade his guards. Why are you still in this godforsaken place?"

Her defenses bristled. "Venezuela is a beautiful country. The landscapes alone… Have you even seen the forests and the mountains and the beaches? What about the birds? There's like fourteen-hundred bird species here. Oh, and the dolphins. Have you seen the Amazon river dolphins?"

She hadn't seen any of those things, but often when she sat alone in her apartment at night, she imagined what it would be like to leave the slum and become an explorer. Or maybe go to a university and become one of those scientists who discovered new plants that cured diseases.

"You're not here for the damn dolphins." He prowled toward her and leaned down, bracing his hands on the couch bed and caging her in. "You're going to leave with us. I'll take you straight to Camila and—"

"No." Panic rose, and she pushed at his chest, unable to move him. "I can't."

"Why the hell not?"

"If Camila thinks I'm dead…" Anguish swelled against the backs of her eyes, magnified by a blooming migraine. "It needs to stay that way."

"That's not gonna happen." He straightened, scanning the room until his gaze landed on a burner phone. "I'll call her right now so you can tell her yourself."

"Listen to me, goddammit." She leapt from the couch and grabbed his arm, digging her nails into muscle. "She already mourned my death once. Please, if you love her, you won't put her through that again."

"What are you saying?" His voice took on a lethal bite, making her shiver.

"You can't tell her I'm alive." She strode toward her weapons on the kitchen table.

With a disbelieving laugh, he stayed on her heels, breathing down her neck. "You need to give me a lot more than that, sweetheart."

"I'm living on borrowed time." She reached for her guns.

He knocked her hand away, and in the next breath, he had her pinned against the wall with a fist wrapped around her windpipe.

"You answer to me now. You're under *my* protection." He put his face in hers, his lips so close she smelled toothpaste on his breath. "You will leave with us—gagged, blindfolded, shackled, whatever it takes." He glanced at Van. "You good with that?"

"Sure." Van reclined on the couch bed, with an arm bent behind his head.

"What's it going to be, Lucia? The easy way? Or…" He tightened his fingers against her throat, cutting her airflow. "The hard way?"

She couldn't breathe, couldn't pry his grip away. The urgent need for oxygen grew stronger and more desperate, but did it really matter? She was alone in the darkness save for the strong grip around her throat. She couldn't think of a better way to die than fading beneath his beautifully ferocious eyes. But those eyes were traps, the possessive gleam in them compelling her mouth to soundlessly form two words she'd held back.

"What?" He yanked his hand away, freeing her. "Say that again."

"I'm dying." She wheezed, clutching her throat as her attention snagged on the paling sky beyond the window. "Shit, I have to go."

"Dying?" He exchanged a startled look with Van then scanned her up and down, pausing on her midsection. "How? Is it your injury from the crash in Peru?"

"I don't know." It was a terrible truth, one she should've figured out by now. "But if I'm not where I'm supposed to be by dawn, I won't get my medicine. And if I don't get that injection, I'll be in respiratory failure by lunchtime."

He went still. So still the air around him thinned and charged, sweeping over her like a blanket of static and raising the hairs on her arms.

He looked floored, volatile, teetering on the brink of eruption.

"Tate—"

"You're telling me you're terminally ill." Denial flexed at the edge of his voice.

"Yes."

"But you don't know what's wrong with you?"

"No, I… I don't know the medical diagnosis."

"How can you not—?" He swiped a hand down his face and glared at her. "Tell me the symptoms."

"I don't have time for this."

His eyes were as deep and turbulent as the ocean, his lips perfectly arched despite the pressed line of disapproval. Muscles twitched across his bare chest and broadcasted his impatience. But it was his demeanor that demanded her attention.

He rendered her immobile simply by standing there, looking utterly self-possessed and cavalier, like a saintly king or a gallant warrior. Or a sociopath. Whatever it was that made him so damn compelling seemed to glow like a backdrop for his powerful legs, broad chest, and brutally gorgeous features.

He was strong enough, assertive enough to take her burdens so she wouldn't have to carry them by herself. It was his presence that spoke to her, commanded her at a cellular level, and she obeyed.

"The symptoms vary, but what I experience most is chronic nausea, abdominal pain, hematemesis, migraines, bradycardia, tremors, ataxia, seizures, muscle paralysis…" She released a breath of exhausted pain.

"Fucking Christ." He lowered his head and squeezed the bridge of his nose. Then he was staring at her again, his expression dangerous. "Are you experiencing any of that tonight?"

"Some, yeah."

"Told you she was too thin," Van said from the couch.

Tate tossed him a warning glare and softened his eyes as he looked back at her. "Badell gives you medicine? It helps?"

"His doctors developed a treatment. The injection is the only thing keeping me alive."

"Did *he* tell you that?"

"Yes, and I know what you're thinking." With trembling hands, she snatched her guns from the table and holstered them in her waistband. "Sometimes he lets me see just how close to death I can get. I've tasted it, Tate. Felt its icy breath suck the life from my body. Have you ever experienced that? The abject, black void of extinction? The dismal nothingness? There's no bright light at the end of the tunnel. There's no fucking tunnel. When your heart stops, there's *nothing*."

"You're leaving with me, Lucia. Right now. We'll go directly to the hospital."

"I'll be dead within hours. Long before they can diagnose me."

His nostrils flared. "Badell knows what's wrong with you?"

"Of course. As long as he keeps my condition a secret and the antidote locked in his safe, I can't leave."

"Have you tried to find—?" He swore under his breath. "That's why you asked me if I was a doctor."

Tiago owned every medical practitioner in the neighborhood. Moonlighting at the sex club twice a month was her only opportunity to furtively search for visiting doctors. She just hadn't had any luck.

"If I had more time…" She glanced at the window, where the graying sky signaled the coming of dawn. "I'd tell you all about my attempts to escape, my failed visit with a doctor, and the bloodshed that followed."

She strode toward the door, opened it, and wobbled on the threshold.

"You can't fix this, Tate. Go home. And tell my sister…" Keeping her back to the room, she swallowed the heartache shredding her voice. "Tell her I'm already dead."

Forcing one foot in front of the other, she walked out and closed the door behind her.

ELEVEN

The door shut, slamming Tate's pulse into overdrive.

"Goddammit." He spun, searching for shoes, a gun, his phone... "She's not walking away from me again."

"She just did." Van threw a bullet-resistant shirt at him and shoved on his own shoes.

"I need you to stay here." He dressed at breakneck speeds and grabbed a burner phone. "Watch the guards from the window and call me if there's trouble."

"You're going to get yourself killed." Van gripped the back of Tate's waistband and wedged a gun against his butt crack.

"Dude, get your dick beaters away from me." Twisting away, he moved the weapon from his ass to the front of his jeans.

"Dick beaters?"

"Your fucking hands, man. We're gonna talk about boundaries when I get back."

"Are you sure you want to put the gun there?" With the arch of an impish brow, Van stared at Tate's groin. "It would be a shame if you shoot your dick off."

The thought made his balls shrivel, but it was a helluva lot quicker to draw a gun from the front than to reach around the back.

"My dick isn't your concern." He crouched to lace his boots. "I'm going to follow her, find out how she enters her apartment, and come right back."

Cole had said there was only one way in and out of her unit, but that couldn't be right. How did she slip past the guards at her door?

She had too many secrets, but he'd find a way to unwrap her, crack her open, and expose all her mysteries.

I'm dying.

That one had hit him sideways, and he still felt off-balance and outraged from the blow. And doubtful. She seemed pretty fucking resigned to die, but he wanted proof, validation from a professional, someone *not* connected to Badell. There were ways to go about that, but the logistics would be tricky and could put her at risk.

"Now we know why Cole couldn't find medical records on her." He tied the second boot and stood.

"Badell figured out how to hold her captive," Van said, his voice eerily calm, "without locks or shackles."

"Doesn't mean I can't get her out."

Maybe he could get a blood sample and ship it to a lab? Could it be that easy? *Not likely.*

Gun, phone, armored shirt… He had everything he needed and raced to the door, pausing with his hand on the knob. "Did you record her symptoms?"

"I captured the entire conversation." Van held up a small recording device. "What about you? Any luck with the tracker?"

"I stuck one on each of her Berettas when she handed them to me." He opened the door and scanned the vacant hall.

The trackers—courtesy of Cole—were also listening devices. A spy camera on her body would've been ideal, especially since Tate had no choice but to let her return to Badell this morning, but wearable cameras were bulky, and the battery life was shit.

Putting audio transmitters on her weapons was risky enough. If someone discovered them, Lucia would pay the price.

"Try not to die," Van called after him as he closed the door.

Down the stairs, out the main entrance, and along the empty street, he sprinted to catch up with her. The half-light minutes just before dawn was the sleepiest time in Caracas. There were fewer gunshots. No passing motorists. No people anywhere. Just the pound of his boots hitting concrete and the heave of his lungs.

He rounded the first corner of his building, ran a block toward her apartment, and slowed at the next bend. If he turned right, he'd walk into her alley and the guards who waited for her.

Removing his phone, he pulled up the tracking program and pinpointed her location. She'd gone around the block? Why? Maybe to circle the rear of her apartment complex to enter a side door? But how would she get in from there? He'd seen the blueprints of the building and her one-room unit. The front door was the only way into her living quarters.

He followed her moving location, veered left, and ran two blocks out of the way, which spit him out at the rear of her *T*-shaped building. Sticking to the shadows, he kept his senses sharp and aware. But he couldn't watch his back while sweeping the shadows in front of him.

And that was how he ended up with the unmistakable press of a gun against the back of his head.

He froze, spine twitching and pulse thrashing in his ears. For a hopeful second, he thought Lucia was behind him, aiming a Beretta with irritation twisting her gorgeous face.

Couldn't be her, though. This gunslinger was a mouth-breather, hacking air with a scratchy throat and reeking of cigarettes.

The string of words that followed were spat in Spanish. A man's voice. A tall man, given the height and direction of sound. His impatience was evident in the jab of the gun against Tate's head.

Each shout and jab made his muscles tense to react, to knock the man on his ass. But he forced himself to remain still and think through the best course of action.

He'd practiced this exact scenario with Cole before they left the States. A little movement to the side, just a quick-second shift would remove his head from the path of the bullet. But he wouldn't have time to pause after that. It had to be a single flow of motion. Shift to the side, reach back for the gun while dropping, turning, drawing his own gun, and firing without hesitation.

Christ, it was a shot in the dark. Literally. The odds of turning before he ate a bullet weren't in his favor, but it was the only shot he had.

Breathe in. Breathe out.

Then he moved.

A gunshot rang out—a single jarring bang that resounded in his chest, disorientating him. He blinked at the gun in his hand, at the finger that never made it to the trigger.

The scent of blood clotted the air, so sharp and acrid he could taste it. Was it coming from him? His stomach turned to ice as he ran a numb hand over his head, seeking a wound.

It took him a second to register the overweight man at his feet, sprawled in a dark puddle of gore and leaking from a hole in his temple.

Whoever fired that shot had impeccable aim and could've just as easily hit Tate.

A chill swept over him, and he quickly put his back against the building, surveying the perimeter. No movement. No apparent witnesses. The shooter had to have been Van or Lucia.

Another minute passed before the slender form of a woman emerged from behind a car across the street. *Lucia.*

With a heavy exhale, he seated the gun in the front of his jeans, right next to the delicious ache clenching in his groin. Because fuck him, she was all legs, perky tits, and fearless beauty charging toward him like a warrior princess.

There was nothing sexier than a woman with a gun. But Lucia was more than that. Strong, stunning, and gutsy as all hell, she was badass personified. And to think, she was sick. *Dying.* She didn't let it show in the square of her shoulders or the jut of her chin. She looked for all the world like she was bulletproof. Impenetrable.

Except he'd penetrated her, impaled her deeply and thoroughly, and fuck if he didn't want to do it again.

By the time she reached him, he was so goddamn hard he had to step back and fold his arms across his chest to stop himself from falling on her like a rabid animal.

"Are you pissed?" She crouched beside the body and rifled through the pockets.

"Pissed?" He lowered his arms, dumbfounded. "You saved my life."

"No, I didn't." Pocketing the dead man's money, she tossed the empty wallet on the ground. "You moved your head. His bullet would've missed you. With your gun out and the way you turned so fast, you had the shot." She glared at the corpse. "Sorry I took that from you. I've wanted this kill for years."

"Why? Who was he?"

"One of Tiago's stooges." She rose to her full height and spat on the body. "A serial rapist."

The pain simmering beneath her voice triggered his protective instincts.

"He hurt you?" He gripped her arm.

"Not anymore." Pulling away from him, she strode down the alley behind her apartment building.

He wished he would've been the one to shoot the fucker. He'd killed before, right alongside Lucia's sister, and enjoyed every second of it. Evidently, he had an unquenchable thirst for the blood of the guilty.

"What about the body?" he asked her retreating back.

"Leave it."

He trailed after her, lengthening his strides to catch up. "The police—"

"They can't touch me." She set a moderate pace, her steps even and eyes straight ahead. "Tiago, on the other hand, would punish me for killing one of his men."

His jaw clenched. "Punish you how?"

"Death." She lifted a shoulder and veered around a dumpster in the narrow alley. "But hey, I didn't do it, right? I mean, I've been in my apartment all night with guards on my door."

"Jesus, Lucia." He tipped his head up, probing the dark second-floor windows. "Someone might've seen you."

"Maybe, but it's their word against that of his two best guards and his favorite girl."

His favorite girl?

What kind of relationship did she have with Badell? When he gave her medicine, what did she have to do in return? The only information Tate had was the video of her at the compound and Cole's words.

Her job is to inflict physical and emotional pain. Torture. Sometimes she rapes them.

If she raped the victims, why did she have such a grudging reaction to the rapist she just killed? It didn't make sense, and he desperately needed to understand.

It would be daybreak in about ten minutes, and they'd reached a bend in the alley where the three arms of her building came together. Her apartment would be right there.

He didn't know how she would get in from back here, but first, he needed to settle this one thing.

Grabbing her waist mid-stride, he swung her around and held her against him, chest to chest. "How are you his favorite girl?"

She stared into his eyes for a span of several heartbeats, her face an emotionless mask.

"Does he fuck you? Or force you?" He wrapped his fingers around her neck and forged his voice with steel. He wasn't angry with her. He was angry *for* her. "Answer me."

A muscle bounced in her cheek. Then slowly, reluctantly, her aloofness shuddered and broke away. Uncertainty creased her forehead. Disquiet twitched her lashes. Concession sighed from her parted lips.

"You're possessive." She raised a tentative hand and traced the corner of his mouth.

His lips felt a little weak and a lot hungry. "I told you you're under my protection—"

"I don't mean *me* specifically. You're possessive as a general rule." She moved her finger along the seam of his mouth, exploring with achingly sweet curiosity. "It's a quality I've never given much thought to...until now. It looks good on you. Like really fucking good."

Her breath whispered against his face, weaving with the flutters of her featherlight touch. A touch he felt all the way down to his balls.

She caressed a path across his cheek and slid her fingers through his hair, all the while inching closer. Hovering her lips just out of reach. Leaving a hairbreadth between *stay* and *go*. A sliver between *yes* and *no*.

It all blurred together as he leaned in with single-minded focus. Maybe it was just the perfect combination of feminine seduction—the sultry look in her eyes, the drugging feel of her touch, the warm scent of her skin—but he felt buzzed, utterly drunk on this woman, and he needed to kiss her like he needed air.

Only she shifted back. He chased her mouth, and she evaded again, blocking the next advance with a finger against his lips.

He reached up to remove her hand, but her words stopped him.

"I've never had sex with Tiago Badell." She didn't give him time to respond as she lifted on tiptoes and pressed her lips next to the finger she held against his mouth.

Then she stepped back, pushing against his chest until he released her waist. "Goodbye, Tate."

Oh, fuck that. He gave a humorless chuckle. "Can't get rid of me that easily. I'm walking you home—"

"And you did. Thank you." She turned to the nearest apartment door and removed a key from her pocket.

Given the vicinity of the door and his recollection of the building's blueprints, she was accessing her next-door neighbor's unit.

She unlocked the door, and the yap of a tiny dog on the other side confirmed it. There must've been a hidden cut through between the two apartments?

He moved to follow her in, but she flattened a hand against his chest.

"I really love how protective you are." Her voice was gentle, but it felt like she was fighting tooth and nail to hold herself together. "Camila's lucky to have you."

Her face was ghastly pale, and her legs trembled to keep her upright. Christ, she didn't look well at all. It killed him to let her out of his sight, but he didn't have the medicine she needed. She had to go to Badell.

"I'll be here when you get back."

"No. You need to go." She met and held his eyes as the first light of dawn reflected in hers. "Take care of Camila. Please."

Then she shut the door in his face.

TWELVE

Lucia must've looked like death by the time she arrived at the compound, because Tiago gave her a narrowed glance and immediately led her to his room.

The short walk wasn't short enough. She kept her expression impassive while dragging her listless feet and fighting the urge to retch. She hadn't eaten since Tiago's dinner last night, but her stomach buckled anyway, trying to empty its emptiness.

Her misery had long ago passed the point where she thought she couldn't endure more. Knowing her days were numbered broke her even further. With each staggering step, she heard the distant beat of her dying heart, felt it weakening, fading, taking her with it. Then she blacked out.

When she came to, she was being carried, undressed, and separated from her weapons, her consciousness flickering in and out through it all.

She stirred at the familiar prick of a needle. As the medicine trickled warmth through her thigh, she knew she'd live to loathe another day.

Tiago was there, holding her on his lap and stroking the edges of her panties—the only thing she was permitted to wear in his room. It was always the same. Injection in the morning. Dinner with Tiago at night. Torture, ransom, and debilitating pain scattered throughout the day.

"Why are you keeping me alive?" she murmured.

He set the syringe aside and smoothed his hands along her body. "I enjoy you."

The erection swelling against her backside said his enjoyment was sexual. *Without sex.*

"I don't have much time left." She rested her head back against his shoulder and closed her eyes. "What's wrong with me, Tiago?"

He cupped one of her bare breasts and rolled the nipple between his fingers. "You're perfect."

Over the course of a thousand mornings, in his room, on his lap, she'd grown indifferent to his touch. The caress of his hands, the absence of her clothes, the arousal in his voice—it was all just part of her daily medicine.

But this morning was different.

The feel of his fingers sliding across her skin set her teeth on edge. She didn't want him touching her, resting his gaze on her nudity, or telling her she was perfect.

What she wanted was Tate. Him on top of her, around her, locking her in the circle of his arms, and keeping everyone else out. Just him and her and the heady glide of their lips.

She'd said goodbye to him, but he wasn't going anywhere. She was certain he wouldn't leave until he got what he came for.

Her.

Not a future with her. No, his dream of the future was Camila.

Lucia just wanted a future. Period.

They were both fucked.

"Tiago?"

"Hm?" He nuzzled her neck.

"What if there's a cure your doctors aren't aware of? If you'd let me see another physician—"

"Did you know seventy percent of plants with anticancer properties exist only in the Amazon?"

Her blood turned to ice. "Cancer?"

"You don't have cancer." He slid a hand to her collarbone and traced the shape of it. "I'm feeling generous this morning. Would you like to hear a story?"

She doubted anything he told her would bring her comfort, but information was a weapon. "Yes. Please."

"My father was a pharmacist and an expert in medicinal botany. When he died, I brought his medical team here, to work for me."

Why would his doctors go from saving people to assisting him with kidnappings and torture? Maybe they were never the *saving* kind of doctors.

Except they'd saved *her.*

"The rainforest," Tiago said, "produces thousands of variations of seeds, berries, roots, leaves, bark, and flowers that have healing attributes. Only a small percentage have been discovered by modern man. But as you know, my doctors aren't modern."

The medical team of four men were in their sixties and seventies, with thick indigenous accents native to a land she couldn't place. Their skin, the darkest pigmentation she'd ever seen, bore picturesque scarification — different designs and words than that of Tiago's, but the welts appeared to have been cut with the same brutality. They reminded her of an ancient civilization, rich in culture and ceremony.

"My doctors know what ails you." He dragged the backs of his fingers across her abdomen. "And they've developed the only known antidote for it. Keep that in mind next time you try to seek a second opinion."

She already assumed he had the only antidote and often wondered if her illness was a byproduct of the crash in Peru. While chained in the back of a truck with a dozen other slaves, she'd felt the jolting, crashing fall as they tumbled off a cliff, heard the twisting of metal and agonized screams, and smelled the blood. After that, she remembered nothing.

The year that followed had been a drug-induced haze of surgeries and coma-like sleep. She had a scar across her abdomen but didn't know what damage lay beneath the marred skin.

The strange part was that her illness didn't surface until three years ago — seven years *after* the last surgery. Maybe the fix Tiago's doctors put in her was failing? The medicine erased the pain, but she couldn't go longer than twenty-four hours without another injection.

"What did you learn at the sex club?" Tiago asked.

"It was a quiet night." She'd been too busy riding a blue-eyed god to overhear the conversations around her.

"Tell me about the men you were with."

"There was just one. One of my usuals." The lie floated effortlessly off her tongue.

"Did he fuck you here?" He feathered his touch across her lips.

"Yes."

"And here?" His hand spread over the front of her panties, his fingers pressing against the satin crotch.

She nodded.

"I envy him." His voice, scratchy with desire, rasped at her ear.

Such an odd thing to say, since he didn't do more than touch her. Did he ever have sex? She never saw him with a lover and knew he didn't allow anyone else in his room. Yet he was so easily aroused and constantly hard.

He was also distrustful and paranoid and never took unnecessary risk. Maybe he thought sex was too risky. It was, in a way. At the peak of climax, when the body let go and the mind lost all reason, a man was at his most vulnerable.

If she could lure him to the edge of orgasm, she'd use his

distraction to stab her thumbs into his eyes and crush the sockets. It was a plausible way to kill a man, right?

Problem was, after spending eleven years with him, he hadn't shown a single moment of weakness.

Twenty minutes had passed since she received the injection, and the pain had retreated into the sickly place inside her. Her heart rate found a normal tempo, and feeling returned to her legs.

Tiago, who was always attuned to her state of health, nudged her off his lap. "Let's go see to our newest victim."

Her insides twisted anew.

He led her to the hall and waited as she dressed. When she tucked the Berettas in her jeans, she let her hands linger on the grips.

She could shoot him. His guards would fire immediately, probably before she even squeezed the trigger. But maybe, just maybe she could get a shot off before she died.

It was a hopeless paradox. On one hand, she wanted to die, ached to end the endless misery. On the other, if one of his guards aimed a gun at him, she wouldn't hesitate to shoot the traitor to protect Tiago.

If Tiago died, she couldn't access his safe, didn't know how to locate his doctors, and wouldn't be able to find a cure before her organs failed. His death would bring the onset of hers, and as much as she wanted that, there was a brighter, stronger yearning inside her.

She wanted to live.

Her contradictory train of thought circled back to the armed guards. If she were willing to shoot his men to save Tiago's life, the same must've been true for them. This wasn't an operation rooted in loyalty. She suspected Tiago's men were indebted to him somehow, and like her, it was in their best interest to keep him alive.

Tiago's gaze fell to the vicinity of her hands on the Berettas at her back, and she tensed.

A ghost of a smile, deprived of amusement, touched his lips. "Try it, Lucia."

"I'm not stupid." She lowered her arms to her sides and stood taller.

"No, you're not that." Offering his arm, he escorted her to the basement and the kidnapped victim who waited.

THIRTEEN

Two hours later, Lucia left the sobbing victim chained to the floor in the chamber. As she stepped into the hall and tossed the condom in the trash, she tried to embody the cold precision of a blade, sharpening her expression and steeling her posture. But despair swelled an unwieldy pressure behind her eyes, and every breath was a fight to keep the tears away.

Armando had been the cameraman, and as he followed her out, his probing, over-staring eyes produced a stampede of goosebumps across her nude skin.

"When are you going to milk my nuts?" he asked in Spanish.

The gun was already in her hand, so it only took a fraction of a second to aim at the nuts in question.

"Another time then." With a grin, he lumbered toward the stairs.

She waited until he was out of sight before lowering the Beretta and pulling on her clothes.

Today's victim was a middle-aged married man and father of five, who had come to Venezuela on a religious mission.

And she'd just raped him.

If she had any humanity left before she'd stepped into that room, she didn't now. But despite the man's wretched crying, he wasn't broken. If his wife paid the ransom within three days, he'd live.

Lucia dragged the balaclava off her head and let it fall to the floor. She was the one who was broken, and if she lived three more days, she wouldn't deserve it.

Footsteps approached from the stairs. She holstered both guns in her jeans and turned to find Tiago strolling toward her, flanked by two guards.

He gave her a cursory once-over. "Was it convincing?"

The victim had wept prayers to his god, begged for his virtue, cried for his wife to forgive him, and in the end, ejaculated in the condom, inside her, with a self-loathing howl. As far as torture went, he was emotionally wounded, and the camera caught every second of it.

"Yes." She breezed past Tiago, anxious to escape the basement. "If his wife has the money, she'll pay it."

"I know why you did it."

Her breath caught. Did what? Rape that man? Or did he know about the one she killed this morning? Oh God, did he find out about Tate?

She slowed her steps, arranged her features into a detached visage, and pivoted to face him. "What do you mean?"

"Leave us." He swept a hand at the guards without looking at them.

The two armed men retreated to the stairs and closed the door, leaving her alone in the dark hall with Tiago.

The guns at her back suddenly felt heavy and threatening, like foreboding shadows looming behind her. There wasn't a single time in eleven years when she was permitted to keep her weapons in Tiago's presence without his guards. If this was a test, she was guaranteed to fail.

"Come here." He snapped a finger at the space before him.

Heart hammering, she held her arms at her sides and closed the distance. When she reached him, he slid his hands around her waist and rested his fingers on the grips of her guns.

She closed her eyes as everything inside her froze. This was it. He was going to shoot her with the guns she'd earned in his employ.

"I know why you petitioned me to use your method of torture," he said at her ear.

Oh. A ragged breath fled her lungs.

When she was initiated into this job, her role had been to hold the camera as Tiago exacted ungodly pain from the skin of his victims. She'd been weaker then, her stomach unbearably sensitive to the sight of blood and sounds of anguish.

She'd also been naive enough to believe rape was a mercy over the flesh-cutting cruelty Tiago inflicted.

The victims only needed to look distressed for the video, mistreated just enough to convince a family member to send money without hesitation. Rape had been her solution.

And that was the flaw in her logic. When was rape ever a solution?

But in her idiocy, she'd persuaded Tiago to use her vile approach instead of his. Not only had he agreed, he'd designated *her* as the resident torturer of the male victims.

It was on the tip of her tongue to tell him she'd been wrong, that her way wasn't as effective. But could she really go back to watching him carve up the bodies of innocent men? *Men.* He never tortured women in that way. She didn't think it was out of chivalry. Quite the opposite. He'd told her once that his art of mutilation was a *man's* rite of passage.

"You're trying to make a difference in the kidnapping world." His mouth hovered over hers, his breaths warming her lips. "And you're doing it with sex."

"Rape." She ground her molars.

"Whatever you want to call it, Lucia. You could've begged me to abandon my ruthless line of work."

"You would've killed me."

"That's right, and you can't make a difference if you're dead, yeah? So instead, you suggested what you believed was a gentler method of torture. A suggestion that didn't make you appear weak to me or my men."

Her method was psychological and emasculating. His was physical, gruesome, and barbarous. Whether one was better than the other was debatable.

"I feel nothing in particular for the victims." He squeezed the grips of her guns, pressing them against the rise of her backside. "Except maybe pity. It's their own stupidity that brings them into my kingdom. But that wasn't the case with you. Taken from your home, left to die in a fatal crash… None of your choices led you to me. Do you know why I kept you imprisoned all those years? Why I didn't just kill you then?"

She tried not to think about her first eight years in his compound—locked in a room on the upper floor, the unbearable isolation and fear, the news of her parents' deaths, Camila already gone. In those darkest years of her life, she lost parts of herself she would never recover.

Her illness developed over that time. When she became too sick to go without daily injections, Tiago had a new way to cage and torment her.

"No." She met his heartless eyes. "I don't pretend to know why you do anything you do."

"I hope you never give me a reason to kill you." He slid the Berettas out of her waistband and glided the metal frames along the outsides of her arms. "No matter how ill you are or how intolerable I make your life, you manage to keep something in your possession, something I lost long ago." Lifting one of the guns, he trailed the barrel across her cheek. "You still have compassion."

Her throat tightened. It was the closest he'd ever come to saying anything sentimental without making it feel sexual.

It was also possible that he said shit like this just to fuck with her head.

"I live in an ugly world," he went on, "and you're... You're a pretty little flicker of compassion, begging to be extinguished. Sometimes I'm tempted to do just that. But I like you like this. You remind me how weak and foolish it is to cling to humanity."

Her nostrils flared.

"You can retrieve your guns from my guards." Without a backward glance, he ambled toward the stairs with her weapons. "You're free until dinner."

Free.

She wished for nothing, prayed to no one, and had zilch to lose. If freedom was a state of mind, she was hopelessly liberated.

FOURTEEN

"She's leaving the compound." Tate paced through the apartment, his pulse wound up and nerves shot to hell.

The tiny microphones on Lucia's weapons broadcasted to a receiver on his phone. He'd listened to her activities all morning while burning through a pack of cigarettes and seething every shade of rage.

Without visual confirmation, it was difficult to understand exactly what was happening. But from the sounds and conversations, he knew she'd passed out, was separated from her weapons for a while, then used a stairwell to the lower levels of the compound. That was when he'd sent his fist through the wall.

"You're gonna give yourself a coronary." Van reclined on the couch, tracking his movements with a narrowed glare.

Van was notorious for his explosive temper, yet he'd remained chillingly calm when they'd listened to her rape a sobbing, pleading man. Maybe it was because Van had been in a similar situation and was the one person who could empathize with her.

Tate, on the other hand, had gone ballistic when she was in that basement chamber. His imagination had created all kinds of graphic images to fill in what he couldn't see. It wasn't until he'd heard the pain in her voice during her conversation with Badell that his vision cleared, and his head stopped pounding.

She was stuck in a living nightmare, and there was fuck all he could do about it when he couldn't get to her.

But she was on the move now, stepping onto the street outside of the compound and turning…

"She's not heading toward her apartment." He strode toward the door, phone in hand and weapons concealed beneath his clothes.

Without a word, Van followed him out of the building and trailed a safe distance behind.

The tracking signal led Tate to a street market fifteen minutes away on foot. Although the tents were crowded with people, it didn't take long to spot her raven-black hair amid the throng.

A thin shirt hung from her shoulders, the wide neckline clinging to the delicate peaks of her tits. Flat stomach and toned legs encased in denim, she had the body of a young girl, but she wore it like a woman. A woman who would fuck rigorously, unapologetically, in every position and manner he wanted.

And he wanted.

He wanted to feel her fall apart on his cock, hear her cry in relief, and see a glimmer of happiness on her face. But more than that, he wanted her safe and healthy and out of this city.

Her guards wouldn't be far, so he kept his distance, marking her as she moved from stall to stall, touching the produce and staring at the meats. Jesus, she looked hungry, her gaze crawling over the food with ravenous longing, yet she didn't buy anything.

Watching her poke through the market empty-handed produced a protective twinge in his chest. She was too thin, too alone, and given the dark circles around her eyes and the sag of her shoulders, too goddamn sad. Every bone in his body thrummed to take care of her.

As he slipped deeper into the market area, the sweet smell of slow-cooked meat and fried dough saturated the air. He paused within a few paces of her and directed his eyes on the hanging rope of bananas she'd caressed.

She must've sensed him, because she turned at the edge of his vision, and that deep brown gaze warmed the side of his face.

Knowing her guards were watching, he held out some bills to purchase a few bananas and gave her no reaction.

With a casual twist of her neck, she scanned the perimeter, likely searching for his backup.

Van stood at his nine o'clock across the street, and the moment she spotted him, her chest hitched with a sigh. Then she continued to the next stall.

From there, they eased into a wordless interplay. She touched or glanced at the foods she liked, and he bought them—bread, pork, strawberries, coconut cookies. When she reached the last tent, she selected a paper bag of tea and handed it to the merchant.

Tate sidled in behind her, fighting the impulse to rest a hand against the small of her back. He couldn't touch her, but she was close enough to infuse his senses with hints of citrus and gun oil, sunshine and city air.

He didn't look at her as he paid for the tea and whispered against her hair, "You're not alone."

Before she could respond, he left the bag of food on the table in front of her and strolled out of the market.

For the rest of the day, he sat in his apartment, listening to the receiver. The silence on her end stretched for miles while she sat by herself across the street. Hopefully, she was sleeping since she hadn't slept at all last night.

He took a short nap, but it was restless, as his hearing was constantly tuned into the receiver. So he gave up and used the time to research her symptoms, leave messages for doctors in the States, and order the most comprehensive home blood test kit he could find online.

"Is that your plan?" Van gnawed on a toothpick, scrutinizing him. "An online blood test?"

"Got a better idea?"

"No. I just want to make sure you're not planning to storm the compound and steal the medicine."

He laughed, because dammit, it'd crossed his mind. "I'm not that reckless."

"I don't know. You have a crazy look in your eyes."

"I'm going to start staying with her at night." He paced to the window and surveyed the alley until he located her guards. "I need to learn everything she knows about her illness, the injections, the doctors, her injury... There's so much she hasn't told me. Maybe the solution isn't as hopeless as it seems."

"And if it is? Hopeless?"

"I'll draw her blood and send it off to a lab. Maybe figure out a way to bring a doctor here to her."

"If she has a terminal illness, Tate, there's little you can do."

"I know." He pivoted away from the window and dragged his hands down his face. "I know."

They'd been in Caracas for eleven days. The trip could extend twice that or longer. Van never mentioned his wife, but he was so damn smitten with her the distance must've been eating at him something fierce.

"I could be here another month." Tate crossed his arms and met Van's eyes.

"I know. I'm with you till the end." Van gave him a soft, genuine smile.

The human side of Van was an anomaly. Witnessing its rare appearance wedged something deep inside Tate, crowding out some of the cynical, mistrustful feelings he'd harbored for so long.

"I'm sorry I haven't said it before, but thank you." He released a slow breath. "I'm glad you're here."

"I know." Another smile from Van, this one twisting with his standard wickedness. "Wanna mess around? This dry spell is brutal."

He closed his eyes and pressed his fingers against his brow. "And there you go, ruining it."

"You make it too damn easy." Erasing the few feet between them, Van stepped into his space. "Just so you know, I'm going to rid you of your homophobia."

His hackles went up. "I'm not homophobic."

"You have a problem with men fucking men."

"No, Van. I have a problem with *you* fucking *me*."

"Well, then let me clear that up." Van braced a hand on the window behind Tate and pressed close enough to exchange breaths. "I love my wife, and I'd cut my dick off before I cheated on her. I like to fuck *with* you, but I don't want to *fuck* you. Feel me?"

He'd rather not feel Van's breath on his face, but... "Yeah, I feel you."

"Good boy." Van patted his cheek and held the touch there, cupping his jaw for a defining moment before strolling away.

The familiar touch paired with the murmured words should've triggered a flashback of those agonizing weeks in the attic. But as Tate tempered his breathing, he felt strangely...peaceful.

"All teasing aside, you seem more comfortable around me." Van lowered onto the couch, his expression serious. "You're healing."

Tate nodded absently, thinking. Being cooped up with Van in a small apartment and depending on him for protection might've been a much-needed catharsis. He could honestly say he trusted the perverted psychopath. He might even like him, but he wouldn't admit that out loud. So he left it at a nod.

"Good." Van grabbed a bottle of tequila and poured two glasses. "Let's drink to that."

A few hours and shots of tequila later, Tate watched from the window as Lucia left her apartment to meet Badell for dinner.

Armed and ready to go, he left Van behind to keep a lookout on the alley.

When he hit the street, the sky was dark enough to cloak the buildings in shadows. He kept his head down, gait swift, and managed to arrive at the rear of her building unmolested. After a quick *I'm here* call to Van, he knocked on the neighbor's back door.

The middle-aged woman looked as harmless as her little dog when she answered, but she refused to open the door farther than a crack. When he slipped a few bolivars through the opening and said, "I'm Lucia's *amigo*," she was more than happy to escort him in and show him the hidden cut through in the closet.

It was too easy. Giving up Lucia's hidden door to a total stranger meant she'd do it for anyone willing to bribe her.

"What's your name?" he asked.

She stared at him blankly.

Well, shit. He'd only picked up a few Spanish words. "Uh...*nome?*" No, that wasn't right. "*Nombre?*"

"Franchesca."

"Franchesca, don't let..." *Damn language barrier.* He needed a translator. "Hang on."

He dialed Van, who had grown up in a border town and spoke fairly decent Spanish.

"Miss me already?" Van rumbled through the phone.

"Nope. I need you to translate. Tell Lucia's neighbor to never let anyone in the back door. Never show anyone the passage through the closet. Never, no one, under no circumstances. You get the idea. Use your threatening tone."

"I have a threatening tone?"

The innocent act was bullshit, so he decided to poke the sleeping bear. "You used to, but you've grown soft. And gay. So gay your pretty wife is at home right now bouncing on a harder, straighter dick."

"What the fuck did you just say to me? You're going to find out exactly how gay I am when I fuck your skull through your asshole, motherfucker. You're fucking dead."

"Yeah, *that* tone. Here she is." He handed the phone to Franchesca.

As she listened, her breath wheezed, and her eyes grew wide. When she handed the phone back, he disconnected and placed a larger bill in her trembling hand. No translation needed for *hush money*. It was a universal language in this town.

He left her staring at the money and slipped into Lucia's unit through the closet.

Other than the muted glow from a night light in the wall, her windowless space was dark. He did his best to seal up the passageway. She needed a lock or something to brace against it. Something to keep trespassers like himself from breaking in.

At least, she wouldn't be sleeping here alone anymore, and when he left Caracas, she would be with him.

Switching on the ceiling light, he scanned the barren room, which entailed a single-person mattress, mini fridge, sink, toilet, and shower head that aimed at an open tiled space.

Her boots and a small stack of clothes sat in the corner. On the counter was the bag of tea, a toothbrush, toothpaste, and a generic bottle of hair and body wash.

That was it? A lump formed in his throat. Everything she owned would fit in one small bag.

There were no cabinets or pantries, so where was her food? Her dishes and cookware? Hell, she didn't even have a stove.

His attention zeroed in on the fridge, and he yanked it open. The scanty contents wobbled on a single shelf—a sandwich of bread and pork, strawberries, bananas, and coconut cookies. The only food in her possession was what he'd bought her.

She has nothing.

No one should live like this.

A restless pang clenched behind his sternum, and his muscles burned to do something, anything, to fix this.

But he couldn't fix it. Not without risking her life.

Phone in hand, he paced the room, back and forth, back and forth, staring at the screen.

It was time to call Matias. The cartel capo could find the best doctors and bring them here. According to Cole, it would take weeks, but Tate could at least get that ball rolling.

Drawing a calming breath, he dialed the number by memory and hovered his thumb over the button that would connect the call. And he hesitated.

I'll be dead within hours. Long before they can diagnose me.

Lucia knew how resourceful Matias was, yet she'd begged Tate not to call him or Camila. She was fucking stubborn in her conviction that Badell held the only antidote.

Then there was Cole's warning that Matias wouldn't have enough men and sway here to fight Badell.

Fuck! He erased the number on the phone and slumped against the wall. He needed to talk to Lucia first. Then he'd call Matias.

Over the next hour, he listened to her dinner conversation with Badell. Strange how she was allowed to keep her guns in his presence. Though there was a span of time this morning when it sounded like they'd been taken from her. Was it when she received her injection? If she was given medicine, Tate didn't hear it happen.

As long as he keeps my condition a secret and the antidote locked in his safe, I can't leave.

Where was the safe? Did she have access to its location? Were guards posted in every room?

There might've been guards where she met Badell for dinner, but it was just the two of them talking and eating. The discussion focused on business—police activities, competitor secrets, and weapons suppliers. If Tate were a government spy, the information would've been gold. But he didn't give a shit about Tiago Badell's dirty affairs.

The entirety of his concern focused on the brown-eyed beauty who was sitting with a man who could kill her on a whim. Meanwhile, Tate paced her apartment with knots the size of Texas tying up his insides.

When she finally left the compound, he turned off the light, stood behind the front door, and listened to her footsteps through the receiver. When Van called to tell him she was in the alley, he silenced the phone and waited.

The seconds felt like a marathon—sprinting pulse, labored breaths, the urgent need to cross the finish line.

She was his finish line, and when she opened the door, it took every ounce of his self-control to remain silent and still.

Close the door, Lucia.

The instant she did, he launched…right into the barrel of a gun in his face.

"It's me," he whispered into the darkness.

"What are you—?"

Without warning, she dropped the Beretta in his hands and covered her mouth. Then she ran through the unlit room, falling with a thump near the toilet.

"Lucia?" He holstered the gun and searched for the light switch.

When he found it, the sound of retching shuddered the air.

FIFTEEN

"Shit." A surge of panic sent Tate racing toward Lucia's doubled-over body as she emptied her dinner into the toilet.

The guards would be outside on the street, probably out of hearing range. But just in case, he would have to keep his voice soft.

"Did you get your medicine this morning?" He dropped to his knees beside her and gathered her hair.

"Yeah." She moaned weakly with her head in her hands and elbows wobbling on the seat. "Nighttime is always the worst."

He stroked her back, vibrating with anger at his own helplessness. "What can I do?"

She vomited again, and tears streaked down her pallid face. "I'm sorry."

His chest caved in. Why the fuck was she apologizing?

Her arms dropped, and her head hung over the toilet, swinging back and forth and plopping tears into the bowl. "I raped a man this morning."

Fucking Christ. This was wrong. Wrong timing. Wrong place. Wrong everything. As each wrongful second passed, he felt more and more useless.

"You just puked the only thing you've eaten today." He hit the toilet lever and glimpsed specks of blood before it flushed away. "Goddammit!"

There was no drug store. No urgent care. Nothing in this apartment to help her. There wasn't a goddamn thing he could do. *Nothing!*

"Please, don't be mad," she whispered.

"I'm not mad." He was so fucking livid he couldn't think straight. "What hurts?"

She sat back on her heels and wiped her mouth. "I probably look like the living dead, but I feel better."

Her complexion was ghost-white, her eyes sunken and bruised, and she appeared to have lost ten pounds she didn't have to lose. But despite it all...

"You're beautiful." He touched a knuckle to her chin.

Her pretty, pixie-like features contorted in misery, and her chest heaved in sudden bursts, as if she were swallowing down a sob. "You're lying."

"Lucia—"

"Don't." She made a wretched sound and pushed him away.

He wouldn't budge and instead reached for her.

"I don't want you to see me like this." She twisted, giving him her back. "Please, Tate. Just go. Go back to Texas."

"You're fucking crazy if you think I'll leave you." He shifted around her and got in her face. "We're doing this. Together. *Us*. Get that through your stubborn head."

She laughed, a painfully broken sound that sent more tears skipping down her hollow cheeks.

"What?" he asked softly.

"*Us?* What does that even mean?"

"It means I'm staying—"

"For how long?"

He wanted to sling her over his shoulder like a damn caveman and take off tonight, right fucking now.

She must've read it in his eyes, because she heaved a frustrated breath. "Let's say I left with you. *Hypothetically*. What happens next?"

"I'll take you wherever you want to go." His pulse accelerated as he edged closer and brushed the hair out of her face. "We can stay with your sister in Colombia or go home to Texas. We'll get you healthy and safe."

"Then what?" More tears brimmed her eyes.

"Then we can...I don't know...get a Netflix subscription, rescue a dog, take a road trip to wine country, whatever people do. I don't give a fuck as long as you're well and we're far away from here."

"You talk about *us* and *we* in terms of a relationship. In terms of always."

Goddamn, woman. He wasn't prepared for this conversation.

"You're in love with Camila," she said.

"This isn't..." Jesus fuck, he wasn't pursuing a relationship with anyone. His focus was on here and now and keeping Lucia alive.

"It's not what?" she asked.

"We're not doing this right now." He gripped her elbow. "Can you stand?"

"You just said we're doing this. Together." She stared at the floor and didn't move. "I want to understand."

"You're right." He closed his eyes and gave himself a second to calm down. "We can talk about the future, but right now, I'm focused on your health and the danger you're in. You're hurting, and it's..." Helpless rage locked up his fists, and he breathed through it. "It's not in my DNA to sit back and let you dictate how this will go."

"Okay," she said numbly.

"Tell me what you need." He bent down to capture her gaze.

Her chin trembled, and she hugged her waist, shaking her head. "Why do you have to be so nice?"

It looked like she needed a hug more than anything else.

He pulled her onto his lap and embraced her tightly. "You're about to spend some time with me, and you'll find out just how *not* nice I am."

"You might be crazier than I am." She looped her arms around his neck and buried her nose against his throat. "Thank you for the food."

It was comforting, in an unfamiliar way, to hold her like this. It was also exactly what he needed, and he hadn't even realized it. She had the ability to hurt his heart and put it at ease all at once.

"I'll bring you more to eat," he said. "I'm also going to install slide bolts on both of those doors."

"You don't need to—"

"I'm sleeping here from now on. Until we leave."

Her muscles tensed, as if she were bracing to argue. Then she seemed to deflate with her next exhale. "I need to brush my teeth and take a shower."

He carried her to the sink and prepared her toothbrush. "Did you sleep today?"

"Yeah. How did you know I was at the market?"

"I'm watching you, Lucia. Get used to it."

She surprised him with a simple nod and turned her attention to the toothbrush.

As she cleaned her teeth, he slid the heels off her feet, removed the gun from her waistband, and grabbed the second Beretta from his. Then he set everything beside her clothes in the corner.

The bugs on her guns were too conspicuous. It was only a matter of time before she or someone else noticed them. They also had a limited battery life and would need to be recharged every few days.

A glance over his shoulder confirmed she was bent at the sink with her back to him. He removed the bugs, pulled a fully charged one from his pocket, and adhered it to the arched underside of her heeled shoe.

The location was less noticeable, and since the audio quality was so good, he could adjust the receiver to tune out the tread of her footfalls.

If he told her about the listening devices, it would add another burden on her shoulders. He didn't want her walking into Badell's domain every day worrying about being wired. He also didn't want her filtering her conversations.

With the new bug on the sole of her shoe, he moved the mattress to butt up against the front door, checked the lock, and set his gun and knife beside the bed where he would sleep.

"The guards never come inside," she said from the sink. "They don't even stand near the door."

After watching the alley from his apartment window, he knew the guards usually hung out down the street. But he wasn't taking chances. If someone tried to push their way in, the door would bump the mattress and wake him. He would also make sure they kept their voices at a whisper.

Moving to the shower, he turned it on and adjusted the water temperature.

There was no curtain, no privacy whatsoever, but did she need that with him? She'd had her mouth on his cock, his cock in her pussy, his hands and lips all over her body.

"Has the nausea passed?" he asked.

"Yes."

"I'll help you with the shower."

"I'd rather you didn't."

Dignity. Despite her frailness, she glowed with it.

"I'm not leaving." He stared into her honey-brown eyes.

"I know." She stared right back.

Gripping the hem of her shirt, she pulled it over her head. The bra and jeans went next. Then she hooked her thumbs under the elastic of her black panties, slid them off, and carried them under the spray of the shower.

He meant to turn away and give her space, but he couldn't unglue his shoes from the floor, couldn't avert his greedy gaze from her body.

Bones protruded along her ribs and hips, but toned layers of muscles flexed in her arms, abs, and legs as she washed her panties.

She's washing her underwear in the shower?

"Is that the only pair you own?" He glanced at her skimpy stack of clothes and didn't see undergarments.

"The other pair ripped, so..." She stared at the worn scrap of satin and shrugged. "This is it."

"Give them to me."

When she handed them over, he scrubbed them in the sink, taking care with the delicate, thinning fabric. Then he hung them on the doorknob to dry. "Anything else need washing?"

"Not tonight." She lathered bubbles through her hair and over her fragile curves, spreading the small dollop of soap impossibly far.

The impoverished way she lived seemed so disturbingly normal to her, but she hadn't been raised this way. Her parents had been successful citrus farmers and had given her a comfortable upbringing. *Until they sold her into slavery.*

It infuriated him to think that over the past eleven years, she'd adapted to hardship to the point that it didn't even faze her.

As she continued her shower, watching him watch her, a fog of complicated questions hung between them. Questions he wasn't ready to answer.

Did he want to get to know her romantically?
Could he be with her without thinking about her sister?
Would she resent his feelings for Camila?
Was it wrong to want her on such a carnal, animalistic level?

He couldn't stop thinking about fucking her again. Her gorgeous tits looked so damn appetizing. Round and firm with stiff pink nipples, they were perfect for biting and pinching and bruising.

His mouth watered, and blood surged to his cock, swelling his length at a painful angle behind the zipper.

"You're staring," she said.

He snapped his gaze to hers and glared unapologetically.

"What are you thinking about?" She ran her hands through her hair, rinsing the soap.

"You don't want to know."

"I can guess." She gave his erection a pointed look. "Tell me."

A conversation about her and him and Camila was a minefield he didn't want to tread, but sex was different. Lust was simple and clear-cut.

He clasped his hands behind him and gave her an honest answer. "You have great tits."

She glanced down and made a face. "I imagine they're a lot smaller than Camila's."

Well, that fucking backfired.

"They fill my hands," he said. "What more do I need?"

"Camila's?"

He pulled in a long breath. She wasn't going to let this go. If it made her happy, she could ask her questions, and he'd answer them. But first, he wanted her comfortable and fed.

"Time's up." He shut off the water and searched the room for a towel. "What do you dry off with?"

"Air dry." She squeezed out her hair and swiped the water off her arms.

Swallowing a string of explicits, he yanked off his shirt and used it to dry her shivering body. "You can't live like this."

"I get by."

With his hands grazing across her soft skin and her pussy inches from his face, he would've been wildly turned on under other circumstances. And he was. But his mind was stuck in a whirlwind.

She had a partial roll of toilet paper, toothpaste, soap, and a razor for shaving. She needed shampoo, underwear, basic pain medication, a fucking towel, and... What about feminine products?

"Where are your tampons? Pads?" he asked.

Her hand flew to his, where he wiped the wadded shirt across her stomach.

"I don't..." She made a sound in her throat and stepped out of his reach. "I don't need that."

A fist of dread clamped his insides. "Why not?"

"I haven't had a period since the accident." She grabbed a t-shirt from the pile of clothes and pulled it on.

No period in eleven years? Were her female organs damaged? Removed? Or was it stress? Malnutrition? An IUD? Having been raised in a brothel, he had an in-depth knowledge of monthly cycles, hormones...all the female stuff. If she couldn't conceive, the destruction would reach far beyond a physical injury.

Everything inside him thrashed to demand answers, but he remained silent, motionless. It was one of those instincts he depended on, and it was telling him not to push her on this.

She seemed to have shut down, moving robotically through the apartment, straightening and organizing with no purpose. Pausing at the sink, she ran hot water until steam floated into her face. Her hand trembled as she reached for a paper cup and tried to unwrap a pouch of tea.

He went to her, taking over the task. The water wasn't hot enough to steep the leaves, but it was the only option. Once the tea was prepared, he lifted her onto the counter, set the cup in her hand, and molded her fingers around it. Then he fixed her something to eat.

Her silence pressed against him, but at least she was drinking. Dehydration was one thing he could control in this fucked-up situation.

There were no plates, so he arranged the sandwich and strawberries on the counter beside her. Then he crowded into her space, pushing against her knees until she spread them.

Wedged between her legs, he lightly stroked her damp hair and waited.

She drank half of the tea before she set it aside and closed her eyes. "I remember the crash in Peru. The falling sensation as we rolled. The bodies slamming against me. Bones being crushed. The sharp scent of blood." Her fingers skated over her midsection, shaking as she traced the scar. "And the pain…"

He felt it, the terrible hurt in her voice, as if he were living in the memory with her. It hit him right in the chest, and he clenched his jaw until his molars protested.

"I blacked out before I saw what impaled me." Her tone flattened, becoming detached. "I don't remember much of the next year with all the surgeries and sleep-inducing drugs. After that, Tiago kept me locked in a room. A suite in the old hotel. He didn't let me out for eight years."

"He what?" Fury hit him like a thunderbolt, ringing his ears and scattering his breaths.

"I was a prisoner." She lifted a shoulder. "He could've killed me. God knows why he didn't."

The impulse to hit something simmered beneath his skin. The next best thing would've been a cigarette, but he couldn't smoke here and risk the smell alerting the guards.

He pulled away from her and paced.

"He visited me every day," she said. "Always ate with me. Dinner was our thing. Still is. It's like he doesn't have anyone to talk to, no one he trusts anyway, and I was a safe ear since I was locked in a room with no contact with the outside world."

"When did you get sick?"

"During my isolation in that room. After the accident, the abdominal pain never went away. Then it spread, and new symptoms emerged. The headaches, nausea, muscle paralysis… It started happening about once a month. Increased to once a week. Then daily. Some days were better than others. It took his doctors months to diagnose me and develop a treatment. When Tiago eventually freed me from that room, I was sick every day and… Well, I was never free. Not with the guards." She gestured at the door. "I've made several attempts to escape, only to get hauled back and deprived of medicine until the only thing that could save me was a ventilator."

His nostrils widened with the force of his seething breaths. "Lucia…"

"I made contact with a doctor once, someone who didn't have his hands in Tiago's pockets. I met him at his house outside of the neighborhood. A gentle, kind man—he was willing to help me for free. But we didn't get past the medical questions before Tiago's men showed up and…" She clutched the hem of her shirt and stretched it to her knees, covering her thighs. "They cut off his arms and made me watch as he bled to death."

His heart ached for her. She'd endured so much and had done it alone. How could she not be defeated and despondent and at the end of her limit? Her luck was in the red, her strife ceaseless. She had a never-ending shortage of anything good in her life.

Yet here she was, asking him about *us* and the future. She hadn't given up, and it left him awestruck and overwrought with admiration.

"I think the antidote is derived from Amazon plants." She told him Badell's father had been a pharmacist and what little she knew about the team of indigenous doctors. "They're experts in medicinal botany."

"They're also surgeons?" He stepped toward her and touched her shirt over the scar.

"Yes. Tiago won't tell me what organs were damaged or removed, or how the sickness is related to the injury, or if—" She sucked in a hard breath, her expression blank. "Or if I can bear children. But hey, at least I don't have periods."

Her smile was hapless and heartbreaking, so utterly void of humor it tore him apart.

"I want you to do something for me." He held her face in his hands and forced her to look at him.

She sawed her teeth together, and a glimmer of fight lit her eyes.

"Tonight," he said, "I want you to not be so damn tough. Let it go. Give it to me. Let me be your strength."

"Tate—"

"One night, Lucia. Everyone needs someone. Even me. Tonight, I'm yours. Your someone."

"My person?" she whispered.

"Yeah."

It was a sluggish, circumspect unraveling, her entire body shuddering, fighting the turmoil that rose behind her eyes. She visibly wrestled with it, battling an inner storm he couldn't comprehend. But when she finally gave in, he was there, his arms around her, his lips in her hair, and his whispered words swaddling her in truths. *You're resilient and brave. I respect you. You're not alone. I'm here for you.*

She wept quietly, gracefully, and with every tear, he felt her muscles loosen and her joints give until she was pliable and spent and maybe even relieved.

As her tears slowed, he chased them with his lips, kissing them away one by one. He'd never been so moved, so absorbed in the emotions of a woman. He loved Camila, but she didn't need him. She'd never needed him. Not like this.

And that wasn't all. The taste of Lucia's tears, the provocative scent of her skin, the directness in her questions, the glimpse of vulnerability beneath her strong exterior — it turned him on like nothing else. This woman was everything he never knew he was attracted to.

When her eyes dried, he leaned back and inspected her exquisite face for signs of pain. "How do you feel?"

"Better." She placed a hand on his bare chest and idly stroked the muscle there. "Thank you."

"Your stomach?"

"Settled."

"Eat." He placed the sandwich in her hand and stepped back.

She nibbled on the bread, ate a strawberry, and after a few more bites, she tore into the pork with voracity.

Satisfied, he rested his fingers in his pockets and caught her gaze. "You have questions about Camila and me. Ask them."

SIXTEEN

The last bite of the sandwich stuck in Lucia's throat under the force of Tate's stare. The intensity in his ice blue eyes, assertive growl in his voice, stillness in his confident posture—everything about his pushy, take-charge style made her blood throb and heat in places that had no business reacting at all.

He towered over her, a head taller and shoulders twice as wide. His expression was that of a man restraining his need, one who seemed to have everlasting patience. He adjusted his fingers in his pockets, shifting the front of his jeans to accommodate that huge, relentless erection—an erection that had been tenting his zipper since she removed her clothes.

Chemistry was an effortless thing between them. Last night at the club left no doubt in her mind about that. But this was more than sex.

He'd washed her panties.

Kissed her tears.

Held her as she'd cried.

Offered to be her person for one night

And he loved her sister.

Her gaze faltered, bouncing around the room until it collided with his once again.

You have questions about Camila and me. Ask them.

"Does Matias know?" She swallowed down the last of the tea and slid off the counter.

"Know what?" He caught her arm, steadying her.

"That you love her?"

"Yes."

And Tate was still alive? Maybe Matias wasn't threatened by him, though that seemed impossible. Tate would have a shameless effect on any woman he set his sights on, including her lovesick sister.

Lucia was thoroughly intimidated in the shadow of his powerful body and plundering gaze, but she also felt protected. And lucky. Without him here, she would've spent tonight like every other night — starving, homesick, heartsick, *sick* sick, and so terribly alone.

His hair was a sexy mess of short blond spikes. Black roses tattooed one muscled arm, the rest of his upper body a landscape of unmarked skin and ripples of definition. Though he wore a deep scowl and seemed to enjoy staring her down in a condescending way, he was also tender and possessive.

He was a man to love. If Camila hadn't already belonged to Matias, she would've given her heart to Tate without hesitation.

"Was it hard to...?" Did she want to ask this? She sat on the mattress on the floor and pulled the shirt down to cover her thighs. "Was it hard to have sex with Camila then let her go?"

"I wouldn't know."

"You mean...?" Her heart thundered. "You haven't...?"

"I've never so much as kissed her." With a sigh, he sat beside her and stretched his legs along the floor in front of them. "When I met your sister, I'd just spent ten weeks with Van. I wanted her instantly, but I was..." He wiped a hand down his mouth, his fingers lingering on his barely-there beard, his expression pensive. "I needed time to come to terms with what happened in that attic. We both did. I lived like a monk for the next two years, waiting for her and... Maybe I was waiting for myself. To feel worthy of her. To feel like a man again." He dropped his hand on his lap. "When I was finished waiting, the very night I decided to go after her, Matias showed up." He laughed a sharp sound that wasn't a laugh at all. "I knew then that I didn't have a chance in hell with her."

He must've had superhuman staying power. To wait for Camila like that only to lose her in the end? Lucia commended his patience.

"You haven't tried to move on?" she asked. "With another woman?"

"For the last four years, I've fucked everything that moved."

An ice-cold jolt knifed straight through her chest. Is that what she was to him? Something that moved? "How's that working for you?"

"It's..." He stared at his dusty brown boots, his brows knitting. Then he huffed another non-laugh. "It's been utterly joyless." He turned toward her, head cocked and eyes squinting. "You asked if it was hard to have sex then let her go. Are you worried about that? With us?"

Us.

She looked away, an involuntary reflex she immediately regretted and forced her gaze back to his. "Am I worried because we had sex?

Because I might not want to let go of something you found *utterly joyless?*"

"We didn't just have sex. We had great fucking sex." His perfect lips formed the words with natural seduction, making her shiver all over. "You enjoyed it as much as I did."

Her nipples hardened beneath the shirt. He zeroed in on her chest, and something flickered in his eyes.

"If I could make you happy..." He unlaced his boots and pulled them off. Then his socks. "Even if it's just a fleeting happiness..." His hands went to his jeans, unzipping and shucking them off. "I'll do whatever it takes."

"A pity fuck won't make me —"

She was pinned beneath him on the mattress before her next breath. He was so heavy and solidly built his weight was alarming.

"Does this feel like pity?" He grabbed her hand and shoved it between them, molding her fingers around his cock.

Trapped in his tight briefs, his swollen length angled toward his hip, so damn thick and long the cotton barely contained it. It definitely didn't feel like pity. He felt ruthless.

"Don't ever mistake my desire for you as a mercy." He ground himself against her hand. "I don't care if you're sick, sweetheart. I intend to exhaust my need for you until you forget where you are and how many breaths you have left. How's that for a nice guy?"

It was arousing, electrifying, stimulating and lubricating the deepest, hungriest part of her.

"I've never come as hard as I did when I was inside you." His breathing sped up, his lips parting and brushing against hers as he rocked his hips in the *V* of her thighs. "I know you felt it — the crazy consuming shock of it. I'm going to take you there again and again, until you never want to let go."

"Never let go of you?"

"If that makes you happy."

His response confused her, and given the creases on his forehead, it confused him, as well.

"Be careful, Tate." She stroked the line of his sculpted jaw. "It's just sex, remember? We'll have to let go eventually."

Considering the state of her health, it would be sooner rather than later. But for now, she wrapped her arms around him and held tight.

"We'll see about that." He took her mouth in a kiss that stole her thoughts and bowed her spine.

The instant his tongue met hers, sparks of energy flashed through her body. He must've felt something similar, because he gasped against her lips and leaned back. His eye contact was brief yet poignant before he tangled a fist in her hair and returned to her mouth with an explosion of passion.

It was a full-body fusion—legs entwining, hips grinding, chests heaving, and hands groping and clutching. He shaped her to him, like heat melting glass, and she softened, liquefied, inhaling when he exhaled, moaning when he groaned. It was the best kiss she'd ever experienced, and he kept it going for a lifetime, letting her feast, savor, and soar.

When he pulled back, she blinked at him, dizzy with hunger.

His lips were wet and swollen, his pupils huge and breaths careening out of control. Knowing he was as affected as she was only made her want him more.

"Arms up." He shoved her shirt toward her head and yanked it off.

Then he was on the move, his chiseled torso and hard cock shifting out of reach as he settled his shoulders between her legs.

"I fucking love your cunt." His fingers slipped through her wet heat and circled her opening. "You're dripping."

"Tate…" She wriggled beneath him, hating and loving the way he spread her flesh open and bared her to his eyes.

"God, I can smell you." He buried his nose in her pussy and inhaled. "The sweetness of your skin mixed with your arousal… You're a goddamn sinful temptation."

He pushed a finger inside her and turned his head to nip at her inner thigh. His strokes kissed along her inner walls, rubbing with wicked precision and setting her on fire. Her hand fisted the blanket, the other flying to the silken strands of his hair.

As he fingered her cunt and licked along her thigh, his thumb danced over her clit, swiveling and whisking and making it hum.

With his long digit curling inside her, he rested his lips against her mound and captured her gaze. "Did you use a condom this morning?"

Shame punched her in the gut. During her delirious puking episode, she'd told him she raped a man. *I've raped so many innocent, married men.*

The reminder swelled a sob in her throat and sent her scrambling to get away from him. She was humiliated, so fucking disgusted with herself, she couldn't bear his touch or whatever look was on his face.

"Stop." He caught her swinging arms and restrained them above her head.

She fought him for a useless moment before falling still. The struggle had shifted her fully beneath him with his legs straddling her hips and his huge body bent over her.

"Why are you doing this?" She glared up at him through a sheen of tears. "You can have your pick of untainted, *clean* women."

"I'm not asking for me." Holding her wrists in one hand, he

removed three condoms from the jeans on the floor and tossed them on the mattress. "I need to know if you're protecting yourself."

"When I can." Her voice broke into a flat, dead sound. "Sometimes I'm not given a choice."

His eyes clouded, darkening with understanding. Like her, he'd been forced by a man. He didn't just grasp the ruin. He'd lived it. But unlike her, he'd never inflicted that ugliness on another. Her crimes were hypocritical and heinous.

"How can you stand to look at me?" she asked. "Let alone touch me?"

"Do you enjoy raping them?"

"No!" A flood of misery crumpled her face. "I'm hurting them, and I don't want to. I thought…" Guilt spilled from her eyes and down her temples, tickling along the curves of her ears. "I thought it would be better this way, but it's not. It's insidious, disgusting abuse, and when they…" She gulped down a sob and evened her voice. "When they come, I see the destruction in their eyes. They hate themselves as much as they hate me. I'm doing that. I'm—"

"Listen to me." He gripped her chin and held her head immobile. "You didn't do it for yourself. You did it for them, and doing so hurt *you*. Dammit, Lucia. I know you know that."

"I'm not a martyr." She clenched her teeth. "Not even close."

"Doesn't matter. It stops now."

Her breath hitched. "What? I can't—"

"You're dying, right? So be sick. Fake the symptoms if you have to. Vomit. Pass out. Do whatever you need to do to avoid that torture room."

"He'll hurt them! He has this…this razor thing he puts on his finger, and he…" Her stomach rolled with nausea, thickening her words. "He cuts and mutilates their bodies."

"We can't save them." His fingers tightened against her jaw. "But I can save *you*. You're my only concern, and I want you out of that room. Understand?"

She swallowed, and swallowed again. "Yes."

"I'm waiting on a medical test kit. It should be here in a couple days." He released her and propped his elbows on either side of her shoulders. "I'll draw your blood and test for STDs."

"I'm clean." She averted her eyes. "No STDs. Tiago's doctors test me regularly."

"Okay. Good." He lifted up and gazed down the length of her nude body, chewing on his lip. "I don't know if the blood test will tell us anything. But while we wait for the results, no more torturing. And I'll be here every night…"

He dragged a knuckle over her breast and down her trembling stomach, pausing on the short hairs above her pussy. He had that look in his eyes, the prowling predator look that told her in no uncertain terms that he wasn't finished with her.

But the conversation they'd just had left her feeling raw and loathsome. She killed a rapist today only to turn around and inflict the same evil on someone else. Yet Tate stared at her as if she were the loveliest woman he'd ever seen. It was appalling.

"I can't do this." She shoved at his chest with enough force to knock him off balance.

Then she fled. Off the mattress, across the floor, she didn't make it to her feet before he seized her ankle and yanked her back to the bed.

"You're a fighter." He shackled her wrists in the unbending clamps of his fingers, holding her down on the mattress. "But you want me to fight back. You want me to punish you and use your body to get myself off. Because that's what gets you off."

"That's not—"

"I saw you with that man at the club last night. The pleasure on your face while he caned you was undeniable." He spread her legs wider with his knees and brought his mouth to her ear. "You're a dirty, kinky girl. Tell me I'm wrong."

The protest stuck in her throat. He wasn't wrong. Punishment and capitulation balanced her horribly unstable world, and she needed that now—the liberation that came with pain and pleasure and willing surrender.

"You're right," she whispered.

He hauled in a rough breath and blew out slowly.

"If you move your arms," he said, pressing her wrists to the mattress above her head, "I'll flip you over and fuck your ass."

SEVENTEEN

I'll flip you over and fuck your ass.

Heat flushed through Lucia's core, and her legs fell open, unbidden.

"Ah, fuck, baby." Tate's hand shot to her pussy, stroking the soaked flesh. "You like that, don't you? You want me inside your ass."

She'd never had a pleasant experience with anal. It had always been forced and blindingly painful. But she ached to feel him there, knew he would do it with care, and nodded her consent.

"You're killing me." He stole a deep, heart-pumping kiss. Then he gathered the condoms and lined up the three foil wrappers along her breastbone. "I'm going to use all of these tonight and wish I'd brought more."

Instead of sheathing his cock, he slid his hands beneath her butt and lifted her pussy to his mouth.

The first lick followed her seam from bottom to top. She throbbed against the hot greeting of his tongue, fighting to keep her arms above her head. He buried his face, and she moaned, jerked, and choked on her own breath.

As he sucked and licked with ferocity, his scratchy jaw burned a trail of fire along her thighs. His lips covered every thrumming nerve between her legs as he gripped her ass cheeks and spread them so he could roll his tongue around her rim. She bucked against his unyielding mouth, drenching his whiskers with her arousal.

At some point, the condoms tumbled away, and her hands moved on their own, pulling at his hair and clawing his scalp.

He knocked her fingers away. "Your ass is mine."

Tossing her to the side, he flipped her to her stomach and covered her back with his body.

She panted in response, wanting him to fuck her there but also scared shitless. "It's going to hurt."

"Probably." His mouth teased her ear, his breaths hot and shallow. "If it's not the good kind of hurt, I'll stop. Trust me to take care of you."

Trust. That was a thing she gave no one. But as he tore open a foil packet with his teeth, she found herself relaxing beneath him, savoring the heat of his body on her back and the flex of his hand rolling on the condom.

"Breathe." He notched himself against her pussy.

Not her ass?

When she exhaled, he clamped a hand over her mouth and thrust.

Everything inside her stretched as he slammed against the back of her cunt. She screamed against his palm, sucking hard through her nose and writhing against the invasion. His cock was impossibly huge and vicious and *oh my fucking fuck fuck fuck*, he pounded her into the mattress, breaking her open and stabbing her darkest depths.

He grunted with the exertion of his hammering hips, his fingers digging into her cheek and his other hand chasing the lines of her body, squeezing and kneading and scratching her skin.

But there was pleasure amid the savagery, an unlocking sensation that set her breaths free and her skin ablaze. When her cries turned to moans, his hand slid from her mouth to her throat, pressing lightly and turning her neck. His lips were there, feeding from hers, licking and biting with the voracious tempo of his breaths.

She was so turned on she felt it in her veins—that wild, erratic, reckless thrill she hadn't experienced since she was a teenager. She'd forgotten what that was like, to just live and play and love. Tate had returned that feeling to her. With his cock ramming brutally, powerfully inside her, he treated her like a desirable woman instead of a dying invalid. He reminded her how to be herself again.

"Is that all you got?" She arched her back and wriggled her ass against him.

He let go of what little restraint he'd held back, thrusting harder, deeper, faster, as if trying to drive himself right into her heart. With the hug of his arms around her and the caress of his lips on her neck, maybe he'd already buried himself deep within her existence and left his mark. Fuck it, she didn't care. He felt too damn good, too perfect.

He fucked without mercy, working himself in and out with brute force. But the caress of his hands on her body was an intimate communication. Each touch made her feel sexy and loved. Every stroke thrummed with appreciation.

It didn't take long for her to shoot off with a gasping, electrifying, body-tingling release that fired her nerve-endings from her hair to her toes. She was still groaning when he pulled out, and she missed the stretch of him instantly.

He slid his fingers inside her, lubing them up before slipping them out and back, right into her forbidden hole.

"Christ, you're horny." His breathing was tight, bursting sharp gasps past his lips. "You're opening right up for me."

She didn't feel the usual pain. Not even a pinch. Just a tingling swirl of desire and warmth. She was so sated and drugged on pleasure maybe she didn't have the wherewithal to tense. "Can't believe how good that feels."

"You're nice and relaxed." He thrust his fingers in and out of her ass.

"Only with you."

His touch vanished. "When you say things like that…" He leaned down and spit on her clenching ring of muscle. Then he pressed the wide flare of his cock against the moisture. "Makes me really fucking possessive, Lucia."

"You're already possessive."

"Not like this." He pushed, just enough to stimulate her nerves. "Can you keep quiet?"

"Yeah." She breathed deeply. "Fuck me, Tate."

He grabbed her waist with both hands and kicked his hips, tunneling his massive shaft straight through her.

She choked on the sudden burn, but it only lasted a second. The incredible fullness that followed was unlike anything she'd ever felt. Intense. Consuming. It stunned her how much she welcomed the dark thrilling feel of him inside her like this.

A groan vibrated in his chest as he buried his length and thrust slowly. Bending over her, he trailed a shaky hand up her spine and rubbed her back. If he was trying to soothe her, she didn't need it. Maybe he was calming himself.

His hands roamed, teasing every exposed inch of her before clutching a fistful of her hair.

"I'm not going to last long." Using that grip, he yanked her up until her back hit his chest.

On their knees with him seated fully in her ass, he wrapped a hand around her throat while the other slid up her thigh and sank three fingers in her pussy.

Then he fucked her, plunging and retreating with the speed and stamina of a machine. He held her tight to his body and pumped his fingers as his cock drove viciously, greedily in her ass.

His grunting, erotic breaths revved her up and made her insane with need. He was a beast, untamed and wild, as he shoved himself deeper and deeper. She felt every ridge and bump of his cock, and his muscled physique generated so much heat she was certain he would reduce her to ashes.

She couldn't move or meet his thrusts, but she could put her hands on him. As he slammed into her tirelessly, she reached back and palmed the flexing brawn of his butt. He continued to thrust, burning red-hot aftershocks through her body, and she held on, moaning, panting, and taking exquisite pleasure in the ride.

When his fingers slipped from her pussy to work her clit, she knew she would climax like this. And she did moments later, anchored by his cock and the hand around her throat. Her eyes rolled back in her head, and she came and came until white flashes blotted her vision. It was ecstasy. Nirvana. Total attainment of everything right in the world.

"Fuck, Lucia. I'm coming." He jerked his hips and released a long, deep groan that penetrated her chest. "Oh goddamn, fuck!"

His hand slipped from her neck, and his head dropped to her back. He stayed that way for several heaving breaths before smacking a stinging palm against her ass.

"You wore me out." He fell to his back and gasped at the ceiling. "Go drink some water and eat more of that fruit."

"Bossy." With a grin, she removed the rubber from his softening cock and obeyed his orders.

A few minutes later, she stood at the counter, eating strawberries and tingling all over with a rhapsody of sensations. She felt full and glowy and utterly ravished.

His footsteps approached from behind, stretching her mouth into a smile. Then his hands were on her, cruising her hips, slinking around to her abs and cupping her breasts.

"Still hungry?" He kissed a trail of electricity from her shoulder to her neck.

"Not for food." Molten heat curled through her belly, burning hotter with each stroke of his hand and brush of his lips.

The sound of a foil packet caught her ear—the only warning she got before he pushed himself inside her from behind.

"I can't get enough of you." He rocked into her and nibbled on her neck.

"We have all night."

"I need more than a night, baby."

He fucked her against the counter. Then the wall, the floor, in the shower, and back on the bed. Over the next few hours, he made good on his promise to use all three condoms before collapsing on top of her, winded and spent.

"I think you broke my dick." He pressed his face into the crook of her neck, his chest rising and falling, and his cock softening inside her.

When he lifted to move away, she hugged him to her.

"Don't pull out."

"I'd stay here forever if the damn rubber wasn't strangling me." He kissed her lips and left the bed to dispose of the condom.

"Those things don't fit you."

"It's fine." He strode back to the mattress, unabashed with his nudity.

Even flaccid, he hung longer and thicker than the average erection. God, he had a glorious cock. It should never be covered in latex.

"Feels like I'm chapped." He stood above her and ran a hand along the length, glancing at it.

"Maybe I can help." She lifted onto her knees and gently kissed along the soft, warm skin of his thick shaft.

"I wasn't complaining, but..." He released a happy breath and twitched against her lips. "That's nice."

His hand went to her hair, sliding through the strands from the roots to the tips. His cock filled with blood, but he seemed content to just let her nuzzle and tease with chaste kisses.

Without an inch of fat on his body, every sinew and vein stood out in stark relief beneath his taut skin. She traced the lines of his narrow hips and the sexy cuts and ridges that formed the *V* of his abs. He was beautifully formed. So powerful and manly, and if she touched him much more she might beg him to fuck her without a condom.

She sat on her heels, and he knelt beside her, nudging her to her back.

"How are you feeling?" He guided her legs apart and probed his thumbs around her swollen tissues. "Sore?"

"I'm good."

She brushed his hands away, but he was relentless, inspecting and touching and shifting down to examine her rectum.

"Tate, stop." She twisted away from him. "I'm better than good, okay? Better than I've been in years."

"Yeah?" He flashed her a grin.

"Yeah."

He reached up and flicked off the light switch, leaving the dim illumination of the night light in the wall outlet. Then he prowled toward her on hands and knees, his blue eyes glinting. Unsure of his intent, she didn't know whether to sigh or tense up.

His arm caught her waist, and he dragged her against him. She clung to his shoulders as he rolled and adjusted until they were on their sides, chest to chest, snug under the blanket.

"We're going to sleep?" She slid her fingers through his hair, stroking.

"Yep."

He was so close she smelled all his distinctive aromas — salty skin and warm sex and musky masculinity.

She felt high on his scent, the deep sounds of his breaths, and the euphoric heat of his body tucked against hers. "Are you still awake?"

He laughed, a rumbling delightful sound. "I doubt I'll sleep tonight."

"Why?"

"I want to enjoy this." He twined his legs around hers and rubbed her back. "Feels too good."

Her chest fluttered and stretched with his words. "Tell me about you. Your full name. Age. Childhood. Anything."

"Tate Anthony Vades. Twenty-five. I grew up in a whorehouse."

"No way."

"Yes way."

His gravelly voice drifted around her as he told her about The Velvet Den, the traumatic way he lost his virginity, and his admiration for the woman who raised him.

She talked about the citrus grove and her favorite memories of Matias and Camila.

He spoke about the roses inked on his arm and the whores he spent his childhood with.

Then she explained how Tiago administered her injections — in his room, without her clothes and weapons, with the safe only a few feet away. Locked. Inaccessible. She'd never seen inside it.

As the night crept by, they got to know each other through words. And kissing. He kissed her often. Lazy, unassuming kisses without urgency or intention. Kissing for the sole purpose of expressing affection.

He told her about his house and his roommates — four men and a woman. Then he kissed her again, his hands never leaving her body and his arms tightly wound around her back.

"I want to call Matias," he breathed against her lips.

She knew why. In just a couple short hours, she would be back with Tiago where Tate couldn't protect her, couldn't control what happened to her, and that didn't sit well with a man like him. But if he made that call, Matias would come to Caracas and risk his life and that of his men to extract her from Tiago's world. And for what purpose? To free a dying woman?

She couldn't even consider threatening Camila's happiness until she knew there was a chance of survival.

"Wait for the blood test," she said. "If it reveals a diagnosis and treatment, I'll go wherever you tell me to go. How long will it take to get the results back?"

"Several days." His jaw flexed against hers. "I don't like this."

"I know." She snuggled closer, burrowing against his chest. "But I like *this*. I've never slept in a bed with a man."

He hummed a growly sigh and squeezed her butt. "I'll be your first and your last."

What did that mean? She lifted her head. "Why?"

"As long as I'm alive, I'll be the only man in your bed."

She stared at him, lips parting, and blinked.

"Close your mouth and go to sleep." He gripped her neck and pressed her cheek to his chest.

"You're a Neanderthal."

"I've been called worse. Now sleep."

And she did. It was the best sleep she'd ever had, and so was the next night, and the next.

For the next five nights, it was just him and her and the protective bubble he built around them.

She went to the compound for her injections in the mornings and the mandatory dinners in the evenings. While in Tiago's presence, she exaggerated her illness, moaning and stumbling and feigning vertigo until he sent her home.

And Tate was always there, waiting for her.

He stocked her apartment with food and necessities, added discreet bolts on the insides of the doors, and drew her blood when the test kit arrived.

Now it was a waiting game, a delay of action until the results came back. They bided their time in her tiny windowless space, talking, eating, sleeping, and exploring each other emotionally and physically.

His hunger for her was insatiable. They fucked daily and nightly, in every manner of motion, mood, and position. And holy hell, the man loved to kiss. She was kissed more in those five days than in the previous thirty years of her life.

It was five days of intoxicating, Tate-induced bliss. She never wanted it to end.

But like all good things…

The old adage got it right.

Except her good thing didn't just come to an end. It ripped open and bled out in a devastation of pain.

EIGHTEEN

"Feeling better tonight?" Tiago studied Lucia from across the table in his private dining room.

She let him see the trembling in her hand as she pushed away her empty plate. "No."

It was the truth. Tonight was going to be a bad night. She felt it simmering inside her — the queasiness, the tremors, and the pinpricks numbing her lower body.

The last time she lost mobility, he left her on the floor in the common area of the compound, paralyzed, vulnerable, unable to move her legs to walk home.

"I don't feel well at all." She shifted to the edge of the seat and craned her neck for a better view of the hall outside the dining room. "I'm ready to go home."

Armed guards lined the corridor. Three times more men than usual. Restless energy buzzed through them as they fidgeted and whispered to one another. Something was wrong.

"Did something happen?" Dread curled in her gut, aggravating the nausea.

"There's a spy in my neighborhood." Tiago set his utensils down, casually dabbed his mouth with a napkin, and imprisoned her gaze. "Do you know anything about that?"

"No."

It took every ounce of discipline she could muster to moderate her expression. Meanwhile, her heart clambered the rungs of her ribs and pounded a terrified howl in her throat.

Did he capture Tate? Was he holding him in the basement

chamber to await an unspeakable night of torture?

Saliva rushed over her tongue, bringing with it the urgent need to throw up. Her sickness, nerves, fear—all of it rose up and contorted her face.

But Tiago didn't notice, his attention locked on the man striding into the room.

Armando, her fellow torturer, paused beside Tiago's chair and said in Spanish, "We have him."

Her stomach bottomed out, and her blood turned to ice.

No, please, God. This can't be happening.

The guns holstered in her waistband grew hot and heavy, begging her to reach for them. But a guard stood at her back, and two more bracketed the door.

"*Muy bien.*" Tiago stood and offered her his hand. "Shall we?"

Terror held her frozen in the chair. She could fight, but they were physically stronger. She had weapons, but they had more. If she died in this room, Tate would die, too.

He's dead no matter what.

She needed to get the fuck out of there and alert Van. He could contact that Cole Hartman guy and... She didn't know, but it was the only option she had, and Tiago was waiting.

She made her legs work, putting her weight on the heels as she hoisted herself from the chair. Her knees locked, and she took a wobbly step.

"Tiago... I think I'm..." Dizziness swept her into a spinning fog.

She clutched the table, careening sideways and catching herself before she hit the floor.

Fucking hell, she was going downhill quick. Her abdomen spasmed and clenched, and her head pounded. Her throat was so tight she couldn't swallow. It felt like her insides were being wrung out and tied up. Everything hurt.

Tiago stared at her from a foot away, his bored expression growing blurrier with each heavy blink of her eyes.

Fuck him. I can do this.

Resisting the urge to puke, she pushed through the pain, straightened to her full height, and stepped toward him.

Only her legs didn't move. She couldn't feel them. Couldn't feel her hands or her heartbeat. She swayed in the whirling room, battling to stay upright, and willing her body to cooperate.

Don't give up on me. Please, not now. I can't—

The floor fell out beneath her, and she plummeted into the black void of nothingness.

NINETEEN

Lucia woke to the sound of bloodcurdling screams. The strident howling echoed at a distance, but she knew it was coming from only feet away. Garbled and frothing with spit, it sounded like a dying animal. But as her senses focused and disorientation burned away, she realized it was a man in unfathomable pain.

Tate.

Fury snarled though her veins, surging her upright. The sudden motion knocked her off-balance, and she teetered, falling with the hard smack of her cheek against the concrete floor.

Pain burst behind her eyes. Overhead lights burned into her skull, and the scuff of rubber soles sounded near her head. She recognized the floor, the unforgiving glare of the fluorescents, and the reek of death that lived in the walls.

She couldn't let the basement chamber claim its next victim.

Must get up. Protect him. Save him.

Rolling to her back, she immediately noticed her guns were missing. She tried to move her legs and couldn't. Tried to focus her eyes and couldn't. Tried to sit up and only made it to her elbows. The room was empty before her. All the activity was at her back—the guttural screams, the scrapes of multiple shoes, and the rattle of chains.

Swimming in a thick soup of lethargy, vertigo, and nausea, she mentally prepared herself. Given the rawness in his voice and the scent of blood and urine, the torture had been going on for a while.

"Welcome back." Tiago stood behind her, bending over her head so he could smile at her upside down. "Still can't move your legs?"

She couldn't fucking feel her legs, and she was two seconds from retching all over his shoes.

He prowled into her line of sight, his shirt smeared with crimson stains and his index finger tipped with a razored claw.

The claw he used to carve pictures into flesh and muscle.

She despised him with such deep, searing, vile hatred it vibrated her bones and popped blood vessels behind her eyes.

"What have you done?" She choked on the bile rising in her throat, blinking back tears as she fumbled to shift her useless body toward the scene behind her.

Blood. It was everywhere, dripping from deep cuts in the hanging slab of breathing meat. The dissection was gruesome, and though she'd seen his macabre handiwork before, she still went into shock. Her nervous system shut down. Her lungs froze up, and her mind struggled to process the rivers of red and the stench of carnage.

She looked away and forced herself to move. Crawling on her belly, she dragged her legs behind her and lost a heeled shoe in the process. Desperate to get to him, she couldn't stall the burning tears, the wretched sobs, and the violent shaking in her arms as she inched forward with strenuously slow movements.

Too much blood. I'm too late.

When she reached the sticky dark pool at his feet, she angled her neck to look up, up, up and...

She stopped breathing.

The slaughtered body was too thin, the hair too long and black, and the trousers too baggy and unfamiliar.

Not Tate.

Not Tate.

That man isn't Tate.

Her relief was so profound and overwhelming she lost control of her stomach and vomited across the floor.

"You never appreciate my artwork." Tiago stepped around her, easing her away from the puke and onto her back. "You look like hell."

"Fuck you."

His chuckle was worse than any response he could've given. She was here for a reason, and like all the other times she'd been in this room, she wouldn't leave unscathed.

The man's wails weakened, ebbing into silence. He must've passed out. Or died. With his back to the wall, his head hung toward his chest, eyes closed. Chains wrapped his wrists and suspended him from the ceiling, and his chest... She was certain if she looked close enough she'd see bone in the trenches of some of those cuts.

She glared up at Tiago. "You're a monster. A butcher."

"You're a whore. Now that we got that out of the way..." He

gestured toward the door. "Armando is waiting."

Horror spiked through her heart as she followed his gaze.

Tall and pear-shaped with an overhanging belly, Armando caught and held her glare. He smoothed a hand over his greasy hair, his grin a rictus of yellow teeth.

"Waiting for what?" Her question didn't need an answer. She knew. Deep in the pith of her miserable existence, she knew.

"He discovered the spy." Tiago approached the mutilated man and inspected the carved designs. "This was one of my new recruits. Turns out, he works for the competition. Came here to steal from me."

He pulled a gun from his pants, aimed it at the man's bowed head, and fired.

She averted her gaze as the bang reverberated through her chest, making her shoulders twitch.

"To reward Armando for bringing him in," Tiago said, holstering the gun, "I told him he could have anything of mine for one night. Guess what he chose?"

Me.

She closed her eyes and tried to temper her runaway breaths. Spasms ignited in parts of her butt and midsection, but feeling still hadn't returned to her legs. There would be no running. She wouldn't even be able to kick in defense or clench her thighs together.

She calmed herself with the reminder that it could've been worse. It could've been Tate hanging there, carved up and dead. She wouldn't have survived that.

But she could survive this. *Just like all the times before.*

"I know you're sick." He crouched in front of her and slid the other heeled shoe off her paralyzed foot. "But you're a trooper, Lucia. Spread those pretty legs and show him a good time."

She didn't have use of her legs, but she had a wealth of aggression in her bones. Her body was dying, but her spirit sang with life. Her muscles would give, but her mind would not.

Armando would rape her while Tiago watched. She would spit and punch and cry until Armando hit her hard enough to knock the wind from her.

Then they would do it all again.

No matter how hard she fought—and she would—the result would be the same.

This was happening.

Because that was the way of things.

TWENTY

Hours later, Lucia hung upside down with a shoulder jabbing her unbearably sore stomach. Her body was too broken to obey her commands, so one of the guards had to carry her to the apartment.

She'd been punched in the gut so many times the nausea had gone silently numb. Every bone, tissue, and tendon throbbed with fire. Her legs were heavy dead things attached to joints made of sand and dust. Her skull pounded rhythmically. Her swallows felt like serrated blades, and molten lava tunneled between her thighs and buttocks.

Armando had brutally violated every hole in her body. He'd bitten her breasts and thighs, kicked her ribs and face, and repeated the torment until she lay curled in the fetal position with her arms around her head.

His cruelty had been so severe Tiago had to interfere several times to stop him from crossing the line.

But lines had been crossed. All of them. The wreckage was so complete, so excruciating, her body didn't feel like it belonged to her. It'd become a burdensome, pulsating prison of pain. It had failed her. Over and over again.

Her arms dangled toward the oily pavement, and the shadows of surrounding buildings rocked with the guard's heavy-booted steps.

Then those boots paused, and an impatient hand dug through her pockets and found her key.

The scraping sound of her door urged her to move her limbs, but she couldn't. She'd left the last of her strength on the floor in that basement chamber.

But it'll be okay now. Tate would be waiting for her inside, like he did every night.

At that thought, her traumatized heart stirred to life, beating with urgency. She needed Tate so badly. Needed the protection of his arms, the comfort of his voice, and the affection in his kisses.

He was smart enough to stay hidden until she was inside with the door shut. So she didn't worry when the guard stepped in, dumped her on the mattress, and set her guns and shoes out of reach on the floor.

When the door clicked shut behind him, she released a shredded breath and listened.

Silence.

"Are you there?" She didn't hear Tate's footsteps, didn't feel his touch, didn't sense his imposing presence in the dark.

"Tate?" she whispered, rolling to her stomach with a painful heave.

The continued silence closed in around her, swelling her throat and heating her eyes. "Tate... Please, I need you."

She knew he wasn't here, but she kept calling for him, kept hoping.

Where was he? Was he safe? What if he'd left town? Maybe her test results had come back and there was nothing he could do for her. Would he return to Texas without saying goodbye?

He wouldn't do that. It was just the voice of misery inside her, taunting her while she was down.

And she was down, face in the mattress, trapped in a dying, throbbing body. Everything burned and trembled as her injuries set in. There would be bruises, swelling, and possible scars around her rectum, but the surface stuff was negligible compared to the damage wrought inside.

"Tate... Tate, where are you?" She lay immobile, lifeless, as the tears welled up. She didn't bother blinking or rubbing them away. There was no one here, nothing to see.

She was alone.

Alone was her normal. She learned long ago how to fend for herself, fight for herself, and endure by herself. But she didn't want to be alone anymore. She was exhausted, hurting, and...done. She was so fucking done.

So she let the tears fall until she was emotionally bankrupt. Until all that remained was the hollow husk of a battered body.

Eventually, her eyes dried, and her vision cleared, bringing her guns into focus on the floor across the room.

One bullet. It was all she needed.

It would erase the pain. Eradicate the illness. End the loneliness.

Her arms moved without hesitation, elbows grinding against the hard floor as she hauled her body toward the end.

She was afraid to die, afraid of the terrible nothingness that awaited. But more than that, she was terrified to live, to endure another day of this vicious circle. She didn't want to fight anymore.

As she lugged her body toward the guns, her mind traveled to a better place. She smelled the citrus grove, the sunshine, and the fertile soil. She felt the warm breeze in her hair and the tickle of long grass on her legs. She saw her sister — her beautiful, laughing, vibrant baby sister. Camila and Matias would have such adorable, brown-eyed children. Their love for each other was so strong it would carry through generations.

Then she heard Tate's voice, his breathy whispers at her ear. A tearful sigh billowed past her bloodied, cracked lips. She ached. God help her, she ached to see him one more time.

He had a magic about him, an allurement that went beyond his model-perfect looks. He'd experienced the kind of brutality that would destroy a man, but he'd ridden it out and stood taller, stronger, despite it.

She felt the strength of his fingers around her throat. Smelled the clean scent of his breath on her face. Tasted his possessiveness on her lips.

For a moment, she thought he was actually here, but there was only the empty room and the gun that was now within her reach.

Her hand shook as she lifted the metal frame, her entire body screaming in agony from the effort it'd taken to crawl there. It was a heavy trigger, but she would have just enough determination left to pull it.

With her cheek on the floor, she positioned the gun in front of her face and stared into the barrel.

It would bring her peace.

It would bring the end.

She wanted it to end.

She needed the end.

End it.

End it.

End it.

TWENTY-ONE

A stinging slap across Tate's face woke him from a violent dream and shoved him into a goddamn nightmare.

"Wake up."

The heartless voice magnified the ringing in his ears, and a furious roar burst from his throat. Except the sound was deadened, muffled by the wad of cloth in his mouth.

That motherfucking, psycho, bastard fuck!

He jerked forward, vibrating with rage and out for blood. And he went nowhere. Because he was fucking duct taped to a kitchen chair.

He glared at the man who had bound him there. *I'm going to kill you.*

"You made me knock you out." Van sat in front of him on the couch, all casual and calm, despite the bloody, swollen mess of his face.

Tate's cheekbone pulsed with its own swelling pain, his knuckles split and sore. He and Van had beaten the shit out of each other, and he seethed to do it again.

After Lucia is safe.

He hadn't heard everything that had been transmitted from the bug on her shoe, but he'd heard enough. The dinner, the torture, and *Armando's reward.*

Listening to her being assaulted, violated, and forced by that man had been a horrifying, inconsolable hell. In a fog of murderous wrath, he'd holstered his guns and stormed toward the door intent on raining death and destruction on the compound in his effort to save her.

But Van had stopped him with a fist. Then they fought with more fists, putting holes in walls and breaking furniture. Until one of Van's swings caught him on the temple and *lights out.*

How long had he been unconscious? He tried to bellow the question, but the gag garbled his words.

"She's in her apartment." Van lifted a phone and held it near Tate's face. "Alone and quiet."

He strained his hearing until he caught the distant sound of her raspy, wheezing breaths.

His blood boiled anew, steaming through his veins and clouding his vision. He thrashed against the tape across his chest, desperate to get to her.

Let me go! Let me go! Fucking release me!

"Calm down." Van stood and paced through the room, picking up broken pieces of the coffee table. "I saved your life."

Fuck off. He growled low and deep in his chest, heaving against the gag.

"You're here for her. I know that." Van dropped the splintered wood in a pile and stepped toward the window to peer down at the alley. "But I'm here for *you.* To protect you. To keep your stupid ass alive."

Tate closed his eyes and drew a sharp breath through his nose. Maybe Van had saved him from a bloody, unproductive death. And maybe he would thank Van later. But only if Lucia was still alive.

He still didn't have the blood results back, and the lab wasn't returning his calls. He'd talked to Cole Hartman earlier today and explained Lucia's situation. Cole could bring a doctor to her, but it was going to take two weeks.

She didn't have two fucking weeks.

"What's it going to be, Tate?" Van prowled toward him and gripped his jaw, forcing his head up. "Are you going to be smart? Or dead?"

TWENTY-TWO

Something soft and warm whispered across Lucia's lips, rousing her. Arms slipped beneath her body and lifted her from the floor, jostling swollen joints and pushing against bruises. Pain blasted through her bones, and she cried out.

"Shh." The satiny sensation returned to her lips, making gentle sounds and infusing her inhales with a clean, minty, familiar scent.

"Tate?" She opened her eyes to a crystal blue dream.

"I'm so sorry." He brushed his mouth against hers again, lingering over the cuts on her lip. "I would've been here, but…"

He raised his head and glared at something across the room. The glow of the night light illuminated a crisscross of gashes on his cheek and around his eye.

"What happened?" Her pulse kicked up, and holy fuck, it hurt.

Her heart, her head, her stomach, everything hurt so badly. She still couldn't move her legs, but she summoned the strength to turn her neck and follow his gaze.

Van. He folded his arms across his chest and leaned his butt against the counter, his scowl as puffy and battered as Tate's.

"We had a disagreement." Van narrowed his eyes. "Why were you sleeping with a gun pointed at your mouth? With your finger on the trigger?"

Her thoughts imploded with painful sparks. Flashes of the Beretta in her hand. Echoes of her dismal hesitation. She'd wanted to die, had even tried to squeeze the trigger. But she hadn't tried hard enough. Hadn't wanted it bad enough. She must've passed out.

She focused on Tate, on the swirling depths of his vigilant gaze. "I couldn't do it."

Now would be a good time to tell him what happened with Armando. But as his entire body shook against her, vibrating with barely-contained fury, she decided not to throw salt in the wound.

"If I'd been here, I wouldn't have allowed you to even consider it." Another death glare at Van. Then he lowered her to the mattress and stretched out beside her, cradling her against his chest.

He was so close his short beard tickled her chin. His fingers combed through her hair with agonizing tenderness, and his exhales incited her to breathe.

He was here. This was real. She was *breathing*.

Those merciful thoughts swarmed in with the ugly ones — her abused body, her necessary return to the compound in the morning, and the inevitable fate that awaited her at the end of this.

But for now, she had him, his arms around her, his hand stroking her hair, and his unspoken intent to take care of her.

Tears leaked from her eyes and dripped into the cuts on her lips. It was neither sadness nor contentment, but rather the overwhelming weight of the past eleven years finally catching up with her.

He kissed her cheeks, nuzzling her skin. Then he shifted and cupped her head in his hands to position her on her back. The movement triggered an explosion of agony so sharp she thought she might puke.

"Fuck." He bent over her, caressing her hair, and glanced over his shoulder. "Van."

Footsteps approached, and the mattress dipped on her other side beneath Van's weight.

"Where does it hurt?" Van slung a backpack off his shoulder and removed a huge zippered pouch with a medical logo on it.

"Everywhere. I think..." The constant pain trembled her voice, and she swallowed. "A shower would be nice if I had help."

He glanced at Tate, and something passed between them.

"We don't have time." Tate feathered his fingertips across her stomach and paused on the hem of her shirt. "We're leaving. But first, Van's going to examine you and make you as comfortable as possible to travel." He lifted her shirt, inching it toward her head without moving his eyes from hers. "I called Matias."

"What?" Her lungs slammed together. "Camila knows? She knows I'm alive?"

"I just called him, but yeah, I'm sure she knows now."

Anger shuddered through her. Not because Matias would take her away from her medicine. Her death was inconsequential. But she didn't want Camila to experience it. *Again.*

The thought jabbed into her wounds and tore them open. "You

shouldn't have done that. Camila can't—"

"Camila isn't a fucking factor in this." The harshness in his tone contradicted the delicate way he inched her shirt up and off.

"That's bullshit." Her frail voice failed to express her distress. "You're here for her."

"Not anymore." The loaded press of his gaze sent her heart into a tailspin.

With a coughing smirk, Van left the bed and turned the water on at the sink.

"What does that mean?" she asked, aching to hear Tate say it, to taste the hope.

"I'm here for you and you alone."

Just like that, her wish for death was laid waste in the promise that hovered between them. Maybe she could find a cure. Maybe she could see Camila again, and her sister wouldn't have to mourn her death a second time.

Maybe Tate would love her the way he loved Camila.

She dreamed of a life where she could explore possibilities with him, where she could nurture their connection, grow it, and pour the entirety of her being into it. To do any of that, she needed to live.

He kissed the corner of her mouth, the injury on her cheek, and the trickle of tears spilling from her eyes. "The quickest Matias can get here is eight hours by helicopter. But he can't get into the neighborhood. We have to go to him."

Eight hours and she would be rid of this place.

Eight hours and I'll be dead.

"I have time for one more injection if—"

"No. You're not going near the compound." He focused on her jeans, releasing the fly and gingerly sliding them off. "Are you still not able to feel your legs?"

"No, I can't..." She searched his eyes, confused. "How did you know about that?"

Van returned with a wadded wet shirt and bottled water and removed two pills from the medical bag.

"For the pain." He helped her swallow the medication while exchanging a silent look with Tate.

What were they not telling her?

She stared into Tate's bloodshot eyes, wincing at the cut swelling his eyelid. "Why were you fighting?"

"I know what happened to you tonight. I was listening." He worked his jaw, his expression pained. "You've been wearing a bug."

He told her about the listening devices, how he planted them, how they worked, and why he hid them from her. His hands flexed as he detailed what he'd heard tonight and the fist fight that followed with Van.

"I can't tell you how sorry I am for failing to protect you." His voice broke beneath a tide of torment.

Desolation flooded his expression, and it hurt her to see it. She let her eyes drift shut and tried to process everything he'd said.

She didn't feel anger or resentment about being spied on. She felt…relieved. Safeguarded. Maybe even cherished. He didn't have to watch over her like that, but he did. Because he was here for her.

"Thank you," she whispered.

He gave her hip a gentle squeeze and ghosted his fingers along the edge of her panties. "I need to remove these."

She kept her eyes closed, knowing there was dried blood and come between her legs. Since he'd heard her struggle and ultimate defeat in the basement, he wouldn't be surprised at what he found.

Once she was bare, he didn't make a sound as he used the warm wet shirt to clean her. Then he and Van worked together, washing and nursing the worst of her injuries. The gash on her cheek needed stitches, as well as two across her ribs. Brutal knuckles, the concrete floor, the steel toe of a boot… She didn't know which cruelty caused which wounds, but Van sewed them up. Considering he used to torture people for a living, she supposed he was an expert at tending injuries inflicted by a sadist.

As Van stitched, Tate wove his fingers through hers and kissed her hand. "Your paralysis is concerning, Lucia."

She cracked open an eye. "What time is it?"

"Just after midnight. If you usually get your medicine at dawn, we have enough time to go to the nearest hospital and—"

"All three hospitals in Caracas are infiltrated with Tiago's people. The doctors won't treat me. He would kill them if they did."

His eyes flashed dangerously. "Then we'll find a hospital outside of the city."

"Waste of time."

"Dammit, Lucia. I'm not giving up."

"This isn't about giving up. The country is in a major health crisis. The shortage of medical supplies and hospital beds is so awful women are giving birth in the waiting rooms. Patients are dying on the bloodstained floors of hospital hallways after waiting days to see a doctor. I've seen the newspaper headlines. They have three percent of the supplies they need to treat people. *Three* percent, Tate."

"Because of the limitations the President put on importations?" Van clipped the final stitch and packed up the medical bag.

"I think so," she said. "As a result, the hospitals have *nothing*. I'll be dead and cold long before I even get into an exam room."

The simple act of talking had stressed her body. Parts deep inside her stabbed and burned, but she didn't know what was damaged or how irreparable the damage was. The burning sensation in her gut spread outward, blanketing her skin in violent, sweaty chills. Her breathing labored, and her pulse weakened, as if her organs were shutting down. Soon, they would be of no use to her.

"I'm dying."

"Not if I have something to say about it." Tate released her hand, and his large frame retreated in the blotches of her vision.

As unconsciousness tried to claim her, his voice thrummed at the edges. He was on the phone, making angry demands and pacing through the room.

She floated in and out of awareness, shifting restlessly on the mattress in an attempt to escape the persistent pain. Tate's voice continued in the background as Van dressed her. She welcomed the warmth of clothes, until she became too hot, too clammy. She was burning up.

Then Tate's hands were there, smoothing back her hair and easing a cool damp cloth around her face.

"I just talked to Cole Hartman." He touched a kiss to her lips. "He's going to find a doctor outside of the city. Someone we can trust."

Her chest lifted, filling with lofty wishes and greedy reveries. She wanted to scream her excitement and hug him until they both grunted with laughter, but the most she could offer was, "'kay. Thank you."

"He'll call back and let us know where to go. But we need to move. Get out of this neighborhood. Are you ready?"

"Can't walk." Her words sounded garbled and slurred.

"Shh. I have you." He pulled a gun from the front of his jeans and twisted toward Van. "I'll follow you out."

Van stepped toward the passageway in the closet with a gun in his hand and a huge pack on his back.

Tate bent to lift her and stopped. "Did you hear that?"

The silence that followed strangled like a chokehold. Then Van said, "No—"

A deafening bang rattled the front door, and it blew open in an eruption of splintered wood.

Her heart stopped, and guns fired. A man screamed. More men swarmed in. Assault rifles and handguns and street clothes. Tiago's guards.

Tate stood over her, shooting, dodging, ducking, and shouting something at Van. Boots scuffed near the door. Bullets pelleted the wall. Then glass popped, and the lights went out.

Her vision fuzzed in the darkness, her brain sluggish, her entire body convulsing with panic and helplessness. She couldn't stand, couldn't defend him, and fear ate away her alertness.

She blindly stretched an arm across the mattress, seeking her Berettas as the gunfire began to slow.

"Van!" Tate lurched off the bed and slammed into something just as a shot rang out from the doorway.

Then silence.

Icy, dead, ominous silence.

She broke out in a cold sweat, trembling in her effort to stay conscious. "Tate?"

The rustle of clothes, tread of boots, beam of a flashlight—there were people in the room. Was Van among them?

"Tate?" She blinked, but her eyes wouldn't work right. "Answer me."

Where was he? What happened?

He'd called to Van, jumped, and a shot was fired.

He was hit.

Her heart collapsed, and the roar of blood thrashed in her ears.

No no no no no. He can't be hurt. He can't die. He can't. He can't. He can't.

Shadows moved in around her. Then footsteps. A lot of them.

She turned her neck and felt a cool hand on her cheek.

"Tate and Van." The low rumble of a man's voice. Tiago's voice. "I know a lot more than their names."

"Help." She cringed away from his touch, but his hand stayed with her. "I think Tate was shot."

"He was definitely shot." His fingertips crawled across her lips. "Directly in the chest."

She couldn't breathe. This wasn't real. Her body locked up, and her mind screamed in denial. "I need to see him. Let me see!"

A phone rang. Muffled and cheerful, the chirp sounded close. Somewhere on the floor.

Cole Hartman. He was supposed to call back with an address for a doctor.

The hand on her lips slipped away. A moment later, the chirping grew louder, clearer. Then it died.

"Who's calling him?" Tiago's voice drifted from above.

"I don't know."

It didn't matter. That call was an invitation for believers and dreamers. There were no dreamers in hell. Only sufferers and tormentors, prey and predators, and she epitomized both sides.

She was also a fool. Because dammit, she still hoped.

She hoped Tate was alive as Tiago carried her away from him and out of the apartment.

She hoped to live as he sat her in the backseat of a car and drove her to the compound.

She hoped for strength as he hauled her into the basement chamber.

But as she trembled on the concrete floor, it was hard to hang onto hope. The pain in her body became intolerable when her muscles began to spasm and a seizure thrust her into the black void.

Voices and footfalls ricocheted around her, but her mind was a mass of wool. She couldn't focus. Couldn't fight. They would do whatever they wanted to her, and the slow pulse of time would be a new kind a torment.

At some point, her brain disentangled, and her senses came online. A pillow, hard and thick, bolstered the back of her head. She lay face up, squinting against the harsh lighting. And hurting. The pain concentrated in her stomach, constricting and twisting and threatening to take her under again.

Oh God, it hurts. Make it stop.

She shifted her gaze away from the lights and focused on what was directly above her. Broad chest, thick biceps, and a scarred and swollen face with silver eyes. As her mind sharpened, she realized her head was on Van's lap. With his back against the wall and his arms chained to a horizontal beam behind him, he watched the activity on the other side of the room.

Her heart rate exploded. If Van was here…

She gathered the strength to turn her neck and collided with the crystal blue fury engulfing Tate's eyes.

He's alive.

Her breaths seized, and her arms quaked to hold him.

Shirtless and heaving, his chest bore a ghastly wound that bled beneath the skin. But it wasn't the critical, penetrating type of injury she expected from a bullet. It looked like someone had swung a hammer as hard as possible against his ribs.

If he was in pain, he didn't show it. His red-hot expression suggested he had so much adrenaline and testosterone pumping through him he felt nothing but violent rage.

"He took a bullet in the chest for me," Van said quietly. "Saved my life. Only reason he's alive is because he was wearing an armored shirt. His ribs are probably broken."

She knew his soft tone was meant to calm her, but beneath the whispered words shivered something she knew too well. *Fear.* She felt it, too. Dread. Terror. The horrifying grip of doom.

Tate hung from chains that encircled his wrists and connected to the rafters, his feet bare and raised on toes, as if to ease the strain on his arms. It was the same place, same position, same fate as the man who died there only hours earlier.

Standing beside him, Tiago held a phone in one hand and Tate's shirt in the other. He spoke in a low voice to Armando — the only other person in the room. When he tossed the shirt on the metal table in the corner, that was when she saw it.

The lethal razor blade curved from the end of his finger like a claw.

An artist's instrument.

His favorite weapon.

"No." A mangled keening sound wailed from her throat. "Tiago, please, I'm begging you. Don't do this. I'll do anything."

"You'll do anything for *him*?" He tipped his head toward Tate, holding her gaze.

"Yes. Anything."

"Hm." He teased the claw across Tate's pecs. "I'm more interested in finding out what he'll do for *you*."

TWENTY-THREE

The scent of blood stung Tate's nose. Not *his* blood. The death from earlier tonight hovered in the air and stained the concrete floor. He'd heard the man's tortured screams through the transmitter and could now see the source of that agony glinting on the end of Tiago Badell's finger.

The blade looked lethal enough to carve through muscle, and as it lightly scraped across his chest, he was certain it would.

His heart drummed a furious tattoo. Chains restrained his arms, and broken ribs made every breath excruciating. He had no defense, no way to protect Lucia and Van. No way out of this.

Fear should've been a hulking presence inside him, but it was crowded out by unholy rage. Lucia lay on the floor in dangerous need of urgent care. She'd just surfaced from what must've been a seizure, one that had convulsed her muscles so violently it banged her skull against the concrete. Van, with his arms shackled, had managed to wedge a thigh beneath her head. Meanwhile, Badell had stood there and watched her suffer like a morally depraved psychopath.

How would they get out of this? With Van and him shackled and Lucia clinging to life, they needed a fucking miracle.

It would be eight hours before Matias realized there was trouble, and even more hours to organize a rescue party. Maybe Cole would suspect something since his call went unanswered. That wouldn't help them, though. He was in another country.

"There are no contacts stored on your phone." Badell set it on the metal table and met his eyes. "No call history."

At Cole's request, Tate had meticulously kept the burner phone wiped clean. Thank fuck for Cole's counsel. The man had laid out plans for every emergency, including instructions in the event Tate was captured.

"I can give you a contact." He hardened his expression, masking the pain in his ribs. "Call my brother." He rattled off a predetermined phone number that would alert Cole of foul play. "You'll get your ransom money."

"Your *brother?*" Badell casually strolled through the room, clasping his hands behind him and twitching that deadly finger blade. "Your shirt repelled a bullet, and your companion" — he glanced at Van — "doesn't carry a phone."

Tate had destroyed all the phones but one before they left the apartment. He'd also had the foresight to protect their friends and family in anticipation of repercussions for taking Lucia out of Caracas. If Badell were to discover Tate's identity, his friends' lives could be threatened. So when he'd called Matias, Matias vowed to send his local guys to collect Liv and Josh, Amber and Livana, and all of Tate's roommates. They should be safely on their way to Matias' Colombian estate at this very moment.

"You have high-tech weapons and medical supplies." Badell paused before him, head cocked. "But no IDs. No passports. Nothing to connect you to anything or anyone. We both know you won't be providing your *brother's* number."

A knot formed in Tate's throat. He'd given Badell too many reasons to be suspicious. The man might've been clinically insane, but he was smart. There would be no ransom demands, because he smelled the trap.

Across the room, Lucia's whimpers grew louder. She rolled off Van's lap and pulled herself across the floor, grunting and sobbing in her determination to get to Tate.

"Lucia, don't." He jerked uselessly against the restraints. "Stay where you are."

"No." Her legs dragged behind her, slowing her down, and she cried out in frustration.

It was gut-wrenching to witness, cracking things inside him that hurt far worse than broken ribs.

He gave Badell the deadliest glare he could manage for a man hanging in chains. "She needs medicine. A doctor."

"Whether she gets that is up to you."

"What do you want?"

"Tell me why you're here. In Caracas."

Given Tate's weapons and the bullet-resistant shirt, Badell knew this wasn't a pleasure trip. He also knew it was personal. He only needed to watch Lucia as she hauled herself toward Tate. Her anguished cries shuddered with heartbreak. And *love.*

Love.

She loves me.

The intensity of that realization sent waves of pain through Tate's fractured chest. At first, he didn't understand it. It made him feel desperate and terrified, but underneath the panic was something new, something wholly unexpected.

When she smiles, I feel a peace unlike anything I've felt in my life.

Van's words hit him with soul-deep comprehension.

Lucia's smile was his responsibility, his goal, his everything. Her life, her health, all of her was his to protect.

She didn't belong to Matias or Badell or any other man. If anyone even thought to lay claim to her, he wouldn't step aside. He wouldn't back down. He would fucking fight for her with every breath in his body. She was his.

I love her.

Not the kind of love he'd flirted with before. What he felt for Camila paled in the dense, feral glow burning in his chest. This was deep, consuming, world-changing love. His past, present, and future, his entire existence took on new meaning.

His reason for everything was right here, in this room, dragging herself toward him. Her pain was his pain. Her tears, her happiness, her fate—all of it was his. Protecting her wasn't an obligation. It was his purpose.

It was the most significant thing he could ever do.

In that moment, he knew he would endure anything to make sure she smiled again. He would kill, bleed, cry, break, and die for her. There was nothing, absolutely fucking nothing he wouldn't do for her.

Fortitude built in his mind and girded his spine. It wasn't just a willingness to fight for her. It was an insistence.

"You know why I'm here." He leveled Badell with a look that encapsulated the depth of his conviction. "As for finding out what I'll do for her, the answer is yes."

"Yes?" Badell's eyebrows rutted together.

"Get her and Van out of here. Give her the treatment, let them go, and my answer is yes to anything you want from me."

Lucia burst into a sobbing wail and sped up her harrowing crawl.

"Fascinating." Badell stepped out of her path, studying her as she closed the distance.

"Tate." She collapsed beneath him and slid a trembling hand over his bare toes, along the arch of his foot, and curled cold fingers around his ankle beneath the jeans.

His eyes burned, and his heart rate skyrocketed. God how he wanted to cradle her against him and console her. He wanted to clutch her hair and press his face to hers and smell her and hold her and kiss her. His inability to do so filled him with such maddening anger he couldn't form words over the scalding heave of his breaths.

Across the room, Van wore a bleak expression, but there was something else in his eyes. His strength and redemption was rooted in his love for his wife. He understood.

"The human spirit intrigues me." Badell closed the blade on his finger and pocketed it. Then he leaned down and gripped Lucia's hips, lifting her until she was eye-level with Tate. "Show me what you want, Lucia."

Her hands immediately slid around Tate's torso, and tears streaked her ashen cheeks as she tried to pull herself against him.

Badell adjusted his hold, hooking an arm across her stomach and giving her what she sought—contact, connection, togetherness.

Tate clutched the chains that suspended his arms and pressed toward her, chest to chest, breathing her in. Their lips met, and he fed her what they needed. Commitment and unity. Substance and meaning. Promise and love. His tongue rubbed against hers, dedicated, possessive, licking away the salt of her grief as everything inside him roared with desperation.

It was a kiss that would carry them through the night. A kiss that hoped for tomorrow. A kiss that would survive the end of time.

Too soon, Badell pulled her away and carried her back to Van.

"No! No, please!" She sobbed, thrashing her head and feebly wheeling her arms. "Let him go! Let him go! You can't do this."

She continued to cry as Badell positioned her on her side with her cheek on Van's thigh, facing Tate. The placement was deliberate and cruel. He wanted her to watch.

"You think you love her." He returned to Tate, his dark eyes gleaming with morbid curiosity. "I'm not convinced."

"Do we have a deal?" He gritted his teeth.

"She's a beautiful woman. And compassionate. If you're into that kind of thing."

"Give her the medicine, Badell." He yanked at the chains, coughing against the agony in his ribs. "She needs it now!"

"I understand your urgency." Badell cast her a passing glance. When he turned back, the indifference in his expression faded, replaced with impatience and a hint of anger. He sucked on his teeth, his voice dropping an octave. "Once I'm convinced of your feelings, when I fully understand the lengths you'll go for her, I'll give her the medicine. Then I'll let her leave. I'll set her free."

Lucia screamed her protests, her words too hoarse to be discernible.

"How can I trust you?" His heart stammered, dying a thousand deaths.

"Lucia?" Badell called over his shoulder. "Have I ever broken a promise to you?"

"No," she wept weakly, miserably.

"We should get started." He removed the blade from his pocket and attached it to his finger. "She doesn't have much time."

TWENTY-FOUR

Tate memorized the delicate lines of Lucia's face, the fall of glossy black hair around her tiny shoulders, and the love glistening in her deep brown eyes. He devoured her pain and beauty, anchored himself to it, to *her*, as hands grabbed him and spun him toward the wall.

The hands, as he'd learned when he was driven to the compound, belonged to Armando. Badell's torturer. The man who raped Lucia just hours earlier.

While Armando adjusted the chains, Tate played out all the slow, agonizing ways the rapist would die. Didn't matter the method. Blood would spill. More blood than that which coated the wall inches from his face.

Why was there a sheet of wood on this wall and not the others?

"The chains usually prevent movement." Badell tested the links that ran from Tate's wrist to the ceiling. "But you're a big guy. Strong."

His hand vanished from view, and his footsteps shifted behind Tate.

A featherlight scratch moved across his shoulder blade. Chills swept through him, stealing his breath.

It's the razor. He knew it. His clenching muscles knew it, and he tried to relax, to convince himself to accept it. But dread turned his body into a shaking block of ice.

"Nooooo!" Lucia screamed just as shocking, fiery pain seared through his skin and muscle.

His head fell back as violence and fury roared from his throat. It was so excruciating his limbs convulsed and slammed him against the wall.

Fuck, fuck, fuck. Breathe. It was just one cut. Just one. I'm better than this.

"See, if you buck like that, you'll rip the chains from the ceiling," Badell said at his ear. "I can't have that."

He was still heaving with blinding pain when Armando wrestled his forearm against the wood above his head. Blinking away the spots in his vision, he watched in horror as Armando stabbed an icepick through his arm and pinned him against the wood board.

The pain was unimaginable, shooting through him in shocking quakes of agony. His head hung on his shoulders, and his knees buckled, causing his weight to pull on the arm nailed to the wall. Nausea rose, and his vocal chords shredded. He tried to stifle his screams, but they were constant. Or maybe it was Lucia. Her anguish had become one with his own.

When I fully understand the lengths at which you'll go for her, I'll give her the medicine.

He needed to breathe. Breathe. Breathe. In and out. Stay alert. Focus. He was strong.

As his lungs found their pace, he planted his feet beneath him, lifting on toes to minimize the movement of the icepick through his arm.

"Why do you care if I love her?" he growled in a thick, guttural voice. "What do you gain from this?"

"Your loyalty to her intrigues me. I want to examine it. Challenge it." Moving into his line of sight, Badell studied him with a pensive expression. "To truly understand the veracity of love, a man must be tested. He must pay for it."

What is the price you're willing to pay?

Cole's question repeated in his pain-addled mind, and he spat the words. "I'll pay, you son of a bitch. Just name the price."

"The price of love is devastation."

"How the fuck would you know?"

A muscle bounced in Badell's cheek. "I've paid it a thousand times over."

The sick fuck wasn't capable of love. Not that it mattered. He was lord and king here, Hell's monarch in human flesh. There would be no mercy.

And so it began.

The blade sundered his flesh from neck to waist, striping, curving, digging, cutting. Cutting. Cutting. Hours of continual pain immersed him in a bottomless pit. He went into shock, but it didn't numb the insufferable misery.

He kept his feet firmly beneath him and cheek pressed against the wood, staring at the metal handle protruding from his forearm. Every breath caused slight movement, shifting tendon and bone around that spike.

Everlasting fire incinerated his back, his ribs, his arm. Dizziness dulled his thoughts. But at the outskirts of his senses, he tracked the clang of Van's chains and marked the moment Lucia's weak cries dissolved into wheezing breaths. God willing, she must've passed out. He couldn't imagine what his back looked like and didn't want her staring at it.

How much blood could a person lose? Was he reaching his limit? It drained from his arm in steady red rivulets, leaving tracks down his bicep and ribs and soaking his jeans. The same wet warmth flowed from his back beneath the relentless slice of the blade. There was so much blood his feet slipped in the sticky pools cooling on the floor.

"How long have you known her?" Badell traced a soft finger through the agony along his spine.

He swallowed, tried to clear his head. Five days? That was when they met. But he'd known her for six years through photos, Camila's stories, and the depths of his investigations.

"Long time." He choked on a throat full of phlegm and bile and spat it out.

"And Van? How do you know him?"

Another stroke of that finger down his back, a gentle taunt that fired muscle-flinching pain. But Badell wasn't cutting. Conversation meant a reprieve from the blade.

Tate tried to make his mouth work, to give an answer that would delay the torment. Words eventually slipped out, but they were strangled and unintelligible.

"I kidnapped him," Van said from across the room.

"Explain." Badell shifted, creaking the stool beneath him.

Van outlined the sex trafficking operation, focusing on the training and the network of slave buyers. His words were carefully chosen, avoiding details that might've suggested they had friends or family. He also didn't explain why or how it ended. As far as Badell knew, it had been just Van and Tate and a dozen other faceless slaves.

He wasn't sure why Van shared any of it. Maybe Van was angling to connect to their captor in a companions-in-kidnapping way.

Badell listened, but he wasn't distracted from his mutilated canvas. The vicious, incessant cutting continued, shoving Tate into a hazy fog of gasping, retching distress. He vomited everything he'd eaten in days, heaving until blood vessels burst in his eyes. His suffering was so acute he felt every twitch of the blade, every notch, slash, slice, and cleave.

He was cold. So fucking cold he feared he was nearing the dark dismal nothingness Lucia had talked about. His lungs produced weak, shivery sounds, and the breaths trembling from his throat cracked his dry lips.

But he still had his mind, and he let it travel to the quiet woman across the room, absorbing himself in hallucinations — the softness of her hair as he ran it between his fingers, the ferocity of her expression as she argued, and the sweet perfection of her submission as he commanded her to kneel. A man could get lost in a dream like that, and he did, for a time.

Badell and Van continued their conversation while the dissection stretched over the expanse of his back. There wasn't an inch that hadn't been carved. He'd been in excruciating pain for so long he'd forgotten what relief felt like. The razor penetrated again and again, and he no longer had the energy to tense or resist. The fight had bled out of him. His life would soon follow.

It must've been nearing dawn when the last of his alertness faded. His groaning had become a heavy, hollow drum in his ears, booming in the black cavern of his mind. He was stuck there in that desolate vacuum, unable to escape the throbbing pressure. It was the only thing that existed. One continuous, torturous throb.

Throb.
Throb.
Throb.

Then he was cold again. A suffocating, liquid kind of cold that washed over his face and seeped into his nose. He choked and hacked, fighting for air.

I'm drowning.

It wasn't real. He wasn't under water. He just needed to return to that room. To Lucia.

Open your eyes.
Wake up.

More icy water. He coughed, taking the cool liquid into his mouth. His throat filled with shrapnel.

"Open your eyes." A deep voice breathed at his ear. *Badell.*

He blinked, moaning against the bright light as he tried to find his bearings.

Pain flared and flamed everywhere, but the pressure on his arms was absent. Nothing cinched or tore at his wrists, and his legs weren't pulling him down. He was weightless.

I'm on the floor.

Concrete pressed against his cheek and shoulder. He lay on his side, his good arm stretched toward the closed door. The other arm extended from beneath his torso and tucked against his stomach. He refused to glance at it, couldn't bear to see the ruin from the icepick.

And his back... Fucking God, his back felt skinless and exposed, as if the flesh had been shaved off and the muscle had been torn from bone.

Grisly images of a bared spine and vertebrae flooded his mind.

Footsteps circled around his head as he tilted his neck back, aching, needing, searching…

There she is.

Eyes glazed, face blotchy, and frail body shaking violently, Lucia reached for him from a few feet away. Her fingers stretched toward his, too far, and her head lolled on Van's lap.

She was still alive. He was still alive. They still had a chance. *What time is it?*

He tried to ask, but his vocal chords had been reduced to rock and gravel. "T-t-time?"

"An hour till dawn." Badell crouched in his line of sight, blocking his view of her.

Then he lifted a bucket and trickled cold water over Tate's face. When the rest was dumped on his back, the frigid drops felt like razor blades slicing across his skin. He bit down on his tongue, trapping a godawful bellow.

"You are my greatest masterpiece." Squatting with his sleeves rolled to the elbows, Badell rested scarred forearms on his thighs. "I haven't decided your fate. Quite frankly, I loathe the idea of destroying such a beautiful creation. If you live, you might one day come to value the artwork." He ran a hand along the welts covering his own arm. "Took me twenty years to appreciate mine."

Since he didn't wear a mask, Tate could identify him. The nutjob had no intention of letting him go.

"You promised," he ground out. "Meds." *Her medicine. Give her what she needs.*

"My promise was," Badell said, setting the bucket aside. "Once I know how far you'll go for her, I'll give her the medicine." He stood, slid his hands in the pockets of his blood-stained trousers, and paced the room. "I was going to have Van fuck her while you watched, but after hearing the history between you and him, I have a much better idea."

Profound relief mixed with overwhelming dread, curdling a venomous concoction in his stomach. The darkness in Badell's expression was sinister. Haunting. Whatever he had in store would threaten to break Tate's mind. He was certain of it.

He shifted his gaze across the floor and found Lucia staring back. Silent tears spilled from her eyes, and her mouth trembled with heartbreaking fragility. Her arm still lay outstretched toward his, fingers twitching to close the distance.

His chest heaved as he strained toward her, extending useless joints and failing to erase the inches between them. Goddammit, he just needed to touch her. Fury rose above the anguish, hardening his body into stone.

"Make your demands, Badell." He flexed his jaw, battling the never-ending pain that dotted his vision.

"One more trial." Shiny, blood-splattered shoes paused inches from his face. Badell lowered to a crouch and rested a hard, cool hand against Tate's jaw. "Van will take his pleasure in your body. Then you will take pleasure in his. Come inside him, allow him to release in you, then I'll know how far you will go."

"No-no-no-no-no…" Lucia chanted in a scratchy, tear-choked voice.

The hammering bang of his heart drowned out her cries. He was sprawled on the floor with his cheek against the concrete, frozen in place, silent and breathless as his vision lost focus.

Deep down he knew it would come to this. Badell wanted a trial, one Tate was sure to fail.

Hot moisture dripped from his unblinking eyes and traced a sodden stripe across his face. Such a strange sensation, that warm soundless trickle. He couldn't remember the last time he cried.

He would never be able to perform, let alone ejaculate. Not with a mutilated body. And not with Van.

But it was better than the alternative. If Van were forced to rape Lucia, Tate wasn't sure he'd ever get back up again.

Was that why Van had volunteered so much information about Tate's time in the attic? Perhaps he'd predicted Badell's plan for Lucia and steered him in a different direction. It took a sadist to know a sadist. Van probably saw the blood-smeared writing on the wall from a mile away.

Shifting his gaze, he sought the man who'd become his friend.

Van sat against the wall with his arms shackled, head tilted back, and eyes closed. Tate didn't have to be a mind reader to interpret the conflict twisting his face.

If Van participated in this, it would be a betrayal to Amber. If he didn't, they were all dead. He and Tate were probably dead regardless. But Lucia had a chance.

With her cheek on Van's thigh, she silently shook with full-body tremors. Tate gave her intense, meaningful eye-contact that said all the things he couldn't. *I'll kill for you. Die for you. You'll be okay. You're the strongest woman I've ever met.*

Van lowered his head and shared a look with Tate, a miserable moment of commiseration. Then Van acceded with a single nod.

Tate closed his eyes, steeling himself. He felt completely and utterly defeated, his body a broken, worthless mess. He could handle the physical damage. He could survive it. It was the emotional blows that would bring him to his end.

He needed a mind-over-matter pep talk. If he were brave enough, the strength of willpower would help him overcome. He'd survived ten weeks beneath Van's thrusts. He could endure a few minutes, or hours, however long it took.

Reciprocating, however, was something entirely different.

"I found your limit." Badell stood and leaned against the wall. "It seems you won't, in fact, do everything—"

"Yes. The answer is yes," he whispered. "Send her out of the room."

Badell straightened, his brow lifting in shock before he emptied his expression. "She'll witness your undoing. That's nonnegotiable."

He stepped to the door, opened it, and spoke quietly in Spanish to whoever waited on the other side.

With a hard swallow, Tate returned his attention to Lucia, focusing on their hands and the dismal inches that separated them. "I'm sorry. I don't want you to see this."

Her mouth moved, and her chest rose and fell with the effort to speak, but nothing came out. She directed her eyes at her fingers, where they stretched toward his, and returned to his gaze.

"Shh. I know." His breathing accelerated, and he fought to calm himself down. "I'm here. No matter what happens, I'm with *you*. Only you."

The door closed, and Badell prowled toward him with three armed guards in tow. The men went to Van, two aiming rifles while the third unlocked his shackles.

Once free, he pulled his arms in front him, rubbing his wrists.

Please, Van. Don't do anything stupid.

Van thought about it. Tate saw the calculation in his silver eyes as he glared at the weapons pointed at his head. Then he turned to Lucia and lifted her fully onto his lap.

The guards kept their guns trained as he stood, taking her with him. Badell didn't stop him as he carried her closer and placed her on the floor, on her back, aligning her body against Tate's.

Thank you. Tate edged toward her with deliriously painful movements until the only thing separating them was his injured arm.

The press of her skin against the wound ignited unfathomable anguish, but he didn't care. He held the arm against his stomach and wrapped the other across her torso.

Fuck, how he'd needed to hold her like this. He needed *her*. More of her. More touching. More talking. More smiles. More time.

Their five days together had been the best days of his life. They'd lived in dearth and turmoil in a windowless room, yet they'd craved nothing but each other. It was confounding the way he connected to her so effortlessly, the way she fit so perfectly in his arms, against his body, and inside his heart.

Five days hadn't been enough. He wanted to laugh with her, fight with her, make up with her. He wanted a life with her. A lifetime. A forever.

Sweat beaded on her sallow face and drenched her t-shirt and jeans. Van had dressed her in those clothes while Tate had been on the phone with Cole. It felt like an eternity ago.

For the past five days, he thought he had this rescue mission under control. He'd sent off the blood samples and just needed a couple more days to receive the results. But it was too late for that.

He should've called Matias the moment he made contact with Lucia. Her illness, though... It was an endless, looming threat. Not even Matias had the means to cure her in time. Without the medicine, her fate was dire.

After she was raped, however, all bets were off. Tate had contacted Matias sometime before midnight. If dawn was an hour away, he'd been in this room for seven hours.

And so had she.

He called forth the energy to hug her tighter, savoring the flow of her breaths, the sweet scent of her hair, and the pulse in her throat as he kissed her neck. He ached to see her healthy and smiling and free. It would be the greatest gift, the ultimate definition of happiness.

"I love you," he whispered.

Her eyes squeezed shut, and her face crumpled with a weak nod.

Badell moved to the far side of the room and perched on the stool. His shoes left deep footprints in the thick puddles of blood.

My blood.

It ran from his body to the wall. There was so much of it on the floor, the wood board, and his jeans, he didn't understand how he was still breathing. He wasn't just physically spent. His emotions had run the gamut for hours, churning from intense trauma and helplessness to scathing wrath and hatred. The latter simmered anew as he met his tormentor's soulless eyes.

"You'll give her the medicine and let her and Van leave Caracas alive and unharmed." He lifted his chin with might and rage, eyes hard and breaths seething with vehemence.

"You have my word." Badell curled a hand beneath his chin, watching him, as if studying a curious object.

He looked away, vanishing the demon from his sight and his mind. As far as Tate was concerned, Badell and his guards were no longer in the room.

That left Van, who circled his feet and lowered to the floor behind him. "Stay where you are."

It wasn't like he could go anywhere. The constant state of his throbbing, bleeding torment would prevent him from getting his legs beneath him.

"I don't want to do this," Van said in a dead tone.

"I know."

"It's karma. I've carried this debt for so long. For the crimes I committed against you." Van leaned in, whispering at his ear. "When this is over, you and I are even. No more bad blood between us."

Tate nodded, but his thoughts were elsewhere, wholly occupied by what was about to happen.

"Give me permission." Van rested a hand on the button of Tate's jeans.

There had been a time when Van got off on taking without consent. And while every fiber in Tate's body screamed in horror, there was only one answer. "You have it."

"I'll only touch you where I need to." A crack in Van's monotone voice.

The hand on Tate's zipper moved efficiently, opening the jeans and pulling them down with the briefs to gather at mid-thigh. Then he lifted Tate's leg as far as the denim would allow and rested his thigh across Lucia's.

"Too heavy." Tate groaned through horrendous tremors.

"Stay." Lucia's whisper was barely audible as she curled a weak hand around his leg.

He wouldn't deny her the closeness, but once this began, there would be no eye contact. If he survived the night, he didn't know how she would be able to look at him the same. He couldn't bear to see that shift in her gaze now.

Van leaned away, leaving Tate's body wrapped around the side of hers. His cock and balls lay exposed and lifeless against her denim-clad thigh, his legs slightly spread, and his backside bare and vulnerable.

With his bleeding arm trapped between them, the pain was a sharp, constant presence. But it was nothing compared to the unholy dread amassing inside him.

Van's zipper sounded at his back, followed by the slapping of a fist against flesh. Van was stroking himself to get hard, and there was a measure of comfort in that, knowing his friend wasn't aroused.

"Tate." Her lips trembled through words that found no voice.

He tried to read her mouth.

Me… Look at me…

He didn't need to look at her to see her, sense her, feel her. She was inside him, part of him, embedded in his being. Curled around her delicate frame, he kissed her cheek, buried his face in her neck, and waited.

Several minutes passed before he heard Van spitting. Then a wet finger forced its way into his rectum.

Unbidden, he tensed up and stopped breathing.

"Was I the last person here?" Van asked quietly.

Six years ago. More than enough time to physically heal.

"Yes," he grated through clamped teeth.

"Don't clench." Van removed his finger and replaced it with something much wider. "You remember what to do."

Breathe. Relax. Push back.

The instant Van pushed in, Tate couldn't help it. He fought. The instinct to buck, kick, spit, and punch was uncontrollable. But he had no stamina, no energy, and Van easily subdued him.

"Hold still." With a grip on his hair, Van pushed his head toward Lucia, pressing his face into her neck.

Then the hand was gone, and all that remained was the invasion.

Slow and cautious, Van buried himself to the hilt. The burning fullness was much like Tate remembered, but also different. Maybe because his back, his ribs, his arms, everything was on fire. Or maybe it was the comfort of Lucia's hand on his leg and the rasp of her breaths at his ear.

Van held his body away as he drove in and out, no part of him touching Tate's back. Fingers clutched his hip for leverage, but this wasn't a dominant fucking. It wasn't taunting or cruel with the purpose of degradation.

It was efficient, merciful, and far gentler than anything he'd ever experienced with Van Quiso.

But it still hurt. A shameful, defenseless, lasting hurt that annihilated a man's dignity in one desecrating thrust.

He clung to Lucia, rubbing his lips against the tears that found their way to her neck. Her tears. And his.

Then it was over.

Van quickly pulled out and rolled to his back. Silent. So quiet it didn't sound like he was breathing.

"Show me." Badell leaned forward on the stool, craning his neck.

He wanted to see evidence of Van's release.

With a shaky hand, Tate reached behind him and spread his cheeks to expose the wetness Van left behind.

"Very good," Badell said. "Now switch."

Switch places.

He lay like the dead, half on top of Lucia's body, no doubt crushing her damaged organs. He didn't have it in him to move, let alone do what Badell demanded.

His physical self teemed with brutal spasms and fever. But his mind was numb. Detached. Unresponsive.

Unending pain, exhaustion, and humiliation had taken its toll. He'd finally reached the limit of his ability. He couldn't even will himself to look into her eyes.

"I failed you," he whispered.

Her head twitched side to side, knocking more tears free. The hand on his leg squeezed, and her other one fumbled between them.

When she bumped into his punctured arm, he swallowed an agonized roar. She whimpered and sucked in a breath, reaching her hand lower, sliding along his thigh until she found what she sought.

Trembling fingers encircled his flaccid cock. Then she began to stroke.

He couldn't. Even if he were able to send blood to that part of himself, how would he thrust? How would he stay hard inside of Van's body?

But she was determined. Why was that? She wouldn't push him into this depravity just to save her own life.

Suspicion aroused his senses.

Shifting his hand from her shoulder to her jaw, he turned her head and leaned up. Vertigo threatened to knock him sideways, and the cords in his neck quivered to hold up his skull. But he pushed through the pain and met her gaze.

Something flashed in her eyes, a fierce spark of perseverance.

If he were somehow able to satisfy Badell's demand, she would leave this place. She would have to leave him behind. But that wasn't what her expression conveyed.

He let his head drop, returning his mouth to her ear. "Don't you dare put your life on the line for me. Understand?"

A feeble nod.

"I can do this." He reached between them, nudged her arm away, and took his cock in hand.

The task was grueling. Each stroke aggravated the mangled muscles in his back. Every exerted breath squeezed the cracks in his ribs. There was no pleasure in it. And no blood. His dick refused to harden.

Then her hand was there again, wrapping around his, sliding in tandem, and lending him strength. He focused on her touch, on her slender weight beneath him, and on the sigh that parted her lips. He narrowed all his concentration on the pleasure and filled his mind with one image: Her pussy.

Her soft pink folds swelled so beautifully when she was aroused. She was too small for him, and he had to work himself in, but she was a greedy little thing, and she would spread her creamy thighs and welcome him, gasping and trembling as he seated himself to the root.

Christ, she turned him on. Her exotic beauty, resilience, and submissive nature was a trifecta of perfection. She was his ideal mate in every way.

She was his.

He slid his fingers over the top of hers and rocked into her fist. His breathing sped up. His pulse accelerated, and fuck him, but he stirred to life. It was medically impossible and beyond disturbing, but he had an erection and intended to keep it.

Grinding harder against her grip, he angled his neck until his lips found hers. The kiss was clumsy and languorous, but holy hell, her taste. The salty sweetness of her mouth aroused him further, heating his blood and driving his hips.

"I want you," he breathed against her lips.

"Van," she gasped weakly and looked at the man leaning over his back.

Van. That was who he needed to want right now. How? How the ever-loving fuck would he do this?

She tightened her hand around his shriveling erection and hardened her eyes. Goddamn, he loved her spirit, but it was going to take a lot more than a glare to push him past the physical and mental blocks.

"I have to rearrange us." Van moved to kneel on the other side of Lucia, with his jeans partially zipped up. "Lucia, he'll need his good arm to brace himself. Keep him hard and…positioned."

Her chin trembled as she attempted a nod.

Van looked at Tate with an expression that didn't belong on his face. Even in his worst moments, he was power and passion and dominance. But now… Now, he wore a mask that didn't fit. A facade that buttoned up his emotions and sucked the life from his eyes.

"When we start, don't look at me," Van said coldly. "Keep your eyes closed. Focus on her hand. I'll do the rest."

Shame coiled inside him, and it quickly spiraled into rage, whipping his heart against broken ribs and chopping his breaths. He gnashed his teeth, hating this for Van and hating himself for being so goddamn weak.

"Listen to me, dickhead." Van's voice was sharp and menacing—a tone Tate hadn't heard since the attic. "You're going to stop being a pussy and power through this. Close your fucking eyes and don't open them until you come."

He clenched his jaw and squeezed his eyes shut. *Her hand, her hand, her hand…* He felt the stroke of her fingers, appreciated it, and wrapped all his thoughts around it as the sounds of shuffling moved around him.

The comforting press of her body slid away. Then her touch was gone, too. He kept his eyes closed and tried not to imagine how this would work. Van used to arrange his captives in all sorts of vulgar positions. It was difficult not to think of that as limbs and bodies bumped against him.

He balanced on his side with his head on the floor, his throbbing arm pressed against his stomach, and his limp cock in his hand. Someone shifted close against his front, and he knew it wasn't Lucia. The breathing was too controlled, the physique too wide and hard.

As he tried to stimulate his dick, his knuckles brushed against skin and rigid muscle. Given the position and shape, he didn't have to open his eyes to see Van's bare ass. He suspected Van was face down beside him, with Lucia on the other side of Van.

Her hand wrapped around his shaft, her arm stretching over Van's backside. He didn't look as she rubbed and fondled him. Didn't open his eyes as she coaxed the blood back into his cock. He kept his thoughts on her and her alone, fantasizing about every dip and curve on her body, the taste of her lips, and the noises she made when he got himself off inside her tight cunt.

It took a lifetime to bring him to hardness, and by the time he was stiff enough, he'd fucked her in his mind in every position, in dozens of places and scenarios.

She held onto his erection as he shifted his weight and crawled over Van's prone body. The muscle tone, the masculine scent, even the feel of the t-shirt was wrong. Add to that the blazing pain across his back and down his arm, and he started to soften.

But he'd made it this far. He just needed to…lift…adjust… His good arm shook like a bitch as he braced it between Van and Lucia and supported the weight of his torso.

A sheen of sweat formed on his face, and his lungs huffed and wheezed with agonizing effort. He held his useless arm against his chest and dragged his knees into the V of Van's spread legs beneath him.

Then the real torture began.

Lucia, who was right beside him now, put all her strength and energy into rousing him. When he hardened, she lined him up. When he softened, she went at it again, stroking, squeezing, and encouraging with determined fingers.

Van must've already lubed himself with spit because his opening was wet. But Tate couldn't get it done. Every time he pressed in, his semi deflated.

Minutes passed. Too many to track. The countless starts and stops and position adjustments put enormous stress on his already weak body. He'd lost so much damn blood. Eventually, his muscles tired. His arm gave out, and he collapsed on top of Van's back.

Then he opened his eyes.

Van lay face down on the floor beneath Tate, braced on elbows with his head bent and his face pressed in the cup of his hands. Discomfort and strain flexed across his back beneath the shirt. His entire body was a concrete slab of tension.

This man wasn't a bottom. Not even close. He'd been sexually abused as a child and probably hadn't taken a man this way since he escaped that trauma.

"I'm so fucking sorry." Tate rested his cheek against Van's spine, his eyes burning with regret.

"Don't." Van pulled his arms beneath him and slowly lifted to hands and knees.

The position slid Tate to kneel behind Van, the weight of his upper body resting on top of Van's back.

"Instead of apologizing," Van said in a cruel voice, "think about all the times I pounded you into the floor. All the times I held you down while you begged me to stop until your throat was raw and your ass was bleeding. Think about that, Tate, while you fuck me."

The first time Van forced him was forever branded in his brain.

His insides ripping and tearing around Van's ruthless thrusts.

Arms and legs restrained.

Mouth gagged.

His body no longer his own.

He'd wanted to kill Van then, but beneath that sinister wish lurked even darker thoughts. So many times, in the isolation of that attic, he'd imagined doing to Van all the things Van had done to him. He'd imagined fucking his captor until his cock dripped with blood.

He didn't want that now, but he harnessed those feelings — the vengeance, the violence, and the brutal urge to reclaim his dominance, to reclaim himself.

He wasn't a pussy. He wasn't emasculated. He controlled how this ended.

With a surge of empowerment, he balanced on his knees and grabbed Lucia's hand, showing her the speed and pressure he needed to get hard. It took a while. Fuck, it took goddamn forever, but he stayed focused, clear-headed, and finally hard.

He sank into Van's body in a single stroke, pushing with a grunt that made Van gasp and shudder. He found Lucia's eyes, gripped her hand, and held onto both as he gave into the forbidden pleasure and chased his release.

It was the longest minutes of his life. The climb was a battle of concentration. The peak was short-lived and cathartic, and the downward spiral dropped him into guilt-ridden hell.

He fucked, and he came, and he despised himself for it.

Van lowered him to the floor on his side as Badell stepped toward them and examined the evidence.

Every cell and nerve in Tate's body shivered with scorching pain. A shroud of darkness tried to pull him under, and he fought it, rapidly blinking as he sought Lucia.

When their eyes connected and locked, the spinning, wobbly world righted itself. He fucking loved her, and as long as she lived, everything would be okay.

"You did well." Badell's voice reached his ear, distant and muffled.

"You made a promise," he tried to say. His lips felt numb.

"I will honor it." Badell lifted Lucia's lethargic body from the floor and carried her out of the room.

TWENTY-FIVE

Lucia lay on the mattress in Tiago's room, feigning sleep as her mind whirled and panicked.

A few feet away, Tiago grunted through an upper-body workout. Dumbbells lifted and hit the floor. His footsteps paced. Then he started again.

She'd passed out before she received the injection, then again after. Though she'd been awake for the last hour, she'd held herself still and quiet, waiting for the medicine to saturate her system. Waiting for her strength to return and her brain to fire on all cylinders. With her eyes closed and the desperation to get to Tate gnawing at her nerves, the wait had been brutal.

But she was fully alert now. Perhaps eighty-percent back to health. Very little pain in her abdomen. No paralysis.

She was alive.

Physically.

Emotionally, she'd died a hundred times over. Died every time the blade had made a new cut in Tate's flesh. She'd died in that torture chamber and continued to do so.

The monstrosity inflicted upon his back, the icepick in his arm, his screams, the blood, the sodomy, the heartbreak… It replayed and fermented and thrashed inside her, crushing her chest and blackening her thoughts.

Whether Tiago let her go didn't matter. He would never free her heart.

Her person.

The man she loved.

The man who proved his love in the most excruciating ways imaginable.

Tears simmered beneath her eyelids. She willed them away, relaxed her face muscles, and continued the ruse of sleep.

Tiago had imprisoned her for eleven years. He would do the same to Tate just to rest his gaze on his macabre artwork every day. That knowledge had plagued her in the basement, and she'd spent those gut-wrenching hours devising a different ending.

She would walk out of the compound today, and Tate and Van would be with her. She knew exactly how she would do it.

Except she hadn't expected to wake on Tiago's bed. She needed to be near the chairs, so she could use one as a weapon.

There were other surprises, too. Tiago never lifted weights in her presence. Never allowed her in his room for this long. And never, never, never permitted her to wear clothes in here. The fact that she was dressed meant he'd been in a hellfire hurry to give her the injection.

But she didn't have her guns.

The thud of a dumbbell against the floor resounded through the room. If one of those was twenty or thirty pounds, it would be light enough for her to lift. And heavy enough to crush a skull.

She peeked across the room from beneath barely raised lashes.

Tiago hissed through a set of curls, his bicep flexing with each heave of the dumbbell. Covered in sweat and dressed in a tank top and athletic shorts, he was angled toward her with his eyes down and his brow creased.

He was disgustingly handsome, sculpted all over, and evil down to the morrow of his bones.

She hated him with a seething passion that clouded her vision and poisoned her blood. Murder was the only way to relieve the pressure swelling behind her eyes. When she killed him, she wouldn't feel an ounce of remorse.

Multiple dumbbells of various sizes scattered around his feet, and several of those looked like the weight she needed.

She twitched the muscles in her legs and arms, testing responsiveness. Everything moved as it should.

The plan will work.

Her insides tangled in a heap of nerves, making it harder and harder to initiate the first step. Once she alerted him she was awake, it would be go time. No turning back.

She pulled in a deep breath, sharpened her mind, and deliberately released a sickly moan.

The dumbbell paused mid-curl. He lowered it to the floor and prowled toward her. The mattress sloped beneath his knee, and his hand cupped her face.

"How do you feel?" His fingers, sweaty and vile, crept along her jaw.

"Where's Tate?" She widened her eyes in a semblance of panic and wheezed a cough from her throat.

"You need to rest." He gripped her chin, a gentle pressure.

"No." She bowed her back and flailed as if trying to sit up but couldn't.

Except she could. The flexing of muscle in her core and limbs gave her hope. She was strong enough. Definitely determined enough. She could do this.

"I want to leave." She shot him a fierce look, one he'd come to expect from her. "You promised."

"I'll let you go, *after* we have a conversation."

Restlessness trembled through her. She didn't want to spend another second with this man. Didn't want any part of his slippery tricks or mind games.

"You're going to leave Caracas without Tate." He tightened his fingers on her face, as if expecting her to jerk away.

She didn't have to fake the quiver in her lips. If her plan failed, Tate and Van would never see outside of these walls again.

"You care for him." His touch softened, ghosting across her cheek. "You might even love him. Those feelings will eat at you and consume you and you'll return to Caracas with a half-cocked rescue plan. You'll probably attempt to kill me, and you'll die trying."

Her jaw clenched. *He has no idea.*

"I won't. I'll stay away." She made her voice shake. "Please. Just let me go."

"I investigated your friends." He stood from the mattress where it lay on the floor and paced away. "I learned that Tate Vades and Van Quiso are missing persons, living under the radar in Austin, Texas."

Her stomach folded in. Tiago had been with her the entire night. An investigation like that would've taken time.

"How long have you known?" Her voice fractured.

"Six days." He shot her a disapproving glare. "I investigate every man you fuck at that club."

Oh God, oh God, oh fuck. Did he know she'd sneaked out the back door that night? Or that she spent five days with Tate? Or that Tate was close to her sister and her sister was alive?

Why did he wait six days to capture Tate?

Because he loves his twisted mind games.

"I know Van Quiso's married," he said. "But I didn't know about his criminal history until he told me."

Van's married?

Her fingers clenched at her sides. The forced sex between Van and Tate had been harrowing enough. The fact that Van was married made it even worse. She wanted to scream and kick at the unfairness of it, but she kept herself lethargic. She needed Tiago to believe she was too weak and defeated to be threatening.

He went on to describe Tate's roommates, their house, and the two-hundred-acre property Van shared with his wife. Not once did he mention Camila or Matias. He either hadn't made the connection between Van and Camila or he was deliberately fucking with Lucia's head.

The scariest part was his discovery of Van's wife and Tate's friends. Tiago knew where they lived and was vindictive enough to go after them.

Even more reason to kill him.

"I'm relocating." He stood in the center of the room, arms crossed with a knuckle resting beneath his pensive frown. "I found something…a new interest I'm pursuing."

That was fucking cryptic. And inconsequential. He wouldn't be leaving this room alive.

"When I let you go," he said, "you can try to come back for Tate, but he won't be here. I'm taking him with me."

The hell he was.

He stared at her like he expected a reaction, and she was more than ready to give him one.

In a series of intentional movements, she surged upward, swayed dizzily, and tumbled back down like a rag doll.

"Lucia." He watched her in that way he always did, head tilted and eyes tracking her with unfeeling curiosity. "You're not ready to get up."

Swinging her legs to the floor, she exaggerated every motion as she climbed to her feet. With staggering steps, she made her limbs look cumbersome and awkward.

While she didn't glance at the dumbbells, her senses narrowed on the one she wanted. Each weaving, uncoordinated stumble brought her closer, closer…

Close enough.

She let her ankle twist without injuring it, pretended to lose her balance, and angled her fall so that she landed with her fingers next to the dumbbell.

"Always so stubborn." He strolled toward her with his hands behind him.

Lowering into a crouch beside her hip, he trailed the softest touch down her spine. The glide of his fingers became a rubbing hand that traveled the length of her back. The same hand that had tortured and scarred Tate without mercy.

She lay still beneath the affection, pushing air in and out of her lungs noisily and intentionally. If Tiago would just lower his head a little more, she wouldn't have to swing so far.

"I've treated you badly." He smoothed his fingers through her hair, gently and rhythmically. "Sometimes, I wish I could undo the things I've done. I wish..." His hand paused, and he let it fall to the floor beside her shoulder. "Well, I can't change my plans for Tate, but *you* have the power to give him what he wants most. You can start over, stay alive, and move on. He wants you happy, and you can be that for him. His survival is up to you."

She would do better than that.

With a sweep of her hand across the dumbbell, she curled her fingers around the bar and jerked it from the floor. It was heavier than she expected, and she gritted her teeth, accidentally releasing a warning grunt before swinging it toward his head.

It connected with his temple, and his eyes widened with a gasp. The heavy force of the momentum sent him backwards, and his arms flew up to grab her. But she was ready for it, dodging his hands, rearing back, and striking again.

The second hit landed higher up on his skull, with a crunch of bone, a wet smack, and a dead fall to the floor. He slumped on his back, eyes closed, with his legs bent beneath him. Blood saturated his black hair and spread a slick red pool beneath his head.

I did it.

The weight fell from her shaking hand, and her breath hung in her throat. She waited for him to rise up and attack. Waited for the guards to rush in. Waited for this to not be real.

I actually did it.

I killed him.

I fucking killed Tiago Badell.

Bile rose up, and she dry heaved. No sound. No vomit. Just cold, paralyzing shock.

And sorrow.

It stitched through her chest in pinprick stabs, causing her to double-over.

She didn't want to feel a damn thing for him, didn't want to dwell on the tenderness he'd shown her or the soft words he'd whispered. She needed to slam the weight against his head over and over until his face was as mutilated and unrecognizable as Tate's back.

But she couldn't.

She wasn't a monster.

You're a pretty little flicker of compassion, begging to be extinguished.

She scrambled away from his lifeless body and ran toward the safe in the closet. The detour would be a waste of time, but she couldn't leave without checking.

Her hands fumbled with the lock's dial, spinning through number combinations and testing the lever. She would never guess it, and every second she delayed was a risk to Tate's life.

She stepped back. Leaving behind the medicine had been part of her plan. She couldn't do anything to change that.

With a resolved breath, she pivoted and faced the body.

The sticky puddle beneath his head had doubled in size. The sight of his slack face, matted hair, and gory wound on his skull made her feel sick. Villainous. Her stomach knotted, and her scalp tingled with unease.

She'd killed him in cold blood.

So much for not feeling remorse. God, I'm so fucked-up.

Turning on her heel, she strode toward the door.

She still wore her boots, jeans, and shirt. Dried blood stained her chest and arms. Tate's blood. If Tiago's death had splattered on her, it wasn't noticeable.

At the door, she rested a hand on the knob and checked the line of sight between her position and the body. The guards wouldn't see Tiago unless they pushed the door all the way open.

It would be easy to enter the hall without being questioned by them. She did it every morning after every injection, and Tiago rarely followed her out. Today would be the same.

She swallowed, emptied her expression, and turned the knob.

Her Berettas weren't on the bench in the hall. Being unarmed would suck for the next few minutes, but it worked in her favor.

The guards gave her a cursory glance. She returned one of her own as she slipped out, shut the door behind her, and made her way down the hall.

All they had to do is peek inside his room. If they were suspicious or simply had a question for him, the door was unlocked. With just a turn of that knob, they would know what she did. And they would kill her.

Fucking hell, she trembled. Her hands shook, and she clenched them. Her heart beat so fast she felt dizzy and overloaded with tension.

She didn't know what Tiago's plans had been for her once he released her. But on a normal day, two guards would be waiting in the lobby, watching for her so they could escort her back to the apartment. Escaping them wouldn't be an option. She would have to neutralize them quietly and discreetly.

She weaved through the labyrinth of corridors, passing countless men—thieves, kidnappers, murderers, rapists. The worst of humanity.

And they had no idea she'd killed their commander.

As the lobby came into view, she veered to the left and slipped into the kitchen.

Food and cookware scattered steel counter tops without a single person in sight.

Yes! I lucked out.

She rushed toward a rack of utensils and snatched the biggest knife. Then something moved in the pantry behind her, the squeak of sneakers on tiled floors.

Quickly and carefully, she concealed the blade in her boot and spun toward the sound.

"*Qué buscas?*" Roberto, the oldest of Tiago's chefs, paused in the doorway of the pantry.

If he'd seen her steal the knife, she would have to kill him. More blood. More death. She braced herself for it.

"I'm hungry," she said in Spanish.

He strode toward her, carrying a bag of rice while eying her from head to toe. His graying mustache twitched with the roll of his lips.

"You eat when everyone else eats." His Spanish dribbled with disdain as he thrust his chin at the door. "Get out."

Gladly.

She fled the kitchen, fighting the urge to glance down and make sure the knife was hidden until she stepped into the vacant hall.

The stairs to the basement waited just around the corner. She kept her gait even, casual, as she walked, turning the bend and—

A hand clamped onto her shoulder, propelling her heart to her throat.

"Are you ready to leave?"

She didn't recognize the masculine voice but knew it was one of her Spanish-speaking guards before she turned to face him.

"I left my Berettas in the basement," she said in Spanish and stepped out of his grip with a racing pulse.

Her guns were probably still at her apartment. If this tattooed, baby-faced thug had been involved in the gunfight last night, he would know that. Unfortunately, she'd been in too much pain and shock to recall the details of Tiago carrying her away.

She held her breath as he studied her with bloodshot eyes. She could really use a 9mm with a silencer. Most of the guards carried them, but not this one. The sawed-off shotgun on his hip wouldn't help her if it alerted every gang member in the compound.

"Fine," he said in Spanish and pulled a cigarette from his shirt pocket. "Be quick."

Forcing her boots to move as if reluctant and bored, she shuffled toward the stairwell.

TWENTY-SIX

There were benefits of being a high-ranked gang member for Tiago Badell. One, Lucia had access to every hallway, room, and dark corner in the compound and no one questioned her. Two, she had deep insight into how Tiago ran his security.

Since there were two prisoners, there would be two guards in the basement. No more. No less. They would be armed and separated. One at the door to the basement corridor and one at the entrance to the chamber.

She was so damn nervous her shoulders tried to hunch around her ears. The tension in her neck tightened to the point of pain.

I can't fail. I can't fail. I can't fail.

With a steeling breath, she opened the door to the stairwell and found the dank, narrow space quiet and empty.

So far so good.

Closing the door behind her, she grabbed the knife from her boot and flattened the blade against the side of her leg. There was no way to conceal it, so whatever happened next needed to be swift and soundless.

The almighty pound of her heart threatened to liquefy her knees as she rounded the first bend in the staircase. Her senses buzzed on high alert, making every step more arduous than the last.

One more corner to go.

Her soft treads whispered along the stone walls, but there were other sounds, too. The rustle of movement. The faint rasps of breathing. There was definitely a guard waiting at the bottom door.

The knife handle slicked in her clammy fist. She squeezed her fingers, shifted it out of sight behind her thigh, and edged around the last bend.

Perched on the bottom few stairs, the guard pulled his attention from the phone in his hand and glanced over his shoulder.

Armando.

Panic, disgust, vengeance—all of it blazed through her, feral and venomous.

His eyes widened. "*Donde esta* Tiago?"

Where's Tiago?

He's dead, and you're about to join him.

He knew, even as he'd asked the question, something wasn't right. He'd been in the torture room and witnessed her despair. He knew she was here for no other reason than to rescue Tate.

It happened so quickly—that realization on his expression and her sudden lurch forward. He tried to rise to his feet, but his movements were too slow, his belly too big, and she was faster.

Her higher elevation on the stairs gave her an advantage as she jumped and collided with his back. The strength and direction of her attack knocked him off balance. He stumbled, bumped against the wall, and went down. She followed him to the floor, clapping a hand over his mouth, wrenching his head back against her shoulder, and thrusting the blade upward, right into the soft part beneath his jaw. She pushed hard and fast, aiming for his brain until the hilt met his throat.

Hot blood soaked her fingers as he sagged. Soundless. Breathless. Dead.

She held onto the knife, frozen and listening for footsteps over the thrash of her pulse.

Blessed silence.

His phone lay on the floor at his feet. A 9mm with the extended barrel of a silencer sat on his hip. She needed both and waited several torturous seconds, concentrating on her surroundings. When she was certain no one had heard, she pocketed the phone and chambered a round on the gun.

That was the easy part.

Any second now, the guard upstairs would finish his cigarette and come looking for her.

With trembling hands, she positioned herself on knees at the bend in the staircase and raised the gun, ready to shoot anyone who rounded the corner.

The wait lasted an eternity as her mind swam through worst case scenarios. If Tiago's guards checked on him, she would fail. If multiple men entered the basement and outnumbered her, she would fail. If the gun in her hand misfired, she would fail.

Tate's fate rested entirely on her ability to not fucking fail.

When the door at the top of the stairs finally scraped open, every pore in her body beaded with sweat. Her lungs froze, and her limbs locked up.

Breathe, dammit.

The sound of footfalls grew louder, clomping, descending, speeding up. One threatening gait. Only one.

He would see Armando's body the moment he turned the last bend, but she wouldn't give him enough time to react.

Resting her finger on the trigger, she breathed in, timed his steps, and waited, waited...

His chest came into view, and he jerked to a stop, spinning toward her.

She squeezed the trigger on her exhale, point blank range, right in the chest.

The bullet casing pinged against the stone wall behind her, and the report of suppressed gunfire ricocheted through the stairwell. The echo sounded like a metal ball bouncing on concrete.

It's too loud!

The guard was dead before he hit the floor, but the racket would've been heard in the basement. She didn't have time to pause.

Stepping over the bodies, she cracked the lower-level door and spotted a man charging toward her, maybe ten feet away. He reached for the gun in his waistband, but hers was already aimed.

She fired at his torso, and the suppressed bang reverberated through her.

He dropped before he pulled his weapon, but his hand was still moving, reaching for it.

Adrenaline kicked in as she sprinted toward him and shot again, directly through his heart.

His arm fell to the floor with the slump of his body, his eyes fixed, glassy and frozen, at the ceiling.

This was far from over. Even with a silencer, those three shots had made noise. If the reverberation had reached the main floor, she didn't have much time.

She raced toward the chamber where Tate and Van waited and slammed to a stop mid-stride.

Keys!

Spinning back to the dead guard, she grabbed his 9mm and unhooked the keyring from his belt.

Then she ran, stretching unused muscles in her desperation to get to Tate. At the door to the chamber, she released the bolt and rushed into the room.

The overpowering scent of blood hit her in the face, causing her to stumble. Van sat against the wall, arms shackled to the beam. Tate lay on his stomach beside him, free of restraints because...

Oh God, his back was a gruesome tapestry of tattered flesh and gory illustrations too shocking to focus on. With his cheek against the concrete and his wounded arm lying like a dead thing beside him, he didn't move, didn't react.

Waves of heartbreak crashed through her, wrenching a whimper from her throat.

His eyes were open but glazed over, expressionless, utterly catatonic.

With panting breaths, she forced her feet to keep moving, skidded to her knees beside Van, and set the guns on the floor.

"We have to hurry." She fumbled with the key in the locks, losing precious seconds before the chains fell loose.

"Badell?" Van pulled his arms free and grabbed one of the guns.

"Dead. In his room. No one knows. *Yet.*" From her pocket, she handed him Armando's phone. "I'll get us out of the compound, but we need help leaving the city. This won't be a stealthy getaway."

"Matias should be close, but I don't know how to contact him." Van inched toward Tate and stroked a hand over his unmoving head. "Tate? I need Matias' number."

Tate's lashes twitched, followed by a sluggish blink. The muscles in his jaw bounced, like he was trying to respond and couldn't.

Her heart shattered, and it took every ounce of willpower she had left to keep her emotions in check.

"He's been unresponsive since you left." Van stood, stepping out of her way.

"Tate." She stretched out on the floor beside him and put her face in his. "We're getting out of here, but we need Matias' number."

His eyes tried to track her voice, focusing and clouding over. Then his lips moved, whispering the digits slowly and painfully in a shredded voice.

As Van made the call, she moved down Tate's legs. His jeans gathered just beneath his butt, as if the task of righting them had been interrupted. She carefully dragged his pants into place, focusing on her hands rather than the horror painting his back.

"It's Van Quiso," Van said into the phone. "We're in trouble."

Tate groaned weakly as she slid a hand beneath his hips, tucked him inside the boxer briefs, and zipped the fly as much as she could manage.

Van quietly and efficiently outlined the situation to Matias. A few seconds later, he turned the ringer off the phone, pocketed it, and rested those sharp silver eyes on her.

"He's twenty minutes outside of the neighborhood." He crouched at Tate's side. "We need to head north, and he'll meet us at—"

"M-mmeh…" Tate inched his hand toward her, dragging his injured arm along the floor and hissing, "Medsss…you…"

"I got the medicine." She caught his hand in hers and found his swollen blue eyes, blinking back tears. "I'm good, Tate."

"Extra?" he slurred. "More mehhs…sinnn?"

Extra medicine?

Despite her efforts, her strung-out misery flowed down her cheeks in hot streaks. She couldn't imagine the amount of pain he was in, yet his concern was entirely focused on *her.*

She knelt over him and put her mouth against his. "The syringes are locked up, but it's okay. Matias will find me a good doctor." She kissed his cracked lips, lingering, savoring the connection. "I have twenty-four hours. Plenty of time." *Not near enough time.* But she wouldn't dwell on that. "Van's going to carry you. We need to go."

Tate closed his eyes, his expression contorted in pain. When he refocused on her again, he looked fiercely determined and brutally handsome.

Flattening the hand of his good arm against the floor, he tried to push up. Van was there, lifting and adjusting to position Tate's body in a fireman's carry. Though Tate didn't make a sound, his agony was palpable in the tenseness of his muscles and the creases on his bruised face.

She lost her breath through the grueling process of dragging him to his feet. His back was one massive, open, chewed-up wound. His ribs were broken, and the hole near his elbow slicked his forearm and hand in fresh blood. Moving him without causing extreme pain was impossible.

Sliding behind Van, she cupped Tate's jaw and kissed his mouth, tasting his torment and love and wetting his lips with promises.

"Netflix, a rescued dog, and a road trip to wine country." Squatting beneath the droop of his upper body, she kissed him again. "It's all waiting for us."

The corner of his mouth twitched—a heartbreaking attempt at a smile.

"Lay out the escape plan." Van hitched Tate higher on his shoulder, with the guard's gun held tightly in his hand.

Thank fuck he was strong, because Tate wasn't a small guy. Carrying him through the compound would be a feat in and of itself.

"There are two ways in and out." She strode toward the door, trembling violently with nerves. "We'll take the stairs up, turn right down the hall, and go out the back exit. Less guards."

She opened the door and peeked down the basement corridor. Other than the dead man, it was empty.

"Since I have the silencer, I'll do the shooting." She checked the magazine in Armando's 9mm. "Five rounds left."

"When we make it out, what then? Is there gate in the rear?"

When not *if*. She could've hugged Van for his confidence.

"No gate. Just guards. It's a service entrance. We'll have to shoot and run." She rested a hand on Tate's backside, where he hung over Van's shoulder. "Can you manage?"

"I've got him." Van gripped the door, opening it wider. "We need to head north. It's quicker and easier for us to leave the neighborhood than for Matias to fight his way in."

He gave her the address of the meet spot, which was about a fifteen-minute sprint. Half that if they stole a car.

Her stomach turned to ice as she led him down the hall and into the stairwell. She paused at the bodies long enough to snatch the sawed-off shotgun and holster from the dead guard. She strapped it on her hip and crept up the stairs with Van at her back.

At the top, she met his eyes and whispered, "Don't let him get hit."

"I'm more concerned about you," he whispered back. "He'll kill me if something happens to you."

Tate released a low, deep sound in his throat, and her lips quivered in a smile.

She stroked the back of his leg, her chest aching with an outpour of things she wanted to say to him. But this wasn't the time.

We'll make it out. Then she would have a lifetime to tell him how much she loved him.

She cracked the door to the main floor and scanned the empty hall through the opening. "Clear."

They ran. Down the long hall, guns raised, footsteps soft, the sprint zapped the air from her lungs and turned her stomach to lead. Adrenaline soared through her blood, and her hair flicked against her face as she swung her neck side to side to watch their backs and fronts.

A shadow moved across the wall of the intersecting corridor up ahead, and an all-over tremor shook her aim. She locked her elbows and honed in on the approaching threat.

The guard stepped from around the corner and paused in her sights. He gasped, and she fired. The bullet hit his chest, and he dropped just as another man emerged behind him.

This one managed to release a warning bellow and draw his weapon before she shot him in the face.

Fucking shit and damn! The back door was close now, only ten paces away, but the commotion was too loud. Soon, they would be swarmed by armed men.

A glance behind her confirmed Van was on her heels. She grabbed a gun off a dead guard, shoved it into her waistband, and cut the corner.

The din of distant footfalls pounded behind her, intensifying the terror that gripped her neck and shoulders. They were feet away from the exterior door when two more guards entered the hall at the opposite end.

"Go, go, go," she shouted at Van. "Get outside."

Breathless and sweaty, she ran past the exit and fired three shots at the men. One guard went down as Van threw open the door and slipped outside with Tate.

The second guard fired back, missing her by inches. Tate's hoarse roar sounded over the bang of gunfire, and she fired again.

A hollow click stopped her heart. *Out of ammo.*

The man at the end of the hall had paused to check on his friend. But he was moving now, running toward her with his pistol aimed.

A bullet pelleted the plaster beside her head as she dropped the silencer, drew the short-barrel shotgun, and blasted a huge hole through his chest.

Her ears rang with the explosive noise. She tossed the gun and pulled the pistol from her jeans, needing the 9mm to cover the distance between her and the throng of men tearing around the corner.

She backed through the doorway and into the sunlight, angling around the door jamb and spraying bullets into the chaos inside.

More gunfire ricocheted behind her, spiking her heart rate. She turned and found Van shooting down two approaching men in the alley. He crouched beside the open rear door of a small car. Tate lay face down across the backseat.

"Let's go." He scanned the barren street and ran toward the driver's side.

Can he hot wire that car?

She didn't have time to ask. More men flooded the corridor. Too many to shoot down. She slammed the steel door shut and hauled ass toward the car. Van bent under the steering wheel and yanked on wires as she pulled Tate's feet into the backseat with her.

"Hurry!" She closed the door and ducked just as the window exploded in shards of glass. Bullets pinged the side of the car, and the report of gunfire shuddered the air.

"Van!" she shouted, petrified. "Can you do it?"

The car roared to life and jerked forward, slamming her against the seat back and tossing her on top of Tate's prone body.

Van sped out of the alley, sideswiped another car, and bounced over a curb. Bullets rained down upon them, blowing out the rear window and riddling the metal exterior.

Keeping as low and concealed as possible, she curled up near Tate's head and rested his cheek on her lap. His lower half hung off the seat, his knees bent on the floorboard at an awkward angle.

"Which way is north?" Van swerved around a pedestrian and hit the gas.

"Left." She craned her neck to look between the front seats. "Not this street. Turn left at the next one."

He followed her directions, and as her panting breaths slowed, so did the bullets and yelling behind her, until…nothing.

We lost them.

We escaped.

The glory and relief in getting away settled through her in great shivering waves. She combed a hand through Tate's hair and bent to rest her lips against his feverish brow as she caught her breath.

But they weren't out of the woods yet.

"They have motorbikes," she shouted at Van over the gusts of the wind through the windows. "They'll catch up."

He took the corners at high speeds, lurching in and out of traffic, and whipping her around the backseat with the starts and stops of g-force.

The pungency of fuel and burning rubber saturated the cab, and the taste of blood soaked her tongue from her stabbing teeth.

"It's going to be okay. We're going to make it." She whispered the chant at Tate's ear.

She didn't have medicine and probably wouldn't live through tomorrow, but she had today. She had Tate, and he would survive this. He had to.

His eyes were closed, his lungs laboring for every intake of air. Clots of blood coated his back in a gruesome reminder of the prior night, and beneath the gore lurked a picture carved into flesh and muscle. Through the shimmer of tears blurring her vision, she could make out images. A massive gate opening outward and… Was that a silhouette floating through it?

"We're close, right?" Van pointed at the motorway that emerged up ahead.

"Tiago's domain ends there. Just a few blocks away."

She twisted to see out the broken rear window. No one chased them. No motorbikes. No speeding cars. No guns.

Dread buckled her stomach.

The escape was too easy. Even if Tiago's men had discovered his death, they wouldn't just let her go. Something was wrong.

"Call Matias," she said urgently. "Tell him where we are."

"A little busy." Van's laugh strained with tension as he swerved the car side to side, dodging motorists.

She cradled Tate's head and scooted forward to reach between the seats and search for the phone in Van's pocket.

"Fuck!" He slammed on the brakes, throwing her back against the seat. "Fuck, fuck, fuck!"

Up ahead, police cars skidded onto the street, blocking their path.

"Turn back!" Her pulse exploded as she twisted around, searching for a side street. "Take that one!"

She caught Van's eyes in the rearview mirror and pointed at the alley behind them.

"We can't trust these cops?" He shoved the car in reverse and sped backward. "What happens if they catch us?"

Tires squealed behind them, followed by the rumbling sounds of motorbikes. Her scalp crawled, and a chill spread through her cheeks as she looked back and found a roadblock of armed officers.

"Get to that alley." She gripped tight to Tate's head and shoulders, shaking and nauseous. "They wouldn't be here unless Tiago called in a favor."

"What?" Van spun the car around and veered into the alley — the only way out. "I thought Tiago was dead."

"He is." Her breath came in wheezing pants. "I smashed his head in with a dumbbell. I thought... Oh God, I didn't check. I couldn't..."

His pulse. I didn't check his pulse. Was he still alive?

If the police caught them, they would die in prison. Or they would be taken back to the compound, where they would be tortured before they died.

"If they surround us, we're dead." She tightened her arms around Tate's limp body.

"Goddammit." Van slammed the shifter through the gears and recklessly weaved around dumpsters and metal stairs in the alley.

The motor revved, and the end of the alley glowed like a beacon. Police on motorbikes zoomed in behind them, but there were no barricades up ahead.

They can make it. They can make it. Go, go, go...

The air vibrated with a rumbling reverberation right before the end of the alley filled with half a dozen police on bikes.

"Hold on." Van accelerated.

Twenty feet, ten feet... Holy fuck, he was going to plow through them.

Heart pounding, she bent over Tate's head, wrapped her arms in a death grip around him, and braced for impact.

A ringing sound split her eardrums, buzzing with the clamor of gunshots and Van's shouting. Then sirens.

Sirens on a police car, in the alley, careening toward them head-on. The alley was too narrow, and they were traveling too fast and close to avoid collision.

Van jerked the car, hit the side of a building, then slammed into something else. The world spun, and time became heavily compressed and fractured.

The jarring impact catapulted her to Peru, shackled in the back of a transport, falling, rolling, flailing in the memory of twisted metal, broken bodies, crushed bones, and the scent of blood.

TWENTY-SEVEN

Tate surfaced to a muffled symphony of pandemonium. Banging, shouting sounds pulsed in and out, as if trying to penetrate the cotton stuffed in his ears. He lay twisted in a mangled car, covered in glass and throbbing in excruciating pain.

Lucia was there, her tears drenching his face and her hand stroking his hair. Her agony was unbearable, her fear palpable. He couldn't swallow, couldn't breathe as he tried to make sense of the clamor around him.

He remembered gunfire and running and the speeding car. The front hood was bent against the broken windshield. The dash was too close to the front seats, and the pungency of coolant, gasoline, and burnt chemicals fumed the air. They must've crashed.

Black spots dotted his vision as he dragged his good arm beneath him and lifted. He blinked. And blinked again.

Multiple rifles pointed through the shattered window beside Lucia, aimed at her head. The armed men shouted something, and she screamed back at them, sobbing and shaking uncontrollably.

His pulse raced, and his senses sharpened. The men wore helmets and uniforms with arm patches and name tags. They surrounded the car, training rifles through every window and shouting in Spanish.

Where was Van? The airbags were deployed, and the front seat was empty.

Overpowering pain tore through his body and stole the strength from his neck. His head dropped onto her lap, and his muscles trembled with never-ending agony.

This wasn't him. He wasn't weak or puny. He was physically fit, stubborn, aggressive. He was a survivor. He needed to get the fuck up. He should be able to protect her.

The door beside her opened with a godawful squeal of grinding metal. Hands dove in, yanking her out of the car. She fought and kicked and screamed his name, but he couldn't reach her. His arms wouldn't respond to his urgent orders.

"Lucia." Seething with pain, he tried to scramble after her.

His limbs wouldn't cooperate, moving sluggishly, inch by inch across the seat. He reached his working arm through the open door and clawed at the pavement, yanking himself forward in a fevered frenzy of ripping flesh and dizzying anguish. He felt things tearing and breaking inside him, but he was separated from his body, completely fixated on getting to her and nothing else.

With his torso hanging out of the car and his legs caught within, he watched uniformed men with guns haul her away. Police cars and motorcycles filled the alley, and at the far end, several cops wrestled Van into the backseat of an armored transport.

If they were incarcerated, she wouldn't see a doctor. Wouldn't have access to medicine. Maybe Matias or Cole would find them and grease the right palms to get them released, but it would be too late for her.

She would be dead by tomorrow.

A roar ruptured from his throat as he twisted around, searching the car for a weapon and coming up empty. A seat belt tangled around his leg, and he wasted miserable seconds and precious strength to free himself. Then he crawled on one arm, rolling onto the pavement and nearly blacking out. He muscled through it, compartmentalizing the pain and fumbling forward, scraping his chest along the ground.

She thrashed and swung her legs in the clutches of the men who carried her. When she found his eyes, her expression hardened, and she redoubled her efforts. But she was outnumbered, and he was too slow, too fucking weak.

He couldn't reach her, couldn't touch her, couldn't save her.

But he tried, and tried, and kept trying.

Goddammit, he would never give up on her.

TWENTY-EIGHT

Crammed inside a cell in the municipal police station in eastern Caracas, Lucia struggled to breathe amid the sweltering heat and the reek of body odor, shit, and urine.

She didn't know where the police had taken Tate. Didn't know if Tiago Badell was orchestrating their fates. Didn't know if Matias would be able to find them or if he even had the power to get them out of this place. Her nerves were shot, and with every hour that passed, she felt the tendrils of despair taking root.

When she and Van were thrown in here, they were shell-shocked and manhandled. The guards took his shirt and shoes and her bra and boots. But they let her keep the rest of her clothes. Then they were shoved to the back of the prison cell by dozens of restless, hungry prisoners.

Van had dragged her through the crowded bodies, fighting his way back to the front to yell at the guards through the bars. Though he spoke good Spanish, his pleas for a doctor fell on deaf ears. He'd tried to explain her illness and her need for medical attention, tried to argue for her human rights, but there were no rights here. Within the walls of the *calabozo*, no one was human.

Shirtless men and barely-dressed women stood shoulder to shoulder against one another, with no room to sit. They took turns resting on hammocks made from sheets tied to the bars. A few managed to squat along the back wall.

Every hacking cough was a reminder of the diseases that lurked among them. Tuberculosis. HIV. Influenza. Not to mention the red scabies-like rashes that blistered the arms and legs around her.

A small window outside of the cell sat high on the wall. The sun had set forever ago. The guards had changed twice. Dawn would come soon.

She stood with her back to a corner. Van had wedged her there, using his body to separate her from the others. With his arms braced on the walls above her head, he worked his jaw rhythmically.

Neither of them had eaten, drank, or gone to the bathroom in over twenty-four hours. Her bladder cramped painfully, but relieving it would require peeing in a plastic bag while everyone watched. She would have to submit to that eventually, but she wasn't mentally ready.

"Still no symptoms?" Van asked for the hundredth time.

"No."

There were some nights, though rare, when she didn't experience nausea, abdominal cramps, or any pain at all.

Tonight, she felt a different kind of pain. A deep, emotional torment that festered and cramped in every part of her.

Tate was probably in a prison cell like this one, alone, unable to stand or defend himself. Were prisoners stepping on him? Was he bleeding out on the filthy floor? Would he take his last breath while prisoners stood on him unaware and unconcerned? She couldn't stop imagining it, and it was slowly killing her from the inside out.

Beside her, a man leaned his back against the wall, sobbing as he pulled on his hair and scolded himself for robbing a merchant to feed his starving family.

"I can't believe places like this exist," Van muttered, staring at the man. "That's saying something, considering I grew up in the shittiest shit hole on Earth."

Her chest pinched. "I'm sorry you got pulled into this. This wasn't your fight."

"I volunteered." He bent his knees, bringing his scarred, bruised face into her line of sight. "I've committed so many crimes, and this is the first time I've been behind bars. This is justice, don't you think?"

She shook her head. "You're a good man."

He laughed and returned to his full height, looking away.

"No." She gripped his bicep and pulled him back down. "What you did for Tate last night, especially knowing you have a wife—"

"How the fuck do you know about her?"

She yanked her arm back and swallowed. "Tiago knows. I'm sorry. I don't know if he'll go after her or—"

"She's safe." His entire body turned to stone, and he dragged a hand over his face, breathing through his nose as if trying to rein in his temper. "Matias has her. He's protecting everyone connected to Tate."

Oh, thank God.

She closed her eyes and inhaled. Then she looked up into his silver-bladed gaze. "I probably won't make it through the morning—"

"Lucia," he growled.

"I just want to thank you for what you've done for him. You didn't have to come to Caracas. You didn't have to participate in Tiago's demands last night. If you hadn't done those things, I wouldn't have made it this far."

"*This* far? To a prison?"

"I had five days with him." Her voice quivered. "I got to experience love. Do you know that feeling?"

"Yeah." His eyes closed briefly, and when they opened, they glimmered.

Jesus, this mean-looking ex-kidnapper was head over heels in love. Who would've thought? She certainly wouldn't have recognized it before, but now... Now that she knew what it felt like, she sensed this man's love for his wife all the way down to her toes.

Neither of them was in a position of hope, and maybe that was why she felt the need to say, "Promise me you'll see her again."

"Easy." His expression hardened with conviction. "I'm counting every breath until I see her again. I promise." He cupped the back of her head and held her face against his chest. "Your turn."

"I'll see him again." *In my memories. His face will be the last thing I see before I die.* "I promise."

TWENTY-NINE

Four nights. Three days. One room.

Tate marked the loss of time by the ebb and flow of sunlight through the cracks in the wood walls. He lay face down on a thin blanket, his muscles trembling and his back a throbbing, burning, spasmodic ripple of pain.

His prison was a windowless shack with a dirt floor, a bucket to shit in, and a door that locked on the outside.

After Lucia had been taken from him in Caracas, the police put him in the trunk of a car. He'd traveled about a day in that dark cramped space. When he arrived here, he was blindfolded and carried into the shack by two men he couldn't see.

During those few seconds outside, he'd felt the warmth of the sun on his skin and the dry heat in the air. It smelled like a desert—dusty, hot, barren.

Maybe he was near the coastline, but he didn't hear the tide or the sea birds or any insects. He didn't hear anything at all through the walls of the shack.

Except when the doctor came.

Twice a day, a car rolled up outside. The bar slid from the door on the shack, and an old man shuffled in to tend to his wounds.

Always escorted by two armed guards, the black-skinned doctor spread a numbing cream into the cuts on his back, cleaned the stitches on his arm, and bathed him from head to toe. Then he was fed broth and tea.

One guard emptied the shit bucket while the other patrolled the door. Tate could barely crawl, let alone stand. But they weren't taking chances.

DEVASTATE

No one spoke. In those first couple of days, Tate couldn't, either. He wasn't sure any of them knew English. The guards resembled the thugs in Badell's compound, and the doctor matched the descriptions Lucia had given him of Badell's medical team, down to the scarification welts on his arms.

My back will look like that someday.

If I live.

Though he'd heard Lucia say she'd killed Badell, he knew the gang leader was the reason he was here. Either someone had taken over the operation or Badell was still alive.

When Tate could finally manage raspy words, he badgered his visitors with questions about his location, Badell's whereabouts, and Van and Lucia.

Where's Lucia? was the question he demanded most, and during the visit this morning, one of the guards had given him a single English answer.

Went to prison.

He'd blown a gasket when he heard the response, seething and thrashing and reopening wounds in his fit of rage. The guards had to restrain and gag him while the doctor patched him back up.

If he counted the day it took him to travel here, it'd been four days since he'd been separated from her. If she was imprisoned, she would be dead now.

His brain struggled to process that. His heart flat out refused.

He ran through a range of conflicting emotions in his isolation, from fury and guilt to determination and hope, and chief of all was helplessness. He'd failed her. Failed to protect her. Failed to rescue her. Failed to make her smile.

His shame and self-pity made him resent the healing of his injuries. He resented every fucking breath he took. Why bother?

But what if she lived?

He wore himself out trying to stand. Felt the wounds on his back tearing when he tried to stretch. He was imprisoned in a horizontal position, lost in the destructive fabric of his thoughts.

In hopeless conditions, the mind deteriorated. He knew that was happening, knew he needed to shut down parts of it to survive.

So he did.

THIRTY

I'm still alive.

Lucia didn't know how or why her illness up and fucking vanished, but she hadn't experienced a single symptom since the night Tate was tortured. Tiago must've given her a cure in the last injection. It was the only logical answer.

She and Van spent a week in that overcrowded jail, living in a cesspool of feces, disease, and despair. Now they were on a prison bus, being transported to a permanent penitentiary. There were no phone call allowances, no lawyers, no judicial process. No human rights. This was the underworld, and corruption pulled the strings.

She wasn't sure if their case had even made it to the courts. She still didn't know what they were being held for. Tiago was behind this. He was powerful enough. Vindictive enough. She expected nothing less after bashing him over the head with a dumbbell. Killing her would've been too merciful for his brand of revenge.

Did she regret attacking him?

Maybe he'd truly meant to give her freedom.

Freedom from him.

Freedom from her illness.

But without Tate, she would've never been free.

The only thing she regretted was not bashing him again and again until his brains spilled onto the floor.

She sat beside Van on the bus, hands and legs shackled with a chain between the restraints to limit movement. Dozens of prisoners crowded in around them, all traveling to the same horrific fate.

Sadness hung like a fog in the humid air. The entire bus smelled like defeat. But she refused to subscribe to it. Her feelings had been all over the place for the past seven days, but she hadn't let herself break. She hadn't given up. Eleven years ago, she'd entered Tiago's world much like this and worked her way to the top. She would do it again.

But could she do it with a broken heart?

Thinking about Tate, missing him, craving him, loving him — her need for him didn't come and go like her illness. It was a building, growing, continuous escalation, and she couldn't break away from it. She didn't want to. She'd never experienced such deep-seeded torment in her life. But it was *her* torment, and she would endure it for as long as she was separated from him.

About an hour into the drive, the bus rolled through an urban town. High-rise buildings lined the street in a mishmash of historical and modern architecture.

There were over a hundred prisons in Venezuela, and she didn't know which one they were assigned to or where this town was on the map. But as the bus stopped in front of a towering office building, it didn't feel right.

She exchanged a confused look with Van.

"Where are we?" he asked.

"Hell if I know."

The driver rose from the seat and opened the door. The two armed guards in the front also stood.

Footsteps announced someone boarding the bus. She craned her neck and spotted a mid-thirties Caucasian man. His short brown hair was a military-type cut. He wore aviator glasses, a black leather jacket, and dark jeans. Strong jawline and muscled physique, he looked like a hot DEA Special Agent from the States. *Wishful thinking.*

Why was he talking to the driver?

She glanced at Van, who watched the man with a grin tugging at his lips.

Her heart rate skyrocketed. "Do you know him?"

Without looking at her, he gripped her wrist above the chains and squeezed. Hard.

Oh my fucking God. He knows him!

Was it Cole Hartman? The man who helped Tate locate her? Who else could it be?

The bus hadn't been forced to the side of the road. This was a preplanned stop. An arrangement negotiated in advance.

A rescue.

One of the guards turned and strolled down the aisle. Her lungs crashed together as he stopped beside Van and unlocked the restraints from the seat. He did the same for hers and stepped back, motioning for them to go.

Her legs trembled, and her pulse hiked as she followed Van off the bus. The man in sunglasses led them into the building without a word, his gait efficient and quick. Too quick for her shackled, shuffling feet to keep up. Van managed only slightly better with his stronger legs.

Once they were inside the vacant lobby, the stranger crouched before them and unlocked the chains with a key.

"Where's Amber?" Van kicked his feet free.

"With Matias." The man unlocked her shackles and rose to free her wrists. "I'm Cole Hartman."

Her heart tumbled and flipped.

"Do you know where Tate is?" She dropped the last of her restraints and sucked in a breath.

"Tiago Badell has him." He freed Van's hands, strode to the bay of elevators, and pushed the *up* button. "I don't know where."

Her heart shattered into a million pieces. "Is he alive?"

"I don't know," Cole said. "When I leave here, I'll find him."

"Who's funding that?" Van prowled toward him, head cocked.

"You are." Cole smirked. "Your wife approved it. Matias is chipping in on the extraction fee."

"Extraction." Her voice cracked with tears, and she cleared it. "You know he's alive?"

"I don't want to get your hopes up."

"Hope?" She gripped the front of her shirt, drawing his attention to the dark red stains. "I've been wearing his blood for over a week. I left him crawling in an alley with broken ribs, his back carved to hell, and a hole from an icepick through his arm. Hope is all I have left."

"Okay." Cole's brows drew in, and he stood taller. "What I know of Tate Vades is when he's determined to do something, he does it. If he wants to live, he will."

The elevator dinged, and the doors opened. In a swirl of tears and long brown hair, a beautiful woman shot out of the lift and collided with Van's chest.

He grunted a noise that sounded a lot like a sob as he yanked her up his body and buried his face in her neck.

"Amber, you were supposed to stay upstairs." Cole stiffened as he scanned the street through the glass doors. "It's not safe."

She wrapped her legs around Van's waist, crying as she peppered his face in kisses.

"Where's Livana?" Van caught her chin and stared into her eyes.

"She's in Colombia. Liv, Josh, they're all there, except Kate. Matias has a team of men looking for her."

Kate. Tate had told Lucia about his roommate, but he never

188

mentioned Livana.

Amber went back to kissing his face, covering the length of his scar and the bruises around his eye. When their lips met, he kissed her hard and deep, eating at her mouth with a passion that heated Lucia's cheeks.

"Who's Livana?" she asked Cole.

"Van's daughter. Get in the elevator." He shooed her in.

Van has a daughter?

She didn't move. "I'm not going anywhere without Tate."

"We'll discuss it upstairs." He gripped Van's arm, guiding him onto the lift with Amber in his arms.

"Lucia." Cole lowered his voice to a threatening tone. "If you die in this lobby, you won't be able to help him."

She gritted her teeth and stepped onto the lift. He pressed the button for the top floor, and the elevator started its slow crawl upward.

"Who gave you a black eye?" Amber cupped Van's face as tears streamed down her own.

He kissed her again, pressing her back against the wall and tangling his hands in her hair.

Watching them together ripped open the hole in Lucia's chest. She'd been kissed like that once. For five days. Not only had Tate given her a blissful taste of happiness, he'd also fought for her, bled for her, and reopened his own emotional wounds. For her.

She owed him her life, her freedom, and she intended to pay that debt. She wouldn't neglect it or abandon it. She would never walk away from him.

"What's on the top floor?" When she glanced at Cole, her horrific, puffy-eyed face reflected back in his sunglasses.

"Helicopter," he said. "Matias is taking you to Colombia."

Camila might be here with Matias, but it wouldn't change anything. Lucia's mind was made up. "I'm not getting on that helicopter."

He slid the sunglasses to his hairline and pinned her with the intensity of his brown eyes. "I didn't just spend seven days getting you out of a Venezuelan jail to let you stay here."

"I'm going with you."

"No. Absolutely not." He set his jaw. "I work alone."

"Work alone then. I know Tiago better than anyone. I'll find him on my own."

The elevator bounced to a stop, and the doors opened to a waiting room filled with half a dozen people. Some she didn't recognize—Matias' cartel members by the look of them and the weapons they carried. But there were two familiar faces.

Sitting on a couch beside Matias, Camila lifted her head toward Lucia. Their gazes caught, locked, and connected in a way only two sisters could.

Camila stood, and Lucia stepped off the lift, her legs numb and throat tight.

I'm not going to cry. I will not cry.

Tears welled in Camila's huge dark eyes. God, she was beautiful. Gone was her sweet baby face and spindly limbs. She'd bloomed into a curvy, toned beauty with long black hair and a healthy glow that radiated around her like a halo.

She paused within arm's reach of Camila and tentatively touched her soft hair and tear-soaked cheeks.

"You're as tall as me." Lucia laughed through a sob. "I told myself not to cry."

It'd been twelve years since Van had taken Camila from their citrus grove. Twelve years since Lucia last saw her. But it felt like only yesterday when they were running through the maze of orange trees, laughing and screaming as Matias chased them.

"You're thinner than me, bitch." Camila grinned through her tears.

"And you're still bitchier."

They reached at the same time, crashing together in a hug that constricted her ribs and wrenched a sob from deep inside her.

"I thought you were dead." Camila cried, soaking Lucia's neck.

"I thought you were dead, too. This doesn't feel real, does it?"

Camila shook her head and tightened her embrace. "I'm taking you to Colombia with me. You need food and a doctor and... Goddammit, Lucia." She leaned back and wiped her cheeks. "I'm so sorry. I should've looked harder. Done more. And Tate..." Her face crumpled.

"Don't do that." She brushed Camila's tears away. "Tate told me all about your vigilante work. I'm so fucking proud of you."

Matias stepped in, nudging Camila aside to wrap his arms around Lucia. "So damn good to see you, *bella*."

"You, too." She hugged him back. "Thank you for taking care of my sister."

"She's my life." His head turned toward Camila.

She followed his gaze and watched Camila pull Van into a tight embrace. His hands hung awkwardly in the air for a moment before they slid behind her and patted her back.

"I still want to kill him," Matias growled.

"Give him a second chance. We all deserve one."

"I'm trying."

Camila pulled away from Van and returned to Lucia, encircling possessive arms around Lucia's waist.

"Let's go home," she said to Matias.

He stared at her for a suspended moment, sharing a private smile that lit up his face.

He was even more handsome than Lucia remembered, with his thick black hair, powerful frame, and hazel eyes glinting in the sunlight from the windows. Thank God, he and Camila had found each other again.

"The helicopter's ready." He gestured at the ceiling. "Head up to the roof. I need to talk to Cole for a —"

"I'm not going." Lucia stood taller, bracing for an argument.

"Oh." Camila stepped back, her expression etched with hurt and disappointment. "Okay... I... Well, we can get you back to Texas. I just thought —"

"I'm not leaving Venezuela without Tate." She wouldn't apologize for her feelings. They were real and honest, and Camila of all people would understand. "I love him."

A smile wobbled across Camila's lips. "I bet on my life he loves you, too." She gripped Lucia's hands. "But you need to see a doctor. You've been so sick."

Tate must've told Matias about her illness, but that would've been a week ago.

"I'm doing okay now." She rested a hand over her stomach. "I don't know why, but I haven't felt any of the symptoms."

Camila and Matias turned toward Cole Hartman, who leaned against the wall on the far side of the room. He straightened, shoved a hand through his hair, and approached.

"I intercepted the blood results Tate was waiting on," he said. "I had them reviewed by a doctor I trust."

She stopped breathing, and everything inside her went still. "What is it?"

Camila clutched her hand and squeezed. Clearly, everyone knew but her.

"There were traces of something like hemlock in your system." He held a fist against his brow, as if trying to think. "I don't have the report in front of me, but it was a poison that behaved like hemlock, derived from a plant the doctor couldn't identify. He found compounds or alkaloids or whatever that causes ascending muscular paralysis. I guess it starts at the legs and works its way to the respiratory muscles. Did you experience that?"

"Yes. Exactly that." A sudden coldness hit her core. "What are you saying?"

"Tiago Badell was poisoning you with an unknown venomous plant. You had dinner with him every night, so I assume he put it in your food. Every morning, he injected you with an antivenom."

She swayed as the past few years came crashing down upon her. The mandatory dinners, the nighttime cramps and nausea, the instant relief after the medicine—it all fit. And she hadn't been sick since the last time she ate at his table.

"I don't have a terminal disease." She clutched her throat as she tried to absorb the impact. "I'm not going to die."

"Not today." Cole smiled. "As far as the doctor can tell, repeat exposure to the poison didn't cause lasting damage. Your overall blood work is healthy. But you need to have tests ran, a full examination. Not to mention your injury in Peru…"

His voice faded beneath the heavy thud of her heart. Tiago poisoned her. *For years.* That sick, disgusting, depraved son of a bitch. How could he do that? And now…

"He has Tate." Her pulse raced, and pain stabbed through her chest as she turned to Camila. "I need a loan. I'm sorry to ask this, but I just need some money for…" *Lodging, transportation, food, clothes, weapons— the list is endless.* "I have to find him, and I promise to pay you back."

"Lucia, calm down." Matias slid into her line of sight. "Cole will find him. He knows what he's doing and—"

"What would you do?" She moved around Matias and confronted her sister. "If Matias was taken by a man like Tiago, what would you do?"

"I'd put everything I had and everything I was into finding him." Camila's eyes dampened, and her voice broke. "I'll give you whatever you need."

"Stop." Cole pinched the bridge of his nose and cursed under his breath. "Here's the deal. I'm not babysitting you, and I'm not fucking kidnapping anyone."

"Okay." Lucia held her breath.

"Say your goodbyes." He rubbed the back of his neck and lowered his hand. "We leave in ten minutes."

THIRTY-ONE

Standing on sturdy legs, Tate lifted a soaked sponge over his head and squeezed. Cool water sluiced down his nude body. It was neither refreshing nor painful. It was just...water. He plunged the sponge into the bucket and repeated the task with robotic movements.

Lift. Squeeze. Plunge. And don't forget to scrub beneath the ankle cuff.

They'd taken his clothes away when the doctor had stopped bathing him. It must've been weeks ago.

Was it weeks? Or months?

Time didn't exist within these walls. It didn't speed up or slow down. It didn't move at all. Because it was dead.

Sometimes his mind weakened, and he thought about the lost weeks. He could track them if he wanted to. He only needed to take inventory of his injuries. The stitches in his arm had been removed, and his hand had some mobility. His back didn't feel as tight when he paced the dirt floor, dragging the heavy chain behind him. Pain still lingered in his ribs, but it was muted. Dull.

Dull like the water trickling over his skin as he bathed.

Dull like the stew and porridge they brought every day.

Dull like the beat of his heart when he forced himself to face the truth.

She's dead.

He hurled the sponge into the water, snatched the bucket from the ground, and shoved it toward the guard waiting at the door.

It was always the same two silent scowling men. They were about as happy to be here as he was.

The guard reached for the bucket, and Tate yanked it back.

"Where's Lucia?" he demanded.

Always the same question. Always the same non-response.

When the man pinned his lips, Tate threw the bucket at his feet, splashing the man's trousers with water.

"Where is she?" he bellowed.

The guard's face turned red-hot. A beating would follow. A fist in the face. A boot in the ribs. Didn't matter if he taunted them or not. They seemed to get off on boxing a shackled man who was too weak to defend himself.

But Tate always fought back, and he was growing stronger. He fought until blood leaked into his eyes and clouded his vision. Until his lungs wheezed, and his ribs screamed in protest. Until the bastards knocked him out.

He fought because it made him feel alive.

Today would be no different.

The second guard entered the shack and cracked his knuckles. They never brought weapons in. Nothing Tate could use against them. If he managed to kill them bare handed, what would he do? His fucking ankle was chained to a fucking pike buried a mile into the fucking dirt floor. The damn thing wasn't budging. He'd bloodied his hands trying to dig it out.

He stepped to the center of the shack, as far as the chain would allow, and squared his shoulders.

But the guards didn't attack.

"Where's Lucia?" He gnashed his teeth.

When they didn't respond, he spat at their feet. "Fuck off then."

They didn't fuck off. Why were they just standing there?

A moment later, an electronic buzzing sound broke the silence.

Buzzing.

Like a phone.

One of the guards reached into his pocket and removed exactly that.

He hadn't seen a phone since the night he...

He tried not to think about that night.

His attention locked onto the phone as the guard connected the call on speaker and held it out of his reach.

"Hello, Tate." The deep voice sliced across his skin like the edge of a blade.

Tiago Badell.

He tried to step closer to the guard, but the chain jerked his leg back. "Where's—?"

"If you ask about her," Badell said, "the call ends and you'll never hear from me again. You'll spend the rest of your lonely existence locked away in that shack, wondering why I called and what I was going to say."

His molars clamped together so hard he felt the pain ripple through his skull. "I'm listening."

"I would be there in person, but I haven't been feeling well. I'm sure you know why."

Lucia thought she'd killed him. She must've injured him, and Tate hoped the bastard's dick had been removed during the attempt on his life.

"I wanted to offer you something," Badell said. "Let's call it a last request. Anything you want. This doesn't include information, and it must fit inside the shack."

What the fuck? "What is this? Like a last-meal request? Am I on death row?"

"I'm offering more than a meal, Tate. You can choose anything—a bed to sleep on, a girl to fuck, a drug to numb your mind. I'm sure you can come up with something creative."

"Why?" He paced the dirt floor, and the chain slithered after him. "What do you want?"

"I've already taken my payment. Consider this a thank you."

He slammed to a stop, and the pound of his heartbeat thrashed in his ears. "What did you *take*?"

"Not Lucia. I left her to die in prison. What's your last request, Tate?"

A hot ember formed in his throat and sank slowly, agonizingly into his chest, where it spread like fire, consuming him in excruciating heartache. His vision blurred, and despite the inferno charring him from the inside out, his skin felt cold, his limbs heavy, and his eyes gritty with hot sand.

He lowered to the blanket and stared at his empty hands. He had nothing. If she was truly gone, he wanted nothing. Yet his mouth moved, voicing the question before his brain caught up.

"Do you have a photo of Lucia?"

"Yes."

There was something. Something he could ask for, and as he closed his eyes, it was all he could see.

So he said it out loud.

He told Badell his final wish.

THIRTY-TWO

Three months later…

"Stop the car." Lucia grabbed the binoculars, her pulse hammering and her mouth arid dry.

As Cole Hartman rolled the jeep to idle on the dirt road, she adjusted the focus on the lenses and scanned the parched horizon.

There weren't any big trees to provide a canopy in this part of Venezuela, and with the blistering temperatures, wavy heat lines distorted the landscape.

Where are you, Tate? I know you're out there.

Woody-stemmed shrubs dotted the salt-crusted earth. Between the widely spaced out cacti with their spiny slender arms, there was nothing but rocky sand and bare dirt as far as she could see.

"According to the old man," Cole said, leaning forward with an elbow propped on the steering wheel, "the monastery is supposed to be twenty kilometers the other way."

They'd already driven twenty kilometers in every direction, chasing one of the hundreds of possible locations where Tiago might've been holding Tate.

"This has to be it." Sweat beaded on her brow as she shifted the binoculars and dialed in on an obscure formation in the distance.

"What are we doing, Lucia?" He grabbed a bottled water from the backseat. "We're wasting time on the musings of a senile man."

"He said there was a gate, and I'm not moving on until I find it."

With a scowl, he snatched the stack of papers from her lap and held them up. "There are two-hundred and seventeen places with gates. We'll never get through all of them."

Her desperation to find Tate might've pushed her past the point of insanity, but she wasn't stopping, wasn't budging. She would find him, dammit, and he would be alive. She refused to accept any other outcome.

"This one feels right." She glared at Cole's cocky aviator sunglasses and held her ground. "It's a hunch."

"You said that the last three times. This whole damn operation has dissolved into a *hunch*." He gulped back the water and tossed the capped bottle onto her lap. "This isn't how I do things."

Her chest constricted with pressure and insistence. "We spent three months doing things your way."

Three months chasing dead ends and all they knew was Tiago had left Caracas the day she attacked him. How he survived the head injury, where he went, and what he was doing—all of it was one big fat mystery.

Meanwhile, Tate was missing and alone, his body beaten and susceptible to infection. She couldn't stop obsessing over it, couldn't eat, couldn't breathe, couldn't think straight. Every second without him was another second he spent in misery.

Cole had hunted down the cops who had apparently tossed Tate into the trunk of a car. But the corrupted police didn't know where he'd been taken or who'd been driving. Any clues leading to Tate had been so thoroughly buried not even Cole could bribe, threaten, or wrestle the information into the light.

But she knew Tiago, knew how his unshakable mind worked, and she couldn't stop thinking about the night Tate was tortured. It had been a trial, a disgusting experiment that put Tate's love to the test.

Over the past few months, she wondered if this was *her* test. Tiago wouldn't just throw her in a prison to die. His god complex demanded that he challenge, control, and weigh everyone around him, including her. He'd challenged Tate, and now it was her turn.

So many times, she replayed her conversation with Tiago right before she attacked him.

You have the power to give him what he wants most.

His survival is up to you.

There had been a lot of mumbo jumbo twisted into his words, including his suggestion that she move on. But there was something deeper at play. He never eluded to it, but he'd left her a clue.

He'd carved an image into Tate's back.

For her.

He tortured countless men that way, leaving scarred welts on the arms, chests, and legs of those who lived. But his designs tended to be more primitive—geometric lines, whorls, and simple shapes. What he'd sliced into Tate's skin was altogether different. It was a detailed illustration. Hours of gruesome cutting that painted a place with gates and a human-like figure floating through them.

Tiago had given her a way to find him. A depraved challenge to test her determination and love. Yes, it was just a hunch, but it sat heavily and deeply in her gut, howling and bucking and refusing to be ignored.

Then she met the old man.

She and Cole had comprised most of their list of gated places by talking to people, such as historians at universities and locals in small villages. They'd traveled the breadth of the country, and that was how she met the elderly man in an impoverished town an hour's drive from here.

In thick Spanish, the man had told her about a monastery called *Medio del Corazón*. Translation: *Middle of the Heart*.

Abandoned a century ago, it was left in rubble and ruin. He said the gate still stood to protect the dark secrets that loomed behind its bars. Secrets about a high-ranking monk who had fallen in love with a village girl. The religious order condemned their relationship, separating them. But the lovers had found a way to steal a night together, and within the sacred walls of the monastery, they'd killed themselves.

The old man claimed the lovers could still be heard in the crumbling foundation. He called it *a silent, unified heartbeat in the midst of devastation.*

She knew it was just folklore. Whispered words among superstitious locals. But the story resonated with her. If Tiago put Tate behind gates, it would be those gates. She believed it down to the bottom of her soul.

Problem was, the old man wasn't exactly sure how to find it. He'd never been there, and his directions were approximations. She and Cole had been circling the desert for days.

"Find a road that goes that way." She pointed at the formation on the horizon.

With a sigh, Cole handed the papers to her and shifted the jeep into gear.

An hour and several wrong turns later, he slowed along a rocky road that ended on a hill. At the top of the incline stood two towering pillars of stone. And between them hung a massive wrought iron double gate.

"This is it." Her heart slammed against her ribcage, and her hand shot out to grip Cole's arm. "Those pillars... I remember them on his back."

She couldn't breathe as she fumbled with the door handle, shaking all over with urgency.

"Lucia, wait." He caught her wrist, stopping her from scrambling out of the jeep. "If he's here —"

"He is!"

"—there will be guards. Security. We don't know what's up there, and they probably heard us approach."

With panting breaths, she opened the glove compartment and removed a 9mm gun.

"I'm going in alone." He drew a pistol from one of the many holsters he wore. "Stay in the car."

"Not happening."

After spending three months together, their power exchanges had fizzled into a laughable waste of time. He barked orders. She barked back. Then he stormed off, grumbling about how he should've never taken this job. Which he did now as he slid out of the jeep, tossed a backpack over his shoulder, and crept up the hill with his gun raised.

The sun beat down on her neck as she followed behind him. Then they separated, seeking the concealment of the pillars on either side of the gate. The gun rattled in her hands, and the atmosphere was so dry it burned her lungs.

Beyond the heavy black bars sat clumps of simplistic, boxy structures made of stone. A passage of archways cut through the largest building at the center. Two wings of corridors spread out from there, connecting smaller, one-room buildings. No doors. No bars or glass on the windows. And from this vantage, there didn't appear to be a roof on the main belfry.

She scanned the perimeter. No cars. No people. No signs of life whatsoever.

Her gaze locked with Cole's where he stood on the other side of the gate.

No one, she mouthed.

Muscles bounced along his jaw, and his shoulders loosened. The disappointment on his face made her stiffen. He'd already decided they had the wrong location.

"I'm not leaving until I look around." She stayed alert as she sidled through the two-foot opening in the sagging double gate.

Arms locked in front of her with the gun trained, she made her way to the ruins on silent feet. Cole trailed at a distance as she crept through the largest building.

The scent of dust and baked earth permeated the air. Loose gravel crunched beneath her boots, and birds took flight in the open rafters. Very few plants grew in this region, but something twiggy and leafless had vined its way up the stone walls toward the open sky.

The altars and benches and pots were long gone. There was nothing. No indication that anyone had been here in decades.

Desperate and tense, she continued moving, passing through the decaying corridors and rooms that would've slept rows of monks on spartan beds. A century later, this monastery only housed families of birds. Nests made of spindly shrubs lined what was left of the rooftops.

She searched everywhere for a hidden door, a basement, someplace that could house a prisoner. When her quest brought her back to the main tower, she let her head fall back on her shoulders and stared at the pale sky peeking through the rafters.

Why isn't he here?

She'd been so certain. So damn amped up with hope.

The thud of her heart drummed in her ears, growing stronger, louder in the silence.

A silent, unified heartbeat in the midst of devastation.

A tear trickled from her eye. Then more fell, tracing sluggish, crooked lines down her cheeks and clinging to her throat.

Goddammit, Tate. Where are you?

She wiped her face and lowered her chin. Then she saw it.

An arched corridor led to the rear of the monastery and opened to a barren landscape of shrubs and sand.

Standing at this angle, she could peer through the arches and see something in the distance. A small structure. Maybe fifty yards away.

"Cole." Her whisper echoed like a roar through the cavernous space.

"I see it." He stepped to her side and gripped her shoulder. "I'm right behind you."

She took off, sprinting over gravel and fallen rock in the passageway. The sun blinded her as she burst outside and raced across the field of sand and stone. Her legs burned. Her lungs heaved, and her muscles worked overtime to cover the distance.

As she grew closer she could make out a shed. A tiny, single-room shack made of rustic wood, with a steel bar across the door.

He's in there. He has to be.

But for how long? They were in the middle of nowhere. How did he eat? Who took care of him? What if he was left there to die?

Her pulse went crazy, and by the time she reached the door, her entire body was shaking uncontrollably.

Cole skidded to a stop beside her and helped her lift the steel bar from the supports.

As she moved to push open the door, he clamped his fingers around her arm, halting her. Then he cast her a look that said, *Brace yourself. You don't know what you'll find in there.*

A vicious battle erupted inside her, a tug-of-war that seesawed between terror and exaltation, ramming against her breastbone like an earth-shattering hurricane. This was it, the moment that could salvage her life or utterly destroy it.

She pulled her arm from his grip, drew in a ragged breath, and opened the door.

The next breath came in a gasp as her heart dropped out of her chest and tumbled across the dirt floor.

Tate stood near the back wall, with a dirty, paper-thin blanket tied around his waist. The rest of him was nude, his skin pale, his entire physique emaciated. A full beard covered his face, and his hair hung in clumped strands around his crystal blue eyes.

"Tate." The violence of her emotions and the overwhelming happiness spiking through her staggered her forward steps.

He jerked back, bumping into the wall. "You're not real."

"I am." She covered her mouth with a hand to stifle her sob. "This is real."

Behind her, Cole spoke quietly into his phone, probably arranging transportation with Matias.

Trusting him to watch the door, she inched closer to Tate. He went rigid, lifting his chin at an angle and glaring at her with a menacing look in his eyes.

A metal cuff encircled his ankle, the skin beneath it torn and red. A chain connected the cuff to a spike. The hard, moistureless dirt floor had been dug away from it, revealing a block of concrete underneath.

He'd tried to escape at some point, and though he looked stunned and distrusting, he was still in there somewhere. She just needed to be patient.

"You're an angel," he rasped, his voice dry as dust. "Not real."

"Do angels have scars?"

His brows pulled together, and he shook his head.

With a trembling hand, she lifted the hem of her shirt to expose her abdomen.

"I doubt I'll be chosen for heaven, but if I am..." She traced a finger along the marred flesh from her breastbone to her hip. "I don't intend to take this with me."

He stared at her scar. The longer he stared, the faster his breaths came, until his chest heaved with whatever was building inside him.

She held impossibly still, waiting for him to make the first move, to say the word, to give her an indication that this moment was sinking in.

When he finally lifted his eyes and found hers, she saw him. He was right there, clear and bright and alive.

"Lucia." He swallowed and took a step forward.

The chain clanked against the ground, but he wouldn't need the length of it, because she was running, reaching. Her fingers tangled in his long hair, and she lifted on tiptoes to press her nose against the pocket of his throat.

He wrapped his arms around her back and held her tight against his chest. He felt different, so much thinner, but the embrace was the same—protective, strong, *possessive.*

"God, I missed you." She couldn't stop the tears from coming, couldn't hold back the whimpers or the clench of her fingers in his hair.

"The memory of you was the only thing that kept me alive." His deep voice whispered over her, threading with unimaginable pain. "How long has it been?"

"Three months." Cole crouched beside them and dug through his backpack. "It'll take me a second to pick the lock on your shackle. Are you expecting visitors?"

"Two guards bring food at nightfall." Tate dragged his nose through her hair. "How are you alive?"

"Long story." She stepped back and glided her hands up his arms. "Let's get you out of here first."

Her fingers bumped a patch of strangely rough skin on his bicep, drawing her attention to it.

What the—?

She'd been so focused on the drastic changes in his appearance—his beard, loss of weight, the healing skin on his injured arm—she didn't notice until now that his tattoo had grown, stretching above his elbow and covering part of his shoulder.

The inked roses he had before blurred into something new. A portrait of a woman with straight black hair, holding her finger against the profile of her lips.

Her breath caught. "Is that—?"

"You." He glanced at it and returned to her eyes with a flicker of light in the brilliant blue of his. "Badell gave me a last request. Since I couldn't have *you,* this was the next best thing."

He asked for a tattoo of my face on his arm?

Tingling warmth seeped through her limbs, sparking a sudden release of all tension. Her chest expanded. Her heart overflowed, and every whirling, erratic, out-of-control piece of her life snapped into place.

"Got it." Cole stood and tossed the chain away. "I'll run and get the jeep."

"I can walk." Tate twined his fingers with hers and strode to the door.

"It's rocky—" She was jerked forward by his grip on her hand and stumbled to keep up.

He crossed the hot, rugged terrain on bare feet with his free hand shielding his eyes. He didn't wince or slow, his gait matching Cole's in strong, efficient strides. The only thing he wore was a small blanket, and as her slower pace put her behind him, his back moved into her line of sight.

The image was just like she remembered, only cleaner, free of infection, and healed. The raised skin from each cut formed an artistic illustration of pillars along his sides, a double gate hanging between them, and a silhouette of a woman levitating in the opening with the arc of the sun behind her head.

It was terrible and beautiful, summoning extreme reactions from horrific agony to profound wonder.

"You're staring at it." He glanced at her over his shoulder.

"Have you seen it?"

"No." His tone held deep anger, and he tugged her forward.

Cole explained the history of the monastery as they passed the stone structures, including the tragic love story that had compelled her to come here.

She and Tate didn't speak, but they watched each other, their eyes sharing three months of loss, one night of lasting torture, and a future that didn't need to be defined. Wherever they went from here, they would go there together.

When they reached the gate, he stopped abruptly and released her hand.

"What's wrong?" she asked.

"That's..." He stared up at the towering wrought iron bars and reached behind him, sliding his fingers over the welts on his back. "I've felt this so many times, trying to figure out... That's it, isn't it? He carved those gates on my back?"

Her chin trembled as she nodded. "I think he did it to see if I would find you. That's why it took me so long. I've been searching for gates and—"

"There's something else." He moved his hand up his spine.

She edged back, watching as his fingers traced the feminine figure.

"It's a silhouette," she said on a serrated breath. "A woman."

"Show me." He pointed at the gates before him. "Walk through them."

A swallow lodged in her throat. She glanced at Cole, who waited patiently behind her, surveying the perimeter. Then she moved to stand in the opening of the gate, facing Tate exactly as it was depicted on his back.

The sun sat high in the sky. If it were a few hours later, it would've been at the right height behind her head.

"It's..." His chest rose and fell with a deep breath. "Beautiful. You're absolutely stunning, Lucia." He twisted to look at Cole. "Is that what my back looks like?"

"Pretty much." Cole flicked his gaze between the gate and the illustration. "It's uncanny, really."

Tate regarded her for an endless moment before he lowered his head and stared at the ground.

"Okay." He anchored his hands on his hips and made a sharp sniffing sound that almost resembled a laugh. His lips twitched, and he met her eyes. "Let's go home."

"Where's home?" She reached her arm toward him, stretching her fingers.

He caught her hand and squeezed. "Wherever you are."

THIRTY-THREE

Four days later, Tate exited the physician's room in Matias' extravagant estate in Colombia. His muscles twitched with restless energy, and something in his chest pinched, urging him to go look for Lucia.

He couldn't bear to be separated from her. Every time he left her side, it felt as though his limbs were being ripped from his body. He needed to get over that. Missing her was one thing. Smothering her was unhealthy.

He'd visited Picar, the old crusty resident doctor, three times now. But this meeting had been his last, because Picar had just given him a clean bill of health. No infections. No STDs. And other than the scarring on his back and the twinging discomfort in his arm, there was no permanent damage to his body.

He stepped onto the causeway and strolled through an open terrace sitting area. There was no one around, so he allowed himself a moment to enjoy the warm breeze and breathe in the aroma of loam and thriving vegetation.

The estate was expansive and luxurious, ensconced in the Amazon rainforest and protected by the best security available. He'd been here many times, and it always felt like paradise. But it wasn't home.

When Matias' helicopter picked them up in Venezuela, Lucia offered to go back to Texas with him. He would've preferred that, but she needed to spend time with Camila. She needed a reprieve from the bustle of reality. So he insisted they come here.

From the moment she floated into the shack like an angel, they'd been inseparable. But they hadn't spent much time alone, without others around. She had twelve years to catch up on with Camila, and he wanted that for her.

She was probably with Camila now, and as much as he craved her and ached to have her in his sights, maybe he needed a moment, too, just to...*be.*

The last four days had been a whirlwind of reunions and conversations. Everyone was here—Van and Amber, Liv and Josh, Livana and his roommates. Everyone except Kate.

Kate had disappeared the night he was tortured. A month later, she called Liv from an untraceable number and said she didn't want to be found. She'd demanded that no one look for her.

Lucia had recalled Tiago Badell saying something about relocating. That he'd found a new interest he was pursuing.

Then there was Tate's phone conversation with him.

I've already taken my payment. Consider this a thank you.

What did you take?

Badell took Kate. There wasn't a doubt in Tate's mind. Cole Hartman was out there looking for her. Tate would've gone with him, but Lucia had begged. She'd pleaded with tears in her eyes for him to stay.

He would do what he could for Kate and help with the investigation. But Lucia came first. She didn't want him putting himself in harm's way, so he wouldn't.

Leaning against the railing of the causeway, he soaked in the sunlight. What he felt for Lucia was all-consuming. It itched and vibrated beneath his skin. His pulse soared, and his cock hardened just thinking about her, but they hadn't shared a single sexual moment since before that night in the basement.

They spent the majority of the past four days talking. They analyzed Badell's mental health, his cruel romanticism, and his motivation for bringing them together in such a brutal way. Tate told her everything he remembered during his time in the shack. She recounted her attack on Badell, their escape from the compound, the prison, and her three-month quest to find him.

She'd also spent some time with the cartel's cantankerous doctor. The poison Badell had been feeding her was completely gone from her system, but the crash in Peru had resulted in the removal of her uterus. She'd taken the news in stride, turning to Tate to say, "You were a child without a mother once. If you want a baby, I would love to save one."

Her tenacity and bravery awed him to no end. Several times, he found himself lying beside her on the bed in their room, face to face, content with simply staring at her as she stared back. Christ, he fucking loved her.

She slept beside him every night. She kissed his face when they were in the company of others. She caressed his back every time he removed his shirt. She held his hand when they strolled along the causeway. Every glance she cast in his direction made him want to shred her clothes like an animal and fuck her against the wall. But he held back.

His body didn't feel like his own. He'd shaved his face, cut his hair, and scrubbed his skin with scalding hot water. But he was wearing borrowed clothes and sleeping in a borrowed bed. He was still underweight, still overwhelmed, and so fucking out of sorts.

On the bright side, he'd completely lost the craving for cigarettes.

So he'd made use of Matias' gym. His strength would eventually return, but his mind... He wasn't broken. There was just something stuck there. Something he needed to un-stick.

Part of it had to do with his feelings of failure and the misery Lucia had gone through when he was too weak to protect her.

The rest of it had to do with Van. He'd seen the man around the estate and chatted with him about anything, everything, except what had happened that night in the basement.

He needed to talk to Van privately. And soon.

Decision made, he turned toward the common area to search for him.

"Tate." Camila's sweet voice drifted over his shoulder.

He pivoted, grinning instantly at the sight of her huge brown eyes. "Hey."

"Hey." She gave his clean-shaved face a quick caress. "Much better. I hated the beard."

"Yeah?" He rubbed his jaw, silently agreeing with her. "Where's Lucia?"

"Matias is showing her the citrus grove."

"Citrus grove?"

She bit down on her smile and hugged her waist. "He grew it for me a long, long time ago."

Because Matias loved her. He'd loved her his entire life, and apparently, Tate had to go through hell and back to truly understand the meaning of that.

"You know..." He gripped the back of his neck. "The feelings I had for you —"

"I know."

"It's different now."

"I know." Her eyes glistened as she smiled.

"You're my closest friend. That isn't going to change."

"Dammit, Tate." She pressed the heels of her hands against the corners of her eyes. "Don't make me cry."

"Come here."

He held his arms out, and she stepped in for a hug.

"Lucia's pretty fucking amazing, isn't she?" she mumbled against his chest.

"Yeah, she really is." He nudged her back and held her teary gaze. "We good?"

"Yeah," she said softly. "Thank you for finding her. Words can't express—"

"You're welcome." He appreciated her smile, but it wasn't the one he craved. His heart hammered, begging him to go find Lucia, but first... "Do you know where Van is?"

"Did you check his room?" She motioned toward the east wing. "He doesn't let Amber out of bed."

He chuckled. "Okay, I'll check there."

Ten minutes later, he stood at the door to Van's room, fist raised to knock and a million thoughts clashing in his head.

Just say what you need to say. In and out and move on.

He drew in a breath, slowly released it, and rapped on the door.

A few seconds passed before Van answered. Dressed in only a pair of jeans that weren't fully zipped, he glanced behind him before opening the door to let Tate in.

As Tate stepped through the doorway, he caught a glimpse of Amber crossing through the far side of the room, wrapped in a sheet and her hair a tangled mess of just-got-fucked.

Camila hadn't been joking.

"If I'm interrupting," Tate said, pausing in the entryway, "I can come back."

"Let's go out to the patio." Van turned and strolled toward the back door.

Tate followed him. The guest rooms were set up like hotel suites, with kitchenettes, sitting areas, private bathrooms, and artfully decorated beds and furnishings.

It never ceased to amaze him how much wealth could be amassed through corruption. He didn't know what the Restrepo cartel was involved in. No one knew but Camila. That said, Matias spent a great deal of time and money fighting a war against human slavery. Tate admired the man deeply for that.

The room reeked of sex. Several belts lay on the king-sized bed, and clothing scattered the floor as if they'd been stripped in a hurry.

A shiver crept up his spine as he entered the private patio and lowered onto the chair beside Van. It was blissfully hot outside, even at dusk. Moisture infused the air, so unlike the parched heat of the desert.

"How long will you stay?" he asked Van.

"Until I know my family will be safe in Texas."

That wouldn't be the case until Tiago Badell was six feet in the ground.

Matias had brought in a private teacher for Van's daughter, so she was probably getting a better education here. But Liv and Josh would lose their jobs if they stayed much longer.

"Spit it out, Tate." Van shifted his gaze from the tropical landscape and rested it on him.

Out of the corner of his eye, he saw Amber moving through the living area and decided to start there. "Does she know what happened?"

"Of course. I don't just fuck my wife. I confide in her, lean on her, and trust her. I tell her everything."

Tate nodded, letting that settle through his rioting nerves. "How did she take it?"

"She cried." Van's frown twisted into a smirk. "Then she demanded I talk to you when you returned."

"I'm not good at this." Tate leaned forward, bracing his elbows on knees. "I think what's been digging at me the most is the damage I might've done to you."

"Well, you have a huge goddamn cock, and I felt every inch —"

"You know what I mean."

"Right." Van heaved in a heavy breath and leaned back in the chair. "I was raped as a child. You don't really get over that, but you get *through* it. I've done that, and so have you." He removed a toothpick from his pocket and set it between his teeth. "What happened between us in that basement might not have been willing, but it wasn't violent or cruel. You didn't abuse me the way I abused you all those years ago. You understand the difference?"

"Yeah."

"The hardest part for me was betraying my wife." Van twisted in the chair and tracked Amber's movements through the window. "She sees me at my weakest, and she still loves me."

"You weren't weak in Caracas. What you did for me —"

"I was messed up in my head when I returned to her, but she has this deep well of sympathy in her, an ability to identify with how and why I do the things I do." He rolled the toothpick between his lips. "Don't know what I did to deserve her, but she's stuck with me, for better or worse. So to address your concerns, there's no damage on my end. What about you?"

He laughed uncomfortably. "The sex was the least painful part of that night."

"But the most painful to come to terms with." Van softened his voice. "Have you fucked her since you returned?"

"No." He set his jaw. "I can't get out of my damn head."

"Go fuck your girl, Tate. The second you're inside her, controlling her in the way you both need, the mental blocks will disappear." Van rose from the chair and held out a hand. "No bad blood."

He stood, ignoring the offered handshake, and pulled Van into a one-armed hug. "Thank you for everything you did in Caracas. We're more than even. No bad blood."

"Good to hear."

Tate left Van's room, hellbent on taking care of Lucia in the way she deserved—deeply, passionately, and thoroughly. The intimacy he'd wrongfully denied her, the urgency to connect with her on every carnal level possible, and the cravings he felt every time she was near—it all swelled to hard, pulsating life.

The breath of his soul had been a distant whisper for so long he thought he'd lost it. But he heard it now, felt it growing closer, coming back to him. Maybe it hadn't been his body that was different, but rather his spirit. That was the part of him that had been severely wounded, reduced to damn-near nothingness.

He found her on the veranda, surrounded by Camila, Matias, and several men in the cartel he couldn't name.

As he approached Lucia's back, his emotional aches retreated, fading into the background of his thundering heartbeat.

He stopped behind her chair and brought his mouth to her ear, "Come with me."

She spun around with a huge grin, and the tabletop candlelight danced behind her, sharing his excitement.

A casual red dress molded to her curves and flirted with her knees as she stood.

His breath stuttered. Three months of poison-free health looked so fucking good on her. Sun-kissed skin, glossy black hair, full tits, a Latina ass that didn't know when to quit, and their room was a five-minute walk away. He was so fucking hard there was no way he'd make it there.

He clamped a hand around her arm and led her out of the dining area and toward the causeway.

The air around them sparked with hunger—his *and* hers. She didn't ask where they were going. She saw it in his expression and fed from it. He didn't have to be an empath to sense her desire. It materialized in the gasping hitch of her breath, the pebbling nipples beneath her dress, and the look in her eyes that didn't stray from his face.

He tried to focus on steps. One foot forward. Turn left at the next hall. Pass the kitchen. Watch the wet spot on the marble.

Wet spot. Short skirt. Long, sexy-as-fuck legs. Panties, pussy, tight heat...

Fuck this. He hooked an arm around her waist and shoved her back against the nearest wall. His hands went under her dress. His fingers found the satin crotch of her panties. Her mouth slotted against his, and they crashed into a frenzy of kissing, licking, biting need.

He ground his hips against her, letting her feel the swollen length of him. Then he yanked her panties down and buried his fingers inside her.

Her moan vibrated against his mouth, and goosebumps dotted her arms. The warm, wet clasp of her body sucked on his fingers, clenching and taunting as he imagined her sliding along his cock. Her pussy was the hottest thing he'd ever touched, and it was even hotter when she climaxed.

It'd been three months. Three harrowing months without the taste of her lips and the squeeze of her cunt.

He kept his tongue in her mouth, panting and feasting as he thrust his hand harder, faster, mindless in his pursuit to feel her come. He needed it. Goddamn, he'd missed her so much.

Footsteps approached the corridor, slowed to a stop, and moved on. He didn't care. Her nails scored his shoulders, and her moans intensified. Her orgasm was within reach.

"Give it to me, Lucia."

She quivered, ignited, and combusted on his hand, drenching his fingers and throbbing rhythmically. Her tits bounced with the heave of her chest, and her pupils dilated as she stared up at him, burned into him.

"You're so getting fucked right now." He unzipped and pulled himself out while fingering her and holding her on that euphoric edge.

She kicked her panties away and reached between her legs, sliding her fingers over his where they sank in and out of her.

"Hold on." He lifted her, pinned her back against the wall, and pushed inside her silky cunt in one motion.

"Fuck." He groaned, shaking with the deep-reaching flood of sensations. "Christ, your pussy… So fucking tight. Every bump and ridge is gripping me."

"There's nothing between us." She cupped his face, smiling as she searched his eyes.

No condom. He'd never had consensual sex without one. And as he kicked his hips to meet her body, he vowed to never wear one again.

Nothing felt like this. Nothing. It wasn't just the bareness between them. It was her. The staccato of her hungry whimpers, the submissive give of her body, and the love shining in her honey-brown eyes.

He pressed tighter against her chest and worked his mouth frantically against hers, his movements unhinged and desperate. It had been too long, and they'd been through too much to put restraints on this. He let his desire take over, driving his thrusts, drinking in her kisses, and digging his fingers into her beautiful skin.

The caress of her hand traveled over his ass, squeezing and

kneading before dipping beneath the waistband to finger the cleft of his cheeks. Then it rose, slipping under his shirt to trace the scars he neither loved nor hated. They made her sad when she looked at them, but they'd brought them back together. They meant nothing to him. And everything.

Their lips slicked together, his tongue sliding over and around hers in a kiss that amplified every physical and emotional sensation vibrating through him. He was lost to her, a crazed and starving goner with everything he ever wanted in his arms.

His muscles were whipcord taut, his lungs pumping with the speed of his thrusts. Each stroke invigorated his body and nourished his heart. He couldn't get close enough to her, deep enough. He wanted to fuck her soul.

With his hands beneath her knees, he hitched them higher, wider, opening her to him as he pistoned between her legs, pounded her against the wall, and devoured her every gasp.

Then he broke the kiss to look deep into her eyes, gazing at her beautiful, healthy face. Her skin sheened under the dim lighting. Her lips parted, plump and wet, and her hair tousled around her graceful neck and shoulders. What a glorious sight.

Arousal loved her.

"Tate." A throaty, greedy whisper. The most seductive sound he'd ever heard.

"I love you." He drew his hips back and surged again and again, filling her, stretching her with an urgency that chopped his words into grunts. "Love you so damn much."

There was a natural rhythm between them, a pace and angle that had a way of bringing them to climax together. He didn't know how many times they'd had sex during their five days together, but he'd found their rhythm then and rediscovered it now.

His hips moved instinctively, impulsively, as he savored the slow build of yearning low in his back. Just the possibility of it, the relief of being inside her, and the knowledge that he would be here, in her, every day for the rest of his life — it was more than he could ever hope for.

He sensed the surge of pleasure inside her, the promise, the moment they reached for it at the same time.

Then he rode them over the edge, staring into her eyes and coming with her in powerful spurts that pounded his heart into a mold around hers. A unified heartbeat. It was the song in his ears and the barometer of their future.

She stared up at him, dazed and breathless. "We needed that."

Lowering her feet to the floor, he kissed her lips. "I won't ever deny us again. I'm sorry I—"

"Whatever you're about to say, stop." Her eyes flashed. She

snatched her panties from the floor and pulled them on. "You endured things most men can't even think about, and you're apologizing for taking four days to heal?" She framed his face with her hands. "Take as long as you need, Tate. I'm not going anywhere."

He knew that, but hearing it from her lips freed something in his mind, un-sticking the final pieces of his mental baggage.

"What I need is *you*," he said, brushing a knuckle across her cheek, "and we've only just begun."

Ten minutes later, he stood by the bed in their room and ordered her to strip. Then he spread her gorgeous nude body across the mattress and worshiped every sensual inch of her skin. He kissed and licked until she bucked her hips, offering up his journey's end.

His body vibrated with need as he shifted between her legs. But he took his time, drawing out her panting breaths, making her wait for it. Her head snapped up, and when her eyes found his, he ran the tip of his finger with taunting slowness up the seam of her soaked pussy.

He teased her with his touch, stroking, rubbing, plunging in and out, all while imprisoning her with his eyes. She orgasmed on his hand. Then she orgasmed on his tongue. And he was nowhere near finished with her.

Kneeling between her thighs, he slid the head of his cock up and down her slit, torturing them both in the best way possible. He controlled her pleasure, and he didn't need chains or belts or any kind of physical restraint to do it.

She surrendered to him as he sank inside her. She yielded to the demands of his body. She relinquished her heart in connection of their lips.

He spent hours inside her, trying to slack a need that would never burn out. When they finally collapsed in a tangle of limbs, she laughed. She rolled to her back and laughed deep belly laughter with her knees pulled up and her arms around her waist.

He laughed with her, because fuck him, her smile. It was a huge, bursting, mystical entity inside him—an energetic, unpredictable live wire of happiness stretching out beneath his skin.

Snuggling up against her side, he tossed a leg over hers and cupped the side of her face. "What is it?"

"Joy." She met and held his gaze, glowing with life. "This feeling, you, us... It's laughter and soul-deep joy."

Her answer was everything. No matter where the future took them, he would make sure she never stopped laughing.

"Tell me about your dreams." He circled a finger around the luscious curve of her breast. "Your fantasies, your hopes and aspirations."

Rolling toward him, she gave him a heart-melting smile. "It starts with you, a bottle of wine, and a Netflix subscription..."

THIRTY-FOUR

One month later…

Lucia reclined on the couch in Tate's house in Austin, flipping through the movie selections on Netflix. She smiled as the sounds of shuffling footsteps and heavy grunts drifted from the kitchen.

"Fucking hold still," Tate growled from around the corner.

Maybe she should go in there and help him, but it would only frustrate him more. The man loved to be in control.

When they left Colombia a few weeks ago, they made a stop in California wine country. The threat of Tiago lingered, and they kept their wits about them always, but deep down, she believed he'd moved on from Tate and her. He'd played out his mind games and got his revenge.

Whether she and Tate went after him was still up for discussion.

Tate's roommates had stayed in Colombia, working with Camila on her war against slavery. Cole was still searching for Kate.

Cole Hartman, as it turned out, was an interesting man. She'd learned a lot about him during their three months on the road together. Hardworking and highly motivated, he lugged around a tragically broken heart. It gave him a perspective that few people could appreciate.

He never collected on the money Tate owed him, and she doubted he intended to bill Van and Matias. Cole had become part of their family, part of the Freedom Fighters.

The scamper of skidding feet tore out of the kitchen, and in the blink of an eye, her lap was filled with the long, awkward legs and huge muscled frame of an eight-year-old rescued greyhound.

Kingo stumbled and staggered like a newborn deer on her thighs, his feet slipping and tripping between the cushions, until he hopped off and collapsed onto his side on the floor.

"He got mud all over the kitchen." Tate stepped into the room and gave her a once-over. "And you."

She glanced down at her muddy clothes and shrugged. "He's still learning how to be a house dog."

They were fostering Kingo, until they were ready to make some permanent decisions. Stay in Texas, return to Colombia, search for Tiago Badell, explore the Venezuelan rainforest—all of it was on the table.

Tate disappeared in the kitchen and returned a second later with two glasses of wine from their trip. He set them on the coffee table and motioned for her to stand.

She did so with a smile, holding still as he removed her muddy shirt and jeans. Clad in a bra and panties, she sighed as he kissed her. His seeking tongue, his greedy hands on her body, and his clean, heady breath against her lips, he was so familiar and intoxicating and *hers*.

He was her everything.

He lowered her to the couch and positioned her where he wanted her. Then he stretched out behind her, tucking her backside against his groin and stroking his fingers through her hair.

Heaven.

As she sipped from her wine and cued up an action movie on Netflix, she felt a depth of joy that could only be earned through blood and tears.

There was a tilting, cracking, end-of-the-world transformation that happened inside of people who experienced extreme terror and hardship, abuse and tragedy, shame and forgiveness. Those who suffered the most held the greatest appreciation for movie subscriptions, rescued dogs, and a glass of red from wine country.

Maybe she and Tate would give up those things to pursue new quests together and reunite with old friends. But they would always remember what they'd endured and how they fell in love. They would always find solace in the dark and the pain, in a hand around the throat, or a last request in a shack, or a seedy sex club, or a ransom payment, as well as antivenom injections, scarification, Venezuelan prisons, monastery ruins, and tragic love stories.

Without the bad stuff—the trauma, the fall, and the crash—joy wouldn't exist. Maybe something like it would be in the background, like an echo of the real thing. But it wouldn't have strength and impact. It wouldn't be felt in every bone, tissue, and organ.

It was the bad stuff that breathed vivid life into the good.

Sorrow existed to breed happiness.

Pain gave rise to pleasure.

Loss brought about exploration.

Through a story of suicidal lovers and a gate carved into skin, it was grief that had led her to Tate.

They found each other in tragedy.

A silent, unified heartbeat in the midst of devastation.

TAKE

PAM GODWIN

Book 5

ONE

Kate had been watching the storm gather strength for two days. Turbulent clouds collided beyond the barred window, howling and banging against the concrete walls of her prison.

The wind wanted in as violently as she wanted out.

She'd been here before. Not in this dingy stone building or in these exact restraints. This place was utterly foreign, the scratchy rope on her wrists too primitive to be real.

But dammit, it *was* real. And intimately familiar. So much so it hadn't taken her long to shake off the shock of being kidnapped. *Again.*

The last time she found herself in shackles was four years ago. Back then, she was just a clueless eighteen-year-old girl. She hadn't understood who had taken her, what they wanted, or how she — a nobody from nowhere Texas — could be of interest to anyone.

But this time was different.

When two men captured her at gunpoint behind the diner where she worked, she'd guessed why, how, and *who* was behind it.

That was a month ago.

She'd been locked in this room for a goddamn month and still hadn't glimpsed her captor. Not once had she heard his name whispered on the guards' lips.

That didn't stop her from shouting her assumptions from the rafters.

"Tiago Badell!" Her hoarse roar echoed down the dark corridor, aimed at the door that remained closed at the end. "I know you can hear me!"

She'd grown bold in her isolation. Impatient. Desperate. And reckless.

"Show yourself, you fucking coward!" She yanked at the rope on her arms and glared at the end where it secured to the steel beam overhead and out of reach.

With her hands bound together in front of her, she couldn't loosen the knot between her wrists. God knows, she'd tried. Weeks of gnawing on the rope shredded her lips, her fingernails broken and jagged from useless clawing.

She was being held in a second-floor antechamber to another room. Beyond the reach of her leash were two doors. One at the end of the hall. The other led down to the main level and the armed guards who patrolled the property.

The rope allowed her access to a mattress and a doorless bathroom with no mirrors. There was no furniture. No objects that could be fashioned into a weapon.

Hygiene, clothes, and food — the basics were granted and nothing more.

She ached for fresh air, exercise, her friends, human contact... The list was inconsolably long. But what consumed her thoughts more than all else was the dark, elusive door to the other room.

Someone lived in there, and she was certain that someone was Tiago Badell.

Three times a day, an elderly man delivered two servings of food. With skin the color of midnight, he floated through her chamber like a shadow, never speaking, never meeting her eyes. He always set one serving before her, just within reach. The other he carried to the room down the hall.

He wasn't mute. Sometimes, voices drifted from beneath the door in a language she couldn't decipher — the old man's raspy accent and a deeper, richer timbre.

When she first arrived, the old man would linger in that room for hours. Lately, his visits had grown shorter. He would slip behind the mysterious door and emerge shortly after with empty platters.

He was in there now, having just dropped off her dinner.

Steam rose from the tin plate on the floor. Rice, chickpeas, and grilled meat — the spicy aroma made her mouth water, but she was too focused on the corridor to eat.

Lightning flashed, illuminating the window and strobing the stone walls of her prison. She strained to hear voices from the other room but couldn't detect a word amid the thunder.

"Tiago!" she screamed at the top of her lungs. "Come out, goddammit! Tell me why I'm here!"

Didn't matter how often or how loud she yelled. He never came out.

Was he sick? Hiding? Protecting his identity? She still didn't know what he looked like.

A few weeks before she was taken, her close friend, Tate Vades, left for Venezuela's Kidnap Alley to penetrate Tiago's compound. It was an insane undertaking, but not unexpected. All her roommates — Tate, Ricky, Martin, Luke, and Tomas — had a habit of running headlong into danger. After escaping Van Quiso's shackles, they banded together to take down as many human sex traffickers as possible.

Camila Dias had been the first to escape. Although she no longer lived with them, she continued to lead their vigilante group of Freedom Fighters.

Tate's latest mission focused on rescuing Camila's missing sister, Lucia, who allegedly worked for Tiago Badell. As if Tate's endeavor wasn't risky enough, he took Van Quiso along as his backup.

How the hell could Tate trust the man who had enslaved and raped him? Sure, Van expressed regret for the hell he rained down on her and her friends, but it was too little, too late. Kate would never forgive him, and she sure as fuck didn't trust him with Tate's life.

The fear she had for Tate before he left was nothing compared to what she felt now.

Now, she was petrified.

Tiago wouldn't have taken her unless Tate's mission was compromised. How else would Tiago know she existed?

That left some devastating questions.

What happened to Tate? Was he still alive? Was he imprisoned within these very walls, gagged and forced to listen to her screams?

Despair crushed her heart in a suffocating vise.

She never mentioned Tate, just in case she was wrong about his connection to her kidnapping. Instead, she spent the past month telling herself he successfully rescued Lucia and escaped unscathed. If he'd bested Tiago, it made sense that Tiago would go after Tate's loved ones in retaliation.

Of all the people in Tate's life, she was the most vulnerable. The loner. The weakest fighter. The only woman without a companion. Of course, she would be the one to get snatched.

That must've been it, but she needed to know for sure.

"Tiago!" She faced the corridor and raised her voice. "I want answers, and I won't shut up until I have them!"

The door held still.

Restlessness twitched her muscles, reaching into her bones and rattling her sanity.

She paced toward the window and halted a foot short from the glass. It was as close as the rope would allow, but the angle supplied a view of the dusty, barren landscape.

Two stories up, she couldn't see the exterior of the building or any other structure in the vicinity. Two cars sat off to the side, where a burly man loitered, smoking a cigarette with a rifle strapped to his back. Farther out, a dirt road meandered around woody shrubs and cacti before fading into the sandy horizon of nothingness.

She didn't know if the guards lived downstairs or somewhere else. They seemed to come and go in shifts. Five men and one woman, by her count. All heavily armed.

Her journey here had been foggy, muddied by sedatives and shrouded by a blindfold. Multiple transfers between cars, a long flight on a private plane, and more blindfolded car rides had obliterated the odds she was still in the U.S.

Venezuela was the logical assumption.

But this wasn't Kidnap Alley.

While Tate had prepared for his mission, she saw videos, photos, and maps of the slum where he was headed. This wasn't it. Not this arid, desolate wasteland.

She knew her friends would never stop looking for her, but how would they know to come here? *She* didn't even know where she was.

Her throat closed around a hard lump of reality.

There was a good chance she would never be found.

The day she arrived, two guards brought her to this room, stripped her down, and took everything. The cheap necklace from around her neck. The fitness watch from her wrist. The ponytail holder from her hair. They stole her damn dignity.

Then they bound her arms and left her with nothing but a handmade, strapless dress thing to wear.

How long would she sit in this room before she endured the real reason she was here? Her captor wouldn't have gone through the trouble of transporting her unless there was something in it for him.

His specialty was kidnapping. For ransom.

She learned through Tate's intel that Tiago's goons tortured and raped their captives, sent video footage of the brutality to family members, and demanded payment in exchange for the victim's release.

God, how she hoped this was a ransom deal. She and her roommates had plenty of money — *millions* — thanks to the peace offering Van Quiso had given them. If there was a price for her freedom, her friends would pay it.

But in the month since her capture, there had been no mention of payment. No torture. No video recordings. Other than the rough handling during her transport, the guards didn't touch her, talk to her, or visit her room.

If this wasn't a kidnapping for ransom, it was something worse.

She didn't have to imagine the *worse*. She'd lived it. In a windowless, soundproof attic, Van Quiso had whipped her into an obedient slave. An object to be sold for sex. Not to take pleasure but to give it. With her hands, her mouth, and her pain.

Her virginity had been a valuable commodity then. Maybe that was still the case?

Would Tiago sell her virtue to the highest bidder?

Or would he take it for himself?

It was her biggest fear. Her heaviest burden.

At age twenty-two, she should've explored her sexuality like a normal, healthy woman. But she wasn't normal. When she escaped Van, her virginity was all she had left. A precious mercy, and she didn't want to squander it. She longed to give it to someone she trusted. A man who would appreciate the significance.

The naive notion resonated a hollow thud in her head, silencing all other sound.

She managed to escape Van without getting raped. So what? She wasn't stupid enough to believe that would happen again.

Outside, the wind picked up, and with it came the first plops of rain. It would be dark soon, and she'd be forced to endure another night without answers.

She stepped away from the window and shouted, "Tiago—"

The door creaked open, shooing away the shadows in the corridor.

Footsteps sounded. The clink of dishes. Then the elderly man emerged, balancing empty plates as he closed the door behind him.

"Why won't he come out?" She rushed forward and jerked when the rope caught. "I just want to talk."

He ambled past her, keeping to the farthest wall, beyond the perimeter of her tether.

Vertical scars marred his face, two old cuts on each cheek, perfectly aligned, almost decorative. It was as if he'd them put them there intentionally.

With a blank expression and eyes fixed on the door to the stairs, he moved in that direction, giving her no acknowledgment, not a twitch, like she wasn't even there.

"Just tell me what he wants." Blood pounded in her skull.

He reached the exit and uttered a foreign word. A command not intended for her.

Locks clanked on the other side. The door opened, and a scruffy-bearded guard stepped to the side.

Instead of leaving, the old man turned, lifted his wrinkled face, and rested glassy eyes on her.

"Please." She pulled on the rope. "Untie me. Just let me go."

For the first time since she arrived, he opened his mouth and addressed her in a heavily accented voice. "He's ready to see you."

No shit?

Oh, shit.

Shit, shit, shit.

Her body went taut against an ice-cold shiver, and the hairs on her nape stood on end.

Don't freak out. Don't fucking lose it.

Sweeping her gaze to the dark corridor, she drew in a slow breath.

This was what she wanted. A conversation with the dickhead in charge. Answers. Reassurances. Negotiations.

But none of that was a guarantee. After watching those videos with Tate, she had only one certainty to go on.

Tiago Badell tortured his prisoners.

A tremor unfurled inside her, crashing its way along her arms and legs.

How badly would he hurt her? How long would it last? Hours? Days? Would he let her live? Would she want to?

The elderly man mumbled something that sounded like Spanish, prompting the guard to step into the room. The massive man strode toward her, removed a pocket knife, and before she could blink, he sliced through the rope between her wrists and the ceiling.

Her arms dropped, and the sudden freedom made her gasp.

As the guard returned to the stairwell, she tensed at the opportunity to attack him from behind. Should she do it? *Could* she overpower him and get away?

He was twice her size, armed with a knife, and her wrists were still tied together. The old man hovered in the doorway, physically frail, but those cloudy eyes watched her with unsettling strength, as if reading her thoughts.

The odds stacked against her, but whatever happened, she wouldn't go down without a fight.

On the heels of that thought, she flung herself toward the guard, her bound arms raised to loop around the guard's neck.

He turned before she made contact, his hand already flying. Meaty knuckles met her jaw and sent her head whirling sideways.

She staggered, momentarily stunned by the jolt of pain. After a soundless choke, she recovered, found her bearings, but not quickly enough.

The door shut with a resounding click.

"Fuck." She raced toward it and yanked on the handle.

TAKE

Locked.

"Fuck you!" she screamed. Then groaned. *Not helpful, Kate.*

That left the other door.

She trembled to summon movement in her legs, her ears pricked for footsteps in the corridor.

He's ready to see you.

Thunder boomed. Rain pelted the window, and her heart drummed an unruly dirge in her ears.

Apparently, Tiago was too high and mighty to come to her. Whatever. She would go to him, because her curiosity demanded it. But she refused to trudge in there with shaking limbs and hunched shoulders. If he was anything like Van Quiso, her fear would give him a hard-on.

A shudder rippled through her, and she snapped her spine straight.

The only power she possessed here was that over her own emotions. She allowed Van to use her terror to control her and wouldn't make that mistake again.

Rolling back her shoulders, she stood taller, closed her eyes, and breathed deeply.

She survived Van's cruelty. The experience didn't break her. It made her sharper, tougher, and really goddamn *angry.*

Fuck Van for molesting her, beating her until she bled, and ordering her to suck his dick day in and day out. And fuck Tiago Badell for ripping away her freedom, shoving her into isolation for a month, and summoning her like an object.

Rage scorched through her veins and spurred her into motion.

Her bare feet slapped across the gritty stone floor, her body clad in one of the sleeveless, unfitted rags they provided. The thin gray linen covered her from chest to knees, but if she stood in the right light, the fabric would be transparent.

Nothing she could do about the clothes. If Tiago wanted to strip her bare, she wouldn't be able to do anything about that, either. Except fight. *That* she would do.

Hands clenched around the severed rope, she stormed down the corridor and turned the door knob.

She expected luxurious furniture, plush fabrics, and perhaps the fatal end of a rifle waiting on the other side. But as she stepped in, none of that greeted her. The room was as empty as her prison.

The only source of light glowed from a shadeless lamp on the floor beside a small mattress. Rumpled blankets and a dented pillow suggested recent use. A large duffel bag of clothes sat open near a bathroom door, as if the room's occupant didn't intend to stay.

As for the occupant…

Her breathing stalled as she tracked the reach of light to the farthest, darkest corner.

A man sat on a two-foot-tall steel safe, his lower body illuminated enough to reveal heavy boots, dark slacks, and a posture that could only be described as an arrogant sprawl. He lounged with his back against the wall and legs spread, his body language insinuating he didn't care whether she entered or not.

The rest of him melted into chilling blackness. His chest, shoulders, face—none of his upper half was visible. He probably positioned the lamp at just the right angle to give the illusion of a predator lurking in the dark, just to ramp up the fear factor.

No illusions needed. She knew what he was, and her knees wobbled with the impulse to cower and beg for her life. But a meek and submissive demeanor would only earn her extended torture. She'd learned that the hard way.

She would rather die quickly than draw out the torment.

Her heart rate accelerated, and she swayed beneath the spinning weight of vertigo. She didn't want to die. But if her life was taken from her, if this was her last stance in the world, she would face it with ferocity and bitter rage.

Shoving back her shoulders, tight as they were, she strode into the room.

"Welcome, Kate." His low, deep baritone curled a shiver around her spine. "Come closer. I know you've been anxious to meet me. Everyone on this side of the continent has heard you begging."

"Cut the shit, Tiago." She paused outside the lamp's glow and swallowed her nerves. "I haven't seen your face. I can't identify you. Let me go, and I'll forget the whole thing."

"Step into the light." Rich and rumbly, his accent swirled with hints of South America and something indefinably exotic.

"You first."

"This will go faster if you follow orders."

"Am I keeping you from something?" She cast a pointed look around the spartan room. "What have you been doing in here for a month?"

The silence that followed closed a fist around her windpipe. It lasted a minute, then several more, until she could no longer bear it.

"Are we in Venezuela? What is this place?"

More silence.

"If you're not going to talk, I might as well head back to the isolation in the other room." She meant to sound bored, but the shakiness in her voice ruined the attempt.

His hand stirred on his thigh. Fingers tapped, *tap-tap-tap*, and fell still. When the shadow finally spoke, it chilled her to the bone.

"Do you want to live, Kate?"

She choked on a whimper. "Yes."

"Are you worthy of mercy?"

"Yes."

"Convince me."

Her nostrils flared, and her neck ached with tension. "I make an honest living and help people in need. I've certainly never kidnapped anyone and locked them in a room for a month." She couldn't disguise the contempt in her tone. "I haven't done anything to you!"

"Feel that high sense of value and superiority? That's pride, little girl. One of my favorite sins."

She drew in a sharp breath. "You asked—"

"I know what I asked. And since you know my name, you know it's not synonymous with mercy."

TWO

No surprise that Kate had been right about *who* had abducted her, but it didn't calm the tremors in her belly. Because let's face it. There was nothing remotely comforting about being held captive by Tiago Badell.

As one of the wealthiest crime lords in Venezuela, he smuggled guns and drugs, kidnapped tourists for ransom, controlled the police force, and made a living off other people's misery. Tate's intel had given her a harrowing overview of the operation, but how would that insight help her? Tiago probably wanted to kill her just because of her association with Tate.

Even if that were true, she wouldn't mention Tate. Not until she better understood the landscape and the man who reigned over it.

Why was he just sitting there in the shadows? Was he aiming a gun? Coiled to strike? Trying to keep his face anonymous? Or maybe he was just a dickhead and wanted to get a rise out of her?

The steel safe he used as a chair was the freestanding variety, with a combination lock and heavy-looking door. It was probably bolted to the floor and stuffed to the brim with artillery, cash, and enough criminal evidence to earn him a top spot on the *Most Dangerous Men in the World* list.

A quick scan of the room confirmed there was nothing she could wield as a weapon. Except the lamp. Unplugging it would plunge her into darkness. She could use the cord for strangulation or the wooden base as a bludgeon. But not effectively with her wrists tied together.

If she stepped closer, she might be able to see his features. It would also put her directly in the light, with the outline of her body backlit by the lamp. A minor vulnerability, but not one she was willing to concede without negotiation.

"Tell you what." She lifted her bound hands. "I'll come to you, if you remove the rope."

A grunt scuffed from his throat. "With your hands free, you assume I'll wait here while you grab the lamp and swing it at me?"

When he put it like that, it made her sound foolish and predictable.

She clenched her teeth, and another idea struck. It wouldn't help her escape, but she went with it.

Circling backward, she paced away from him, toward the lamp, and approached it from behind. The rope squeezed her wrists as she clutched the base and raised it above her head.

With it tilted in his direction, the light stretched to his chest, revealing a white collared shirt, unbuttoned at the throat and tucked into black slacks. Sleeves covered his arms, the crisp fabric clinging to broad shoulders and defined pecs. Every thread on his body looked perfectly fitted for his tall, lean frame.

Narrow hips, muscular thighs, seemingly hard all over—his athletic physique was unfortunate. She might've been able to outrun an out-of-shape man.

What was with the fancy clothes? Did he dress up for her or was he expecting another visitor? Other than the old man who delivered the meals, no one had entered this room in the month she'd been here. Not even the guards.

"I feel underdressed." She glanced down at the thin dress. At least, she wasn't illuminated from behind.

He didn't move or make a sound, not even as she hoisted the lamp as high as the cord allowed. Because he knew. No matter how she positioned it, the glow wouldn't reach his face.

"Are you finished wasting my time?" He stretched out a leg, reclining farther into the shadows.

"Why am I here?"

"Someone took something from me, so I took something in return." A smile surfaced in his voice. "I took you."

The implication settled through her, loosening her chest. Tate must've succeeded. He must've taken Lucia from Tiago and fled.

They were safe.

Sweet mercy, what a relief. After an eleven-year separation, she couldn't imagine how overjoyed Camila must've been to reunite with her long-lost sister. This was great news. Fucking fantastic.

Except for Kate's part in it. For that, she had no one to blame but herself.

Tate had demanded she not take the job at the diner. All her overprotective roommates were against the idea because they couldn't keep an eye on her. But she wanted her independence. Her freedom.

Now, she had neither.

She readjusted the light, moving it side to side, desperate to see her captor's eyes. "Are you holding me for ransom?"

"No." The gruff syllable punched from the darkness and hit her in the chest.

No ransom. No negotiations in the works to release her. She was fucked.

Her arms lowered as fear rose to the surface, tightening her face and hunching her spine. She set the lamp on the floor and inched away from it, seeking the cover of darkness.

"I have money." She pressed her back against the stone wall, struggling to quiet her quickening breaths. "A lot of money. I'll pay—"

"*You* are the payment."

Her stomach collapsed. "You're going to rape me."

"If you're offering, it wouldn't be rape."

"I would *never*—"

"You presume I'm interested."

She assumed a lot of things. Sodomy, mutilation, slow excruciating death… Any manner of evil was on the table, in any order and degree of agony.

"I'm not," he said.

"Not…?" Her brows pinched.

"Not interested in fucking you."

Her breath caught and held. She should've felt relief, but she'd seen the videos and knew what he wasn't saying. "You'll let your guards rape me."

He didn't answer, and God help her, the wretched silence made her blood shiver.

"I have powerful friends." She licked dry lips. "Dangerous allies who are looking for me right now. When they find me, you'll beg for death. You'll beg each time they cut off a piece of you. They'll use fire and chop and cook until there's nothing left but burnt ends and shit stains." She stood taller, her voice stronger. "Let me go, and I'll let you live."

He chuckled, mocking her. "Your friends are cannibals?"

"No, they're…" She clamped her molars together, cursing her bungling attempt to threaten him. "They're coming for me."

"You're a remarkably stupid woman. You know what I am, yet you walk in here, spewing nonsense, as if you actually believe you can control your demise."

Needles pulsated behind her eyes. "So that's it? I'm going to die?"

"Everyone dies. Some more painfully than others."

TAKE

His cold, callous tone validated her assumption. This wouldn't be a quick execution. He intended to make her suffer.

Terror trickled down her spine, freezing her in place.

Don't just stand there. Move. Run. Fight, for fuck's sake.

She unlocked her legs and bolted toward the door.

Two steps was all she managed before the lamp turned off and pitch-black darkness swallowed the room.

Her heart rate exploded as she strained her eyes. How the fuck did he kill the light?

She couldn't see her hands in front of her face. The exit hovered somewhere to the right, so she crept in that direction, listening for his footsteps amid the eruption of her gasps.

She tried to move slowly and soundlessly, so he couldn't track her. Then her scalp tingled. The air shifted against her, around her. Panic kicked in, and she burst into a blind sprint.

Heart racing, she made it a few more feet before something thumped up ahead. The sound of the door closing, of air being pushed out as it sealed. Then the lock slid into place.

She froze, her lungs shriveling with ice. Energy bounced against her, a disturbance of atmosphere. He was close, but where?

"Turn on the light." She swerved backward, spinning, her bound arms throwing her off balance as she swung at nothing.

He made no sound, yet his presence squeezed in on all sides, taunting her with her fear of the dark.

Her hair ruffled, and she pivoted. Was he circling her?

She whirled back, disoriented. Where was the door? Straight ahead? Behind her? She darted forward, and her throat slammed into an iron bar of muscle. His arm. He fucking clotheslined her.

Pain exploded in her larynx, and she staggered backward, expecting a hand to fly out of the blackness. But it was his boot that hit next. Directly in her stomach.

The excruciating impact sucked the wind from her lungs and knocked her flat on her back.

She landed on the mattress, gulping for air, and in the next heartbeat, he was on her. Powerful legs straddled her hips. His hand collared her throat, and the other pinned her arms above her head.

He was too heavy, too strong. Too fucking close.

"It doesn't matter what you want, who your friends are, or what you think you know about me." His calm breath feathered her face. "You have no opinions here. No privilege or power. Apparently, you didn't learn that the last time."

Her heart crashed against her ribcage as she bucked and twisted beneath his weight. "The last time?"

"Four years ago."

Oh God, he knew her past. He'd done his research.

"That's right." He flexed his thighs against her writhing hips, holding her to the mattress as his hands moved along the rope on her arms. "I know all about Van Quiso and his training."

"Don't do this." She didn't need her vision to know he was tying her to something on the wall. All-consuming fear jangled her insides, violently shaking her. "Let me go!"

"Try not to shit yourself. If you make a mess in my bed, I'll make you sleep in it. Not because I'm into that kind of thing. It's fucking disgusting."

Her jaw fell open, and a stunned whisper tumbled out. "What the hell is wrong with you?"

"We're not going to get into that. Right now, we're focusing on what's wrong with you." He put his mouth at her ear. "It's safe to assume Van Quiso did a number on your head. But instead of learning from the experience, you went and got yourself captured again. Let's be honest, Kate. That was really careless on your part."

"Careless?" she shrieked. "*You* kidnapped—"

He clamped a huge hand over her face, covering her lips and part of her nose. "Another outburst, and my next strike will break something important."

THREE

Kate wrestled for air beneath the press of Tiago's fingers on her face. He already kicked her hard enough to turn her stomach black and blue by morning. If he adjusted his grip by a millimeter, her airway would be completely closed. She had no choice but to heed his threat.

Commanding the rigidness to leave her body, she sank into the mattress and blinked in the darkness.

He released her mouth, then her hands, but his weight remained on her hips.

With her arms stretched toward the wall above her head, she yanked hard. No give. Just as she assumed, the rope was tied to something immovable.

"Now, where were we?" His deep rumble penetrated her chest.

"You were pointing out my faults." She bared her teeth, not that he could see her with the lights off.

"So I was. Among those faults is this withering scorn you carry around." He gripped her jaw, gave it a painful squeeze, and let go. "You're sick of being the underdog, the victim. So you charged in here wearing a cloud of righteous anger, because fuck the man, right? And by man, I mean every prick who's treated you unfairly. The father who abandoned you. The brothers who bullied you. The roommates who didn't protect you. The scar-faced bastard who tried to sell you to some fat fuck with fetishes more unspeakable than his own. Then there's me. You don't even know what I have planned for you."

Horror consumed her, constricting and pulling. He just dissected her with all the boredom of a man playing a child's game. She had no defenses against him, physically or emotionally.

Nothing would stop him from grabbing her throat and ripping out the meat of it. Or breaking her legs so she couldn't flee. Or he could go for her unprotected core. Her abdomen trembled right there between his thighs. He could pummel her until she bled internally.

Any or all of it was possible, and the thought shoved her into a fresh hell of panic.

What about her friends? Would he go after them next? How did he know so much about her life? Her father was dead. But her brothers... No one knew about them.

Except Van.

Tiago coasted his fingers over her hair, slithering a chill across her scalp. "I appreciate your bravado, but it's a portal to make-believe land. It'll get you nowhere." His hand retreated. "It won't save you."

Her head hammered, her eyes wide and unseeing. She might not know anything useful about him, but she knew his type.

Living with five alpha males, she was accustomed to the overbearing display of dominance. The vibration of confidence close to the skin, the puffed-up chests and unwavering eye contact—every action demanded respect and submission. Which begged the question...

"Why did you turn off the light?" She waited through a span of silence, strangling beneath the press of his proximity. "If I'm going to die, it doesn't matter if I see your face. If you're the one in control, why are you hiding in the dark? You've been holed up in this room for a month. Who are you running from?"

"Now *that*," he breathed at her ear, "is the smartest thing you've said."

The light flicked on, and the sudden brightness blotted her vision. As her eyes adjusted, she glimpsed a remote in his hand. He set it aside, and her gaze tripped along a muscled arm to the column of a masculine neck.

Stubble shadowed his chiseled jaw and outlined sculpted lips. A prominent nose, bladed cheekbones, and eyes so dark they could've been black—the squared cut of Hispanic features formed a ruthless, shockingly attractive face.

As she took in his unexpected beauty, the corners of his mouth levitated in a macabre smile.

He was madness with straight, white teeth. Corruption with glowing skin. A nightmare in a designer suit.

Dipping his head, he brought his eyes into the angle of light. Holographic hues of brown glittered in his irises, but it was the intelligence in that stare that jolted electricity through her heart.

His gaze was deafening. As jarring as a crack of lightning in the night. But instead of chaos writhing in his eyes, she found the steady pulse of self-control and calculation.

He watched her closely, deliberately, as if he knew it unsettled her, and that knowledge gave him pleasure.

His smile widened.

An increase in pressure and temperature swept the room. Her chest rose and fell, fighting for each shallow gasp.

He was so fearsomely, horrifyingly beautiful she had to look away, her focus landing on the only weakness she could find.

A bandage. Multiple bandages, taped in a row from his temple to the back of his head. Thick layers of gauze concealed what lay beneath, but from the size of the wrap, the injury had been severe.

Severe enough to debilitate him for weeks.

"That's why you haven't left this room." Her mind swam as she glanced around at the sparse space, homing in on the duffel bag of clothes. "You fled Kidnap Alley to recover here, to remain hidden until you regained strength. Have you been unconscious all this time?"

"In and out. An inconvenient side-effect of pain killers."

She was surprised he answered so candidly. Did someone shoot him? Knife him? Was it Tate? She returned her attention to his head, scrutinizing the wide swath of shaved scalp. How serious was the damage?

"You want to see under the bandages." His voice purred with provocation, licking a hum across her skin. "You're dying with curiosity."

"Dying is a poor choice of words, considering." She pulled harder on her arms and craned her neck to find her hands tethered to a cast iron pipe on the wall. She returned to his eyes, and a deep inhale helped her maintain that contact. "What happened?"

"Lucia Dias." A twitch feathered along his jaw. "She went vigilante on me with a forty-pound dumbbell."

Camila's sister attacked him? He still hadn't mentioned Tate. Was the attack part of Tate's rescue mission? Did he and Lucia make it out? Were they alive?

Tiago watched her steadily, devouring the trepidation she couldn't hide on her face. If he didn't already know Lucia's name meant something to her, he knew now.

"What happened to her?" A swallow solidified in her throat.

"You tell me."

Was he fucking with her? She didn't know how to play mind games with a psychopath, but she needed to try. Since she couldn't overpower him, she would have to outsmart him.

How had Lucia survived eleven years in his ranks? She worked for him, but no one understood why. There were so many pieces Tate hadn't puzzled out. So many unanswered questions. Hell, he'd traveled to

Venezuela uncertain if Lucia would welcome him or shoot him on the spot.

"I don't know her." She held Tiago's intimidating gaze. "I assume you provoked her? The fact that she succeeded in injuring you means you didn't see it coming."

He nodded, eyes narrowing, losing focus. "She was a special circumstance. As fierce as they come. She survived in my outfit longer than any of the men, and that kind of resilience was rare. It made her useful. Worth having around."

Every past tense word struck her like shrapnel, shredding her hope that Lucia was still alive. "How did she catch you off guard?"

"I never trusted her, but we had an agreement." He absently stroked the medical tape on his temple. "I allowed her to live, as long as she followed my rules."

Bashing his head would've been the opposite of following his rules.

"Where is she?" She struggled beneath him, attempting to unbalance his straddled position. "What did you do to her?"

"I let her go."

"You…" Wait. *What?* "You said someone took her from you."

"That's not what I said." He scowled hatefully. "Pay attention, Kate."

"You're speaking in riddles." Her arms pulled at the shoulders, and her hips twinged beneath his weight, compelling her to twist about, seeking distance. "Please, get off me. You're fucking heavy."

He pondered her request for a moment before adjusting his legs and lifting some of that bulk off her lower body.

She released a slow breath, contemplating his cryptic words. "You said someone took *something* from you."

"Yes. I never had her loyalty, but I possessed something more effective. Her *fear.*" He tipped his head, his gaze invasive. "You, of all people, understand how every aspect of a person's life can be controlled through terror."

No use denying it. Four years ago, her crippling fear gave Van Quiso power over her entire being. Lucia must've experienced the same with Tiago. Until she attacked him.

"Someone took her fear from you," she said.

"That's right." He flashed an unnerving grin and traced a finger along the gauze near his eye. "I haven't seen her handiwork. Boones says it's healing, but he won't remove the bandages."

"Boones?" She shook her head. No one entered this room, except… "The elderly cook?"

"He's a doctor. A damn good one, despite his motherly approach to my care." He fingered the medical tape, picked at the corner. "Fuck it."

He gripped the edge of the bandage and ripped it off. She winced as he forcefully tore at the pieces, pulling out strips of hair in the process without a twitch of pain on his face.

"Be honest." He gave her his profile and smoothed a hand along a jagged, puffy laceration. "How bad is it?"

She stopped breathing as her gaze locked on the damage.

Jesus. Lucia hadn't just hit him with a dumbbell. Somehow, she'd managed to hit him *twice.*

The first gash sat so close to his eye it was a wonder he survived the blow. The orbital bones around his eye socket should've shattered under the impact. Maybe they did. A yellowish hue discolored his cheekbone where bruises must've lingered for weeks.

The second wound carved a huge crescent-shaped groove along the side of his skull. This one appeared deeper and would've required more stitches, the skin around it still raw and scabbed over, taking longer to heal.

That side of his head was shaved to the peak above his temple where hair tended to retreat. But there was no threat of a receding hairline. Thick black strands fell over the non-injured side in finger-raked textures, accentuating his rugged features and whiskered jawline.

He was in desperate need of a haircut, one that evened out the sides. The messy-all-over, renegade style no longer worked for him, because hair would never grow in over the deep gouges that ran diagonally from his temple to the back of his head.

Together, the marks would leave a permanent map of scars the length of her hand and almost as wide. A hit like that was meant to be fatal. No doubt he sustained multiple skull fractures.

Too bad it didn't mash his brain to pulp.

She returned her gaze to his and found him watching her, waiting for an answer.

How bad is it?

It didn't diminish his disgusting masculine beauty. If anything, the scars made him even more arresting. But she didn't give a fuck what he looked like. She wanted him to suffer.

"I can't really see from this angle." She bent her neck and squinted. "Can you lean in a little closer?"

As he shifted, she reared her head back and slammed it forward. Aiming for his wounds, she hoped to reopen them with the ram of her skull.

In a blur, he dodged left, fisted the hair at the back of her head, and ruthlessly yanked her flat against the mattress.

"Not exactly the spice of originality." He forced her neck at a painful angle. "I'm disappointed."

She should've known. After Lucia got the drop on him, he'd be hyper-vigilant about strikes to the head.

"You said I don't have an opinion." She squirmed, unable to relieve his eye-watering grip on her hair. "Then you asked me to be honest about your wounds. Excuse me if I'm having trouble with your contradictory rules."

She needed to figure out a different way to fight him. If she could reach him with words, say something he found intriguing, maybe he'd keep her alive.

A heart-pounding smile wrenched his lips. So disturbing, that mouth. As it fell into a slack line, his sudden lack of expression produced a sick, buckling sensation in her stomach.

He released her hair, straightened his seated position on her pelvis, and removed something from his pants pocket. "You might think all human skin cuts the same beneath a blade."

Her pulse quickened as he slipped a small metal instrument onto his index finger and unfolded the tip. It opened like a switch blade and curved into a lethal claw.

All the air vacated her lungs. She couldn't unfreeze her gaze from the glinting steel, couldn't feel her heart beat or move her hands and feet. Her fear was brutal, her mind a torture chamber of the grisly things to come as she fast forwarded the swipe of his finger, the sharp edge slicing her from neck to gut, and the slick gush of blood that would bathe her final moments.

He tilted the razor inches from her face, causing light to dance across the surface. "Cutting a woman, it's different than cutting a man. The blade must be held with a passionate hand, and when feminine skin separates, it doesn't just bleed. It weeps."

Throbbing pressure built in the back of her throat and swelled behind her eyes. His words, the clinical apathy in his voice, the unfeeling look on his face... He was deeply deranged, inhumanly evil, and it scared the living hell out of her.

Tremors crashed through her body. She wanted to believe she was a strong person, that she could endure the worst of his depravity without breaking. But she wasn't and couldn't. She couldn't even rein in her emotions at the sight of his blade.

As she shoved down the panic, it bubbled back up. As she blanked her face, the muscles in her cheeks contracted and quivered. She swallowed ugly, miserable sounds, but they broke through, fracturing the silence and exposing her fragility.

It was such a helpless feeling—the choking breaths, the godawful constriction in her chest, the inconsolable horror. Her chin trembled, chattering her teeth. She blinked rapidly, tried to stop the worst of it before it spilled from her eyes, tried to hold herself together with invisible arms. There was no comfort to be found.

She couldn't remember the last time she was this terrified. Everything inside her twisted and swelled to the point of unraveling. She ached to surrender to it and mentally played out what it would feel like to give in to the tears, to the uncontrollable sobbing, to abandon the fight and let defeat pull her under. She longed for that, to give up and accept her fate. God, the relief in letting go would be extraordinary.

But when her meltdown was over, there would be nothing left. He would still be here, getting off on her pathetic show. He wouldn't even have to cut her. Her misery alone would feed his sadism. It would make him stronger.

He didn't see her as a person. She was an object, a thing to play with and torment. Eventually, he would grow bored and toss away her pieces like a broken toy. Then he would find another.

Fuck that.

A heavy stillness fell over her. A purpose. She wasn't dead yet. That meant she could change her fate, rewrite the ending. But how?

He ghosted the razor's edge along her brow, just a whispered touch of steel that put every nerve in her body into cardiac arrest.

With great effort, she dragged her attention away from the blade and focused on the shadows in his eyes.

What made him become so vicious? Was he born into a life of crime? Did he have any loved ones? Anyone important to him?

He seemed to respect Lucia, said she was fierce and resilient. But Kate wasn't fearless, and he already scolded her for trying to be brave.

There was something broken inside him. That much was obvious. She had no clue how to decode his fucked-up mind, but after her experience with Van, she'd been drawn to documentaries and psychiatric studies about violent criminals.

There was evidential research that linked personal trauma to the making of a murderer. Not all serial killers were victims of abuse, but many experienced brutal childhoods. She couldn't diagnose him or pretend he was anything other than a criminal, but maybe she could reach him in a way no else had tried?

With the glide of his finger, he curved the razor along the side of her face. His gaze followed the movement, and his breathing picked up.

She held still, paralyzed beneath his deadly touch. "You don't want to do this."

His eyes flicked to hers and tapered with warning.

It was a powerful, overwhelmingly desperate moment when the mind recognized that death was only seconds away.

"I can give you something." She swallowed. "Something no one else has offered."

"Don't be naive. You're smart enough to imagine the range of pleasures women offer me." He scanned her body with zero interest on his face.

"Not that." She organized her thoughts and carefully chose her words. "I get the feeling you've suffered things. Unspeakable, horrible things that left a deep impact on your life."

His expression emptied, giving nothing away.

Was she digging her own grave? Her hands slicked with sweat, her lungs shriveling on the cusp of hyperventilation. "Maybe I'm just projecting. When Van Quiso took me, I experienced my own trauma. Whatever happened to you, I can empathize. I don't forgive you for kidnapping me, but I'm capable of compassion." She softened her voice. "Surely, that means something to you?"

"Compassion?" He laughed. "I've heard of it, but not in this world. Not where joy is nonexistent, and integrity is a luxury." He hooked the blade under her throat, skyrocketing her pulse. "In this world, the weak are crushed."

Her chest heaved, and her entire body convulsed with overwhelming horror. Oh God, she didn't want to die. Not like this. She wasn't ready.

But what hope did she have? There was no ransom, no way to locate her, and no white knight riding in on a horse.

What if death was her only escape?

"Okay, Tiago." She wheezed, eyes wide and burning. "I'm scared. Is that what you want? I'm fucking terrified. But I won't give you the pleasure of watching me fall apart. You want to kill me? Go ahead." She raised her chin and pushed against the blade, shaking violently. "You have my fear. You've taken my freedom. I have nothing left to lose."

"That's not true. There is something."

The blade retreated, and he folded it shut. Her heartbeat reeled as he pocketed it and pulled out a phone.

"I have something you and Lucia want." He unlocked the screen, tapped it a few times, and met her eyes.

"I don't understand." Or maybe she did, but denial was easier to swallow.

He turned the phone and showed her the screen.

A live video of a nude man streamed across the display. He stood in a shack with his back to the camera and a sponge in his hand. He was bathing, using water from a bucket at his feet. Even more crude was the shackle connecting his ankle to a chain that snaked along the dirt floor.

What was on his back? She leaned closer to the screen.

Holy fuck.

Blood pounded in her ears, and ice skewered her veins.

Who would have the stomach to carve up that man's back so gruesomely? Her gaze shot to Tiago, her thoughts spiraling to the razor in his pocket.

Dread hardened her gut as she returned to the screen.

The mutilation spanned from the man's shoulders to his waist, the cuts welted and red, but not fresh. Not only that, there were pink scars on opposite sides of his arm, as if something had been recently stabbed straight through it.

God, the pain he must've endured… She couldn't imagine it. Couldn't take her eyes off the video. She pored over his brown hair, his muscled mid-twenties physique, and the unfinished tattoo on his bicep.

Her breath hitched. *Oh, please, no.* She knew that tattoo.

"As it turns out…" Tiago's deep voice broke through her. "Lucia fell in love."

"No, no, no." She shook her head, denying the truth even as it forced itself upon her. "That's not Tate. It can't be."

"It's him, and the man holding the camera has been instructed to kill him, if I don't call in…" He tilted the phone to check the time. "Five minutes."

Her heart catapulted to her throat. "Call him!"

He regarded her, head canted and expression composed, as if he had all the time in the world.

Everything inside her snapped. She thrashed and spat and went fucking feral as he watched her with a sick kind of curiosity.

"Please!" She kicked her legs, bucking beneath the straddle of his knees. "What do you want? I'll do anything."

"Anything?"

She looked at the phone, at the brutality marring Tate's back, and her stomach sank. "Lucia loves him? And he loves her back?"

"Yes." The corner of his mouth bounced. "They risked their lives to be together, and if they're lucky, they'll die together."

"What are you saying?"

"I have a weakness for tragic love stories. It's the only reason I didn't kill them immediately." He shut off the phone, a scowl darkening his inextricable eyes. "Lucia will find him, unless you fuck it up."

"Don't put this on me," she seethed. "I'll do whatever you say. Just make the call."

FOUR

Fucking Christ, Tiago's head hurt. He wasn't in the habit of physically restraining people, especially not while recovering from a fractured skull.

He preferred other means of control, as Kate would soon find out.

"I'm going to remove the rope." He pulled the finger blade from his pocket. "Be a good girl."

Her watery gaze stayed with the phone where it sat out of reach. Her fear for Tate was palpable, paling her pretty face to a ghostly shade of white. She would really lose her mind if she knew her friend was being held within walking distance from here.

Tiago didn't relish the thought of ending Tate's life. It would ruin everything he'd put into place.

But he would follow through on his threat if Kate didn't behave.

"Hold still." He cut through the thick rope on her arms until the fibers unraveled enough to fall away.

She rubbed her wrists, the skin red and raw. A little rope burn was nothing compared to the hurt she would endure before she died. She might as well get used to it.

He rolled off her slender body, and she instantly tried to scramble away.

"Stay." He pointed the blade at the spot beside him on the mattress.

She froze with a foot on the floor and glared back at him. "You're going to call your guy? Stop him from killing Tate?"

He tapped the mattress where he wanted her.

Her shoulders slumped, and she crawled to the far end, putting her back to the wall and her eyes on his phone.

Another wave of queasiness hit him sideways, and he braced a hand on the bed, catching himself.

Christ, he needed something for the double vision. Being bedridden for a month left him dizzy and weak. Wrestling a pint-sized woman made it worse.

It was time to start working out again. The sooner he rebuilt his strength, the sooner he could return to Caracas and reestablish his reign there.

First, he needed to deal with his prisoners.

"If you make a single sound, Tate will die." He unlocked the phone. "Tell me you understand."

Her blue eyes flashed, and her teeth sawed through the words. "I understand."

He dialed Arturo, the guard who sent the video, and didn't wait for a greeting. "Put Tate on the phone."

Sounds of movement rustled down the line, followed by an angry rush of breaths.

"Hello, Tate." Tiago set the phone on speaker, so Kate could hear the conversation.

Tate made a stricken noise. "Where's—?"

"If you ask about her, the call ends, and you'll never hear from me again."

It had been a month since Tate and Lucia saw each other. Tate asked about her relentlessly, but his questions went unanswered.

Tiago needed him to assume the worst. "You'll spend the rest of your lonely existence locked away in that shack, wondering why I called and what I was going to say."

Kate sucked in a breath, her expression murderous.

"I'm listening," Tate said.

"I would be there in person, but I haven't been feeling well. I'm sure you know why." As he spoke into the phone, he held her gaze, wordlessly reminding her to keep quiet. "I wanted to offer you something. Let's call it a last request. Anything you want. This doesn't include information, and it must fit inside the shack."

"What is this?" Tate asked. "Like a last-meal request? Am I on death row?"

She tensed, her fingers biting into the mattress.

He shook his head, admonishing her. "I'm offering more than a meal, Tate. You can choose anything—a bed to sleep on, a girl to fuck, a drug to numb your mind. I'm sure you can come up with something creative."

"Why?" Suspicion laced Tate's voice. "What do you want?"

"I've already taken my payment." Given the rancor in her eyes, he might have to kill her before the call ended. "Consider this a thank you."

"What did you *take*?" Tate whispered harshly.

"Not Lucia. I left her to die in prison. What's your last request, Tate?"

Kate pressed a hand against her lips, smothering a whimper.

Tiago had spoken the truth about Lucia, but not the *whole* truth. If Kate sat there and kept her mouth shut, maybe he would enlighten her.

Returning his attention to the phone, he digested the silence on the other end.

Right about now, Tate was likely hitting a very cold, inconsolable rock bottom. Tiago knew too well what that felt like. The suffocating, dire weight of helplessness pulling through the body. The endless chill hardening organs and arteries. The grip of desolation overshadowing self-preservation. An emptiness so profound and consuming there wasn't enough air to return from the dead.

To have and to hold the entire world, then to watch it be violently ripped away... There was no greater suffering.

Kate was right. Some experiences cut so deeply it gutted a man. *Or twisted a good man into a criminal.*

Tate's rasp vibrated the speaker. "Do you have a photo of Lucia?"

"Yes."

"My request..." He coughed, his voice hoarse. "I want to finish the tattoo on my arm, feel her face on my skin, with me always."

Tears welled in Kate's eyes, her nostrils pulsing above the hand she held against her mouth.

Tate had more than proved his love for Lucia in the basement of the Caracas compound. Having her inked into his skin would add a layer of commitment that made his devastation that much more meaningful.

The idea moved Tiago, sinking deep into a graveyard of memories and resurrecting ghosts. He harbored an ugly past, one that made him fixate on rare and beautiful things, like the mutual devotion between two people.

Wrenching Tate away from Lucia had been as cruel as carving a portrait into his back, but that was the point.

The strongest love rose out of the greatest hurt.

With regard to the logistics of Tate's request, it just so happened one of the local guards was a tattoo artist.

"Very well." Tiago switched the call off speaker. "Return the phone to the guard."

After making the necessary arrangements with Arturo, he disconnected and glanced at Kate.

"Can I see another video?" She wiped her damp cheeks. "Proof that your guard isn't killing him?"

"No." He locked the phone and tossed it aside.

Her lashes lowered, and another tear slipped out. "Please, let him go."

If she thought he kept a watchdog on Tate, she was wrong. The few guards Tiago had with him were needed here, watching the perimeter of the house.

When he was carried out of Caracas a month ago, he was comatose and bleeding from two fractures in his skull. Only Arturo and Boones came with him — the two men who saved his life.

Boones had taken care of everything, treating his injuries and transporting him to this isolated area in the Venezuela desert. Tiago owned this land and had decided days before Lucia's attack that Tate would be captured and brought here. Boones followed through on that plan perfectly.

Only five other guards joined them here, all of which were pulled from Tiago's other domiciles around the country.

His outfit in Caracas didn't know about this place, and he intended to keep it that way. He had countless enemies and trusted no one. Except Boones.

Every day, the old doctor delivered Tate's meals and nursed his wounds. Only then did a guard go near the shack, and that was for Boones' protection.

If Tate managed to free himself from the ankle cuff, no one would stop him from escaping.

Tiago reclined against the wall and captured her gaze. "When Lucia finds him, he's free to go."

"You said Lucia's in prison." Her brows gathered. "You also said you let her go."

"You may not believe this, but I haven't lied to you. I did let her go."

"I don't know what to believe."

"Good, because you have no—"

"Opinions. I heard you the first time." She looked away, giving him the profile of her willful chin.

Why hadn't he sent her back to her room? He wouldn't need her until later, if at all.

He'd captured her to send Tate and his friends a message. *Fuck with the most powerful gang leader in Venezuela and pay the consequences.*

As for Kate's fate, it wasn't pretty. He would offer her to his enemies as a bribe. Or give her to his guards as a reward for their loyalty.

Or he would just kill her.

He tilted his head and let his gaze wander over her, really taking her in for the first time.

Blond hair hung in wild waves to her elbows. Bony shoulders, smallish tits, she was skinnier and shorter than the average twenty-two-year-old.

For all the profanity and thunderous noise her face produced over the past month, he'd formed a completely different picture in his head. Between bouts of unconsciousness and listening to her bellow in the other room, he'd imagined a tough Amazonian beast of woman. Someone tall and strong with meat on her bones.

Not that he had complaints about the image before him. That was the problem. Kate was a goddamn knockout.

Her fair complexion, ethereal figure, graceful legs, and fuck, her eyes… As vivid as the ocean and too deep to measure, those bottomless blues could enchant a man, make him change course and lose his way.

He should just kill her now and be done with it.

With a slow breath, she sat taller, pushed back her shoulders, and faced him. "Will you tell me what happened? With Tate and Lucia?" Her eyebrows knitted together as she faltered over her next question. "Is Van Quiso alive?"

Interesting how she asked about everyone else while her own life hung in the balance. And Van Quiso no less. The sex-trafficking rapist enslaved her for weeks, no doubt violating her six ways to Sunday. He didn't deserve her concern.

One might argue that Van couldn't hold a testicle to the crimes Tiago had committed. Nevertheless, Tiago felt a strange itch to answer her and found himself wondering how she would weigh in on his decision concerning her fate.

His train of thought baffled him. She was nothing more than a prisoner. A soon-to-be-dead prisoner.

Her death would be a waste of a gorgeous body. Most men would sell their souls for a night between her legs. But the lure of a beautiful woman had no power over him.

Lucia spent eleven years at his side, naked in his room, and dependent on his mercy. He'd allowed himself to touch her, to indulge in the feel of her every dip and curve. But he never fucked her. That was his rule. His self-imposed penance.

Kate was no different.

He ran a hand along the cuff of his shirt, unbuttoned it, and did the same with the other sleeve. "After a month of bed rest, this is the first time I've put on clothes. Unfortunately, when my bag was packed for me, my casual attire was forgotten in the rush."

Her mouth parted, her eyes bright and watchful. He knew she'd wondered why he'd dressed up. The fact that he answered her unspoken question surprised him as much as it did her.

TAKE

"I've been straight with you." He rolled up his sleeves, taking his time with each one. "Your life is forfeit. A penalty paid for Tate's stupidity. It's in my best interest to kill you quickly."

She fell unnaturally still, her gaze focusing on nothing. He wasn't sure she was breathing.

Then she blinked and locked onto his eyes. "Do you have anything to drink?"

Her calm response gave him pause, and in that unexpected moment, he found her...spellbinding.

"There's a bottle of tequila in my bag." He nodded at the luggage. "Cups are in the bathroom."

"I'll pour us some shots."

As she stood, her arm wrapped around her stomach where he'd kicked her, her face etched in pain.

He should've killed her the moment she entered his room.

Why didn't he just do it now? As long as she was alive, her friends wouldn't stop looking for her.

She shuffled through the small space, grabbing the tequila and pulling his concentration along with her. The white-gold of her hair, the unintentional sway of her ass, the irresistible flex of muscle there—the sight of her made him burn, hardening him until there was nowhere to go in his fitted trousers.

He deserved the discomfort, had earned the torment of looking at her without touching. Twelve years ago, he made the gravest mistake of his life and lost everything that made him human. But he still had a working dick, and the damn thing wanted out.

She returned to the mattress, watching him watch her. "Why is killing me in your best interest?"

There were many reasons, but he gave her the one that would hurt her most.

"You said it yourself." He lifted the tequila from her hand, filled the cups, and handed one to her. "Your army of *dangerous* friends is looking for you." He took a hearty draw from the mug, hoping the alcohol would numb his perpetual headache. "I'll leave your body where they can find it."

She tossed back the tequila, gulping it down between hacking coughs.

"Sit." He motioned at the mattress.

She wiped her mouth with the back of her hand, sat at the farthest end, and held out the empty mug. "If you kill me, they'll come for *you*."

"Not with the same urgency or persistence." He refilled her cup. "What will they sacrifice to avenge your death? How long will it take before they refocus their efforts on those they can save? That's what they

247

do, right? They free human slaves."

She averted her eyes, jaw clenched, and looked back at him. "You don't know them."

"When Van Quiso and Liv Reed ran a sex trafficking ring, you were their seventh slave. But they put all that behind them, and now they co-parent the child who came out of their twisted relationship. Van married Amber. Liv married Josh, and they're all one big fucked-up family. You are not their priority."

"Where did you get that information?"

"Then there's Lucia's sister, Camila Dias. She's not only the leader of your little army. She also happens to be married to the capo of the Restrepo cartel. She made quite a leap from Van's attic. Or a fall, depending on how you look at it." He finished off his tequila and poured another. "While Matias Restrepo has the resources to take me out, his focus is and always will be on Camila. If she died by my hand, he'd tear the universe apart in his fury to make me suffer. But I took *you*, and you are not his. You're not his priority. Not his concern."

"Whatever you think." She lifted a shoulder, and the trembly motion ruined her attempt at indifference.

"As for the men you lived with, they're currently seeking refuge in Colombia, under Matias' protection."

"They're afraid you'll come after them. If you kill me, they *will* retaliate."

"Which roommate were you fucking? Martin? Luke? Tomas? All of them?"

He'd investigated the entire crew the moment he discovered Tate Vades sniffing around his domain. While he didn't know who was fucking who in Tate's household, he'd learned enough to determine that Kate was the ideal target.

She wasn't married. Didn't have a romantic partner or monogamous lover. There was no one in her life who would travel to the end of hell and back to avenge her death. And that was where he was headed after he killed her. Back to Caracas. Hell on Earth.

"All your assumptions can fuck right off." She guzzled her drink and shoved the cup aside.

"Your friends might be outraged by your death, but they don't love you. Not the way a man loves his soulmate. You are no one's other half. No one's number one."

She closed her eyes, tucking away her reaction. But he felt the moment his words penetrated. The mattress shook beneath her perch on the edge, her body quaking so loudly and intensely he marveled at the strength of her despair.

Her gaze moved to the exit. Would she make a run for it? If she did, she wouldn't make it past the antechamber. The door to the stairway required a key from the inside, which he kept in his locked safe.

He poured another drink, stalling the inevitable task. She wouldn't be the first life he took. Nor was this the first time he hesitated.

As if she sensed the direction of this thoughts, she turned and gave him her full attention.

Perspiration formed along her hairline, her breaths choppy and rough. "I don't want to die."

FIVE

Smooth tequila, a gorgeous woman, and the thrum of rain on an old roof…
Tiago hadn't felt this relaxed in a long damn time.

He didn't want to kill her. Not tonight.

Maybe the month he spent in this room softened more than his
muscles. With a grumpy old man as his only visitor, he ventured to guess
he was lonely.

He hadn't seen his guards since he arrived. Even though they'd
been carefully vetted and handpicked for this job, he didn't trust them in
his personal space, let alone his headspace.

He longed for conversation, and Kate wanted answers. He could
give her that much.

Wetting his lips with a sip from the mug, he let his mind drift to
the past. "Eleven years ago, my men pulled a smuggled slave out of a
deadly crash in Peru."

"Lucia," she breathed.

"They found her chained in a truck with a twisted piece of metal
protruding from her abdomen."

By some miracle, she'd survived. But barely.

The same could've been said about him at the time.

"When they brought her to me, I knew I'd have to kill her. It was
the easiest solution."

"But you didn't."

"I hesitated." He reached for his boot and untied the laces. "It
wasn't a matter of morals. I've been taking lives since my early twenties."

Killing was a job requirement, then and now.

Her face paled. "How old are you?"

"Thirty-seven."

Fifteen years her senior.

She touched her throat, eyes round with shock. "You're older than I thought."

He felt old. Too fucking old and jaded to have a meaningful conversation with a girl from the suburbs. But he wanted to tell her about Lucia, needed to get it off his chest.

Removing his boots, he leaned back against the wall, with his legs stretched off the mattress. "Lucia came to me at a time when I needed a distraction."

It had been the worst year of his life. He'd lost everything, moved halfway across the world, changed jobs, and stripped his identity down to the black remains of his soul. All he had left were nightmares and chaos, and he needed to balance that with something constant, something he could control.

And there she was. A woman he could save.

"Boones and his medical team operated on her," he said. "She went through several surgeries and a long recovery."

"He has a medical team?"

"Three other doctors. They followed me to Venezuela twelve years ago to work for my organization. But they're old, older than Boones, and it was time for them to go home. They left the night Boones transported me here."

"Where is *home?*"

Tiago didn't originate from Eritrea like Boones and the others, but their quiet African village on the Red Sea was the only place he ever called home.

His chest constricted. What bound him to Eritrea was a collection of pervasive, melancholic memories. His life there ran the gamut from extreme joy to unendurable tragedy. None of which he was inclined to talk about.

When her gaze dipped, he realized he was scratching the scars on his forearm.

Lowering his hand to his lap, he skipped over her question. "I didn't keep Lucia alive out of the goodness of my heart. She's attractive and ferocious, and I wanted to mold those attributes into a weapon I could use." He chuckled in remembrance. "She became an invaluable spy, but it took *years* to tame her."

Kate stared at him as if he just told her he ate the hearts of human babies.

She wasn't far off the mark.

He was a self-made felon, feared and abhorred by all walks of life. "I could've killed her. Maybe I should have. Had she fallen into the hands of another drug lord, that's exactly what they would've done. Let's not forget, she was found in a truck full of slaves, destined for a life much worse than the one I gave her."

"She was taken from her home by those slave traders. How did you keep her from running back to her family?" She absently rubbed the red marks on her wrists. "Did you tie her up for eleven years?"

"I poisoned her."

He unraveled the details of his deception — how he'd secretly tainted Lucia's food and made her chronically ill, how he counteracted it with daily injections of the antidote, and how it led her to believe she had a disease that only he could cure.

"My medical team monitored the poison, ensuring the doses weren't fatal," he said.

"That's sick." Kate shook her head, her face scrunched in revulsion. "And unacceptable."

"It was more humane than keeping her in shackles."

"You could've let her go."

He didn't expect this naive girl to understand. Her ordeal with Van Quiso was nothing compared to what existed in the bowels of the criminal underworld.

"I assume she figured out you were poisoning her," she said. "Is that why she attacked you?"

"No. Matias Restrepo was the catalyst for the recent chain of events."

"Matias? How?"

"A week before I took you, Tate initiated contact with Lucia. He approached her in a sex club and fucked her. Or maybe it was the other way around." He smirked. "I knew about their hookup but didn't consider him a threat until her routine changed. She started acting cagey. That's when I dug deeper and discovered his connection with the Restrepo cartel."

"You didn't know Matias was Lucia's brother-in-law?"

"No, and neither did she. It changed the stakes. I was no longer dealing with some clueless American sneaking around my turf. Tate's presence was attached to a cartel, a notoriously ambitious one. I didn't know if they meant to wage war against me, try to seize control of my smuggling routes, or something else. So I took you."

"As payment."

"And to send them a warning."

Kidnapping and murder, business as usual.

"Matias isn't interested in taking your business." Her breathing accelerated. "Lucia is his family. He just wanted her back."

"To that end, he would've gone to war." He cocked his head. "He sent men to the states to gather everyone close to Tate and bring them to Colombia. But when they arrived at your diner to collect you, they were an hour too late. You were already in my possession."

A whimper left her before she cut it off.

"The night you disappeared," he said, "was the same night I captured Tate and Van."

While she was being transported from Texas to Venezuela, he was putting Tate through eight brutal hours of trials and torture.

He gave her a graphic account of the evening — the icepick through Tate's arm, the carving on his back, and the forced sodomy between him and his former captor.

"What?" She gasped, her cheeks damp and bloodless. "You made Tate *fuck* Van? Why?"

"Justice is rarely pleasant, and Van had it coming."

"How is that justice? Tate wouldn't have wanted that. He'd already forgiven Van."

"Are you sure? Have you made peace with Van?"

She glanced away. "Why do you care?"

"I don't like him."

Van was a reflection of himself. Scarred. Splintered. Heartless. There was a reason he never looked in a mirror.

"Is Van still alive?" she asked quietly.

"Yes."

He detailed the events of Lucia's incursion with the dumbbell, her escape with Tate and Van, the gunfight, and car chase. "After they fled, Arturo found me on the floor in my room. By the time I woke, your friends were already recaptured."

"How could you orchestrate that with your head smashed in?"

"Boones arranged things on my behalf, leveraging the police on my payroll. Lucia and Van went to prison, and Tate was taken to the shack as part of the original plan."

"You didn't let her go." She ground her teeth.

"She's free, right now, because I allowed it. While she sat in prison for a week, I could've had her executed or returned to me at any time." He tapped a finger on his thigh, questioning this compulsion to explain himself. "She escaped prison, and I allowed that to happen. I let her go. Her and Van both."

"Why? I mean, I'm happy they're safe, but I don't understand the change of heart."

"I want her to find Tate."

"Then release him! It makes no sense." She tucked her limbs close to her torso, keeping her legs covered by the thin dress. "You poisoned her, tortured him, and separated them when all they want is to be together.

Do you hurt people just for the hell of it?" A swallow bobbed her throat. "Because you get off on their pain?"

"You want to know if I'm a sadist." It was a query he didn't mind examining. "I suppose the label fits. Delivering pain is an expression of art. It's inspiring, inherently satisfying, but only when the hurt has meaning, when it serves a purpose beyond cruelty."

She slowly drew her head back, shrinking away from him. It was a sane reaction. Sitting within arm's reach of the man who would end her life, she was probably crawling out of her skin to run far, far away.

He'd told her she had no opinions here, but that was bullshit. He couldn't control the thoughts in her head, and after talking with her, he wasn't sure he wanted to. She was a good listener and spoke her mind, even if he didn't like what she had to say.

It was refreshing.

Her stare lasered onto his, narrowing, analyzing, before traveling down his arm to linger on his scars. "Your cuts are self-inflicted."

"Hm." He didn't move his eyes from her face.

"The lines on your left arm are straighter, cleaner. Because you're right-handed."

Impressive.

She glanced at his head wounds and returned to his arms. "When you asked how bad your injury looked, I thought you were concerned about infection or something. But that's not it at all. You regard scars the way a painter beholds a painting."

He leaned forward, hanging on her words.

"*Delivering pain is an expression of art.* That's what you said." Her nose twitched. "I assume that means you prefer to be the giver of scars, not the receiver. But you gave *and* received those." She nodded at his arms. "I don't know what to make of that. Do you?"

He could explain it, but he chose not to.

At his silence, she drifted closer, inspecting his welted skin with those huge blue eyes. "The designs are incredibly detailed. I can make out a few of the abstract shapes, like the sunset and mountain range. Some of the symbols are animals, but the other marks... They're esoteric." She looked up and met his gaze. "Every cut means something to you."

"Yes." He felt himself warming to her, wanting to give her more than a night to live.

"The image you put on Tate's back..." Her neck stiffened. "I couldn't see it clearly. What is it?"

He described the illustration of the double gate hanging between pillars and the woman floating through the opening. "Lucia was there when I carved it into his back. When she realizes it's a picture of the location where he's being held, she'll find him."

TAKE

Kate's jaw fell open, her glare livid. "Why won't you just let him go? That's a whole lot easier than cutting a map into his body." She speared a hand through her hair and pulled at the strands. "What you're doing to them... It's insanity."

"Love is insanity."

She blinked. Blinked again. "Okay?"

"Tate and Lucia were an experiment. I wanted to learn the limits of how far they would go for each other. As it turns out, the thing between them is unstoppable. He's alone in a shack under the assumption she's dead, and his only request is a tattoo of her on his arm. She hasn't seen her sister in eleven years, but instead of going home, she's scouring the country day and night. I'm certain she won't give up until she finds him. It's fascinating to watch."

"You're playing God."

"I'm helping them."

"Helping? *Jesus Christ*," she muttered under her breath. "You're interfering in destiny. Manipulating it."

"Destiny is a power far bigger than my mortal reach. I'm simply providing obstacles for them to overcome, to make them stronger."

"Sounds like a veiled excuse to deliver pain." Emotion leaked into her voice, raising it a few octaves. "Does their agony inspire you? Do you get hard thinking about it?"

"Stop being so goddamn narrow-minded." His pulse quickened, firing through his veins. "Adversity builds character."

"And feeds the sadist."

"Careful, Kate." He hardened his eyes, gripped by an irrational need to make her understand. "If you love someone and they don't reciprocate, what happens? You love them harder, deeper, more obsessively. Roadblocks don't diminish desire. They intensify it. Obstacles heighten the obsession."

"Fine." She blew out a breath, sagging in defeat. "I get what you're saying. Love is insanity. No one can control it."

"Not even me." He felt the glimmer in her eyes, the lingering heat and thrill from arguing.

"Just because I gave the devil his due on one point doesn't mean I agree with your demented methods."

"I don't give a fuck whether you agree or not."

With a harrumph, she tipped her pretty head, studying him. "You're not...quite what you seem."

"Explain."

"Well, you seem to be a romantic, for one. I didn't see that coming. *Wait.*" She straightened, staring at him with a startled expression. "Is that what happened to you? You had your own love story and—?"

255

"Do you actually believe a woman could love a man like me?"

Her lips parted as she exhaled a slow puff of air. "Am I supposed to answer that?"

He grabbed the tequila and empty mugs and rose from the bed. "We're finished here."

She touched a nerve, and he didn't bother hiding it. He wanted her out of his room.

Heading to the bathroom, he set the bottle on the counter and rinsed out the cups.

The sound of her footsteps approached from behind, pausing outside the door. "Why are there no mirrors in the bathrooms?"

They were removed for reasons that were none of her business.

She sighed into the silence. "Can we talk about the elephant in the room?"

The ever-growing burden of what to do with her unsettled his stomach. With his back to her, he mindlessly dried the cups while making a decision.

If he sent her back to her room and waited until tomorrow, she would spend the evening agonizing over her fate. Unnecessary cruelty wasn't his thing.

He needed to kill her now. No more delaying.

SIX

Some murderers claimed that killing was the same as having sex. Others argued it wasn't about lust. It was about feeling that last breath of life leave a woman, looking into her eyes, and being God.

Tiago didn't have a god complex. Nor did he derive sexual pleasure from killing. He especially hated taking a woman's life, but occasionally things happened.

If he had any human qualities left, he would get to know the stunning woman glaring at his back. He would date her, seduce her, and fuck her until neither of them could walk.

Instead, he was contemplating where to dump her body and how badly it would rot before her friends found it.

"You have four options." Kate's voice strummed with nervous agitation.

That raised his brow. He turned and rested his backside against the counter.

"One. You can let me go." She wilted beneath his glare and hugged her waist. "But that would make you appear merciful and weak. Can't have that."

He let his silence affirm her words.

Drawing a breath, she released it slowly. "Two. You can keep me locked up. But my friends won't stop looking for me as long as I'm alive."

He slid a hand in his pants pocket and fingered the casing of his blade, the only solution.

Her eyes followed the movement, and a tremor rippled through her. "Three. You can kill me, and maybe my friends won't put a lifetime of effort into hunting you down. Like you said, there are other priorities, stronger passions than avenging my death. But killing me will make them your enemies. It's a small world, and when you cross paths with the Restrepo cartel, they'll remember."

It was a weak argument. His treatment of Lucia ensured that Matias Restrepo would forever be an enemy. "You said there were four options."

"I can make a phone call."

"No."

She cleared her throat and closed her eyes. When she looked at him again, a strange transformation rolled over her, loosening her posture. Her shoulders eased, and she stood taller, lengthening her height with grace and confidence.

"Liv Reed is my closest friend." She smiled, and it glowed so beautifully across her face it was disarming. "I can convince her I'm safe, that I haven't been hurt or touched against my will. Since I've been here for a month, that's plenty of time to get to know you." Her eyes beamed, lashes fluttering flirtatiously. "I enjoy your company. You're ridiculously handsome and protective, and you make me feel things I've never felt. I know it's crazy, but I want to stay. I need this. It's a chance to get away for a while and figure out my life. So there's no need for anyone to look for me. I don't want to be found." She released a shaky breath. "How was that?"

Fucking hell, she was good. Not a hitch or tremble in her voice. She sounded and looked so goddamn sincere he almost believed the lies.

"Did Van teach you how to do that?" He prowled toward her, captivated.

As a trained slave, she would've received lessons in obedience and decorum so that she wouldn't embarrass her Master in public.

"Did Van whip you until you learned how to maintain that pleasing disposition?" he asked. "To hold that smile through the godawful pain?"

"Yes," she spat, all traces of sweetness gone. "I bet that puts joy in your hateful heart."

"Not at all." He circled her, stepping so close he felt a shudder vibrate her tiny frame.

"Shall I grab your phone?" she asked warily.

He kept untraceable burners in the safe. If he went with the *phone a friend* option, what was the risk?

She couldn't tip them off on anything useful. She didn't even know her location. If she meant to deceive him and started begging for help while on the phone, he would just end the call and kill her.

Liv Reed would be skeptical no matter what Kate said to her. But a believable performance would leave her friends wondering, hoping. Just hearing her happy, healthy voice would take some of the urgency out of their need to find her.

"Do it again." He moved in closer, crowding her back and breathing in the gentle scent of her hair. "Talk through the conversation you would have with her."

With a deep breath, she re-acted the call. Every word and inflection in her voice was just as convincing as the first time. She made references to him throughout, praising his good looks and weaving a tantalizing tale of budding romance and exciting adventure.

Her enthusiasm was so persuasive it drew his body tight, heating his skin and tempting him to touch. The strapless dress exposed her shoulder blades, the top half of her back, and all her delicate arches of feminine bone and muscle. He couldn't resist.

Sweeping her hair to the side, he rested his fingertips on the soft, warm curve of her nape.

Goosebumps rose beneath his hand, but she didn't flinch or stutter. It was a testament to how badly she wanted this phone call. She was determined to prove she could do it, with or without distractions.

As he feathered his touch down the sinuous line of her spine, he interjected questions that Liv would ask. Kate answered with quick-witted untruths and seamlessly redirected the conversation.

She could absolutely pull this off.

He drew his hand away and stepped back. Anticipation hummed through his body as he stalked to the safe and removed one of the phones.

Keeping her alive introduced new problems and temptations, but the challenge excited him. *She* excited him.

He locked the safe and returned to her. "If you're playing me, there will be repercussions."

"I'm not." She picked at her fingernail, avoiding his eyes. "Before I make this call, I need you to promise me two things."

He could guess her demands. "Choose one."

"But—"

"Only one, Kate."

Pressing her lips together, she stared at her bare feet. Crossed her arms. Lowered them. Then she lifted her gaze, decision made. "I need your word that Tate will go free."

"When Lucia finds him—"

"I want a deadline." She raised her chin. "Promise me you'll release him if she hasn't found him in one week."

"One year."

"What?" She gasped. "He's chained in a shack, sleeping on a dirt floor, without a bucket to shit in."

"There is a bucket."

"Please, don't say —"

"To shit in."

Her neck went taut, and she gritted her teeth. "One month, tops."

"Six months."

"Three months."

"Six months. I'll keep him fed and cared for. No harm will come to him."

Her mouth quivered. "Six months is too long."

"That, or we forget about the phone call and go with option three. What will it be?"

"Damn you." She pinched the bridge of her nose, inhaled deeply, and dropped her hand. "If Lucia doesn't locate him in six months, you'll release him, alive, and never hurt him or touch him again. That includes you or anyone under your command. Promise me."

"You have my word."

She gave a stiff nod, set her gaze on the phone, and rattled off a phone number.

He dialed and put it on speaker.

A dulcet, feminine voice answered on the first ring. "Who is this?"

"Liv? It's Kate."

"Kate? Oh, thank God." Movement sounded through the speaker. "Are you okay? We've been worried sick. Where are you?"

"I'm fine. Everything's fine."

She ran through her spiel, her voice as strong and mesmerizing as her eye contact. She smiled and motioned energetically with her hands, one-hundred-percent committed to misleading her closest friend. "So you can stop looking for me, okay? I don't want to be found."

"Wow, I…" Liv released a heavy breath. "I'm relieved to hear your voice, but we really need to see you. Just tell me where you are and —"

"You'll what? Check things out to make sure I'm not screwing up? Don't assume you know what's good for me."

Tiago clenched his hand around the phone, his nerves on high alert.

"You're calling from an untraceable number," Liv said cautiously. "I know I'm on speaker phone. Is he there? Listening to our conversation?"

"You have every reason to hate him." Kate gave him a firm look and held up her palm, staying him. "He poisoned Lucia, mutilated Tate's back, and the thing he forced Tate and Van do together… It's unforgivable."

"He told you about that?"

"Of course. He tells me everything. I know he has issues. God, they're never-ending."

He narrowed his eyes.

She narrowed hers right back. "But we're working through them. *Together.*"

"He kidnapped you, Kate, and it's not uncommon to become attached and feel affection toward your captor. It's a psychological response, the mind's way of surviving."

"Is that what happened with Josh? You kidnapped and tortured him, so his feelings toward you are just survival tools? Marrying you was his coping mechanism for the hell you put him through?"

"Don't you dare," Liv snapped. "You were there, and you know damn well what he and I mean to each other." Her fuming breaths rattled the phone. "Where's Tate?"

Tiago hovered a finger over the end button and shook his head.

"I don't know." Kate pressed a hand against her breastbone. Her eyes brimmed with tears, but she kept the emotion out of her voice. "I love you, Liv, but I'm going to hang up now. Don't look for me. Don't worry about me. I'm exactly where I want to be."

"Kate, wait—"

He disconnected the call and pocketed the phone, monitoring her expression.

The facade she'd maintained for Liv gave way to a heartbroken stare and hunched shoulders.

"She'll worry. They all will." She inched backward in the direction of the exit. "But they won't look for me."

He let her continue her tentative retreat through the doorway, holding her teary gaze until she turned away in the corridor. When his ears perked to the soft, distressed sounds she tried to swallow down, he stalked after her.

"Kate." He leaned a shoulder against the doorframe and folded his arms across his chest.

She paused in the hallway with her back to him, her posture curling in on itself. The call to her friend marked the point of no return. A decision that would haunt her until she died.

She made a deal with the devil, and in the end, the devil always won.

"You wanted two promises from me." He rested a hand in his pocket and touched the finger blade. "The one you chose guarantees Tate's freedom while sentencing you to a lifetime in captivity. Or worse. Nothing is stopping me from killing you and hiding your body. Your friends will be none the wiser."

"I know." Her rigid back contracted with the heave of her breaths.

"That was your second request, the promise you didn't choose. You wanted my word to keep you alive after the phone call."

"Yes."

She didn't beg or cower. Didn't turn around to see if death was coming. Instead, she placed one foot before the other, eyes forward, and slowly walked to her room.

From his stance in the doorway, he watched her crawl onto the mattress and curl up on her side. With a strange pinch in his chest, he closed the door to his room and locked it.

Tomorrow, he would release her from the confinement of the second floor.

But she would never be free.

If she tried to run, he would kill her.

SEVEN

The next day, Tiago woke before dawn with a sense of levity pulling at his lips. The pounding in his head had abated. His vision was clear. No signs of dizziness. For the first time in a month, he didn't feel like an invalid.

More than that, he had something to entice him out of bed. Something beyond the obligations of running a criminal organization.

His gaze clung to the door as he rose to his feet and stretched. Was she still asleep?

He envisioned all that golden hair fanned out around her serene face. As he showered and groomed, he imagined what her fair skin and angelic blue eyes would look like in the daylight.

By the time he slipped on his boots and stepped into the hall, he was starving for a glimpse of her.

The sun had just risen, spilling faint light into the antechamber, where he found Kate on the bed. Not asleep.

The mattress sat on the floor, and she knelt at the end of it. With her back to him, her hair fell in wet tangles from a recent shower.

"Come on, dammit." She bent over her knees, scrubbing the bed with a towel. "Fucking shit."

He prowled closer, craning his neck to see around her. "What are you doing?"

Her hands froze, and her head shot up. She didn't glance back or meet his eyes as he moved to stand beside her.

She returned her attention to the bare mattress and the red spot at the center, working the towel over the blotch. All her huffing and rubbing only made the stain worse.

"What happened?"

"What's it look like?" She threw the ruined towel aside. "I started my period."

"Is this the first time?"

She shot him a bland look.

His groin tightened. Her bitchiness did nothing to negate how goddamn striking her eyes looked in the sunlight. Iridescent shades of blue glimmered beneath long, thick lashes. As he continued to stare, her delicate nose twitched, and her full, pouty lips curved downward.

"Answer the question." He strode to the doorless bathroom and checked the supplies. Shampoo, soap, toothpaste, toilet paper...

She climbed to her feet, watching him rummage through the shit under the sink. "This is my first period since I've been here."

It had been a lifetime since he'd given any thought to a woman's cycle. "You've been here for..."

"Thirty-six days." She blew out a breath. "Stress fucks with the body, in case you didn't know."

Boones would've prepared for this, though he'd done a piss poor job of dressing her. She wore another one of those strapless rags, the linen thin enough to reveal the dusky color of her nipples. The style had been practical when her arms were bound, but *Christ*.

He forced his gaze away, irritated by the distraction.

"We'll eat downstairs." He headed to the door and removed the key from his pocket. "You're free to explore the house and grounds."

Her eyes bulged, her whisper a halting, disbelieving exhale. "Really?"

"If you try to run or attack anyone here, you'll pray for death long before I'm through with you. Get me?"

"I get you." She swallowed. "Does Tate know I'm with you?"

"No." He unlocked the door and found Arturo waiting on the other side, as expected.

The six guards on-site spoke both English and Spanish. Tiago was fluent in many languages but primarily used English.

"When she's outside of this room, she doesn't leave your sight." He strode past Arturo and took the stairs to the ground floor.

The wooden steps groaned beneath his boots, and dry heat seeped from the cracks in the stone walls. More stone greeted him on the main level. Old and musty, the building was erected to withstand the arid climate, without comfort in mind. It was barely habitable, let alone anesthetically pleasing.

When he purchased it years ago, he updated the utilities and brought in enough mattresses to house an army. The isolation of the desert made it ideal for a temporary hideaway, and its solid stone exterior should hold up against gunfire. Hopefully, the latter wouldn't be tested during his stay.

A peek through the gap in one of the covered, barred windows confirmed everyone on patrol was positioned appropriately. Spread out around the perimeter, three men vigilantly watched the horizon.

He crossed the main room, passing a row of mattresses. The night shift occupied two of the beds, both guards sleeping soundly.

The large space opened to the kitchen, where Boones sat at the table with his gaze on a laptop.

"You're still on bed rest," the old man said in perfect English. His eyes didn't lift from the screen as he switched to Tigrayit, the Afroasiatic language of his people. "Go back to your room before I—"

"Before you what?" he asked in the same tongue. "Are you going to hit me with those brittle, antique sticks you call arms?"

"Idiot. Suit yourself. When you die—"

"Yeah, I know. You're taking all my money and moving to Florida."

Boones laughed softly, a deep comforting sound. "Where's the girl?"

"Bleeding all over the bed."

The laptop slammed shut, and Boones shoved to his feet. "You've been out of your room all of five minutes, and you're already butchering—"

"She's alive, asshole." He smirked, enjoying the opportunity to rile Boones. "She bleeds every month."

Boones studied him with dark, incisive eyes. Had things gone differently with Kate last night, they would be having a different conversation. Nevertheless, Boones knew her life still hung on a fragile leash. He didn't like it, but it was the way of this world. He accepted that the day he fled Eritrea.

"I'll take care of it." Boones approached, his expression morphing into that of a doctor as he looked over Tiago's head. "You need to sit."

"I need clothes, for her *and* me." He remained standing. "Jeans, t-shirts…"

Boones made a humming noise and prodded a finger around the skull wounds. "Any dizziness this morning? Double vision?"

"No. Add gym shorts and running shoes to the list."

"I didn't approve exercise. Your body needs time to heal and—"

"I need my strength back." He pulled away from Boones' examination. "Stop coddling."

The stairs creaked, and he turned toward the sound.

Kate descended with tentative steps, her eyes taking in her surroundings as Arturo followed closely behind. When she reached the kitchen, Tiago gestured at the massive man at her back.

"Arturo will be your constant shadow when you're out of your room." He clamped a hand on the old man's bony shoulder. "You met Boones."

She offered a tight smile that faded quickly.

"I have a closet stocked with supplies," Boones said in English and motioned for her to follow him to the back wall.

She trailed after him, her movements lissome and unintentionally seductive. She was surrounded by violent criminals, her future dark and nebulous, yet she held her shoulders back and spine straight.

As Boones filled a plastic bag with feminine products, she stood beside him, discreetly scanning the kitchen from beneath the veil of her hair. It wouldn't be hard to find knives, scissors, or any number of things scattered around that could be used to stab or strangle.

Arturo would be on her before she managed to slip even the smallest needle beneath her dress. But Tiago appreciated the fight blazing inside her. He savored it, riveted by the way her hand twitched at her side and how her small toes gripped the stone floor. She had grit.

"I put some weights in the backroom," Arturo said, breaking his trance. "When you're ready to work out again."

Boones glanced back at that, the wrinkles around his eyes deepening with disapproval. But he bit his tongue. He never berated or argued with Tiago in front of others, because he understood the importance of setting an example. Respect was paramount in running a gang.

When Boones shooed her away, she carried her supplies back to her room with Arturo on her heels.

Tiago waited for the door to shut upstairs and switched back to Boones' native language. "Do you have an update on Lucia?"

"She's still working her way along the coast."

"With Cole Hartman?"

"Yes." Boones ambled through the kitchen, setting out a skillet and gathering eggs.

"I need to speed up her search." He explained the promise he made to Kate and the phone call to Liv Reed. "If Lucia doesn't find Tate in six months, I have to release him, which defeats everything I set into motion."

"Let go of this fixation, son. It's not healthy."

He crossed his arms, refusing to engage in another argument about this.

"All right." Boones cut his eyes at him. "What are you suggesting?"

"Leave some bread crumbs. She's looking for the picture on Tate's back. Pay some of the locals in the surrounding towns to tell the story about the *Medio del Corazón* monastery to anyone asking about gates. Once she hears the folklore, she'll know to look for him there."

"Very well. Anything else?"

He ran a hand over his partially-shaved head and eyed the gray fuzz that Boones kept religiously trimmed on his scalp. "Where are your clippers?"

"Bathroom." Boones thrust a thumb over his shoulder.

He strode down the hall, found a zippered black pouch of barber supplies, and exited the bathroom without a glance at the mirror. When he returned to the kitchen, Kate was on her way down the stairs.

She ate her eggs and toast in silence while he conferred with Boones and Arturo about business in Caracas. As they conversed in languages she couldn't interpret, Boones seemed more interested in her presence than Tiago's month-long absence from the city. His questions about her were relentless.

What do you plan to do with her? Will she return with us to Caracas? Is she a replacement for Lucia?

Since Tiago didn't have answers, he didn't give any and instead shifted the conversation back to border issues and smuggling routes.

As they wrapped up the meal, one of the night shift guards climbed out of bed and shuffled into the kitchen, scratching his bald head.

"I thought I smelled breakfast." The man did a double-take at the table, his tattooed eyes fixed on Kate before darting to Tiago. "*Jefe.*" He straightened and held his arms at his sides. "It's good to see you up and around, sir. You look well."

With a nod, Tiago turned to Kate, who sat stiffly beside him with her jaw hanging open. "Kate, this is Blueballs."

"Blueballs," she echoed, staring at the man's blue eyeballs.

Blueballs grinned and widened his eyes to give her a better look.

"How did you...?" She pointed at the freakish coloring of ink that turned the whites of his eyes bright blue.

"The dumbass tattooed his sclera." Boones stood and carried his dishes to the sink. "He's lucky he's not blind."

"Hey! I'm a professional." Blueballs shifted back to Tiago. "Speaking of... I'll get started on Tate's tattoo today."

"What?" Kate gasped. "Is he here?"

Tiago clenched a fist under the table, seconds from cutting the tongue out of Blueballs' blabbing mouth.

"No, he's..." Blueballs paled, gripped the back of his neck, and recovered quickly. "It's a long drive, so I need to head out soon."

When he dared a glance at Tiago, his stupid blue eyes didn't blink. He'd fucked up, said too much, and knew the consequences. He wouldn't be walking out of here alive.

Kate slumped against the back of the chair, watching Blueballs with a downcast expression. "When you see Tate..." She sniffed and rubbed her nose. "Please, be kind to him. He's suffered enough."

If she hadn't bought the lie about Tate's location, she would've shown signs of edginess and glanced at the door, itching to escape and save her friend. She wouldn't need to run far to stumble upon the gates of the monastery and the shack behind it.

But she believed Blueballs, and her gullibility just saved his life.

"You heard her." Tiago turned back to his breakfast. "Better get going."

"Yes, sir. Thank you." Blueballs made a beeline out of the house.

Without another word, Kate moved to the sink and started on the dishes. During her preoccupation with the task, she didn't notice the container of food Boones slipped into his medical bag.

A moment later, he left without announcing his departure. She had no idea he was on his way to deliver breakfast to Tate.

Keeping her in the dark about Tate's location wouldn't be easy. If she knew he was less than a mile away, there was no telling what she would risk in her attempt to see him.

The solution was to return to Caracas as soon as possible, take her with them, and leave someone here to care for Tate. But Tiago couldn't return until he built some of his strength back. He needed to be able to run when necessary, hold a weapon without tiring, and trust that his vision wouldn't crap out on him.

He needed another week of recovery. Maybe two.

She finished the dishes and turned away from the sink, staring at him expectantly. "I'd like to step outside for some fresh air."

"You'll cut my hair first." Tiago nodded at the trimmer kit on the table.

"Me?" She shrunk back in revulsion and glanced at Arturo. "Why can't he do it?"

Arturo leaned against the wall, supervising her every move with a deceptively bored expression.

"I said you're doing it." He cast her a hard glare.

"You want to put scissors in my hands?"

"Yes, unless you know another way to cut hair." He unzipped the black pouch full of barber accessories.

She stepped forward, eyes zeroing in on the shearing tools. When she reached his chair, her fingers floated over a pair of sharp blades, lifting them.

"Use this on the sides." He removed the cordless clippers and set it on the table beside her.

She edged closer, but not close enough. He gripped her waist and tugged, wordlessly ordering her to stand in the *V* of his spread knees.

Her rigid, narrow-shouldered body felt surprisingly curvy beneath his hands. He pulled her another step into his space, and the tantalizing scent of her skin met his nose.

Goddamn, she smelled fantastic. His position in the chair put his face inches from her chest, and at this proximity, the white linen dress was see-through. If she knew he was ogling the supple rings of pink around her nipples, she would be mortified.

She had a modest way of holding herself, as if unaware of her beauty and the power it held over the opposite sex. Her innocence only made him harder.

As she lifted her hands near his head, the round shape of her tits filled his view, drying his mouth. A glance lower revealed the apex of her thighs and the shadowed patch of hair there. No panties. *Fucking torture.*

The dress fell to mid-thigh, and her bare cunt was right there for the taking. The idea locked things up inside him and scrambled his brain.

He jerked his attention back to her face. Her gaze narrowed on his hair, calm and astute. Her fingers flexed around the scissors, her hands hovering out to the sides.

"Do you know what you're doing?" he asked.

"Sometimes, I shave my asshole. This isn't any different."

Arturo choked on a laugh and coughed into his fist.

The mention of her asshole painted a glorious picture in Tiago's mind—her body spread out before him, her little pucker taking his cock, clenching and dripping with his come.

She called to his testosterone, summoning the most primal part of him to mount, fuck, bite, cut, carve, and make her bleed.

He bit down on a groan, his skin hot and itchy. Christ, he was starting to sweat and needed to get a handle on this. *On her.*

Reaching up, he yanked down the top of her strapless dress and held the fabric tight around her waist.

"What are you doing?" She shrieked and flailed her arms.

He caught the hand that held the scissors, plucking them from her fingers.

"Stop!" She flattened her palms over her exposed chest and twisted, trying to escape his grip on her clothes. "Let go."

He wrangled her arms down and restrained them behind her, holding her wrists in one fist. All that soft, feminine flesh was so damn tempting. He wanted to sink his teeth into her heaving tits, mark her, claim her. But that wasn't how he did things.

Maybe he'd allow himself to touch her, but if anyone fucked her, it would be his guards.

"Do you think she's pretty?" he asked Arturo.

"Very much, *Jefe.*"

She shook her head rapidly, her breaths coming hard and fast, bouncing her gorgeous rack.

He traced the scissors across the slope of one breast, taunting her as he asked his guard, "Do you want to fuck her?"

"More than anything." Arturo stood straighter, interest smoldering in his eyes.

"No, please. Don't do this." She fought harder in his hold.

He yanked her against him and pressed the closed blades of the scissors against her pussy, with only the thin layer of linen between her delicate skin and the steel edge.

"If you cut me, draw blood, or disobey me in any way, Arturo will fuck your ass." He adjusted his grip, angling the sharp tip against her tight, little opening. "When he's finished, I'll yank out that tampon and fuck your cunt with the scissors."

EIGHT

Oh God, oh fuck, oh fuck.

Kate's breath escaped in a shuddering wave, and her heart banged painfully in her chest. Tiago's ruthless grip on her wrists made her bones ache, but it was the scissors he held against her vulnerable flesh that had her shaking to the point of nausea.

"I won't disobey you. I swear. I'll do whatever you say." She lifted on tiptoes, unable to escape the bite of steel between her legs. "Please. You're scaring me."

"Good." He set the scissors on the table, released her hands, and combed his fingers through his hair. "Even up the sides and trim the top."

Black spots blotched her vision, and she swayed on wobbly legs. Wrapping her arms around her waist, she fought the compulsion to cover her exposed breasts.

The malicious glint in his eyes promised every horror he'd mentioned if she dared to hide her body.

She'd spent weeks in Van's attic, crawling naked on the floor in front of Van, Liv, and Josh. It'd been four years since then, since *anyone* had seen her nude, but she hadn't forgotten how to cope with the humiliation.

Lowering her arms, she focused on facts rather than feelings. She wouldn't die from embarrassment. Tiago pulled down her top to degrade her, but it wouldn't kill her.

She needed to be more resilient and think twice before striking back. For every awful setback and torment he put her through, she would just have to stand stronger, aim higher, and remain true to who she was and what she believed in. He could cut her open and mangle her body, but he could never destroy *her*.

Slowly, her breathing returned to normal, and the tremors faded from her limbs. When her heart settled into a calmer rhythm, she picked up the scissors.

The first brush of her hand through his hair made her sick. She didn't want to touch him, didn't want to give him a damn thing, especially not a haircut with her tits hanging out.

But she powered through it, ran numb fingers through the thick, inky strands, and started clipping.

Growing up in poverty with three older brothers, she used to cut their hair all the time. Basic styles. Practical. Nothing sophisticated or attractive, like what a man with Tiago's wealth and power would expect.

He dressed like a billionaire playboy in his crisp collared shirt, open at the neck, and dark fitted slacks. The cuffs of his sleeves buttoned neatly around strong wrists, his long fingers resting on his thighs.

He didn't have a bulky build, not compared to Arturo or Van Quiso, but he was solid and *tall*. She had to stretch to see the crown of his head, even in his seated position.

As she carefully measured and snipped each section of hair, he didn't leer at her bare chest or grab her ass. He was too controlled for that, too debonair and confident.

But put a weapon in his hand and all bets were off.

The more hair clippings that fell to his shoulders, the more she feared him. If he hated the style, he would kill her. If she accidentally nicked him or bumped his injuries, he would kill her. If she took too long and overextended his patience, he would kill her.

She was a human being with an expiration date, just like everyone else. But her expiration jumped closer with every movement she made. By the time she finished trimming the top of his head, her nerves were frayed and brittle.

His hair spiked in tousled, voluminous layers, each shiny black strand perfectly cut and finger-raked. She still needed to clean up the sides, but damn, it looked professional. The shorter, textured style made the angles of his shadowed jaw seem squarer, his eyes deeper and darker.

Those eyes beckoned like mysterious doors. As she gravitated toward them, they dipped, focusing on her mouth with too much attention.

She looked away and set down the scissors. "What happens if you don't like it?"

"It's just hair." His fingers captured her nipple in an agonizing vise, wrenching her gaze back to his. "If it looks like shit, shave it all off."

She pretended to ignore the stinging burn he'd inflicted on her breast and considered his words.

TAKE

He wouldn't kill her over a haircut? That was a relief, *if* he was telling the truth.

Last night, he said he wasn't interested in fucking her. But his fingers told a different story as they meandered along the material gathered around her waist. His other hand joined in, and he inched the top of the dress lower, lower, baring her abdomen and the tips of her hipbones.

She held her breath as he lightly placed a palm over the reddish area on her stomach where he'd kicked her. His gaze lifted, narrowing on hers as he pressed his fingers against the soreness.

Her breath rushed out, but she didn't whimper or show signs of distress. Maybe he wouldn't rape her, but that didn't make it easier to share the same air as him.

He was an aficionado of pain, and she was here to absorb the hurt, to wear the bruises of his *art*, until she escaped or died.

The thought was crippling.

She grabbed the cordless clippers and threw herself into completing the task. He sat quietly as she trimmed, shaped, and scattered tiny hairs to the floor. To avoid grazing his wounds, she had to lean in, which felt like she was putting her face next to the jaws of a lion.

He even smelled intimidating. With her nose so close to his neck, she detected notes of cypress, vetiver, and leather, all bound up in the heady scent of an alpha male.

She stepped back, unable to endure another whiff of Tiago-infused air. But there was no escaping his presence. He was everywhere, all around her, overwhelming and watchful. Always watching with those dark, dangerous eyes.

"I'm finished." She glanced around for a mirror, her throat tight. "Do you want to see it?"

With a grunt, he skimmed a palm over his scalp.

"Feels fine." He stood and unbuttoned his shirt as he addressed Arturo. "If she goes outside, keep her within eyeshot of the house. I'll be in the backroom."

She'd overheard Arturo mention something about weights. What were the chances she could slip in there while Tiago worked out, steal a dumbbell, and finish the job Lucia had started?

He loosened the cuffs of his sleeves and stripped the shirt. The tank top underneath followed, revealing a heart-stopping landscape of muscle and scars.

The welted designs on his forearms stretched around his biceps and faded at his shoulders. His slacks hung low on narrow hips, his torso a scar-free, concrete wall of virility.

This man had spent the past month in bed? Impossible. He didn't have an ounce of fat on his body. No flab or loose skin. Nothing that resembled weakness or poor health. The last thing he needed was a damn work out.

God help her, she was in trouble.

When she'd stormed into his room last night, she'd been blinded by rage, empowered by the possibility that he was old and out of shape, and floating on the hope that her friends would come. She had none of that now.

Her future rested on the whims of a criminal. A crafty, cold-hearted, beautifully-sculpted criminal, who would end her life without a second thought.

His gaze grabbed hers as he shook out his shirt, draped it over the chair back, and lowered his hands to his belt.

She gave him an incredulous look. If he needed to remove his pants to lift weights, why couldn't he wait until he was in the backroom?

Watching her unnervingly, he slipped the strap from the buckle and emptied his pockets. Keyring, phone, wallet—everything went on the table. Then he toed off his boots and lowered the zipper of his fly.

She didn't want to do this with him. She didn't want him to remove his pants while gazing into her eyes. It felt personal. Intimate. She couldn't breathe.

But looking away would be a sign of submission. Van had taught her that.

So she held fast to that eye contact. She stared as he slowly closed the distance between them. She stared until he ducked his head and dragged his nose across her cheek, her jaw, her mouth, *smelling* her.

She pinned her lips together and remained motionless as he lifted the top of her dress and straightened it into place.

Once her chest was covered, he stepped back and dropped his pants. An arrogant smirk kicked up the corner of his mouth.

She winged up a brow, refusing to glance down or give him a dramatic reaction.

His smirk transformed, curving into a handsome, breathtaking grin. It softened his eyes and altered the very air around him, making him unrecognizable. One smile, and he could be mistaken as human. A hot-as-fuck human with the capacity to shift and melt things inside her.

Holy bejeezus. When he wasn't scaring the piss out of her, he was sucking her in with his glowing charisma.

Lucifer had charisma. It was easy to be both repulsed by evil and drawn to its power. She would do well to remember that.

He tossed his pants on the chair beside the shirt and glanced at Arturo. "Inform Boones that my clothes are covered in hair."

"*Si, Jefe.*"

TAKE

She waited for him to give her a parting command or threat, but he didn't. He turned away without acknowledging her and strode down the hall, taking every molecule of energy with him.

His command, his influence, his damn magnetism — it created an intoxicating aura around him, freezing her in place as he ambled toward the backroom.

She couldn't look away if she tried. Couldn't stop her gaze from following the ridges of his chiseled back to his trim waist and the fit of the tight briefs across his flexing ass. An unwanted fever heated her skin, and frantic little flutters erupted in her belly.

Why was she checking him out? He was deplorable, mean as hell, and mentally unstable. Pure poison beneath that superficial beauty.

He turned the corner and glanced back, his gaze spearing hers.

Letting her head tip to the side, she plastered on a stoic expression. He already inspired fear in her, and he knew it. She wouldn't give him the impression he was enticing, too.

When he slipped into the backroom and out of view, she glanced around for something she could swipe without Arturo noticing. The scissors on the table? The bread knife near the stove? The keys on Tiago's keyring? His locked phone?

Arturo didn't take his eyes off her as she strolled through the kitchen. She loitered for a few moments, waiting for a distraction, but that only prompted him to shift closer and watch harder.

Giving up on that, she padded through the front room and spied a sleeping woman on one of the mattresses. The sight of the feminine form gave her a sense of comfort. Not that she could trust anyone working for Tiago, but if she had any chance of making a friend here, maybe that woman was an option.

At the front door, Arturo breezed past and led her onto a concrete porch. The shade from the overhang offered little relief from the dry heat.

She stepped off the stoop and lifted her face to the cloudless, sun-bleached sky. Without shoes, the rocky ground burned the soles of her feet, but she didn't care. It'd been a month since she felt direct sunlight on her skin.

There were no sounds, no traffic, no roaring of ocean waves, no signs of civilization in any direction. Unmarked nothingness embraced her with empty arms.

She paced a circuit around the house, examining the barred windows and probing for weak exit points. If she decided to run, the front door would be the only way out. Not that she would make it two feet with the silent, intimidating barricade hovering at her elbow.

Arturo's presence made her skin crawl, especially after hearing him admit he wanted to fuck her *more than anything*.

A shudder gripped her as she returned to the porch and sat on the steps.

"Are we in Venezuela?" She squinted at him.

He leaned against the awning support and said nothing. At six-foot-and-too-many-inches tall, his thirties-something gladiator build backed up the combative vibes that emanated from him.

"How long have you worked for Tiago?" she asked.

No response.

"I'm not comfortable with what you said about me inside." She rubbed her neck. "Please, tell me you weren't serious."

He grunted a huff, and his pockmarked cheeks bounced with sick amusement.

"So it's true." Her face turned to ice, despite the suffocating heat. "He lets his guards rape his prisoners."

"He likes to watch."

NINE

Kate's stomach plunged to her feet.

Tiago liked to watch his men rape women. Of course, he did. He was a criminally insane psychopath.

And she'd been sleeping next to his room for the past month.

Her heart sprinted as she honed in on the car parked thirty feet away. What were the odds she could outrun Arturo, hop into the front seat, and find a key in the ignition?

Not a chance in hell.

She slumped. "Where did Boones go?"

One of the cars was missing, and she hadn't seen the doctor since breakfast.

Arturo stared at the hazy horizon, as if she weren't speaking.

"What animal best represents your personality?" she asked, trying to startle a reaction from him.

His eyes narrowed, but he didn't glance at her.

"I'm thinking a bear." She tapped her chin. "But could you survive in the wilderness?" She sighed at his muteness. "A teddy bear, then."

A raping, murderous, gangster teddy bear.

He crossed a booted ankle over the other and rested his fingertips in the front pockets of his baggy jeans.

"What do your clothes say about you?" She pursed her lips, frustrated by his refusal to talk. "Say something. I dare you. No, really. I totally dare you to utter one word."

He was a statue. A voiceless, expressionless sentinel.

Over the next two hours, she continued to toss out questions, hoping he would bite. She wanted him to slip up and tell her something useful. But the comment about Tiago watching his guards rape prisoners was the only information she managed to coax from him.

The sun beat down on the cracked earth, brutally hot and smothering. Nevertheless, she remained on the shaded porch, preferring the limited freedom of outside to the stale confinement of the stone walls indoors.

Eventually, Boones returned.

As he parked the sedan and climbed out, Arturo straightened, assuming a more attentive stance. She didn't know how many weapons the massive man concealed beneath his clothes, but she wouldn't try to steal car keys from Boones and risk a bullet from Arturo.

Her escape would require more stealth than a grab-and-run.

"Help me with these." Boones handed her several shopping bags and carried the rest into the house and up the stairs.

There were stores nearby? Close enough for Boones to buy all this stuff and return within a few hours? She still didn't know what country she was in. Maybe there was a receipt with an address in one of the bags?

Arturo relayed Tiago's message about the hair-covered clothes in the kitchen. Then he hung back in the stairwell as she followed the old doctor through the antechamber and down the hall to Tiago's room.

Boones heaved the bags onto the mattress and removed the contents. Running shoes, active wear, jeans, t-shirts, underwear... As he separated the clothes into two piles, she realized one of the stacks was meant for her.

She emptied the other bags and helped him sort, unable to locate a receipt or anything that identified her location. "Are we staying here? In Venezuela?"

"This place is temporary." His cloudy eyes glanced at her sidelong. "But we won't be leaving Venezuela."

Finally, an answer!

"Why is this temporary? Where is he going next?"

"You'll have to ask him," he said in a foreign syllabic rhythm she couldn't place.

"Is your accent Hindi?"

He snorted. "No."

"British? South African?"

"No."

"Caribbean?"

"You're getting colder." He shifted back to the clothes. "No one ever guesses correctly."

"You're not going to tell me."

"No."

With a frown, she lowered to the mattress on the floor and helped him remove the tags. "Why doesn't Tiago sleep on a real bed?"

"He prefers to live modestly."

"But he's wealthy?"

A low chuckle creaked in his throat. "He has more money than God."

How much of that money came from blood, drugs, and ransom payments? She gritted her teeth. "Is that why you work for him? He pays you well?"

"Loyalty keeps me here." All humor vanished from his wrinkly face. "Tiago means a great deal to me, and I'll remain at his side for as long as he needs me."

There was a story there, thickening his accent with deep emotion.

"Your markings…" She motioned to the vertical welts on his cheeks. "Tiago has them on his arms. Did he give you those?"

"No." Boones pushed up the sleeves of his linen shirt, exposing a faded tapestry of scars on his dark forearms. "Where I'm from, we believe scarring connects us with our ancestors. It's an ancient tradition, one that's rarely practiced anymore."

"Where are you from?"

"That, I will not say."

Somewhere in Africa, if she had to guess. "Did Tiago adopt the practice from you?"

"I taught him, but his scarification has nothing to do with tradition." He lowered his sleeves and turned back to sorting the clothes. "For him, the scars convey a message."

"What message?" She leaned closer. "What do his scars mean?"

"Beware, there is pain in the world, and you cannot run from it. But if you endure it, if you accept the suffering, it will stop."

"Oh." She let that soak in. "You're talking about emotional pain."

"*All* pain. He carries more than most." He gave her a sad smile and handed her the stack of women's clothing. "Take these to your room and change out of that dress."

She did as he instructed, anxious to wear something other than a transparent rag.

It was interesting how easily Boones talked with her when she couldn't pull a word from Arturo's pinched mouth. Was Boones trying to make her sympathize with Tiago's actions?

Clearly, Tiago had a different relationship with Boones than he did with his guards. He and the old man shared a bond, a history, that piqued her curiosity.

After slipping on cotton panties, jeans, and a soft gray shirt that fit her perfectly, she returned to Tiago's room and helped Boones fold the remaining clothes.

She favored Boones' company over Tiago's, but it didn't stop the monster from occupying her thoughts.

Was he still working out? In his underwear? If she asked him to show her another video of Tate, would the request infuriate him?

She lifted a pair of gym shorts and eyed the new running shoes on the floor. She could take the clothes to him as a gesture of kindness and weigh his mood.

The thought of seeing him made her insides float and drop in a roller-coaster of sensations. He provoked every emotion at its extreme. Terror, excitement, hatred, curiosity, attraction... She really hated herself for that last one.

The reality was she couldn't avoid him. She was stuck here, stuck with him, until she found an opportunity to escape.

"I'm going to run these down to him." She didn't look at Boones as she gathered the exercise gear and headed out of the room.

Arturo waited at the top of the stairs. He let her pass before trailing on her heels.

In the living room, the mattresses sat empty. Where did the woman go? Where was everyone else? She strained her ears, listening. Then she heard it. The deep, gravelly rumble of Tiago's voice in the backroom.

He was speaking to someone in Spanish, the words flowing so melodically it sounded like a sensual song. She followed his timbre, marking the pauses between sentences. He must've been on the phone.

She hit the hallway with Arturo in tow, passing a bathroom. Then a bedroom, where a mattress sat in the corner on an actual frame. Was that where Boones slept?

Moving on, she stepped through the last doorway and slammed to a stop.

Tiago stood near a rack of free weights, one hand braced on the wall in front of him, and the other holding a phone to his ear. With his head tilted back and eyes closed, he intoned a string of Spanish between heavy breaths.

He wore only a pair of tight black boxer briefs, his muscles pumped, veins bulging in his arms, and sweat clinging to miles of shredded, bronze skin.

It was a carnal, painfully arousing sight, potent enough to send her into cardiac arrest. But that wasn't what stopped the blood from pumping to her brain.

A woman with short black hair knelt before him. Her mouth pressed against his abs, teeth scraping skin and tongue tracing the V-shaped indention near his hipbone. Her hands wandered everywhere, gliding down his back, kneading his ass, and trailing his waistband back around to the swollen bulge between his legs.

Every muscle in Kate's body tensed to turn heel and run. Her vision clouded, and adrenaline flooded her system. If he wanted to fuck his security guard, fine. Good. Better that woman than Kate. But why leave the door open? What the fucking fuck?

She burned to smash his face in. With one of those heavy barbells. At the same time, she trembled to scurry away like a simpering, prissy, little virgin.

Fuck.

She hovered in the doorway, holding his sneakers and gym shorts, while Arturo breathed down her neck. Her chest hurt. Her throat filled with cement, and nausea seared her stomach.

There was no rational explanation for her raging disgust. But as his breathing grew deeper and roughened his voice enough to affect his phone conversation, she saw red. The whole fucking thing was making her stabby as hell.

The woman lowered her hand to stroke along his rigid length, and thoughts of murder were eclipsed by the need to vomit.

Tiago's eyes snapped open, and he stepped out of the woman's reach before she made another pass over his cock. Then his gaze flicked to the doorway, locking on Kate.

Fuck him.

She rolled her shoulders back, lifted her chin, and stepped into the room.

He barked a few Spanish words into the phone and tossed it aside.

"Sorry to interrupt." She set the clothes on the rack beside him and met his hungry stare head-on. "Boones got you some clothes, and… You should really wear foot protection while working out."

What the fuck was she saying? She needed to get the hell out of there.

She turned toward the door.

"Kate." His stern voice pierced through her. "Come here."

Her ribs squeezed, and her fingernails pierced into her palms. After a few slow, deep breaths, she relaxed her hands and forced herself to face him.

"This is Iliana." He glanced down at the kneeling woman. "Stand up."

Iliana didn't just rise to her feet. She slithered up his body in a sexual undulation of hips and tits. With a nip at his chest, she pivoted and held out a hand to Kate. The same hand that had rubbed his dick.

No, thanks.

"Do you shake hands with all the prisoners?" Kate asked.

"No, I…" Iliana dropped her arm. "I guess not."

She smiled sweetly at Kate. It seemed genuine. As did the lust in her eyes when she sidled up to Tiago and tiptoed her fingers across his flat stomach.

The woman embodied all the allure of a gorgeous Latino fantasy. Fit body, great skin, beautiful hair, exotic accent, and sexual confidence. She and Tiago looked outrageously perfect together.

"You didn't come in here to bring me clothes." He grabbed the shorts, lifted them for inspection, and slid them on. "Tell me what you want."

She wasn't inclined to ask for anything in front of his lover, but Iliana didn't appear to be leaving.

"I was hoping…" She smoothed a hand over the coarse tangles of her hair. "I want to see a live video of Tate."

"No." He shifted away, punctuating the finality of his answer.

Making the rejection even more unbearable was the woman pressing up against his back and pawing at his body.

Hatred sizzled in her gut like a hot ember.

She hated him.

Hated Iliana.

Hated her illogical jealousy.

She held tight to that hatred, let it carry her out of the room and into the hell that followed.

TEN

Every day was the same. Same prison. Same guards. Same hell.

The ruler of hell spent most of his time working out. When he wasn't grunting and clanking weights in the backroom, he was holding meetings with Boones and his minions in languages Kate didn't speak. Every foreign word was meant to exclude her, to keep her isolated and uninformed.

Her hatred for him endured, strengthened, and all that animosity sharpened her focus.

The problem was, while she never took her mind off escape, her captors never took their eyes off *her*.

Arturo trailed her relentlessly. The other guards formed a vigilant wall around the property. Then there was Tiago. He ate his meals with her, shared the second-floor with her, and watched her with an awareness that raised the hairs on her neck.

Even if she managed to sneak past his sentinels, he would hunt her down before she made it to safety. Then he would kill her. Slowly and horrifically.

She thought a lot about her phone conversation with Liv. Had she been *too* convincing? Had her friends completely given up on her? They probably had all their resources tied up in looking for Tate, as they should. Thinking about him sitting in that shack made her heart hurt.

"A penny for your thoughts?" Iliana sat across the kitchen table from her, smiling over the lip of a coffee mug.

"Nope." She pushed the syllable past the thousand vindictive things she wanted to say.

A week had passed since she walked in on Tiago and Iliana. Every time she saw them together, Iliana had her hands on him, touching him in a suggestive way. He tolerated the attention to a point.

When she tried to kiss him, he jerked away. If her fingers dipped below his belt, same response. But none of that was required for fucking. Which they were doing. Why else would they be in the backroom together every day?

Iliana didn't hide her intentions. She was obnoxiously flirtatious, not just with Tiago but with everyone, including Kate. Sex dripped from every glance and gesture, but Kate sensed something reserved and steely behind the bawdiness.

"You have great tits." Iliana cocked her head. "Every time those little nipples harden, I get wet."

The wardrobe Boones had bought didn't include bras. It wasn't her fault she nipped out, and whenever Iliana brought attention to it in front of Arturo, Kate wanted to rip out the woman's tongue.

Pushing away from the table, she grabbed her dishes and rinsed them in the sink.

"Hey." Iliana caught up with her, leaning close to tuck a lock of hair behind Kate's ear. "I'm sorry."

"Don't touch me." She ground her molars.

"Shit, Kate. It's just…" Soft brown eyes blinked beneath long lashes. "You're so beautiful. I totally get why he's crazy about you."

"What?" Her pulse quickened. "Who?"

"*El jefe.*" Iliana scraped a hand over her black pixie cut and sighed. "Your naivety makes you even more desirable." She glanced at her watch. "Damn. Gotta run, babe. I'll see you at dinner." She turned and winked at Arturo. "You, too, handsome."

Kate gripped the edge of the sink and waited until the front door shut before releasing a heavy breath.

"She has no off switch." She peeked over her shoulder and met Arturo's eyes. "Are you fucking her?"

He shrugged, expressionless.

"Well, your boss is fucking her, too, so enjoy those leftovers." She twisted to face him. "Why did she say he's crazy about me?"

The only thing that moved was his eyes. One slow blink.

"I'm not naive, Arturo." She crossed her arms. "Tiago doesn't get crazy about people. He's just crazy. Period."

No response.

"Great talk." She swiveled back to the sink and tackled the rest of the breakfast dishes.

A few minutes later, something thumped in the hallway. Footsteps sounded, staggering from that direction and closing in. She turned just as Tiago stumbled into the kitchen.

TAKE

"*Mierda*." He gripped his head, his face creased with pain. "I need..."

He pitched forward with a lurch. She tried to jump out of his way, but he landed against her, trapping her back against the counter.

Did someone attack him?

She scanned his sweaty, half-naked frame for blood and found none. "What do you need?"

"Goddamn head. Fucking kills." He let his weight slump against her, holding his skull in one hand while swinging the other across the counter behind her and knocking dishes to the floor. "*Agua...*"

He looked like he needed more than water. He'd pushed himself too hard. Even the healthiest man would eventually collapse beneath the rigorous exercise he'd been putting himself through. But what did she care?

"You're crushing me." She shoved at his steel chest.

"Jusss a *minuto*," he slurred, dropping his brow to her shoulder and breathing heavily.

His proximity saturated her senses, the length of his body smothering her from head to toe. His thighs against hers, the cage of his arms holding her in place, she couldn't evade the heat of his flesh, the stroke of his breath on her neck, and his scent...

Sweet hell, he radiated the scent of a man when the exertion of work warmed his early washed skin. She tasted the potency of it on her lips, breathed him into her lungs, and somewhere low in her core, she *throbbed*.

"Drink." Boones appeared out of nowhere, holding a glass of water to Tiago's mouth.

Tiago pushed off her and gulped down the fluid as Boones rattled off a string of short, unfamiliar words. Despite the calmness in his voice, the old man's eyes flashed with ire.

A conversation ensued between them. It sounded casual to the ear, but she sensed the undertones of a heated argument. It ended with Tiago staggering toward the stairs alone.

Boones watched him go and gripped her arm. "I'll make lunch, and you'll deliver it to him."

"I'd rather not."

"That's an order. *His* order." He pointed at the far cabinet. "Grab the medium pot."

Fifteen minutes later, she trudged into Tiago's room, carrying a tray of heated soup for two, crusty bread, bottled water, hot tea, and various pills.

Her stomach tumbled as she searched the empty space and paused on the bathroom. Steam drifted from the doorway, bringing with it the aroma of masculine soap.

"Tiago?" She willed him to be dressed, even as her mind entertained erotic images of his sculpted, nude physique.

He emerged from the bathroom and leaned a shoulder against the doorframe, his hair wet and body clad in sweatpants.

"Where do you want this?" She held up the tray, staring too long at the mist beading on the hard ridges of his chest.

He gestured at the mattress and gripped his forehead. A hiss pushed past his clenched teeth.

"There's some medicine for the headache." She set the tray on the floor near the lamp and backed toward the door. "I'm sure Boones will come—"

"Sit. You're eating in here." He made the short walk to the bed, dropped to his knees, and collapsed with his face in the pillow. "Fuck."

"Maybe you just need to sleep." She lingered by the exit, rubbing clammy palms on her jeans.

"I won't repeat myself." He angled his neck to glare at her.

"Fine." She strode toward him, grabbed the food, and sat beside him on the mattress. "I don't understand why Iliana isn't in here with you instead?"

"I don't trust the guards in my personal space."

She jerked her head back. "But you trust me?"

"Not at all. Pass me the water."

He drank, refused the pills, and after some grumbling in Spanish, he accepted the soup.

They ate in silence, and with each bite, the pain lifted from his face.

Over the past week, he seemed to be on the mend. She'd caught him holding his head a few times, but he hadn't slowed down his workouts or shown any signs of weakness. Until now.

"Why are you exercising so much?" She collected the empty dishes and set the tray aside.

"I need strength to return to Caracas." He rolled to his back and closed his eyes. "Too many people want me dead."

Her friends included. Except they weren't looking for her anymore.

"You don't have to go to Caracas." She considered his wealth and all the places he could live. "You can go anywhere, do anything, right? Why not retire?"

"I chose this life. End of." He rested an arm across his brow, his expression relaxed, almost sleepy.

She'd never seen him asleep. He kept his door locked at night and was downstairs before she woke most mornings.

TAKE

A peculiar blanket of warmth settled over her, and her fingertips tingled. Why did she suddenly feel so weird?

What were they just talking about?

She blinked, trying to remember as a strange pull urged her to stretch out beside him on the mattress. Something was wrong.

"I think Boones drugged the soup." Holding her hand in front of her face, she marveled at its weightlessness. "I feel stoned."

"Probably. He knew I wouldn't take those pills." He patted the mattress beside him. "Lie down."

"That doesn't make you mad?" She gave in to the heavy weight in her limbs and lay on her side, facing her captor without a twinge of worry or panic. *How weird.*

"Can't be mad at Boones." He shifted to his hip, bending an arm beneath his head and mirroring her position. "He cares."

Fringes of thick lashes swept downward, hooding his brown eyes as he reached across the space between them. The pad of his finger rested on hers, barely a touch, yet it shivered every nerve ending in her body.

She held still, studying his slack expression. He seemed different, less threatening. Normal. Like a person capable of having a conversation without kicking her in the stomach.

"How do you know about my brothers?" she asked.

"Public records mostly." His gaze lifted to hers. "Are you aware all three of them are in prison?"

"No." She waited for a simmer of emotion behind her breastbone and felt only a brief pinch of anger. "For drugs?"

"They were smuggling *cocaína* for a Mexican cartel. Someone ratted them out."

They deserved it. After her mom died, they were supposed to be her protectors. Instead, they turned her childhood home into a crack-house, exposed her to a world of drug dealers and addicts, while chasing away every boy who showed interest in her in high school.

In the end, they were the reason she fell onto Van's radar. He'd overheard them talking about their little virgin sister in a bar, *bragging* about how they'd protected her virtue. Van followed them home, abducted her, and she hadn't seen or talked to them since.

Her hand curled into a fist. "Fuck them."

He pried her fingers open and rested his huge palm over hers. "Tell me about your time with Van Quiso."

"I don't want to talk about that." She slid her hand away.

"I'm not asking." He caught her wrist and used it to yank her chest against his.

She shrunk back, straining to hold a sliver of space between them. "What do you want to know?"

"Everything."

Why not just tell him? He probably already knew the details anyway.

With a deep breath, she talked through the ridiculous requirements Van had beaten into her. Kneeling, eyes down, constant nudity, perfect dick-sucking techniques… She was vague about the sexual training, and Tiago didn't press for details. Just mentioning *blow job* seemed to put him on edge.

His fingers tightened around her wrist with bruising pressure. "I despise that ceremonious BDSM bullshit."

"There was nothing sane or consensual about it." She twisted her arm in the shackle of his fist. "You're hurting me."

He released her, and she rolled away from him. But his arm hooked around her midsection and hauled her back against his chest.

"What are you doing?" She shoved at the bar of muscle across her stomach, unable to move it an inch.

"Go to sleep." His breath caressed her hair.

"Release me." She squirmed in his grip. "I'll go get your girlfriend, and she'll make it real good for you."

God, she sounded snarky, but she couldn't stop picturing him fucking Iliana, pile-driving her against a wall or whatever they did together. Her jaw stiffened, and her insides boiled. She needed that venom to remind her she didn't want to be here, cuddling with a gang leader.

"You're jealous." He dragged his nose along her neck.

She flinched at the sensation, confused by his gentleness. "Captives don't get jealous. They get Stockholm syndrome."

Soft laughter vibrated his chest. "Tell me about Texas."

A safe topic. She calmed down, as much as she could in the iron bands of his arms, and shared some impersonal details about home, highlighting scenery, culture, and local food.

She missed it, her friends, the simplicity of everyday life. The more she talked about it, the heavier her heart grew. He listened without comment, and eventually, the effects of the drugged soup pulled her into a heavy sleep.

When she woke, Boones was standing over the bed with a peculiar look on his scarred face. Tiago stirred behind her, his arm still locked around her waist.

"I brought dinner." Boones pointed a gnarled finger at the tray of tacos on the floor and squinted at Tiago. "Rate your pain on a scale of one to ten."

"What's the rating for *drugged*?"

Boones flattened his lips and blinked. "You're staying in bed."

"Good idea." He pulled her to his chest, fitting her buttocks tightly against his hips and upper thighs. His cock, neither soft nor swollen, rested along the crack of her ass.

And so that was how it went for days. Every hour sanded away the distance she so desperately tried to maintain. She couldn't avoid him, couldn't breathe without his eyes on her.

Because he didn't just confine himself to his room.

He locked her in there with him.

ELEVEN

Kate's demands to leave his room were met with silence. Tiago Badell and his goddamn smugness incited a level of anger unlike anything she'd ever felt. But she'd agreed to obey him. The night she met him, she'd agreed to do *anything* in exchange for Tate's freedom.

For days, he abstained from exercise and limited his activity to eating, showering, and napping. There was no Iliana. No business meetings or phone calls. And no fucking freedom.

It wasn't the confinement that made her feel restless and trapped. It was him.

This lazy version of Tiago was suspiciously pleasant, talkative, and sometimes, he was clingy. Not clingy in a dependent, insecure way. But in a growly, aggressive, bring-your-ass-here way.

The next three days came with some startling revelations. Behind the face of a crime lord was an intelligent conversationalist. They talked for hours on end, analyzing Venezuelan politics, arguing about American football, and while finishing off the tequila, he shared his thought-provoking views on religion, extraterrestrials, and the future of technology.

She philosophized with him late into the night, floating in a bubble of complacency, where she let her guard down and basked in his company.

When he flashed that infectious smile, her bitterness dissolved. When he held her tight against the heat of his skin, she didn't pull away. At some point, her brain decided he wouldn't hurt her, not here in this quiet one-room world inhabited by two.

Even as she knew he hadn't earned that kind of trust, she

struggled to maintain distance. Meanwhile, he seemed to have no trouble keeping his defenses in place.

He napped with her tucked in the curve of his rock-hard body, but he didn't sleep soundly. Whenever she thought he'd fallen into a deep slumber, she would move ever-so-slightly, and those sinful eyes would pop open without fail.

Like now.

"I thought you were asleep." She lay on her side, her legs trapped beneath one of his, and his mouth so close she smelled mint tea on his breath.

He grunted softly and stroked a knuckle along her cheekbone. Heat rolled off that touch, and the air around him vibrated with power and dark suggestions. Her body tightened in response, fearing what he was while aching for what he could offer.

"Christ, you're stunning." He said it spontaneously, vehemently, his expression unguarded.

"Thank you." Captivated, she leaned closer and hovered a hand over the wound near his eye, too scared to touch him. "How's your head?"

"Fine." He curled his fingers around her wrist. "Ask my permission."

The words clogged in her throat, her mouth parched. It was in these suspended moments that he posed the most danger to her, when he made her want things she should never want from him.

Something had happened to him in his past, something deeper and more painful than the wounds on his head. Though he refused to discuss his life prior to Caracas, she ached to show him compassion. She just didn't know how.

"I'm growing impatient." His hand clinched around her arm, fingers biting into bone.

Her eyes felt too wide as the question fell past her lips. "May I touch you?"

He gave an inviting growl and guided her palm to his cheek.

Thick stubble shadowed his face, and beneath the tickle of hair, his jaw felt like solid metal. Not clenched. Just...*hard*.

Were all men so sharply cut and rigid to the touch? She'd only put her hands on Van Quiso and the few boys she fumbled around with in high school. The sensations from those encounters weren't worth remembering.

She let her fingers dip, roving past the squared underside of his chin to explore the column of his neck. Sturdy and so very masculine, he felt as strong as oak and granite, any of nature's most durable materials.

Her gaze darted to his, and the intimacy in that eye contact stole her breath.

"Don't you get sick of looking at me?" She withdrew her hand.

"You have one-hundred-and-ninety-three eyelashes on the top lid of your right eye."

"You did *not* count them." She rubbed the lashes in question.

"Stop." He gripped her arm and drew her gaze to the single brown eyelash stuck to her fingertip. "Now it's one-hundred-and-ninety-two."

A profound *happening* pulsed between them, a metamorphosis she couldn't explain away. It flapped loudly in her chest and sizzled static across her skin, refusing to be ignored.

Maybe she was having a mental breakdown.

"You can't say things like that." She wiped her hand on her shirt.

"Things like what?"

"I don't understand why I'm here."

"We talked about this. You're a payment—"

"No. Why have I been in this room for the past three days? Am I one of your experiments?"

"What does your gut tell you?"

"I only hear my captor, and not once has he told me I'll survive."

His expression closed off, and he rose from the bed. "I need to take a shower."

He wore jeans today, and off they went on his way to the bathroom. Kicking them free at the doorway, he disappeared around the corner, wearing only boxer briefs. A moment later, the shower turned on.

Panic crept in. She'd pricked the bubble they'd been floating in and sent them plunging back to reality. This wasn't some profound happening. He was her captor, holding her against her will. That was the ugly truth.

She climbed from the bed and paced, eying the door to the corridor, the door to the bathroom, and pausing on the jeans he left on the floor.

Her pulse sped up. It wasn't uncommon for him to leave his clothes unsupervised within her reach, as if he thought she were too afraid of him to try anything. Well, fuck that.

She raced toward his pants on silent feet and searched the pockets. Phone, finger blade, keyring, wallet—it was all there.

The splash of water around the corner announced his movements in the shower. She focused on the phone, tried to unlock the screen and make an emergency phone call. It required a code, and after too many attempts, the keypad prompt locked her out.

Shit!

She tossed it aside, removed the cash from his wallet, and shoved it into her pocket, along with the finger blade. Arturo would follow her down to the ground floor. If she could lead him outside, catch him off guard with the blade, cut his throat if she had to, she might be able to make a run for it.

Her heartbeat shot into overdrive, nearly exploding. It was a risk, one that would either set her free or end her life.

Palming the keyring, she bolted out his room, down the hall, and paused at the door to the stairs. Pipes groaned in the old walls. He was still in the shower.

Her hand grew slick around the keyring. One key unlocked this door. The others could've been for the cars, the house, a safe? She didn't want to tip off Arturo, so she tried the handle first.

It gave beneath her grip, and she sucked in a breath. Then she opened the door.

Arturo stood on the other side and leveled his eyes at her. Then they lifted, pointing at something behind her.

Sinister energy crept over her back. The hairs on her arms prickled, and her stomach rolled over in violent waves. Reaching through the paralyzing dread, she gathered the courage to peek over her shoulder.

"You disappoint me, Kate." Tiago's gaze, black as coal, burned into her face from a few feet away.

Dressed in the jeans she'd ransacked, he prowled toward her, holding a bundle of rope. His hair was dry. Not a drop of moisture on his shirtless chest. Yet the sound of water still ran through the pipes.

The fake shower, the discarded jeans… It had been a test. One she failed.

"I'm sorry." She whirled to face him and inched back. "I was scared and —"

The cold, sharp edge of steel caught her beneath the chin, driving her head upward. With a gasp, she dropped the keyring, grabbed Arturo's arm, and teetered back against his chest.

"If you speak or move a muscle without permission, Arturo will slice you open from ear to ear." Tiago tossed the rope at her feet. "Drop your arms."

Tears burned the backs of her eyes and scorched down her throat as she obeyed.

He gripped the front of her shirt with both hands, ripped it down the front, off her shoulders, and flung it aside. When his fingers bumped her bare chest, she bit down on her lip and tasted blood.

She trembled to scream, beg, bargain, to do anything to remove that heartless, frightening look on his face. But it was too late for that. She'd fucked up and wrecked their imaginary peacetime.

Crouching before her, he removed his belongings from her pockets. Then he yanked down her jeans and panties, stripping the last of the clothing from her body.

A feverish chill swept through her, simmering into convulsions that wobbled her knees and dotted her vision.

He didn't grope her or stare at her nudity, didn't so much as look at her.

"Take her downstairs." He picked up the rope and tossed it to Arturo. "Tie her to the table."

TWELVE

Four limbs tied to four table legs, Kate lay face up and stretched open, her nude body arranged like an X-shaped centerpiece for the sick and depraved. She shook so viciously the table rattled beneath her. Because she knew what was coming.

He lets his guards rape his prisoners.

He likes to watch.

When Arturo had dragged her into the kitchen, Boones took one look at her and disappeared into the bedroom down the hall. Tiago hadn't come downstairs yet, but there were two others in the kitchen, staring, *anticipating.*

Iliana perched on the chair to her right with a hand gently massaging Kate's wrist near the rope. If the touch meant to calm her, it was a wasted effort.

Sitting at her left, Arturo braced his elbows on the table and held the tip of his knife against her neck. Dishes cluttered the tabletop around her, emitting aromas of fried meats and stomach-turning spices. She was going to throw up.

Her mouth flooded with saliva, and she swallowed, battling the fear that attacked her so cruelly. She hadn't spoken, hadn't moved without permission, acknowledging the verity of Tiago's threat in the blade at her throat.

Arturo and Iliana didn't speak, either. The entire room held its breath, waiting for *el jefe.*

Too soon, the tread of boots sounded on the stairs, triggering a fresh surge of shivering panic. He strolled into the kitchen, showered, and decked out in black dress pants and a white collared shirt, unbuttoned at the throat.

Trenches rutted his wet black hair from his fingers pushing through it, his jaw cleanly shaved and hard as stone.

Approaching the table, he paused at her feet. A short conversation with Arturo followed in Spanish. Then he looked down and helped himself to an eyeful of her spread thighs and everything intimate and vulnerable in between.

Liquid fire filled her eyes, blurring her vision and spilling from the corners. She glued her gaze to the ceiling, pinned her lips together, and bit back the sounds of her grief.

Since the night she'd been taken from the diner, she knew it would come to this. The past forty-six days had only dragged it out, delayed the inevitable. Crying about it wouldn't change a damn thing.

That was exactly why she'd jumped on the opportunity to steal his weapon and escape. She wouldn't regret the boldness of her actions. She only wished she could dredge up some of that bravery now and face her punishment.

The soles of his boots scraped the stone flooring as he stepped closer and leaned in. Bent over her, he braced his hands on either side of her hips. The heat of his gaze ghosted across her pebbled flesh, his presence a smothering, inescapable force.

Now would've been the time to beg, but a mere swallow jogged her throat against Arturo's blade. Her heart thundered, every thrashing beat a plea to survive.

She didn't want to look into the eyes of the crime boss, but she needed to know. If there was any trace of the man who counted eyelashes and snuggled during naps, maybe she could connect with him, make him remember she was a person.

With agonizing effort, she inched her gaze to the buttons on his shirt, up to the bronzed skin of his throat, and higher to his sculpted lips, straight nose, and the coldest, darkest eyes she'd ever seen.

There was no soul in the depths, no humanity or mercy as he silently commanded, *Don't move. Don't make a sound.*

How could something so evil be so enticingly, flawlessly beautiful?

She'd fallen for the devil's trickery, and now she would pay the price.

Letting her muscles go slack in the restraints, she conceded. There was no escaping his intent, and she would need her strength for it.

"Let's eat." He lowered into the chair between her bound feet and filled his plate.

The meal was an eternal hell. The chewing, the leering, the laughter from discussions in a foreign language… They carried on while she slowly died inside. The one time she glanced down the length of her body, she found Tiago with a knife in his hand, cutting his meat and glaring at her pussy.

He was a psycho with the face of a model in a men's fashion mag. *Please, make this end.*

When utensils finally clattered to empty plates, Arturo started clearing the table.

Tiago turned to Iliana, his lips lifting in a chilling smirk. "Remove your clothes."

A growl clawed up Kate's throat, and she trapped it behind her lips.

Iliana rose from the chair, eyes smoldering as she slowly peeled away her shirt, jeans, and everything underneath.

No matter how hard Kate tried, she couldn't look away. The woman had a body that wouldn't quit, all hourglass curves, heavy breasts, and toned, tanned flesh.

She sashayed toward Tiago and wriggled her way between his chair and the table, blocking Kate's view of what they were doing.

If he intended to hurt her by fucking Iliana in front of her, then... Yeah, that would do it.

Her hatred for him stabbed punishing heat through her veins, spawned from a jealousy that made no sense. She hated him too much to want him. She hated him for making her think that wanting him was even a possibility. She hated him for fucking with her head so thoroughly she didn't know what to do or feel.

Don't give up. How about that? Pull your sniveling shit together and stay strong.

There was nothing stronger than the human spirit. She needed to stop underestimating herself. She'd survived horrors worse than this. She'd obeyed Van's countless rules and restrictions, watched him fuck Liv for weeks, and came out of that experience smarter and tougher than ever. She would survive this.

"Turn around and bend over the table." His deep, husky voice sent her fingernails into her palms.

Iliana twirled in place and leaned into the triangle of Kate's bound legs, with her nose right there, up close and personal.

Kate screwed her eyes shut, but her imagination choreographed Iliana's ass in his face, his fingers between her legs, and his hard prick straining beneath his zipper.

In a burst of anger, Kate jerked her arms, her legs, and twisted her hips, fighting against the rope. Until a knife skimmed the curve of her throat.

She flinched, and her eyes flashed open, colliding with Arturo's narrowed glare.

Don't move. Don't make a sound.

She swallowed a whimper and held herself as stiff as a board.

"Put your tongue in her cunt," Tiago said to Iliana.

Kate's mouth opened on a horrified breath, unable to silence the wheezing from her lungs.

Arturo inched back the blade just a little as Iliana edged closer, focused on her target.

Detestation curdled in Kate's stomach. Iliana might've been following orders, but the woman was going to enjoy every second of it.

Refusing to watch, Kate closed her eyes again.

There was no build up. No easing in. Iliana stabbed her tongue inside, fast and deep, with a harsh suck of her lips. A scrape of teeth. A hungry moan. All of it rolled into a rude, nauseating open-mouth kiss.

Enduring the invasion wasn't physically painful, but humiliation and helplessness built a searing pressure in Kate's throat. Tears clamored in, burning their way across her vision and dripping down her face.

She opened her eyes and found Tiago staring at her from behind Iliana's bent position.

Heat inflamed that vicious glare as he watched with an invasiveness that felt more penetrating than the tongue lashing inside her.

He was doing this, commanding this cruel molestation for his own perverted pleasure. His eye contact struck her with the severity of a fist. She couldn't look away, couldn't hear or feel anything but rage as a million rapid-fire heartbeats pounded into the space between them.

If she thought he had a heart, she'd been wrong. There wasn't a hint of humanity or softness in the sharp angles warping the sick perfection of his face.

The slash of that hard mouth parted, speaking to Iliana without looking away from Kate. "Describe the taste."

"Sweet. Lively. Heaven." Iliana leaned up, blocking the view of Tiago as she met Kate's gaze. "The essence of want-to-get-fucked."

Bitch, Kate mouthed.

Iliana laughed, a tinkling sound of joy. She was in her happy place, stark naked between Kate's legs, with her ass arched in his face like a cat in heat.

He stood and moved his chair a few feet away, positioning himself with a sidelong view of the show. "Arturo."

The massive guard pocketed his blade and lumbered around the table to stand behind Iliana. A zipper sounded, and a heartbeat later, Iliana's mouth fell open in a silent scream of rapture.

Good for her.

She writhed and bucked and bounced her breasts in the spread of

TAKE

Kate's legs. Arturo didn't hold back, his gaze locked on Iliana's backside as he slammed his hips and scooted the table across the floor.

Each thrust evoked the groans of impending orgasm. Their bodies heaved and slapped together, but no part of them touched Kate. They didn't have *his* permission.

She didn't look at him. Not as the scent of sex infused the kitchen. Not as five minutes pounded into ten. But eventually, her eyes moved on their own, rolling in his direction.

He wasn't watching them fuck. His stare fixed directly on *her*, his jaw tight and hands fisted on his thighs.

Fire spread through her, chilling her skin and hardening her nipples. She sucked in a jagged breath, detesting the effect he had on her, hating that he hadn't forgotten she was here.

He was just biding time, tormenting her with it, until he could hurt her in deeper ways.

Jerking her gaze to the rafters, she couldn't help the tears that trickled down her temples and collected in her hair.

Eventually, Iliana moaned and trembled through her climax, marking the end of the pre-show.

Kate's pulse detonated. She was up next.

"Move her to the edge of the table," Tiago said, his voice a languid drip of sex and smoke.

Iliana floated around Kate, adjusting the rope for the new position. As the tension on Kate's wrists released, the bindings on her ankles took up the slack.

Calloused hands gripped her thighs and yanked her to the end of the table, drawing her attention to Arturo. He was still clothed, save for the sag of his pants and the angry, wet erection jutting from his open fly.

Bile hit the back of her throat, and her insides clenched against full body tremors.

He couldn't put that thing inside her. He wasn't gentle. Or small. It would rip her apart.

He stepped between her legs, his fingers biting into her thigh as he positioned himself.

The trembling in her chin shook more tears loose.

Why was she so terrified? It was just sex, just sex, just sex. People did it all the time.

She needed to loosen the tension down there, make her inner muscles more pliable. Liv had coached her about that, hammering on the importance of relaxing the rectum during anal. But her body refused to calm down. She felt as though she were careening toward a complete loss of heart function, breathing, and consciousness.

"Shhh." Iliana put her mouth at Kate's ear. "He's gonna feel good, babe. I promise he'll be the best you've ever had."

She'd never had vaginal sex, anal sex, or any kind of sex. Who knew which hole he would tear open? She only knew she didn't want it, not like this. Not tied to a table, against her will, in front of an audience.

"Fuck her, Arturo." Tiago's voice thrummed with impatience. "Make sure she feels it."

She locked her jaw down so hard it throbbed. The pain flared into defiance, and she twisted her neck, giving Tiago the full force of her eyes.

As he met her glare with a meaner one, she poured all her fear and misery into that shared look. He didn't twitch, didn't react with a trace of emotion. There was no moving him.

In a desperate last-ditch attempt, she let a whisper tumble out. "Please, don't take this from me. It's all I have left."

His spine snapped straight, his expression frozen in malice.

Shit. She'd made a sound, broken his rules. This was about to get a whole lot worse.

Arturo's hips bumped her inner thighs, and her entire body locked up on reflex. She sealed her eyes shut, willing the trembling to ease from her muscles.

His breathing grew heavier, closer, and fingers dug into her leg.

"*Basta,*" Tiago barked. Footsteps sounded his approach, and his next words came from above her. "Open your eyes."

She couldn't look at him.

Keeping her eyes squeezed tight, she angled her head away.

His fingers stabbed into her hair, fisting it near her scalp. Then he yanked, wrenching her face to his and forcing her to meet his terrifying gaze.

He looked at her, really looked for an eternity, as if searching for some answer behind the anguish in her eyes.

Whatever he found there slackened his expression. He released her head and stepped back.

"I changed my mind." Gripping his nape, he swung his glare to Iliana, then Arturo. "No one touches her but me."

THIRTEEN

What the fuck am I doing?

Tiago scraped a hand down his face, reeling from shock.

She's a virgin.

It shouldn't matter. It shouldn't mean anything at all.

But it fucking did.

Actually, the only thing that mattered right this second was getting her away from Arturo, who was standing there with his mouth ajar and his dick in his hand.

"Iliana." He gestured at Arturo. "Finish him."

She crooked a finger, and Arturo followed her into the front room. As she pushed him onto a mattress, Tiago didn't miss the suspicious look she flung in his direction.

Yeah, something was definitely off with him. He never reacted on impulse or emotion. Everything in his life was studied, rehearsed, designed with patience and purpose, and meticulously positioned to prevent undesirable outcomes.

Except this.

Kate lay on the table, motionless, watchful, her face pale and soaked with tears. Long golden hair rippled around her head, and full lips bowed downward, conveying all the ways she wanted him dead. As her steely glare held fast to his, he reminded himself to breathe.

She was the fiercest, most exquisite creature he'd ever laid eyes on, and she was his.

His prisoner.

His property.

His only source of light, glowing through a crack in the coffin of a twelve-year purgatory.

Grunting sounds drifted from the front room, breaking his trance. He fished the finger blade from his pocket and tackled the rope on Kate's arms and legs.

The instant she was cut loose, he tossed her over his shoulder.

There was no reason to carry her. But he was operating on instinct, and for the life of him, he couldn't stop.

He left the kitchen, took the stairs, her warm body draped over his as he navigated each step and turn. Her sweet natural scent was so pervasive his skin heated, and he quickened his pace, speeding toward a delirious unknown.

Every movement was unpracticed, every step uncharted. He had no strategy, no agenda but one.

Claim her.

Blood rushed to his cock, making him thicker, hungrier, more impulsive. He charged straight to his room. Shut the door behind him. Locked it. Carried her to his bed.

The second her feet found purchase on the mattress, she attacked.

In a whirlwind of fangs and claws, she went for the wounds on his head.

Knocking her arms away was easy. Sweeping her legs out from under her and dropping her onto the bed with a knee on her chest took less than a heartbeat.

Her eyes illuminated with blue fire, signaling her next move before she swung a balled fist toward his groin. Even with the warning, that bony-knuckled punch required him to jerk back. She missed but kept coming, flinging herself at his chest with a glorious, bloodthirsty expression on her face.

He caught her, rolled them onto the mattress, and landed with her on her back and his weight pinning her down. But she wasn't finished.

With a battle cry, she reared back an arm, and for reasons unknown, he let her have the hit.

Her fist skidded across his jaw and mouth. He tasted blood, a kiss of pain, and grinned. "That's the only one I'll give you."

"I hate you." She bucked and thrashed underneath him.

"I'd question your sanity if you didn't."

With the rope still tied to her wrists, he secured the ends to the cast iron pipe on the wall. She held her murderous rage behind clenched teeth until he finished restraining both arms above her head.

"You're a heartless kidnapper," she spat.

"Can't argue with the evidence."

"You're a murderer."

"Yes." He put his face in hers and smiled a humorless smile. "I'm the reason people lock their doors at night."

She took a breath, one that seemed to go all the way through her, and released it. "What are you going to do to me?"

"Everything you're dreading and more." He pushed off the bed and unbuttoned the cuffs of his sleeves.

A tear slipped from her eye, but she didn't sob or beg for mercy. She simply glared, and in that single chilling look, he knew she was his perfect match.

Bending at the waist, he removed his boots while letting his gaze travel along the porcelain skin of her thighs, the dramatic tuck of her waist, and the delicate curves of her small breasts. His hunger for her was sharp and sick.

She looked like an angel, her body too pure and ethereal to touch. But she wasn't innocent. Even though Van Quiso hadn't fucked her, he'd put her through weeks of hands-on training. She probably learned techniques Tiago didn't even know existed.

"Explain something to me." He removed his socks, his shirt, and stared down at her. "How are you still a virgin?"

"I'm not."

"Lie to me again and there will be consequences." He unlatched his belt.

Her eyes flashed, and a huff gusted past her lips. "Van couldn't rape me. The slave buyer paid for a virgin."

"That was *four* years ago. Since then, you've been free to spread your legs for any man you desire." Cocking his head, he absorbed her blinding beauty, savored every detail, utterly gobsmacked. "You lived with five hard dicks, and none of them fucked you."

Her face turned ten shades of livid. "There's more to life than sex."

"Not for a man. Your roommates are pussies."

"And tying unwilling women to your bed makes you a man?" She dug her feet into the mattress and scooted back against the wall, tucking her knees to her chest. "You said you weren't interested. Then you learned I'm a virgin and changed your mind? Is that your thing? You prefer your victims unsoiled, so you can be the one to plunder and defile them before you cut out their throats?"

He was many things. Many repulsive, unforgivable things, but she was wrong about this. So fucking wrong on all counts. He'd never fucked a virgin in his life, not even when he lost his virginity at sixteen. He didn't understand the appeal.

Even now, imagining hurting her in that way, taking something so intimate and precious brought him no satisfaction.

Worse was the thought of Arturo or any other *cabrón* touching her.

This inconvenient possessiveness wasn't new. He'd successfully ignored it since the night he met her. Didn't matter that he wanted her with every vile, undeserving bone in his body. He never intended to fuck her.

Until he heard her whispered plea.

It's all I have left.

He would die before he'd let Arturo take that from her.

Of all the women who tempted him over the last twelve years — the parade of virgins, prostitutes, and every level of experience in between — he couldn't fathom why this mouthy, petulant, argumentative vixen was the one who had pierced through the tough, shriveled crust of his dead insides.

Of all the goddamn women, why was she the one he wanted for himself?

He had but one explanation, which wasn't an explanation at all. "You're mine."

"Oh, for the love of caveman clichés." Her mouth twisted into a snarl. "Just kill me already."

Brave words, but she didn't mean them. Her will to survive blazed in the molten core of her being. Not even he could douse those flames. And he wouldn't.

While the rational part of him analyzed all the reasons why he couldn't wrap his life around this woman, the rest of him didn't fucking care.

This wasn't him. This wasn't how he operated.

He flexed his hands, seconds from putting a fist through the wall. He wanted to hear the bones crunch, feel the hot gush of blood between his fingers, and remember the paralyzing pain. He needed to remember his penance.

Tipping his head back, he stared at the rafters, exhaled roughly, and leveled his gaze back on her.

Those destructive blue eyes fired a barrage of animosity and judgment. He could drown in her hatred and rise out of death in the intensity of her passion. Because she wasn't just malice and vengeance. There were so many facets to her he wanted to carve her open, bleed all her layers, and preserve her strength in a canvas of beautiful scars.

Fuck his penance.

He was doing this.

He was going to break his own rules.

Resolve kicked his pulse into a gallop. He whipped his belt free and dropped it. His pants followed. Then he knelt on the mattress, wearing only his briefs.

"What are you doing?" She squeezed her thighs together.

"I'm going to hell, and I'm taking you with me."

TAKE

No mistaking her terror. It drained the blood from her face and saturated the air with the short, frantic sounds of her breaths.

That added another punishing scar to his miserable existence. The past six weeks hadn't been easy for her, and every time he breathed in her direction, he hurt her more.

He regretted what he was and the shit he'd done, but the shame wouldn't stop him. It never did.

A criminal with remorse was still a criminal.

"You're a rapist." She flattened her back against the wall.

"I'm not. But that's about to change."

With her legs free to kick, she swung them wildly, desperately, at his head.

Putting an end to that, he closed his hands around her ankles and pulled. She fought uselessly as he hauled her down the mattress on her back toward his kneeling position. When the rope on her wrists snapped her arms above her, he pinned her knees to her armpits and spread her thighs open.

Everything stopped—his heart, breath, all sound and motion. The room faded until all that existed was the view beneath him.

He stared at her, at her slit, at the dark narrow breach within. His face was just a kiss away as he gazed earnestly, devoutly, memorizing and cherishing her gorgeous design.

The flesh around her tiny holes was so pink and taut he couldn't stop himself from running his nose deep inside the cleft, devouring the scent of sweet torture from her pussy to her ass and back again.

His fingers curled around the backs of her thighs, and all the heat in his body descended south. Fucking hell, he'd never been this hard, this reckless. His mouth watered to taste, eat, and consume.

"Untie me, Tiago. Let me go. Right now!" She jerked her head, the only thing she could move. "I don't want this."

"I know you don't. But I promise, before I finish tonight, you'll experience pleasure unlike anything you've ever felt." He was nothing if not thorough.

"The only thing I'll feel is the seething, poisonous, undying desire to castrate you with my bare hands."

"That's your fear talking. You know I'm right, and the thought of enjoying sex with someone like me scares you more than anything."

"I'm not scared." She sawed her teeth together and roared, "I'm fucking pissed!"

He was going to fuck that temper out of her with only his tongue. It would take a while, possibly hours to thaw her enough to climax. Christ, it had been a long damn time since he put his mouth on a woman. But he had all night to relearn.

Settling in on his chest, he wrapped his hands around her thighs, trapping her legs on either side of her torso.

She went crazy trying to break the position, but he was bigger, stronger, and more determined.

"Be still." He nipped her thigh. "You'll wear yourself out before I get started."

"Fuck you, you miserable piece of —"

He buried his face in her pussy and stole the breath from her voice.

Her back arched as drugging sips of honey flooded his mouth. Her taste, her velvety warmth, the frantic rush of her gasps — she became his entire existence.

Carnal need took over, pulsing through his veins and turning him into a mindless starving animal.

His tongue delved into her depths, curling, licking, and moving on its own. He couldn't control his aggression, and she was too tense to enjoy it, fighting and spitting through every second of it.

She would continue to fight until he drove her to exhaustion. Only then would her anger retreat long enough to free the sexual energy that buzzed beneath her skin.

Eventually, he reined himself in and eased into a pace he could maintain for as long as it took.

Teasing a finger around the entrance of her cunt, he marveled at her silky heat. It felt unreal. Impossible.

He hadn't planned for this, hadn't even allowed himself to fantasize about it. Yet here she was, every inch of her beauty exposed beneath him, legs spread wide, with the intoxicating scent of her sex in his lungs. It wasn't just a new feeling. It was monumental and absolutely necessary.

He had to physically restrain himself from plunging in and decimating the depths of her body. "How often do you fuck yourself?"

"Rot in hell."

He caught her clit between his finger and thumb and squeezed until she screamed. "Answer me, and be specific."

"I...I used to do it all the time. Every night. Before you took me."

"Did you put things inside you? Toys? Your fingers? I don't want to hurt you more than necessary."

"Oh, is that right?" Her tone grated with resentment and hostility. "You want to force yourself on me the non-painful way? Instead of the fun, bind-and-torture-because-it-makes-you-feel-like-God way that rapists luxuriate in?"

He pinched the swollen nub harder.

She jerked beneath him, unable to escape the pain. "Jeeesus, stop! Fuck! I use a dildo. My fingers. Whatever. Just... Please, stop!"

Good, so there was no hymen to tear.

He released her. "You come that way?"

"Yes."

Thank fuck. He didn't have the know-how or finesse to teach a virgin how to orgasm.

Snugging closer into the juncture of her legs, he lightly stroked her inner lips with his tongue, around and around, following the edge of her opening without penetrating.

She was wet with his spit, not with arousal. Using his mouth, he lubricated a finger. Then he kissed her cunt again, deeply, voraciously, leaving enough slickness to slide a digit into the hot, sucking glove of her body.

As he slowly pushed in to the last knuckle, he groaned at the inconceivable tightness, the heat, while battling the overwhelming instinct to climb on top of her and rut like a raging beast.

Her pussy quivered and shuddered against his mouth and hand. Her breathing accelerated. The lobes of her ears turned pink, and far quicker than he expected, her cream began to soak his finger.

Her brain didn't want this, but her libido was powering up, humming to come undone.

He teased her with one finger, then two, determined to send her over the edge before he fucked her. The firmness of his purpose pulsated between his legs, hot and swollen, so damn stiff and trapped at a painful angle against the mattress.

The steady stream of her gasps wove through the room, spurring his tongue deeper as he focused on her pleasure. His teeth scraped in his urgency, and he fell into a zone, lost in her addictive beauty, the sublime fragrance of her skin, and the breathy sounds of her cries.

He ate her for so long his mouth became one with her body, sealed to her delicate, delicious heat. He'd never been so blindsided by desire, so overcome by the need to lick every crease, kiss every curve, and plumb every hole. Her pussy, her ass, no inch between her legs was neglected by his tongue. He couldn't get enough.

He kept the thrusts of his fingers slow and consistent, careful not to overstimulate, chafe, or scare her so much she completely shut down. He could finally taste her arousal, the crisp, intoxicating tang of it telling him her body was reacting.

When her hips lifted toward his mouth, that tiny reflex compelled him to move in closer and sink deeper. He was spiraling, falling, and fucking God, he didn't want it to end.

Where did his infatuation with this woman come from? Somehow, she'd reached straight into his chest and dug up something so vital and needy there was no turning back.

His entire body shook with ravenous energy, his hips grinding against the mattress, breaths panting, and hands clenching so tightly his fingers imprinted on her legs. Nothing compared to this. To *her*. Just the feel of her satiny flesh against his lips drove him to madness.

Time ceased to exist as he kissed her cunt the way he burned to kiss her mouth, as he devoured her soaked flesh until his jaw wore out, as he gorged on her again and again. Now that he accepted this indomitable attraction, he was possessed with it. Ensnared. He would never quit.

Eventually, he lowered her spread legs, let her tired muscles relax, and flexed his stiff fingers. She sagged onto the mattress, boneless and breathless, too exhausted to fight.

With her thighs resting on his shoulders, his hands were free to roam. He caressed her slender hips, her high round breasts, every part of her he could reach, and all the while, his tongue continued to worship her cunt.

He fucking loved her body, especially her tits and the perfect way they fit his hands when he palmed them. He curled a thumb over a nipple, tormenting the taut bud as she rocked her head on the pillow and gulped for air.

But she still wasn't with him. Amid her husky moans snapped the cutting words of *no* and *stop* and *hate you*, reminding him she didn't want this.

He needed her to want this. In fact, his need for her to want this became the most important thing in the world.

"Kate." Her name scraped from somewhere deep and echoed outside of him like a prayer in an empty church. "Let go."

Her glistening gaze crept down the length of her body and landed on his. When their eyes met, it was a connection so welcome it trembled through his chest.

Shifting his mouth to her clit, he flicked his tongue. Drew the nub between his lips. Sucked gently. And never looked away.

That was when he sensed it. The shattered sigh she couldn't hold in. The softening in her bones and muscles. The tiny twitches along her inner thighs. The reluctant longing in her expression.

Her crumbling resistance.

He finally had her.

FOURTEEN

Under duress, a woman would do whatever she could to cope with the pain and justify its cause. Kate could endure physical abuse and all its malicious faces, and she had, many times over. But this? She had no defenses against Tiago's gentle manipulations.

The blade of his tongue ravished her relentlessly, weakening her willpower. The suction of his mouth was cruel in its devotion and so damn pleasurable her eyes blotted with wet stars.

She would die if she didn't come soon.

She would hate herself if she did.

But she might not have a choice. Not with her clit caught between those wicked lips as he suckled and tortured and plotted her ruination.

"Stop." Her chin quivered, and she twisted her arms in the rope, too bone-tired to put up a real fight. "Enough."

The wound beside his eye twitched with the flex of his jaw. It was a reminder that even he had weak moments, that he could be hurt, that he could bleed, just like other people.

All thought vanished as his tongue knifed between her legs, slicing from her pussy to her ass and spearing both holes. His mouth was hot enough to melt iron and tenacious enough to liquefy every ring of muscle he kissed, loosening every opening he violated, and consuming her with one. Simple. Lick.

Don't come.

Don't come.

Everything below her waist felt like warm butter — soft, wet, melted, and gooey. He'd reduced her to a throbbing puddle of lust, and at this point, he could fuck her without resistance. There would be no reflexive tensing, no self-preservation. Her body was enervated, wide open, soaked to the needy core, and humiliatingly primed for him.

Frenzied sparks of electricity swept through her nerve endings, replacing her torment with a passion that answered his.

Good God, he had never-ending passion. Every time he touched her, fevered energy rolled off him and caught her up in the surge. With her arms bound above her, she could only lay there and absorb the frantic caresses of his lips, the trembling reverence in his hands, and the intensity in his dark wolfish eyes.

His hunger blanketed the room, smothered her senses, and turned her body against her. His tongue laved. His fingers adored, and his breathing ran away from him. He was climbing, building to a crescendo, and taking her with him.

Her inner muscles found a rhythm, pulsing, squeezing, knotting, needing. Soon, every part of her locked onto that steady throb, matching it, heightening it, until all she felt was one banging heartbeat against his mouth. It propelled her toward the precipice, gathering, contracting, and launching her in the wrong direction.

No, no, no, no, no!

Tears hit her eyes, clogging her voice. "I won't give this to you."

"Then don't." He reached beneath his hips and shoved off his briefs, the last of his clothing gone. "Take it, Kate. Take it from me."

He set his vicious mouth over her clit, clamped back on, and sucked, hellbent on forcing her surrender.

Her body engaged, glued to those lips, everything inside her heating and tightening without her permission.

Seized by resentment, she glared into the face of the beautiful monster as it bored down upon her, tunneling in with fingers, teeth, and tongue. She scrambled away from the edge. Tripped. Lost her grip. Spiraled.

And fell into his dark hell.

He groaned as she plunged, and goddammit, she groaned back, shaking, writhing, unable to stop the orgasm. Then she screamed, and the world exploded as her consent ripped away, and a ballistic eruption of heartbeats blew apart the darkness in shimmery bands of color.

She came until his breath broke. Until his hot mouth left her pussy to the cool air. Until his bare chest appeared over her, his hands tangled in her hair, and the penetration of hard, heavy fullness raided her body.

She was still coming as he thrust, slamming his hips against hers. It happened so quickly. A single swift stroke, and that was that.

He took her virginity.

Buried to the root, he didn't move, didn't shift those arresting brown eyes from hers. His fist hung tightly in her hair, as if forgotten amid the joining of bodies. His mouth parted, but there was no breath, as if he were paralyzed by shock.

It didn't hurt. She wished it did, so she could focus on the pain. The anger. But all she felt was confusion and sadness. And pressure. The pressure of all of him inside all of her.

His girth swelled against her inner walls, stretching her to the point of discomfort. There was so much of him she didn't think she could hold him in any longer. But instead of feeling the need to push him out, she willed him to move, to slide and rub inside her like her dependable dildo.

Her reaction was so fucked up and shameful she could never speak it aloud. But there was one thing she needed to say.

"Put on a condom." She squirmed beneath him. "Please, don't get me pregnant. You don't want that."

She didn't want that. It would be the worst possible outcome, outside of death.

"I can't have children." Pain slipped into the creases of his eyes and vanished just as quickly. "I'm sterile."

"Oh." Startled, she glanced away, blinking, stalling, and looked back. "What about—?"

"I'm clean."

Of course, she was, too. Clean as a virgin.

But her virginity was gone. The one thing she had left was no more. She couldn't stop herself from mourning the loss of it, couldn't stop the ache in her eyes or the silent stream of tears that ran into her hair.

He watched her, his gaze inches away, chillingly still, barely breathing. Was that look on his face one of contrived regret? Or was it genuine sympathy as the reality of abduction, abuse, captivity, and manipulation rode on the waves of pleasure?

How messed up was she that she craved that pleasure? Not the kind she gave herself at home alone. But a pleasure so filthy and twisted it could only be derived from a rapist's tongue, lips, fingers, and cock as he invaded her body, weighing her down with his sickness, ruining her in the best and worst way possible.

Staring down at her, he just held himself there, his thick cock firmly seated inside her, with a strange expression on his face. He didn't speak, but his eyes didn't shut up, the depths crowded by a storm of churning thoughts. She couldn't read him, not for the longest time. Then he blinked.

"This means something." His breath carried the bladed words, slashing them against her lips.

"No. You're wrong." She didn't want to hear this and shook her head, knocking more tears loose.

"It means something to *me*." He gripped her chin and wrenched her face back to his. "You have no idea."

Then he moved. Tiny, shallow, shaky thrusts. Mouth parted, cords straining in his neck, his eye contact was deafening, broadcasting something she didn't understand.

Soft, secret grunts reverberated from a hidden place inside him. The sounds shivered into strangled noises, reminiscent of fragile things breaking apart. Noises she never imagined coming from such a hardened, vicious criminal.

With a hand in her hair and one framing her face, he fucked her slowly, delicately, as if committing every sensation to memory. He fucked her as if this were his first time, too.

What a ridiculous notion. He hadn't gone down on her like a novice, and he certainly didn't fuck like one, either. But there was an innocent attentiveness in every thrust. A thoughtful slide of motion that implied this was more than sex to him, that it was grave and significant.

She knew she was just reading into his deceptive words and strangling herself with misguided trust. No doubt he fucked Iliana with the same dedication.

"I hate you." She yanked on the rope, desperate to break free.

"Ah. We're back to that." A smile twisted the aroused male's gorgeous features.

His skin was on fire, burning against her. His weight, solid and hard as cement, tacked her to the bed from chest to feet. She registered every point of contact, every quiver that ran through his muscles, every hitch in his breath. All of it affected her deeply, the intimacy shredding and destroying her. She wanted this to be different so badly it broke her fucking heart.

"You're raping me." Another shameful tear slipped out.

The hand on her face glided through the wet track, wiping it away, stroking with too much tenderness. "If you need to hate me, then hate me. Use me. Take pleasure from my body."

"You're confusing me."

"I'm a bad man, Kate. Never confuse that."

She should've nodded her head emphatically. But she could only stare at the stunning paradox of beauty and atrocity that embodied Tiago Badell.

Was he really as terrible as he claimed? Did true evil admit to being evil?

What was she thinking? He was the absolute worst. He'd poisoned Lucia, mutilated Tate's back, kicked Kate in the stomach, locked her in a room for a month, tied her to the dinner table. Raped her.

But he raped her gently.

Gently?

Could that word even be used in this situation?

She was losing her goddamn mind.

"Hate is a feeling." The warm wetness of his mouth brushed against hers. "As long as you feel something, you're with me. I need you with me."

"Fuck what you need." She gnashed her teeth, aiming to bite off his tongue. "Go talk about your *needs* with someone who cares."

His cock jerked inside her, triggering an unwelcome clench in her pussy. He lowered his head, and her pulse jumped through her veins. She tasted his minty breath before his mouth closed over hers.

She tried to fight, lips pinched and neck arching away. But the hands in her hair held her to the pillow, trapping her face exactly where he wanted her.

Then he plundered. Just like when he put his mouth between her legs, this assault wielded the same skill, potency, and seduction. Demanding full lips coaxed and pried until they caught her bottom lip between them, tugged roughly, sucked deeply.

His teeth joined in, nipping in warning, biting when she tried to pull back. The longer she refused to kiss him, the harder his hips plowed against hers. He wouldn't allow her to escape his gaze, his kiss, or the toxicity of his presence.

"Give me your mouth." His voice dropped low, his heavy cock sliding in and out, faster, deeper, scrambling her mind.

She searched for a breath, unable to catch it through her nose. When her lungs burned, she had no choice. She gulped, gasping, and he dove in.

Sweeping past her lips, his tongue hunted hers, lashing, curling, claiming in a vigorous ambush of breathy kisses. He moaned into her mouth, and rumbling vibrations spiked through her, annihilating her pleasure zones.

Her body yielded. Melted. Sighed.

Because the man knew how to kiss. Sweet hell, he knew exactly how to own her.

Every nibble and lick carried just the right tickle, taunt, and floaty, languorous pull. The stubble on his jaw inflicted just the right burn. The firmness of his lips created just the right cushion to caress and bruise. And his taste... Oh God, his mouth burst with flavors that were uniquely him. A fusion of sharp mint, warm caramel, and dark, bold decadence. He tasted like sin.

He didn't just kiss her. He devoured her with his entire body. His hands were everywhere, kneading her ass, coasting up and down her thighs, palming her chest, her neck, her face, and tangling in her hair. All the while, his hips never stopped moving, a constant piston of endless energy and forbidden pleasure.

Frenzied ripples of sensation swallowed her resistance as he stroked his length along her walls, digging in, reaching deep, jerking, and stirring. Tongues locked, hands trailing, cock stabbing, he meant to own her. And in that moment, he did.

It was the kiss. His fucking kiss had the power to crash walls, fuck minds, and bleed souls. It threaded between vulnerable and arrogant, selfless and greedy, polished and primal, silken and brutal, and she sucked it from him helplessly, needfully, knowing it was wrong, which only made her want it more.

He didn't dominate with just one technique. He mastered them all, licking the corner of her mouth, sinking his teeth into her lips, sipping at the seam, sweeping deep into the recesses, quick pecks, long deep perusals, and everything in between.

He kissed her, and kissed her, and kissed her until she couldn't feel her tongue, couldn't unlock her jaw, and couldn't taste anything but him.

When he finally came up for air, she floated in a fog that smelled only of him — his breath, the swollen flesh of his lips, the skin on his masculine face. Even his whiskers had a warm, rough, comforting scent.

Comforting? No, it was…

Familiar.

She'd been naked with him for hours, *with* him in ways she'd never been with anyone else. He was the most familiar thing she'd ever known. The kind of familiarity that cultivated a sense of safety and attachment.

A vein of fear ran through her, sharp enough to shake her from his spell. "This isn't real."

"It feels good and ugly, painful and fucking extraordinary. That's life, Kate. That's *real.*" Lines formed between his dark eyes as he searched her face. "It doesn't get more real than this. I know you feel it."

"It's Stockholm syndrome."

"Don't give a shit what you call it." His accent thickened, sliding across her skin. "Doesn't change what it is."

The frantic wallop of her heart rang in her ears. "What do you call it, then?"

"Ours." He drifted closer and stabbed his hands in her hair, holding her lips to his. "You and me. Wide awake. Alive. This is all we have left, and it's the only *real* we'll ever need."

He captured her mouth in a brutal attack, sucking her in, commanding her heart rate, possessing, always taking. His tongue controlled hers, hot and strong, feral and unstoppable. His terrifying power curled around her, summoning her darkest shame. Promising to fulfill every depraved fantasy. Vowing to hurt and cherish her in equal measures.

Diabolical hands found the flesh of her ass and squeezed aggressively, achingly. Palms inched over her hips, fingers splaying as they skimmed up her ribs to her chest and continued along her arms.

The kiss didn't slow as he reached the rope around her wrists, tugging at it.

He was untying her?

The restraints loosened and fell away, and her breath caught.

She stared into his eyes, her hands lowering, free to grip the first thing she encountered—the hard bulges of his shoulders. She meant to push him away, but he was too big, too heavy, too overwhelming.

She held on, sinking fingernails into puckered scars.

Yanking one of her legs around his hip, he pressed his weight into her body and effectively trapped her against the mattress.

His eyes narrowed, and ruthlessness strewed across his handsome face. "I'm going to fuck you now."

"What? You already—"

"Don't let go."

Then he went off the rails.

FIFTEEN

The moment Tiago relinquished his self-control, Kate realized just how much he'd been holding back.

She lost track of time as he fucked, kissed, and tumbled her over every inch of the bed. It was nothing like before. This was a rebellion of chaos and mastery, thunder and liquid smoke.

His thrusts trailed fire. Fingers bruised flesh. Teeth caught lips, and his sounds lost all traces of strangled vulnerability. He growled and grunted from some deep chasm in hell, roaring like a majestic beast in battle, pounding his cock inside her, fighting to get closer, raging, rabid, and petrifying.

Shredded muscles rippled and pumped beneath her hands. Sweat squelched in the creases of their bodies. Her arousal leaked to her legs and spread between their grinding hips. His, hers, they were drenched in wetness, sliding together and burning up.

His broad torso blocked her view of the room, the lamp light, the entire world as he bowed over her, pommeling into her body with the stamina of a fully-charged machine. Ramming. Heaving. Groaning. Kissing.

His kiss owned her soft parts, her compassion and humanity. But this… This brutal, unruly savage of a man owned something darker, something innately carnal and animalistic inside her. He'd woken her from dormancy, ripped her away from shelter and safety, and preyed on the hunger she couldn't hide from him.

A turbulence of conflict tore through her gut. She feared him down to the marrow of her bones. Desired him with every fiber of her sexuality. Cursed him to the ends of her pride and back.

TAKE

She shouldn't have to remind herself this wasn't consensual, yet as he took her mouth with those fierce, unapologetic lips, she fell in, aching for more, drowning in the overload of his terrible beauty and passion.

"Fucking goddamn." His huge hand cupped the side of her face, stealing her breath and pieces of her soul. "Feels so good, Kate. So fucking honest and real. I need to come. I need..." He pushed deep inside and choked. "I can't hold off much longer."

Hold off? He'd been fucking her all night.

He shoved up just enough to reach between them and rub her clit. His fingers had gravitated there countless times since he began, constantly focused on that overly-sensitive nub. He'd loved it so hard it hurt to the touch.

Then it dawned on her. "You've been waiting for me to come?"

Stormy, hungry eyes hardened and flared, as if he had the right to be offended by her ignorance.

"Well, don't!" She slapped his hand away from her abused clit. "In case you forgot, I was a virgin, and I don't want this. I'm not willing. You've pounded my insides into hamburger. I'm sore, raw, and bruised, and I will *not* come for you."

"You came on my tongue."

Shame. It crashed in from all sides and collided in her gut.

"No more." She pushed at his shoulders, unable to move his bulk. "Please, just stop. Or finish. I don't care. Just do it without me."

"Only with you." His hoarse, gravelly voice brooked no argument.

"I'm with you in all my hatred and venom."

A huff released from his throat, and she heard the relief in it, the smile.

She didn't expect him to relent so easily, but as he folded his arms beneath her back and pulled her deeper into the heat of his body, she felt the twitchy, fiery fatigue in his muscles.

With a hand flattening on her spine and the other cradling the back of her head, he rested his brow against hers and began to drive into her with purpose.

Flexing his hips, he caught a fast, steady rhythm. The warm softness of his tongue traced her lips. His heartbeat thundered against her chest. Breaths heavy, grunts deepening, eyes locked on hers, he chased his release.

She hadn't moved her hands from his shoulders since he'd freed her, but his unguarded expression compelled her to move them now.

Feathering fingertips along curves of biceps and brawny ribs, she suppressed the moan that rose in her throat. Feeling brave, she sought out his hip bones, and around to his lower back, marveling at the sinewy strips of muscle and sculpted grooves she would never find on her own body.

Dipping lower, her fingers bumped the cleft of his ass. Tentatively, she explored the tight divide between rock-hard glutes. Hot and sweaty, his buttocks squeezed with the smack of his hips. Each cheek formed a globe of steel wrapped in silky satin skin.

What a magnificently built man, all bold lines and chiseled strength. And so responsive. He groaned and shivered as she caressed his backside. She knew it was wrong, stroking such a private part of him, especially since she didn't want this.

But she reveled in the feel of his body, feasted on his reactions.

How incredible that her fingertips could alter the tempo of his breathing and spread goosebumps across his flesh. It felt powerful and strangely addictive.

Four years ago, she'd learn how to touch and please a man in every way. Van Quiso had seen to that. But he'd never responded to her hands, and she'd never responded to him.

Why was this so different? The circumstances were the same. Captor and captive. Abuser and victim.

The difference was the man behind the sins. The soul beneath the skin.

The heart of Tiago Badell lay hidden under blood, teeth, and vicious threats, but it was there, calling to her, beating for her. She felt it every time their eyes connected.

Like now.

"Kate." He clutched her neck and tilted up her chin, his thumb stroking the hollow of her throat as he stared, pupils wide, his pelvis slamming her into the bed. "I'm going to blow my load. Fucking fill you up with my come. Tear up that pussy." His accented English stumbled into Spanish, rolling together syllables that sounded like a vulgar plea to God. "Fucking fuck, fuuuuuuck!"

His hips lost rhythm, jerking wildly, and his jaw turned to stone. He pushed up, his gaze dropping to where they were joined as he pumped, coming without sound or breath, the length of his body shuddering, stiffening, strung like a bow.

Then he groaned, long and deep, his eyes finding hers and his lungs releasing in a guttural whoosh. "Jesus, fuck."

She'd never experienced anything like that and didn't know what to expect or how to react. So she just lay there, motionless, quiet, and invisible.

He pulled out and stared at his flagging erection soaked in their combined fluids. Her first glimpse of his cock didn't leave her gasping at the generous length and thickness, because she already knew it so well. She'd felt every fat inch inside her.

Sitting back on his heels, he dragged his gaze over her flushed body, probing, scrutinizing, heating her skin anew. Hadn't he seen enough?

The only blanket had been tossed out of reach. With nothing to cover herself with, she pressed her arms to her sides and met his hooded eyes.

Without looking away, he cupped a hand between her legs. Placing his other over the juncture between her shoulder and neck, he curled his fingers around her nape. A covetous hold. Possessive and weighty.

Neither of them spoke. There were only the sounds of their breaths, the slam of a door downstairs, the wind whistling across the thin roof. And something else. The stillness between them. It swelled with hurtful words, conflicting thoughts, and promises she didn't want him to make.

With his hands at her throat and pussy, he held her there for a long moment as his gaze made a vow he didn't need to voice.

He would never let her go.

Then his face blanked. He pulled away and shifted to the foot of the mattress. There, he lowered to the floor beside his clothes but didn't pull them on.

He sat with his back to her, unabashedly nude, with his legs bent and his arms dangling over his knees. He seemed to be finished with her. At least, for tonight.

What now?

She wasn't restrained, didn't have anything to wear or cover up with. Every part of her ached and burned from hours of his brutal attention. She just wanted to curl up in bed by herself and escape into sleep.

Staring longingly at the door, she started to climb to her feet.

Until his low, creaky rasp shuddered the air.

"My wife was murdered twelve years ago." His voice lapsed to a monotone, and every word pulled his shoulders down, slumping his powerful body. "I walked in while it was happening. Too late. Too slow. Couldn't put her back together. Didn't save her. I failed her in every way."

Ice trickled down the base of her skull, and her throat tightened around a hot ember.

His wife.

He was married.

She couldn't wrap her mind around it, even as she'd known there was *something*. Something horrendous that had left a bleeding scar on his life.

Tucking her thighs to her bare chest, she hugged her legs and watched the painfully slow break down in his posture.

An elbow wobbled on one knee, his head sinking toward his chest with a hand over his eyes. She guessed they were closed, his expression lost in memory. Or maybe his face was as tortured as his body language.

She hated that she couldn't see his eyes, but she didn't dare move.

He was quiet for so long she didn't think he'd speak again. When he finally stirred, it was a jerky movement. His arm moved out to the side, sifting through the pile of clothes and disappearing in front of him again. He shifted, shoulders twitching, his hands fidgeting or doing something out of view.

His silence loaded the space between them, a roaring freight of heaviness, too loud in her ears.

She swallowed. "What was her name?"

His back tensed, relaxed, and he raked a hand through his hair. "Semira. She was a doctor, like her father. Grew up in a small village in…" He cleared his throat, his tone strained with pain. "In a faraway place."

"What happened?"

"Someone I trusted turned on me. An assassin came. Gutted her from hip to hip. Let her insides just…spill out. He made sure I saw her bowels hit the floor as I walked in the door."

"Why?" An outcry of emotions tangled in her chest, and she pressed a fist against her mouth to keep it all in.

"Why does anyone rape and butcher innocent women? Why am I hurting you? Everyone has their reasons. Pain is constant and everywhere. All you can do is endure and fucking accept it."

God, that was heavy. Some of it echoed her own sentiments, slicing like hot knives in her chest. But he didn't just accept the pain in the world. He added to it, made it worse. She couldn't reconcile that.

"Before Semira died…" He hunched forward, further hiding his expression from her line of sight. "I was what society considered a *good man*. I had a lawful job, paid my taxes, and followed all the fucking rules. But there were conversations I should've had with my wife. I should've asked her if she was conflicted about the things I did and the man I was."

So many questions piled up, most of which she knew he wouldn't answer. "Why would you become like the man who had her killed?"

"I didn't. He was my colleague. When he betrayed me, I became the opposite of him. I became his enemy."

"It doesn't make sense. What was your job?"

"This isn't about the job. It's always been about her."

"I don't understand."

His arms twitched with movement, his torso blocking her view. What was he doing with his hands?

"When she looked at me," he said, "she saw what I was. What I am. I didn't even know it was there, this egregious thing inside me. But she saw it."

Had his wife seen the rapist, the murderer, the gruesome artist who carved images into living victims?

She squinted at the back of his head. "You said you were a good man."

"Whatever she saw when she looked at me was neither good nor evil. It just *was*, and it killed it for her. It killed the love she wanted to feel for me long before that knife killed her." He drew in a breath and let it out. "Some men simply have something inside that makes them impossible to love."

"I don't believe that. All humans are capable of giving and receiving love. Everyone has a *someone* out there."

"Semira believed the same when she married me. I loved her deeply, and no matter what I did to earn her love, her feelings never developed. It was hard for her to bear, knowing that while I cherished her above all else, she couldn't bring herself to reciprocate. She wanted to fill that void with children, and I would've done anything to give her that. But I couldn't. It was another part of me that didn't work. Another thing for her to resent."

Jesus. He had years to dwell on this, to let it eat at him, and now his infatuation with the romance between Tate and Lucia had an explanation. It seemed his own failed relationship had fostered a fascination with happy endings.

Was it possible that he craved love?

She wanted to know about his wife's death. It seemed that was the key to everything. "Why did your colleague betray you?"

"Because the good guys aren't always the good guys. Integrity isn't a guarantee, just because you're fighting on the right side of the law."

"So your colleague was a traitor?"

"I can't talk about the fucking job." His voice vibrated with so much threat it stopped her heart.

"Will you just explain one thing?" Swallowing hard, she sat taller and glared at his back. "You went from a straight life to that of a crime lord. It changed when your wife was murdered?"

"Yes."

"You said it isn't about the job, yet the job was connected to your wife's death. You must hold resentment for everything that life represented—the legitimacy of it, the paid taxes and moral righteousness. Could it be that if you let go of that grudge, you might—"

"Be a better man?" He barked out a self-depreciating laugh. "When I held Semira in my arms, with her intestines in her lap and her life spilling through my fingers, it was neither love nor hate that shone from her eyes. The last look she gave me was saturated with pity. Pity for a husband she couldn't love, even in death. Pity because she knew that without her, I would forever be alone, because no one would put as much effort into me as she did. I hated her for that. I hated her pity to the depths of my soul, and I made damn fucking sure no one would ever give me that look again."

He became a monster.

In a deranged, fucked-up way, it made so much sense. Monsters were abhorred and feared, but never pitied. In that, he'd succeeded.

Kate had never felt bad for him. Never felt sorrow or disappointment. Not even now. Because it was inconceivable to think of him as weak or helpless. He didn't evoke that oh-you-poor-thing, head-patting kind of emotion from anyone.

What she did feel was compassion. That innate goodness that most people possessed was what compelled her to sway toward him, filling her with the perverse need to comfort him for the pain *he* had inflicted on *her*.

Talk about messed up. But the more she thought about it, the more she understood. For the first time, she felt a real sense of hope.

Hope for him.

He was a self-aware bully, open-minded and regretful, imperfect and *human*. She could work with that, relate to it, and maybe, just maybe, she could convince him to let her go.

"A terrible thing happened to you." She quietly inched to the side of the bed. "But it doesn't have to be this way. You can change the course of your life. Stop kidnapping and terrorizing people."

His neck slowly turned, bringing the intensity of his eyes over his shoulder to grab hold of hers. "I'll stop being heartless when you stop looking at me like it's the only thing I am."

She emptied her expression but couldn't clear the guilt. It stuck in the press of her lips, accusing and judgmental.

"Or don't stop." He jerked back around. "Either way, it doesn't change your circumstances."

Reality crashed in, banging in her chest. What was she doing trying to reason with her captor? He just fucked her ruthlessly, while she screamed *no* until her throat bled. He didn't give a shit about her.

Except something was happening deep in her gut. She felt this coiling, fierce objection to putting him in a category marked *Irredeemable*. He was so much more than a bad man, and she'd only scratched the surface.

Or maybe she really was just suffering from Stockholm syndrome.

Why had he shared his past with her? Was it a call for help? Was he begging her to see past his imposing, brutal good looks? Or was it a trick? A ploy to engender feelings from her so he could use them against her later?

An unusual sound broke through her introspection.

The plop of wet drops hit the floor near his position.

Plop. Plop-plop.

Was the ceiling leaking? It appeared dry.

Was he crying?

She craned her neck, straining her senses, listening.

The wet sounds sped up. More liquid. A slow trickle.

"What is that?" Chills swept across her scalp as she stood from the bed.

Scanning the room, she scrambled for the closest thing she could grab. His shirt. She spread the crisp material against the front of her body and slowly stepped around him. And lost her breath.

Blood.

Oh God, it was everywhere.

Rivers of crimson snaked along his forearm, forking stained lines down his fingers and dripping to the floor.

Hot red splatters. There were so many dots between his feet they overlapped.

She teetered, lightheaded, and focused on the source of the bleeding.

A razor. He wore that damn finger blade like a claw, dragging it over old scars.

"What are you doing?" she whispered.

He was cutting and not answering her, because it was a stupid question.

She took a shaky step closer. "Why?"

"Punishment." His voice lacked all emotion, and the blade continued to carve.

Balling a fist in the shirt, she clutched it tighter against her chest. "Punishment for what?"

"You."

She flinched, and her gaze flew over the scars on his arms. So many marks. Faded ones. Newer ones. "Do you do this every time you fuck a woman?"

The razor paused. He lifted his head, his expression empty, voice emptier. "The last person I had sex with was my wife."

"What?" Her naïveté plummeted to the floor and shattered. "That was—"

"Twelve years ago." He returned to his cutting.

"You haven't had sex in twelve years?"

"That's what I said."

She recalled how incredibly experienced he was in bed and stared at him in disbelief. "You're lying."

His nostrils flared, and he dug the razor deeper into his arm.

Thick droplets oozed free, flowing off his skin and soaking the flooring.

Dark red against dark wood.

The scent of copper in the air.

She wished it would stop. She needed it to stop.

"Tiago, can you just…" Now within reach, she stretched an arm toward him and held the other against her chest, trapping the shirt. "Please, just stop for a second and talk to me."

He looked up, stared blankly at her face then her outstretched hand. She wanted to yank her arm back, but she refused to look scared, even if everything inside her screamed to run.

His bladed finger twitched as he raised his slashed arm and curled a bloody hand around her wrist. He pulled, forcing her to shuffle into the space between his legs.

The soles of her feet sopped up the gore on the floor. She tried not to think about that, and instead focused on what he'd said.

"You fucked Iliana." She held her arm still in his grip. "In the backroom, every day."

"I've *never* touched that woman."

Cycling through her memories, she couldn't identify a single time he put his hands on Iliana. Not even tonight in the kitchen. It was always the other way around.

"She's all over you," she said.

"Iliana throws herself at everyone." His fingers tightened around her arm. "She will *never* touch you or me again."

"What about Lucia?" She squinted. "She was your captive for eleven years. You can't tell me nothing happened."

"I touched her body and imagined my wife, but I never kissed her. Never fucked her."

He released her wrist and yanked the shirt from her grasp. Blood-soaked fingers curled around her hip, and he lowered his head, touching his brow to her stomach.

Was he staring at her pussy? Or were his eyes closed? She kept her attention on his bladed finger and held her breath.

"When I was with you tonight, I didn't think about Semira. Not once." He pressed his lips to her belly button. "Celibacy was my penance for failing her. It was my choice. Until you."

He broke his twelve-year abstinence. For her.

It means something to me.

As if pulled by an invisible string, her hand floated toward his head, where his soft hair lay against her abdomen. Before she made contact, she snapped out of the enchantment and dropped her arm. "Why me?"

In a swift glide of powerful muscles, he unfolded his body and rose to his full height, towering over her, completely nude. "You're mine."

Mine. That fucking word set her teeth on edge. He could say the same about this house, his security guards, the stupid blade on his finger. He could take his property and all his precious little possessions and shove them up his ass. She refused to be one of his belongings.

Stretching her spine, she tried to add length to her height, to stand taller than eye-level with his chest.

"Why did you cut yourself?" She lifted her face. "What was the punishment for?"

He narrowed his eyes.

She narrowed hers back. "For everything you've done to me?"

"No, Kate." He cocked his head. "For everything I'm *going* to do to you."

SIXTEEN

The heat in Kate's cheeks gave way to numbing chills. She didn't have a chance to stammer a response before Tiago grabbed her hand and hauled her into the bathroom.

"What are you doing?" She dug in her feet, slipping in the blood that trailed him.

"Get in the shower." He pushed her in the general direction. "Back against the wall. Hands at your sides."

He didn't need to flash the blade on his finger. His tone was sharp enough to send her running.

"What did I do?" She pressed her spine against the shower wall and pinched her arms close to her ribs. "If I angered you—"

"You meant to. You'll fight me at every turn." He set the razor on the counter and prowled toward her with a terrifying glint in his eyes. "I look forward to it."

"Don't hurt me." Her breathing quickened, knocking her chest into a heaving jog.

"Too late for that." He stepped into the shower and wrapped both hands around her neck, forcing her head back with his thumbs beneath her chin. "I fucked you thoroughly and completely, and I've only just begun."

Warm blood dripped from his arm to her chest, and she shivered. "You need to get Boones. Let him look at your cuts."

"Tell me you care if I bleed out."

"No." She set her jaw. "I don't care."

"So fucking honest." He leaned in and licked her lips. "Tell me more."

"You're a possessive, duplicitous, unreasonable nutjob."

"Your insults make me so damn hard." He dropped a hand to her ass and squeezed it painfully. "*Me encanta tu culo.* When I put my mouth here..." He wedged a finger into the crack, making her clench. "When I lick this tight rim, tell me you hate it."

She couldn't. Just thinking about it hardened her nipples. She knew it was happening when he glanced down at her chest and grinned.

"I waited twelve years for you." He touched his mouth to the corner of hers.

"Don't say that."

The wet sound of dripping drew her attention to the tile floor. Red splatters hit the drain. One heavy drop landed on her foot and worked its way between her toes. They both stared at it.

"I've seen a lot of shit in my life. What's normal to me would be shocking by society's standards." He wiped a hand over the cuts on his arm, collecting a palm full of blood. "Don't move."

He set that hand against her stomach and smeared the scarlet wetness across her hips, her thighs, and between her legs.

Horror hit her in a surge of tears, trembling her chin and burning through her sinuses. She closed her eyes, desperate to unsee the blood he was rubbing into her pussy.

"I've been a voyeur for twelve years." His hands cupped her face, warm and sticky. "Always watching from the front row, close enough to smell the tang of a soaked cunt, to hear the hungry slap of balls. I collected a lot of fantasies, and the things I've imagined... The dirty, filthy fucking things I've played out in my head never had an outlet."

Until now.

Until *her.*

She kept her eyes squeezed shut and bit down on a sob. But it found her vocal cords and vibrated in her throat.

He moved in closer, his wet palms sailing downward, lingering on her chest, tweaking her nipples, then continuing south to her waist and hips. No inch of her was left untouched. He was so attentive that way, achingly affectionate, and it fucked with her head.

Reaching her balled hands at her sides, he pried them open and guided one to his groin.

"Let go of your self-imposed restrictions, Kate." He forced her fingers around his heavy testicles.

When she tried to pull away, his free hand flew to her throat and applied pressure.

"Let go of every preconceived notion you have about sex." Holding her neck in a threatening restraint, he slid her hand to his cock and molded her fingers around the girth. "Fuck the stigmas and labels and society's definition of what's proper. Stop thinking about what you *should* do and fight for what you *want*."

"You know, maybe I'd feel more liberated if the roles were reversed." She swallowed against the collar of his fist and opened her eyes. "I have no power here. I'm completely at your mercy, and as you already pointed out, you have none."

His lips split in a feral smile, a menacing spark lighting up his eyes. "Fucking love your mouth."

The hand on her throat crept into her hair, and he clutched a hunk of it to yank her lips to his.

Stubborn as she was, she tried to resist. But she just couldn't. Not with his hot, beautiful cock in her hand, his fingers holding that grip, and his mouth setting her on fire.

The kiss went from playful to starving in seconds. Her body craved him. It recognized his touch, his mouth, the scent of his skin, and the rumbling sound of his voice. Didn't matter how selfish or cruel he was. The brainless, fleshy parts of her loved the way he made her feel.

While his tongue chased and licked hers, he guided their hands along his shaft, angling to rub the head between her legs, touching her, touching himself.

It was erotic and tantalizing and so fucking wrong. She loved it. She hated that she loved it. He was corrupting her, and her mind seemed hellbent on rationalizing and justifying every illogical reaction.

"You're right in that you have no power here," he breathed against her lips. "Not while I'm holding you against your will and you're constantly looking for an escape. But you have the power to take from me. When we're together like this, you can take as much pleasure as you want. Deviate from everything Van taught you. Break free from your hang-ups. Explore whatever you desire without judgment."

She wanted that, but she didn't trust it. Not with him. He was spinning her around so fast she didn't know which way was out.

Her eyes fluttered closed. "I don't know how."

"Look down. Look at us."

She lowered her gaze, taking in her bloodstained body, his hand holding hers around his cock, and the semi-hardness of it gliding between her thighs, seeking entry.

He adjusted his grip to drag a finger along her slit, collecting the ejaculate he'd left there minutes ago. Then he smeared that into the blood on her thighs.

It didn't feel forced or planned. He wasn't pretending to be something he wasn't. This was Tiago, the man no one else saw, in all his crude, natural, horrifying glory.

No one had ever captivated her the way he did.

"You're covered in me." He tipped her head back to stare into her eyes. "You're wearing my spit, sweat, come, and blood. Give me *your* definition for that. The first word that comes to mind."

"Raw." Her brows pulled together.

"Yeah." The corner of his mouth curved up. "Raw isn't a bad thing, Kate, and I'm not finished."

He swooped in and caught her lips, stealing choppy breaths from her lungs.

What did he mean he wasn't finished? Would he cover her in his tears next? Or… *Oh, God.*

A hot, wet stream flowed down her legs. The length of his dick rubbed against her hip, warm and half-hard in their hands. His mouth moved over hers, distracting her with the potency of his assertive tongue and sultry lips.

But she knew what was happening. A steady rush of liquid warmth drenched her lower half, tickled her feet, and stirred an appalling reaction between her legs. He was peeing on her, shamelessly pissing on her body, and her pussy *throbbed.*

It wasn't the shocking dirtiness of it that turned her on. It was the intensity of his arousal from it. The quicker his breaths grew, the faster her heart panted. He kissed her harder, more frantically, and she met him lick for lick, bite for bite.

She clung to the sounds of his groans, the confident way he held his cock in their hands, and the sensation of his body's hot fluid soaking her skin. It was the rawest form of intimacy she could've ever imagined.

Urinating wasn't much different than climaxing. There was a need for privacy while doing either action. The urge to hold it, stall it, then the tightening, building internal pressure, until the burst, the gushing flood, and the overwhelming relief. It made her want to release her bladder and orgasm all at once, just to share in the freedom he was experiencing, to let it all go without the judgment of prudes in the outside world.

Because a prude was one thing Tiago was *not.*

As the warm trickle slowed, he sighed as if he'd just jerked himself off on her legs.

"Look at you." He swayed back enough to let her see down the length of her defiled body. "So goddamn beautiful."

"Yeah." She unraveled her hand from his as modesty and shame crowded in. "I'm a glowing matriarch for women's rights."

Somehow, she'd forgotten to scream and fight him off while he was peeing on her.

"Hate me all you want." He clutched her chin and put his face in hers. "But never hate your desires. Never be ashamed of what you want."

"You pissed on me. I can't want that."

"Says who? You? Or the world you were raised in?" He released her to turn on the faucet and adjust the water temperature.

"It's dirty," she said lamely.

"I don't have an infection." He positioned her under the shower head. "It's sterile enough to drink."

"Where do you draw the line?"

"No shitting and no sharing." He grabbed a bar of soap. "Those are our limits."

"You can't tell me *my* limits."

"I just did."

He proceeded to wash her body. Then his own. His dick, fully erect now, jutted from the apex of his powerful legs. But he ignored it as he focused on cleaning away the blood and urine.

She was at a loss. Part of her warmed at the thought that he didn't want to share her. When he'd offered her to Arturo in the kitchen, it had been the worst possible scenario. Worse than Tiago finishing the job himself.

Why was that? Wouldn't a quick fuck by a random guard have been better than the hours she endured with Tiago?

The voice in her head screamed no.

"Do you still want to kill me?" she asked quietly.

"No." Grasping her hips, he spun her to face away. "Put your hands on the wall."

Exhaustion sluiced away her resistance. She flattened her palms on the tiles and let her head drop between her arms. "But you'll kill me if you need to."

"I should've killed you weeks ago." He set the soap aside and ran lathered hands up and down her back and shoulders. Then his fingers curled around her throat. "There are other forms of punishment if you try to escape."

"Torture."

"I have endless energy when it comes to you." He lowered his other hand to her abdomen and sank his fingers between her legs, pushing one inside. "I can torture your pussy for days. If you lose consciousness, I'll dunk you in cold water and start again, sucking, licking, biting, fucking, and never letting you come." He thrust that long digit in and out, racing her pulse. "If that doesn't convince you, you should know I won't hesitate to hunt down your friends."

The implication he would kill them slammed into her gut, but he didn't voice it. He didn't need to.

I hate you leapt to her tongue, and she bit it back. She'd said it so much it'd become trite and predictable.

"What are the rules?" she asked. "How do I guarantee their safety?"

"Don't try to escape and no murder attempts against me or those in my employ."

"But I can defend myself? I can fight and disobey you if I don't like what you're doing to me?"

He leaned his chest against her back and put his mouth at her ear. "Be my guest."

Strength revisited her muscles and joints. Determination wound around her spine. As he kicked her feet apart and sped up the finger inside her, his intent was clear.

She pulled in a breath, knowing he expected her to start struggling. Instead, she held still, anticipating the right moment.

He seized her from behind, banding both arms around her. His teeth went to her neck, and she dropped like a rock to the floor, breaking the hold. He lurched after her, but she was already swinging.

Her fist collided with his erection and the meaty sac of his nuts. She put all her strength into it, certain the hit was hard enough to drop him.

Except he remained on his feet. He didn't even let out a grunt or reach down to cup himself. Pain drew his lips into a flat line, but that was it.

She gave him a point for barely reacting, knowing full well that behind that stoic expression, he was battling the need to double-over and roar.

Water rained down upon her, and she blinked through the deluge, watching him, terrified.

After several heartbeats, he glared down at her and blew out a swift expulsion of air. His body seemed to widen before her eyes, flexing with testosterone and aggression, his nostrils flaring with a surge of heavy breaths. Like a bull preparing to charge. To fight, fuck, and maul.

Instead of attacking, he tilted his head and considered her. "I didn't give you that hit."

"Yeah, well, I took it." Point for her.

Begging for forgiveness was her best option at this point, but she wasn't feeling apologetic. So she swung again.

This time, he caught her fist and wrenched her to her feet. The shower stall spun around her, and her cheek smacked against the tile wall. His body pinned there, his hand at her throat, cutting her air.

He was teaching her a lesson, proving he had the upper hand. He could crush her throat—her trachea, esophagus, and whatever else she needed to stay alive—with nothing but a squeeze of his fingers.

Pain pulsed beneath his grip, and she pawed at it, eyes watering and lungs burning for oxygen. Her fear was deep and cold, stinging without mercy. He said he wouldn't kill her, and she hung onto that promise as dots blackened her vision.

"I'm going to take you right to the edge, Kate. Over and over again." He let go of her.

She gasped, clutching at her throat and savoring the weightlessness of unbridled breath.

Wrapping his arms around her from behind, he pressed his mouth to her jaw. "You hate me for it now, but someday, if I earn your trust, that razored edge will set you free."

He was completely unhinged if he thought she could ever trust him.

Grabbing her hands, he placed them on the wall before her. Then his fingers slid between her legs.

He worked her the way she knew he would — passionately and persuasively. Every touch rubbed salt in the wound of desire. His lips at her neck wobbled her knees. His hard, long cock against her backside coaxed cravings she didn't want.

Engaged in a constant war, with him, with herself, she was tired. So goddamn tired.

As he sensed her body begin to yield, he braced his bleeding arm on the wall beside hers and guided her other hand between her legs. She was wet, not just from the shower but from her treacherous arousal.

Twining their fingers together, he glided them through her folds and around her clit. He stroked himself, stroked her, his foreplay an endless night of mind-fucking torment.

By the time he stuffed his cock into her from behind, she was grinding in his arms and panting raggedly.

He banged her against the wall, with his hand trapping hers where they were joined. Just another of his wicked tortures, forcing her to feel his strokes with her fingers, using their hands to caress each glide of his length as he thrust.

That erotic touch brought an awareness to the connection she couldn't ignore. Sparks of pleasure shimmered across her fevered skin. Pleasure that belonged only to them. She couldn't fight it, didn't want to.

Greedy and mindless, she surrendered to the climax, moaning and rocking and clawing at the shower wall.

He pulled out, spun her around, and took her again, chest to chest, mouth to mouth, hiking her up his body, so he could kiss her as deeply as he pounded into her. He came fast and hard, roaring her name and shaking from head to toe.

"Never letting you go," he whispered long after he finished, still buried inside her, still chanting her name as he caught his breath.

It wasn't the last time he fucked her in the shower. Over the next two weeks, he took her there, on the mattress, the floor, and everywhere.

TAKE

He moved her into his room, made her sleep in his bed, and spent more time inside her than out of her.

His headaches came and went. Some days, he exercised downstairs. Every day, he worked out in her body.

When she found the energy to fight him, he restrained her with rope. When she felt herself slipping under his seductive spell, she remembered Tate.

Tate, sitting alone in a shack, with a bucket to shit in and a tattoo of the woman he loved.

That reminder helped her cling to her hatred. But she knew she wouldn't be able to hold onto the anger forever.

Tiago was inside her, possessing her like a demon and cherishing her like a man.

She saw the truth in the devoted way he kissed her, in those breathless moments when she returned his passion with a fire of her own, in the homage that scratched his voice as he said her name.

The chemistry between them burned so hot she had to shield her eyes and look away. But she still saw it. It was Tiago who didn't know it went both ways.

She told him she hated him, and he never doubted it. He didn't know about the times when she felt herself swaying, softening, falling.

Someday, Tate would be free, but she would still be here, staring at the crime lord who stood at the edge of hell, with his arms open, waiting to catch her.

SEVENTEEN

Tiago pushed through his work out, tossing up weights and annihilating his cardio routine with a nourishing burn in his lungs.

His strength had returned, his headaches completely gone, his health back to normal.

He might've been fifteen years older than Kate, but he'd spent the past two weeks fucking her like he was in his twenties.

With a grunt, he grabbed a heavier weight and heaved it through a set of bicep curls. He should've been focused on his upcoming return to Caracas, but his thoughts constantly wandered back to her.

What was she doing right now? Was she staring at the front door and plotting her escape? Or was she caressing the lush curves of her greedy body and thinking about his hands?

She despised him with every breath she took, but she loved the way he touched her, kissed her, and moved inside the tight clasp of her cunt.

"Goddamn." His skin tingled and heated.

He dropped the weight and dragged a towel down his face.

They were leaving for Caracas in just a few days. He didn't want her anywhere near the cesspool of his organization, but he would never leave without her. Hell, he couldn't even bear being in a different part of the house than her.

Finished with the work out, he exited the backroom and stepped into the hall.

Iliana had stayed out of his way since he set the record straight. She and the other guards received the same message two weeks ago.

He and Kate were off-limits.

No more touching or flirting.

No sharing.

Kate would be treated with the same respect as Boones. Keeping her and the old doctor safe was his top priority, and he made certain his security team knew it was theirs, too.

As he prowled down the hall toward the kitchen, the sweet sound of her voice reached his ears. He peered around the corner and found her at the table with Boones.

Arturo stood in the front room. When Tiago gave him a nod, he soundlessly headed down the hall in the direction Tiago just came from.

With their backs to the doorway, Kate and Boones didn't notice the change of guard.

"Who is she?" She leaned over a crinkled photograph in Boones' hand, the one he always carried in his pocket.

Boones stroked the black-and-white image of the gorgeous Eritrean woman. "Her name was Semira."

On a stunned exhale, Kate whispered, "Tiago's wife." Another gasp. "She was your daughter?"

"My only child."

"I'm so sorry for your loss."

In the doorway behind them, Tiago stared at his feet as a mace of memories formed in his stomach, all sharp, pointy spikes, piercing and heavy.

Semira wore a traditional Tigrinya dress and gold head jewelry in that picture. Tiago had been behind the camera, capturing the snapshot of the mischievous smile she'd so often thrown at him. As beautiful as she was strong, she'd ripped his heart out of his chest the first time he'd seen her.

"He told you about her?" Boones clutched her arm, his toothy smile glimmering with hope.

"He shared some of the painful highlights but was rather stingy with the details. I'd love to hear more." She entwined her fingers with his. "How did he meet your daughter?"

Tiago silently shifted back into the hallway and let his head rest against the wall. He trusted Boones to share only the parts that were safe to speak out loud. Her question was one Tiago would've answered himself. But she hated him too much to ask him directly.

"Tiago met my daughter when his family moved to my country," Boones said. "His father originated in Venezuela as a pharmacist, and that's where Tiago was raised. When Tiago finished school and took a job in America, his father moved his mother and younger brother out of Venezuela. His father's expertise in medicinal botany brought him to..." He coughed. "My village."

"Why is the location of your home such a big secret?"

"Tiago has enemies from his old life, as well as this one. Now that my brothers have returned home, he can't keep them as safe as he would like. He doesn't want anyone to know where to look for them."

"Wait. Your brothers? They're the other doctors on your medical team?"

"Yes. Semira, her uncles, and me. All doctors."

"So Tiago was raised in Venezuela? And when he returned, you and your brothers followed him back here?"

"Of course." A sad smile sifted through his voice. "We're his only family."

"That's why he's so protective of you." Realization softened her tone. "His parents...? They're not alive?"

Tiago ran a tense hand through his hair, fighting the impulse to make his presence known and end the conversation.

"They died," Boones said. "His father was my dearest friend. We worked together for years, while Tiago was off traveling the world, immersed in his career. But Tiago visited my village often, mostly to court my daughter. He loved her."

"He said she didn't love him back."

Boones sat quietly for a long moment. Tiago didn't need to see his father-in-law's scarred face to read the troubled thoughts in his head.

"She fell in love with his looks and the safety he could provide," Boones finally said. "He has a big presence, powerful and handsome, but you already know that."

His military background in America was what drew Semira to him. The political climate in Eritrea wasn't good, hadn't been good for decades. Repression ran rife throughout the country. Citizens lived in constant fear, unable to speak out against the government. News outlets were closely controlled. Everything was locked down.

For Semira, Tiago had represented freedom. A way for her and her family to escape the repression.

He'd been in the process of moving them out of the country when she was attacked. How ironic that instead of keeping her safe, he was the one who got her killed.

"She never loved him the way he loved him." Boones' voice carried years of regret. "We fought about it, she and I."

"Because *you* love him," Kate said.

"Like a son."

Tiago closed his eyes. The best thing that came out of Eritrea was that stubborn old man. Boones had stuck by his side through the worst, brought him back to life multiple times, watched him do things no one should ever have to witness, and not once did Boones give up on him.

TAKE

"You have to understand," Boones said. "Tiago didn't just lose his wife that day. He lost his father, mother, and little brother. His entire family was slaughtered in front of him."

Her gasp cleaved through Tiago, but it was Boones' next words that twisted the knife of shame.

"He needs a woman's love."

Enough of this.

Tiago charged into the kitchen, circled the table, and stood on the other side to glare down at Boones, then Kate.

He braced himself for the pity she wouldn't be able to hide in her honest eyes, but when he peered closely, he didn't find it.

She tilted her head and raised a brow, her lips pursing as if she were annoyed by his intrusion.

Fucking incredible.

He turned his gaze to Boones and spoke in Tigrayit. "I don't need love, you meddling old fuck."

"Idiot," Boones said in the same language. "You need it more than ever now that you have brain damage."

"You said the injuries didn't damage my brain."

"I changed my mind."

Irritation slithered beneath his skin. He switched to English. "Tell her what happened after I watched my family die."

Boones bit down on his thin lips. He didn't like this part.

"That's okay." Kate patted Boones' arm. "I have a pretty good idea."

"I don't think you do." Tiago paced around the table, his hands clasped behind him. "I killed everyone involved. Those who coordinated the attack on my family and everyone associated with those people. I murdered handlers, operatives, and officials, which put me on wanted lists for multiple countries and all the three-letter agencies."

Her face paled.

"I didn't just walk away from my job." He paused beside her and leaned down, gripping the edge of the table. "I went rogue, killed a bunch of important people, and took Boones and his family down with me."

"Don't you start on that." Boones stood and pointed a finger at Tiago. "We demanded to go with you."

"I shouldn't have allowed it." He'd ruined their lives, tainted their gentle souls with his filth.

Boones slammed a fist against the tabletop, his body stiff with rage as he turned to Kate. "I was as close to his father as he was. We were all close, his family, my family. The day they died, we *all* changed. My brothers and I needed revenge just as badly as Tiago. That's why we went with him." His accent thickened, vibrating with vehemence. "We followed him from city to city, waited as he took each life, and patched up his broken bones and wounds. Then we followed him here to Venezuela." He cut his eyes to Tiago, the white scars on his cheeks glowing against his black skin. "I made my own choices. You don't get to take credit for my crimes."

He gave Boones a tight nod, willing to give the man anything he wanted. The last twelve years had been painful for both of them.

"Thank you for sharing that with me." Kate glanced from Boones to him and squared her shoulders. "I didn't mean to open old wounds."

"Don't worry about that. Tiago has been opening a lot of wounds lately." Boones pointed his cloudy eyes at the cuts he'd treated on Tiago's arm two weeks ago.

Tiago hadn't touched his razor since then, but he wanted to. He longed to draw blood, fantasized about it constantly, and it wasn't his flesh he imagined cutting.

His gaze shifted to hers, and his groin tightened.

Boones ambled toward him, obstructing his view of blue eyes and flawless skin.

A bony hand gripped Tiago's neck and dug in with surprising strength. "Let her see you," Boones said in Tigrayit. "All of you. Even if it invites her pity. Then she can decide whether to love you. And you'll know if she's worthy of the man in here." He tapped Tiago on the chest.

His hackles bristled. "Semira was worthy. She was just ambitious, focused on her career. She was a good woman."

"I loved my daughter, but she wasn't good for *you*."

With that, Boones left the kitchen and slipped out the front door.

"I'm willing to bet some of that exchange was about me." Kate rose from the table and gathered the dishes from lunch. "It's rude to talk about people in a language they don't understand."

"Leave that." He snatched the platters from her and held out his hand. "Come with me."

Ignoring his command, she walked past him and headed for the sink. "I figured out why there are no mirrors upstairs."

He caught a fistful of her hair and yanked her around. He wanted to look into her eyes while she called him out on his shit. "Tell me."

"You hate your reflection." She jerked in his hold, swinging and kicking until he released her. "Not your appearance. You know how damn…" She growled and waved a flippant hand in his direction. "You're ridiculously good-looking. It's not that. You don't like what you see in your eyes. The cruelty. The hypocrisy. Your family was murdered, and what did you do? You went to Caracas and became a kidnapper and murderer. Your cold eyes are windows into that hell, and I have to stare into them every time you fuck me. Because you hold my head and make me look and…" She spun away, fists clenched at her sides. "You're pure evil."

Fucking Christ, she was fiery today, itching for a fight.

There were no guards around to witness her disrespect, so he let her continue the rampage, because she wasn't wrong.

She stormed to the sink, clanked a few pots around, and charged back. "And another thing. I'm over the whole *mine* declaration. That's something an insecure guy says to a girl when he doesn't want her fucking other guys. When you say it to the woman you abducted, it's psychological warfare. Not sexy."

He laughed, loud and deep, because fuck him, this woman had balls. Huge fucking lady balls. "I don't give a fuck whether it's sexy. You won't be fucking anyone but me."

Her spine went straight, and her cheeks burned into an angry shade of red.

But this wasn't anger. She was scared. Beneath her surly bravado lurked a deep sense of dread. She feared what it meant to belong to a man like him. She feared for her friends if she tried to break free. And she feared the day she would stop thinking of escape and yield to the force that knotted them together.

Every time he entered her body, he wanted their roles to disappear. But how could he move them away from being captor and prisoner when he was unwilling to let her go?

He didn't just want to keep her. He wanted to bind her, spank her, cut her, and fuck every hole. He wanted to share every depraved fantasy with her and earn her trust at the same time.

He didn't need a woman's love. He'd survived thirty-seven years without it.

But he ached for *her* to love him.

Him, a thing that couldn't be loved.

He wanted the impossible.

All humor gone, he extended his hand again. He'd told her to come with him, and he wouldn't repeat himself.

The atmosphere shifted and tightened. She stared at his mouth, his chest, his hand, and shifted her weight from one foot to the next.

Then she ran.

EIGHTEEN

Kate bolted toward the front of the house, the perfect curves of her ass flexing in denim shorts, and all that blond hair swinging around her tiny waist.

Energy swelled, heating Tiago's muscles. His cock lengthened and hardened for the chase. The thrill of the hunt.

She veered around mattresses and tripped over backpacks, her noisy breaths spurring him into motion. When she reached the front door, she fumbled with the handle, and it cost her.

He caught her from behind, an arm against her stomach and a hand around her throat.

"What did I say about trying to escape?" He sank his teeth into her shoulder.

"I wasn't! I just need…" She twisted in his hold, an attempt to break away, but ended up with her chest against his and her mouth so close he tasted lemon tea on her breath. "I just need some air."

"What's wrong with the air in here?"

On an exhale, a pleading look seeped into her eyes. "You."

Gripping the backs of her thighs, he hitched her up his body. The position forced her to hug his neck and hook her legs around his waist.

"Explain." He tangled a hand in her hair and seized her molten blue gaze.

"How can I explain *you*? This?" She feathered her fingers along his whiskered jaw, cupped the side of his face, and touched her forehead to his. "You make me crazy."

"Goes both ways, Kate."

"Then let me go."

TAKE

"Never." He turned and climbed the stairs.

Her limbs tightened around him, and her breathing accelerated. She thought she knew what would happen when they arrived in their room, but she didn't have a clue.

"I won't surrender," she whispered fiercely against his mouth.

"You always say that."

"I don't want this."

"Always say that, too."

She lowered her head to his shoulder, resting her cheek there, with her warm lips against his neck. "I'm tired, Tiago."

Tired of fighting him.

She'd been here for two months and spent every second of it resisting, defying, spitting, and fighting. Always fighting.

He didn't intend to break her down or defeat her. He wanted her arguments, her wrestling matches, and her rebellious spirit.

"Don't give up." He pressed a kiss beside her ear.

"Never."

There's my girl.

In the bedroom, he locked the door and set her on her feet.

"I need to use the toilet." She backed away and vanished into the bathroom.

While she did her business and washed her hands, he removed the rope and blade from the locked safe. Then he grabbed the bag of medical supplies Boones kept near the door.

When she stepped back into the room, Tiago was sitting on the mattress, holding his phone.

She stood there in little jean shorts and a tank top, with her arms rigid at her sides and her head held high.

Just like the first time she walked in here and raised that chin at him, he was sucker-punched with the fiercest, rawest form of perfection. She was so much more than he could've ever fathomed.

Except now, he knew that devastating beauty ran through the deepest parts of her, and his heart longed for it, hammering and stretching to sink inside of hers.

He could make her come on his mouth and fall apart on his dick. But he couldn't make her love him. He couldn't even hope for such a thing.

Nevertheless, he wouldn't stop fighting for it, knowing he would lose in the end.

Turning his attention to the phone, he opened a screen and held it out to her.

"What is it?" She inched closer, her long lashes hooding the curiosity in her eyes.

"I had a camera installed in the shack."

She erased the distance in three running strides and snatched the phone from his hand.

Arturo had placed the solar-powered recording device on the roof and angled the lens through a hole to capture the interior. Tate didn't know it was there, and no one would spot it from the outside.

"Oh my God." She clutched her throat, eyes wide and glued on the live streaming video. "That's Boones. How is he with Tate?" Her gaze snapped up and landed on his, the depths clashing with relief and accusation. "Tate must be close by."

"Within walking distance. Come here." He leaned against the wall, stretched out his legs, and opened his arms.

She came right to him, somewhat absentmindedly as the video held all her attention.

Gathering her on his lap, he tucked her back against his chest. With a hand stroking through her hair, he watched her watch the live footage.

"That's where Boones goes every day." She pulled in a serrated breath and released it. "He's been taking care of Tate."

"Yes."

On the screen, Boones knelt behind her friend and applied a balm to the man's back. He would do the same with the arm injury, the new tattoo, and check for any health issues.

"This is so much better than I've been imagining." Her fingers tightened around the phone. "It's still horrible and inhumane, but knowing he has Boones, that he's so close, it means everything."

"I installed the camera so you can check on him. Before we leave for Caracas, I'll take you to see him."

"What?" She spun on his lap to face him, dropping the phone in her excitement. "Really?"

"I can take it away just as quickly as I've given it." He locked the device and set it aside. "Remember that."

She looked up into his face and adjusted her legs to straddle him, to stare a little closer, a little deeper, with a strange tumult of emotions flitting across her expression.

"You tortured my friend and chained him in a shack for two months. I can't forgive you for that. But..." She swallowed, breathed in slowly through her nose, and placed her soft hands on his jaw. "It's funny how you throw me a few scraps, a video, a chance to visit him, and follow it up with a mean threat, and all I can think is... Here's a glimpse, a tiny peek of goodness. This is the moment when I don't see the fearsome, ruthless gang leader you created twelve years ago. I see *you*, the man who mourns his wife and family. The man I want to know. The man I want to kiss."

Erratic and unstable, his pulse careened through his veins. "I'm not a good man, Kate."

"No, you're definitely not that. But you're not the one-dimensional creation you show the world, either."

"I believe your exact words were *pure evil*."

"I was angry."

"And now?"

"I'm moved."

She leaned in slowly and skimmed her fingers into his hair. A puff of breath. A gentle brush of lips. Everything inside him clenched and locked.

It was the first time she initiated intimacy, and the kiss was so delicate it shivered with fragility. It took every bit of strength he could muster to stop his hands from flying to her head, to stall his tongue from sweeping in and taking over.

She was such a sexual creature she couldn't breathe without radiating the sizzling, ignitable energy that lived beneath her skin. His entire body recognized it, fed on it. But he wrestled down the need to control this and closed his eyes, savoring the tenderness, the exquisite affection.

The peaks of her supple, braless tits dragged against his chest. The heat of her cunt burned against his cock through their clothing. Her tongue found his with licking, curling, divine sweetness, and perspiration formed on his spine. She was killing him.

Then she grew bolder. Her hands wrapped around the base of his skull, bringing him closer, angling his head for a deeper kiss. Her tongue slid over his, tasting, exploring as she panted against his mouth.

It was the most exhilarating, most sensual kiss he'd ever experienced. All his senses telescoped to her lips, her soft, wet tongue, and the maddening way she tunneled her fingers through his hair.

She transported him into a fantastic dream and smothered him in layers of emotion. She didn't just kiss with her body. She fused to his mouth with her whole being, all tongue and breath and deep, swirling feelings.

When she broke for air, her fingers clung to his neck, pupils blown, and lips swollen. For a moment, she seemed disoriented, stunned. Then she blinked, and her expression glowed with wonderment. Maybe even fondness.

"I like you like this." She stroked a thumb along his bottom lip. "Kind and unassuming."

His stomach hardened.

She thought she was looking at him, but she was staring at a stranger. He wasn't a man who let a woman straddle his lap and dole out vanilla kisses. There wasn't a docile breath in his body.

He needed pain to feel alive. Perversion to stay focused. He needed the razor-sharp edge.

Let her see you. Then she can decide whether to love you.

"You're only seeing what you want to see." He touched her cheekbone and traced a path to her perfect mouth.

"I haven't forgotten what you've done or why I'm here."

"You don't know the half of it."

She ghosted a hand along the scars on his forearm. "What haven't you shown me?"

His brutal cravings.

His darkest hunger.

His deepest hurt.

He pointed his eyes at the rope and blade beside the mattress, and she followed his gaze.

"No." She tensed and started to pull away, shaking her head. "You don't need that."

He yanked her back by her hair. "There's a lot of pain in the world. You can't avoid it."

"If you endure it, accept it, it will stop."

His breath caught. That was *his* mantra, something he'd only ever repeated to…

He narrowed his eyes. "You've been spending too much time with Boones."

"I adore him."

"He had his scars deliberately put on him. Does that disgust you?"

"Not at all. They're an important part of his culture." She circled a finger around a raised welt on his wrist. "Did your wife wear scars, too?"

"No. She thought it was outdated and crude. But many of the women still practice the art. I find it seductive, exotic, and beautiful." He met her eyes. "I've never cut a woman."

In his mind, he'd carved countless elaborate illustrations on Kate's body, but there was one in particular that made his fingers twitch for the blade.

"You haven't?" Her head flinched back. "But you said cutting a woman is different than a man. Something about a passionate hand and weeping and…" She choked on a gasp of realization. "You were referring to your wife. When she was…"

"When I watched that knife slice her open, I *felt* it. I felt myself bleed. I heard myself weep. Then all I knew was rage. I emulated that exact cut on the man who killed her, the men who killed my family, and all the others associated with the attack. The more men I sliced, slashed, and carved, the more I liked it. *Craved* it. So much so I became less discriminatory about my targets."

"You turned the blade on innocent people. Like Tate."

"Yes. But I've never cut a woman." He opened his expression and let her see every nefarious intention in his mind.

"No." She scrambled off his lap so fast she tumbled to the floor. Scooting backward on hands and feet, she screamed miserably, "Stay away from me!"

He sprung after her and seized her ankle, yanking her back to the mattress.

She went crazy, all flailing fists and snapping teeth. He held her to the bed and snatched the rope, making quick work of the knots around her wrists and the cast iron pipe.

Then he sat back on his heels, his legs straddling her hips, restraining her lower body in place. The position reminded him of the night they met, the first time he tied her up.

"We've been here before." He planted his hands on either side of her face and leaned down, biting her lips.

She tried to bite him back, missing his mouth in her outrage. "Let me go!"

"I need you to listen."

A tremor rippled across her jaw. "Are you going to cut me?"

"With pleasure."

"Fuck that." She thrashed. "Fuck you. I won't let you do this!"

"Stop." He grabbed her chin and held her head still.

"Please, don't kill me." Tears spilled from her liquid blue eyes.

He loosened his grip and glided his fingers along the side of her face. "I can't lose you."

It was the most honest, vulnerable thing he'd ever admitted aloud.

"But you're going to hurt me?" More tears escaped.

"God, yes." He bent down and ran his mouth over her wet cheeks, kissing away the pain he'd caused her.

"Why?" She gulped air and swallowed back her sobs, a noble effort to pull herself together.

"It's a need that drives me. A comfort I can't live without."

Cutting was a purging, an outlet for the nightmares inside him. As much as he cut himself, it wasn't the same. He needed the connection to her pain.

Her arms trembled in the rope. "Does it arouse you?"

"With you? Yes."

"You're a sadist. I get that. It's part of what makes you so intense, unusual, and terrifyingly captivating. But Tiago, there's a difference between hurting a woman who gets off on it and hurting a woman against her will."

It was a moot point. He didn't ask permission when he fucked her, and he wouldn't ask permission for this.

"I won't surrender to that blade. Not ever." Her lashes fluttered, and her eyes flicked back and forth before pausing on his. "But I'll make a deal with you. We're leaving for Caracas in...?"

"Three days."

"What will you do there? Kidnap more people? Torture them and hold them for ransom? Kill them if their families can't pay?"

She knew what he did. He didn't need to fuel her hatred with a response.

"Retire." Her expression morphed from fearful to determined. "You don't need the money."

"No."

"Can't or won't?"

"Both."

"Then change your business model. You want to live a life of crime? Fine. Stick to victimless crimes."

He laughed heartlessly and stopped short when he realized she was serious.

"No more kidnapping. No more hurting innocent people. Make me that promise, and I'll..." Her nostrils widened with a slow, deep inhale. "I'll be whatever you need me to be."

"No deal. I want you exactly as you are."

"If you don't make me that promise, all you're going to get from this point forward is a plastic, hollow version of me." She leaned up, as much as the rope allowed. "Don't forget. I was trained how to please a sadist. I can make this a memorable experience for you or I can turn it into a robotic musical of fake moans and cheap quivers."

"You said you wouldn't surrender." He rubbed his brow. Christ, this woman. Why was he even entertaining this conversation?

"I can't surrender to this. Pain doesn't turn me on. At all. But I can give you the real me." She pulled on the restraints, trying to lift her face closer to his. "I know you, Tiago Badell. You need this to be mutually honest. No games. No bullshit. Just you and me."

Heat surged to his balls and swelled his cock.

She jutted her chin. "Stop. Kidnapping."

"What you're asking for is ridiculous." He sat up and hardened his eyes. "Caracas is the kidnapping capital of the world. You don't survive Kidnap Alley without playing by the rules."

"If you're the king, you can do whatever the fuck you want."

NINETEEN

No more kidnapping.

Was it as easy as just deciding to stop? Tiago never had a taste for abducting people off the streets, but he had a reputation to uphold and hundreds of powerful men in his pocket, including law enforcement and politicians. If he so much as appeared weak, he wouldn't just lose their protection. They would turn on him and everyone loyal to him.

The deaths of his family had led him to this corrupt life. His last revenge kill was in Caracas, and when he finished, he stayed.

He'd slunk into the deepest, darkest corner of Kidnap Alley and became one of them. One of the irredeemable who lurked in the shadows, smuggling contraband, kidnapping tourists, and killing at will. Within a year, he'd become their leader.

His fate was sealed. He was hunted by government agencies, cartels, crime lords, influential people. They wanted him imprisoned, tortured, dead, dismembered, his head on a stake in town square. Didn't matter. They wanted him gone.

If he left his life in Caracas, he left the protection of his crime syndicate. Walking away was the same as walking toward death row.

But he could make a minor change to the business. If he refocused his efforts on gun smuggling and expanded his routes, he could make the argument to his money-hungry constituents that it was more lucrative than kidnapping for ransom.

He could give her this one thing. He wanted to, and not because he was receiving something in return. He wanted to give her this because it was the right thing to do.

It might be the only good thing he could ever offer her.

"No more kidnapping." He ran featherlight fingers down her neck, eliciting a shudder in her breath. "Consider it done."

"Thank you. And you'll take me to visit Tate before we leave."

"You have my word."

All she had was his word, and he could break it at any time. But he wouldn't. She seemed to know that. She trusted it.

"Untie me." She stared at him, a silent bid to trust *her*.

"No." He climbed off the bed and collected the blade and Boones' medical bag.

The air between them assembled and charged, a palpable battle of her fear against his anticipation. As he readied the supplies, her anxiety pressed against him, the shallow sounds of her breaths accelerating his.

She deserved so much more than the sickness inside him. But she would remind him of that. The hatred in her eyes, the derisive words from her mouth, she would never quit fighting. He counted on it.

Moving back to the bed, he climbed over her and shimmied her tank top over her head, up her bound arms, and left it gathered around her wrists. Then he lowered his hands to the button on her shorts.

"Do you already know the design you're going to cut into me?" A sheen of wetness spread over her eyes.

"Yes." He released the fly and dragged the denim and panties down her legs and off.

"You planned this."

"Weeks ago."

"Of course." Her jaw set, and a quiver raced along her nude body. "How big will it be?"

"The size of my hand." He splayed his fingers over her thigh, magnifying her shivering. "It'll wrap all the way around your leg."

This twenty-two-year-old, petite wisp of a woman, whose hair tangled wildly around her bare chest and bound arms, didn't flinch.

Life hadn't been kind to her. She was abandoned by her parents, betrayed by her brothers, tortured by Van Quiso, and now this. Life should've broken her, but instead of shattering, she became her own hero. She didn't even realize she'd saved herself. And in doing so, she saved him.

He cleaned the blade with Boones' antiseptic and rubbed the homemade compound into the skin on her thigh, something he never bothered to do with anyone, including himself.

And because he couldn't control the impulse, he leaned down and kissed her pussy, dragging his tongue through her velvety flesh and taking generous sips of her intoxicating essence.

Her hands fisted around the rope, her eyes never leaving his as he worshiped her body.

He needed her in ways he didn't understand. She satisfied every sexual craving, but this wasn't just lust. He needed her strength, her defiance, every nuance of her ferocious spirit.

If there was ever a woman mighty enough to break her restraints and stand as his equal, she was it.

She was the one.

With the preparations finished, he fitted the sharp blade onto his finger. The custom-made scalpel extended like a claw, enabling him to cut detailed swirls and precise lines.

Kneeling in the spread of her legs, he lowered the blade to her thigh.

His nerves fired and exploded with excitement. He wanted this too deeply, too vehemently. He could see the finished image in his mind, imagined her wearing his scars for the rest of her life. He was overcome.

"It's beautiful." Her shaky voice drew his gaze to hers.

"I haven't started yet."

"Doesn't matter. I have a choice. I can spend the rest of my life loathing the scars every time I remove my clothes. Or I can decide right now they're as beautiful as the ones that cover you and Boones." Her eyes flashed. "I already made up my mind about it. Every time I look at the scars, I'll remember that a crime lord gave up kidnapping in exchange for art."

Fuck him, she was remarkable. Rare. Perfect.

Mine.

"Hold still." He steadied his hand and spread her skin taut beneath the scalpel. Then he drew the first cut on her upper thigh.

Her bleak blue gaze creased with pain, but she didn't look away. Didn't twitch or scream. She watched him with the eyes of a tortured goddess. Proud. Fierce. Distressed, but not defeated.

Gathering the gauze he'd set aside, he went to work, focused on the design, and dabbed at the trickles of blood.

He dragged the blade the way a tattoo artist dragged a needle—hunched over, breaths calm, eyes glued to the art, every mark deliberate and meticulous.

Cutting Kate was different than cutting anyone before her. He felt the vibrations of her labored breaths, the wetness of her silent tears, the very fluid of her life slicking over his hands.

Time became irrelevant. Seconds leaked into hours. He was lost in it. Lost in the passion of creating, the release, the bleeding.

The bleeding.

The bleeding.

It was flowing too fast. He held the gauze to the deepest slash, but no matter how much pressure he applied, blood gushed between his fingers, pooling under his hand, drenching his arm, the bright ruby rivers quickly darkening, tangling, growing thicker.

Organs spilled. Ropes of viscera. Heavy, wet things. The pungent scent of bowels. And blood. God, the blood oozed from everywhere and nowhere, staining everything it touched.

How did he get here? Did he kill someone?

Silence crashed in, thumping hollowly in his ears as he watched Semira die again and again, the pity in her eyes vivid and alive, making him pay.

His pulse went berserk, the agony hitting in waves and turning the blood to acid. All he could do was rock in place, the occasional whimper ricocheting off the walls.

"Tiago!" A faraway voice pleaded with him. "Look at me!"

Everything sharpened, narrowed to a pinpoint of purpose.

Kill.

A flash of glinting steel.

Destroy.

Deadly shades of red.

Slaughter.

"Tiago, dammit! Stay with me!" That voice again. That heavenly voice.

He jerked his head up and looked into the eye of his storm. She stared back, gaze glowing, expression soft, his perfect calm and clarity.

"What happened?" She tilted her head.

"Nothing."

"That wasn't nothing. You look like you're seconds from blowing a gasket, and I don't want to be under that blade when it happens."

He glanced down at his hand, at the razor on his finger. Blood didn't flow. Organs didn't tumble.

What he saw was her pale, toned leg across his lap, her skin etched with the birth of a painting, a carved outline, and the budding blooms of something beautiful.

The sight of his design heated his soul to burning.

"Untie me." She kicked him in the hip with her free leg, her voice gentle. "Let me touch you. The contact might help."

Pain would've been deep within her thigh now, stinging and smoldering, as if the bone had caught fire. She couldn't veil the agony on her face, her lips stretched taut, and her forehead beading with perspiration.

But it was the concern in her eyes that moved him up her body. This woman, whom he'd hurt so ruthlessly, had the capacity in her heart to help him.

It made no sense, but he didn't question it. Instead, he untied the knots on her wrists.

She tossed the rope and tank top from her arms and grimaced at her leg.

"I'm not finished." He shifted back into position, resting her thigh across his lap.

"I know." She lay back and gripped the arm he held across her midsection. "I'm not surrendering."

"I know."

She turned her gaze to the ceiling, and he returned to the design, cutting a braided pattern across her thigh.

"You had a flashback, didn't you?" Her body quivered beneath the blade, her teeth sawing the hell out of her bottom lip.

"Yeah." He reached up and tugged on her chin. "Stop that."

"Does it happen often? The flashbacks?"

"Never." He nudged her to her side and continued the lacerated braid to the back of her leg.

"Maybe this is helping?" She whimpered as he carved along a tender spot.

"Helping with what?"

"Your terrible personality."

He glared at her through his lashes without lifting his head.

"Yeah, you're right." She glared back. "Your personality can't be fixed. But maybe reliving your past is better than bottling it up. It should be cathartic."

"This, us, *you* are cathartic."

She fell silent after that but never removed her touch.

An hour passed before another flashback sneaked in.

She sensed it before he did, and her hand sank into his hair, fisting, pulling, until his gaze latched onto hers. "Stay with me."

And so he did. He focused on the warmth of her fingers against his skin, on the way they trembled and flexed with her pain. He marked the rapid pace of her breaths and paused often to let her calm down, kissing her body during each break, his lips on her knee, her chest, and everywhere in between before starting again.

Blotting each drip of blood, he felt that flow of life roll through his veins like lava. Soon, he fell into a rhythm, a sensual slide of his hand, the scalpel seamlessly slicing her gorgeous flesh.

Dark, depraved pleasure circulated through his system. Indecent and drugging, sensations swarmed his nerve endings and heated his skin. Christ, he'd needed this.

He flipped her to her stomach to finish the back of her thigh. Numbing balm went into the incisions as he went along, and he forced water to keep her hydrated.

Dinner had long passed by the time he sat back and wiped off the blade. She'd stopped watching a while ago but not once had she withdrawn her touch.

He marked the heavy sag of her eyelids and the slackness of her mouth. "Where are you, Kate?"

"Floating on hatred."

More like floating on endorphins, high on spikes of pain and stress, exhausted from hours of shivering, and probably lightheaded from the burn out of an adrenaline rush.

She looked ready to pass out, and he was hard as a rock. Cutting her had aroused him to the point of distraction. But this was Kate. Every time he touched her, his cock lengthened.

"Finished?" She inched her gaze to his.

"Yes." He set aside the supplies. "Ready to see it?"

"It's beautiful." She closed her eyes.

"Bullshit." He gripped her under the arms and lifted her to a sitting position. "I know you made up your mind about it, but you're going to give me your honest opinion."

"Fine." She blew out a resigned sigh and looked down.

As her gaze flicked over the design, her sexy bowed lips separated. She leaned forward and twisted to see around the sides and underneath.

Her bright, glossy eyes and appreciative noises shifted things inside his chest.

"My God. It's... I have no words." She hovered a hand over the design, as if itching to touch it. "Why did you choose this? What does it mean?"

"The image will be clearer as it heals. It's a rope, coiling around your thigh."

"With a flower trapped under it?"

"Not trapped. It grows out from beneath it, blooming despite the confinement." He ran a hand along her calf, cupping it to drag her closer. "There are twenty-two petals on the flower, each representing a year of your life."

"Why?" She blinked, and a tear skipped down her cheek.

"You're the miracle that grows in the smallest crack of sunlight. The bloom that never gives up."

"Tiago." A teary hiccup teetered to her lips, and she smothered it with the back of her hand.

"There's something that thrives within all living things, a force that drives us to want to live more than anything else. You're the essence of that. The purest example of resilience. No matter what direction you need to grow — out of the darkness of an attic or from beneath the constriction of braided rope — you do it fiercely, tenaciously, and without fail." He clutched the back of her neck and brought her face to his. "There's nothing more vibrant, more beautiful, or more treasured than the flower that blooms in hell."

"That's... I don't..." Her voice creaked, and she feathered fingertips around the perimeter of cuts on her thigh. "How long will it take to heal?"

"Two months. It'll fade to pink. With time, it'll be completely white and blend in with your pale complexion. But unlike a tattoo, it has a tactile element."

"It'll be raised like yours." She tickled a hand over the welts on his arm, but didn't look down at his scars. Those huge, glistening eyes fixed on his. "I like the way they feel."

Compelled by a force he'd only ever felt with her, he ducked his head and kissed her, running his tongue along the seam of her lips the way he'd imagined for hours.

Soft and wet, her mouth opened for him, salty with her tears, warm with the gust of her breaths.

He plundered her with urgency, devoured her with hunger. Hauling her onto his lap, he took her mouth with feverish strokes, his body moving of its own volition, grinding against her, mindless with desire.

The need between them swelled, and he didn't hold back. They were an explosion of motion—hands gripping, tongues battling, breaths heaving, hearts pounding. All of it burst into a consuming, soulful integration of her and him.

Her mouth dove to meet his in a kiss that was so unexpected he groaned and shook to his core.

She was unexpected, yet it felt as if his entire life had been building to this. Every tragedy, every crime had brought him here, to this woman, who kissed him with all the hatred and goodness inside her.

Her fingers lifted to his hair as his hands lowered to her chest, cupping and caressing her nude flesh. She rocked on his lap, and he gripped her firm ass, jerking her body harder, faster, until he felt wetness bleed through his gym shorts.

"Kate." He grunted against her greedy lips. "Kate, wait."

She pulled back, dazed.

"Your leg. Hang on." He swept her onto her back and fumbled for the package of gauze. "Don't move."

He re-cleaned the incisions and dressed her thigh in soft bandages. She watched his movements with labored breaths, her cheeks flushed, and eyelids at half-mast.

Then her brows pulled together, the depths of her gaze flickering with an inner war.

At any moment, the words *I don't want this* or *I hate you* would fire out, but instead, she reached for his face and traced the line of his jaw.

He lowered his body into the cradle of hers, falling. "You're wrecking me."

"You deserve it." She hooked her legs around his hips.

Shoving down the elastic band of his shorts, he slid the head of his dick along her slit. "You're mine."

A pretty growl vibrated her throat. "Shut up."

"You want my cock."

"Not even a little."

"You want to come all over it."

"Lies."

Her body didn't lie. A sweep of his finger through her cunt released a gush of arousal. She made a strangled sound and pressed her hands against his bare chest.

When he pushed back, her fingers caught his nipples and locked on, pinching with an alarmingly strong bite.

He choked, seated his cock against her pussy, and shoved home.

With a yelp that rivaled his throaty groan, she wound her arms around his neck.

"So fucking wet." He rotated his hips, grinding into her soaked heat, teasing her. "Hear how sloppy you are? You're creaming all over me."

"You're a good kisser, okay?" Her hand speared through his hair and clenched. "I still hate you."

"You want to hate me, but I don't think you do."

Her eyes shuddered, and she looked away. "I want my freedom back."

"Can't release you." He shifted to his side, taking her with him so that her bandaged leg rested over his hip.

"Then, for now, I'll take a different release." She rolled her hips, catching a slow ride on his cock. "We both need this escape. You can take from me. I'll take from you, and just for a little while, let's get lost in it."

Her words gripped him deeply, every part of him bowing toward her. An honest touch from her fingers could sustain him forever.

"No more resistance," he ordered.

"No more restraints," she ordered back.

He palmed her ass and drove harder inside her. "No more holding back."

"I'm sick of fighting this." She gasped on his next thrust. "But I won't stop fighting everything else. Especially when you're being a total dick, which is pretty much all the time."

"Except now."

TAKE

She raised her face to his, her expression drunk on desire. "This is a good moment."

Lying on their sides, he wrapped his arms around her. Then he fucked her gently, taking, giving, fusing them together. She cried out, her mouth agape as he drove into the hot, tight fist of her body.

Hands down the best thing he'd ever felt. Soft lips on his mouth. Thick blond hair against his arms. Lush, toned curves beneath his fingers. Wet, warm pussy sucking in his cock. Heaven. Salvation. She made him feel again.

She made him want to be a man she could love.

Wrapping up the length of her hair in his fist, he forced her gaze to his. Slowed his pace. Stroked in and out in a steady, desperate grind.

Eyes locked, mouths connecting and separating, the connection was raw, unhurried, and heavy. Every kiss thrummed with what-ifs, every touch a climbing step to something huge and unstoppable.

A fever of lust.

A bolt of energy.

A blissful fall.

He came with her, syncing their orgasms by eye contact alone.

Her body clamped down on him, spasming, squeezing, as unholy pleasure hit him from all directions. Her hungry mouth crashed down over his, stealing her name as it rode on his groaning breaths.

After, he lay on his back with her body splayed across his chest and her eyes losing the fight against sleep.

When her lashes stopped fluttering, the fringes spread over her cheeks, he started counting each one.

His heart knocked an unusual beat.

Relaxed.

Peaceful.

Happy.

But it wouldn't last.

In three days, he would come out of hiding and take Kate with him.

There was no way around it. He'd been holed up in the desert for two months. Eventually, his enemies would find him, and here, he only had the protection of a handful of guards.

He needed to get his ass back to Caracas, where he would be surrounded by the fortification of his neighborhood and the hundreds of loyal criminals who worked for him.

But once he arrived in the city, his enemies would know.

Twelve years ago, he killed some important people and painted a target on his back. That had never mattered to him. Until now.

Until Kate.

There were so many ways he could lose her. So many fucking enemies. DEA, FBI, local crime lords, the Mexican government, neighboring cartels who fought for his smuggling routes, and of course, Lucia's brother-in-law and capo of the Colombian cartel, Matias Restrepo.

The biggest threat, however, was Cole Hartman.

Hartman had steered Tate directly to Lucia, and now he was helping Lucia locate Tate. Once that job was finished, he would come after Kate.

If anyone could separate her from Tiago, it was that fucking guy.

A tremor attacked his muscles, the barbs of dread sinking in and shredding his insides.

Tightening his arms around her, he pulled her closer against his chest and buried his nose in her hair. In her sleep, she burrowed into the shelter of his body and sighed.

When he lost Semira, he surrendered his humanity.

If he lost Kate, he would surrender everything.

TWENTY

Tiago woke with a start, his pulse pelting against his throat as the hum of a distant car engine lingered in his mind.

Had he dreamed it? Or had he heard it in his sleep?

The sky hung beyond the barred window like a black velvet blanket, hours before dawn.

No one should've been coming or going. Not the guards. Absolutely no visitors.

He held himself motionless, his hand possessively gripping Kate's perfect ass beneath her panties.

He didn't wear a stitch of clothing. No weapons within reach. He could only stare across the dark room in the direction of the locked door and listen.

The pitchlike silence heightened his paranoia, making him twitchy.

Seconds pounded by. Minutes. His hearing strained against the hush. No sounds. No movement.

Probably just remnants of the dread he'd carried into sleep.

But he couldn't shake the feeling something was wrong.

Reluctantly, he untwined his arms and legs from Kate's slender limbs, despising the separation from her soft, warm skin.

Moving quietly in the dark, he was careful not to wake her. But as he unfolded from the mattress, her groggy whisper floated up.

"Where are you going?"

He lowered back to the bed and kissed her parted lips.

"Getting some water." He traced the scalloped hem of her panties and fingered the bandage on her thigh, checking that it hadn't unraveled.

"Need anything?"

"More sleep." She rolled away, her breathing instantly falling into an even rhythm.

He ran a hand down her spine, smoothing the oversized shirt. *His shirt.*

He'd fucked her so many times last night she hadn't been able to keep her eyes open. Eventually, he'd put her in the panties and his shirt, because sleeping beside her nude body...

His dicked jerked. Started to harden.

Yeah.

Rising to his feet, he navigated through the dark room, located his bag of clothes, and pulled on the first thing he found. A pair of sweatpants.

Then he grabbed his phone and checked his messages on his way to the stairwell.

Just after three in the morning. No notifications. No missed calls. A quick peek at the live video of the shack confirmed Tate was safe and asleep.

At the bottom of the stairs, he scanned the main room. Muted light from the kitchen illuminated one occupied mattress. Arturo.

No reason to wake him. Not yet. The other guards would've been outside, patrolling the perimeter.

Except there should've been more of them asleep at this hour. Three on the day shift. Three on the night shift.

But only Arturo was required to sleep inside as a last layer of defense for Boones.

Pacing to the covered windows, he peered through the slit of one and probed the shadows.

The cars sat where expected. Stillness stretched to the horizon. Too dark. He couldn't see shit from this position. He would have to go out there to investigate.

He slipped into the kitchen on silent feet and grabbed the largest knife from the butcher block. Then he headed to the hall and made a beeline to Boones' room.

The door stood ajar. He stepped in.

The faint sound of snoring drifted from the bed, but it wasn't enough to calm his nerves. He needed to *see* Boones alive and free from harm.

He approached the bed and crouched beside it, straining his eyes in the dark until he could make out sheared gray hair, black skin over sharp bones, and the rise and fall of a scarred chest.

He exhaled a sigh of relief.

The snoring stopped.

"What's wrong?" Boones asked in his native tongue.

He lowered the butcher knife out of view. His scalp tingled, his senses telling him a tendril of unrest was creeping toward the house.

Or, most likely, it was just his overactive paranoia taking shape in imaginary noises.

"Just checking on you." He rested a hand over the welts on Boones' sternum, finding sanctuary in the thumps of a strong heartbeat. "If you die in your sleep, I'll have to find someone else to make breakfast in the morning."

"I spit in your eggs." Boones smacked him away, a smile in his voice. "Shut the door on your way out."

He did more than that. As he slipped into the hall, he turned the handle and engaged the lock from the inside without sounding the click and worrying Boones.

A hard kick would break the door, but it would take an extra second or two to bust in.

In the front room, he returned to the gap in the window. Outside, the landscape was a black tarp of empty silence.

Nothing moved. No guards in sight, which meant they were stationed where they were supposed to be, spread out around the property, watching the perimeter from every angle.

Still, he couldn't shake the tingling along his nape. His senses hummed on high-alert, the hilt of the knife hot in his hand.

He prowled through the front room, listening, waiting, second-guessing the foreboding feeling in his gut.

"*Jefe?*"

He turned toward the sound of Arturo's gruff voice and squinted at the silhouette sitting on the mattress. "Who's on watch right now?"

"Blueballs, Iliana, and Samuel." Arturo rose to his feet and said in Spanish, "Or maybe it's Alonso, not Iliana. I don't know. They switched up the schedule last night." A pause. "Juan was in here when I dozed off."

Alarm spiked his heart rate, hardening his body into battle mode.

"The guys rarely sleep in here." Arturo scratched his whiskers, wearing only a pair of boxers. "The desert is making them restless."

Tiago strode into the kitchen and removed all the bottom drawers in the cabinets. Behind each one waited a stash of weaponry and ammo. He grabbed a .40 cal pistol, two loaded magazines, and glanced down at his pants.

No pockets. No shoes. No shirt. He wasn't dressed for combat.

Tension stifled the muggy room as he loaded the magazine in the gun and set the extra one aside. Then he grabbed the knife, both hands armed.

Silence buzzed in his ears, a haze of muted light shining down from the ceiling. His skin itched, sticky with sweat, his pulse thick in his throat.

"What is it?" Arturo approached, zipping up the fly of his jeans. Eyes wide and alert, he loaded his own weapon. "You hear something?"

"Not sure. I'm going to take a walk outside. I need you to stay here with—"

The boom of gunfire sounded in the distance.

He froze, blinked, and in a blur of sharpness, he sped in the direction of the stairs.

Except Boones was down the hall.

His footsteps faltered, skidded.

Kate or Boones.

Kate or Boones.

Indecision cost him half a second.

He swung toward Arturo, pointing the knife. "Go to Boones. No matter what happens to me, you'll protect him with your life. Don't let him out, and do *not* leave his door. Swear to God, Arturo, if any harm comes to him, I will haunt you long after I'm dead."

The hard edge of his voice sent Arturo running toward the hall, carrying an armful of artillery.

He swiveled back toward the stairs.

Kate.

Flying into a sprint, he made it halfway through the front room before the windows exploded in a shower of glass and lead.

He shielded his face with an arm and ran into the shrapnel, hunching low to avoid a wayward bullet.

The front door crashed open, followed by a stampede of boots. Then the rapid firing of popped rounds and ear-splitting, disorientating chaos.

His military training kicked in, revving his pulse, sharpening his awareness, and focusing his mind on one objective.

Kill.

The Glock in his hand held fifteen rounds, and he used every bullet to clear a path to the stairs. When the pistol clicked empty, he whipped it across the face of the nearest intruder and threw it at the head of the next one.

Down to the knife, he slashed it along a heavily muscled arm. The man's firearm dropped out of reach. Tiago slashed low and opened the man's gut.

Five intruders left. Two swept up the stairs.

Kate.

Fury flogged him, but he couldn't chase them. Three men were already on him, punching, kicking, and swinging knives.

He tackled the only one with a gun, gripping the man's arm and guiding the automatic weapon as the fucker squeezed the trigger.

The spray of bullets went wild, punching a zigzagged line along the floor, up the front wall, and taking out one of his own guys.

He swept the man's legs out and wrestled him to the ground.

Gunfire sounded from the direction of Boones' room, ramping his pulse to a dangerous level, distracting him.

An elbow slammed into the back of his head. He coughed a pained grunt and lost his balance.

Adrenaline flooded his veins as he rolled, swept the blade wide, and cut a deep gash across the man's chest. Hardened eyes rounded in shock then tapered with the drive to kill.

With a grunt, Tiago flipped to his feet and spun as another guy jumped on his back. A backward stab with the blade relieved him of the threat behind him.

He rammed his forearm against the throat of one in front, pinning him against the wall.

Footsteps erupted on the stairs, descending at a run.

He swiveled his neck and marked two men making an escape from the second floor.

One of them carried Kate, her unconscious body dangling over a bulky shoulder, blood dripping from her face.

Heat smothered his brain and blinded his vision.

She'd put up a fight and received a knockout punch for the effort, which meant this wasn't a rescue attempt. It was a kidnapping, and he knew exactly how it would play out.

Her chance of survival was nil.

Rage detonated in his chest and hit the air in a blistering roar. He seethed, breaths shaking, teeth cutting the insides of his cheeks.

With a surge of strength, he pushed harder against the throat beneath his arm. Holding the knife in his other hand, he buried it in the man's skull, pushed it in to the hilt, and yanked it free.

The body dropped, and he launched for the stairs. Until someone slammed into him from behind.

The wind evacuated his lungs as he collided with the floor, his shirtless chest skidding through shards of glass beneath the weight of the man on his back.

He trained his eyes on the front door, where those dead motherfuckers had just carried out his whole fucking world.

They knew it, too. They knew exactly what she meant to him, because one of his own goddamn guards had tipped them off.

Someone had told them to head straight for the stairs.

An arm hooked around his neck from behind, the heavy drive of a knee against his spine. He shoved his upper body into a push-up, dug in his toes, and dove into a somersault. The man lost his grip and came up swinging.

Fists flew. Elbows. Shins. Bone-crunching smacks. Tiago wouldn't feel the pain from those hits until later. Right now, all he felt was pure, raw aggression, scorching his blood and driving him forward, toward her.

If he didn't get her back, he would burn the whole fucking country to the ground.

Venom seared through him, powering his punches, propelling each strike harder, faster, spraying blood, breaking teeth, bone, and cartilage, until the man slumped to the floor.

Legs quaking, heart thrashing, he grabbed a pistol off a dead body and bolted out the door and into the night.

At the end of the drive, taillights glowed red in the blackness. They already had her in the van. Already driving away.

Bullet holes littered his cars. Tires deflated. Hoods ablaze with fire.

He was too late.

Grief tried to suck him into the earth, but he pushed forward, throwing himself into a burning sprint.

Serrated air sawed in and out of his lungs. He pumped his legs and leveled the gun on the van's tires. Fired. Missed.

As he emptied the magazine, the van sped away, vanishing into the darkness.

He careened to a stop, braced swollen, bloody hands on his knees, and attempted to stymie the insufferable pain closing around his heart. If he let in the anguish, it would kill him.

This wasn't over.

He couldn't fail her.

Her captors would contact him, before or after they killed her. It depended on who they were and what they wanted. He had an hour at most to organize an attack.

First, he needed to find out where the fuck they were taking her.

Spinning, he raced back to the house as his mind pored over what he knew and everything that had just gone down. He recalled faces, accents, weapons, and fighting styles.

They were Mexican cartel.

When he burst through the front door, he barreled into Boones.

"What are you doing out of your room?" He ran his hands over Boones' shirtless torso, front to back, shoulders, legs, his frenzied search fueled by fear.

"Calm down." Boones gripped Tiago's arms, hindering his hunt for injuries. "I'm fine. Not a scratch."

His hands shook as he stepped back and locked onto Arturo's eyes behind Boones. "Search the property for survivors and bring the old truck around from the back. We're going to need it."

"*Si, Jefe.*" Arturo headed toward the door with a rifle.

"Arturo." He waited for eye contact, trying his damnedest not to fall apart in front of his guard. "Thank you for keeping Boones safe."

With a stiff nod, Arturo lumbered out the door.

"We need information." He combed the room littered with dead bodies and found one breathing.

The man lay on his back, his face and stomach soaked in blood as wet gurgling sounds wheezed from his mouth.

Boones stared down at the injured man and ambled toward the kitchen. "I'll get the sharpest knife."

Twenty minutes later, every inch of skin had been flayed from the squealer's chest. He didn't survive the torture, but Tiago now had a location and an identity.

The orchestrator of the attack was the *comandante* of a Mexican cartel. Hungry for money and power, they operated without borders, trafficking worldwide in drugs, prostitution, stolen cars, and contract murders. But it wasn't enough for them.

The *comandante* wanted Tiago's gun smuggling routes. Tiago had refused every offer and negotiation over the past couple of years, and thus, infuriated the ruthless, brutal man.

A man who now had Kate in his custody.

Tiago rose to his feet and stared down at the gore he'd strewn across the floor. Boiling rage lined his insides and scalded his throat, the taste of death coating his tongue.

During the skin-flaying session, Arturo had returned carrying Blueballs, the only survivor. The tattoo-eyed guard had been shot in the stomach and lived long enough to explain that he, Samuel, and Alonso were on the night shift.

Iliana and Juan had wandered off to fuck when the attackers arrived on foot. While Tiago's guards were picked off one by one, a van showed up. The occupants captured Iliana as she tried to race back to the house.

The same van that had taken Kate.

Blueballs had managed to wheeze out every detail while Boones worked tirelessly to save his life. When he died, Tiago knew Blueballs hadn't betrayed him.

Another concern was Tate, but a check on the video footage of the shack verified Kate's friend hadn't been touched.

The cartel had known exactly *who* to target. They knew Kate's capture and ultimate death would hit the deepest, most vulnerable part of Tiago.

There would be no negotiations.

The *comandante* would make contact in the form of body parts. Proof of Kate's death.

Normal behavior for a violent, power-hungry criminal group.

"You'll get her back." Boones cleaned away the blood from Tiago's trembling hands and shoved a clean shirt against his chest.

Tiago looked at him and Arturo, the only two left standing.

They seemed nervous amid the storm whipping off him, as if waiting for him to pull his shit together, anxious for a plan.

"Right. Okay. This is what we'll do." He outlined a strategy, called in fifty of his best men in Caracas, and sent them to a small town a couple of hours away, where Kate would be held.

Then he strapped on as many weapons as he could carry and rose out of hiding.

TWENTY-ONE

Taken.

Again.

Kate might've laughed at her absurd misfortune if she weren't so fucking terrified.

Handcuffs shackled her arms behind her, and the hood over her head confined her within a black, sightless world.

Sweat coated her skin, made worse by the chills that came in feverish waves. She licked her cracked lips, tasting blood. Probably from the fist that had knocked her out in Tiago's room.

Where was she? Who had taken her? What happened to Tiago?

She'd woken in the back of a moving vehicle. It had traveled another hour or so before stopping here.

Here was some kind of city, an urban area. She couldn't see through the hood, but she smelled the asphalt, felt the heat of it beneath her bare feet. The sounds of motor traffic rumbled nearby, as well as in the distance.

Men surrounded her, marching along in heavy boots, their deep voices firing words in Spanish.

Her insides buckled to the point of nausea. Her lungs couldn't gather enough air.

The cold metal of guns prodded at her from both sides. When her toes caught on a curb or a crack, someone pushed her from behind.

After a few minutes, the crumbly concrete underfoot smoothed into polished cement, and the scuffing of boots echoed off walls that closed in around her.

She'd just entered a building.

Ushered forward by barking shouts and urgent hands, she was forced into a jog. She imagined a winding hallway with countless turns and stairs going up and down.

With her hands fettered behind her, it fucked with her balance. The whole thing was a stumbling, falling, slipping all-out run to some unknown destination.

Eventually, calloused fingers yanked her to a halt.

More voices. The same ones, new ones, all yelling in Spanish. The scent of motor oil and gasoline permeated the hood, tickling her nose.

"Who are you guys?" She spun around, blind and winded. "Where am I?"

A hand caught her neck, squeezing her airway, strangling. Hot breath saturated the outside of the hood, seeping through the material and heating her face.

Her mouth gulped for oxygen. She couldn't breathe, couldn't escape the choking grip.

He held her there, waited as the very end of her life crashed toward her in a chest-squeezing, lonely, black wave of nothingness.

Alone.

She would die alone.

The collar of fingers released her with a vicious shove that sent her careening across the floor on her back. Boots shuffled out of her way. One of them kicked her into a corner.

She pressed herself there, curling into a ball, gasping for life, and swallowing silent tears.

Time passed in frantic heartbeats. Her pulse hammered for an hour. Maybe two.

The cement floor grew unbearably hard beneath her butt, grinding against her bones. Her legs bare, her body covered in only a shirt, she was overly exposed and unarmed. But still alive.

Not once did she let herself consider the possibility Tiago was dead. He was too untouchable, too impervious. Too goddamn mean to die.

He would hunt her down. Find her. Hopefully, before it was too late.

Footsteps came and went. Others scuffed around her, lingering, guarding. The men never shut up, their voices charged with energy, fear, excitement.

Then she heard a word she recognized.

Comandante.

A horrible feeling overtook her, running chills down her spine. She was already in the worst situation she could imagine. But hearing the mention of a *comandante*, she knew this was either a rebel group or a cartel.

She wouldn't escape this alive.

TAKE

That suspicion solidified when another set of boots entered the room and paused before her.

The hood lifted, and florescent lighting blinded her eyes. She blinked through the brightness as the cold press of steel caught her beneath the chin.

Her heart stopped.

Holy fucking goddamn, that was a huge fucking knife.

The man holding it crouched before her. Black hair and a mustache, pockmarked cheeks, and soulless eyes, he smelled of cigarettes and torture.

She scanned the surrounding shelves that lined the wall, taking in stacks of machinery, tools, a random tire, and things made of steel. A supply room full of automotive parts? A mechanic shop, maybe.

Nothing within reach to slam into his face. Not that she could with her arms handcuffed at her back.

Another man stood beside her and gathered a fistful of hair on her crown, pulling, elongating her neck.

And she knew.

They were going to cut off her head.

Her insides turned to ice as her mind spun, quickly forming an idea and weaving a bogus story.

"I've been waiting for you guys." She met the eyes of the man with the knife.

He arched a brow.

"Do you speak English?" she asked.

"Yes."

"Take me to the *comandante*." Her bladder threatened to release beneath the force of her almighty fear.

"I am the *comandante*."

Oh God, oh God, oh God.

With a deep breath, she raised her chin above the knife. "I work for Matias Restrepo. Do you know—?"

"Everyone knows Restrepo." His gaze pulsed with interest.

"He planted me inside Tiago Badell's organization. The assignment was to grow close to Badell, become his lover, and wait for your infiltration. Matias Restrepo knew you would capture me, and that you would feel inclined to…uh…" Her teeth chattered. "To send my head to Badell."

The man grinned with yellow teeth. "Go on."

"Restrepo wants you to contact him."

"Why would I do that?"

"Because I have information. Intel I've been gathering on Badell. And because you just extracted me from the hands of Restrepo's enemy, he's now in your debt." She hardened her jaw. "Call him. Tell him you have Kate, and you'll be generously rewarded."

It was a risk. He could just as easily torture her for the intel she boasted about. Of course, she didn't know shit about Tiago's business dealings, so it would be a slow, bloody, horrifically gruesome way to die. Much worse than getting her head sawed off.

But she was offering the *comandante* an opportunity to join forces with Matias Restrepo, an offer no one ever received. She didn't know who this man was in the underground world, but she hoped her bullshit story carried some weight.

If only for a little while.

She just needed to buy some time until Tiago arrived.

Swallowing against the blade, she held the *comandante's* oily gaze. After an eternity of wordless torment, he lowered the knife.

It took everything she had not to pass out in relief.

He rose to his feet and barked a string of Spanish words. The room erupted in a scurry of squeaky boots. Everyone evacuated except the man fisting her hair.

His hand tightened, yanking her forward. She fell with a yelp, her cheek pressed against the cement as he unlocked the shackle on one of her wrists.

Oh, thank fuck.

She rolled her stiff shoulders, started to rise, and heard the clicking sound of handcuffs latching onto something.

"You just saved your head." The *comandante* lingered in the doorway, staring down at her. "Until I reach Restrepo, you are ours to enjoy."

He slipped into the hall, and her stomach turned inside out. She scrambled away from the other man, but the snap of her arm yanked her back.

The son of a bitch had handcuffed her to his wrist.

"This is a mistake." She scooted on her back and stretched her free arm out to the side, floundering for something to grip, a heavy piece of steel, something sharp, anything she could brandish as a weapon. "Restrepo will kill you if you rape me."

Her fingers gripped the leg of a steel shelving unit. She pulled, and he pulled her back by her leg, dragging her across the floor.

At the center of the room, he dropped her feet near the door, dove on top of her, and ripped off her panties with a violating fist.

"No!" She thrashed beneath him, smacking at his greasy face and kicking her legs. "No! Stop! Get off me! You'll regret this."

He was thinner, smaller than Tiago, but still twice her size. She couldn't get leverage, and even if she did, she was fucking handcuffed to his arm. Where would she go?

Didn't stop her from putting up the biggest fight of her life. She went crazy, bucking, screaming, scratching, and biting. She lost her mind, flailing in a fog of desperation and horror.

Seconds felt like hours, and her body started to give out, draining energy fast.

He forced her thighs apart with his knees and unzipped his pants. She released a blood-curdling roar, and his hand clapped over her mouth as his other fisted his swollen dick.

She sank her teeth into his fingers. He bellowed, face red, and reared back his arm.

Her heart slammed. She saw it coming and instinctively closed her eyes, knowing she couldn't dodge the impact.

He made a choking sound, and a hot wet drizzle dripped across her thigh.

She opened her eyes to a sharp object protruding from his chest.

Her brain couldn't make sense of it, and he seemed to share her confusion as he stared down at the serrated steel edge that stuck out several inches beneath his breastbone.

Then it moved, slicking upward in a vertical line, cutting his torso from bottom to top.

Blood poured in a bright red stream from the wound, from his mouth, bubbling down his chin.

She gulped, gulped, gulped, with no sound. No air. Her pulse throbbed so loudly it created a vacuum in her ears.

The blade pulled free. Life leaked from the man's eyes as he tipped to the side and hit the floor, unblocking her view of the door.

Tiago stood over her, glaring at the dead body before leveling her with force of his terrifyingly potent presence.

A machete dangled from his hand, magnifying the fury and testosterone pouring off him. Brown eyes darkened into hues of feral. Speckles of red splattered the shadows on his face. God, that strikingly beautiful face, all brutal angles, sculpted lines, and dangerous scars.

The air left her lungs in trembling gasps.

He'd abducted her, fucked her, pissed on her, scarred her.

And saved her.

She squeezed her legs together and shook beneath the press of his power. The most arresting kind of power—lawless, savage, protective.

He wore a black leather jacket and jeans, both stained in blood. No telling how many people he'd slaughtered on his way here.

"I've never been more happy to see you." She pulled her feet under her but couldn't stand. Not with her arm handcuffed to the dead body.

Tiago knelt between her legs and trapped her fingers between his and the floor. Then he swung the machete, cutting off the man's hand.

Bile hit her throat. The sight and aroma of so much gore numbed her brain and chilled her from the base of her skull to the tips of her toes.

Wriggling the handcuff from the severed limb, he circled the rotating arm all the way around, which left it unlocked and hanging from her wrist.

"I'll remove this later." He gripped the cuff still attached to her.

"With a key, I hope."

A big hand lifted to cradle the side of her face, commanding her gaze to his.

"I almost lost you." He swallowed hard.

The jog in his strong, muscular throat reminded her this brutal, hardcore criminal was human.

She'd been taken from him, nearly beheaded and raped, and the starkness in his eyes told her he knew. He knew exactly the sort of horrors she'd just evaded.

"You weren't too late or too slow." She touched her forehead to his, replaying the words he said about his wife's death. "You don't need to put me back together. You didn't fail."

Tilting her chin back with his finger, he scanned her face with a flicker of vulnerability in his eyes. There and gone in a flash, his handsome Venezuelan features went from gentle to stony.

"I killed the man who hit you." He prodded a thumb around the cut near her eye. "Got him on my way in."

"How do you even know—?"

"Did he have a crucifix tattooed on his neck?"

Yeah, he sure did. Tiago must've identified him while she was transported out of the house.

"Don't we need to go?" she asked.

"Arturo," he called over his shoulder.

The burly guard poked his head into the room, held up a finger, and returned to the hall.

"We're waiting." He slid off the backpack that hung from his shoulder and removed a pair of shorts and running shoes. "Put these on."

"Waiting for what?" She pulled on the shorts, sans underwear.

As she shoved on the sneakers, his hand wandered to her thigh, smoothing over the bandage where he'd cut her.

"There's a gunfight outside." He withdrew his touch and glanced at the door. "Not taking you out there until the numbers have dwindled."

"Gunfight?" She listened for a moment and was met with silence.

"We're deep within the warehouse." He grabbed her hand and stood, lifting her with him. "One of their chop shops."

TAKE

"Cartel?"

"Yes."

"The *comandante* – "

"Killed him, too."

Before or after the man called Matias Restrepo? Didn't matter at this point. Matias might've been in route here, but he'd still be hours away.

"Hold onto my waistband." He pulled out two handguns and swung the backpack behind him. "We're going to run into some resistance on our way out. Stick to me like glue until I tell you otherwise. Understand?"

"I want a gun."

"No." He turned toward the door.

"Why not?"

"Because you have me," he growled.

"But –"

"If you shoot me in the back, accidentally or deliberately, your chances of escape drop to zero."

Well, shit. She didn't like it, but she understood. Those were his guys out there, fighting and dying under *his* command. They were loyal to him, not her. If he died, she was fucked, with or without a gun.

"We're not returning to the desert, are we?" she asked.

"No."

"Is Tate –?"

"*Jefe.*" Arturo appeared in the doorway and lowered a phone from his ear. "It's time."

"Tate is safe." Tiago gave her his back and adjusted his grip on the pistols. "Hands on my belt."

She curled her fingers around his belt loops, registering the small gun between his tailbone and waistband. Multiple knives strapped to his hips, legs, and boots. Loaded magazines filled every pocket and holster. He was a walking armory.

"Let's go." He charged into the hall.

She did her best to keep up with his long-legged strides. Arturo stepped in behind her, pacing backward to cover the rear.

Her breathing sped up, tripping in her throat as Tiago navigated a maze of never-ceasing turns and stairs.

The muffled report of gunfire alerted her they were getting close, and she silently thanked him for coming for her.

His body felt like steel beneath her hands, shifting and flexing through a seamless glide of muscle. Her gaze traced the sinewy cords in his thick neck, taking in the strength of it, the harsh cut of his rigid jaw, and the profile of a face chiseled in stone.

He was such a devastatingly sexy man. If he were normal and this was normal, she might've told him he was the most beautiful man she'd ever seen.

The boom of guns came in bursts, slowing between each report but growing louder as he crept to a doorway. It opened to a massive garage crammed with more luxury cars and motorcycles than she could count.

Armed men patrolled the space. Just outside the wall of garage doors waited more men, who fired off sporadic rounds and shouted at one another.

"This is the only way out," he whispered so low she had to strain her ears. "I need to clear the room."

Before she could draw a breath, he was on the move. Arms stretched out before him, he trained the pistols and sidled along the back wall, using his body as a shield in front of her.

The men in the garage didn't spot him creeping amid the shadows. Arturo veered off in the opposite direction, rifle raised, headed toward the huge garage doors.

Her pulse pommeled, her stomach a block of ice, as her fingers dug into Tiago's hips.

He reached a wall covered with small hooks holding keys. Flicking his gaze over it, he examined each one.

What was the plan? Would he steal a car?

He snatched a key, apparently the one he was looking for, given the glimmer in his eyes. Then he pivoted, gripped her arms, and shoved her into a nook between a workbench and concrete wall.

"Stay," he mouthed.

She locked her legs as he spun and blitzed through the garage toward the enemy, his guns up and firing.

Two men went down. Others shot back. He found cover behind an engine block, but the shooters closed in, surrounding him.

On the far side, Arturo hoisted one of the rolling garage doors, letting in a flood of morning light.

The distraction allowed Tiago to fire off another kill shot. But more men flooded in, through the open door and from the other side of the garage.

Her heart pounded so hard it made her lightheaded. She felt helpless, useless, her hand clutching her throat as she watched without breath.

Arturo volleyed bullets from the shadows, taking down the men Tiago missed. But there were too many.

They were outnumbered.

Bullets pinged off steel casings and pelleted beautiful cars. Glass shattered. Dying groans sounded from fallen bodies.

Arturo let out an enraged shout, dropping beneath a flurry of fists and losing his gun. A moment later, he found his feet and launched into a bloody brawl with multiple men, punching and choking and spitting blood.

She searched the space around her and spotted a tire iron. Dropping to hands and knees, she crawled to it, curled her fingers around the cold metal, and waited with her heart in her stomach.

Tiago must've run out of ammo, because he chucked his last gun and reached back to free the machete from his backpack.

In a blur of incredible speed and strength, he ran through the half a dozen attackers, taking down the ones with guns.

The din of bullets fell silent, replaced by the panting grunts of hand-to-hand combat.

She trained her eyes on the open garage door and spotted a clear path.

Gripping the dangling handcuff against the tire iron so it wouldn't rattle, she drew in a deep breath and ran.

The shadows along the back wall concealed her escape. No one noticed her. Those who were still alive were fighting to stay that way.

Twenty feet from the exit, Arturo bent over a man, pummeling his fists, over and over. Farther away, Tiago took on three others, slashing the machete with the skill of a professional assassin.

She reached the exit and peered outside.

Bodies scattered the parking lot. The gunfight had moved down the street, and the number of shooters seemed to have been drastically reduced.

Buildings lined the narrow roads. Plenty of places to hide and provide cover as she fled this nightmare.

This was it.

She could make a run for it and find a way to contact Matias.

Her hand slicked around the tire iron as she stepped into the parking lot and tasted the bright light of freedom.

Another step and the space between her shoulder blades itched.

He had come all this way for her. Protected her. Shielded her with his body. And she was bailing on him?

Her chest squeezed, and her throat closed.

Fuck!

She couldn't leave. Not without looking back. Not without seeing him one more time.

TWENTY-TWO

Twisting her neck, Kate scanned the garage behind her. As she honed in on the powerful body laid out on the floor, a sudden coldness hit her core.

She'd expected Tiago to be the only one standing, not face down in blood with a man pounding fist after fist into his ribs.

Her hand squeezed around the tire iron, clanking the handcuffs.

She needed to leave.

Right now.

Tiago stretched an arm toward the machete, but it lay too far out of reach.

Her shoes turned into blocks of cement.

Fucking goddammit!

Across the garage, Arturo wrestled another man in and out of a choke hold. The rest were dead or too injured to move.

Tiago continued to lie there as that fucker pounded fists into his back and ribs. He just took it, his legs twitching as he absorbed every strike.

Her heart cried out, and her molars slammed together, grinding hard enough to break enamel.

Before her brain caught up, her legs were moving, carrying her toward him as fast as she could run.

She was neither stealthy nor strong. But she was quick, approaching the man's back and smacking the tire iron into his head before he knew what hit him.

He toppled over, and she continued to swing, slamming the metal rod into his skull, again and again. She didn't stop hitting until strong arms banded around her, yanking her back, pulling her away.

The weapon fell from her hands, and she turned, stunned so completely she felt as though she were floating outside of her body.

Lifting her head, she stared into Tiago's impossibly gorgeous eyes and swayed. Or maybe the room was swaying.

No, it was him.

She grabbed his leather-clad arms and steadied him. "Are you okay?"

"I am now." He tiptoed ice-cold fingers along her jaw, leaned in, and stopped before their lips made contact. "Got a lot to say and do to you, but we need to go."

A scream sounded from an office-like room in the front of the garage. A woman's scream.

His face tightened, and he bent down to snatch the machete from the floor.

On the other side of the room, Arturo snapped up his head, where he stepped through piles of carnage, stabbing anyone who still lived.

"Who is that?" Kate shifted toward the office.

A slender figure emerged in the doorway. Short black hair. Seductive mouth. Iliana.

Why was she in that room and not fighting alongside the others? Was she hiding?

Iliana spotted Tiago and ran toward him. "*Jefe,* oh my God! You made it!"

He gave Kate's hand a squeeze and prowled ahead, toward the approaching woman, slowly, stiffly, letting the machete hang from his lolling fingers.

Was he tilting a little to the side?

Blood covered him from head to toe. His clothes were an utter mess and would need to be burned, but there weren't any concentrated stains. Nothing to indicate the blood was coming from him.

As she studied his gait, he seemed steady. Strong. He'd taken a helluva beating and was probably in a world of hurt.

"I was so afraid they got you." Iliana raced toward him and raised her arms, as if to embrace him.

Two steps away, he stopped, flexed his hand. Then he ran the blade of the machete through her stomach and out the back.

Her mouth gaped, eyes wide with shock as she doubled over the hilt.

He twisted it, gave it a hard shove, and yanked it free.

Kate cupped a hand over her mouth to smother a whimper. What the unholy fuck?

When Iliana hit the floor, he wiped the blade on her shirt and jeans until it was clean. That done, he rose and stalked toward Kate.

Her heart pounded as she shuffled back. "Why?"

"She betrayed me." He strode past her, grabbed her hand, and hauled her with him. "She took you from me."

"How do you know?"

"Why do you think she tried so hard to get in my bed?" He veered toward a row of motorcycles, his gaze sweeping over each one. "She was feeding information to the cartel."

"Why would she do that?"

"Money. Protection. Who knows? Maybe they were holding something over her." He punched something into his phone and pocketed it.

"That's how they found you in the desert."

"And how they knew you were important to me."

Her chest constricted. "You knew she was a traitor all this time?"

"No." He paused beside the biggest, meanest-looking bike and inserted the key from his pocket. "I'm suspicious in nature. Never trusted her. When she vanished after you were taken, I knew."

So he killed her.

There was a time, not too long ago, when he would've run that blade through Kate.

He removed the backpack from his shoulders, stored the machete in it, and strapped it onto her back.

"Arturo!" he shouted across the garage. "You good?"

"Never been better." The guard strode toward the open garage door, his face a mask of blood as he took off in the direction of lingering gunfire.

Tiago mounted the motorcycle and fired up the engine. "Hop on."

"Helmets?"

"Afraid not."

"Shouldn't we take one of the sports cars, instead?"

"If we're chased, this is the best option." His eyes turned flinty. "I'm getting impatient."

Grateful he'd brought her a pair of shorts and shoes, she swung a leg over the huge hunk of steel and scooted in behind him.

The handcuff on her wrist caught against his leather jacket as she wrapped her arms around his chest.

He tensed and adjusted her hold to squeeze him lower around his abs. Then he zoomed out of the garage, polluting the air with a hard rev of the engine.

Turning in the opposite direction of the gunfight, he hit the narrow streets at a speed that stole her breath.

Her hair whipped around her head, her body bending with his as he ducked low, his face protected by the small windshield.

TAKE

She tucked in tight against his back and squinted her eyes away from the blasts of air. The sun sat just over the horizon, the humidity clinging to her pores despite the constant lashing of wind.

He didn't slow. Not through stop signs or intersections. He raced out of the small, concrete town scattered with sagging buildings and minimal traffic and arrowed into a thick copse of trees.

The winding road snaked through a jungle-like terrain. Twenty minutes in, asphalt turned to dirt, and civilization faded behind her.

Did he know where he was going?

She clenched her arms around his waist, blinking through the windblown tangles of her hair.

Another twenty minutes zipped by, taking them deeper into the tropical wilderness of massive trees and hanging vines.

He'd stopped maintaining a constant speed. The motorcycle slowed, sped up, teetered a little, and thrust forward again.

Why did he feel so rigid in her arms?

Slipping a hand under his zipped jacket, she followed the grooves of his hard stomach to his chest. He felt really cold and sweaty through the shirt. His breaths heaved shallowly, erratically against her palm.

Then her fingers encountered wetness.

She yanked her hand back and held it up.

Blood.

"Tiago!" She grabbed his arm. "Stop the bike."

"Almost there."

"How far?" she shouted into the gust.

"Two hours."

"You'll be dead by then!"

He hit the gas, refusing to stop. The next mile blurred by. And another. Then the bike wobbled.

She held onto his waist, eyes closed, bracing for impact. But he kept them upright and found a turnoff, veering onto a trail and slowing through overgrown foliage.

Woody branches scratched her bare legs as he eased them to a stop without crashing.

She jumped off and spun in a circle, scanning the surroundings.

Trees. More trees. So much green and buzzing insects and endless nature. They were in a fucking jungle, without doctors or medical supplies.

"What the actual fuck, Tiago?" She whirled on him. "Were you shot? Stabbed?"

He killed the engine, slid off the bike, and walked to a nearby clearing. "Just need to sit for a second."

His gait was wrong, lacking his usual power and confidence. He stumbled into a lopsided step, and she raced to his side, hooking his arm over her shoulders and lowering him to the ground.

Kneeling before him, she shrugged off the backpack and inspected his face.

Clammy complexion, pained eyes, sinful lips, he looked so damn beautiful, even in agony.

"Where's your phone?" She patted the front pockets of his jeans. "Need to call Boones."

"Already sent him an alert. My phone has a tracker. He'll find us."

A smidgen of relief loosened her shoulders.

"I have to remove your jacket." She yanked down the zipper.

The instant she wrangled it off his arms, her heart plunged to her sneakers.

Multiple stab wounds gouged his shoulder, and it looked like a bullet went through the side of his chest. And the blood... God, she could taste the gravity of it on her tongue.

No wonder he'd moved her arms to his waist when she mounted the bike.

"Why didn't you tell me?" She ripped his t-shirt down the front, carefully removed it from his body, and shredded strips of it to use as bandages.

"The knife wounds are superficial, and the bullet just grazed my side."

"Why is there so much blood?"

"You were going to run."

The rapid change of subject stammered her breath, and she dragged her gaze to his. "What?"

"At the warehouse. You started out the garage door. But you came back. You chose *me*." His voice broke on the last word, at odds with the smug look in his eyes.

"Don't misunderstand me. I want my freedom back." She tore open the backpack and dug through weapons, searching for medical supplies. "Do you have anything in here —?"

The *click-click-click* of metal yanked her attention to her wrist.

The open end of the handcuffs, which had hung from her arm a moment ago, was now shackled around his.

She pulled, and his hand came with it, snug within the cuff. Locked. "You did *not* just do that."

"I'm not letting you go." His eyes hooded, heavy with pain, but his timbre carried all the weight of a possessive, overbearing man.

"Where's the key?"

"Don't have it."

"What if you die?" Outrage screeched into her voice.

"Not gonna die."

"You're bleeding all over the fucking place, and I don't even know if the bullet is still in you."

"Check the jacket." He lowered to his back and dropped his unshackled arm across his forehead.

She snatched the pile of leather, swinging his cuffed hand around with hers as she hunted for a bullet hole.

There it was, a tiny tear in the back of the jacket. How had she missed that?

A knife had cut up his shoulder pretty good, but the leather wasn't torn all to hell. The jacket must've been hanging open, which meant he'd zipped it later to hide the wounds from her.

Grinding her teeth, she ripped up the rest of his shirt and stared at the battlefield on his chest. "I don't know what to do."

"There's a first-aid kit at the bottom of the backpack."

He talked her through how to clean and dress the injuries. There was enough gauze to wrap the wounds, and his instructions were precise and calm. Given the number of scars on his body, he knew his way around an injury.

"How long before Boones arrives?" She wadded up the jacket and propped it under his head.

"Don't know." His voice took on an edge of pain. "An hour-ish. Maybe more."

"What about Arturo?"

"He went to the desert with another guard. Need them there to look after Tate."

Tiago could've just freed Tate and eliminated that complication, but this was neither the time nor place for that argument.

"Can we call someone else?" She used the extra pieces of the shirt to clean his mouth, cheeks, and neck.

"No." He lay on his back and stared up at her, the look on his face *not* like a man who lost a lot of blood.

His tongue peeked out, wetting his lips, his gaze alert and watchful. Always watching, staring as if he were seconds from swallowing her whole.

"You must be hurting." *And delirious.* She rummaged through the first-aid kit. "Do you have anything to dull the pain?"

"You."

"Get real."

"*You* are going to take the edge off."

She let out a tight laugh and glanced down. He wasn't even hard.

His eyes lost focus through a long, slow blink, as if he were fighting to stay awake. "Sit on my cock."

"You've lost your damn mind. How can you think about that right now? You just killed like fifty men, drove an hour on a motorcycle while bleeding and half-dead. Not to mention you don't even have enough blood in your body to get it up. Oh, and we're probably surrounded by snakes, spiders, and random other venomous—"

"Shut the fuck up, Kate." His pale lips failed to form the *T* in her name.

"Shit." She reached for the red-soaked gauze on the side of his chest. "You're still bleeding."

"Apply pressure." His voice was weak, reedy. He was fading fast.

Flattening her hands against the wound, she pressed hard and held it. His lashes lowered, hiding the agony in his eyes.

"Tiago." She didn't know if his injuries were life-threatening, but keeping him awake seemed important. "Stay with me, dammit."

His eyes snapped open, sharpened, drilling into hers. "Need to tell you something."

"What?"

"I love you."

Her heart skipped. "You're insane."

"Love is insanity."

Desperate to keep him alert and talking, she leaned in and asked, "What do you love about me?"

"First off…" He lifted his unshackled hand to her face. "Everything."

His eyes fluttered shut, and his arm dropped.

Passed out.

TWENTY-THREE

I love you?

Kate blew out a ragged breath.

Maybe those words would've meant something if Tiago weren't caught in the delirium of blood loss, but right now, he didn't know what he loved.

"Tiago." Pressing against his wound with one hand, she pried open his eyes with the other. "Wake up."

Nothing.

Her nerves rioted, quickening her pulse. "Tiago!"

When he didn't stir, her anxiety burned to anger.

She was shackled in the middle of a jungle in Venezuela. At any moment, she could be ambushed by a rebel group, attacked by a man-eating panther, or strangled by an anaconda.

If he died…

She eyed the machete sticking out of his backpack, recalling how he'd freed her from the last dead body.

Fucking hell, she didn't have the stomach for that.

"Wake up!" she shouted in his face.

Was he even breathing? Her heart raced as she scanned him for signs of life.

"Damn you, Tiago. Nothing says *I love you* like handcuffing me to your dead body." She pressed shaky fingers against the pulse point on his throat, panicking. "This is sick and fucking twisted, even for you."

A breath huffed past his lips, and he cracked open an eye.

"I'm not dead." He shifted, groaning in pain. "Would drag my ball sac through ten miles of broken glass for another chance to be inside you."

"Oh my God." She groaned with a mix of relief and annoyance.

"You're so beautiful." His eyes glossed over and faded beneath the descent of thick lashes.

"No, no, no. You need to stay awake."

"Did you fuck me unconscious?" The corner of his mouth crooked, but his eyes remained closed.

"You wish. Where's your phone?"

"Boones will come." A slurring whisper.

"Before or after you die?"

No answer.

She gripped his square jaw. Too slack. Too cold.

Too unconscious.

Fuck.

If he survived this, she was going to kill him.

She eased the leather jacket from beneath his lolling head and located his phone in the pocket. It was locked, of course, with a passcode she couldn't hack. She couldn't even tell if there was a signal.

What if they were in a dead zone? Was cell service required for tracking?

She checked the bullet wound, and it appeared to stop bleeding. Turning her attention to the backpack, she removed all the knives and tried each one on the handcuffs. None of them made a dent in the chain. Not even the machete.

She tried to pick the lock. That only ended in cursing, screaming hysterics.

Her mouth felt like stale toast, despite the mugginess in the air. There was no water, no way to hydrate. She hadn't had anything to drink since last night.

Out of options, she turned her anger to the unconscious man at her side. "I hate you."

The words tasted sour and made her stomach hurt.

She needed to hate him, but she couldn't. She needed him to live, because if he didn't, she would feel that loss in ways she didn't want to examine.

An ache burned the backs of her eyes, and her chest caved beneath the constriction of fear.

"Don't die." She stretched out beside him and snuggled in under his uninjured shoulder, pressing herself so tightly against him she felt the slow thud of his heartbeat.

"Don't you dare give up." She buried her face into his neck and let the tears fall.

With her free hand clinging to the hilt of the machete, she forced herself to stay awake, her awareness heightened with every rustle and buzz in the jungle.

As the residual effects of adrenaline abandoned her, exhaustion barreled in. She fought the overpowering need to close her eyes, perking her ears, watching the trail, waiting.

When the rumble of a distant engine broke the silence, she shot to her feet and heaved the machete out in front of her.

Her pulse exploded as the vehicle approached. It could be anyone. Someone more interested in killing Tiago than saving his life.

A van emerged through the trees, slowing on the road at the entrance of the trail. Twenty feet away.

Only the front of the vehicle had windows, and through the glass, she made out two faces.

Faces she didn't recognize.

Her hands shook as she planted her feet on either side of his body, crouching over him and holding out the machete.

The arm connected to hers limited her range of motion, but she had a weapon. Multiple knives. They would have to go through her to get to him.

The doors opened and shut. Her muscles trembled with enough force to stop her heart.

"Don't come any closer!" She adjusted her grip on the hilt and bit down on her cheek, sawing through tender tissues.

Footsteps approached. Big men, wearing sunglasses, heavy boots, and armed to the gills with holstered guns and knives.

They didn't run at her. Didn't free their weapons and start shooting.

"Who are you?" she shouted. "What do you want?"

A creak sounded near the van. The back door closed, and a tall, gray-headed, black man emerged on the trail.

The warm, familiar face swarmed her with overwhelming emotion. The surge crashed through her so violently she nearly fell beneath the weight of it.

The machete tumbled into the foliage, and she buckled over, giving into the sobs that piled in her throat.

Boones reached her side and gripped the handcuffs on her wrist, staring at the link to Tiago's arm. She didn't know what she expected, but it wasn't the laughter that burst from his chest.

The comforting sound of it combined with the gentle squeeze of his fingers around hers reduced her to a hot mess of sobbing, laughing, maniacal hiccups.

"He's lost so much blood." She sobered and quickly walked him through the gruesome points of Tiago's injuries.

The other two men gathered the backpack and weapons, and two minutes later, they had Tiago in their arms, up the trail, and laid out on his back in the rear of the van.

The handcuffs pulled her along. Boones joined her in the cargo space, which was loaded with multiple medical bags and equipment.

As much as she wanted the damn manacle off her wrist, she didn't mention it as Boones went to work on Tiago's wounds.

The light in the roof illuminated his steady scalpel and meticulous stitches, his face aglow with remarkable concentration.

She found a case of water amid the supplies and guzzled three bottles. She used another to wet Tiago's lips and clean the blood from his body.

As Boones taped on the bandages, she filled him in on the events at the warehouse, explaining how things ended with Iliana.

He caught her up on what happened during the attack at the house. The news that Arturo was the only surviving guard hit her harder than she expected.

When Boones finished the last bandage, he nodded at the driver waiting in the front seat.

The engine rumbled to life, and the van shot into motion, speeding toward Caracas.

She took in Tiago's rapid breathing, slack face, and bruised body, willing him to look at her. But his lashes didn't stir.

It tightened her chest. "Is he going to live, Dr. Frankenstein?"

Boones cut his eyes at her, his expression disgruntled.

"You didn't create the monster." She clutched Tiago's limp hand, linking their fingers. "But you've been patching him up for twelve years."

"He's not a monster."

Flashbacks of the past few hours peppered her mind in blood and bullets. "He is when he needs to be."

His face softened, relaxing the scars on his cheeks. "I've been his accomplice through it all. He will always have my support, even when he makes mistakes."

"He's made a lot of mistakes, Boones. Just in the past couple of months. With *me*."

"Yes, but he'll learn from them. I don't always agree with his actions, but I believe in him." He crooked a finger at her. "Let me look at you."

She scooted around Tiago's body and let Boones clean the injury on her face. Then he removed the bandages on her thigh. His body language gave nothing away as he cleaned the swirling cuts and applied a tingling cream.

"It's beautiful, isn't it?" She searched his eyes.

"Yes." He redressed her leg with clean bandages. "You're healing him."

"What do you mean?"

"He's been hurting for a long time. I can only heal the body. But you..." He clutched her hand and placed it against Tiago's chest. "You heal the rest."

She didn't know about that, but there was one milestone she could share with him.

"He's giving up the kidnapping business." At the widening of his eyes, she felt a shimmer of pride. "He made that deal with me last night."

Boones studied her with an unreadable expression. Then a smile broke through. "See? You're good for him."

She nodded, accepting the truth in that. "So how about helping me out of these handcuffs?"

"Not a chance." He turned to his medical supplies and started putting things away.

"Why not?"

"He secured you that way for a reason, and they will stay until he decides to remove them."

Dammit.

"You didn't answer my first question." She took in Tiago's pallid complexion and the bandages that covered half of his torso. "He's going to live, right?"

"He's very lucky. If the bullet hit anywhere else on his chest, even just slightly to the left, it would've damaged organs or bones. Surgery in a van is less than ideal."

"He would've died."

"Yes."

"What about the blood loss?"

"No arteries were nicked. He'll be weak for a while, but he'll recover. The priority right now is getting him to safety."

The hairs on her nape lifted. "Are we in danger?"

"He's a wanted man." He stared down at Tiago's face with a troubled look. "There will always be danger."

She considered the long list of enemies he'd acquired over the years. No matter what he did going forward, he would never escape what he'd done.

"He can't leave this life, can he?" She swallowed. "Even if he wanted to?"

"When he avenged my daughter's death, he was labeled as a criminal and forced to live like one. He's safer here, among other criminals, than out there in normal society. Here, in the heart of hell, he's protected."

She shivered at what his words meant. What they meant for *her*. If she didn't escape, his violent world would become her life. If she managed to get away, she would lose him.

"Are we going to his compound?" she asked. "That's where he lives, right?"

"He *did*."

"What does that mean?"

"I'm taking you to his penthouse in Caracas."

"He has a penthouse?" She couldn't imagine it.

"It's a luxury he owns but never indulged in. He kept it for my brothers and me. He didn't want us sleeping in the filth of his slum, and he doesn't want you sleeping there, either."

"No more mattresses on the floor?"

"He has a very nice, very large bed in the penthouse that has never been slept in." He cast her a knowing look. "Or used in any way."

She refused to acknowledge his response and held up her shackled arm. "What happens when we get there and I need to pee?"

"Hold it or release it. The handcuffs stay on."

TWENTY-FOUR

Tiago woke to the immaculate face of an angel. She floated over him, her vivid blue eyes backlit by a halo of golden hair. The seam of her cupid lips separated, and he wanted nothing more than to hear her voice, taste her kiss, and lose himself in her ferocity.

"I must be dead." Confusion poked at his muddled brain. "Except angels don't exist in hell."

"Not dead." The angel scowled. "But you should be."

Kate.

Alive.

Relief cut through the dull pain in his chest. "Where are we?"

"The garage of your penthouse." She leaned to the side, revealing the interior of a cargo van.

At the rear, Boones stood in the open doors, flanked by two men. Tiago didn't know them, but he trusted Boones to choose only the best for his personal security.

There would always be traitors, but Iliana's death should serve as a deterrent for the time being.

He flexed his arms and rolled his neck, testing his strength and mobility. Muscles protested, but the pain didn't make him want to hurl his guts. Definitely an improvement from the jungle.

"What's the damage?" He glanced down at his torso but could only see clean bandages.

"You'll live." Boones stepped back and motioned at the men. "They're going to carry you up."

"Fuck that." He pushed to a sitting position and swayed beneath an onslaught of vertigo.

"Tiago." Kate gripped the metal bracelet on his wrist and tugged at the other half still attached to her. "Remove the handcuffs. It'll be easier if you're not dragging me along beside you."

No way would he release her until she was safely locked behind the doors of the penthouse.

Shifting to the rear of the van, he lowered his boots to the ground, rose to his full height, and waited for the dizziness to pass.

The walk to the elevator was a short trip of staggering steps, grabbing hands, and glowering disapproval. Most of the scowls came from Kate, but her fingers gripped his arm with the kind of support no one could give him but her.

By the time he entered the top floor, his body was drenched in sweat and the pain had morphed into a fire-breathing entity inside his chest.

"Idiot," Boones said in his native tongue and walked past him, heading toward the master bedroom.

"If the roles were reversed..." She trudged along beside him, surveying the contemporary interior of the penthouse. "I'd be draped over your shoulder like a caveman's whore."

"Give me a couple of hours, and I'll carry you like that again." He caught himself on the doorframe of the master bedroom.

"A couple of hours?" She gaped at him. "You're going to be in bed for days. Maybe weeks."

He refused to admit she was right.

The rush of water sounded from the master bath as he forced his heavy feet across the bleached wood flooring.

Bold, colorful artwork punctuated the white walls, and the sleek, minimalist furniture satisfied his modern aesthetic. The penthouse didn't drip in gold accents or conform to the lavish styles of a moneyed Venezuelan, but it was exorbitant, nonetheless.

"I ran a hot bath." Boones stepped out of the en suite. "Use it, but keep your chest above the water."

A bath sounded perfect, especially with the woman handcuffed to his arm.

"You can't leave the penthouse." Boones ambled toward the hall. "No one knows you're in Caracas, and it needs to stay that way until you're recovered."

Because of Kate.

Word of Tiago's return would spread, and when that happened, Matias Restrepo and Cole Hartman would learn her location.

Tiago had planned for this complication upon his return, but those plans hadn't included getting shot and stabbed.

He needed to meet with the biggest, most powerful constituents in his network, attend their parties, and prove to them he was still strong and undefeated. Only then could he petition them for their support in keeping her friends out of Caracas. If he didn't, Matias Restrepo would snake his way in and turn the entire city against Tiago.

"I want you in bed after the bath." Boones gripped the doorframe, looking as tired as Tiago felt. "Breakfast will be brought in shortly."

"Thanks, Boones."

The penthouse had a full-service staff, such as an on-site maid, cook, and personal guards who had been here for Boones since the beginning.

Tiago owned the entire building, and the security was the best money could buy. No one could penetrate these walls without getting blown to bits in the process.

He made his way to the desk in the corner of the bedroom, with Kate keeping pace at his side. She angled toward the nearby window that overlooked the violence, poverty, and despair of the slums below.

"It's weird." Her brows pinched as she took in the view of crumbling concrete and rusted metal roofs. "The top floor of this building feels like a palace, and it stares down at *that*. It feels wrong."

He agreed, which was why he'd never stayed a single night here. He deserved to be down there amid the strife and misery, but she didn't.

"When the economy went to shit, many of Venezuela's aristocratic families moved to Miami, including the untouchable *enchufados*." He dug through the desk drawer and grabbed a paper clip. "I bought this abandoned tower for a steal and fortified it to keep Boones and his brothers safe."

"Do you think Boones will ever go home to be with his brothers?"

"No. I've tried to make him leave. He's stubborn."

She nodded, her expression contemplative. "What now?"

"Bath, food, sleep. In that order." Forcing his heavy feet across the room, he pulled her along.

When he reached the massive tub, steam rose from the water, infused with the calming scent of Boones' herbs. She hung back, as far as the handcuffs allowed, and shifted her weight from foot to foot.

"What's the problem?" he asked.

"I need to pee."

He pivoted, somewhat clumsily, and led her to the toilet. "Sit."

"How about you use that paper clip you're hiding in your fist and unlock the handcuffs?"

Christ, she was perceptive. And sexy as fuck.

If he weren't seconds from face-planting on the marble floor, he would plant his face between her gorgeous legs.

Instead, he hardened his expression in silent command.

Her glare sparked with objections as she kicked off her shoes, shoved off the shorts, and plopped down on the toilet with an urgent release of her bladder.

While she peed, he stripped his clothes from the waist down. He was already shirtless, but every movement ignited an inferno in his shoulder. He gripped the edge of the counter and breathed through the pain until it passed.

"If you removed the handcuffs, I could help you into the bath." She hit the flusher and stood.

"You're getting in with me."

A tsunami of resistance came at him, emanating from her rigid posture.

He nudged her to the side, braced a straight arm on the wall above the toilet, and used his shackled hand to angle his dick while he peed.

She watched for a second before pressing her lips together and looking away.

"I want to piss all over your tight little pussy," he said, just to further ruffle her feathers.

She ground her teeth.

"I'm going to cut you again." His tone was flippant, but there was nothing casual about his intentions. He meant every word.

She tensed. "Can we just…not have this conversation right now? I don't have the emotional bandwidth for it and could really use a couple of days without any blood or violence."

The cynical side of him wanted to push her even more, but there was a stronger impulse to do something completely foreign. She needed rest as much as he did, and he felt an overwhelming need to simply take care of her.

He flushed the toilet and led her to the edge of the bath.

Adjusting the paper clip in his hand, he bit the end of it and made a dent. A quick twist inside the keyhole on her bracelet released the ratchets of teeth.

When the cuff swung open, she yanked her arm free and rubbed her wrist.

"Remove the shirt." He picked the lock on his and set the handcuffs aside.

She obeyed without argument and stood before him wearing only the bandages on her thigh.

Crouching to one knee, he peeled away the medical tape and unwound the gauze. A fresh sheen of ointment coated the clean incisions. Boones must've treated her on the way here.

Tiago took his time examining her, admiring his work, and memorizing the stunning contrast of deep red lines against her pale skin.

Then his gaze drifted to the flawless shape of her body, traveling along the sexy curves of her hips and smooth undersides of her pert tits.

He leaned in and skimmed his nose along her flat stomach. Her fingers feathered through his hair, and the soothing contact made him lightheaded.

Too soon, her touch retreated. She stepped into the water and held out a hand, offering to help him in.

The gesture surprised him, and for a moment, he didn't know what to do with it. She was too nude to conceal a weapon. Maybe she intended to drown him. But even in his weakened state, she would never be able to overpower him.

Perhaps she was just tired and wanted to get this over with.

He rose to his feet, gripped her offered hand, and lowered into the water.

Shifting to face him, she fit her legs on the outside of his and straddled his thighs. Then she went to work, lathering a washcloth with soap and cleaning his arms and the exposed skin around the bandages.

Assuaging fingers washed every inch of him, her mouth a kiss away as she finished her task with concentrated focus.

"Careful, Kate." He sank deeper into the water, his body giving into the tranquilizing comfort. "I might get the impression you care."

"Well, don't. I have Stockholm syndrome."

"You sure about that?"

"When I stepped into that parking lot with no guards, no shackles, and no confinement, freedom was right there." A tumult of emotions scrunched her features before settling into the vertical grooves between her eyes. "All I had to do was run. I wasn't even thinking about your threat against my friends. I want to escape that badly. But I didn't." She stared at her hands. "I looked back."

His pulse thumped in memory. He'd sensed her escape from across the garage and started to go after her. The distraction had earned him a knife in the shoulder and a crippling drop to the floor. If she hadn't come back for him, he would still be lying there. Dead.

She lifted her head and wrecked him with her crystal blue gaze. "This isn't real. It's just my mind's way of coping."

A fist of hurt slammed through his chest, one he'd earned through a lifetime of destructive choices. "What do you feel when you're with me?"

"Fear."

"What else?"

"Physical attraction. Desire. But you already know that."

"You don't think those feelings are real?"

"I don't know. It's not just that. I..." She closed her eyes, drew in a breath, and looked at him. "I feel protective of you, like I would choose your life over all else. I mean, I already did. I chose you over my freedom, and it doesn't make sense. If that's not Stockholm syndrome, I don't know what is."

He hated it, fucking despised her assessment of the intrinsic tether between them. But he knew what he was and what he'd done to her. Expecting her to hand over her heart to a warped bastard was inconceivable.

That didn't, however, change his feelings for her.

"You're probably right." He toyed with a lock of wet blond hair that curled around her nipple. "But *I* don't have Stockholm syndrome. For me, this doesn't get any more real."

Her expression fell. "You only feel that way because I'm the first person you've had sex with in twelve years."

"No, Kate. You're the one I had sex with *because* I love you."

A quivering twitch pulled at her mouth, and her gaze dropped to the carving on her thigh. "You can't love me. If you did, you would let me go."

"Bullshit. You're fucking essential, as necessary as water, air, and blood. I can't give you up." He gripped her chin, pulling her face to his. "If you truly love someone, you don't let them go without a fight."

"Even if not letting me go makes me miserable?"

"Are you? Miserable?"

"I have no freedom, no independence, no rights." Resentment leeched her voice, sucking the calmness from her words. "If you loved me, you would at least let me leave the penthouse to take a walk or—"

"Absolutely not. You would be kidnapped within seconds."

"Kidnapped by people like you? Or taken by my friends?"

"Both. If Matias Restrepo found you, do you know what he would do?" He clamped a hand around her nape, seizing her gaze. "He would confine you to his compound in Colombia, with no way to leave, no access to the outside world, no freedom."

"He would only do that so you couldn't take me again!"

"Think through that, Kate. He doesn't want me to take you from him. I don't want him to take you from me. Same. Fucking. Thing."

"He's never hurt me."

"No, he hasn't. He's safe, because you don't owe each other anything. Is that what you want? To spend the rest of your life surrounded by risk-free bets? If that's the case, stay far the fuck away from love. Growing close to someone, becoming attached to them, that shit doesn't come with a guarantee." His voice roughened, haunted by the reality of his past. "There's no guarantee they'll outlive you or love you back. It's a fucking risk that could end in a lifetime of hurt."

Her breath cut off as she searched his face. He didn't expect her to risk anything for him, but he knew she felt something. He wasn't alone in this unfathomable connection.

"I hate when you say things that make sense." Her heavy exhale cumbered the space between them. "It feels manipulative."

Fatigue fanned in lines from the corners of her eyes and hunched her shoulders. The conversation wasn't helping.

"Come here." He guided her to lie against his uninjured shoulder and used the washcloth to clean away the long night.

When he started to shampoo her hair, she took over, lathering and rinsing and teasing him with all that velvety blonde cascading around her arms and back.

She was such a pleasure to watch. The fluidity in her movements, the nuances of her expressions, and the sweeping dips and arches of her nude form—all of it sent a rush through his veins, invigorating him.

"If I knew then what I knew now…" He let his head fall back on the edge of the tub, regarding her beneath the weight of his eyelids. "I would do things differently."

"Like what?"

Everything.

No, not everything.

He would never regret taking her.

"I'm sorry you didn't see Tate before we left the desert." He handed her a towel from the rack beside the tub.

"Me too." She rose from the water and dried off. "I know you can't go back now that the house is compromised, but doesn't that mean he's in danger there?"

"He's safely hidden behind a monastery." He grabbed a towel and followed her out of the tub. "No one will find him unless they're looking for him."

Once they had a full sleep, he would show her another video and ease some of her worry.

In the bedroom, a tray of breakfast food steamed from beneath metal domes. They ate quickly. Then he directed her into the massive bed and slid in behind her. She didn't roll toward him but didn't pull away, either.

Lying on his uninjured side, he tucked her backside into the bend of his hips and held her close.

Within minutes, her breathing evened into the steady rhythm of sleep. Every bone and muscle in his body thrummed to join her in slumber, but his mind refused to shut down.

With his entire world in his arms, he lay awake and made plans.

TWENTY-FIVE

Recovering from a gunshot wound was a bitch.

Tiago should've been thankful the through and through injury had missed bones, arteries, and internal organs. It healed fast, and within three weeks, he could move the damaged flesh and muscle without nauseating pain.

But three weeks of recovery meant no exercise and no leaving the penthouse.

Word had gotten out he'd fled the gunfight on a motorcycle. Since that was the last time he was seen, there were all sorts of rumors in the air about his inability to maintain his power in Caracas.

Many assumed he was too weak or too dead to be a threat. His allies dwindled with every meeting, dinner, and party he failed to attend, no matter what excuses he gave.

His rivals launched attacks against his operational locations and smuggling routes, thinking they could overtake his syndicate. His men managed to hold their ground, but the constant fighting was wearing on them.

Still, he wasn't ready to announce his location. Not until he was one-hundred-percent confident the city and its constituents would stand against Matias Restrepo when the capo attempted to retrieve Kate.

Tiago spent his days on the phone, barking orders, making deals, rallying new supporters, and repairing relationships in the criminal underground. Business as usual.

His evenings, however, belonged to a blonde spitfire.

Blindfolded and naked, she lay face up on the bed, with rope crisscrossing her body from neck to feet.

TAKE

She hadn't gone into the restraints easily. After all her thrashing and cursing, he could still feel the burning scratches from her nails on his face.

"Untie me! Right now!" Her hands flexed under the net of knots as she swung her head, trying to knock off the blindfold. "Where are you, motherfucker?"

Across the bedroom, he reclined against the wall and devoured her sublime anger.

The redder her skin flushed, the faster his heart beat. The louder she screamed, the harder his cock grew. He should go to her, calm her, but he couldn't stop staring at the beauty of her distress.

He might as well have been a psychopath. Most of the time, he could control his urges and find a release valve in his workouts. But without exercise, he didn't have a way to burn off the need for pain.

Did he think about whipping her, spanking her, applying clamps or constriction bands?

Nah. Not his thing.

Did he want to cut her skin, piss on her tits, and insert needles into her tender female parts?

Fuck, yes.

Blood, come, and urine—any or all of it covering Kate's body made him painfully hard.

"Tiago!" She tried to arch her back but couldn't gain a millimeter in the restraints. "I won't surrender to this, you son of a bitch. Let me go!"

Although she had no idea what he had planned, she still wasn't receptive.

In his estimation, it took some level of mental scarring for a person to be open to the indulgences of a sadist.

He didn't buy into the delusion of a power exchange that was prevalent in the BDSM community. People abused those positions of power, and he was no different.

Kate was smart enough to understand this, and maybe that was why she wanted no part of it.

That didn't mean he would change. Not that he could, even if he wanted to. He was warped beyond hell, with warped problems that had no simple solutions.

But none of that mattered tonight. The sexiest, most desirable woman in the world was trussed up in his bed, and he intended to put a smile on her angelic face. And maybe a few tears.

Pushing off the wall, he prowled toward her on soundless feet. With the blindfold on, she didn't sense his approach, didn't know he leaned over her until he fisted her hair and yanked her lips to his.

She gasped at the sudden contact, and he swept his tongue in with hungry lashes, kissing her hard and deep. His need for her raged, and he didn't hold back.

His hands went everywhere, pulling, bruising, and grabbing at her beneath the rope. He consumed her lips, licked the graceful column of her neck, and sucked the rise of her perfect breasts before returning to her mouth.

She whimpered beneath the harsh strokes of his tongue, fighting and yielding, giving and taking, drowning and resuscitating, and no doubt hating him to the end of hell and back.

People like him should never fall in love. His wife couldn't reciprocate. Kate was smart enough to guard her heart. But it was too late for him.

He loved her at a deadly, explosive, unstoppable level.

He came up for air, his mouth hovering a fraction away.

"Please, Tiago." She panted. "I need to see."

"The blindfold stays." From the bedside drawer, he removed the jewelry he'd sterilized and the supplies he needed. "I have three gifts for you. The first one will make you angry as hell."

"I'm already angry." Her chest heaved, causing the rope to pinch her tits. "Gifts are supposed to make people happy."

"This might bring you happiness someday."

"Oh God." Her face paled. "You're going to cut —?"

"Shhh." He pressed a finger against her mouth and sat on the bed beside her hip. "No cutting tonight."

She looked so breathtakingly erotic lying there on her back, with her legs and arms tied to the mattress.

He'd stretched the rope across her torso in an X pattern that made her breasts accessible while preventing movement in her core. She couldn't lift or twist or do anything below the neck.

He leaned down, examining the three new cuts that sketched along the side of her ribs. He'd added those swirls a week ago, without her consent. Nothing like the one on her leg, the small carvings had only taken minutes, just a few quick turns of his blade before he'd buried himself inside her.

"What are you doing?" Fear trickled into her voice.

He pinched her nipples and tugged hard, elongating the peaks. "Tonight, I'm going to pierce these."

"Fuck," she said with a gulp. "Can we talk about it?"

"No." Bending close, he spoke at her ear. "This gift means the most to me, Kate."

"Why? Because it's going to hurt the most?"

"That has nothing to do with it."

Maybe someday he would tell her exactly what he was giving her.

"Stay still." He squeezed her left breast, letting her know which one he was starting with.

Boones had instructed him on how to safely clean and pierce the area. With the preparations done, he didn't draw it out.

Hands steady, he stabbed the back end of the barbell into one side of the nipple. The front of the bar pierced the other side.

The pain was probably so intense she felt it in the pit of her stomach. But she didn't scream or fight in the restraints. Her hands balled in the sheets. Her teeth dug into her bottom lip, and the sinews in her neck stretched taut.

Goddamn, she was devastating.

As he repeated the steps on the other nipple, heat simmered beneath his skin. Just imagining the sharp puncture of her sensitive tissues made his cock swell.

It wasn't a fast pain. He'd never done this before, and each nipple took about a minute to pierce the ruthless rod all the way through.

He thought her stoic composure would snap by the end, but she persevered without crying. Anyone else would've screamed bloody murder beneath his inexperienced hands.

When he finished, he put the antiseptic away and pulled off the blindfold.

Her watery eyes went straight to her chest and widened. "Gemstones? Are they garnets?"

"They're called painites."

The double-prong barbells held a one-carat precious stone on each end. Four stones in total. He had the pieces custom-made so that her nipples would fit snugly between each pair of deep red gems.

"Fucking beautiful." He circled a finger around her breast, eliciting a shiver.

She twisted her neck away and stared across the room at nothing.

"If you don't like the piercings, too damn bad." He roughly cupped her tender breast, making her gasp. "You will *not* remove them. Understand?"

"Yes." Her jaw set.

He turned his attention to the knots and spent the next few minutes untying her. When the rope fell away, so did some of her indignation. She really didn't like to be restrained.

Scooting to the headboard, she sat with her back against it. Her nipples would be sore for a few days, and though the jewelry wasn't heavy, it would feel like a constant bite, an ever-present reminder of him.

"Will there be more?" She pulled the sheet over her lap but didn't try to cover her chest. Instead, she stared down at the piercings with bitter curiosity. "Will you cover my body with jewelry until I look like a pincushion?"

"No more piercings, but there will be needle play in your future."

She closed her eyes and choked. "Sorry I asked."

"The second gift is some news I want to share." He shrugged out of his shirt, grimacing at the tightness in his shoulder.

His shoes and jeans hit the floor next. Then he joined her on the bed.

"I finalized some negotiations today with three of the largest gangs in Caracas." He leaned his head back against the headboard, watching her sidelong. "I traded some of my smuggling routes for their kidnapping operations."

She whirled on him, her blue eyes burning. "You promised you wouldn't kidnap anymore."

"I keep my promises, Kate."

"So you gave them your smuggling routes in exchange for…?" Her gaze flicked over his face, her expression etched in confusion. "For their kidnapping operations? What does that even mean?"

"Their territories are now mine. It's a lot more complicated than that, but the gist is I control the bulk of Kidnap Ally and the surrounding areas. With the exception of a few rogue gangs, I'm the only one who can kidnap in Caracas."

"Except you don't do that…" Realization penetrated her voice, soaking the words with stunned tears. "You found a way to stop *everyone* from kidnapping."

"Not everyone. But I'm working on it."

There was the smile he'd hoped to see. It stretched her honeyed mouth, lifted her cheeks, and glistened in her eyes.

"That's a great fucking surprise, Tiago." She slid onto his lap, enticingly nude as she straddled his thighs. Her fingers braided through his hair. She touched their foreheads together, and her mouth closed over his gently, briefly. "You did good."

"Sometimes I do the right thing, but it's usually by accident."

"How does it feel?" She ghosted her lips along his jaw and softly sucked behind his ear.

"Keep doing that, and I'll skip the third gift and show you exactly how it feels."

"I'm not afraid of you." She leaned back and coasted a hand along the scar on his head. "The cutting and piercing and all the other pain you put me through really pisses me off. But then you do things that surprise me, like abolishing kidnapping in Caracas. Tell me that good deed doesn't feel amazing."

"It feels good to make you happy, Kate." He stroked a thumb along her bottom lip. "That's all that matters."

She made a humming noise and ran her fingers through the messy strands on his head. "You have great hair. Who's your stylist?"

"She's a foxy little thing. Likes to put her tits in my face when she's giving me a trim."

"She also now knows how to stitch up your next knife wound."

"Boones taught you that today?"

"He *showed* me. I haven't actually held a needle."

While Tiago spent the past three weeks running his business from the penthouse office, she passed the time with Boones, learning the basics of emergency medicine. She initiated the instruction, and Boones was more than willing to share his knowledge.

"If you ever decide to become a doctor," Tiago said, "Boones would be an excellent mentor."

"I know." She gave him a small smile.

He clasped her tiny waist and lifted her to fasten his mouth to hers. After a few dizzying sips, he adjusted her legs around his and reached for his phone.

"One more gift tonight." He unlocked the screen.

"I don't think the last one can be topped."

A swarm of energy buzzed in his gut as he handed her the phone. "The video is a couple of hours old."

She glanced at him, directed her eyes on the screen, and stopped breathing.

TWENTY-SIX

Tiago's back rippled with tension as he absorbed Kate's reaction.

She held the phone tightly, her gaze glued to the screen. Face contorted. Lips pinched. Tears breaching the waterline.

The recorded video showed Lucia entering the shack with Cole Hartman. Tate looked at her, and it took a moment for him to come to terms with her presence. But once he did, he pulled her into his arms and held onto her like he would never let her go.

"I've waited three months to see this." A keening sob tore from Kate's chest.

"I know." He hadn't expected to feel so relieved by the reunion. It put a strange warmth in his chest and shifted the shape of his mouth.

"You're smiling." Her own smile trembled beneath streams of drippy tears as she watched the video until the end. "I guess you're happy about your experiment."

"No." He took the phone from her and set it aside, tasting the thick onus of his words. "I regret it deeply."

She traced gentle fingers along his hairline, her eyes bright and wet as she watched his face, waiting for him to elaborate.

"I shouldn't have separated them." He reclined against the headboard, his stomach a hard knot. "If someone did that to me, if I lost you for three months…" He dragged a hand down his face. "I can't even let my mind go there."

Crushed by guilt and unbalanced with relief, he wanted to end the bleed of vulnerability and kiss her until neither of them could think straight.

"He's free." She touched her brow to his and breathed a blissful sound against his lips. "In the end, you did the right thing. You let him go."

But she wasn't free. She wanted autonomy more than anything else, and he couldn't give that to her. He would never let her go.

"Thank you for the video." She touched her lips to his cheek. "For putting a stop to kidnapping." She kissed the corner of his mouth. "For never breaking your promises."

She trailed a sensual path of sucking nips down the line of his neck, across his shirtless chest, and lower, arrowing straight toward his hardening cock.

"Kate." Lust ran riot through his body, tensing muscles and tightening his balls.

She inched down the length of his reclined frame, nipple piercings glinting in the lamplight and blue eyes peering up through long lashes, drawing him in, pulling him deeper.

She'd never gone down on him, and he never forced it. Her ferocious temper and sharp teeth wasn't a combination he'd wanted near his dick.

Her hands slipped beneath the waistband of his briefs, as if to relieve him of that last bit of clothing. But she hesitated, head down, hiding her face.

Images of his cock sinking between her pillowy lips heated his insides to a smoldering boil. He snared her by the hair and wrenched her head back. "Don't fucking tease—"

"I'm not." Her eyes snapped to his, her expression a composition of longing and moxie, at odds with the tears flitting down her cheeks.

"What are you doing, Kate?" He released her hair.

"I don't know." She sniffed and tugged his briefs down his legs, freeing his erection. "I guess I'm trying to properly thank you, but also..." She clutched the base of his erection and gave him a hard, confident stroke. "I want to do this for myself."

His head rocked back, and he gasped for air as his entire body stiffened and throbbed, strumming beneath her wicked touch.

He tolerated it through a few more strokes before he closed a fist around hers and took over. Kicking his hips, he drove hard and fast into the clasp of their hands.

Her eyes found his. She yanked her grip away, and in the next heartbeat, she replaced it with the hot, wet heaven of her mouth.

"Holy fuck." He clutched her head and worked himself deeper into the back of her throat, shaking and thrusting with urgency. "Jesus, Kate. That feels fucking incredible."

It had been twelve years since he'd let anyone suck him. It was long enough ago that even a half-ass blow job would feel extraordinary right now.

But nothing about this was half-ass. The swirling, sucking motion of her lips and tongue delivered the perfect pressure and rhythm, just the right amount of teasing and manipulation to drive him out of his fucking mind.

He couldn't stop his hands from holding her in place as he fucked hard and deep into her throat. She swallowed through it without gagging, but after a few breathless seconds, she smacked her palms on his abs and pushed away.

Leaning up, she got in his face and growled. "I was trained how to do this by a scary, cold as fuck sadist." She wrapped a hand around his length, torturing him with diabolical strokes. "I want to do it *my* way, for *me*, and I don't need your damn guidance."

"Christ, you're fucking fierce." He was so goddamn hard his dick felt like cement beneath the pressure, like any moment he might crack in the vigorous vise of her hand.

"I've never done this without..." Her brows furrowed. "Without giving my consent." She edged back and lowered her head, her gaze locked on his. "Let me do it."

"Okay." He relaxed into the mattress, his head tipped back against the headboard and his hands at his sides. "Do it. Suck me."

She did. She sucked him until every nerve in his body sparked and sizzled with need. The rolling sweep of her tongue brought him back from the dead. The suction of her lips banished the nightmares, and her tear-stained cheeks filled him with an overpowering sense of responsibility.

His love for her resembled a blade, a source of pain, but vital. He would always protect her, however she needed him, even when he was the cause of her suffering.

Their relationship was unconventional, dark in nature, almost unworldly. Although she resented it, he knew she cherished it just as deeply.

He felt it in the veneration of licks along his cock, heard it in the emotion-soaked panting of her breaths, and saw it in the sodden depths of her watchful eyes.

She wasn't just giving him a blow job. She was surrendering pieces of herself. Tiny, rare, invaluable pieces of her soul.

Possessiveness growled in his throat, and his muscles clenched with desire. He wanted to erase her past and be her forever. He wanted to disintegrate everything from her life until he was the only thing she needed to breathe.

He wanted her to love him.

As her mouth moved along his shaft and her gaze clung to his, he could almost pretend she was with him willingly, that she wasn't locked in his penthouse with twenty guards preventing her escape.

Sucking in air, he swallowed the urge to flip her over, sink into her heat, and pound home the message that she belonged to him.

Instead, he simply let go. He let her set the torturous pace, let her add a teasing nip here and there, and let her decide when to send him over.

The moment she took him to the back of her throat and kneaded his balls in the cup of her hand, she knew she had him.

He surrendered, gasping for breath, groaning incoherently, and coming for the woman he wanted to fuck for the rest of his undeserving life.

She swallowed him down, every single drop, and by the time her sexy lips slid free, he only vaguely remembered how he got there.

"*Hostia puta.*" His lungs stuck together, gasping for oxygen. "It's never been that perfect."

"Well, you have no recent comparisons. It's been a while since someone gave you head, right?"

"Twelve years." He stared at her mouth, obsessed with every little twitch within those lush arches.

"I like that." She crawled up his chest and rested her head on his shoulder. "I like that there hasn't been anyone since your wife. But it also feels intimidating, like her shadow is constantly hanging over me. No matter what I do, I'll never be *her* in your eyes and—"

"Stop." He crushed her close, forging them together as her fragile truths winged through his soul. "I haven't thought about her nor will I ever think about her when I'm with you. My past is where it belongs. I don't want it or her, not even a little. I want *you.*"

The fact that she was dwelling on this at all was progress. Huge fucking strides in the right direction. If she didn't care about him, she wouldn't have brought up his sexual history, marriage, or any insecurities about it.

She was jealous, and she hated him. He was possessive, and he loved her. Together, they were a combustion of extreme emotion that burned without boundaries or expiration.

Didn't matter how far he took her or how hard she fought, she was with him, kicking and kissing, punching and fucking, with her heart engaged and her mind challenging him as nothing less than his equal.

He ran his fingers down her side, veered around her hip, and dipped into the valley between the firm globes of her ass.

"Lie on your back and spread your legs." He clenched her buttocks hard enough to make her squeak.

She lifted her head, and it wasn't resistance that glowed in her gaze. It was heat. Desire. Acceptance.

"I want to come." Her lashes lowered, transforming her petite features into pure seduction. "I like that you always give me that."

As she slid off his lap and stretched out on her back, a second heartbeat took up residence between his legs.

The fluidity of her lithe figure made his mouth water. The tight buds of her nipples pinched erotically between the precious stones, and if that weren't enough to make him hard again, she had the brazenness to meet his eyes and open her thighs.

In a blink, he shifted from man to beast. His hands landed on her knees, spreading her wide as he went after her pussy with tongue and teeth.

She moaned beneath the attack, and her body trembled against him, filling his mouth with feminine hunger.

No matter how many times he went down on her, it was always explosive. Her responses, his need—the air crackled and sang with the sounds of fighting, snarling, mating animals.

As she climaxed, she did it with her entire being. She let go of everything—her hatred, her fear, her painful past—and for those few fleeting seconds, he glimpsed a woman who was capable of seeing what he was and loving him despite it.

In that moment, something awoke between them. Something deep and untouchable. On the surface, they were captor and captive, but at the heart of their connection, they were one.

"Tiago." She opened her arms, panting through the remnants of her release.

He prowled up her body, lowered onto her, and buried himself in her hot, tight pussy.

Pleasure zinged through his veins, and he snapped his hips into a frantic, urgent rhythm. She answered with a cry, and her hands gripped the muscles of his ass.

But it was her eyes that held him. Those vibrant oceans of blue called him into the rippling vastness, pulling him in so close and deep he didn't know where he ended and she began.

With his hands tangled in her hair, he thrust again, and again, harder, faster, with a desperation that echoed in his heart.

All his life, he'd been alone. In marriage, he'd been alone in love. In his career, he'd fought his own battles. In hell, he reigned from a solitary throne.

What would it be like to have Kate's love instead of her hate? To have her fighting beside him instead of against him?

The notion was unattainable but not unimaginable. He imagined it every day, in every possible way.

With a low, deep moan, she came undone. Her orgasm swelled

and crashed around him, contracting her inner muscles and tossing him into a delirium of ecstasy.

"Kate." He groaned, holding her tight as she milked him, draining him into exhaustion.

Spent and sated, he rolled to his back and gathered her in his arms.

It was easy to give up everything for her, but there were some things that required time and planning. He was willing to surrender whatever was needed to earn her love, as long as it didn't compromise her safety.

Letting Tate go had been the right thing to do, but it came with a cost.

Cole Hartman was no longer occupied with the search for Tate.

Now he had a new job, a new target, and by this time tomorrow, he would know where to find Kate.

Tiago had to leave the penthouse tomorrow, and she would be at his side. It was a risk to take her to his compound, but it was even a bigger risk to leave her in the care of someone else.

No one would protect her like he would.

If Hartman meant to take her, he would have to pry her out of Tiago's cold, dead arms.

TWENTY-SEVEN

The grungy, menacing atmosphere set Kate's instincts on high alert as she followed Tiago through his Caracas compound.

The bones of what was once a regal hotel hid behind fumes of cigarette smoke, spray paint, and decay. Sheet metal covered the windows. Bullet holes pocked the ceilings. Brown stains blotted the worn carpet, and sweaty, heavily-armed men stood at attention in the dark hallways.

Hard to imagine Lucia had lived within these claustrophobic walls for eleven years.

The absence of light disorientated Kate, but she stayed close to Tiago's familiar frame. Not that he would let her drift out of arm's reach.

He didn't glance at her, hold her hand, or touch her the way he did when they were alone, but the weight of his attention never left her. Whether he was navigating winding passages or briefing dozens of guards on business deals, he knew where she was and what she was doing at all times.

His awareness of her was an unexplainable sense in her gut, one that had evolved from a collection of shared experiences during their inseparable months together.

Strange as it was, she seemed to be constantly aware of him, too, in the warning tingle across her skin, the rash of heat in her cheeks, and the hum of energy in her chest.

Outside his inner circle, however, no one was privy to the constant storm between them. No one knew she was the object of his dirtiest, darkest, most intimate desires, that she wore his scarred artwork, that she slept in his bed, or that he would kill anyone who tried to take her from him.

Her role at his compound was simply to look the part of Lucia's replacement.

When he'd strapped an unloaded gun on her hip before they left, his expression had been strained so tightly with worry it bordered on anger.

He couldn't stomach the thought of leaving her in the penthouse, where he couldn't watch her. At the same time, it terrified him to take her into this world. He told her none of this, but words weren't necessary. She read it in the intensity of his eyes and felt it vibrating from his anxious posture.

Maybe his protectiveness was a symptom of obsession. Or maybe it came from a place of twisted love.

He'd said the words. Three words no man had ever given her. But she couldn't let his declaration sink its poisonous hooks into her psyche.

As long as he was her captor, love didn't have a damn thing to do with it.

But as she followed him through the dark halls of his lair, she soared on wings of gratefulness. After being locked up for months, she was finally out, even if it meant wearing an unloaded gun and pretending to be one of his guards.

None of his men questioned her presence. In fact, they couldn't seem to take their eyes off Tiago.

It had been three months since he'd shown his face here. Three months since they'd seen their leader alive and breathing, and he was really something to behold.

The dark stubble on his jaw accentuated his masculine bone structure as he spoke to them in Spanish, the soft *J*'s and double *R*'s rolling off his tongue with seductive authority.

Inky black hair raked back from his strong brow in tousled, spiky rebellion. Deliberately rebellious, as if every strand had been commanded into perfect disorder. She felt a disturbing urge to tangle her fingers in all that sexiness.

She'd recently trimmed the sides of his head, making the scars stand out in stark relief. They added a dangerous edge to his appearance, as if he needed more of that with his black jeans, leather jacket, and shit-kickers.

Strength and power radiated from him, and it wasn't just for show. He'd returned to full health, exercised daily, and stood before his adherents with all the potency of a confident, merciless crime lord.

And so he was back to work. For the next week, he spent every waking moment at the compound, catching up with his men. She remained at his side from the second they left the penthouse to the moment they returned, sitting through business meetings held in languages she didn't understand.

The night Tate walked out of the shack, Arturo returned to Caracas and resumed his position as her constant shadow. Between him, Tiago, and the hundreds of guards in his regime, escape was impossible.

By the second week, the bustle of Tiago's return had calmed down. He found some time to give her a quiet tour of the old hotel floors, including the basement cells, where he'd held Tate and Van and countless other victims.

As his monotone voice recounted the things he'd done over the years, his expression lacked smugness and aggression. She hunted for hints of regret in his eyes, hoping to glimpse something human during his narration, but he remained guarded and closed-off.

Until he took her to the room where he used to sleep.

"This is it." He shut the door behind her, leaving Arturo in the hall.

She paced through the sparse space, marking the empty safe, the bare mattress, and the wooden chair at the center.

"It's almost an exact replica of your room in the desert." She paused beside the dumbbell on the scarred floor, and her stomach caved in. "Except this."

He leaned his back against the door and tilted his chin down, wearing a pensive, darker-than-usual expression. "She should've hit me one more time and made it count."

"What?" Her head kicked back. "Why would you say that?"

"You think I deserve to be alive?" His jaw flexed, and his eyes lifted, glowering from beneath thick lashes. "Look around. This room sums up the last twelve years of my life."

She scanned the impenetrable lock on the door, the empty bed, the scarred surfaces, the suffocating darkness, utter vacancy, and isolation.

Maybe the space defined his experiences, but it didn't personify the man.

He'd committed unforgivable crimes. Heartless acts. But over the past few months, she'd come to realize Tiago Badell was in full possession of both a conscience and a heart.

Complex, sentient, and deeply honest, he had the capacity to hurt and love in equal intensities. He gave and received all ranges of emotion, more so than any person she knew.

And to think, he spent twelve years in this empty, lifeless, dispassionate cell.

She hated it.

Even as she knew it was a means of self-punishment, it hurt to imagine him sleeping here alone for so damn long.

She rubbed her chest, and her gaze landed on the dumbbell, a symbol of his constant drive to be strong and invincible. It also represented his pain.

Lucia had every right to attack him with it, but from his perspective, it probably felt like a terrible betrayal. His closest confidant had turned on him, and from what Kate understood about his wife's death, it wasn't the first time he'd been betrayed.

"When we leave this room," he said in a rough, heavily-accented voice, "I'm going to lock the door and never open it again."

"Good idea." She stepped toward him. "The past stays in the past, where it belongs."

"I have a lot of regrets, Kate." He rested the tips of his fingers in his front pockets. "Too many to fit inside this room."

Agitated energy, *his* energy, swarmed around her in dizzying waves as he stared at something behind her.

She followed his gaze to the chair. Not just any chair. "That's where you sat with Lucia on your lap every day?"

"Yes."

Right there was where he gave Lucia the injections that counteracted the poison he put in her food.

Her insides constricted.

"You know my sins. I've disclosed them all in detail." He pushed off the door and prowled toward her, quickening her breaths. "What I haven't done is repent for them."

She held still as he circled her, every cell in her body pinging at his nearness.

"I'm sorry for what I did to Lucia." He paused before her and curled a finger under her chin, lifting her gaze. "I'm sorry I kicked you the night we met."

Her lips trembled, and she locked her knees to prevent them from wobbling. It wasn't his words that knocked her off-balance so much as the raw contrition shining in his eyes.

"I'm sorry for letting Iliana touch you." His hand skimmed along her jawline, making her pulse sputter. "I'm sorry for raping you. I'm not proud of it."

She sucked in a slow, shaky breath, bringing the dark scent of leather, cypress, and dangerous man into her lungs.

"I'm not asking for forgiveness." His fingers wove through her hair and clenched. "I just needed you to hear it."

She didn't just hear it. She felt it stretch and pull inside her.

"Why now?" Swaying toward him, she burrowed into the warm den of his jacket. "What prompted this?"

"You." He leaned back and cuffed a strong hand around her neck. "Your eyes. It's impossible to feel heartless when you look at me like I'm not."

"Tiago." Her heart thumped heavily, catching in her throat.

"Also..." He brushed his nose against hers. "I'm in love with you."

Every word was a razor, reopening the cuts on her body. Lancing pain shot beneath her skin, burning, aching, inflaming the wounds.

His confession of love had never hurt before. So why did it hurt so much now?

An inner voice begged her to ignore it, to hold onto her hatred and feed it with her need for freedom.

But he was in her face, infiltrating her breaths, and staring down at her with a foreboding glint in his eyes.

Dark and tempting, indecently gorgeous and sickeningly filthy in bed, he knew he could set her on fire with only the force of his will. He was always just one impulse away from nailing her against the wall and driving her to the sublime edge of pleasure and pain.

His physique alone was a chiseled altar upon which any woman with a pulse would sacrifice her soul.

But he would never touch another woman.

He belonged to her.

Mine.

Well, maybe not *that.*

But he was her protector. Her lover. There.

If you truly love someone, you don't let them go without a fight.

Maybe she needed to be reminded of what she already had and trust that it was all she really needed.

She just didn't know how to separate the horrible things he'd done from those glimpses of goodness she'd seen in him.

"You're not heartless." She sighed. "Just complicated."

"And selfish." He swooped in and stole a greedy kiss from her lips. "Because Kate..." Another kiss. And another. "I know you can't love me, but I'm not sorry I took you. I won't apologize for it." His mouth sealed over hers, devouring her gasp before he pulled back. "If it came down to it, I would take you again."

With that, he released her, leaving behind the hot imprint of his touch on her skin.

As he turned toward the door, a thought tapped at the back of her mind, something she'd been meaning to ask him.

"Tiago?" When he glanced back, she raised her chin. "While we were holed up in the penthouse for a month, I know you were making plans."

"Go on." He shifted to face her and clasped his hands behind his back.

"My friends know where I'm at now?"

"Yes." A muscle bounced in his jaw.

"I assume some of your planning involved keeping them out of Caracas?" She stepped toward him, searching his unreadable expression. "Have they tried to enter the city or make contact?"

"Not yet."

Because of her phone conversation with Liv? She'd told them not to come. "Can I just call them and see—?"

"No. Stop asking."

Same answer he'd given her the last hundred times she asked to contact them.

"If Matias Restrepo comes for you…" He grasped her hand and pulled her into his space. "It won't end well for him."

"What do you mean?"

"I negotiated a deal with the President."

"What? The President of…?"

"Venezuela. His armed forces will not allow Restrepo to cross the Venezuela-Colombia border."

Her stomach sank. "What did you have to offer in exchange for that deal?"

"Nothing as valuable as you."

"You're evading the question."

"For now." He gripped the door handle and paused. "I accepted an invitation to one of his dinner parties. It's a formal affair this weekend. You're going with me."

"You want me to go to the President of Venezuela's party?" She gulped, seized by panic. "Will I be there as your captive? Your whore? Your fake guard?"

"You'll be there as *mine*."

Her growl came out as a choke. "I need to understand the landscape. Will you have enemies in attendance? Will I be expected to hold conversations? I don't know the language, and I definitely need a gun or something to—"

"If I asked any other woman to accompany me to a Presidential dinner, her first and only question would be what to wear."

"I don't give a fuck about that. I'm more concerned about—"

He captured her mouth in a demanding kiss and smiled against her lips. "I'll take care of the dress."

TWENTY-EIGHT

The dress encased Kate's body like liquid gold, as if each shimmering thread had been cut and woven in veneration of the female form. Fashion never meant one iota to her, but holy shit, this gown was empowering.

She paced to the full-length mirror in the master bathroom, nervously fluffing her long hair. She should've pinned it up or curled it or something, but the girly stuff was beyond her expertise.

Anchoring a hand on her hip, she extended a leg through the slit of the dress and gave herself a final once-over.

Her makeup was modest. A little mascara. A glide of lip gloss. But the gown and the heels and God, the whole look… She'd never felt so glamorous.

The satiny material clung to her slight curves from her chest to the floor. The cut up one side reached high on her thigh, enabling normal strides when she walked.

The slit fell along the leg that bore his artwork. No doubt, intentional. With each step, the fading pink welts of rope and petals peeked through the opening of the floor-length skirt.

Tiny shoulder straps held the top in place, and the deep scoop between her breasts exposed the length of her breastbone.

The gown and gold stilettos had been waiting for her in the bathroom when she exited the shower. No bra or panties. Not that she could've worn anything beneath the unforgiving material.

At first, she thought the gold color had been selected to match her hair. But it was much darker, more bronze-ish. Like the metallic hues in Tiago's brown eyes.

She hadn't seen him yet. Hadn't worked up the courage to step out of the bathroom.

Stop stalling.

Adjusting a shoulder strap, she drew in a calming breath and opened the door.

Across the room, he sat on the edge of the bed, dressed in a jet-black tuxedo. Head down, he wrestled with a cuff link, his face pinched in concentration.

"I can do that for you." She strode toward him, stepping carefully in the skyscraper heels, and slowed at the lift of his head.

He straightened. His mouth parted, and his eyes went from wide and stunned to heated and wolfish as he ate her up from head to toe. He made a few more passes, slower each time, lingering on the outline of the nipple piercings beneath the satin.

The heady caress of his gaze touched her everywhere, stroking, tingling, his breaths growing shallow and hungry.

She swallowed back a whimper. Swear to God, if he stared at her much longer, she could have an orgasm. Just from the potency in his eyes.

The tuxedo wasn't helping. Sweet hell, the man wore the fuck out of tailored threads.

The black trousers and white collared shirt fit his hard body with mouthwatering precision. The dinner jacket cut a crisp outline across his broad shoulders. A gold square, the color of her gown, peeked out of the front pocket, and a black bow tie sat at the base of his tanned neck.

Every hair on his head fell together in unruly perfection. His cleanly shaved jaw showed off all his square angles and outrageously handsome Latino features.

Looking at him was a treacherous trap. He was too attractive, too addictive to take in all at once.

Desperate to break his spell, she focused on her feet and approached the bed. "Need help with the cuff links?"

"You're blindingly beautiful." A fingertip skimmed along her collarbone, teased the pocket of her throat, and dipped to follow the line of her breastbone. "I can't think straight."

"I could say the same thing." She peeked at his face, and if she thought she felt pretty before, her self-appraisal didn't hold a candle to the awe-stricken approval shimmering in his eyes.

His hand shifted to cup her breast, a possessive hold that turned wickedly mischievous as he flicked a thumb against the piercing.

Heat flashed through her, and she stepped back. "Let me see your sleeves."

He held out the cuff links and offered his wrists. "I need to be inside you."

"Too bad." She attached the gold links through the buttonholes.

Despite her resolve, she couldn't stop herself from glancing at his lap.

The outline of his cock formed an impressively long, rigid bulge that lay trapped against his thigh. Harder than hard, he looked ready to tear through the tuxedo pants.

A molten fever gathered between her legs, and her nipples tightened, the unbidden reaction further stimulated by the barbells.

She needed to stop melting all over the place and focus. He hadn't answered any of her questions about what to expect tonight. She didn't know what she would be walking into or how to conduct herself.

"Aren't we supposed to be there at seven?" She secured the last cuff link and sidled out of his reach.

"We're going to be late."

"If we leave now—"

A rough hand grabbed her arm, wrenching her into the space between his knees. "I'm going to fuck you."

Flames swept around them, from his gaze burning into hers, his fingers trailing heat up her arm, and the fire igniting inside her.

His other hand slipped through the slit of her gown and sank between her thighs, finding her embarrassingly wet.

"Fuck." He gripped her waist, dropped his forehead against her stomach, and twisted two fingers inside her. "Fucking drenched. Dripping for a cock."

"We're not doing this." She teetered in the heels and caught his shoulder for balance. "We're already dressed, and I'm too nervous about the dinner."

"I'll take the edge off." He thrust his hand, fingering her harder, deeper, until the line between *yes* and *no* blurred, and her thighs clenched together. "Sit on my cock, Kate."

"Stop." Throbbing, aching, and growing wetter, her body betrayed her. "I don't want to ruin the dress or take it off. It took me forever to make everything look just right. And you're wearing black. The smallest stain will glow like a spotlight. Do you really want to introduce me to the President with come stains on your pants? God, I'm already sweating, and you're making it—"

"Hey, Kate." His fingers slipped to her inner thigh and clenched, his voice chillingly quiet. Deadly serious. "Reach into my pants, pull out my cock, and fucking sit on it."

Her gaze dropped to the captivating curves of his bossy mouth, lingering there before lifting to his eyes, to the swirls of brown glowing in the lamplight.

A tremor erupted low and hot in her belly.

The way he looked at her, the piercing glare that cut right through those dark lashes, grabbed her deeply and completely.

She shivered with goosebumps in her heartbeat.

What was it about this man? This scary, stubborn, rude, horribly sexy man? He tied her up in knots, sometimes literally, and she wanted it.

She really did.

She fucking ached for him.

"You want me to fuck you?" she asked quietly.

"That's what I said."

The fact that they were discussing it instead of doing it gave her pause. Usually, he skipped the conversation and went right to stripping her clothes and working over her body.

Something had changed.

He'd apologized for raping her. Did that mean it wouldn't happen again?

She yanked her arm out of his grip and backed away, testing his sincerity.

He remained seated, his lips twisted in frustration and anger as he tracked her retreat to the door.

When she reached the hallway, her pulse pounded, and her muscles tensed, braced for him to chase her.

But he didn't. He slowly lowered to his back and rested an arm over his eyes, breathing heavily.

"You're not going to force me?" She clutched the doorframe.

"I'm trying, Kate." He adjusted the rigid length of his cock. "Go on. I'll be out in a second."

She stepped into the hall, squinting at him.

He would be fine. It was just an erection, and it was good for him to be denied.

Except she was denying herself.

Her need for him dripped and pulsed between her legs. What was the point in opposing something she wanted? Just to be stubborn?

Maybe this was a sick game of reverse psychology? But why would he bother with a mind fuck when he could just pin her down and fuck her like all the other times?

This wasn't a game.

He regretted forcing her, and she felt that at gut level.

They were already late, and the truth was she couldn't leave him like this. It went against every instinct inside her.

Fuck it.

She strode into the bedroom and shut the door. "I feel like the flakiest woman in existence."

He raised his head and lifted to his elbows, his gaze following her approach, pupils flaring.

"I changed my mind."

"Thank, fuck," he growled.

"But I want this on my terms." She glided her hands along the back of the gown, trying to locate the invisible zipper.

"What are your terms?"

"I get to be in control." Her skin heated, and her body bloomed into a galloping throb, fortifying her decision. "Can you handle that?"

"I don't know." He watched her hunt for the zipper and gripped his dick through the trousers. "Leave on the dress."

After a few more seconds of searching, she gave up and reached for the floor-length hem.

There was a lot of material to collect, and as she gathered it up her legs, his hands ghosted up the backs of her thighs, caressing, urging her to move faster.

Once the dress was ruched around her waist, he held it in place while she crawled over him and opened his fly.

He lifted his hips as she dragged the pants and briefs to his knees. His cock jutted upward, beautifully shaped and leaking a clear bead of moisture from the slit.

She wanted to taste it, ride it, and come all over it. Maybe that was wrong for someone in her situation. Maybe it was a psychological condition. But it didn't change how she felt.

"Don't just stare at it." He dug his fingers into her thigh.

She clutched him, enclosing both hands around the thick, turgid, burning hot length.

A groan rumbled in his chest, his thighs flexing as he pushed himself into the squeeze of her fists.

"Fuck, Kate." His hand enclosed hers, tightening her fingers the way he liked it. "Goddamn, I need you. Come here."

"Stop bossing." She inched up his body and straddled his hips, careful not to mess up his tuxedo. "We're going to do this quick. I'm worried about our clothing and—"

"Shut up, and put me inside you." His hand guided her fingers up and down his cock, angling his hardness to fit at her entrance.

She knocked his arm away and took over, stirring his plump crown through her folds, readying her body, making herself wetter, hungrier.

His fingers joined in, stroking her pussy and rubbing her arousal over the head of his cock.

What now? She'd never done this before. What if she bent his dick when she sat on it?

"You're ready." His voice cracked, his bedroom eyes reading the expression on her face. "Just slide down. You won't hurt me."

He laced their fingers together, and his other hand went to her waist, pushing down with impatience.

"I've got this." She braced herself on the twitching bricks of his stomach. "Relax."

His grip loosened on her waist, and she lowered her body, taking him in inch by hard inch. His jaw stiffened, and the cords in his neck strained taut as he groaned deep and long in the back of his throat.

"Holy fuck, Kate. So good." He kicked his hips, thrusting to get deeper. "*Mierda*, you feel sinful."

"Stop moving." She pressed a hand on his thigh beneath her, trying to calm his need to dominate. "Let me do this."

"Then do it. Fuck me."

Holding their entwined fingers against her midsection, she flattened her other hand on his abs and rocked her hips.

Each movement wrenched a groan from him. When she lifted and lowered, sliding him in and out in languid rolls and undulations, he started to pant.

His hungry responses spurred her faster, harder, until their gasps became one. She threw her head back and writhed on him, losing herself in the pleasure, until his fingers closed around her nipple piercing and painfully tugged.

"Eyes on me." His accent rolled over her, as thick as the Venezuelan humidity.

She met his gaze, and in one look, he obliterated everything between them. There was no air, no fear, no words.

It was a monumental moment. She was on top of him, controlling the pace and rhythm, fucking him into the bed. Something he'd never allowed anyone else to do and would probably never allow again. It was all there in his eyes, drowning her in the gravity of it.

"Give me your mouth." He caught her neck and yanked her to him.

She fumbled around his tuxedo coat until her arms found a safe place to land. Then she leaned up, her chest flush with his, and kissed him.

He let her take a few gentle licks before he annihilated her easy pace with his aggressive, sinful tongue.

That tongue was a weapon, wielded by a wicked, kinky, eternally horny man, who was wrinkling the hell out of his formal wear and thrusting his hips like he didn't have a care in the world.

No, that wasn't true.

In a disturbing, deeply moving way, he cared about *her*. She felt it in the massage of his fingers on her thigh, heard it in the unbridled rush of his breaths, and saw it in the beautiful, extraordinarily thoughtful design he'd carved into her skin.

She'd never been this close to anyone, physically or emotionally, and she felt forever bound to him. Not by handcuffs or threats or the cock inside her. This connection ran deeper, beyond anything she could touch with her hands or see with her eyes.

They were joined on an inexplicable level, and it scared the hell out of her. Because nothing was more terrifying than the beautiful, dangerous threat beneath her and his total and utter possession of her senses.

Pressing closer, she ate his mouth with all the confusion and passion burning inside her. Her hips moved with abandon, chasing the release they both needed.

Tongues moving in tandem, hands kneading and clinging, they groaned together and came up for air.

A pained sound pushed past his lips. The muscles in his face pulled taut, all those gorgeous, masculine angles unable to conceal his discomfort.

"What's wrong?" She froze. "Did I hurt you?"

"Trying not to come." He captured her hand and pressed it between her legs. "Touch yourself."

That she could do.

Sitting up, she circled her fingers around her clit and quickly found the right pace and pressure. Swift, consistent movements, in sync with the snap and twist of her hips.

His gaze smoldered, bouncing between her eyes and her touch, back and forth. He licked his lips, bit down on the bottom one, and his legs began to tremble.

He was fighting it, trying to hold back his orgasm, waiting for her.

Watching his groaning, shaking effort was enough to send her over. The climax tore through her in dizzying, magical ripples of electricity.

"Kate," he moaned, clutching her waist and staring into her eyes. "I'm coming. Ahhh, fuck!"

With a guttural groan, he jerked into her erratically and buried himself deep, holding her against him as he filled her with his come.

"Fucking amazing," he said on a long, languorous sigh. "Thank you."

"That's a first." Twitching with the sparkling remnants of ecstasy, she collapsed on his chest.

"Which part?"

"*You* thanking *me* for anything."

"I'm working on rectifying that." He brushed her hair behind her ear and blew out a breath. "We need to go."

"I'll get a towel to clean us up." She lifted, letting him slip from her body.

"Don't." He straightened his pants and tucked his dirty cock behind the zipper. "You're going to wear my come to dinner."

"How romantic."

He rose to his feet, pulling her with him. His hands smoothed over the dress, straightening and adjusting, and all the while, she could feel his ejaculation leaking down her legs.

She would just have to use the bathroom on the way out and clean up the mess.

As if reading her mind, he sneaked a hand under the gown and smeared the come down her thighs and in her pussy.

She gasped. "What the—?"

He rubbed those same fingers across her mouth. "Let's go meet the President."

TWENTY-NINE

During the two-hour drive to dinner, Kate fretted over whether she reeked of sex or had a wet spot on the back of her gown. As it turned out, the President of Venezuela was in no position to notice.

Not only was he a busy man, life hadn't been kind to him in the hygiene department.

As Tiago clasped his outstretched hand in greeting, she had to hold her breath and stifle her gag reflex.

The elaborately-decorated, so-called dictator smelled like a burnt cigar soaked in the anal gland discharge of a dead skunk. She wasn't even sure which part of his body the offensive odor was coming from.

Maybe it was best she didn't know.

Thankfully, the introductions lasted just long enough for a handshake, a distracted smile in her direction, and a brief conversation with Tiago in Spanish. Then his brigade of uptight assistants ushered him off to the next partygoer.

Tiago hooked an arm around her back and touched his mouth to her ear. "The air is safe to breathe again."

"Jesus," she whispered on an exhale. "What was that?"

"The aroma of corruption and power." He steered her toward the bar.

"You don't smell like that." She smirked.

He smirked back before calling out his drink order to the bartender.

On the way to this majestic beachfront mansion, he'd explained they were going to a private island owned by one of the President's diplomats. The last jog of the journey had involved a car ferry from the mainland. She hadn't been able to see the ocean in the dark, but for the first time in her life, she'd detected the scent of salt and brine and heard the roll of waves.

They'd only been on the island for thirty minutes, entering the main hall at the end of dinner. The hundreds of tuxedos and gowns in attendance had been too busy stuffing their faces to pay any attention to the late arrivals.

But she felt their eyes now.

Pinched-faced, scowling men and women filled the ballroom, all of them glaring at the man at her side. Apparently, they didn't like the King of Caracas in their presence.

"Some of these people are staring so hard," she said under her breath, leaning back against the bar, "when you leave tonight, your ears are going to be on fire."

"They want my city." With his body facing the bar, his assertive hand glided across her stomach and closed around her hip. "And the gorgeous woman on my arm."

"Pretty sure they just want you dead." She spotted Arturo at the entrance of the ballroom, his gaze ever-watchful.

"That, too. But we're safe tonight. No one will try to kill each other with the President's armed forces on the premises."

If there were armed guards in the room, their weapons were concealed beneath tuxedos. Arturo was the only face she recognized, and he didn't have a gun. Every visitor in this house had to go through a metal detector.

She'd asked Tiago a thousand questions during the drive, and he'd only answered a few. While he was hunted by American government agencies and Mexican cartel, he'd assured her the President of Venezuela had more enemies than he did.

That did nothing to calm her nerves.

The bartender handed him the finished drinks. Tiago kept the tumbler of clear fluid and offered her the wine glass.

"What is this?" She took a small sip and widened her eyes.

"*Vino Pasita*. Wine made from bananas."

"Wow." She swallowed another greedy gulp and licked her lips, savoring the burst of sweet, fruity flavors. "This is heaven."

"You only get one. The hangover is a slow death of agonizing pain." He clasped her hand and guided her through the crowds of formal wear, his whisper a caress at her ear. "I need to rub some elbows and finalize a few deals. Enjoy your *vino* and don't leave my side."

For the next hour, she remained on his arm like a silent gold ornament, mesmerized by his sensual Spanish parlance as he hobnobbed with politicians, Venezuelan celebrities, and random powerful bad guys.

During each introduction, he announced her as Kate. Some of the faces she recognized. Others she knew by name. If she had a phone, she would've been burning up the Internet in an attempt to learn about these people.

After another hour of standing around in six-inch heels, her feet throbbed. Her delicious wine was long gone, and maybe she was just overstimulated by all the conversations, but something niggled. She felt edgy. Almost paranoid.

Her scalp tingled, and the constant itch between her shoulder blades had her searching the crowds at her back every few seconds.

Arturo hadn't moved from his position near the door. Nothing seemed amiss.

She needed another drink.

With no servers in the vicinity, she lifted Tiago's tumbler from his hand. He glanced at her while continuing his conversation with the Minister of Foreign Affairs.

She gave them a soft smile and sipped from the glass.

Well, crap. He was drinking water? Useless.

A younger man stood beside the old politician. She couldn't remember his name, but she didn't like his eyes. Especially when they fell to her chest. It was quick. A dip down and back up. But it happened, and Tiago didn't miss it.

His neck rolled, and his biceps hardened, crushing her fingers in the bend of his arm.

Desperate to diffuse his temper, she glanced around the room, and an idea struck.

"Sorry to interrupt your conversation." She set his glass aside and rubbed a soothing hand over his clenched fist. "Will you dance with me?"

"Yes." He said his goodbyes through gritted teeth and escorted her across the room to the dance floor. "Trying to distract me?"

"Absolutely."

"Do you know how to dance to this?"

Dozens of couples spun to the fast, creole-like music. Hands clasped, they faced each other, making small, stomping steps. They all moved in the same speed and style, using waltz turns and sweeping foot movements. She'd never seen anything like it. Maybe it was the fandango. Definitely not the tango.

"I have no clue." She didn't know how to dance at all.

"It's the joropo, the national dance of Venezuela." He led her to the side of the dance floor where the band congregated.

At least twenty musicians played guitars, maracas, harps, mandolins, and multiple other instruments she couldn't name.

He whispered something to the maestro, and a moment later, the music segued into a slow Spanish number.

"Better?" He stared at her mouth and brushed a thumb across her lower lip.

She nodded. "I think so?"

He guided her to the center of the dance floor and held her tight against the front of his body. Then he swayed into an easy rhythm, keeping his steps simple and slow, as if he knew she didn't know how to dance.

If the room was watching, she didn't notice. She was only aware of the strength of his arms around her back and the heat of his breath on her neck.

She ran her hands up the strong column of his neck and spoke against his mouth in an almost-kiss. "I like you like this."

"That so?"

"Yeah." She pressed her smile against his cheek, delighting in the scratch of stubble that had grown in within a few hours.

"Then I'll dance with you every night."

He carried her through another song, gently rocking, pacing the rise and fall of her breaths. But something started to shift under his skin. A tension that wasn't there before.

Or maybe it was just her earlier unease seeping in?

She ignored it for a few moments, until his muscles grew tighter beneath her fingers, and his movements stiffened with each note of the song. He was bracing for something.

"What's wrong?" She looked around and didn't register anything out of place.

"Let's take a walk." His fingers intertwined with hers, and he strolled off the dance floor with a nod to the maestro.

Panic seized her as he wove through the room, keeping his gait slow to accommodate her clicking high-heels. His expression was too calm, too blank. What was he hiding beneath that emotionless mask?

He didn't make eye contact or stop to talk to anyone. His gaze flitted between Arturo and the side door, where he was leading her.

She pinned her lips tight, knowing not to ask questions or draw attention with so many people around.

"This way." He directed her into a quiet corridor and around a few clusters of mingling partygoers.

Stalking down the hallway, around the corner, and past a vacant dining room, he seemed to know his way around. She glanced back and found Arturo trailing at a distance.

"Are we in danger?" she whispered.

"Just one more meeting. Then we'll leave."

"That's not an answer. Where are we going?"

"Not sure." He flicked a finger at the wood flooring. "Following the beer."

"What?" She squinted in confusion. "The beer?"

He stopped and lowered to a crouch. With a swipe of his thumb, he collected a tiny drop of wetness from the floor and held it to his nose. "A trail of beer."

"Why? Who left it?"

He rose and touched his lips to the sensitive skin beneath her ear, shushing her. "Through here."

With a hand at the small of her back, he turned her into a dark, empty service kitchen.

"Where is everyone?" She craned her neck, searching the shadows amid commercial appliances. Her pulse skittered out of control.

"The main kitchen is on the other side of the house." He ushered her toward an industrial steel door.

An entrance to a walk-in freezer?

A beer bottle sat on the floor in front of it. He moved it out of the way and shrugged off his tuxedo coat.

In the doorway to the hall, Arturo stood with his back to the kitchen, keeping watch.

"Tiago, you're scaring me." She rubbed her arms. "Tell me what's going on."

"It's going to be cold." He draped the jacket over her shoulders and pulled the lapels together at her chest.

With a hard, tense kiss against her lips, he turned and opened the steel door.

A blast of frigid air punched through her, but that wasn't what froze the breath in her lungs.

Standing at the rear of the walk-in freezer was a man she never expected to see.

Dressed to the nines in a black tuxedo, he looked like an apparition in a swirling cloud of wintry air.

She gasped. "Cole?"

THIRTY

Kate blinked rapidly, struggling to believe her eyes. Her pulse thundered, and her palms slicked with sweat, despite the frosty air.

"Kate." Cole Hartman folded his hands behind him, shoulders back, as if he were *expecting* her. "Are you okay?"

"I'm kind of freaking out." Her gaze snapped to Tiago as he shut the freezer door behind him.

Not a hint of surprise or anger on his stern face. What the almighty fuck?

Her mind reeled to make a connection between the two men. They seemed to look at each other with familiarity, and that kind of made sense. Cole had appeared on the video with Lucia when she found Tate in the shack.

But Tiago had never mentioned Cole's name to her. Did he know Tate had hired Cole to locate Lucia?

In all likelihood, Cole was here for *her*. To rescue her.

What if he'd sneaked in a gun? Would he shoot Tiago?

Were her friends here, too?

Elation and terror jolted through her, trembling her limbs and making every breath a workout. "Are you alone?"

"Yes." Cole narrowed his eyes at Tiago.

"Don't kill each other." She gripped Tiago's hand and squeezed. "We can figure out whatever this is without spilling blood."

Cole stared at their entwined fingers, and lines formed in his brow.

She would have to explain her relationship to him, even if she wasn't sure how to explain it to herself.

First, she needed answers.

"You purposefully left a trail of beer to this freezer," she said to Cole. "For Tiago?"

"Yes."

She stared up at Tiago's unreadable expression. "How did you know he did that?"

"I spotted him while we were dancing, and he tipped his beer bottle at me. A helpful clue." He scanned the ceilings and shelves of frozen foods. "Is this—?"

"I did a sweep." Cole's words rode on a flume of white steam. "The area is clean."

"Clean of what?" She glanced between them, taken back by the way their eyes connected so...comfortably. "I'm sorry. Do you two know each other?"

"*Clean* means no bugs. We're not being recorded or spied on." Tiago banded an arm around her back, pulling her against the heat of his body. "And yes, we know each other."

"Took you long enough to mark me." Cole cocked his head. "I've been here all night."

"I was distracted." Tiago stroked a thumb along her arm.

"You shouldn't have come out of hiding," Cole said.

"We both know I didn't have a choice." His jaw hardened. "How's Trace?"

Cole crossed his arms over his chest, nostrils flaring.

"Who's Trace?" She adjusted Tiago's tuxedo coat tighter around her, shivering.

"He was our handler." Tiago turned, putting his dark eyes inches from her face. "Cole and I have known each other for a long time."

"What?" Shock strangled her voice. "How?"

"We worked for the U.S. government."

Her mouth fell open, closed, and opened again. "But you're Venezuelan."

"My mother was American. I was born in the U.S. and raised here, in my father's country."

"Were you military?" She recalled what little she knew of Cole and the fog of secrecy surrounding the man's credentials. "Or some kind of spy or assassin?"

His gaze slid to Cole, and they exchanged an indecipherable look.

"He can't discuss the job." Cole's lips slanted in a harsh line.

"But you both knew this Trace guy?" She trembled uncontrollably, fighting to keep warm in the subzero temperatures. "You worked together? On the same side?"

Her whirling thoughts jumped to FBI, CIA, top-secret espionage stuff. Except weren't those the very organizations that were hunting

Tiago?

The night he told her about his wife, she'd asked him why he became like the man who had his family killed. His response hadn't made sense at the time.

I didn't. He was my colleague. When he betrayed me, I became the opposite of him. I became his enemy.

"Many years ago, Cole and I had the same employer, on the right side of the law." Tiago tugged her against his chest and enclosed his arms around her, running a hand up and down her back to create warmth. "We didn't work closely together, but we both reported to Trace. He was the handler who gave us our orders."

Just...mind-blowing.

"Trace is also Cole's best friend. Or *was*." He shot Cole a cruel smirk. "Is he still banging your fiancée?"

Cole bared his teeth. "He married her, you fucking asshole."

"Then he's definitely banging her."

"You know, you weren't always such an insensitive dick." Cole lowered his arms to his sides, and the hard lines of his face smoothed away. "I'm sorry about Semira and your family. Had I known what was happening, I swear, Tiago, I would've warned you. I would've done something to stop it."

Her throat tightened, and she grabbed Tiago's hand. God, they really did know each other. No wonder Cole had located Lucia so easily. Tate would shit himself if he knew about this crazy connection.

"The job came with risks." Tiago said softly. "They told us no attachments. No spouses. No weaknesses. We knew that going in, and we walked away losing everything that mattered to us."

"You were both betrayed?" Her mind churned to fit the pieces together. "It sounds like you were the good guys, fighting on the right side, and that side fucked you over. Is that what happened? You lost a fiancée, a wife, and a family because people you trusted turned on you?"

"Something like that." Cole stared at Tiago.

"Explain it to me," she said.

"There was a defection in our ranks." Tiago flexed his hand around hers. "Two of our colleagues—a man and a woman—defected from the agency and leaked our personal information to known enemies who were willing to pay a small fortune for it. The female traitor threatened Cole's fiancée, but his best friend protected her."

Did the best friend fuck her before or after he protected her? Maybe there was more to the story, but holy crap... Poor Cole.

"The other defector was responsible for the deaths of my family." Tiago's voice scratched, and he cleared it. "He sold classified information about me to an enemy, fully aware it would turn my home into a bloodbath. It wasn't personal. He just wanted the money."

"That's why you both switched sides."

Cole straightened. "I didn't—"

"I know for a fact you did a job for Van Quiso." She glared. "Which side do you think he's on?"

"Given your friendship with the capo of the Restrepo cartel," Tiago said, "it's safe to assume you're no longer working for the American people."

"Right." Cole blew out a breath. "Sometimes I work for criminals and walk a blurry line. But I don't murder or kidnap innocent people for money. And when I was betrayed, I didn't go on a ruthless killing spree. I faked my own death, went into hiding, and lost my goddamn soul mate."

"Good for you." Tiago laughed hollowly. "I guess that makes you a better man than me."

"No." Her hackles flared, and she grabbed Tiago's arm, turning him toward her. "I've never condoned the things you've done, but you know what? Cole didn't lose his parents and only brother. He didn't watch someone heartlessly gut his wife. There is *no* comparison. I don't know him that well, but if someone murdered his fiancée in front of him..." She jabbed a finger at Cole. "I think there would be a very different man standing there."

"You're defending him?" Cole asked with more hostility than she appreciated. "Do you know what he did to Tate and Lucia?"

"Yes." She jutted her chin.

"Are you free?"

"What?"

"Are you free to walk away from him? Right now?"

A numb, paralyzing thud echoed in her ears, and her neck ached to shake her head. Now was the time to tell him, to let him know she couldn't escape.

Tiago would never release her. He would never let her see her friends, or pursue a career, or carry a loaded gun, or go for a walk alone. Cole needed to know this. He could help her. But her muscles wouldn't work, and her voice deserted her.

"She's not free." Tiago's fingers shackled her wrist as he shoved open the freezer door. "If she wants to go with you, I won't allow it. If you try to take her—"

"You'll kill me. I figured as much." Cole flicked his gaze to her. "This isn't over, Kate. I'll get you out."

"The fuck you will." Tiago ushered her out of the freezer, into the warm kitchen, and toward the hallway, where Arturo waited.

"Hang on." She dug in her heels, trying to slow his long strides so she could explain the situation to Cole. "I just need to—"

TAKE

An enormous explosion erupted somewhere in the house. The percussion was so forceful it reverberated in her ribcage and rang in her ears. She lost her balance in the heels, and in the next breath, strong arms came around her and her feet left the floor.

Tiago hoisted her against his chest and swung back toward Cole. "Tell me that isn't an assassination attempt on the President."

"With that bomb? It must be." Cole raced past them and poked his head in the corridor. "It probably dropped from overhead."

"Drones." Tiago's entire body turned to stone. "Goddammit, there will be more. We need to get the fuck out of here."

She choked down the sound of undiluted fear as it tried to escape.

A cloud of dust shook from the ceiling. Alarms, shrill and deafening, blared to life, and in the distance, the blast of gunfire rent the air.

"Opposition activists." Cole shoved a hand through his brown hair. "I heard a rumor the Colombian president was rallying an attack."

"And we're caught in the middle of it?" Her heart lurched.

"Gonna need you to run, Kate." Tiago lowered her feet to the floor. "Kick off your shoes."

He supported her balance as she toed off each heel. Then he guided her arms into the sleeves of the jacket still draped over her shoulders.

At her questioning look, he said, "In case there's any flying debris, the jacket is better than nothing."

"The rear exit is blocked by the gunfight." Arturo appeared in the doorway. "We'll have to leave out the front with everyone else."

"Mass fucking exodus." Tiago pulled her into the hall and laced their fingers together. "No matter what, don't let go."

The flashing, screeching alarms in the ceiling fucked with her bearings. By the time she scrounged up a nod, he was already dragging her at full speed toward the ballroom.

Cole and Arturo stayed on their heels. Until the second bomb hit.

It detonated so close it threw her against the wall. The acrid scent of smoke burned her nose, and she tasted the grit of dust as she coughed.

Given the noise of glass, the ear-splitting howls of people, and the rush of nearby footsteps, the explosion must've blown through the ballroom. If her sense of direction could be trusted, that was just around the next bend.

"Keep moving." Tiago hadn't let go of her hand and pulled on it roughly, urgently, propelling her forward again.

Her pulse thrashed past her ears as she sprinted to keep pace with his strides. Around the corner and through a doorway, they burst into what was left of the ballroom.

429

Dirt and smoke scattered into the atmosphere, creating a nebulous, eye-burning fog. Windows shattered. Shards of glass and twisted steel continued to drop in a groaning, deadly rainfall from the huge bite that had been taken out of the far side of the room.

Furniture tipped upside down, legs in the air. Debris and breakage covered the dance floor, the musicians gone. And the partygoers...

Some lay on the floor in fetal positions, trying to protect their ears and organs. Most ran toward the exit. Others stood off to the side, shell-shocked and unmoving. The rest had been tossed amid the blast, at least a dozen dead.

Tiago spun toward her and gripped her shoulders, shouting with his eyes. His mouth barked commands, but she couldn't hear him over the deafening noise.

He surveyed the glass-covered floor, glanced at her feet, and scooped her up into his arms. It was a considerable distance to carry her over the wreckage from one end of the demolished ballroom to the other, but gratitude overrode her stubbornness.

Wrapping her arms around his shoulders, she pressed her face into his neck and held on.

She assumed Arturo and Cole followed behind, but she was afraid to look. A barrage of closely spaced gunshots broke out around them, firing close enough to damage her eardrums.

The President's opposition might've been here to assassinate him, but if they were willing to bomb a house full of people, they didn't care who they hit in the crossfire.

Tiago tucked her close to his body, bowing over her with his head ducked as he ran like hell.

She wished she had a gun, so she could shoot back. She wished they'd stayed in bed and skipped the fucking party. But wishes wouldn't help them. They needed a fucking miracle.

The din of the surrounding chaos redlined her heart rate. The blaring alarms, panicked screams, and approaching gunfire pounded from every direction. She lifted her head.

Twenty feet from the exit. Almost there.

As every nerve ending in her body stretched toward that door, a great thunderous clap blew apart the world.

One second, she was in Tiago's arms beneath a vaulted ceiling. The next, she was airborne under the open nighttime sky.

Then everything went black.

THIRTY-ONE

Kate floated in a painless state of silence and disorientation. Every few seconds, a series of flashes burst through, like the intermittent vibrations of a dying heartbeat.

She couldn't hear anything. Not her cries or her breath. Was her head detached from her body? Or her limbs? That didn't make sense. But why couldn't she move?

"Tiago." His name chanted from her mind, but she wasn't sure her voice touched the air.

The floor shook violently beneath her. More explosions, farther away. Alarms strobed, but the wailing didn't penetrate her ears. People stumbled and ran, but she couldn't hear their screams.

As she attempted to recover her senses, a blanket of hellish heat saturated the front of her body. Blinking through semi-blindness, she stared up at a pillar of fiery smoke and dust. It rushed out through sections of the roof that had been destroyed by the blast.

Blackened orange flames billowed from the rubble near the exit, baking the startled air. A pressurized wind swept through the room, pulling on her, as if trying to draw her into the fire.

"Tiago!" She struggled to turn her neck and found herself lying by a wall some distance from where he'd been carrying her.

Panic tortured her heart, and her muscles refused to respond. It was so dark, so confusing. Why couldn't she see him? Or feel his hands on her? He would never leave her behind.

The blackness shuddered with jarring flickers of light. Bullets ricocheted, kicking up dirt across the floor. She tried to sit, until she felt the reverberation of approaching feet.

She held still, her stomach clenching as a dozen black-clad men with guns ran past her, their boots stepping close enough to bounce the broken pieces of wood beneath her.

Her hearing detected fragmented sound within her body, like the whooshing of blood and crackling static. Was she hurt? She couldn't sense pain or time, and her brain didn't seem to be working right.

Consciousness shriveled to a pinprick of light, and she strained for it, desperate to stay alert.

After a while, something touched her. Frantic hands, shaking her shoulders and rousing her awake.

Oh God, she'd passed out? For how long?

She opened her eyes, her mouth, struggling to identify the face hovering over her.

Brown hair, blue bow tie, American features—none of the details she ached to see.

Cole Hartman jostled her limp body, his lips moving without sound.

"Where's Tiago?" She braced a hand against the splintered debris beneath her and pushed up. "Where is he?"

Her head pounded something fierce, and sporadic noises filtered in, making the pain unbearably worse.

She must not have been unconscious for very long, because the same chaotic level of disorder raged around her—the fire, the gunfight, the exodus of terrified people.

Tiago was nowhere in sight.

They were on an island. Did that mean there wouldn't be fire crews or ambulances? Where the hell was the mob of people running to? Where would they go?

Away from the fire and spraying bullets.

As Cole tried to speak to her, she focused on reading his lips.

Can you stand?

Are you hurt?

We need to go.

She wasn't going anywhere without Tiago.

Shoving off the floor with trembling muscles, she staggered to her feet and scanned the darkness. "Have you seen him?"

A rush of adrenaline accelerated her pulse, shaking away the crippling shock that had pinned her to the floor during those long, wasted minutes.

Cole's arms wrapped around her, lifting her off the floor and forcing her with him. She pushed against his chest, trying to get down, to stand on her own.

He tightened his hold and took her away from the rubble where

Tiago must've been buried.

"Nooooo!" She screamed in horror, frantically searching the destruction for his body. "I'm not leaving without him!"

Cole didn't slow as he veered around crumbled piles of masonry, wood, and steel. With each step, her hearing returned. As did her determination.

"Go back!" She thrashed in his unbending arms. "Take me back!"

A shooter sprinted past, sweating the room with bullets. Cole took cover, dodging the gunfire while fighting down her flailing hands. Then he burst into a sprint, carrying her through a demolished doorway and into a thick haze of smoke.

"Tiago!" She choked through the suffocating smog and realized the blackness overhead was the sky.

He'd taken her outside and wasn't stopping. His legs ate up the ground, hauling her farther and farther away from the burning mansion.

No, no no!

A sob opened her throat, and a flood of wailing screams fell out.

"Can't leave him! Put me down. I have to go back!" She couldn't stop crying. Couldn't see through her blinding panic and tears.

She howled and writhed until his hand clapped over her mouth and his furious eyes came into view.

"You're going to get us killed," he whispered harshly. "Shut the fuck up."

She shoved his hand away. "But Tiago—"

"He's dead or missing." He ran down an embankment and jumped onto a small deserted dock. "If you run back there, you'll be dead, too."

He dumped her in a waiting speedboat. Before she had a chance to scramble out, he slipped the tether free, fired up the engine, and shot into the black expanse of the ocean.

The sudden momentum knocked her into one of the vinyl seats. She twisted toward the rear, gripping the headrest as the island drifted away.

Rags of fire whipped along the skyline and wafted plumes of smoke above it, making the darkness even darker. The boat crashed against the waves, and as the distance stretched, reality clawed its way in.

Tiago was in that inferno, and she'd left him there.

Grief consumed her, wracking her body with violent, shuddering sobs. She'd abandoned him, something he would've never, ever done to her. He would've launched himself onto an exploding bomb before he let someone drag him away without her.

Because he loved her.

Not once had she said those words back to him, and the thought only made her more miserable. Guilt lashed in her stomach. Defeat bunched her shoulders around her ears. Despondency pounded in her head, and emptiness carved out her chest. She was utterly wretched and inconsolable.

Cole must've thought she'd completely lost her mind. She didn't know how to explain her feelings, but she had about thirty minutes to figure it out before he stopped the boat.

He killed the motor, and waves lapped around them. The ocean bled into darkness. Nothing to see or hear for miles.

After checking something on his phone, he turned his angry gaze to her.

"I don't extract unwilling people." He rose from the driver's seat and approached her in the rear of the boat. "Tell me I didn't make a mistake."

"You made a mistake." She was numb. Depleted. Heartsick. "Turn the boat around. Take me back."

"You want to go back to the man who poisoned Lucia for eleven years, mutilated Tate's back, shackled him in a shack for three months, and held you against your will?" He crouched beside her and softened his tone. "Did he rape you?"

An ugly mass of emotion swelled in her throat, and she looked away.

"You care about him." A sigh billowed past his lips. "It's okay, Kate. You have Stockholm syndrome. I see it all time in these situations and—"

"What if it's not that? What if my feelings are real? And I just…" Another sob rose up. "I just left him there to die."

"He received the same military training I did. If he's alive, he'll get out." His brows knitted together, and he glanced down at her thigh, where her scars peeked through the slit in the gown.

He spent the next few seconds examining her for injuries. Cuts and bruises marred her body. Her ankle was sprained, and he claimed she had a concussion.

She felt none of it. Nothing but emptiness.

"You've been through a lot. You need safety and friends and time to heal." He checked his phone and returned it to his pocket. "Your ride will be here any minute."

"What ride? Who's coming?"

"People who care about you." He removed a small device from another pocket. "I need to do a sweep for transmitters. Did Tiago put anything on your body? Like a small chip under your skin or maybe a piece of jewelry?"

"You mean a GPS chip?"

434

"Yes. You can't go to the Restrepo estate until we're certain you're not being tracked. The location is a highly guarded secret."

Her heart slammed as a fresh wave of sorrow washed over her. Tiago would've absolutely chipped her, and she knew exactly how. She didn't even care if he meant to track her. In fact, she loved that about him.

She loved his possessiveness.

She loved his bossy mouth, his sexy Spanish accent, his cruel eyes, and his addictive masculine taste when he kissed her. She loved everything about him, and so what if that made her a head case?

"He hasn't put anything on me." She rolled her shoulders forward so the material would hang more loosely across her breasts. "We have to go back for him, Cole."

He narrowed his eyes and waved that device right over her breasts until it sounded a low beep.

Her molars crashed together.

"You have piercings." He removed a tiny flashlight from his pocket. "I need to see them."

"I'm not removing them." She hardened her voice. "Take me back to the island."

"Not going back, Kate." He pinched the bridge of his nose and exhaled. "You can take out the piercings or leave them in. I don't give a fuck. I just need to see if there's a tracker on them."

"The thing beeped, so you already know."

"It detected metal. You'll get the same response when you go through an X-ray machine at the airport."

"Oh." She released a breath.

If he needed to see them, he would have to do it while they stayed in.

Without removing Tiago's tuxedo coat, she wriggled the straps of the dress down her arms. When her breasts hit the warm air, he powered on the flashlight and angled the beam on the glimmering red stones.

"The fuck?" He leaned in, eyes bulging as he stared at the jewelry. "It can't be."

"What?"

"Did he tell you what these stones are?"

"Uh… Pawneets… Or no, it was pennet…"

"Painites."

"Yes. Painites. Why?"

He barked out a strangled laugh and sat back on his heels. "That son of a bitch."

"What's wrong?"

He shook his head and gripped the back of his neck, his eyes fixed on the piercings, as if he couldn't believe they were real.

"Did you find a tracker?" She straightened, startled by his strange reaction.

"No. The barbells are too small. It's not that. It's just…" He scrubbed a hand down his face. "You can fix your dress."

Tiago hadn't put a tracker on her?

Her breath stuttered as she put the gown back in order. "Is it the stones?"

"Yeah, Kate. Those fucking stones…" He shifted to the seat across from her and rested his elbows on his knees. "Painites are one of the rarest gemstones on the planet. Extremely valuable. But that's not important. It's…"

Something thundered in the distance, a clap-clap-clap whir of noise that grew louder, closer. In the next breath, she recognized the sound. A helicopter was coming.

"That's your ride. Listen…" Cole ran the device along the rest of her body as he spoke. "There's a rumor going around in the criminal underground that Tiago Badell sold his entire syndicate to some unknown investor in exchange for…" A swallow jogged in his throat. "Four rare painite stones."

"What?" Her face chilled, and she pressed a hand over one of the piercings.

"That sort of hearsay runs rampant in his world, usually conceived as a means of subterfuge and rarely accurate. I didn't even bother fact checking it. But the evidence…" He glanced at her chest and cleared his throat. "Jesus, Kate. If those gemstones are real…"

"He wouldn't give me fake gems and call them real. Not his style."

Cole nodded, his voice stunned. "You're wearing the last twelve years of his life. His entire goddamn livelihood."

"What does that mean?" Tears welled in her eyes as the whomping sound of the helicopter sped closer. "Did he give up his organization?"

"It appears so."

"But he gave the stones to me a month ago, and he's been going to the compound every day, conducting meetings with all his men."

"Meetings about what?"

"I don't know. They're always in Spanish."

"He was probably transitioning everything. Or dissolving operations."

"Oh my God." She jumped from the seat, rocking unsteadily as waves slapped at the boat. "Take me back. I need to go back!"

The helicopter swept in above her, swallowing her voice and enveloping her in a mist of ocean water. She covered her ears against the god-awful noise, unable to make out its silhouette against the night sky.

TAKE

No way would she agree to board that thing. How would it even work?

She turned back to Cole and shouted over the wind, "Take me back!"

He gripped her face, catching the hair whipping around her. "I'll go back. I'll find him."

His words didn't reach her ears, but she read them on his lips and saw the promise in his dark eyes.

"I'll go with you."

He shook his head and pointed behind her. "Go."

Steel arms encircled her from behind, and she turned, falling into the warm, familiar eyes of one of her roommates. "Martin!"

A tether ran from his harness to the helicopter. Evidently, he'd been lowered on some kind of pulley system.

Her chest squeezed as she absorbed the worried expression on his handsome face. Damn, she'd missed him, and the roar of the wind made it impossible to tell him as much.

A gust smacked her sideways, and she braced her legs to remain upright. Cole held her in place as Martin quickly attached a belt around her hips, between her legs, and secured the contraption to his. Then he shined a flashlight into the darkness overhead.

The harness pulled tight and his arms even tighter as they were lifted into the air. The blades beat the wind against them like a hurricane.

With her heart in her stomach, she stared down at Cole and demanded with her eyes. *Find him.*

He stared back with a silent vow tensing his face.

Digging her hands into Martin's shoulders, she held her breath and closed her eyes. She had to trust Cole to go back to the island, but it left her feeling completely useless and terrified as that boat sank farther away from her feet.

When they reached the helicopter, hands grabbed, and arms pulled, until she was lying on her back and safely inside the aircraft.

Familiar faces filled her view. Smiles. Cheering roars. Even a few wet eyes.

"Kate!" Camila tackled her as soon as she was disconnected from Martin. "Fucking shit, girl! You've given me a dozen heart attacks."

Matias nodded at her from the cockpit. She caught a glimpse of Luke's red hair, before Ricky hauled her into the seat beside him and strapped her in. Martin plopped down on her other side, and the helicopter's nose dipped as it raced into the night.

The blaring noise from the blades made conversation difficult, but she felt their relief and happiness pouring off them. Four of her old roommates had shown up for her rescue—Martin, Camila, Ricky, and

Luke—and she suspected Tomas and others were waiting at Matias' Colombian estate.

After being gone for four months, it was surreal to be sitting here with them. A consuming, head-spinning kind of surreal that crashed in with a flood of pain.

Her eyes burned with that achy feeling that always came right before she cried. She tried to hold back the tears, but they were persistent and full of so many conflicting emotions—gratitude, fear, joy, desolation, and hope.

She was finally free, and it hurt to the depths of her soul.

The one thing that mattered most in her freedom was missing.

She needed Tiago.

Whether he joined her in her freedom or took it away, she just needed them to experience whatever came next together.

THIRTY-TWO

Eight people have been arrested after Saturday's apparent assassination attempt on the President of Venezuela. The President survived the ambush after several drones dropped explosives on his dinner party at a private residence, an attack he blamed on opposition activists and Colombia's president. Thirty-seven people are confirmed dead. Twelve others are still missing.

Kate powered off the TV and stared at the blank screen, her voice brittle with pain. "Tiago's alive."

A throat cleared. Feet shuffled. Someone sighed.

Sitting in one of the many living rooms at Matias' Colombian estate, she was surrounded by her friends. All of them. Liv and Josh, Van and Amber, Camila and Matias, Tate and Lucia, her roommates—everyone was here, seeking refuge within the cartel's stronghold while awaiting the verdict on Tiago Badell.

No one trusted him, and maybe that was smart. As long as she was separated from him, they weren't safe.

Cole Hartman had returned to the island as promised, but after a night of searching for Tiago and Arturo, he came up empty.

The next day, he went to Tiago's penthouse and slipped past the building's supposed impenetrable security. Everything was still there, but the entire staff had vanished, including Boones.

That was four days ago.

He hadn't been able to confirm the list of casualties on the island. The President had buried that information. No surprise. Most of the names at the party belonged to the sort of unsavory people no president should be associated with.

Cole assured her he would learn who died and who was missing, but it would take time.

Didn't matter. She already decided Tiago was alive. She just needed to figure out how to find him. That was the tricky part.

Tiago had enemies, and now they knew who she was and what she meant to him. The moment she stepped outside of Matias' fortress, they would find her.

It didn't dissuade her. She had powerful friends, and they were extremely protective of her.

Except that was the problem. Her friends were *too* protective.

When she'd asked Matias for a security team to accompany her to Venezuela, he refused. Then he threatened to lock her in a cell if she tried to leave. Her roommates supported that threat.

When she'd asked Cole to somehow get a message to Tiago in the criminal underground, that request was refused, as well. Cole said it would end up in the wrong hands and only put her in more danger.

But Cole kept a diligent watch on Caracas, and he'd been able to confirm one thing.

Tiago was no longer associated with his organization.

Smuggling routes had been dismantled. Rival gangs had moved in. There was even a new leader running what was left of his compound.

He'd given it all up. Forfeited his livelihood. Surrendered his protection.

For the four gemstones he'd attached to her nipples.

The man had a filthy dark sense of chivalry.

"We need to consider the possibility he'll never resurface." Tate paced to the window and stared out at the moonlit landscape of the rain forest. "We can't hide here forever."

"He won't harm you," Kate murmured.

Tate pivoted and tilted his head to the side, regarding her. "Have you seen my back, Kate?"

"Yes." She glided a hand over her thigh, seeking comfort in the scars that lay beneath her borrowed jeans. "He and I made a deal. He promised me he would never hurt you again."

"His promises mean nothing to me."

Her chest was empty, drained of tears and breath. It felt as though she'd left her insides in that fire. Everything under her skin was simply gone. Except the hum of determination. That was still there, rising up from the chasm where her soul once lived, where he used to be.

"He's alive, and I'll find him." She met Tate's eyes. "Unless he finds me first."

He pressed his lips together, biting back a retort.

Every hour that passed reinforced her belief that Tiago was alive. That meant she wasn't the only one hurting. He had vulnerabilities that could only be comforted and healed by her. He needed her, missed her, feared for her as much as she did for him. They were two halves of a whole.

Since arriving here, she'd heard the term *Stockholm syndrome* from every mouth in every conversation. It didn't upset her or make her defensive. Because honestly, how many times had she thrown those very words at Tiago?

How sad that she had to lose him in order to see what had been right in front of her all along.

She knew what she felt was love—not coercion, not lust, not Stockholm syndrome—because it had become an artery that ran through the deepest part of her heart. She felt it beating and knew if she severed it, she would bleed out. She wouldn't survive.

The night she reunited with Tate, she sat down with him and explained this. Since he was so utterly wrapped up in Lucia, he understood the madness that came with love. He couldn't fully comprehend her position with regard to Tiago, but he listened. He was trying.

Then she had a heart-to-heart with everyone else, individually, paired off with couples, and together as a group. It'd been four days of discussing, soul-searching, and analyzing until her emotional shields were eradicated and there was nowhere to hide from their hard questions.

It felt like a form of group therapy. She endured it because she appreciated their life experiences, valued their opinions, and trusted their intentions.

Josh and Amber related to her the most. They'd both fallen in love with their captors, so they understood her on the darkest, most vulnerable level. Their journeys hadn't been pretty, and look at them now. They fucking glowed with happiness.

There was comfort in that. Validation. Hope.

So here they all were, the whole gang sitting together in Matias' estate, talking, monitoring the news, and waiting. Because the man she loved was missing, and that made him a threat to everyone.

On the bright side, she had her friends back. Thanks to Van Quiso, they shared a remarkable bond, one born in shackles and strengthened in survival.

For the rest of the night, they lounged around in the living room, pouring drinks, sharing stories, enjoying one another's company, and musing about the future.

She didn't know what the future held for her, but she never saw herself as a vigilante warrior. Not like them.

She told them she wanted to heal people, and maybe someday, she would become the Freedom Fighters' resident doctor.

A doctor like Boones.

If she located the old man, she would find Tiago.

Maybe Boones had returned to his brothers in his home village? She didn't know where that was, but through her observations, she'd collected four months of clues, including the unique sounds of his native language.

A plan started to form, thrumming through her blood and bouncing her leg.

"I'm going to head to bed." She rose, said her good-nights, and strolled through the maze of corridors in the sprawling, contemporary estate.

Verandas and scenic breezeways led her to her suite. The fortress reminded her of an all-inclusive resort, equipped with every amenity. Commercial kitchens, dining rooms filled with dozens of tables, Olympic-sized pool, and full-service staff... With all the surrounding luxury, she could almost overlook the scary, heavily-armed cartel members who roamed the halls.

When she stepped inside her room, the tread of approaching footsteps sounded behind her.

"Hey, Kate." Martin caught the door before it closed. "Can I come in?"

"Like you have to ask." She strode past the bed, lowered into the armchair, and pulled Tiago's tuxedo coat over her lap, instantly finding solace in the crisp feel of the fabric. "Want a drink?"

Every suite had a fully-stocked wet bar, laptop, sitting area, and private bathroom.

"Nah. Just wanted to check on you." He sprawled on the loveseat beside her.

She grew up with three older brothers, and none of them had been even a fraction as protective as her five alpha roommates.

As he stared at her, a glint of aggression hardened his green eyes before melting away into the shadows of his handsome face.

His model-like features, perfectly-combed blond hair, and muscular build fit the requisite mold of beauty and seduction. They all had that in common.

Over a span of seven years, Van and Liv had captured six beautiful men and two women. Plucked out of the ghettos along the Mexican border, Kate and the others didn't have families who would miss them.

Joshua Carter was the exception, the one who shattered Liv's façade and brought down the entire sex trafficking operation.

Martin had been slave number five. He was also the pack leader among her male roommates.

442

"You sleep with that thing?" He nodded at the tuxedo coat.

"Maybe." She pulled it up to her nose and inhaled the scent of fire and masculinity from the collar.

"You're a fucking mess."

"You should talk. How's Ricky?"

His jaw set. "I'm not touching that conversation."

She loved to pester him about the sexual tension that vibrated between him and his best friend. Ricky was openly bisexual, flirtatious as hell, and had a very obvious, soul-deep crush on Martin.

Martin, on the other hand, grunted and growled like a homophobic every time she mentioned the attraction. He claimed to be straight and banged a different woman every night. But there was so much more going on beneath the surface. He carried a freight load of baggage, most of which had compounded during his captivity with Van.

Everyone knew he wanted to fuck Ricky's brains out. He just hadn't come to terms with it.

"How are you doing with Van?" she asked. "Is it still hard for you to be around him?"

"If I ever get him alone, I'm going to take him for a ride in the country."

"What does that mean?"

"It's what my dad used to say. Whenever one of our old dogs needed to be put down, he'd load up the dog in the truck, drive to an isolated field, and shoot it." A dark smirk twisted his lips. "It's time for a ride in the country."

"Please, don't." Her stomach caved in.

"You're telling me you've forgiven him?"

"No." She nodded. "Maybe. I don't know. Being around him isn't as hard as it used to be. He doesn't scare me."

There was a bigger, meaner, much more terrifying man in the world, and goddammit, she missed his brutal mouth.

"That's good, Kate. It's great." He pushed up from his sprawl and leaned forward to grip her hand. "You're a fucking fighter, you know that?"

"Can't shoot a gun or throw a fist to save my life." She laughed.

"You fight with this crazy, fathomless inner strength. I've never worried about losing you to depression or insanity or…" He squeezed her hand. "A broken heart. It seems you've figured out how to survive the emotional shit better than the rest of us. I envy that."

"Thank you." Her throat tightened.

"You're not going back to Texas, are you?"

She hadn't thought about it, but her answer was certain. "No."

"None of us are returning."

"You're all staying here?"

"I don't know what Tate and Lucia will do, but the guys and I need to be here, with Camila."

It made sense. Camila was their leader in a dangerous fight against human sex trafficking. Most of their missions sent them to South America. There was no reason for them to continue to live in Texas.

"We should sell the house." She gave him a sad smile.

"Agreed." He cocked his head. "This isn't a break-up, Kate."

"No." Her smile turned upward, stretching her cheeks. "It's a merger. The Freedom Fighters and the Restrepo cartel. An unstoppable force to be reckoned with."

"Ricky and I are leaving next week. I don't know when we'll return."

"What's the mission?"

"Camila's planting us in a Mexican prison to gather information on the leader of the inmates. He happens to be the capo of La Rocha cartel. A nasty piece of work. His incarceration hasn't stopped him from running one of the biggest slave trade operations south of the border." His gaze lost focus beneath a cloud of barely restrained fury. "He's trafficking kids, Kate. We have to end that motherfucker."

"You're going into a Mexican prison? Undercover? As inmates?" Her pulse sprinted. "What the fuck, Martin? You can't—"

"Ricky and I have been training for this for months. We know what we're doing."

She closed her eyes, released a breath, and met his gaze. "Please, be careful."

"Same to you, when you capture your captor." He winked.

They talked for a little while longer before she walked him out. Then she took a shower, put on pajamas she'd borrowed from Camila, and slipped her arms into the sleeves of Tiago's dinner jacket.

Maybe sleeping in it every night had taken her desperation too far, but she missed him terribly. It had only been four days, and the pain had become more than she could bear.

To think, he'd been such a dick to her. He'd hurt her, brought her to tears, made her vulnerable, and took away all her defenses.

He'd also kept every promise, showed genuine regret, protected her, and loved her unconditionally. Through his cruelty and his tenderness, she realized she could trust him at the deepest level. And those defenses and freedoms he'd taken from her? She didn't need any of it. Not with him.

She just needed his love.

As she crawled into bed, his absence hit her in a torrent of tears. She pulled the tuxedo coat around her, breathed him in, and silently wept.

"Where are you, Tiago?"

A knock sounded on the door.

After living with five roommates, she'd grown used to late-night visitors in her room. Someone always needed something, even if it was just conversation.

Since Martin had just left, she suspected Ricky would be waiting on the other side. But when she opened the door, Lucia's brown gaze collided with hers.

"Hi." Kate wiped her cheeks, certain all the crying had made her eyes red and swollen.

"Hey, um... I know we don't know each other, but I thought since we have a mutual...acquaintance..."

"You mean Tiago?"

"Yeah."

"He's more than an acquaintance to me."

"Poor choice of words. Look, I just..." Lucia rested her hands on her hips and stared at the floor. "I can't sleep. Tate hogs all your time, and I just really wanted to talk to you alone."

"You want me to tell you about Tiago."

"Yes." Her expression softened, her gaze pleading. "I spent eleven years with him, and I... Shit, I know it's late, so if you want to talk another time—"

"I can't sleep, either." She opened the door wider and motioned for Lucia to enter.

"Is that his?" Lucia nodded at the dinner jacket that engulfed her shoulders.

"Yeah." She ran a hand along the black sleeve.

"I never saw him wear a tux, but I can picture it." Lucia perched on the loveseat. "He's very easy on the eyes."

"He looked devastating that night, especially when he danced with me." Her chin trembled.

"Tiago *danced* with you?"

"Yeah." She took a seat in the armchair. "What do you want to know?"

"Everything."

She started at the beginning and walked through every interaction, every fight, every tender moment, the good and ugly, the brutality and rape, the kindness and beautiful acts of devotion.

By the time she finished, she hadn't left out a single detail from the past four months. Tears streaked her cheeks. A smile rested on her mouth, and she felt wonderfully copacetic.

"Damn." Lucia slumped into the loveseat with her jaw hanging open. "I can't even comprehend him being like that. He wasn't like that with me. I mean, the cruelty? Of course. The threats and the control? He ruled my damn life. But I never saw that devoted side of him. No one did. And what the hell? He was married?"

"Yeah, that took me by surprise, too."

"I'm really fucking in awe of you. That man scares the shit out of me. I spent eleven years in fear of my life. But you? You walk in, and within four months, he's kneeling at your feet. You changed him."

"He hasn't changed, and he certainly doesn't fucking kneel. Believe me, he's just as vicious as ever. Don't forget about the scars on my body, the golden showers, the handcuffs in the jungle. If it hadn't been for those bombs, I would still be his captive."

"True. But he gave up Caracas and the protection it gave him."

"I don't know why. I didn't do anything to make him—"

"He loves you. That's huge, Kate. It's everything."

"Somewhere along the way, I fell in love with him, too. I guess that's why this hurts so badly. Not knowing where he is or if he's okay... I can't even let myself consider the possibility he was injured in that explosion. Or worse..."

"What are you going to do?"

She had over six-hundred-thousand dollars sitting in her bank account. The money Van had distributed among his ex-slaves.

It would take her some time to put all the clues together and pinpoint the location of Boones' village. She would need travel documents, a passport, and maybe a hired security guard. But once she had all that in place...

"I'm going to buy a plane ticket to Africa."

THIRTY-THREE

"Reconsider this trip, Kate." Liv Reed stood at the center of Kate's room, arms at her sides and shoulders back. A pillar of grace and dominance.

"No." Wrapped in Tiago's worn tuxedo coat, Kate sat in the corner of the loveseat, buzzing with nervous energy. "You would do the same thing if you lost Josh."

It had been one month since she left Tiago on that burning island.

One long fucking month.

Cole Hartman had finally acquired the names of the casualties from that night.

Both Tiago and Arturo were on the list.

They'd been counted among the dead.

Deceased.

Gone.

When Cole gave her the devastating news, she could've let it destroy her. But she wasn't ready to curl up and die. She couldn't give up.

So she decided that Tiago had taken a page from Cole's book and faked his own death. There was no evidence to support her claim. Nothing to go on but hope.

Hope was all she had.

She spent the past month hunting for Boones' village.

His scarification, the jewelry and clothing from the photo of his daughter, the sounds of his native tongue, and a thousand other tiny little details led her to Northeast Africa.

She contacted a linguistic specialist at a university in Texas. Weeks of correspondence with the professor helped her narrow down Boones' vernacular to Tigre, an Afroasiatic language spoken in Sudan, Ethiopia, and Eritrea.

The three countries sat together along the Red Sea. She was getting closer, but not close enough.

The language had a lot of dialects, and those unique nuances helped her determine that Boones used the patois of the Tigre people in Eritrea.

That was the break she needed.

He was Eritrean, and they referred to their language as Tigrayit.

She had the country of Boones' home, but nothing more specific. After another week of digging, she hadn't been able to pinpoint a town or village.

Impatience dug in its claws.

Throughout her search, she tried so hard to control the emotions that swarmed inside her. It had been one month. At this point, she didn't think she could survive another day without him.

But she would. She would survive as long as it took.

Her flight departed in four days. Luggage lined the far wall of her room, packed with the essentials for her trip to Eritrea.

She'd worked with Matias' staff to purchase everything she needed — clothes, travel documents, fake passport, and ID. She funded every cost and set every demand, all while keeping her destination as secret as possible.

Those involved knew she was going to Africa. Nothing more. Tiago hadn't shared the location for a reason, and she wouldn't, either.

Liv crossed the room and stood near the window, watching her teenage daughter through the glass.

Livana sat on the veranda of Kate's suite, with her nose in a book. She'd grown into a beautiful girl and seemed to be thriving in Colombia. Matias provided her with private tutors and an education far superior than what she received in the States.

"Have you decided to stay here for good?" Kate asked.

"We're working out the details. Van and Amber want to stay and join Camila's fight. Josh and I are willing to do the same, but the shared custody with Livana's adoptive mother complicates a permanent move."

"You could always fight for full custody."

"Yes, but that would be selfish. Livana was raised by her and —"

An urgent, rapid knock pounded on the door.

"Kate." Van barged in without waiting, and his silver eyes cut through the room until they landed on her. "He's here."

"Who?" She leapt from the loveseat, staggering to right herself as her heart pounded out of her chest. "Who's here?"

But she knew.

She knew before Van said his name.

"Tiago Badell."

A gust of dizziness hit her sideways.

He was here. What did it mean? Was he hurting? Angry? Completely insane?

Her blood pressure skyrocketed as she sucked in breath after breath. She was going to hyperventilate. Or pass out.

She needed to go, run, get to him right now.

"Where?" She sprinted to the door, her voice rising to an explosive shrill. "Which way?"

"The west wing." He followed her into the hall and nodded to the right.

The hairs rose on her nape as she bolted in the direction he pointed her.

She hadn't visited the west wing but knew enough about the horrors Matias imprisoned there. Slave traders, traitors, and rival cartel members — the captives were the worst of the worst and deserved every punishment they received within those walls. She heard that Frizz, one of the men in Matias' inner circle, often sewed up their mouths to match his own.

If Tiago was there, did that mean he'd been captured? Were they torturing him?

Her stomach threatened to empty as she picked up her pace, racing through the halls with no idea which way to go.

The sound of sneakers gave chase, and a moment later, Van caught up with her.

"Turn left at the next bend." He directed her through the halls, sprinting easily alongside her.

"How did Tiago get here?" She panted, her legs burning through the strides.

"The crazy motherfucker broke in."

"What?" She faltered, recovered, and sped up her gait. "How did he find this place?"

"Fuck if I know. Another left here." He raced her down a long corridor, his breathing so much calmer than hers. "He came in with guns blazing, ready to take down the whole goddamn cartel."

Her chest tightened painfully, and her lungs wheezed for air. "Did he get hurt? Is anyone dead?"

"Don't know."

Her limbs trembled with terror and anticipation as she skidded to a stop at the entrance to the wing.

The guards let them pass, and she followed the sounds of shouting through two more corridors.

Up ahead, Lucia leaned her back against the wall with a hand clutching her throat. When she spotted Kate, her eyes widened. "Kate! Wait!"

"Where is he?" She ran to the steel door across from Lucia and peered through the small window.

In the concrete room, Tiago lay on his side on the floor, eyes closed, dressed in only a pair of briefs. He bared his teeth and jerked his arms, going nowhere with his hands shackled behind him.

Her heart splintered, and she grabbed the door handle, shaking it. Locked.

Tate paced through the cell, shouting furiously as he demanded answers about Lucia and everything that had happened over the past eleven years.

Blood trickled from cuts on Tiago's face and chest, but there were no visible bullet or stab wounds.

Why was he bleeding and lying on the floor?

A rabid sound wrenched from her throat. She needed to get to him and hold him and let him know she was here.

"Open the door!" She shook the handle harder, more frantically, losing control when it wouldn't budge.

His eyes opened and unerringly found hers through the glass.

"Tiago!" She pressed her hand against the window, and a sharp burn stabbed through her chest.

He'd lost weight, his muscles radically leaner, his jaw more angular and covered in a full beard. What happened to him?

Tate's hands clenched at his sides, his face and neck bright red as he prowled a circle around Tiago's body. He looked as if he were seconds from murder.

"Let me in right now!" She pounded on the tiny window. "Swear to God, if you hurt him—"

Matias appeared on the other side of the glass and narrowed his eyes.

"Open the door," she screamed, banging her fists against the steel.

He slammed a metal cover over the window, blocking her view. Shutting her out.

She lost it.

In an explosion of rage, she threw her body against the door, yelling at the top of her lungs, kicking, and pounding until Van's arms locked around her and yanked her away.

"They're going to torture him." Tears blurred her eyes, and great sobs shook her shoulders. "They'll kill him."

"Kate, listen to me." Lucia gripped her face, capturing her attention. "Only reason Tiago's alive is because of you. Matias and Tate know you love him. They're not going to hurt him."

"He's bleeding." She yanked on her arms, where Van held them at her back. "Let go of me."

He released her and stepped to the side, studying her with those bladed eyes of his. "He's bleeding because he broke into the secret headquarters of a Colombian cartel and attacked the guards."

"Did anyone die?" she asked Lucia.

"No. But they had to subdue him by physical force."

She wiped away her tears and pulled in a steeling breath. A little calmer now, she stepped back to the door and pressed her ear against it.

"Why won't they let me in?" She couldn't detect sound through the thick steel. "What are they doing to him?"

"Just talking." Lucia stared at the door, her expression tight. "Tate needs a resolution."

Tiago had tortured him, forced him to have sex with Van, and separated him from Lucia for three months. Kate wasn't sure there was a resolution for that.

"Why aren't you in there with him?" She flexed her hands, unable to quell the shaking.

"I've made peace with what he did to me." Lucia leaned her back against the wall and gazed at the door. "Hearing about your relationship with him helped. It gave me a sense of understanding, like maybe everything happened for a reason. I mean, I got Tate out of it."

"What about you?" She turned to Van. "I know what he did to you."

"Hm." He removed a toothpick from his pocket and rested the end between his lips. "I'm the last person to throw stones. I don't like the guy, but I'll get over it. Forgive, forget, move on—any of that is better than holding on to hatred."

He gave her a knowing look, and for the first time since she'd met him, she stared directly into his razor eyes and didn't wince.

She didn't know whether she forgave Van or had simply moved on, but she no longer felt fear or hatred for the man.

"Tate's not in there for himself." Van rolled the toothpick to the corner of his mouth. "He's in there for his girl. He needs to flex his strength, make some threats, and prove to Tiago he's willing to do anything to protect her."

"Men," Lucia mumbled.

Kate shifted back to the door, aching to be on the other side. "Is there a first-aid kit around here?"

"I think so. Hang on." Lucia strode down the hall and returned a few minutes later with a bag of supplies, water bottles, and clean towels.

"Thank you." Kate gathered it in her arms and waited.

Another five minutes passed before the door swung open.

Tate stepped out, and his bloodshot eyes darted to Lucia. As Kate tried to squeeze past him, he caught her around the waist and enveloped her in a hug.

"Get him out of here before I start hating him again." He kissed the top of her head and let her go.

That sounded promising. Kind of.

Matias exited next, his expression brooding as he pressed a keyring into her hand. "He doesn't leave this cell."

Her heart burst into a gallop, and she darted into the room, swallowing down a month's worth of stress and tears.

Don't cry. Don't fall apart.

Matias closed the door behind her and sounded the dead bolt.

Her attention turned to Tiago, and her entire world filled with his harsh, imposing presence.

"Kate."

That deep, rich, dark timbre resonated in her soul. She felt his voice, *really* felt it, and in that moment, she experienced the truest form of freedom.

She had choices, endless choices and paths, and she picked him, willingly, freely.

Sitting on the floor with his hands shackled between his back and the wall, he watched her with an intensity that sucked the air from the room. The weight of his abrasive gaze ground against her, rubbing and heating her everywhere, his silence thick and penetrating, sinking inside her and pulling her toward him.

"What if I told you I tried to let you go?" He licked his lips. "Would you believe me?"

She shook her head, more in confusion than in answer. "Did you try to let me go?"

"Fuck no." He laughed, a cruel, humorless sound. "Never, Kate. Not even in death."

The tears she tried to keep in check rose, blurring her vision as she lowered to her knees beside him.

"I have so many questions. Things to tell you." She dumped the supplies on the floor and fumbled with the key. "I don't know where to start."

"Start with getting me out of these fucking restraints." He shifted, giving her access to his arms. "I need you. Christ, I just need to feel you."

She twisted the key into the metal cuffs, and the instant they fell off, he dragged her onto his lap and captured her mouth with his.

The contact burned flames of hunger and energy around them, powering through her in billows of panting breaths.

Their tongues swept together, connecting, releasing, and chasing in frenzied lashes. Hands sailed everywhere, exploring and reacquainting with every muscle, scar, and curve of bone.

How strange and wonderful to feel his beard scratching her face. To feel his hands on her body. To taste his dark, minty essence on her tongue.

He was actually here.

Alive.

Growling.

Biting.

Mine.

When they came up for air, their gazes clung, neither of them blinking or speaking. There was so much to say, but she wanted to bask in the moment, let it settle through her, and commit every glorious detail to memory.

She sketched a thumb along the puckered, lifted scars that curved from his eye to the side of his skull. Her touch lowered to his beard, scraping through the thick, wiry black hairs.

Questions bubbled up, spooling and unraveling in her throat, but what came out first were the most important words she'd ever spoken.

"I love you."

"What?" He stopped breathing, his expression stark and unbelieving.

"I love you."

His eyes closed, and his head tipped back, as if the impact of her confession was too much.

"I love you, Tiago Badell."

He pulled in a broken breath. Relief melted across his face, and his shoulders and back lost strength and tension.

No lover had ever given him those words. It was perhaps the one thing he'd always wanted and never thought he could have.

When his eyes found hers again, he opened his demanding mouth, but no sound came out. It seemed she'd stolen his voice.

Straddling his lap, she gathered the water, towels, and antiseptic. Then she cleaned his wounds, starting with the cuts on his face.

She glided the towel across his wide shoulders, down the lines of his strong neck, and around the deep cut of muscles that sculpted his chest.

His weight loss was most evident in the flat terrain of his abdomen. Fewer ridges lined his lower stomach, and his hipbones protruded from his narrow waist, sharper than normal beneath the waistband of his briefs.

But the strength of him wasn't defined by bone and muscle. His power circulated behind his eyes and charged through his voice. She'd never come in contact with a more overbearing, viciously beautiful man.

Running a clean towel over every inch of his torso, she mourned the raised bumps of new scars. Some etched into the skin on his chest. Others lanced down his side and leg. Most would've required stitches. All of them hurt her heart.

As she examined him, he did the same with her, his hands caressing and probing, his breaths growing deeper, faster.

"You were injured in the explosion." She traced the slash on his ribs.

"Just cuts. You made it out unharmed?"

"A few bumps and bruises and a sprained ankle. No scars."

"I'm so fucking sorry, Kate. I failed—"

"What happened?" She searched his warm brown eyes. "One second, you were carrying me. Then you were gone. I didn't want to leave you, Tiago, but you were *no where*. It killed me."

"You got out. That's all that matters. And no thanks to me. I was knocked unconscious, unable to protect you." His jaw clenched. "I came to, buried under concrete." He gestured at the scar along his side. "When I couldn't find you and Cole, I knew he had you. You were safe. It made it easier to focus on saving my own ass."

"What about Arturo?"

His eyes shuddered. "He didn't make it."

"Fuck. I'm so sorry."

"Me, too." He tucked a lock of hair behind her ear.

"Cole said your names were on the deceased list."

"How the fuck did he get that list?" His dark eyebrows formed an angry *V*.

"I don't know."

"Jesus, Kate. I didn't want you to think I was dead."

"I didn't. I decided you were alive, because I couldn't... I couldn't accept anything else."

He tangled a hand in her hair and brought her forehead to his lips. "I called in a favor to the President of Venezuela, had him put my name on that list before he released it to the authorities. It's not public information, but my enemies will get their hands on it, if they haven't already. As far as the U.S. government is concerned, I'm officially dead."

"They won't hunt you anymore?"

"No active searching, but I still have to lay low. Change my identity. That's if Restrepo ever allows me to leave this cell."

She flinched. "He's not going to keep you locked up!"

A rueful smile pulled at his mouth. "I know the location of his headquarters. No one walks away with that information."

She would see about that. "How did you find me?"

"There was no question *who* Cole placed you with. Problem was I didn't know where the fuck this place was. Took me a couple of weeks to narrow the location down to this section of the Amazon rain forest. I spent the next two weeks living in the surrounding jungle, tracking activity and listening for traffic."

"That's why you lost weight." She gripped his jaw through the beard, soaking in his dark features and beautiful brown eyes. "You look like a Latino Viking."

A feral growl vibrated in his chest. "I need you."

"I love you." She trailed a path of kisses across his cheek.

"Say it again." His hips lifted, rocking his rigid length between her legs.

"I love you."

"I want you." He wrapped his arms around her and ground her body against his lap.

"Take me."

"I'll never stop."

In the next breath, she was on her back, trapped beneath the hard concrete floor and his even harder body.

An addictive, burning desire inflamed her senses, and she writhed beneath him, desperate for his touch, his kiss, his heavy cock.

He didn't waste time, his fingers fumbling with the fly on her shorts. He stripped her from waist to feet, came down on top of her, and shoved up her shirt and bra, baring her breasts.

His gaze made a greedy sweep across her chest, and a devious grin tugged at the corner of his mouth.

"You kept the piercings." His eyes returned to hers.

"You told me not to remove them." She gripped one between her finger and thumb. "Is it true? Did you give up your entire syndicate for these stones?"

"No, Kate. I gave up everything for *you*."

Guilt pinched her stomach. "I was such a bitch when you gave me the piercings. I didn't know what it meant."

His lips crashed down on hers, hard and demanding. She arched against him, yearning for more contact, needing him closer.

Jolts of electricity shot through her as his assertive tongue swept in and out, doing wicked things in her mouth. Every nerve in her body electrified, and she moaned, grinding against the steel bar of his cock.

She ran her fingers down his strong, smooth back, pulling him closer, and her gaze landed on a black lens in the ceiling. "There's a camera."

"Let them watch." He reached between them, his hand brushing her pussy as he shoved down the front of his briefs. "Thank you for believing in us."

She could only nod. If he didn't fuck her soon, she might start crying again.

He met her eyes and pushed slowly, achingly inside her body.

Blissful sensations rippled through her, stealing her breath and scrambling her brain. Her skin heated. Her nipples hardened painfully, a throb that intensified as he drove faster, harder inside her.

They held each other as close as possible, touching everything at once. She swirled her tongue around his earlobe, inhaling his sinful, masculine scent. He turned his head and took her mouth, devouring, possessing, staking his claim.

"I'm yours." She met every thrust, surrendered every kiss.

"Say it again."

"I'm yours." She twitched, fighting the flood of stimulation, and started to come. "I love you."

He fell with her, groaning her name, jerking his hips, his heavy body shaking with the force of his climax.

As he caught his breath, he rolled to his back, taking her with him.

"That was too fast." His cock pulsed inside her. "Need to do it again."

"We will. But first, I need to get you out of here." With great reluctance, she pushed off him and dragged on her clothes. "Where's Boones?"

"I sent him home." He straightened his briefs and sat up. "Why?"

"Do you have a fake passport?"

"Several." He narrowed his eyes. "Start talking, Kate."

"Well…" She lifted a shoulder. "I have a plane ticket to go see him. I'm going to buy a second seat and have Matias arrange us transportation out of here."

She strode to the door and knocked.

"You don't know where Boones is." He was on his feet with an arm locked across her waist before she could blink.

"I narrowed it down to a small country." She angled her neck back and whispered in his ear, "Eritrea."

"How?" His eyes widened.

"It was the only way I knew how to find you." She twisted in his hold and lifted on toes to kiss his beard. "Desperation makes a woman dangerous."

The door opened.

He flicked his gaze over her shoulder and returned to her face. "Hurry back to me."

"Always."

THIRTY-FOUR

One month later, Tiago leaned against a pillar at the entrance of a fish market in a small Eritrean village. His gaze hungrily tracked the beautiful blonde as she picked her way through stalls of fruits, vegetables, spices, chickens, and bric-a-brac.

The sunlight caught the white-gold strands of her hair as she gripped Boones' arm and spoke animatedly about something she'd found on the vendor's table.

Tiago's pulse hammered, and he scanned the crowd, probing faces and clothing, searching for threats.

She wanted freedom and demanded to take these outings without him.

He was trying to give her that, even if it went against every instinct.

They'd settled in a small fishing village on the Red Sea, several hundred miles from where his family was murdered. Didn't mean his enemies couldn't find him. He could live anywhere, and danger would follow.

But he let her have her shopping trips, her walks alone, and her quality time with Boones and his brothers. Kind of. He always followed at a distance. Always watching. He couldn't stop.

Some people simply couldn't change.

He would always tie her up, fuck her, cut her, and control her every move. And she would always fight him, challenge him, and fill his lungs with air.

Thank fucking God, because he couldn't breathe without her.

Thirty feet away, she stopped talking and went still. He slipped into the shadows as she turned her neck and searched the crowds behind her.

After a few sweeps, her huge blue eyes homed in on his location. Shrouded in darkness, he was certain she couldn't see him.

She bit her lip, said something to Boones, and strode directly toward his hiding spot.

His entire body tightened in anticipation.

A brightly-colored flowery sundress clung to her flawless, slender physique, and her pale complexion glowed beneath the Eritrean sun.

Africa looked fucking stunning on her.

A few steps away, she shook her head and fisted her hands on her hips.

"You." She cocked her sexy head. "Need a hobby."

"I have one."

"Stalking isn't a hobby."

"I call it guarding."

"You're a control freak."

"Control enthusiast." He clutched her neck and dragged her to him. "I want to fuck your ass."

"Of course, you do." Her sassy mouth curved into a grin. "You enjoyed it too much last time."

"So did you." He laced his fingers through hers and steered her in the direction of their home.

"You're a terrible influence." She couldn't contain her smile.

Hand in hand, they strolled toward the beach and followed the coastline. Slipping off their sandals, they let the waves lick at their feet as they walked.

"I love it here." She lifted her face to the cloudless sky and sighed. "I love you."

She was his whole, his entire being, more himself than he was. If she ceased to exist, he would be a stranger, no longer part of this world.

She was his constant, his evermore, not just in the physical sense. She was the inexplainable *something* that made up his soul.

The two-mile stroll along the Red Sea brought them to an isolated beach house tucked away in a thick copse of foliage.

Boones and his brothers lived in the center of the village, with all the conveniences of the local shopping and transportation.

Tiago had installed heavy security in both places, relying on technology instead of the presence of armed men. Maybe none of it was needed, but he would never risk their lives. Never let his guard down. Never again.

He no longer had the protection of his syndicate or its allies in Caracas. Nor did he have the income from that business. But he'd saved a great deal of money over the years, enough to never need to work again.

She wanted to learn how to heal people and talked about pursuing a degree in medicine. Boones was beside himself when she asked for his guidance.

When they left Colombia, she told her friends it wasn't a goodbye. She fully intended to return as a doctor, and Tiago would be with her.

He would take her wherever she wanted to go, as long as she never left his sight. If she could deal with his possessive, overprotective inclinations, he would handle everything else.

"What do you want for dinner?" He opened the door to their two-bedroom bungalow and followed her inside.

"Whatever you're making."

A few hours later, he made an Eritrean traditional stew served with flatbread and a paste made from lentil and faba beans.

After dinner, they lay side by side on a blanket on the beach behind their house. The moon was bright in the sky, the tequila smooth as water, and the woman beside him more beautiful than the majestic landscape that stretched out around him.

"You're always in my mind, Tiago." She stretched out on her back and smiled up at the stars. "Perhaps not always a happy thought. Sometimes I'm plotting your demise. But you're always there, always a part of me." She turned her neck and looked at him. "Is that weird?"

"No." He rolled toward her and slid the hem of the dress up her thighs. "I want to live in your mind, your heart, and—"

"Don't say it."

"—your cunt."

"You said it." She laughed.

"I meant it."

"I know." She drew in a breath and ran a hand across his shaved jaw. "Nothing's ever felt more real than this. It scares me sometimes."

"Surrender to it." He gathered the dress above her waist, and the sight of her bare pussy made him painfully hard. "Open your legs."

She let her knees fall open and looked at him with all the trust in the world. He deserved none of it, but he would spend the rest of his life making sure she never regretted her gift.

Removing the finger blade from his pocket, he fit it onto his finger.

She swallowed. Her eyes glistened. Then she lifted her chin and smiled.

Sweet surrender.

He made small shallow cuts that wouldn't scar, and between each nick, he kissed her cunt until she came.

As the tide rolled in and warm water gathered beneath them, they fused together in a slow dance of seduction and heavy breaths. She stroked his cock. He made love to her mouth. She sucked him off, and he cut her again.

Perspiration slicked their skin, easing the glide of their bodies, the slip of hands, and the drive of his thrusts as they licked and fucked and bled together.

Some might consider their love dark and disturbing, but he thought of it as spiritual, unearthly, and wickedly filthy.

Despite all their fights and trials and mistakes, they never lost their sense of selves.

In the end, she saw something in him no one else had been able to see.

She saw a heart worthy enough to take.

MANIPULATE

PAM GODWIN

Book 6

PART ONE

ONE

Ciudad Hueca, Mexico
Two years ago

What a suck ass day.

To think, it started out so lovely and perfect.

Since Tula Gomez didn't have to go into work, she'd decided to make it a bra-less, drink-wine-at-noon, binge-on-Hellraiser-movies, and masturbate-more-than-once kind of day.

Until her phone rang.

She should've sent her sister's call to voicemail.

She should've let Vera ruin someone else's day.

But she didn't.

She answered the damn phone and surrendered to Vera's demands.

Instead of slumming in her pajamas on the couch, she spent the past six hours on the road, driving toward the last city on Earth she wanted to visit.

When she crossed the New Mexico-Texas border two-hundred-miles back, her mood had spiraled past annoyance and straight into pissed-off.

She eased her Jeep Wrangler forward in the stop-start traffic, trying not to ride the old clutch. If the manual transmission decided to go out, today would be the fucking day.

Wavy lines of heat rose from the scorched asphalt. Horns blared, and some idiot a few cars back blasted his bass so loud it rattled the frame of her poor Jeep.

She grabbed her phone and redialed her sister. "Come on, Vera. Pick up."

As it rang, she inched along with hundreds of other border-crossing commuters lined up at the Mexico port of entry.

The phone continued to ring. And ring. Why wasn't Vera answering her calls?

"Dammit!" Tula gritted her teeth at the sound of the voicemail greeting. "This is bullshit."

She disconnected and gripped the steering wheel, vacillating between turning back home and speeding toward hell.

Home was a one-bedroom apartment two states away in Phoenix, Arizona, where everything in her world was safe, normal, orderly, and stress-free.

Hell was her childhood *colonia* in Ciudad Hueca, Mexico, where Vera still lived. Her younger sister thrived in chaos, drama, and danger — all the things Tula had run away from when she moved to the states.

Her visits to Mexico were infrequent and made only out of obligation to Vera.

She didn't shun her Mexican roots, but it had taken her a long damn time to go through the naturalization process to become a U.S. citizen. She was a proud American and a law-abiding taxpayer, who worked nine to five as a high school Spanish teacher.

Her peaceful, boring life suited her just fine. If she never stepped foot across the border again, she would be just fine with that, too.

But Vera was family. Her only living relative. And her sister needed her.

God only knew what sort of mess Vera had landed in this time. When she called this morning, the shitty connection had chopped up the short conversation into a few staticky words.

Some trouble.

Need you.

Come now.

Bring money.

When the connection had cut off, Tula called back, again and again, with no luck. None of her questions had been answered, and she had very little to go on.

Except Vera's track record.

Last time Vera called, she needed help kicking her thieving loser boyfriend to the curb. The time before that, she'd been abandoned a day's drive from home without money or a ride back. There were dozens of other situations over the years, and Tula always, begrudgingly, came to the rescue.

It wasn't a secret Vera hung out with the wrong people. Living in Ciudad Hueca, it was easy to become entangled with cartels.

Tula's nagging pleas to stay away from them fell on deaf ears, and their relationship became resentful and strained. But at the end of the day, all they had was each other.

She attempted several more phone calls while trudging along in bumper-to-bumper traffic. Rows of cars pressed in on all sides, filled with people whose frustration rivaled her own. Road rage simmered like the summer heat, all of it weighing on her with each passing minute.

An hour later, she made it through the port of entry and took the safest route toward her childhood home.

Not that there was a *safe* route. Ciudad Hueca was going through a volatile time. As a border city, it was perfectly located for drug distribution throughout the United States. This made it extremely valuable to cartels, turning it into one of the most fought-over territories in the country.

Since Vera refused to move to the states, Tula stayed abreast of the local news and crime here. Two violent drug cartels battled for dominance, street by street, to control the lucrative drug-trafficking routes.

Driving through her hometown, alone and unarmed, was dangerous as hell.

She kept pepper spray in her Jeep just for these visits. But no guns. Given her inexperience with weapons, she'd end up shooting herself during an attack.

As a precaution, she'd topped off the gas tank in Texas to avoid an extra stop in Mexico. No lingering. No shortcuts.

The five-hundred dollars in cash she'd stuffed in her purse would have to be enough to fix Vera's mess. Tula planned to stay three hours tops, confirm Vera's well-being with her own eyes, and return to the U.S. before nightfall.

Around three in the afternoon, she arrived at her childhood *colonia* on the outskirts of the city. Rundown businesses, rugged streets, and a few trees encircled the tiny, concrete-block house where she and Vera were raised.

Between the two of them, Vera had been closer to their mother. When they lost their only parent to heart disease five years ago, Vera kept the house.

That was about the time Vera started her downward spiral into trouble.

Tula parked in front of her childhood home and leaned over the steering wheel, inspecting the empty street and surrounding houses. No one lingered around the property. No gunfire nearby or in the distance.

It hadn't always been this unsafe. She left home at age eighteen, and in the ten years she'd been in the states, Ciudad Hueca had grown chaotically. Its tax revenue went to Mexico City, and not much came back. Law enforcement rationed gasoline and bullets. Basic infrastructure — schools, roads, sewers, parks — went to shit.

The city was in a state of disrepair, much like the sagging roof of her childhood home.

She grabbed the pepper spray, her purse, and the house key she still kept on her keyring. Then she bolted to the front door.

The key turned the lock, and she stepped in without knocking. "Hello? Vera?"

Silence hit her, along with the usual weight of nostalgia.

Good times. Bad times. No major tragedy. Just the usual poverty and a mother who was anxious to get Tula grown up and moved out. One less mouth to feed.

She made a quick sweep through the sitting room, kitchen, and two bedrooms before confirming what she already knew.

Her sister wasn't home.

Despite Vera's haphazard approach to life, she maintained a tidy, clutter-free house. Not a single dirty dish in the sink. No dust on the furniture or cobwebs in the corners. Nothing lying around to indicate where she was.

With a sigh, Tula called her again.

No answer.

"Shit." She stared at the front door, tapping the phone against her chin.

Vera usually had a job, but never a steady one. She bounced through employers as fast as she went through boyfriends. If she was at work, Tula didn't know where that was.

Over the next ten minutes, she dared a walk outside, knocking on neighboring houses. Three doors opened for her, and all the responses were consistent.

No one had seen Vera in weeks.

Panic set in.

Why would she tell Tula to drive here, if she wasn't home? Where the fuck did she go?

Indecision sent her pacing through the house, rifling through drawers, and digging in closets. The hunt for clues led nowhere.

"Fuck!" She lowered to the couch and squeezed her fingers around the phone.

Should she leave? What if Vera was on her way here? Maybe she was staying with a new boyfriend and lost her phone after the call dropped this morning?

"Damn you, Vera." Tula slumped deeper into the couch and waited.

And waited.

Three hours later, the sun dipped low on the horizon, signaling the darkness to come.

Vera still wasn't answering the phone. Tula must've left over fifty voicemail messages.

She couldn't risk being caught in the city after nightfall.

Time to go.

Nervous energy trembled through her as she opened the freezer in the kitchen and hid some money in a carton of ice cream. Vera would eventually call, and Tula would tell her where to find the cash.

She kept two-hundred dollars, stuffing the bills into her back pocket, in case she needed it on the drive home.

Then she left.

Taking the shortest route to the U.S. border, she itched to hit the gas and speed as fast as the Jeep would go. But she forced herself to drive the speed limit and keep a low profile through the rougher parts of the city.

Signs of violence and strife haunted every corner. Roadside memorials, flowers, and lit candles marked sites of death. Young men gathered under awnings, buying and selling drugs. Girls, too young to be out after dark, solicited sex on every street.

These people were survivors. She didn't judge them, but she also didn't trust them.

She didn't trust the local police, either.

The Mexican military had been brought in to put a stop to the cartels and the drug war. But they were all part of the corruption.

Everyone and anyone could've been a target. If a police officer decided to pull her over, she would be at his mercy.

As she drove through the heart of the city, she spotted a sedan with tinted windows in the rear-view mirror a few cars back.

Was that the same sedan that was behind her when she left Vera's house? Her pulse sprinted into a gallop.

Stop it. You're just paranoid.

Following the GPS on her phone, she veered down a side street.

The sedan turned with her.

Her heart thrashed in her ears, and a hot lump formed in her throat.

Why would anyone trail her? She was a nobody schoolteacher from Phoenix, driving a worthless hunk of metal.

She turned down another road to see if the sedan would follow. When it didn't, she released a heavy breath.

"Oh, thank fuck." She wiped a clammy palm on her jeans. "Jesus, Tula. Way to get yourself all worked up over noth—"

A car flew out of the intersection in front of her and slammed on its brakes.

She skidded to a stop, narrowly avoiding a collision with it.

Blinking rapidly, she schooled her breathing and stared at the car. Another black sedan with tinted windows.

Dread hardened her stomach, and a chill tingled across her scalp. What the hell was going on?

The sedan blocked her path and didn't attempt to move. The doors didn't open, and the window tint concealed the occupants.

Alarms fired inside her, her instinct screaming to get the hell out of there and fast.

She shoved the Jeep into reverse just as a huge military truck appeared over the hill straight ahead.

Mexican soldiers in helmets, green uniforms, and sunglasses jogged alongside the armored vehicle. They gripped assault rifles and machine guns and headed directly toward her.

She gulped for air, her fingers frozen on the stick shift.

Had she driven into a battle zone? Or was something going down in one of the buildings behind her?

With the gear shift in reverse, she glanced at the rear-view mirror.

Another sedan pulled in behind her, barricading her.

No, no, no.

Her blood pressure careened toward detonation.

She eased out of reverse and dropped her phone into her purse. Hooking the strap over her shoulder, she gripped the pepper spray, prepared to run on foot.

Until the soldiers swept in around the Jeep and raised their rifles.

"Get out!" The man beside her door tapped his machine gun against the window. "Now!"

They were here for her? Why? What did she do wrong?

She dropped the pepper spray and held up her hands, her entire body trembling as she twisted toward him.

Apparently, she moved too slow. He yanked the door open and wrenched her out with his gun in her face.

In a blur of uniforms, she was pushed against the hood of the Jeep, face down with her feet kicked apart. They pawed through her pockets and dug through her purse while other soldiers held her in place.

Her palms slicked with sweat, and adrenaline coursed through her system, shutting down her ability to think clearly.

"What's going on?" she asked in Spanish, her heart pounding painfully. "What do you want?"

"Petula Gomez?" A soldier shoved her passport in her face.

It took her a second because honestly, only her mother had called her Petula. "Yes."

"Gomez?"

"Yes, that's my passport." Ice trickled down her spine. "Why are you asking?"

The man tossed her I.D. into her purse. "Arrest her!"

It happened so fast. One minute, she was bent over the hood of her Jeep. The next, she lay in the cargo hold of an armored vehicle with her arms handcuffed behind her.

Soldiers sat around her, guns in hands, faces stern, refusing to answer her questions.

Terror attacked her in waves, chattering her teeth and locking her joints. She couldn't stop trembling, couldn't catch her breath. She feared for her life.

The truck rumbled into motion, and her heart wanted to rush out of her chest. She'd been pulled into something really nasty, and she had no clue where she was going or what would happen when she arrived.

She traveled five or ten minutes before the vehicle stopped. Cruel hands yanked her out of the truck. When she stumbled, a fist swung from behind and punched her across the face.

Stunned to the pit of her stomach, she gasped through the pain and swallowed down bile.

Another strike hit her tail bone, and she staggered forward, trying to remain upright with her wrists shackled.

Rather than letting her walk on her own, two soldiers dragged her by her arms and hair into an unmarked building.

"Why are you doing this? I didn't do anything!" Her breathing came in frenzied bursts. "Where are you taking me?"

The butt of a gun rammed into her back, knocking the wind from her lungs and sending her to her knees.

She cried out and bit her tongue through the agony. "Please, just give me a second."

She'd been speaking Spanish the whole time and knew they understood her. They just didn't care.

Hoisted to her feet before she was ready, she tried to keep her legs beneath her as they ruthlessly hauled her down a dark hallway.

After a few dizzying turns, they wrenched her into a concrete room.

A man stood beside an old metal table with peeling paint. He wore the same green uniform as the soldiers, except his was decorated with colorful ribbons and gold medallions.

She didn't need to see the merits to sense his superiority. It wafted from his stiff posture, raised chin, and hard brown eyes. A trim beard outlined his squared jaw and thin lips, accentuating his dominance.

A tremor skated through her, stealing her voice. This man was evil, his rottenness so thick it clotted the room.

One soldier removed her handcuffs while the other tossed her purse to the officer, along with her passport.

The officer studied the I.D. and gave her a clinical once-over. "Remove your clothes."

"What?" Her stomach collapsed, and she clutched the neckline of her t-shirt, holding it tight. "Why?"

"*Rápido!*"

His explosive roar stopped her heart. She couldn't make her hands move, every part of her frozen in fear.

Did they intend to strip search her? Where were the female soldiers? She didn't remember the law well enough to understand her rights.

A fist slammed into the side of her head, and she collided with the nearby wall. Her skull throbbed. Her eyes ached with tears, and that was when she truly understood.

There was no law here. No justice. No defense for the innocent.

This was military corruption.

"I'll give you one chance." The officer clasped his hands behind his back. "It's up to you if you want to live or die."

There were no options. If she didn't cooperate, they would kill her.

She closed her eyes and swallowed her modesty. Then she removed her sneakers, jeans, and t-shirt. When she met his heartless eyes, she wore only her bra and panties.

The impulse to wrap her arms around herself made her twitch. But she felt the need to make a stand. No one else would be fighting for her here.

Holding her hands at her sides, she pushed her shoulders back, despite the ungodly terror twisting up her insides.

"Where is Hernandez?" He paced a circle around her. "Garcia?"

"I...I don't know—"

He gripped her jaw and yanked it upward at a painful angle, putting his bearded face in hers. "Where's Cortez?"

"I don't know who you're talking about! I live in Arizona. I'm just a schoolteacher. I don't know anyone by those names!"

"Okay." He released her and stepped back.

Did he think she was Vera? How deeply had her sister entangled herself with the cartel? Deep enough to fall into the sights of the Mexican military?

If this was a case of mistaken identity, Tula couldn't point that out and send them after Vera. She'd come to Mexico to protect her sister, not get her arrested.

There had to be another way.

"I gave you a chance, and you didn't take it." He nodded at the soldiers behind her.

"Wait! Let me call someone."

Who? Who the hell would she call? Her boss? A fellow teacher at work? She didn't have friends or family. No one could bail her out of this.

She was on her own.

The two uniforms grabbed her arms and aggressively wrestled her to the table, bending her over the surface with her chest pressed against the cold metal.

In the next breath, her panties were ripped away, leaving behind an ice-cold quake of horror.

This wasn't a strip search. It was sexual assault.

"I want to call a lawyer!" She bucked against their hold, terrified and exposed with her bare butt in the air. "I have the right to an attorney!"

Hands slammed her face down as the other man shackled her arms to the table legs.

Behind her, it sounded like two pieces of metal were being tapped together. Whatever that was shot violent tremors down her legs.

She craned her neck and glimpsed a metal rod in the officer's hand. A wire dangled from it, and she followed the end to where it plugged into the wall.

Ungodly terror crashed down upon her, sitting over her mouth and nose and crushing her chest. A trickle of air slipped through, just enough to keep her organs functioning, but it was crippling, suffocating.

Boots kicked her feet farther apart. Handcuffs tethered her arms to the table. Then she felt fingers, frigid bony digits separating her butt cheeks and the tender tissues around her vagina.

Before she could scream her objections, the metal rod penetrated her rectum in one brutal shove.

A sharp, ripping burn incinerated her anus. The sound of buzzing electricity warped the air as a jarring, horrendous jolt electrocuted her backside.

The pain was so excruciating her bladder released, spilling urine down her legs. Vomit burst past her lips, and her eyeballs felt like they were exploding out of their sockets. As if every drop of life was trying to find a way to escape her body.

She screamed until her vocal cords bled, until she couldn't draw air into her lungs. Snot bubbled from her nose, and tears soaked her face, sticking her hair to her cheeks and mouth.

The torture was never-ending, striking flames through her anal cavity, over and over. Fifteen to twenty jolts. Five seconds each.

He removed the rod, stabbed it into her vagina, and started again.

471

Back and forth he went, reaming that metal device in and out and frying her insides with punishing bolts of lightning.

She cried for him to stop and tried to jerk away from the source of her pain. The pain... It howled through her body and blurred her vision. She couldn't move, couldn't swallow or gasp beneath the agony.

Buzzing, taunting zaps, scuffing boots—all of it grew distant amid the pounding in her ears. Time ceased to exist. Her face stuck to a puddle of vomit, sweat, tears, and snot. Her body lay wasted on the table, electrocuted to the point of death.

She welcomed the end. Willed it to take her from the torment. Yet her heart kept beating. Her lungs continued to suck air. Her body wouldn't die.

Then the buzzing din of static stopped, and the room fell quiet.

A hand stroked over her head, petting her hair. "Are you ready to talk now?"

"Stop." Saliva leaked from her mouth, her voice raw and ruined. "Please."

She didn't have enough energy to lift an arm. Her throat throbbed from screaming and dry heaving. It even hurt to blink.

"We're going to annihilate La Rocha Cartel." His hot breath brushed her face. "Doesn't matter if you're a small-time player. You need to start talking."

"I don't know anyone in any cartel. I'm. Just. A teacher."

Why were they doing this? Why did they want to hurt her so badly? She hadn't done anything wrong.

"My name is Petula Gomez from Phoenix, Arizona. Please, believe what I'm saying. You have the wrong person."

"You want more?" He patted her cheek. "I'll give you more."

He rammed the rod into her ass and resumed the electrocution.

Fiery waves of voltage shot through her body, causing muscle contractions that were so violent it felt like her bones were fracturing.

Her mind flirted with the edge of unconsciousness, and she reached for it, needing the comfort it would give her. But her awareness hung on, refusing to burn out.

Hours passed. Maybe days. It felt like several lifetimes came and went before they unlocked the handcuffs and kicked her onto the floor.

She lay where she landed, crumpled on her side, unable to move. Silent tears escaped her eyes. Drool tickled her cracked lips, and perspiration clung to her naked skin.

The shaking in her limbs was unbearable, every inch of her drenched in a cold sweat. The pain, the shock, the unholy fear—it gathered in her core and vibrated outward like a jackhammer.

She couldn't escape it, couldn't silence the torment.

Voices sounded from the hallway, and she pried her eyes open.

Three men stood just outside the room — the officer and two unfamiliar soldiers — staring at her passport.

"She doesn't know anything." The officer handed off the I.D. "She's not the woman."

She tried to reach out an arm, form a word, or do something to get their attention. She needed to tell them to call an ambulance.

But they turned and walked away.

The edges of her periphery closed in, shrinking her vision until nothing existed.

She blacked out.

When she woke, the first thing she sensed was the clothing against her raw skin. Someone had redressed her.

The surrounding space felt bigger.

She opened her eyes to a new room, this one filled with at least a dozen people. She lay on the cement floor against a wall. Handcuffs shackled her to the bench beside her head.

They weren't letting her go?

Her chest tightened, her panic deep and internal. The agony between her legs would've made her sob if she'd had the strength. She didn't have enough life in her body to move a muscle.

But she could shift her gaze, and as she looked down, she registered a large amount of drugs in a bag at her feet.

"We apprehended an American." Her torturer stood a few feet away, addressing the room with his hands folded behind him. "Petula Gomez attempted to traffic fifty kilograms of marijuana into the United States."

Her stomach bottomed out.

She had never touched an illegal substance. Never been associated with drugs in any way.

She was being framed.

Incapacitated beyond exhaustion, her body tried to sink back into oblivion. She fought it, desperate to defend herself.

Some of the people in the room tossed out questions. At the edge of her awareness, she sensed the sounds of a flashing camera. A news reporter?

She was too scared, too far out of it to comprehend or open her mouth. Everything inside her felt as if it were slowly dying.

Consciousness slipped in and out. When she woke again, two soldiers were loading her in the rear of an armored vehicle, subjecting her achy eyes to the bright sunlight.

It was morning.

Her heart lurched. An entire evening had passed.

They'd confiscated her purse, phone, and identification. All she had was the clothes on her back.

A twenty-minute drive transported her toward a terrifyingly familiar part of Ciudad Hueca. She knew where they were taking her before the barbed wire walls appeared through the truck's tiny windows.

Jaulaso.

The most violent prison in the nation.

The living conditions in Jaulaso were so dangerous and inhumane there had been several attempts to shut it down. And like many prisons in Mexico, male and female inmates cohabited within its walls.

Her chance of surviving in Jaulaso was zero. Especially as an American woman with no connections or experience. She wouldn't make it the first night without getting raped.

Adrenaline returned to her body, energizing sore muscles and injecting life into her blood. Her heart pumped harder, and her hands clenched in the shackles.

By the time the soldiers dragged her into the crowded halls of the prison, she had enough strength to walk on her own.

The man who booked her led her into a small room with a table and two chairs. He left her there alone, without an explanation or a *fuck you.*

Shivering on the verge of hysteria, she huddled into the metal chair and tried to make sense of what was happening.

Mistaken identity?

That must've been the reason for her arrest. The military had followed her from Vera's house, after all.

She and Vera were only two years apart in age. They shared the same last name, black hair, brown eyes, slender build, and golden complexion. They looked similar.

She couldn't blame her sister for this. The Mexican military fucked up. When they realized Tula didn't know anything, they covered their mistake by framing her.

She was in Jaulaso because of corruption.

What happened to her last night was too overwhelming to process right now. She compartmentalized it, shoved it all down and out of reach.

But she couldn't do anything about the coldness inside her, the deadened sensation in her brain, and her inability to react or function normally. She was in a severe state of shock.

Her gaze drifted to the clock on the wall, and she attempted to calculate the timeline since she'd crossed the border. How long had she been unconscious?

The sandpaper feel of her tongue suggested dehydration, but hunger pangs hadn't set in yet.

It felt like she'd been arrested days ago, though she must've only been detained for one night. Everything hurt. Her body was unresponsive to simple commands, her motor functions clumsy and zapped of life.

After doing some painful guesswork in her head, she estimated she'd been tortured in that room for eight hours.

She lost another two hours waiting at that table before the door finally opened.

A white-haired, pudgy man lumbered in, wearing a wrinkled collared shirt and a crooked tie.

"I'm the U.S. consular here in Ciudad Hueca," he said without preamble and sat across from her.

"They tortured me." Her voice shivered beneath a strained whisper, and she cleared her ravaged throat. "The military… They…they electrocuted…" She couldn't even say it out loud.

"I'm sorry, but we don't have jurisdiction here in Mexico."

She was empty. Numb. Barely alive. "I need to get a message to my sister."

After he wrote down Vera's contact information, he explained her rights in a bored, repetitive tone.

"How do I end this?" A tear slipped down her cheek.

"Declare yourself guilty. Accept the charges. That'll give you the best chance to transfer to the states and conclude your sentence in the U.S."

"Conclude my sentence? That's my best-case scenario?"

"Yes." He rubbed his bulbous nose.

"I'm innocent."

What would happen to her job? Her American citizenship?

He arched a brow and tossed her a *that's-what-they-all-say* look. "Your other option is to fight for your innocence in Mexico."

That was the right thing to do. The only option.

"Okay." She might not have been thinking clearly, but she knew she would never plead guilty to a crime she didn't commit. "I'll prove my innocence."

"Fine." His voice drawled with an unnerving lack of care or compassion. "I'll help if I can, but these things take time."

"How much time?"

"Years."

"No. Impossible." Her breathing accelerated. "I'm innocent. I'll be out of here in a month. Two months at most."

"Good luck with that." He heaved from the chair, grabbed his briefcase, and walked to the door without looking back. "I'll be in touch."

TWO

"We have a new one!" The prison guard shoved Tula through the sweaty, packed halls of Jaulaso. "Hot, fresh meat."

Did he really just announce that?

The blatant leering of filthy men pulled her chin to her chest. She folded her arms around her midsection, eyes on the floor, and focused on putting one foot in front of the other.

The lack of strength in her legs made her stagger, her muscles achy and skin feverish as dozens of inmates whistled and screamed vulgarities at her.

Frailty trembled through her and hitched her shoulders around her ears. Tears hit the backs of her eyes, but she refused to cry. She was still standing, still walking on her own. As long as she didn't fall, maybe she would make it to the safety of her cell in one piece.

The immediate future squeezed a fist around her throat. Until she proved her innocence, she would have to fight for her life, every second of every day, and that fight started now.

The scent of vomit clung to her hair, but the air in the hallway smelled worse. The pungency of urine, feces, and body odor polluted every inhale, making her eyes water beyond her need to sob.

The corridor was so crowded she had to step over half-naked people and weave around piles of garbage and discarded clothes.

The darkness accentuated the humid dampness and overall gloom and emphasized how few lights functioned in the facility. Prisoners with working light bulbs squatted in their cells making crafts or preparing food. Others sat in complete blackness.

It was fucking depressing.

MANIPULATE

Despite the obscurity, men and women of all ages milled around the walkways between cellblocks. The guards were grossly outnumbered, and some didn't even wear uniforms. She struggled to distinguish them from the inmates.

Her escort stopped at a cell, where three men huddled together, whispering. A fourth man rushed out and gripped the guard's arm.

"I'm afraid." His lips pulled back, revealing broken teeth. "My cellmates are gang members. Put me somewhere else. Anywhere."

"Back in your cell." The guard shoved the frail man into the dark cage and continued walking.

She jogged to catch up, craning her neck to check on the man as she passed. The distraction cost her.

The guard propelled her into the next cell, and her weakened, tortured body collided with the grimy wall.

A stained, threadbare blanket lay wadded in the corner. Rodent shit and dead bugs littered the concrete floor.

There was no bed. No sink or toilet. No other inmates. Nothing in the cell except a blanket she wouldn't touch if her life depended on it.

At some point, she would need to empty her bladder and wash the puke from her hair.

"Where's the bathroom?" She glanced back at the guard.

He gestured down the corridor, slammed the barred door, and strolled away.

The door rattled in the frame and bounced open.

A terrible feeling crept into her gut as she rushed forward and tried to bolt the gate.

No lock. No latch. Nothing to keep the door from hanging ajar.

How was she supposed to sleep? She needed the security of a locked cell. She needed to let her guard down and close her eyes, just for a little while.

Two shady middle-aged men sat in the corridor across from her, watching her hold the door closed.

Averting her gaze, she glanced at her sneakers. Desperation moved her into action.

Five minutes later, she backed away from the door and hugged her waist.

Her shoestrings wrapped around the bars, tied in complicated knots, and cinched tight enough to hold the door closed.

The men in the hall had smirked at her while she did it as if she believed a shoestring could protect her. Of course, it wouldn't stop someone from entering, but it would slow them down.

The task had also kept her mind busy. But now that it was finished, she couldn't escape the fear that seeped in with the clamor of shouting and grunting outside her cell.

The deep, rumbling voices of Mexico's worst criminals echoed off the walls and drove her into the corner of her cell.

Reality enclosed her on all sides, weakening her legs and chopping her breaths. Hands clenching with white knuckles, heart pounding, and muscles painfully rigid, she was helpless against the surge of emotions.

She was in the most ruthless prison in Mexico.

Alone.

Unarmed.

Terrified.

If she didn't survive, would anyone know what happened to her? Her sister, her colleagues at the school, her students... Would they learn she'd been wrongfully arrested and left to die in Jaulaso? Or would she become a missing person, never to be found?

Summer break had just begun in the States. She wouldn't be expected back to work for two months.

No one would look for her until school resumed.

No one would be coming to her rescue.

A horrible choking sound rose from her chest and burst past her lips, heaving the air in a series of sobbing gasps.

Her knees gave out, and she slid down the wall, crumpling into a fetal position. She couldn't hold it in any longer. Horror, sadness, panic, and terrible, uncontrollable fear exploded from her in a rain of tears.

She clapped her hands over her mouth and tried to stifle the sounds that would draw attention.

If only she were invisible. Or a time traveler. God help her, she'd give anything to rewind the clock to yesterday morning and ignore her sister's phone call.

But what if Vera was in trouble? Like life-threatening, abducted-by-cartel trouble? Why else would she have not answered her phone?

What if she was dead?

More tears fell, harder now. Louder. Vicious pain wheezed past the fingers she clamped against her mouth.

Her stomach joined in, growling its reminder she hadn't eaten in over twenty-four hours.

She usually ate at the deli down the street. They made the best grilled cheese sandwich with fontina and mozzarella. The tantalizing scent of fresh baked cookies always greeted her when she walked in.

She wished she could smell that now instead of the putrid stench of vomit and misery.

Nausea rose, chasing away her hunger and replacing it with the crippling weight of exhaustion.

Her eyes fluttered closed, and she sat up, fighting sleep as it forced itself upon her.

She won the battle for an hour, maybe two, hugging her knees to her chest, feeling forsaken and panicked in her war against fatigue.

She was doing good until her head bounced with a jolting nod, kicking her awake.

Fuck, she couldn't risk falling asleep. Not until she better understood how to protect herself in this violent place.

She needed to find a friend in here if that were possible. Someone she could trust to watch her back. But she didn't have the confidence or energy to leave her dark corner. Not yet.

As the night dragged on, her body worked against her. Consciousness abandoned her, and pain-drenched dreams pulled her down, down, down.

She woke to the sound of rustling. Metal clanked beside her, and a gust of hot breath washed over her face.

Oh, God. Oh, God. Oh, God. She wasn't alone.

Her pulse slammed into overdrive, and she scrambled backward in the dark.

A cruel hand caught her thigh. Another latched onto her hip and yanked down her jeans.

Her zipper was already open, her shirt shoved to her neck.

Fear found her, whispering to her in a deranged voice. It told her stomach to buckle, her chest to constrict, and her lungs to slam together.

It told her she was going to die.

A scream ripped from her throat as she shoved against the bulk of nude muscle and sticky flesh on top of her.

Whiskers scratched her cheek, and a hot wet mouth covered hers.

She jerked her head to the side and tried to buck him off, but he was too strong, too big.

Meaty fingers shoved her jeans and panties to her knees and wrenched her legs apart.

"No! Get off me!" She yelled louder, an ear-splitting cry for help as she tried to wrestle her thighs together.

His trousers gathered around his knees, his body twice her size, damp with sweat, and flush against the front of her, pinning her to the floor.

The hard jab of his erection pushed against her inner thigh, seeking the bare place between her legs. Her thrashing, frenzied movements wouldn't hinder penetration for long.

She clawed and spat, screamed and tried to shove him off, her hands digging into hairy skin and flexed muscle.

When she felt the leather strap of his belt hanging free, she didn't hesitate to grab hold and yank it from his pants.

He didn't seem to notice, his movements focused on lining himself up to enter her body.

The belt swung free, and her hands moved on instinct as she looped it around his neck and twisted the ends into a noose.

She wasn't a violent person. Never used her fists. Never picked fights. Except that one time when she woke with a scorpion in her bed.

She'd gone ballistic at the sight of it crawling beside her head and grabbed whatever she could use as a weapon—a lamp, a pillow, a shoe.

Once she'd started attacking it, she was committed. She'd turned into something savage and feral, beating the ever-loving hell out of it long after its guts smeared the floor, pieces of it scattered the room, and the carnage no longer twitched.

She channeled that murderous aggression now, operating outside of her body as every muscle burned to choke, maim, and destroy until he lay as dead as that fucking scorpion.

It was the hardest, most grueling thing she'd ever done. Her arms shook with the effort to cinch the belt as tightly as possible for as long as it took.

He fought with his weight, rolling across the floor in a breathless rage. Elbows landed against her ribs. His massive torso flopped and flailed, crushing her against the wall.

But she hung on, mindless in her need to survive, to follow through until the last trickle of life left his body.

"He's dead." A masculine voice drifted from the cell door.

She flinched, heart racing, and whipped her head toward the silhouette.

Dressed in a prison guard uniform, the man leaned against the metal frame, arms crossed over his chest as if he'd been there a while.

"Why didn't you help me?" She released the belt and stumbled to her feet, yanking her jeans into place. "He tried to rape me!"

Oh, sweet Jesus, she killed a man. Were there consequences for that in Jaulaso?

Murderers probably murdered other murderers every day here. Did the prison guards look the other way? Or did they haul the offenders outside in front of a firing squad?

A tremor raced through her as she stared down at the lifeless body. She did that. One day behind bars, and she strangled a man until he stopped breathing.

"It was self-defense." Gulping to catch her breath, she staggered to the farthest wall, away from the dead man and the prison guard who studied her too carefully. "Were you here the whole time?"

"You're from the States." He tilted his head, and a gray ponytail fell over his shoulder. "And you speak Spanish."

"Yes." She hadn't heard or spoken an English word since her arrest. If she hadn't known the local language, she would've been more lost than she already was.

"Your options are limited, but you have some." He sucked on his teeth, watching her. "Money is one of them."

"What do you mean? Money for what?"

"I'll take you to a better place." He held out a hand. "If you pay."

"Pay?" She blinked at his waiting palm. "I don't have—"

"If it was on you during your arrest, you still have it. The military isn't interested in stealing money."

She shoved a hand into her back pocket and pulled out the two-hundred dollars she'd kept at Vera's house.

Her breath rushed out in relief.

She held out the cash to him, but at the last second, she yanked it back. "Where would you take me?"

"Area Three."

She had no idea what that was. "Would I have my own cell with a lock?"

"Maybe, but it doesn't matter. You'll have protection."

"I don't understand."

"You're too pretty." His gaze dipped, flitting down her legs before returning to her eyes. "Prettiest thing Jaulaso has ever seen. You won't make it a week on this side. Pay me, and I'll take you to a safer, more suitable living environment. Area Three protects its own."

How did she know this guard wasn't just trying to scam her out of money?

He leaned in and lowered his voice. "You'll have many luxuries there, including your own toilet and phone."

"I'll be able to make phone calls? To whomever I want?"

"Yes."

For the first time since she was ripped from her Jeep, her chest lifted with hope.

Maybe he was lying. She wouldn't know for sure unless she accepted his offer, which was inarguably better than waiting for the next rapist to sneak into her cell.

She sure as fuck didn't want to hang around until another guard walked in and found her with a dead body.

"Okay." She handed him the money.

"Come with me."

THREE

The prison guard led Tula through the overcrowded corridors of Jaulaso, seemingly oblivious to the fact that every inch of her was shaking against a storm of doubt and fear.

How could she trust this man, who had just watched her fight off a rapist without stepping in to help? It felt like a setup as if he knew she would be attacked, and he was just waiting for the right moment to make her an offer she couldn't refuse.

But if he wanted her money, he could've just taken it. He carried a rifle, for fuck's sake.

The brutal stress of this waking nightmare kinked painful knots in her neck. Her legs wobbled like jelly as she tried to keep up. The reek of cigarette smoke assaulted her nose, the filth in the air so palpable it made her gag.

How did these people live like this? Sure, they were criminals, and most of them probably deserved to be here. But how many were innocent like her? How many had been forgotten and left here to die?

The backs of her eyes grew achy as she fixed them on the long gray ponytail of the guard in front of her.

He ushered her through a metal door and into an outdoor yard, surrounded by two-story walls capped in barbed wire.

Nighttime had fallen, dark and humid. Another day lost.

She'd been gone forty-eight hours. Who would collect her mail, water her plants, and pay her landlord for next month's rent?

No one.

Even *if* she managed to reach her sister on the phone, she couldn't trust Vera to pay her bills. Access to her bank account would be too tempting.

Vera would drain her savings. Not that she had savings. She lived paycheck-to-paycheck, and those paychecks would stop if she didn't show up on the first day of school.

Two months.

She would be out of here by then.

The prison guard escorted her across the yard to another door. A young Hispanic man in civilian clothing stood beside it with a rifle resting on his shoulder.

Was he an inmate? She'd heard stories about how the cartels ruled the prisons inside their cities, but she never imagined their presence being so blatant. This guy was staring down her uniformed escort with an automatic rifle in his hand.

Was it true, then? Did the cartel have more power than the prison guards?

Her stomach tilted. Maybe this wasn't her best option.

The armed inmate knocked on the entrance behind him without removing his eyes from her. Deadbolts sounded, and the door opened to a large indoor common area.

Rap music thumped from somewhere inside. Scantily dressed Latina women danced around a table of smiling men and beer bottles. Guys wearing bandannas and wife-beaters played pool. Others stood around laughing among themselves, not paying any attention to the lost woman in the doorway.

There was no stench of death and despair. No overcrowding. Plenty of room to walk around and keep to herself. It looked like a casual house party with friends. Nothing like a prison.

A man stepped into her line of sight, blocking her view. Dressed in a black shirt and trousers, he wore a wreath of gold chains around his thick neck.

"Follow me," he said in Spanish and lumbered away without waiting.

She glanced back, and her prison guard was gone.

Unease gripped her spine. Curiosity tingled her senses. She knew what lay behind her. Whatever waited ahead had to be better.

She jogged to catch up with the guy in gold chains, relieved that the men in the common area didn't leer or try to approach her.

"We have everything here." Her escort guided her through one room after another, gesturing at sectioned-off areas, each serving a different purpose, like a makeshift marketplace. "We have a bar, laundry, restaurant, outdoor gym, health care clinic, recreation area, and canteen that sells food, water, and things for grooming."

The service stations were sad imitations of real places. Each area was pieced together with crates, scrap wood, mismatched furniture, and whatever they could get their hands on to make it work. But the ingenuity behind it was impressive. It almost felt like a tiny mall inside a hotel. Almost.

As he led her into a maze of corridors, she studied him inconspicuously. His Hispanic features were darker than hers. Darker complexion, browner eyes, blacker hair, and bushy eyebrows.

His whiskered jaw hovered in that awkward stage between a scruffy shadow and a squirrelly beard. Despite his need to sculpt his facial hair, he wasn't terrible looking.

A little bony through the shoulders and rough around the edges, he was probably in his forties. It hadn't been an easy forty years, given the scars marring his arms and peeking through the open collar of his shirt.

"Do you know where you are?" He turned a corner, his strides never slowing.

"Jaulaso." Her brows pinched together.

"Sure, but do you know which side this is?"

"No."

"This is Area Three." He lifted his chin, his expression fiercely proud. "Home of La Rocha Cartel."

La Rocha.

The most aggressive, most organized, most violent cartel in existence.

They were *here*? Inside these walls?

Her shoulders squeezed forward.

The things they did to women... Oh, God. She'd heard stories growing up about how La Rocha members freely raped, maimed, disfigured, and beheaded any female they set their eyes on. They impregnated girls just to crush the babies under their boots after they were born.

She hugged herself at the elbows.

Maybe it wasn't true.

A shiver slid across her scalp. She felt so small, so naive and fearful, just like the helpless, wide-eyed girl she once was, listening to her mother whisper chilling stories meant to scare guileless daughters away from cartel.

"Pick up your feet." The man glared at her from the end of the hall. "Faster."

She hadn't meant to fall behind, but *fuck him*. He was lucky she wasn't sobbing on the floor. That was what she wanted to do. She desperately needed to fall apart.

"Here is your cell." He ushered her into a small concrete room.

In the corner, a mattress sat on a metal frame. Her shoulders loosened at the sight of the fluffy pillow and the clean-looking white sheets folded beneath it.

A blanket spread over the bed with a llama on it. A llama wearing a sombrero and smiling with big teeth. It looked chillingly perverse in the context of its surroundings, but there were no stains or ratty holes in the fabric.

Definitely an upgrade from the last cell.

Moonlight slanted through a tiny barred window near the ceiling. Artificial light flickered from a bare bulb over a single sink that jutted from the wall. Beside it sat a toilet.

The surfaces appeared reasonably clean.

No bugs or mouse drippings on the floor.

No creepy inmates loitering outside the door.

Better yet, the door was solid. She would be able to close it, and no one would see in. "Is there a lock?"

"No." He removed an old cell phone from his pocket and tossed it on the bed. "We control all cell phone use within the prison. That's yours."

"I can make calls to the States? Whenever I want?"

"Yes."

The device was a basic model, the kind that couldn't access email or the Internet. But it would do what she needed it to do. She would be able to call her sister, her boss, a lawyer, and make arrangements for her monthly bills.

She could do this. For a month or two, she could manage her life in Phoenix from the confines of this room. She could keep everything together until she returned. She was going to be okay.

The tension in her body dissolved, muscle by muscle, breath by breath. Until she heard the sound of foil crinkling behind her.

"Now, you pay the rent," he said at her back.

Her heart shriveled, and her lungs lost air. She didn't need to turn around to see the condom in his hand or the expectation in his eyes. She knew exactly what form of payment he intended to collect.

"No." She spun away and stumbled backward across the room. "I'm not doing that. I'll pay another way."

"Maybe you'll come up with something next week, but this is how you pay now." He unlatched his belt. "Get on the bed."

She shook her head wildly, tears rising and burning. This wasn't happening. She couldn't do it. She wouldn't.

"I was promised safety." Her legs trembled uncontrollably, shuffling her away until her back hit the wall. "I paid that guard to bring me to a better place. He said I would have protection here."

She'd been too desperate to believe him, blindly holding onto a grain of hope so that she wouldn't completely lose it.

"You don't like the arrangement?" He charged toward her. "Then you go back." He gripped her hair and hauled her toward the door.

"No! Wait!" She reached for the phone, arms outstretched as the bed blurred by, too far away. "Please, don't send me back. I'll work. I can cook, wash clothes, clean bathrooms. I'll do anything!"

"You do *this*." He grabbed her hips and ground his erection against her backside. "Or you go back and let a dozen men take a turn with you every night."

Bile simmered in her chest, and her breaths heaved through great, choking sobs.

"No. Please, anything else." She thrashed in his arms, her feet scrambling across the floor as he dragged her into the hall. She needed that phone, the private toilet, the soft bed… "Please, don't send me back."

"You pay the rent or go."

His indifference about whether she stayed crushed her willpower. Fighting him only quickened his strides as if he couldn't wait to be rid of her. He'd given her a choice and wouldn't bend the rules. She wasn't worth the trouble.

She was nothing to him.

A low, agony-soaked sound gurgled in her throat as resignation sucked the life from her limbs. "I'll pay."

He didn't give her time to change her mind. Turning back, he hauled her into her cell and tossed her on the mattress, face down. A zipper sounded behind her, followed by the tear of a condom packet.

Violent, full-body tremors chattered her teeth and rattled the metal frame of the bed.

She couldn't move, couldn't bring herself to look behind her. She just lay there, frozen in shock and horror, aching to be anywhere but here facing what was about to happen.

Her body stiffened with the instinct to protect itself, everything inside her screaming to kick, bite, and come unhinged. But fighting him wouldn't get her that phone.

The device lay inches from her face. Her only way out of this nightmare.

As he wrenched down her jeans and panties, her fingernails stabbed into her palms.

As he forced himself into her dehydrated body, something broke inside her.

As he pounded the singed, electrocuted flesh between her legs, she swallowed her cries, buried the anguish, and didn't make a sound.

But her silence came at a price.

The only way to hold still beneath the violation was to shed the pieces of herself that cared. With each merciless thrust, she lost her naiveté, her kindness, and her hope in mankind. She carved up the vulnerable parts that wouldn't survive in Jaulaso and let it all go.

Gentle, sentimental fragments of her existence tore away and crumbled to dust, and she knew she would never get those pieces back. Something hard and unfeeling filled the jagged gaps.

Her mind contorted and adjusted, trying to protect itself, to become immune to the damage. She felt herself grow cold and vacant, hardening like a concrete wall.

But she had fractures. God, they were everywhere, letting in the pain from his thrusts, the anguish of being used so despicably, and the fear of tomorrow, and the next day, and the month after that.

She mentally repaired the cracks, stopped the leaks, and shut out the agony. It was a lonely, excruciating effort. As she toughened herself against the stabbing motion of his hips, her edges started to splinter.

The threat of tears burned her throat. It would be so easy to release her grief in a fit of sobbing cries. Maybe someone would hear and take pity on her. Maybe this man would stop hurting her and feel horrible about what he'd done. Maybe, just maybe, her tears would make all this go away.

That wouldn't happen. No one would feel sorry for her. No one would come to her rescue.

She was in Jaulaso. To survive, she needed to become like them.

Wrapping herself in coldness, she erected shields, closed mental doors, and formed layers of impenetrable resilience.

I will not cry.

I will not show weakness.

I will bear this, bury it, and survive.

A strangled groan sounded behind her, and the weight on her back disappeared.

She looked down at her balled hands and uncurled her fingers. Blood trickled from crescent-shaped gouges in her palms and soaked her nail beds.

The pain didn't register.

She slowly rose, pulled up her jeans with numb fingers, and turned to meet his eyes. "What's your name?"

"Garra." He fastened his pants and ran a hand over his black hair, slicking the strands into place.

"Congratulations, Garra. You forced yourself on an unarmed woman half your size. Your mother must be proud." Her voice echoed in her head with icy detachment. "If you ever touch me again, I'll kill you."

"Welcome to your new home, Petula Gomez." His gaze swept over her with the same detachment. "Rent is due again next week."

FOUR

Austin, Texas
Two years ago

Ricky Saldivar knocked on the front door of Van Quiso's cabin and tore a hand through his hair.

Why had he even bothered styling it? He'd raked his fingers through the gelled pompadour cut so many times on the way here it probably looked like he just crawled out of bed. After hours of fucking.

It was nerves. Completely normal. Not that he was a nervous guy. It was just...

Christ, he was at Van's house. Standing on the motherfucker's front porch. Willingly.

This wasn't normal. Not even in the same realm.

Shifting beneath the overhead light, he squinted at his reflection in the glass door and tried to fix his hair. The longer strands on top spiked in every direction, refusing to be tamed.

Why the fuck was he fussing over his appearance?

Nerves.

Excitement.

Anticipation.

All of it coursed through him in fitful waves.

He knocked again and slipped his hands into his front pockets.

The deadbolt turned. It twisted three more times before the door opened.

Van's wife stood on the other side, wearing a tight red-as-sin minidress and a tremulous smile.

"Hi, Ricky." Amber Quiso chewed her lip, her gaze flitting restlessly over the dark front yard. "Sorry to make you wait. I...I was having a moment. Nothing major. You know, I'm... Sometimes, I slip and... Ugh, save me from this rambling."

"It's good to see you. You look beautiful, as always."

"Thank you." She smoothed her palms down the front of the dress and cleared her voice. "He's waiting."

She didn't move to let him inside, her eyes stark as she directed them at her bare feet.

He'd only met her a couple of times in passing and knew she struggled with some disorders, one of them being a fear of open spaces. Just the thought of stepping outside used to freak her the fuck out. She supposedly had a better handle on that now but still had bad days.

"Amber?"

"Yeah? Shit. Yes. I mean, what?" She seemed to snap out of a simmering panic attack. "Sorry, I was...listening to my heartbeats. *Not* counting them. I wasn't counting. Because I'm okay. Really. I'm just a little off. Not that I'm crazy or whatever you've heard..."

"You don't want to keep him waiting." He nodded behind her, expecting her to let him in.

"He's around back. Outside. I'm supposed to take you." She pointed at the path that led around the side of the house. "The long way. *Bastard.*" She whispered the last word with a huff.

"Okay." He stepped off the porch and waited for her to join him.

She didn't move, her hands balling at her sides and her jaw rigidly locked.

Maybe Van demanded this from her as a form of therapy? Or perhaps he just liked to torment her? He was a sadist, after all, which was precisely why Ricky had requested this meeting.

"I assume Van told you the reason I'm here."

"Yeah." Her gaze lifted to his. "Are you sure you want this?"

"I know what I need. *Who* I need it with is another story." He laughed under his breath but didn't feel the humor in it. "I'd choose anyone but him. Believe me, I've tried. But..."

"He's the best."

The best at beating, tormenting, and fucking someone into the most violent, life-changing orgasms known to man.

The only other person who would even come close to bringing Ricky to his knees was his best friend, Martin.

But Martin was straight.

And homophobic.

An impossible fantasy.

"Yeah." He blew out a breath. "Van's the best at being a real asshole."

"Oh, but he's a beautiful, loyal asshole." She stepped onto the porch and inhaled deeply. "He doesn't want to hurt you. He only agreed to do this because he wants to *help* you."

"I know."

"We're monogamous."

He tilted his face toward the night sky and closed his eyes. "Look, I'm not here to steal your husband." He met her gaze. "I don't even like the guy."

"But you're attracted to him."

"He's...compelling."

Even when Van had hurt him beyond his extremely high pain threshold, whipped him until he passed out, and fucked his throat to the point of suffocation, he thought his captor was the sexiest, most viciously captivating male in existence.

Until he met Martin Lockwood.

Martin and his goddamn megawatt smile, Viking warrior build, overbearing protectiveness, and vigilant pale eyes... Everything about the man kindled a roaring need in Ricky, one that wasn't reciprocated and never would be.

Jesus fuck, get over it already.

"He'll give you what you came for." Amber anchored her fists on the toned curves of her hips. "But he won't fuck you."

"Story of my life," he muttered too low for her to hear.

"What?"

"Nothing."

She raised her chin, her tone barbed with ferocity. "No intercourse and no kissing on the mouth. Those are *my* rules."

"Okay..." He cast her a concerned look. "If you're not comfortable with this, I'll go. I don't want to cause problems."

"I agreed to it." She clutched her throat and glanced around before giving him her eyes. "He raped me, too, Ricky. Whatever you're feeling, the filthy things he planted in your head, his taunting voice in your ear whenever you're alone, the shameful memories... I understand all of it. But unlike you, I get to spend every night with him, working through it and repairing the parts he fractured. If you need this from him, I'm cool with it." She shoved back her shoulders. "As long as you remember he belongs to *me*."

"You're a possessive little thing." He grinned.

"With him? You bet your ass."

"No betting needed, considering I'm about to hand my ass over to him."

"Good." She smiled.

"Good." He nodded at the path. "Shall we?"

She breezed past him, navigating the steppingstones with the grace of a beauty queen.

"No one else has sought him out like this." She peered at him beneath her lashes as she made her way around the side of the cabin. "I mean, other than Camila asking him to help with her vigilante work, you're the only one of his...uh..."

"Ex-slaves. You can call us that."

She nodded. "You're the only ex-slave who has reached out to him. He appreciates your trust more than you know, but I'm curious..."

"Why am I here instead of plotting his death like my roommates?"

"Yeah." She padded along the lit path, her expression pinched with wariness.

"Pain makes you stronger, and time heals all wounds. Blah, blah, blah... I'm sure there's truth in that, but to be honest, I sympathized with him and Liv when I found out they were forced into that life."

Back in the day, long before Van met Amber, Van had a hard-on for Liv Reed. He and Liv had made quite the dysfunctional, human-sex-trafficking duo.

Over six years, they enslaved five males and two females. Camila Dias had been their first. Ricky was slave number two.

The night Ricky was captured, he'd taken one look at Liv and followed his dick. The alluring, irresistible beauty had led him out of the dance club, into her car, and straight into shackles with an unspoken promise of fun, kinky, *consensual* sex.

Unbeknown to him, she'd drugged his beer at the bar, which had caused him to black out during the drive. But that wasn't why he ended up in her car in the first place.

He'd wanted her, despite her scarred face, and when he saw Van with a matching scar, he wanted both of them. Separately. At the same time. Any way he could get them.

Apparently, gorgeous criminals were his weakness. He was shallow and reckless like that.

But at the time, he hadn't known what he wanted. Not completely.

"Before Van, I didn't know I was bisexual." He stopped walking and waited for Amber to glance back. "I always knew I wasn't like other guys, but I didn't know how or why until I was chained in Van's attic."

"Oh." She pulled in a slow breath and turned to face him. "He was your first?"

"I'd been with women, but never with a man. Not until him."

"I'm sorry." She cringed. "I imagine he didn't break you in gently."

"No." He laughed with a grimace. "During those godawful months with him... Jesus, he fucked me up so badly I thought I was going to die. But the experience opened my mind. It forced me to examine my curiosities, desires, and all the socially unacceptable things I would've never explored on my own."

"He broke you and put the pieces back together the way they were meant to be."

"Exactly."

It felt good to talk about this, and she seemed to relate to him on a level most people didn't. Because Van had put her through the same hell.

"Had he not subjected me to the things he did..." He gripped the back of his neck. "I don't think I would've ever acknowledged my bisexuality or my need to be dominated in bed. It's crazy that I feel grateful to him for that, considering the nightmares and years of mental trauma he caused me."

But he had time and distance on his side. It'd been eight years since his captivity. Nine years for Camila. Every day was easier than the last.

That was the only reason he was able to face Van tonight.

His roommates—Tomas, Luke, Martin, Tate, and Kate—didn't have as many years to heal. Not yet. They would come around eventually, and maybe someday, they would forgive Van's cruelty.

Even so, the decision to pick up the phone and call Van hadn't been an easy one. It had taken him a year of dialing and hanging up before he let the call go through.

He didn't know if Van would reject him or if he was even ready to take this step with his former captor. He didn't know if he would ever be ready.

"I'm growing impatient." The deep baritone punched from the tree line behind the house, shooting a delicious shiver down Ricky's spine.

Amber must've felt it, too, because her shoulders gave a little shudder.

"It's not too late to change your mind." She squinted at the trees through the darkness.

Not a chance in hell. But he needed to ask. "Do you want me to back out?"

She shook her head, her lips bowing in a seductive smile. "I've always wanted to know what he's like with a man."

Since sex was off-limits, she wouldn't see Van in all his depraved glory. But one thing was certain. Van would find a way to torture them both, holding them right on that precarious edge between pain and pleasure until they begged for mercy.

"Let's do this." His heart raced as he nudged her across the backyard toward the woods, his gaze probing the shadows, searching for Van's intimidating silhouette.

When he called Van yesterday, they didn't discuss rules or negotiate how this would go, which was ironic considering Ricky had endured months of Van's sexual training bound by a rigid list of requirements. But those had been set by the slave buyer.

Van had no use for rules, laws, principles, or anything that resembled BDSM. He did what he wanted, however he wanted, and it was rarely safe or sane. Tonight, however, it would be consensual.

For the first time, Ricky would surrender to Van's will because he wanted this. He *needed* the relief of an assertive, confident hand.

He'd said as much on the phone when he told Van about his botched dating life, failed foray in the local fetish community, and overall disappointment in male lovers.

He longed to be with someone more alpha than himself. His one-night stands always seemed to fit that mold, until he got them in bed. No matter how many people he fucked — and the list was depressingly long — he hadn't found a lover who could master him on a natural level. It always felt...forced.

After he'd explained all this, he said the words he never imagined uttering to Van.

I need a release, the kind only you can give.

Van's gravelly response had been sharp, swift, and arousing beyond belief.

Come to me.

Ricky shivered as he slowed at the tree line, his gaze connecting with Van's silvery, moonlit eyes in the shadows.

A toothpick lolled at the corner of the imposing man's full lips, his scar etching a monstrous seam in an otherwise flawless face.

As gorgeous as he was terrifying, he was built like a mountain and somehow managed to stare down at Ricky, even as they stood at the same height.

"Van." Blood rushed to Ricky's groin, hardening him behind the zipper.

"Ricardo."

"Don't call me —"

"It's your given name. Grown men don't go by *Ricky*." Van stepped into his space and ghosted the back of a finger across his whiskered jaw. "You've definitely grown since the last time you choked on my cock."

Ricky had added a significant amount of muscle mass over the past eight years. The fact that it hadn't gone unnoticed thrilled him more than it should have.

"Will I be doing that tonight? Choking on your dick?" His breathing quickened, his erection a hot throbbing heartbeat in his jeans.

"No." Van grinned around the toothpick. "I only get hard for my wife. I'll put my hands on you, but you won't touch me. Or her. If you do, we're finished. Understood?"

"Yes, sir."

"Lose the *sir* bullshit. You're not here to stroke my ego."

"God knows it doesn't need to be stroked." Amber stood a few feet away with one brow arched.

Van slowly cut his razored eyes in her direction, and her sassy eyebrow slipped beneath an *oh-shit* expression.

He prowled toward her, gripped her hair, and wrenched her face to his. "How many times did you turn the deadbolt when he arrived?"

Her alarmed gaze flicked to Ricky.

"Don't look at him." Van spat the toothpick on the ground. "Answer me."

She stared up at her husband and licked her lips. "Four times."

"And your knuckles? How many times did you crack them?"

"Zero."

"Good girl." His fist in her hair loosened into a soft, petting stroke.

She nuzzled into the affection and purred so low and profoundly the sound seemed to come from the depths of her soul.

A knot of envy squeezed Ricky's chest, his entire body burning for that soul-reaching touch.

"Sit." Van directed Amber to the edge of a wooden table nestled in the trees.

Ricky hadn't noticed it until now, but the piece of furniture must've weighed a thousand pounds, given the huge chunky legs and wide top. Made of raw wood, the surface was sanded down and sealed with shiny lacquer.

She perched on the ledge, her bare feet dangling above the grass. If she spread her thighs, her pussy would be level with Van's groin. No doubt the height had been designed for exactly that reason.

A closer look at the thick tree trunks around the table revealed hardware—eye bolts, levers, and leather straps—mounted in the bark at varying positions.

With the nearest neighbor miles away, no one would hear a scream on Van's property. The debauchery that occurred here on the regular was probably illegal in most countries.

Amber was one lucky bitch.

Van clasped his hands behind his back and prowled a tight circle around Ricky, penetrating skin and nerves with his intoxicating heat.

"Tell me why you're here," Van breathed against his nape,

"instead of at home fucking your best friend."

"Martin?" His pulse sped up. "Why would you assume we're more than friends?"

"Why wouldn't you be? He's the only one in your house who can give you what you need."

"He's straight."

"No." Van laughed, loud and derisively. "He's not."

"Just because you forced him —"

"He hasn't told you." Van tilted his head, his glare sharp and scrutinizing. "Here I thought there were no secrets between you and your roommates."

"What hasn't he told me?" Ricky ground his teeth.

"How he ended up in my attic."

Martin didn't talk about that. Whenever questions were directed at him about his abduction or the time he spent with Van and Liv, he turned heel and vacated the room.

"I assume Liv lured him," Ricky said.

"Guess again."

"You?" His head flinched back. "You took him at gunpoint?"

"I didn't use a weapon or any kind of force."

"What are you saying?" Suspicion tensed his neck. "Did you manipulate him?"

"Not exactly." Van removed a toothpick from his pocket and set it between his molars. "He's your best friend. Ask him yourself."

"I have. He refuses to discuss it."

"Sounds like trouble in paradise." His smirk oozed with ridicule.

"Fuck you."

Van was on him in a blink, an iron fist around his throat and cutting his air as he was slammed face down onto the table beside Amber.

"I'll tell you the real reason you're here." Van ground Ricky's cheek against the wood.

"Enlighten me."

"You want to make him jealous. Ignite that possessive rage he can't control when it comes to you. What better way to provoke him than to return home, flushed and sated in the afterglow of another man's enjoyment? You'll tell him that man was me just to get a rise out of him. He'll shove you into a wall, bruise you with his strong hands, and you'll eat up every second of that physical contact. How am I doing so far?"

That was exactly how it would play out.

"How about you shut the fuck up and hurt me already?" Ricky bared his teeth. "Make me *feel*."

"Put your arms behind you." Van released him. "Cross them against your back and grip your elbows."

His skin heated as he obeyed without hesitation.

He didn't want to think, question, or second-guess this. It was simple. He had an itch and was seeking out someone who excelled at scratching hard-to-reach places.

Heart thundering, he tracked the tread of Van's footsteps through the trees and around the table until the sound paused near his head.

"I'm not going to restrain you." Van bent down, brushing his lips against Ricky's ear. "You are bound by your own will. If you release your elbows, I will stop and send your ass home."

"Got it." He locked his fingers around the crooks of his arms.

"Amber." Van shifted toward his wife. "Lie back. Palms flat on the table."

She moved into position, face up beside Ricky. He remained chest down with his face angled toward her.

Van gripped her waist and pulled, sliding her along the table until her head hung off the edge, upside down.

Ricky knew where this was going, and so did she, given the swallow that jogged in her throat.

Anticipation lengthened his cock, trapping it at a painful angle between his hips and the table. The sound of Van's zipper made him impossibly harder.

Then he saw it, the long stiff evidence of Van Quiso's arousal.

Van rested his erection over her gaping mouth like an offering, teasing the shaft across her lips.

She licked at it, panting and squirming, all while keeping her hands flat on the table at her sides.

A groan escaped Ricky as Van fed her his dick, inch by steely inch. When he reached the back of her throat, she swallowed rapidly without gagging.

Ricky could've done the same. In that soundproof attic, Van had fucked his face until his gag reflex no longer existed.

"Put your fingers in your pussy." Van thrust his hips, his breathing accelerating. "Work it hard. I want a puddle under your ass."

The blow job lasted forever and not long enough. From inches away, he watched Van's cock sink and retreat, over and over. He lay so close to them the musk of their hunger infused his inhales.

He focused on clutching his elbows and tried to not come. His orgasm hovered right there. If he ground his groin against the table, he would blow.

And this would be over.

Finally, Van pulled free from her mouth and angled toward Ricky. Gripping the base of his dick, he slowly dragged his fist to the tip and squeezed out a bead of pre-come.

He swiped his thumb over it, catching the clear drop, and pressed it between Ricky's lips. "Suck."

Hollowing his cheeks, he sucked Van's thumb the way Van had taught him—hard, consistent, and with a firm tongue.

The subtle tang of Van's essence teased his taste buds. The breathy sounds of Van's groans fueled his need for more.

"Fuck, I haven't forgotten your mouth," Van rasped. "Martin doesn't know what he's missing." He slid his thumb across Ricky's bottom lip. "Don't give up on him."

It was a lost cause. If he pushed Martin much harder, he risked ruining their friendship.

Van circled the table, stopped behind Ricky, and helped Amber into a sitting position.

"So fucking wet, baby." A groan rumbled in Van's chest as he thrust a hand between her legs, fingering her until the squelching sounds of her arousal hit the air. "Jesus, you make me so damn hard. Sit just like that. Don't move."

Van turned his attention to Ricky, divesting him of his shoes, jeans, and everything he wore from the waist down.

A few hard kicks shoved his feet apart, and he didn't fight it. Didn't cower or lose his shit as the sound of Van's leather belt whistled through the air.

The first strike against his ass stopped his heart. He didn't find his breath before the next fiery smack landed on the back of his thigh.

"Fuuuuuck!" He'd forgotten how goddamn hard Van hit.

The son of a bitch didn't hold back, didn't pause for breaks, didn't give a millimeter of mercy. He wailed and whipped and annihilated Ricky's backside until everything burned—his skin, muscle, bone, organs.

With his legs spread so wide and his junk hanging unprotected between his thighs, Van made sure that leather strap caught the back of his ball sac as often as possible. It was torture by fire.

Ricky could release his elbows at any time and put an end to the ungodly pain. Maybe Van would break his promise and keep going until Ricky lay broken and bleeding.

But Amber trusted Van. Camila trusted him, and deep down, Ricky did, too. He wouldn't have come here if he thought he would be powerless.

That was the appeal, wasn't it? To be with Van on an equal playing field? It was something he'd never experienced beneath Van's whip.

But it hurt. Holy fuck, it took everything he had to keep his hands fastened to his elbows and his legs spread, exposing his tender balls.

Just when he thought he wouldn't survive another strike, Van dropped the belt. Clothing rustled, and Van's shirt fell to the ground.

Then the rock-hard terrain of Van's abs lowered against Ricky's arms, where they folded at his back. He wished he were shirtless, too, so he could feel the damp warmth of Van's skin.

Sultry breath visited his ear, followed by the press of Van's erection against the back of his balls, flesh on flesh, heat on heat.

He felt the power in the body mashed against his, the strength of muscle flexing around him. Blood scorched through his veins, a fire Van smoldered hotter and thicker with each drive of his hips.

To accept the touch of a man, appreciate the sound of a deep masculine groan, and long for a presence bigger and more rugged than himself... Ricky hadn't known he coveted these things until Van had shoved his face in it.

Exhibitionism was another turn on, thanks to Van. As much as he despised what had been done to him in that attic, there had been tantalizing moments amid the misery. Moments that had involved Liv.

She hadn't participated in the sodomy, but Van often made her watch. Her presence had changed the dynamics somehow. Made Ricky feel less alone.

He'd started to crave her eyes on him, became addicted to an outsider's attention.

Eight years later, he still hungered for the rare hookup with another couple, when one of them watched for a while before joining in.

Like now.

He angled his neck to steal a view of Amber.

She sat stiffly beside his hips, her gaze fixed on Van's cock and her hand thrusting between her spread legs. Lips parted, she breathed heavily, noisily, breathtakingly stunning in her flushed state of lust.

Leave it to Van to marry the hottest woman in Texas.

What would it be like to spend a night in their bed, naked and grinding between them?

The greedy parts of him ached for a pair of lovers. Wanted them to hold him, kiss him fiercely, fuck him hard, and love him deeply. Rough and sweaty. Raw and honest.

To bask in the unapologetic passion of a man like Van, to experience the possessive love of a woman like Amber... That would be something worth fighting for.

"She's every man's fantasy." Van reached under Ricky's hips and gripped his engorged cock, causing his breath to strangle. "But if you don't take your fucking eyes off her, I'll remove them from your face."

Van squeezed his dick so ruthlessly a roar tore from his throat. It felt as though his manhood—balls and all—was being ripped from his body.

"Okay, stop!" His fingers started to slip from his elbows. He adjusted his grip and turned his face into the table. "Not looking. My eyes are closed. Please, just stop!"

Van's fist relaxed, finger by finger, and began a slow, sensual slide along Ricky's length.

Pain morphed into pleasure as each stroke melted through his groin and tightened his nuts.

"Oh, God." He rocked his hips, thrusting into that strong, confident handhold.

Blissful tremors rippled through him, gathering low and deep, pulsing to erupt. The pressure, the rhythm, and the caress of masculine fingers felt as stimulating as his own hand. Better even. Fucking perfect.

Van had married a woman, but sweet lord almighty, he still knew how to master a cock.

Lowering to a crouch, Van repositioned his grip, reaching between Ricky's legs from behind and pulling his erection backward until it angled toward the ground, parallel with his thigh. Then he stroked harder, faster, twisting his fist along the length.

"I'm not going to last." Ricky grunted, his body shaking in his effort to hold off his release.

"Yes, you will." Van's gravelly voice brushed across his ass.

That dangerous mouth hovered between his legs, taunting him with heavy breaths.

He rocked his forehead on the table, his chest rising and falling in sync with Van's strokes. The rush of orgasm threatened, throbbing toward detonation.

Right there. Oh, fuck, right there.

Van's hand stopped moving and squeezed right below the head of Ricky's cock. His thumb and forefinger applied firm pressure, pushing back blood and forcing the climax to retreat.

A moan hit his throat and stuck there. He struggled for air, wrestled to keep his arms locked in position, while directing his frustration into the pained expression that strained his face.

Beside him, Amber's whimpers grew louder, faster, and he realized Van's other hand was between her legs.

A moment later, that hand moved to Ricky's backside, and drenched fingers sank into the crack of his ass.

There was no teasing, no warm-up, before Van forced a digit deep inside him, using only the lubrication from Amber's arousal.

With a sharp grunt, he lifted on his toes and choked against the wicked invasion.

Another finger penetrated. Then a third. Stretching, pounding, Van impaled his rectum with one hand while the other jerked him off in twisting, merciless strokes.

The assault scorched flesh and nerve endings, shooting trails of fire through his body in every direction.

Teeth grazed his buttocks. Then firm lips and an aggressively hot tongue. Van's mouth was the sweetest torment, tasting his skin, sucking the welts, and licking the crevice between his flexing glutes.

Feverish currents zinged beneath Van's grip and ignited around the fingers that pushed viciously hard inside him. He unraveled, biting down on his moan with clenched teeth until the sound escaped in a guttural growl.

Goddamn, it felt too deep. Yet he wanted more. Hands and fingers weren't enough. He needed more than a touch, more than a night, more than a borrowed lover.

But Van held him there, working his body toward that blissful edge. His legs shook against the force of pleasure, thrumming to burst.

"Now." Van tightened his strokes and sank his teeth into the back of Ricky's balls.

A titanic surge of ecstasy poured out of him. He groaned and lost his grip on his elbows, slamming his hands onto the table as he emptied himself onto the ground.

He collapsed against the wooden surface, twitching with residual tremors, his breaths gusting past his lips.

Behind him, Van rose and slid a hand down the length of Ricky's spine over the t-shirt.

He arched into the caress, clinging to the unexpected tenderness, needing that simple touch more than anything Van had offered him tonight.

Too soon, Van pulled back, straightening his pants and collecting Ricky's clothes.

Nighttime critters sang softly amid the surrounding trees as Ricky dressed and slipped on his shoes. Then he turned toward the beautiful couple.

Amber hadn't moved from the table, her minidress gathered around her waist. Van stood sideways in the *V* of her legs, with his hip pressed against her pussy, concealing her nudity.

She curled around his side, her cheek on his shoulder and fingers toying with the unbuttoned fly of his jeans. He was still hard, his bulge straining the zipper beneath her roving hand.

They weren't finished. Not with each other.

That was his cue to leave.

"Thank you." He glanced at Amber then met Van's steel-colored gaze. "I needed that."

"Come back anytime you want," Van said. "Though, I know you

won't."

He considered arguing and decided against it. "We'll see."

Amber straightened against Van's side. "I'll walk you out."

Van growled at the same time Ricky said, "No. It's cool. You guys enjoy your night."

He ambled away, across the lawn, and as he reached the side of the cabin, her scream shuddered through the darkness behind him.

He paused and peered back, leaning around the corner of the house.

Moonlight illuminated the curves of their silhouettes. Van held her so tightly, so possessively, it was impossible to determine where she ended and he began.

They moved as one, chest to chest, foreheads together, her body on his lap, and her legs hooked around him.

Hungry moans shivered the air. The wet sounds of greedy mouths. They writhed together, enclosed in their own world. A universe where they only needed each other and the fathomless love they shared.

"You won't," Ricky whispered, his chest tight.

Van was right. Ricky wouldn't seek him out again. Not for sex.

What he truly wanted, what he needed, waited for him at home.

FIVE

Martin Lockwood released a slow breath at the sound of Ricky's truck pulling into the driveway. It was anyone's guess where he'd gone tonight. He'd sneaked out before Martin could ask.

Not that Ricky needed a keeper. He was a grown ass man and could do whatever or *whomever* he wanted.

"I can feel you tensing all the way over here." Kate smiled at him from her cozy position on the couch. With her head on Tomas' lap, she tucked her feet against Luke's hip. "I bet Ricky would help you work out that stiffness."

"Kate…" Martin dropped his voice in a warning tone and straightened in the recliner.

"She's right." Tomas absently played with her hair, his gaze glued to the basketball game on TV. "You're glaring so hard I can hear it."

They liked to tease him about harboring romantic feelings for Ricky. It was all in good fun and not even remotely true. He was sick of hearing it.

Luke released a soft snore from the couch, his red hair flopping over his brow with the loll of his head. A mechanic by trade, he'd spent the past twelve hours working on his motorcycle and running errands with Camila.

Camila's voice floated from Tate's bedroom down the hall. She and Tate, always hard at work, were ironing out a strategy to decimate the latest human sex trafficking ring in Austin.

Everyone in this house had a role in their small vigilante group. They had all put in a full day on the current mission and decided to stay in tonight.

Except Ricky. The man had an insatiable sex drive and particular tastes. He was always prowling. Always searching for something.

A key turned the deadbolt, and the front door opened.

Ricky stepped in, and those brown eyes unerringly found and held his.

Martin knew his best friend well enough to discern the meaning behind every expression and subtle movement. The soft look hooding Ricky's eyes confessed he'd just gotten laid. The twitches in his biceps indicated challenge, bracing for whatever Martin might say about it.

Ricky's chest lifted, stretching the tight t-shirt he'd deliberately worn to accentuate his muscled physique. His pretty-boy hairstyle had been disheveled by a night of restless yanking. Not by someone else's hands, but his own. For whatever reason, he'd been nervous.

He was still nervous, yet the cause was different now. He seemed to have trouble holding Martin's gaze.

He was hiding something.

"Hey." He gave Martin a chin lift, smiled at Kate and Tomas, and shook his head at a snoring Luke. "I knew that guy would be passed out before I got home."

"Where were you?" Martin asked casually.

"Out." With a shrug, he headed down the hall.

Frustration curled Martin's fingers against the armrests of the recliner.

Who had he fucked tonight? Where did he meet her? Or him?

Better not have been a *him*.

His heart rammed against the rungs of his ribs, a caged beast trying to escape.

"Three..." Tomas said from the couch. "Two..."

Martin glared at him.

"One." Tomas arched a brow.

He launched from the chair and strode toward the hall, surrendering to his predictable nature with a middle finger in the air. "Happy, asshole?"

"Love you, man!" Tomas called after him, laughing.

He passed the bedroom Camila shared with Kate and paused at the second door, which led to Tate's room. Camila was in there, her voice carrying through the walls as she argued with Tate about which strategy was less dangerous.

She took on more risk than any of them were comfortable with. Hell, they all did. But her mysterious connections made everyone uneasy.

Every time they killed a slave-trading shitbag, some unknown person helped her dispose of the body. Cartel was the most popular assumption, but she refused to confirm it. Tate couldn't even pry the secret out of her.

She demanded they trust her. Which they did. Emphatically.

Martin continued down the hall, stalking through the massive, five-bedroom, ranch-style estate. Tate, Luke, and Tomas had their own rooms. Martin and Ricky shared the master suite.

One of them could've moved into the finished attic, but after being held captive in Van's windowless hell, no one volunteered.

They sat on millions of dollars—the money Van had collected selling slaves. At any time, one of the Freedom Fighters could buy his or her own house.

No one was in a rush to do that. They were secure here. Happy and comfortable. Not because it was the nicest place any of them had ever lived. It was definitely that.

They loved this house because it kept them together. Close. Like a family.

Family was a concept most of them had never experienced. At least, not in a positive way.

Someday, they might find partners, get married, and move out. Until then, all they needed was one another.

At the end of the corridor, he stepped into the master suite and found Ricky exiting the walk-in closet. Ricky's shirtless chest glowed with a deep natural tan, enunciating the definition in his pecs and abs.

Martin averted his gaze. "What was the skank's name tonight?"

"Is that what you think of me? That only a *skank* would hook up with me?"

"No." A vein of possessiveness ran through him, hardening his jaw.

"You know what I find interesting?" Ricky toed off his shoes and kicked them in the direction of the closet. "You support me in every aspect of my life. You're always there for me, always listening and offering advice on anything... Except when it comes to this. I can't mention dates, relationships, nothing related to sex without you looking at me like I'm disgusting and undeserving of someone's company."

"That's not it at all." Guilt hardened his stomach. "No one is good enough for you."

Ricky's Adam's apple bobbed, and he clutched his nape, glowering at the floor between them. "Right." He let out a hollow laugh and pivoted toward the en suite. "Now you're just being a dick."

"It's the truth." He followed Ricky into the bathroom, simmering with irritation. "As if you don't know the effect you have on people. Women flock to you, with your ridiculously ripped physique and suave smile."

The broad muscles of Ricky's back went rigid as he turned on the water in the shower.

"You're fun to be around. Smart and easygoing." *And painfully good-looking.* Martin gripped the edge of the vanity, taking in the sharp angles of Ricky's jawline. "You put so much damn heart into everything you do it makes the rest of us look bad. I don't say it enough, and God knows I'm an asshole on my best day, but I respect the hell out of you. You deserve more than a one-night stand."

Ricky grunted and slowly turned to face him. "You should've led with that."

"Probably." He rested his hands on his hips, his head down, but his eyes remained locked on Ricky's.

"I don't keep anything from you." Ricky unzipped his jeans and shoved them off. "Ask me again." He reached into the shower stall and adjusted the water temperature. "Ask me where I went tonight."

Steam curled around them, saturating the air and making it difficult to breathe.

The question sat on Martin's tongue, trapped behind teeth and dread.

"Ask me who I was with." Ricky pushed off his briefs and leaned toward him, all nude flesh and chiseled muscle.

No tan lines. Not on Ricardo Saldivar. The gorgeous bastard had been born with skin the color of sand on a beach after it rained.

And some stranger's hands had explored every inch of that flawless landscape tonight.

"Who was she?" He tried to cover the rasp in his voice with a jovial remark. "I bet she was hot."

"He. Not she."

Shards of ice hit his gut, and his nostrils widened with a harsh inhale. He felt like he was going to puke. Or break something.

"Why do you look so fucking repulsed whenever I tell you I was with a man?" Ricky narrowed his eyes. "You think I should only date women?"

"Yes."

"Jesus fucking Christ." Ricky glared at him, utterly unabashed about having this conversation in the nude. "Are you really that homophobic?"

He gestured at the shower. "You're wasting hot water."

"Don't give a fuck. Talk to me."

"What do you want me to say?" His pulse hammered in his throat.

"I have sex with men. Tell me why that bothers you."

He leaned his hip against the vanity for support and constructed a truthful response, without revealing the whole truth. "If you fall in love with a woman, you'll still need someone to shoot hoops, talk about sports cars, and drink beer with. There's a place for your best friend in that equation."

"Sexist much? Women can do all those things."

"Not *your* type. You like your women feminine and your men masculine."

"True."

He could give Ricky everything he ever needed — friendship, protection, loyalty, and love.

Everything except sex.

"If you get hung up on a dude..." He crossed his arms over his chest and kept his tone even. "Not sure where I fit into that. The guy in your bed would be the guy you're hanging out with. *He* would become your best friend, and I can't stomach the thought of being replaced."

"Do you know how selfish that sounds? What about my happiness?"

"Fuck your happiness." He exhaled a grunt. "Because you know what? Yeah, I *am* selfish. I don't want to lose you, and what kind of friend would I be if I didn't fight to keep you in my life?"

"Okay, well... First off, I'm not falling in love with anyone." Ricky cocked his head. "And do you really believe I would let a lover — man or woman — wreck our friendship? Your reasoning is ludicrous."

Didn't matter if it made sense or not. He felt threatened by every man Ricky hooked up with. Not just threatened. He felt *murderous.*

"Your best friend is bisexual." Ricky's voice cut like a knife, sharp and penetrating. "Don't ask me to be something I'm not."

"I would never... *Fuck.* You're right." He drew in a slow breath and dragged a hand down his face. "I'm such a prick."

"A possessive prick. Could be worse."

"Whatever. I was out of line, and I'm sorry." He turned to leave. "I'll get out of here so you can shower."

"Tell me about your first night with Van. How did you meet him?"

"What?" His breath left him as he glanced back and met Ricky's eyes.

"How were you captured?"

Shame dug in its claws. "It's in the past. Talking about it changes nothing."

"Why is it such a huge secret?"

"Why are you so hellbent on making it one?"

"Forget it." With a scowl, Ricky spun toward the shower.

His back rippled with muscle and strength, tapering into a trim waist and tight ass encased in tanned skin and...

All the air vacated the room.

"What is *that*?" He lurched forward and gripped Ricky's arm, his gaze sweeping over dozens of red welts. "Who the fuck hit you?"

"I asked for it." Ricky yanked his arm free and set his jaw.

"Who?"

"Calm down. You know I like it rough and—"

"Give me a goddamn name!" he roared.

"Van Quiso."

He stopped breathing. "What did you say?"

"You heard me just fine."

"How did he—?" His heart rate careened into the red zone. "Did he force you? I'm going to kill him. I'm going to fucking—"

"I went to him, Martin. Willingly. I drove to his cabin and told him to hurt me."

His arm moved on its own, catching Ricky around the throat and shoving him against the wall.

"The man who held you captive? The motherfucker who tortured all of us? You gave him permission to *hurt* you?" He seethed, pushing Ricky harder against the tiles. "What the fuck is wrong with you?"

"I'm not afraid of Van."

"Did he fuck you?"

"Does it matter?"

"Answer me!" He shoved Ricky higher up the wall by the throat, putting them face to face, chest to chest, hip to hip. "Did. He. Fuck you?"

"No." Ricky pulled at the fist around his neck. "He's married, remember?"

Relief spread through him, magnified by the proximity of Ricky's six-foot-two brawny frame. The shared heat of skin and sinew evoked sensations—tightening, pulsing electricity—that should've felt awkward, not pleasant.

They'd touched so many times his body craved every fist bump, one-armed hug, wrestling scrimmage, and brotherly pat. But never this. He should've cringed away from such close, intimate contact with his best friend.

Yet he didn't.

Hypnotized by the energy in the air, he held Ricky to him. Foreheads drifted together. Breaths mingled. Tension stretched, waiting for that one twitch or sound that would break the trance and snap them apart.

Ricky's dark brown eyes searched his face as if trying to understand what was happening.

Christ, he didn't know. He didn't know what he was doing or thinking. Instinct had put him in this position. The instinct to keep Ricky away from anyone who might take him. The impulse to possess, control, and protect so that no one could ever hurt him.

"Martin." The hungry glare in Ricky's eyes stole his breath. "Either kiss me or let me go."

He yanked his hand from Ricky's throat and staggered backward, reaching blindly for the exit behind him.

"This conversation isn't finished." Ricky stepped into the shower, his gaze stony. "I'll be out in a minute."

With a nod, he strode out of the bathroom and sat on the edge of his mattress.

The spaciousness of the master suite comfortably accommodated two large beds and a sitting area. The need for privacy had never been an issue between Ricky and him. They didn't bring strangers home. No regular lovers or friends with benefits.

None of his roommates were in relationships. Most of them sought out one-night stands. One of them didn't have sex at all.

He shared the latter category with Kate, even though his roommates thought he was a manwhore. He let them believe the lie because the truth was too painful to explain.

Ricky slept around the most and would jump at the chance to fuck him if he so much as crooked a finger. Ricky's interest in him wasn't a secret, but they didn't let it complicate their friendship.

Their bond transcended sexual urges and uncomfortable moments in the bathroom.

Bracing his elbows on his knees, he waited as Ricky finished showering and dressing in the closet. A few minutes later, his best friend joined him on the bed, perching beside him in the same elbows-on-knees pose.

"Tell me what happened tonight." He studied Ricky out of the corner of his eye. "Start at the beginning."

As Ricky talked, it was hard to hear the details. The phone call to Van, the table in the woods, the leather belt, the stimulation of hands and fingers, and the ultimate orgasm... He despised every provocative word, every hitch in his friend's breath, and every jealous reflex that clamped his own airway.

Why was he jealous? Because Van Quiso could give Ricky what he couldn't? His reaction was unreasonable.

"So you'll go to him again?" he asked quietly. "Make it a regular thing?"

"No. I don't regret it, but it's not what I need."

He didn't expect that and couldn't stop the relief from sighing past his lips. "What do you need?"

"Still trying to figure that out. What about you?"

He grunted. "You know my situation. I can't live like this forever."

Ricky was the only one who knew he hadn't had sex since his

captivity with Van. No matter how many times Ricky pressed for an explanation, Martin refused to burden his friend with the horrors of his past.

"You've been celibate for five years." Ricky gave him a sober smile. "What's another five or ten years?"

"Wow. No jokes about you curing my problem?"

"The offer's always there." The words scraped from Ricky's voice. "Wanna talk about it?"

"Nah. Nothing's changed."

Amnesia would cure him. Until then, the thought of sex would continue to turn his stomach with haunting memories.

"What are we going to do?" he asked rhetorically, not expecting an answer.

"We're going to focus on ridding the world of predators." Ricky rose to his feet, his eyes on the door and head tilted as if straining to hear Camila's muffled voice. "Is she still arguing with Tate about his search for her sister?"

"They moved on to arguing about the trafficking ring." He stood and headed in that direction. "Let's go see if they've made progress."

Ricky followed him out, down the hall, and into Tate's bedroom.

"*Hola.*" Camila paced around piles of dirty laundry on the floor, her black hair swinging around her arms where they folded across her chest.

"Hey." Ricky sprawled beside Tate on the bed and propped his head on his hand. "What's on the agenda for tomorrow?"

"Tomorrow," Camila said, "we start trailing Larry McGregor."

"The mailman." Stepping to the desk, Martin traced a finger along the link chart they'd built on a bulletin board that took up the entire wall.

The chart showed people, locations, jobs, crimes, cars, and so on, each one connected by crisscrossing lengths of colored string. Different colors represented different links—family, friend, colleague—between the suspects.

"We're pretty sure the mailman moonlights as a slave trader for this piece of shit." Camila tapped a picture of an average-looking, middle-aged white man. "And he's not even a big player in the operation."

He trailed his gaze along the strings, following each connection until he landed on the man in charge of it all. "All roads lead to Hector La Rocha."

"The notorious leader of La Rocha Cartel," Camila breathed behind him. "God, Martin. He's responsible for thousands of missing women and children. All abducted and sold into slavery."

"If he's our ultimate target—"

"We can't focus on him right now." She waved a hand over the bulletin board. "We need to pick off the little guys, learn what we can from them—"

"Or we can just cut off the head of the beast and bring down the whole thing." Martin flexed his hands and shifted to face the group, expecting the same murderous spirit.

Instead, Tate heaved a sigh and tossed his phone on the bed. "There's seven of us. What are we going to do? Run into the cartel's city with our little guns and kill his army of thousands?"

"I'll go in." He rubbed his head, thinking through the risks. "Undercover, I can gather intel and scope out the operation."

"And she'll be right there with you." Tate jabbed a finger in Camila's direction. "I can't stop you from risking your life, but I won't let her—"

"You're not my boss, *chingado*." She thrust up her chin, her dark eyes glinting with attitude. "If I want to go—"

"The answer is no." Tate shot her an unwavering glare before setting his gaze on Martin. "We'll work our way up to Hector La Rocha. Right now, we don't even know how to locate him."

Martin shifted back to the link chart, his stomach sinking at the thought of how many children would be lost before they finished this. "It'll take years."

"I know that look in your eye." Ricky appeared at his side, arms crossed, and his gaze on Hector La Rocha's picture. "You'll get him. But you won't be doing it without me."

"Deal."

SIX

Jaulaso Prison
Two years ago

For the next three days, Tula kept her head down and her presence aloof. She trusted no one, evaded everyone, and felt… Her feelings didn't matter, as long as they stayed buried deep beneath her bones.

She dedicated every breath to surviving, proving her innocence, and escaping this nightmare.

The phone became her lifeline, and she used it to make some difficult calls to her landlord, her boss, and countless lawyers.

The principal at her school promised her job would be waiting when classes resumed, *if* she proved her innocence and returned to Phoenix in time. She found an attorney willing to take her case, but she couldn't afford his fees *and* her monthly bills.

She had to let go of her apartment. It hurt like a bitch, but what choice did she have?

The landlord agreed to sell her belongings and use the money as payment for what she owed. Whatever she had left would go toward legal fees.

Tracking down her missing Jeep was a lost cause. Not that it was worth much.

After paying the lawyer's retainer fee, she was broke. That wasn't even the worst of it.

Vera's phone had been shut off, the number no longer in use. There was no way to contact her sister. No way to leave a message explaining her incarceration or how to reach her.

When she made the call to file a missing person's report with the Ciudad Hueca police department, there was nothing left inside her.

The impatient detective on the other end of the phone made no promises to find Vera and no guarantees to call if her sister turned up, dead or alive.

It was up to her to stay on top of it, and she would.

Area Three was the quietest between the hours of three and four in the morning. That was when she showered.

She crept through the halls, stepping around inmates who had passed out after a night of drinking. In the community bathroom, she quickly stripped and washed in private.

She ate just enough to keep her body alive and spent the daylight hours studying her fellow residents. She lingered along the perimeter, trying to make herself unnoticeable while memorizing faces and eavesdropping on conversations.

Whenever someone approached her, she walked in the other direction. For the most part, the prisoners left her alone.

Except Garra.

He didn't touch her, didn't stare at her suggestively, and never mentioned his threat about collecting rent next week. But he was always nearby, following her around and talking in her ear.

"The law is here, protected by a wall." He gestured at the two-story concrete enclosure surrounding the outdoor pound. "We are the law, not the government."

She never spoke to him, but she always listened, committing every word to memory. He seemed to know everything about everyone, including her. He knew her name, where she lived, and what she'd been charged with.

There was no telling what else he'd gleaned about her. Did he know she'd been wrongfully imprisoned? Or that she was born and raised in this city? Or that her sister was missing and possibly connected to La Rocha Cartel?

Asking him questions would require her to be civil with him. Being civil meant accepting what he'd done to her.

She couldn't stomach the sight of him, and she sure as hell wouldn't depend on him for answers.

He crouched beside her where she sat on a cement bench. She didn't look at him, didn't react to his nearness, no matter how badly she wanted to cut off his dick.

"That one is no good." He nodded at the men playing chess at a table on the far side of the yard. "The one with the barbed wire tattoo on his forehead. He's a serial rapist with unconfirmed connections to over fifty missing women. Keep your distance."

It wasn't the first time he told her who she could trust and who she shouldn't. Fucking ironic, coming from him.

What was he in prison for anyway? Drugs? Murder? Rape was the obvious answer.

As a resident of Area Three, he was also a member of the vicious La Rocha Cartel. Though, not everyone in here was on the same side.

During one of his one-sided conversations with her, she learned Jaulaso was run by La Rocha Cartel, the González Cartel, and three gangs. They all lived here, cohabiting in their numbered areas, all the while fighting over control of the prison.

It seemed peaceful now, with men standing around, sharing cigarettes, lifting weights, playing cards, and listening to music. But Garra said it could change in a heartbeat.

There were no police, military, or prison guards inside Area Three. Garra claimed everyone needed a gun here because at any moment, hell could break loose.

Two nights later, it did.

She woke to the sound of gunshots reverberating in her chest. The bursts boomed outside her cell, too loud, too goddamn close. Her blood ran cold.

She leaped out of bed as the frantic din of footsteps and shouting erupted in the hall. Bullets pinged against her door, knocking dust loose from the cracks in the ceiling.

The pauses between each gunshot grew shorter and less frequent, until all she heard was the constant report of full-blown magazines being emptied.

What the hell was going on? Why were they shooting at one another? Was this one of the cartel wars Garra had warned about?

The clothes on her body—jeans and a shirt—were all she had to her name. Everyone in here owned a gun except her. Not that she wanted one. But dammit, she might've felt brave enough to peek her head out if she had a weapon in her hands.

A moment later, the door to her cell swung open.

"We're going to have a riot." Garra leaned in, captured her eyes, and returned his gaze to the sights on his rifle, which he aimed into the hall. "The González Cartel is trying to take control of Area Three."

A riot? Images of fires, hostages, breakouts, and bloodshed caved in her chest. Without the aid of prison security, who would contain it?

The mayhem of stomping boots and gunfire grew closer. Her pulse exploded, and her hands slicked with sweat as she hunkered down and covered her head.

They could kill one another for all she cared, as long as she didn't get hit in the crossfire. This wasn't her fight.

"It's safer upstairs," Garra said calmly and fired off a few rounds down the corridor. "Go!"

Then he was gone.

She clenched her fists. He wanted her to go out there without a gun? Shots were firing from every direction. Why couldn't she just stay here?

Fear trembled through her as she inched toward the open door. A peek into the hallway gave her a view of the stairwell thirty feet away. Beyond that, crowds of inmates ran left and right, plowing one another down.

Some faces she recognized. Others she didn't.

The unfamiliar men swept along the corridor, spraying bullets into every cell they passed. It wouldn't take them long to reach hers.

Paralyzed by panic, she ducked back into her cell. Adrenaline coursed through her system. She couldn't catch her breath.

The attacking cartel would consider her an enemy merely because she was in Area Three. She was a sitting duck.

Dropping to her hands and knees, she poked her head into the hall, waited for a clear break, and scrambled for the stairwell.

Bullets whizzed by overhead, and one tore a hole in the wall right beside her. A scream escaped her throat, and she might've peed a little. She couldn't feel her body amid the violent pounding of fear.

She bustled across the floor, crawling, sliding, falling, and dragging her legs. Her lungs heaved a frantic pace, chopping her breaths and burning her chest.

Almost there. Almost there.

With a knee-grinding lunge, she flung herself through the gap in the open doorway of the stairwell. Her elbows banged against concrete, and her head hit the wall. But she made it.

"Fuck." She released a heavy exhale and flew to her feet, pivoting to race up the stairs.

Gunshots rang out overhead. Multiple shooters. Angry shouting. A firefight waged right above her.

Her stomach flipped inside out.

Goddamn Garra! She couldn't go up there, and she couldn't risk running back to her cell.

Fucking fuck, fuck!

She spun in a circle, jumping at the deafening pops of guns. Shooters were in the stairwell, in the corridor, and she was caught in the middle.

"What are you doing?"

She whirled toward the deep voice in the hall.

Across from her, the door to a cell stood open. An older man with silver-black hair leaned a shoulder against the door jamb, arms hanging at his sides, his expression as calm as could be.

"I...I don't know." She'd seen him a few times in the common area but hadn't learned his name.

"Do you know how to use a gun?"

No. She nodded jerkily.

He removed a pistol from his waistband and tossed it across the hall to her. "The safety's off."

She palmed the heavy weight of metal, turning it over in her shaking hands.

The sound of his door jerked her head up.

He'd returned to his room. *Shit.* She should've told him the attackers were shooting into all the cells.

The stampede of boots broke out in the corridor, stomping in her direction. The report of gunfire on the stairs above her resounded in her ears. At any moment, she was going to get shot.

But she had a gun.

Clutching the grip in both fists, she hunkered low to the floor between the corridor and the stairs and tried not to throw up.

Her nerves wound so tightly the pistol rattled in her sweaty hands. She'd never even practiced on a paper target. How would she shoot a moving person? She didn't have the guts or the skill.

Except she'd strangled a man with his own belt.

Surely, a bullet would be easier. Quicker.

The thought steeled her spine as an army of González members ran past the stairwell.

She backed into a shadowed corner, out of view, and held her breath.

Some of the footsteps slowed at the doorway, but the sound of gunfire upstairs sent them continuing down the hall.

All but one.

A young, lanky guy with a rifle stopped at the door to the old man's cell and tried the handle. It didn't open.

Her pulse rushed in her ears.

The armed man stepped back, trained his rifle on the door handle, and fired.

The bang stopped her heart and echoed in her eardrums so loudly and painfully she wondered if they'd ruptured.

Ten feet from her hiding spot, the shooter raised his gun to fire into the now open doorway of the cell. He intended to kill the old man.

What if the old man had given her his only weapon? She couldn't just stand here with his gun and let him die.

Three running steps brought her into the hall. The shooter swung his gaze over his shoulder and met her eyes. His mouth opened, but she was already squeezing the trigger.

The explosive bang kicked her arms back and jarred her insides. But the bullet aimed true, hitting her target in the back, dead center.

He dropped to the floor.

The gun blast echoed in her head, her hearing momentarily lost as she stared at the unmoving body.

She'd taken another life.

Guilt tried to work its way in, but her relief was too big. All around her, the sounds of gunfire had fallen silent. She was still alive.

So was the old man.

He stood in the doorway of his cell, his expression etched in surprise and gratitude.

Would he want his pistol back? She tightened her grip on it, unwilling to surrender the only thing in this place that made her feel safe.

"It's yours." He thrust his chin at the gun and gave her the first warm smile she'd seen in days.

"Thank you."

With a nod, he retreated into the darkness of his cell.

"It's safe now," someone shouted from down the hall. "You can come out!"

Bodies were pulled away. Furniture was straightened, and stashes of alcohol emerged out of nowhere.

While she was the only female inmate in Area Three, there was no shortage of women. Prostitutes came and went at all hours. Especially tonight. They filed in by the dozens, and with them came the sharp scent of weed.

Music blared. Cocaine covered the tables, and the aroma of grilled food permeated the air.

An hour after the riot ended, an enormous party swung into full force.

She stood in a quiet, shadowed alcove off the main common area, taking it all in with disbelief.

These men narrowly survived a bloodbath with a rival cartel. They lost fellow inmates. People fucking died. Yet here they were, laughing, banging hookers, and getting high.

A familiar presence moved into her space, darkening her corner. She ground her teeth.

"You survived your first riot. Well done." Garra leaned a shoulder against the wall beside her. "The boss wants to see you."

Boss? She scanned the crowd of drunk criminals. A leader lived among these assholes? Who?

"How long is this silent treatment going to last?" Garra tapped his fingers on the wall above her head. "It was just sex. Nothing personal."

Her hand moved to the pistol in her waistband, her fingers itching to blow a hole in his stupid face. But if she killed him, every man in this room would fire a bullet in her direction.

He shook his head, scrutinizing her. "You have no idea who runs this operation, do you?"

Evidently, she was about to meet him, and the prospect chilled her to the bone.

She'd listened to enough conversations over the past few days to know what made people nervous around here.

They didn't trust newcomers. Convicts often paid their way into different areas of Jaulaso to gather information and keep tabs on enemies.

What if the boss thought she was a spy from another gang? Would he confiscate her gun? What if he didn't want her here and kicked her out?

"Come on." Garra strode in the direction of her cellblock.

She followed on shaky legs as he led her away from the party and crowds. He entered the corridor where she slept, and her steps slowed with shock.

"Here we are." He stopped at the old man's cell.

Confusion pulled her mouth into a gaping frown.

The door had already been replaced with a new handle and lock. Well, not *new*. It looked as though the parts had been taken from someone else's cell.

He inclined his head. "This is the private quarters of Hector La Rocha."

Her breath caught in her chest. She couldn't have heard him correctly.

"I see you know his name." He narrowed his eyes. "Do you know he has absolute control of the prison and the city?"

That nice old man? The one who had given her the gun? *He* was Hector La Rocha? How was that possible?

His name alone struck fear in the hearts of every man, woman, and child in Mexico. With an army that outmatched the Mexican military, he was responsible for thousands of deaths every year.

How did he maintain such an atrocious reputation from prison? And why didn't she know he'd been incarcerated?

Oh, God. Even if he didn't expel her from Area Three, how would she sleep at night knowing his cell was only thirty feet from hers?

"Don't be afraid." Garra tsked. "You are here because he allows it. He wants to get to know you."

Why? She wanted to ask, but her lips were frozen in terror.

Garra knocked, and a muscular man with a mean scowl opened

the door. Intimation deepened the shadows on his face and oozed enough menace to make her heart rate explode.

Was *he* the cartel boss?

With a grunt, he turned and lumbered into a room that was four times the size of her cell.

She stepped forward, and Garra closed the door behind her, shutting himself out.

Her feet carried her into the dark quarters, her senses shuddering at the overwhelming scent of spicy food and cigarette smoke.

Some of the interior concrete walls must've been removed to expand the space, though she couldn't imagine how it would've been done.

The first ten-foot section was arranged like a dining room. At the center, the old man sat at a small table, surrounded by platters of steaming burritos, *carne asada*, and rice.

Random pieces of furniture encircled the space. Wooden bookcases, filing cabinets, and antique chairs — the furnishings were nicer than anything she'd seen in Jaulaso.

Stockpiles of guns and ammunition filled what would've been a neighboring cell. Beyond that, a heavy drape hung from the ceiling. The edge of a bed peeked out from behind it.

The scowling wall of muscle returned to the door and stood with his back to it and his arms crossed.

Was he a guard?

"Don't mind Luis." The older gentleman wiped his mouth with a linen napkin, his Spanish thick and hypnotic. "He's my security."

Where had Luis been during the riot? Had he been in here the entire time? Or out there killing people? Maybe she didn't want to know.

"Okay." Her hands trembled at her sides. "I...um... My name is—
"

"Petula Gomez." The syllables rolled off his tongue with old-world eloquence.

He knew her name.

The most feared man in Mexico knew who she was.

Her pulse quivered as reality crashed in.

She was talking to Hector La Rocha, standing three feet away from him, in the room where he slept. Sweet merciful hell, her mother must've been rolling in her grave.

"What do I call you?" Her voice sounded stronger than she felt.

"Call me Hector." A smile touched his gentle eyes. "Please..." He gestured at the seat across from him. "Sit. Eat with me."

Her stomach bucked with nausea. If she ate, it would all come back up.

"I'm sorry. I... I wasn't prepared for this." She rubbed a clammy palm on her jeans and lowered into the chair. "I didn't know you were here. *In prison.*"

"Very good." He lit a cigarette, watching her through a curl of smoke. "I pay a lot of money to a lot of people to keep my location a secret."

Made sense. It would be easy for his enemies to send assassins into Jaulaso. Hector could only run as far as the prison walls.

She stared at his cigarette with longing. She hadn't smoked since college, but the urge crept up sometimes.

It would calm her nerves, maybe make her look tougher than a high school Spanish teacher.

He tracked her gaze and held out a pack of smokes. "Go ahead."

She couldn't hide the tremors in her hands as she lit one. Somehow, she managed not to cough through the first drag.

Silence stretched between them, and he didn't seem to mind. There was no expectation in his warm brown eyes. No judgment in his relaxed posture.

He was nothing like she'd imagined.

The stories she'd heard growing up had painted him as a raping, murdering, blood-thirsty tyrant. Maybe that was true when he was younger. But now? All she saw was a soft-spoken, unassuming gentleman in his sixties.

Silver streaked a full head of black hair, and the few wrinkles fanning from his dark eyes made him look mature and distinguished. Modestly dressed with a lean physique, he was too debonair to be a cartel leader. Too pleasant and fragile looking to fit in with the uneducated, vulgar gangsters who roamed the halls of Area Three.

His cream-colored shirt buttoned neatly over his narrow chest with the collar undone. No flashy necklaces or rings. Nice teeth. Clean hair. Smoothly shaved jawline. He took care of his appearance without coming across as pretentious.

He didn't radiate cruelty like his guard at the door, and there wasn't a trace of sexual interest in his gaze.

So why was she here? Maybe it was a test, one that would cast her out of Area Three if she failed.

But if she were allowed to stay, Garra would attempt to collect rent. She meant what she'd said. If he touched her again, she would kill him.

She desperately needed to belong to a structure that would keep her safe. To survive, she needed to be part of a group, a circle of trust that would support her when she defended herself and protect her when she couldn't.

If Hector La Rocha truly owned Jaulaso, she needed him on her side.

Scanning his belongings, she searched for something that might help her connect with him and wriggle into his good graces.

An old record player sat in the corner next to a stack of vinyl records. Old-fashioned paintings colored the walls in Mexican landscapes. Handwoven rugs brightened the floor, and countless books lined the shelves. Books with Spanish titles about politics, war, technology, and religion.

If he actually read those texts, he was an intellectual. Probably the only person in Jaulaso she could engage in deep conversation. The cleanliness of his private quarters suggested a tidy mind. If nothing else, perhaps she could offer him some mental stimulation.

"How long have you been here?" She took a long drag on the cigarette, savoring the lightheaded calm of nicotine.

"I've served eight years of a life sentence."

"Oh."

"You should eat."

"Thank you. I wish I could. Everything looks so delicious, but my stomach doesn't feel well."

He nodded, and his silver brows knitted together. "I didn't have this as a child." He waved a hand over the aromatic platters of food. "Sometimes, we didn't have anything to eat at all."

"Makes you appreciate it." She crushed out the cigarette. "So much more than someone who has never felt hunger pangs."

"You know this from experience?" He tipped his head, his expression attentive and thoughtful.

"Sure." She lifted a shoulder. "I was raised by a single mother in the throat of Ciudad Hueca. She did her best to provide for us. Some years were better than others."

"The struggle made you stronger." His eyes locked on hers, and a slow stream of smoke trickled from his nose. "You saved my life."

"I don't know about that." She glanced at the cases of guns and ammunition. "You have an arsenal in here."

"Yet I didn't need it."

He watched her with an indiscernible emotion pressed between his lips. Tenderness softened the creases around his eyes. Admiration, even. It made her feel warm and uncomfortable at the same time.

She returned her attention to the bookcases, skipping over manuals, textbooks, and heavy tomes. "You're interested in learning."

"A man is only as great as his knowledge."

As an educator, she appreciated that sentiment.

Her gaze snagged on a beginner's book of English grammar. "You speak English?"

"I trying learning," he said clumsily in English. "Speak little."

There it was. The connection she needed. Her *in*.

She lifted her eyes to his and took a leap. "I'm a teacher."

His face held no reaction.

She didn't want to offend him, but she had to go for it. A chance to win his trust.

"I teach Spanish in the States. I know it's not the same thing, but maybe I could teach you English, if you want to learn."

His nostrils widened with a deep inhale, his expression unreadable.

Crap. Her hands clenched on her lap. "I didn't mean to presume—"

"Yes. You will teach me to speak, read, and write English like a gringo." A smile broke across his face. "You will work for me."

Her relief lasted a fraction of a second before panic swept in.

Work for Hector La Rocha? What had she done?

Once a cartel member, always a cartel member.

But there was no turning back from this. Refusing him would be a death sentence.

Was she in a position to bargain? Probably not, but she had nothing to lose. "Does Garra work for you?"

"Yes."

"I'll teach you, but I ask one thing in return."

"Anything." He stretched out his arms, indicating all his possessions.

"Castrate him." She sat taller. "Remove Garra's manhood."

Silence. Stunned, agonizing silence. He let it build for so long she couldn't feel anything but the ice forming on her spine.

Then his hand slammed onto the table. She jumped a foot off the chair as he burst into laughter.

"Oh, you are a delightful surprise!" He slapped the table again, rattling the dishes.

"You'll do it?"

He blew out his cheeks with a heavy sigh. "Castration is too messy."

"Your reputation suggests otherwise."

"You think so?" He rested his forearms on the table and leaned forward, his eyes hard and unblinking.

"I know so." She stared back with a knot in her throat.

"Luis." He didn't take his gaze off her. "Send in Garra."

Within seconds, the man she hated most in the world stood at attention before Hector.

Nervous energy skittered through the room as Hector puffed on his cigarette. Was he going to do it? Cut off Garra's balls right here in front of her? Or was the whole conversation just a way to fuck with her? Give her some hope, let her relax a little, then cut her throat?

She stopped breathing.

"There's been a change in the ranks." Hector exhaled a cloud of smoke, his gaze on Garra. "Petula works directly for me, and you now work for her."

Her heart stammered.

"Yes, boss." Garra's voice didn't carry a hint of surprise, but the flex of his hand affirmed his displeasure.

"She pays rent to me," Hector said. "You will not touch her or anyone else unless she allows it. No sex, starting now. You will be celibate like a eunuch, yes?"

"Understood." A muscle feathered across Garra's whiskered cheek.

This wasn't castration, but it was emasculating, nonetheless.

She might've sagged with happiness if her insides weren't gurgling with foreboding.

Hector had given her what she'd asked for, but in return, she would be indebted to the notorious leader indefinitely.

"If you want to fuck a woman, you must have Petula's permission." Hector reclined in the chair, his tone chillingly calm. "She is your number one priority. Whatever she needs, you will provide it. If she's in danger, you will protect her with your life."

She couldn't believe what she was hearing. Hector wasn't just removing Garra's manhood. He was demoting the man, binding him into service to her.

A personal security guard would give her more protection than the gun in her waistband or a lock on her door. But tethering Garra to her side was the last thing she wanted.

"It will be my honor." Garra clasped his hands behind him and shifted to face her. "I'm at your service, Petula."

His eyes connected with hers, and in that look, she glimpsed his contempt. It was there and gone in a blink, leaving behind an empty expression.

Hector's command was law. Didn't matter if they liked it. Neither of them could refuse, and they both knew it.

"We will begin English lessons at sunrise tomorrow." Hector struck a match and lit another cigarette. "You may go."

Garra followed her into the hall and along the thirty-foot walk to her cell. At the doorway, she turned toward him.

His face contorted, a furious scowl twisting at the center.

"Could've been worse." She rested her hands on her hips. "I told him to castrate you."

A seething breath slipped past his clamped teeth, and he tried to rein it in.

With a forefinger and thumb, he pinched the bridge between his eyes and dragged in a string of deep inhales. Each one grew slower, calmer, until his shoulders relaxed.

Then he lowered his hand and met her gaze.

A thousand words clashed between them, none of them voiced. In that defining moment of silence, he accepted his role as her guard, and she came to terms with her new reality.

She'd joined the most ruthless cartel in Mexico.

The very cartel her mother warned her against her entire life.

She'd passed the point of no return.

PART TWO

SEVEN

Jaulaso Prison
Present Day

The fun-size package of sex in tight jeans stole glances at Martin from beneath her dark lashes. He didn't have to look at the Latina beauty to feel the caress of her exotic eyes along his skin. But goddamn, did he look. He couldn't stop.

She sat at a table on the far side of the common area, bent over an open book. Each time her gaze lifted, he openly stared back, savoring the view.

Monochromatic tattoos sleeved her arms in a blend of illustrations too detailed to make out at this distance. Perky tits formed an enticing valley in the *V*-neck of her shirt. Full lips begged to be kissed, no matter how hard she pressed them together.

Large brown eyes perused him up and down, taking his measure, weighing his worth. With each pass, her expression softened as if, in her attempt to analyze him, she'd inadvertently let her guard slip.

After a moment, she looked away. Whatever she decided about him made her pull in a breath. Her chest rose with the inhale, squeezing her perfect rack in the confines of her shirt.

Fuck, his dick.

For the past seven years, the thought of having sex again had tortured him into a celibate existence. But after two days in Area Three, watching this alluring woman react to him, he couldn't control the swelling torment between his legs.

He wasn't prepared.

Not for her.

He and Ricky had trained nonstop for months, focusing on combat, weaponry, and cartel politics. In addition to their daily workouts, they spent a good part of the year perfecting their Spanish.

Going into this assignment, they knew the score.

Coke, marijuana, meth... Name the drug. It was here. Prison guards didn't enter this nasty, dark corner of hell, where inmates carried high-powered submachine guns.

Drug dealers with Uzis.

And they were all at war with one another. If a *vato* so much as looked at someone wrong, he was dead.

He and Ricky had three months to complete the mission while living among the worst of the most violent, crazy, and disturbed men on the planet.

According to their intel, there weren't supposed to be female prisoners in Area Three. And certainly not one as hot as Petula Gomez.

"Stop staring, dipshit," Ricky whispered behind the loose curl of his hand.

"Only reason you're not is because your back is to her."

Being bilingual proved exceedingly useful. Since no one in here seemed to know English, he and Ricky used it in their private conversations.

"How did we not know she existed?" Ricky tossed two cards onto the table between them, maintaining the ruse of playing poker.

Matias Restrepo had been their primary resource for information. As the capo of the biggest cartel in Colombia, he kept tabs on all his rivals. When he married Camila earlier this year, her vigilante group of freedom fighters had gained a powerful ally.

Without Matias, they would've never located Hector La Rocha.

Their target.

Matias and Camila had arranged the arrest that planted Martin and Ricky in Jaulaso. Before they were detained, Matias had given them a few instructions.

Pay a prison guard to move you to a nicer area.

Request Area Three.

Try not to get shot or raped in the process.

Never wander off alone.

So far, so good.

In three months, their bogus drug trafficking charges would be dropped. Whatever deal Matias and Camila had negotiated with the Mexican government guaranteed their release from Jaulaso.

They had three months to steal as much information as possible.

Vital information, like the location of the *comandante* who runs the cartel's multinational sex trafficking operation.

That intel would be handed over to the Mexican government and used to put Hector La Rocha out of business.

Martin would give his left nut to kill the crime boss himself. Not an easy feat, considering Hector was surrounded by hundreds of La Rocha members in Jaulaso. Attacking their leader would be a suicide mission.

Not only that, a dead cartel leader would only give rise to a new one. All the heads needed to be removed, and that required cunning.

Penetrating Hector's inner circle was the first step. Martin had a sinking feeling that circle included the female inmate they knew nothing about.

"She's a deviation." Ricky kept his whisper beneath the din of chatter around them. "Deviations from the pattern are never good."

Through extensive profiling prior to the mission, they'd compiled a list of every officer in La Rocha Cartel. All of them were men.

How did no one outside these walls know about her? Who was she?

Rumors on the inside were rampant, leaking from every mouth in Area Three. In the two days he'd been here, he'd heard she could outmatch any inmate in a knife fight, drink the biggest man under the table, and knew every closely guarded secret in La Rocha Cartel.

Some said she strangled a man with her bare hands on her first night in Jaulaso. Others claimed she'd saved Hector La Rocha's life during a prison riot.

The stories were too outlandish to be true. She carried a weapon on her person at all times, but that didn't mean she had the strength to take down a two-hundred-pound convict. She was just a little thing, half the size of the smallest man in here.

His skin prickled, the electric touch of her gaze making it damn difficult to sit here and ignore her. He was confrontational by nature and wanted nothing more than to charge across the room and talk to her.

That, as he'd learned on the first night, was not allowed.

When he and Ricky had entered Area Three, a man named Garra met them at the door. After Garra informed them they would be sleeping on the floor in the common area, he left them with a warning.

Any man who approaches Petula Gomez without permission is a dead man.

Two days of observation confirmed the threat carried weight.

Her fellow prisoners tracked her with hungry eyes, injected her name into conversations, and boasted about all vulgar ways they would *tear up that pussy*. But no one made a move on her.

No one approached her. No one talked to her. Every man in Area

Three gave her a wide berth.

Except her ever-present guard dog.

Rumor had it that Garra was her lover. The only one, given the possessive way he stood between her and everyone else. When he wasn't glaring, growling, and pissing a circle around her, he was poised at her side with his mouth moving at her ear.

She didn't speak, not to him or anyone, but her posture maintained an alertness that suggested nothing slipped past her notice.

"Jesus." Ricky stomped a foot on the ground and lifted it to reveal a pile of bug guts. "Is it just me or are the roaches unnaturally large here? Why are there so many? I don't even know where they're coming from."

"We've been here two days and haven't seen the boss. We have no weapons, no way to contact anyone on the outside. We're surrounded by the most brutal drug cartel in Mexico, and you're bitching about roaches?"

Their eyes met, and a rush of warmth filled his chest. Ricky's mouth curved upward, his handsome face gentling with affection before tensing again.

The impulse to rescue his best friend's smile pulled him forward.

"Remember when we first started sharing a room?" He leaned across the table, erasing the distance. "I changed our Wi-fi name to *I Can Hear You Masturbating*."

"Yeah." Ricky's hard angles softened, and he bent in, closing the last few inches. "The next morning, I changed it to *I Know*."

"It was funny at home, but not here." He trapped his grin behind a feigned glower. "Your chronic fist fucking will attract unwanted attention."

"What are you saying?" Ricky asked, playing along.

"Seeing how we're in pound-me-in-the-ass prison and sleeping out in the open…" He nodded at the corner of the common area, where they'd crashed the past two nights. "You need to cease and desist the nightly hand parties."

"A little self-gratification never hurt anyone." Ricky's mouth twitched.

"Shooting venereal excitement all over the place?" He couldn't stop his cheeks from rising. "Definitely bad for the environment."

Ricky chuckled. "I don't need your permission to beat off."

"No, but you want it."

Ricky's smile slipped.

Fuck, he shouldn't have said that. It'd been all joking fun until he inadvertently hit on the truth.

Silence crept in, and unspoken words caught and held between them. Neither of them looked away.

Throughout their seven-year friendship, he'd accepted his best friend's sexual interest in him. It was never shoved in his face, and he didn't let it make things weird.

They were too close to ever feel awkward around each other. Even now, as Ricky stared at him in a way he couldn't reciprocate — eyes hooded, pupils dilated, lips parted — he didn't resent his friend for it.

But he wouldn't send mixed signals, either.

"Ricky." He hardened his voice. "I didn't mean — "

"I know." With a forced smile, Ricky steered them back to the safety of their banter. "So no solitary sex? For three months?"

"I advise against all sex." He glanced around at the scarred, tattooed faces of Mexico's hardest criminals. "Considering your pool of potential dates."

"What about the smokin' hot chili pepper at your ten o'clock?"

His gaze shifted, instantly locking on her deep brown eyes.

She was watching his interaction with Ricky, a frown pinned on her gorgeous face and the turned page of her book forgotten in her hand.

He could've looked around the room and determined how long each man had been here by the dimness in his eyes. The light in hers hadn't completely faded, but fractures distorted the glow. Broken memories of a different life.

She bore tattoos, carried weapons, smoked cigarettes, and scowled at everyone. But beneath the tough exterior lurked an innocent sort of curiosity that didn't fit in Jaulaso.

Maybe he was wrong, but she hadn't been here very long. Not as long as most of these men.

Her attention pinged between her book and her surroundings, lingering on Ricky and him more than anyone else in the room.

"She's watching you, isn't she?" Ricky asked.

"Watching *us*." He shared a smile with his friend and returned to her.

Her brows gathered, her expression incredulous.

"She looks confused." He smiled bigger. "Like she's never seen a happy person."

"Maybe she hasn't. Certainly not in this shithole." Ricky scanned the perimeter. "Nothing but gray walls and breathing corpses."

"I wonder how long she's in for."

A lot of the prisoners came here to rot, and they carried that hopelessness in their bones.

This was the hardest assignment he and Ricky ever attempted, but it was temporary, just a job, not the end of the road for them.

"We need to talk to her." Ricky put away the playing cards. "Find out who she is."

"We don't need to do anything."

"Because she'll come to us." Ricky sat back and carved a hand through his thick black hair.

"Yeah." Holding her gaze, he gave her a wink.

Her shoulders tightened, and she shut the book. Then she pushed away from the table and strode out of the room.

Garra straightened from his post against the wall. Instead of following her, he made a beeline to their table.

"Incoming," Martin said beneath his breath.

Ricky slowly twisted in his chair, his expression hardening into granite.

He was one of the most laid-back guys Martin had ever met, but when the situation demanded it, he could switch on his primitive drive and turn into one scary motherfucker.

Garra towered over their table, dressed head-to-toe in black, resembling a forty-year-old Antonio Banderas, without the congeniality or charm.

"We're not interested," Ricky said in Spanish, exaggerating the trill of his *Rs*.

"Not interested?"

"Gold necklaces." Ricky motioned at the heavy chains draped around Garra's neck. "Are you not a jewelry salesman?"

"Stupid fucking *gabacho*."

"It's a joke, not a dick. Don't take it so hard. And for the record, calling me a *gabacho* isn't entirely accurate. I'm at least one-eighth Latino."

As if. Ricky might've been born in the U.S., but his mother was an illegal immigrant from Mexico.

With a growl, Garra turned toward Martin and leaned in, his eyes like black marbles. "I don't like the way you look at her."

"What way is that?" Martin rose to his feet, forcing the man to step back.

"You want to fuck her."

"Every man in Jaulaso wants to fuck her. Look around."

Garra didn't move his eyes. He didn't even blink.

"What I want is a meeting with her." Martin knew the answer before it punched through the air.

"No."

"Just tell me one thing." Ricky drew out a long pause, probably just to fuck with the scowling man. "I'm trying to get a jump start on my Christmas shopping and noticed she likes books. What was she reading?"

"200 Ways To Gut A White Boy."

Ol' Garra didn't miss a beat, but neither did Ricky. "If the rumors are true, she doesn't need a book to do that. I hear she's terrifying with a knife."

Ricky didn't believe the gossip any more than Martin did. He was fishing for the truth.

"If you want your balls to remain attached to your body," Garra said, "you'll heed those warnings and stay away from her."

"The depths of your concern make me feel all tingly," Ricky deadpanned.

Garra shot him a parting glare and ambled out of the room.

Martin returned to his chair and switched back to English. "Gonna go out on a limb here and say — "

"Garra has no friends?"

"He's not going to tell her we want a meeting."

"He won't have to." Ricky leaned back and laced his hands behind his head.

She'll come to us.

"So we wait." Martin rubbed the tension in his neck. "And try not to get killed."

EIGHT

A swarm of emotions chased Tula through the halls and caught up with her in her cell. The sharp burn hit her sideways, stabbing through her throat and gathering behind her eyes.

Most days squeaked by without worry or dread or the threat of tears. She'd become one of them, a member of Hector's inner circle, and with that came safety. Any harm directed at her had to go through Garra.

Two years in Area Three and she hadn't sustained so much as a scratch.

She had nothing to fear.

No, that wasn't true. She feared it would all be taken away. If something happened to Hector, she would lose his protection. She would also lose a friend.

She'd developed a close bond with him. Enjoyed his company, even. He never leered at her, touched her inappropriately, or gave her any reason to think he would hurt her.

She trusted him.

But every once in a while, a bad day sneaked in. A familiar scent or melody would spark a memory, and she would wake from the numbness, sweating and gasping for air. In those moments, the veil lifted, and old hurts came rushing back—how she'd arrived here, the decisions she'd made, and everything she'd lost.

Today was one of those days.

It was the new prisoners. They reminded her of home. Not just because she hadn't seen another American in two years. But because they were different. Smart different. Full-of-life-and-hope different.

With their drawling accents and tattoo-free skin, they looked more like the guys she used to date and less like hardened convicts.

They radiated confidence, not arrogance. Their muscled physiques promised pain if provoked, but they didn't seem like the type of men who bulked up because they had something to prove.

Christ, they were gorgeous, the blond hair and blue eyes of one contrasting with the black hair and brown eyes of the other. Together, they were an overload on the senses. Too much testosterone in one place. Too much lethal beauty.

Area Three didn't see a lot of attractive men. There was plenty of brawn pumping iron in the yard, but those honed bodies were attached to twisted expressions, vile tongues, and depraved minds.

The new guys belonged on the cover of a magazine, but that wasn't what captivated her.

It was the endearing bond between them, the way their gazes connected and held so easily. She envied that closeness. Envied how they weren't alone in this place.

Were they brothers? Best friends? They didn't touch each other with the familiarity of sexual intimacy, so probably not lovers.

Whatever their relationship, they'd arrived here together. That meant they were probably together at the time of their arrest. What crime had they committed?

The blond carried himself with a stern sort of reserve and control. The Hispanic guy was more expressive, smiling brighter and scowling darker than his friend.

They kept to themselves and navigated their new surroundings as a single unit—their *own* unit—with no clear loyalties to a race or group.

That was a problem. The white guy was too white, and his friend was too *pocho*. The fact that they weren't born and bred in Mexico was a strike against them. They made it worse by not sucking up to the shot callers.

It was only a matter of time before they got *heart checked*. The biggest predators would start circling them, sizing them up, seeing if they would fight or cower. Respect was established by being fearless.

Maybe they *were* fearless, but unless they gained four-hundred pounds of muscle, punched like Mike Tyson, and grew eyes in the backs of their heads, they might not survive the week.

Then there was Hector. The boss kept tabs on everyone, and if he suspected them of doing anything against his cartel, he would deal with them painfully and permanently.

That bothered her. For the first time in a long time, she felt something other than indifference. Part of her wanted them to make it through this, and not because they were good-looking.

Well, maybe partly because they were good-looking.

She'd spent the past couple of hours in the common area, basking in the glow on their handsome faces and pretending they weren't dangerous criminals. She wanted to sit at their table and make believe they were just a couple of cute, harmless guys in a restaurant. A real restaurant with real utensils.

They would talk about how hot the Arizona summers were, laugh about the silly things they did as kids, and end the night with a kiss that promised another date.

She missed that. Not a date with two men. That was just a fantasy.

She missed dating. And teaching high school, paying rent, grocery shopping, answering calls from her sister...

Vera.

God, she ached to hear Vera's voice.

Two years with no news, no leads, no nothing. The loss of her sister left a hurt inside her so profound and excruciating it was more than she could bear.

Anguish surged through her chest, and her eyes caught fire.

Stop it.

Gulping deep breaths, she pushed it down, shoved it away, locked it up.

No tears. It's a waste of good suffering.

It was her favorite quote from her favorite book. She glanced down at it in her hand, smoothing a palm over the hardback cover.

The Hellbound Heart.

The rare 20th Anniversary Edition had been signed by Clive Barker himself. God only knew how much it was worth.

Hector had given it to her four months after her arrest. A condolence gift, he'd called it, for the news she'd received from her attorney.

She'd been sentenced to five years for smuggling marijuana. The court made the decision without her being there because that was how the penal system in Mexico worked.

Her devastation had been inconsolable.

The attorney tried to get an *amparo,* an appeal designed to protect the rights of the accused.

It was denied.

In the weeks that followed, she'd fallen into abject despondency. She didn't leave her cell, couldn't eat, barely breathed.

She was innocent, serving a sentence for a crime she didn't commit. She was stuck in a cold, dark place of uncertainty and violence with five years on her shoulders.

Then Hector showed up with the book.

Before Jaulaso, she'd never read the literary draft of her favorite

Hellraiser movie. But there it was, a signed copy in his outstretched hand.

More books followed. He filled her cell with novels of all her treasured horror movies. In return, she made a full commitment to the structure of the cartel.

Teaching him English had been her first job, but it wasn't the last.

Three years from now, she would be released from prison. But she would never be released from Hector La Rocha.

She could blame him for trapping her, for manipulating her into a life of crime. She could hate him with every fiber of her being. But it wasn't his fault.

The military put her in Jaulaso. They turned an innocent schoolteacher into a criminal cartel member.

There would be no going back to Arizona or her high school teaching job or the American citizenship she'd worked so hard to obtain. She was in too deep.

A tear slipped from her eye, and she swatted it away.

Crying about it didn't change a damn thing.

And no more fantasizing about the new guys. If there was any goodness inside them, this place would beat it out. Only the meanest, ugliest souls survived Jaulaso.

There was a reason she kept her distance. No investments. No attachments. No losses.

Footsteps sounded in the hall, and she recognized the tenacious gait. Expected it.

She took her time returning her book to the crate with the others Hector had given her. Locating her cigarettes, she struck a match, took a long drag, and another.

Then she gave Garra her attention. "Are you spreading more rumors about me?"

"I do what is necessary to protect you."

"Someday, all those lies will backfire. You need to stop."

"I am one man against two hundred." He stabbed a finger at the doorway. "Two hundred men who want to fuck you, kill you, and fuck you again when you're dead."

She flinched.

"The rumors add a layer of defense." His gaze lowered to her arms. "Just like your tattoos."

"It's just artwork." She ran a hand along the intricate black swirls that held no special meaning or significance.

"They camouflage your softness. Isn't that why you got them? To make you look tougher? Harder? To fit in?"

He was right, of course. One of the things she learned early on was that inmates with smaller builds and passive dispositions became victims of daily beatings and sexual slavery.

She heard the screams, saw the bruises, and knew exactly how deep that pain went.

If a man didn't come into the prison fighting with fists and teeth, he became someone's fuck toy. As such, he was loaned out to other inmates for sex in exchange for commissary goods, such as soup, cigarettes, and other things that replaced currency.

She had no power to stop it, but as long as she had Hector's protection, it wouldn't happen to her.

If she lost Hector...

She shivered at the memory of her first night in Jaulaso. Her tattoos wouldn't replace the shelter Hector provided, but they helped hide her fragility. They gave her confidence.

"The boss called a meeting." Garra glanced back into the hall. "They're starting to gather."

She took a drag on the cigarette and crushed it out. Her presence was required at every cartel meeting. She didn't always participate in the discussions, but sometimes her opinions were demanded.

Sometimes she was assigned a job, small tasks, such as eavesdropping on a conversation, delivering a verbal message, or overseeing a drug trade.

Hector never made her enter another area in the prison, touch an illegal substance, or take a life. But she was part of his criminal operation, contributing to its corruption.

Violence was necessary to maintain order in the cartel. She'd grown numb to it, started to justify it, because it was for the common good of Area Three.

Pulling in a breath, she followed Garra into the corridor. She didn't have to ask why this meeting had been called.

The González Cartel was recruiting people, convincing them that La Rocha Cartel was losing power. Every person who stepped foot in Area Three was under the microscope, even if it was just a short visit.

Most of the men who came in wanted to join this side and vocally declared their allegiance. Others weren't as transparent about their intentions.

The two American prisoners had shared nothing about themselves. No one knew their cartel affiliations or their reasons for coming to this side of Jaulaso.

Were they recruiters for the González Cartel? Spies from one of the gangs? Or random nobodies like her, just looking for a safer place to sleep?

They were the reason Hector had called this meeting.

Their fate was about to be decided.

NINE

The meeting began with updates on business outside of the prison. Tula stood with her back to the room and thumbed through Hector's vinyl record collection, half-listening to the cadence of deep voices.

Behind her, Hector sat at the table with his closest advisers — Garra, Luis, and a loudmouth, heavy-set *vato* named Simone. Hector's eclectic taste in music fascinated her far more than Simone's complaints about a missing shipment of heroin.

As they argued back and forth, she dug to the bottom of the record stack. His collection included everything from Renaissance composers to Latin American pop, but the majority of the albums covered the breadth of 1960's British bands.

She flipped quickly through the ones she'd seen before. *The Beatles, The Who, The Kinks, The Rolling Stones...*

Wait.

She jumped back to the previous record and slid it from the pile.

On the sleeve, a blond lady with bouffant hair smiled beneath the title, *Petula Clark's Greatest Hits.*

Who was Petula Clark?

"The new arrivals are Martin Lockwood and Ricardo Saldivar." Hector's soft melodious Spanish drew her gaze over her shoulder. "They were booked on drug trafficking charges."

"Are they cartel?" Garra rested his forearms on the table. "Did González plant them?"

She abandoned the records and drifted toward the conversation, her attention piqued.

"I don't know." Hector met her eyes and gave her a gentle smile before shifting his gaze back to the group. "We don't have anything on them."

That was always the case. The moment a convict was booked into Jaulaso, the prison guards notified Hector. He was given a name and little else.

Funny how La Rocha Cartel knew their shit when it came to drug peddling and illegal firearms, but when they needed to investigate a guy, they were at a loss.

So they did what they did best. They resorted to violence.

"I don't care who they are." Simone ran a finger along his thick mustache. "We need to get rid of them."

He wasn't talking about eviction. They rarely kicked a man out of Area Three. The rejection wouldn't just send a prisoner away mad. It would incite him to join sides with the enemy.

La Rocha needed to grow its numbers, not send potential members to the other side.

"Remember what happened the last time we killed a new arrival?" Garra arched a black eyebrow. "We can't risk another riot."

Her thoughts exactly. When they made inmates disappear without justification, it caused unrest in Area Three. The inmates started questioning their own longevity within the structure, wondering if and when they were next. That kind of uncertainty bred low morale and weakened loyalties, which often led to an uprising.

After narrowly surviving three riots in two years, she shuddered at the thought of another one.

She paced behind Hector until he pulled out the chair beside him and motioned for her to sit.

"Thank you." She lowered into the seat.

"We need to take them out without anyone knowing it's us." Simone drummed his chubby fingers against his thigh.

"Check this out." Luis leaned in, eyes glimmering. "We'll have a big party. Once the two *gabachos* are drunk out of their minds and everyone else is passed out, I'll go in there and beat them to death."

Everyone laughed but her.

These guys loved to party. A lot of women, cocaine, and alcohol. More than that, they loved to spill blood.

"I'll make it look like one of the inmates did it." Luis smiled proudly. "It's a good idea, yeah?"

More laughter. Several head nods. Everyone seemed on board.

Brawls between inmates were accepted as the norm. Broken bones and knife wounds determined pecking orders and gave the caged animals an outlet to burn off steam. While infighting didn't usually result in death, sometimes it happened.

Luis' ham-handed plan would probably work, but it should be a last resort.

"You don't even know these guys are with the rivals," she heard herself say.

The room fell quiet, and glares hit her from every direction.

Except Hector. He studied her in that fond way he did, with admiration and respect. "You have a better idea?"

She blew out a breath. "You need to be recruiting potential members, not killing them."

"True, but we don't know if the enemy planted them here. We can't rule out the possibility of espionage."

"Then find out who they are and where they're from."

"What do you suggest?" His dark eyes glinted with amusement. "Shall we ask them?"

The room exploded in another round of laughter.

Of course they couldn't ask a spy if he was a spy. She wasn't stupid.

Her teeth clenched. "Tell one of your guys in the city to investigate them."

The ability to access the Internet in Jaulaso was nonexistent, but Hector had endless resources on the outside. Anyone with a web browser could perform an identity search for him.

"I already had a background check done." His lips thinned. "There is no background. No arrest records. No traffic tickets. No history. Nothing on the dark web. Their identities have been wiped."

Oh.

Her stomach sank. "If they're big-time traffickers, they probably paid off people to wipe their identities and make them untraceable. Doesn't mean they work for an enemy cartel."

"Doesn't mean they don't."

"They know Spanish." Simone tightened his fists on the table. "But they whisper in English, so we can't understand what they're saying. They're hiding something."

"Maybe they're just being cautious." She turned back to Hector and asked quietly, "So you're just going to kill them?"

"Yes." He cocked his head, studying her. "Unless you think you can coax them to talk."

"Me?" She jerked back.

"Yes! I like this." Simone heaved forward on his chair, physically interjecting himself. "Put her in a short little dress that shows off her ass and legs with her titties out to here." He cupped the air in front of him. "Send her to the common area, and call up the *gabachos*. When they see her... Boom! They'll want it. They'll want all up inside it."

"No! Absolutely not!" Garra jumped to his feet, his eyes wide and pleading with Hector. "This is not an option."

Her fingernails dug into her palms, her breath stuck in her throat, as she waited for Hector's reaction.

He lit a cigarette, his thoughts hidden behind a blank expression.

"When she gives it to them, she'll pull them in real deep, if you know what I mean." Simone gripped an imaginary body on his lap and thrust his hips.

She clutched her midsection with cold fingers, willing Hector to put an end to this humiliating conversation.

"It's brilliant." Luis slapped Simone on the shoulder and laughed. "A man will do and say anything in a beautiful woman's bed. We'll get them drunk on the pussy and make them talk."

"Stop." A rush of anger swept through her, burning up her cheeks. "I won't—"

"She's not doing it." Garra shot them a harsh squint, his chest thrust-out and jaw tight. "It's too dangerous."

Simone and Luis talked over him, their postures perking up and voices rising as they described the manipulative powers of the vagina.

Luis pulled on Simone's sleeve, dragging him closer. "She can tell them she plans to desert the cartel and needs two strong men to protect her."

What the fuck? She tried to capture Hector's gaze, but his attention remained fixed on his men.

Simone nodded, his eyes flickering. "She'll earn their trust in bed, and they'll be desperate to help her. If they have connections, they'll bring her into their fold and share their confidences."

"What if they're nobodies?" She inhaled through her nose to calm the tremble in her voice.

What if they were innocent? Victims of the wrong place and wrong time? *Just like her.*

Every inmate in Jaulaso claimed to be innocent. Every. Single. One. The Americans would probably say the same thing, and there would be no way to prove it.

"If we confirm they're not working against us," Simone said, "we'll tell them they passed the test and keep them. That'll add to our numbers, just like you said."

She wanted no part of this half-cocked misogynistic plan. Forget the fantasies she had about the new guys. Appreciating their good looks from afar wasn't the same as manipulating them with sex.

They were locked up in the most violent prison in Mexico. Because they were criminals. *Not* the type of men she invited into her bed. Even if it was for the common good of the cartel. Even if they were innocent.

Especially if they were innocent. It was too deceitful, and she wasn't a deceitful person.

But she didn't need to vocalize her objections. Garra did it for her, vehemently rejecting every point with a *No, Fuck No,* and *Over my dead body.*

His duty was to protect her, but his loyalty lay with Hector. Because of that undying allegiance, he was an overachiever in his job as her guard.

The three men continued to debate the advantages and dangers of the proposed plan. Through it all, Hector remained quiet and still, pensively puffing on his cigarette.

Surely, he wasn't considering this? She felt safe with him and trusted he would never force her into doing something as heinous as fucking a man for information.

Within minutes, the conversation shifted from casual to heated. Simone and Luis leaped from their chairs and faced off with Garra, who refused to hear anything they had to say. Volumes rose. Words sharpened, and faces turned red hot.

"What's your problem, Garra?" Simone sneered. "Afraid you'll lose your spot in her bed? She can still fuck you on the side."

The tingling heat of embarrassment crawled up the back of her neck and across her face. As much as she hated Garra's rumors, she never denied them. The pretense of belonging to a powerful man like him discouraged sexual advances.

But, for whatever reason, Simone's accusation sent Garra into a seething rage.

His lips pulled back, and the cords in his neck strained against his gold chains. "Say one more word about that, and I'll kill—"

"Silence." Hector's chillingly calm tone snapped the room into stillness. "Get out. All of you."

She started to rise, but he put a hand on her arm, staying her.

The others left without hesitating, speaking, or glancing back.

The primary rule of Jaulaso was that Hector La Rocha made the rules. His word was law, and disobedience was a capital crime. Anyone who rebelled—like the González Cartel—was considered a sworn enemy and killed if caught.

The Americans... What were their names? Ricardo and Martin? If she slept with them and learned they worked for an enemy, they wouldn't just be executed. Their deaths would be theatrically and gruesomely staged to serve several purposes.

One, it would reassure the residents of Area Three that they were under the protection of the cartel. Two, it would give pause to any rival considering a raid. And most importantly, it would send a message to everyone.

Obey, or you'll end up like this.

She didn't know if Ricardo and Martin had wives, children, or legit lives at home in the States. She didn't know if they were heartless, murdering drug smugglers or clueless tourists framed for a crime they didn't commit. Whomever they were, she didn't want to be responsible for their deaths.

But that wasn't the only reason this plan made her sick to her stomach.

She turned toward Hector and sat taller. "I'm not a whore."

"No." A slow smile built as he switched to perfect English. "These old eyes see an intelligent, respectable woman, who is a pleasure to talk to and easy to trust."

His compliment slipped beneath her guard and softened her voice. "You want me to do this."

"Yes, but I won't demand it." He touched a firm finger beneath her chin and lifted her gaze to his. "It's your choice."

"If I don't do it, you'll have them killed."

"Yes." He lowered his hand.

Either way, their blood would be on her hands.

Unless they were innocent. If they weren't here with nefarious agendas, they would be allowed to stay. She had the opportunity to save their lives.

"You've never concerned yourself with the business." He tilted his head to the side. "Why do you care if the gringos die? Because they're handsome? Mysterious? From your United States?"

"As far as we know, they've done nothing wrong." She lifted a shoulder and looked away. "I don't want to cause the deaths of innocent men."

"So sensitive and delicate. I would protect you from all the ugliness in the world if I could."

He had a way of saying that without sounding condescending. Her ethics were considered a weakness here, but he never patronized or belittled her for it.

She melted in the glow of his warm gaze. "You make it hard to say no to you."

"That's what I hear." He leaned back with a content smile playing at the corner of his lips. "Is that a yes?"

"Yeah." Her pulse quickened. "But I don't have a clue how to do this. What if I can't get them to talk?"

"Then we'll go with Luis' idea."

Throw a party, wait until they're drunk, and beat them to death.

"Super." She gave him a deadpan smile.

"I want updates on your progress."

"Yes, of course." She stood on shaky legs and wiped her palms on her jeans. "Have you heard… Are there any updates on Vera?"

"No. I'm sorry." His eyebrows pulled down, darkening his expression. "My men won't stop searching until they find her."

When she'd told him about her missing sister's possible connection to his cartel, he vowed to look into her disappearance.

"Okay," she said. "Thank you."

As she trudged toward the door, his quiet timbre whispered over her shoulder. "Petula."

She glanced back. "Yeah?"

"You're stronger than you think. You have the courage to do this job, just like when you saved my life. I have faith in you."

Each word loosened the cement around her heart, chipping away jagged pieces until she felt the slow leak of an unfamiliar emotion.

She'd always been grateful for his friendship but hadn't realized how much she needed his approval.

Her mother had kept her at a distance, and she'd never had a mentor or elder to look up to and ask for advice. She needed that. Needed someone to offer guidance on her choices and praise her accomplishments.

Who would've thought Hector La Rocha would fill that role? She should've been terrified of him, but their relationship wasn't like that.

He wasn't a crime boss with her. He was her friend.

The sincerity in his eyes steeled her with determination. She refused to fail. Couldn't bear the thought of disappointing him.

"Thank you." She gave him her fiercest smile. "I won't let you down."

TEN

Back in the hallway, Tula found Garra waiting for her with his arms crossed. She didn't need to tell him what had been decided in Hector's quarters. One look at her and concern sank into the grooves around his eyes and swallowed his glare.

"Don't say anything." She strode down the hall, past her cell, and headed toward the yard for some fresh air. "I get it."

"You get what?" He chased after her, huffing passive-aggressive breaths down her back.

"If something happens to me, you fail your job, and you can't stand the thought of that."

"It's just a job."

"Not to you." She paused at the door to the yard and peered through the grimy window. "See those guys over there covered in tattoos, with the three dots around their eyes and the faceless clocks on their necks? They'll be running in the opposite direction of the trouble you'll be running straight toward. That's why Hector respects you. Because you fear God more than man. You run into battles, outnumbered and undaunted by the outcome, with only loyalty in your heart to your leader."

"That almost sounds like a compliment."

"It's the truth." Her gaze jumped to the gunshot wound on his shoulder, the scarred welt partially covered by his black tank top. "I haven't forgotten, Garra."

He'd taken that bullet for her. During a riot that broke out a year after her arrest, he leaped between her and the shooter.

Before that happened... God, how she'd hated him. She'd made sure he knew it, too, barely speaking to him and forcing him to live that first year like a castrated servant.

When he saved her life, she decided to let go of the past. No more grudges. No more revengeful punishments. She let it all go and gave him a free pass to have sex with whomever was willing.

Maybe that made her a softie. Compared to everyone in here, she was. But when she thought about the compassionate, naive schoolteacher who was arrested two years ago, she knew that woman was gone. None of those soft, sentimental parts remained inside her.

Not even when it came to the man who had taken a bullet for her.

Garra had only been doing his job, and now, she needed him to step back and let her do *her* job. A job that would put her in the arms of a criminal.

Two criminals.

Ricardo and Martin could've been rapists, pedophiles, serial killers, or rival cartel members on a mission to take out anyone close to Hector. She'd agreed to learn who they were by spending an indefinite amount of time with them. Intimate time. *Alone.*

It would be hard enough to manipulate them into trusting her. If Garra were with her, hovering and watching and listening to every word, they would never open up.

She had to do this on her own, through a series of private moments, away from the watchful eye of her guard.

Garra had already come to this conclusion, given the worry lines etched on his face. He knew the gun on her hip would come off during sex, and she wouldn't be able to defend herself.

Not while she was naked.

Spread beneath a hard body.

With a dick thrusting inside her.

Her breath caught. Her pulse sprinted, and a sudden rush of heat throbbed between her legs.

She clenched her thighs together.

Christ, where did *that* come from? She hadn't experienced arousal since before her arrest. She'd almost forgotten what it felt like.

Two years without sex, and now she was supposed to be some kind of femme fatale? It felt impossible.

"I hate this as much as you do." She opened the door and stepped into the sunlight, grateful for the cool breeze. "You don't want to disappoint Hector by failing at your job, and neither do I."

A fire burned in her belly as she crossed the yard toward her favorite bench. She would tackle this challenge with the same tenacity that got her out of the slums of Ciudad Hueca.

She'd put herself through college, graduated with honors, and immigrated to the U.S. all on her own.

She could do this.

What were the first steps? She needed to approach the Americans, let them know they could interact with her. Then she would need to talk to them, without coming across as obvious or desperate.

Where should this happen? She glanced around at the dozen or so inmates in the yard. Not here. Too many ears.

"Garra." She met his eyes over her shoulder. "Why don't they have their own cell?"

"They haven't earned it."

No one paid rent the way she had when she first arrived. She'd realized later that Garra had arranged that special moment in hell just for her.

She turned to face him and lowered her voice to a whisper. "I can't do this with everyone watching and listening. Give them a cell."

"No."

"Then move two beds into mine."

It was a hollow demand. She would never willingly share her cell with a stranger, let alone two strangers. She also knew Garra would never agree to it.

"I'll find them some space," he growled.

"A private cell. With a lock." If this turned into a sexual thing, she didn't want anyone walking in.

"Fine." His nostrils flared.

"Today. Right now."

He drew in a sharp inhale and scanned the yard, likely searching for inmates who might threaten her. A moment later, he stormed off.

She treaded in the other direction. As she neared her bench, a pack of five men came into view around the corner.

All muscle, tattoos, and menace, they walked with cocky swaggers and eyes locked on wherever they were headed.

She followed their gazes to a table, where the two Americans sat alone.

Shit.

Ricardo and Martin were about to meet the welcoming committee, and it wouldn't be gentle.

Her muscles tensed, and she glanced in the direction Garra had headed. No luck.

Even if he were here, he would never interfere in a yard fight. And she had no power or authority over anyone, which was why Garra didn't like to leave her side.

She had no choice but to let this play out.

Her bench sat within hearing range of the confrontation. No one looked in her direction as she lowered onto the sun-soaked seat.

"Hey, *gabachos*." A huge bald man known as Papá approached the black-haired guy, who she assumed was Ricardo. "I have a list for you. Make sure we get everything on it by tomorrow."

The wrinkled paper in Papá's fist probably demanded things like cigarettes, soap, underwear, and other goods that could be purchased or traded at the canteen.

"Sure, can I see it?" Ricardo asked in fluent Spanish and slowly stood.

As Papá handed over the list, Ricardo slammed a fist into the huge man's nose.

"Oh, fuck." Her hand flew to the grip of her gun, knowing full well they would kill her if she interfered.

In a blur of bodies, five men with sledgehammer arms slammed into the Americans.

She expected them to fall beneath the beating. Or run for their lives. Either option would've labeled them as cowards and turned them into permanent punching bags. Or worse.

But they didn't cower.

They hit back, furiously, expertly, and without fear. Even more incredible was the awareness they had of each other. They worked in tandem, one of them punching high while the other kicked low. Their strikes were synchronized, their arms and legs moving as if controlled by one mind.

The way they predicted each other's movements was mind-boggling. They must've trained together. A lot.

Their bodies carried the muscled strength and coordination of men who had dedicated some serious time to the heavy bag. Biceps flexed with every punch. Pectorals contracted and heaved against the stretch of their shirts. Powerful legs delivered blows that sent a massive man like Papá into a stunned lurch of discombobulated limbs.

Make no mistake, the new guys were getting their asses kicked. But through it all, they shared secret smiles as if they weren't engaged in a fight they couldn't win.

She held her breath as the sounds of meaty knuckles pounded flesh, cartilage, and sinew. Grunts rent the air, and Papá's team started to stagger. A couple of the men stumbled out of the throe, bleeding from cuts on their faces.

The instant Ricardo and Martin dropped to the ground, the battle was over.

They lay on their backs, sweating into the dirt and gasping for breaths. Their attackers wiped away blood, straightened their clothes, and limped out of the yard.

There was no heckling, trash talk, or cheap shots as they departed.

The silent exit was a form of praise to the new guys for having enough heart to fight a battle they knew they would lose.

She released a sigh of relief then silently scolded herself for caring.

Ricardo and Martin had just earned respect, but that didn't mean there wouldn't be more tests and harder fights.

Martin pushed into a sitting position, his expression strained, scowling beneath a sheen of blood.

"For our first prison fight," he said in drawling English, "that wasn't bad."

His friend dropped a forearm over his eyes and groaned. "Yippee-ki-yay, motherfucker."

She felt a tic in her cheek. An unfamiliar emotion.

I like them.

The sentiment was neither here nor there. She had a job to do, and it started now.

Drawing in a deep breath to calm her heart, she stood from the bench and made her way toward them.

Martin noticed her first and rose to his feet with a grace that didn't match his rugged, banged-up physique.

He looked like hell, with a bloody nose, fat lip, and his shirt hanging in shreds around his sweat-slick neck. She'd never seen anything sexier in her life.

His blond hair was short on top and even shorter on the sides. He wore dark fitted jeans that hung low on narrow hips and a thin layer of scruff on his chiseled jaw.

His lashes, thick and golden, hooded his deep emerald eyes as he perused her from head to toe.

An unexpected shiver slid across her skin.

"You must be Martin," she said in English and shifted toward the man lying on the ground at her feet. "And Ricardo."

Ricardo moved his arm from his face and stared up at her with velvety brown eyes. "Ricky."

Ricky and Martin.

"Livin' la Vida Loca?" The instant she blurted the question, she felt awkward.

Ricky shot her a stony glare, and Martin's eyebrows gathered.

Of course, they were confused. She'd ignored them for days, and now she was poking fun at them.

Two years in this place and she'd completely forgotten how to socialize.

"Ricky Martin. You know, he sang that song...?" She shook her head. "You do speak English, right?"

"We thought we were the only ones," Martin said in English.

Perfect. That was the language she would continue to use with them. Maybe it would help them connect with her.

"To what do we owe the pleasure?" Ricky rose to his full height, stretching over six feet of gorgeous masculinity. "Petula, is it?"

Well, hello, Tall, Dark, and Handsome.

He was as tall as Martin, dark where Martin was fair, and just as gorgeous close up. She loved the trendy look of his thick black hairstyle, the way the strands tumbled loosely and disorderly on top and faded beneath a severe side part into shaved sides.

Neither man bore visible tattoos, piercings, or track marks from heroin use. No wedding rings, either.

Maybe they were carrying assassination orders in their back pockets. But at first glance, they seemed like they would show up on a first date with flowers. *And condoms.* But not guns.

"It's Tula, and you two look like you could use a drink." She turned away, tossing an order over her shoulder. "Walk with me."

She didn't wait for them to follow, and after a few steps, her nerves tightened. Dammit, they weren't coming.

Way to make a fool of yourself, Tula.

She was in over her head, but she kept walking, one foot in front of the other, chin up.

Then the sound of shoes scuffed behind her. They grew closer and flanked her on either side, invading her senses with testosterone and body heat.

Her eyes wanted to steal greedy glances at them, but she trained them forward and planned her next step.

If they were going to tell her anything, they would have to trust her first.

She needed to make herself vulnerable. Because what man didn't trust a vulnerable woman?

Blood dripped from head wounds and multiple cuts on their bodies, and Martin's swollen lip looked pretty painful. She had the supplies to clean them up and the alcohol to numb the aches.

In her private cell.

That was where she would take them.

For the first time in two years, she was going to open herself up and invite someone in.

She just hoped they wouldn't hurt her the way Garra had.

ELEVEN

Pain coughed through Ricky's battered chest, and every step aggravated his throbbing shins. He had a few scrapes, some cuts, and a bruise on his ego. Nothing he couldn't handle. After a stiff drink and full night's sleep, he would be back in business.

His partner in crime lumbered along with a slight limp, sporting two sexy shiners on his face and a fair amount of blood on his shirt.

Tula strolled between them, setting an unhurried pace with her shorter legs.

He and Martin had noticed her in the yard right before the muscle squad showed up. Just what a guy wanted—a beautiful woman watching him get his ass kicked up between his shoulder blades. Good times.

As she led them deeper into the maze of hallways, he eyed her up and down in his periphery.

The graceful dip of her waist flared into a round, tight ass. The sinuous line of her neck, small tits, and toned thighs in denim formed an irresistible shape.

Everything about her was delicate, from her petite height and slender tattooed arms to her pert nose and small feet. It would take no effort at all to lift her with a hand around her throat and pin her against Martin's chest. Before she could sputter an objection, he would have her separated from her gun and restrained between him and Martin, with his mouth on her lips and Martin's teeth scraping her neck.

Could she take them at the same time? Or was her pussy too tight? They would have to go slow, give her time to adjust to the stretch of two cocks.

Goddamn, just thinking about it made him hard.

Watching her walk next to Martin, seeing them side by side, it was the *only* thing he could think about. Martin's blond hair, chiseled features, and broad chest towering over Tula's head of long black hair, vivid brown eyes, and dainty figure... They were balls-grippingly gorgeous.

She veered into the corridor a few steps ahead of them, and he exchanged a look with Martin.

His friend raised an eyebrow as if to say, *This was too easy.*

He gave Martin a shrug. *Roll with it.*

"We're almost there." She escorted them down a long run, with a two-story wall of cells on one side overlooking a dining area on the other.

Rectangular tables lined up in rows, and large pots of beans simmered on the stove. The scent of kerosene, grease, and cigarette smoke pervaded the air, and rotting garbage strewed the floor where inmates ate.

He and Martin had managed to avoid that unventilated, windowless shithole, choosing instead to buy watery onion broth and tortillas from the canteen.

"How are you making it in here?" she asked.

Jaulaso lived up to its squalid reputation, with its racist cliques, petty hall fights, inedible food, and endless hours of soul-sucking misery.

He grunted. "It's a lot like high school."

"With guns and knives." Martin glanced at the group of armed men they'd just passed.

"This is your first time in prison?" Her dark eyes flicked between him and Martin. "Both of you?"

"Yup." He stepped around a Jurassic-sized cockroach on the floor and shuddered.

"Your ability to throw hands made an impression in the yard." She glanced at Ricky. "That right cross you caught Papá with made his knees go out."

"You mean the bald-headed diesel?"

"Yeah. You hit him so hard he wobbled away like a baby giraffe." She stopped at a cell door and met his eyes. "There's a saying around here."

"Don't drop the soap?"

Her pretty red lips formed a tense line. "An ass whipping washes off. A coward isn't forgotten." She opened the door and waved them in. "Let's get you cleaned up."

His position in the hall gave him a view of women's jeans and shirts hanging from a pipe in the ceiling and floral hair products lined up on the small sink. A single bed sat in the corner, piled with folded blankets.

This was her private cell, and she was inviting them inside? Where was her surly, overprotective guard?

Martin wore an expression that matched the unease in Ricky's gut.

Why had she brought them here alone? Was it a trap she and Garra had set up? Or maybe she'd waited until Garra was distracted so she could lead them here without his notice? For what reason? To fuck around behind his back?

He and Martin knew better than to touch another man's woman, especially in prison.

"Where's your boyfriend?" he asked.

"What?" Her eyes widened. Then she exhaled past a frown. "You mean Garra. We don't… We're not together. He just watches out for me."

"You should tell *him* that." Martin glanced up and down the hall as if expecting Garra to leap from the shadows. "He dishes out threats to anyone who looks at you, like you're his property."

"He wishes." Her mouth relaxed, and the corners curved upward. Her cheeks rose, and her lips parted, setting free a blinding, dick-hardening grin. "That asshole takes his job way too seriously."

Christ, her smile. It possessed her entire body, pushing away the tension in her muscles and illuminating the golden streaks in her brown eyes. Fucking beautiful.

"Asshole, huh?" Martin braced a hand on the wall above her head and leaned down to imprison her eyes. "You're the only female inmate in Area Three, and you're telling us there's no boyfriend? No lovers or anyone who might feel compelled to pump us full of lead for talking to you?"

"There's no one. Even if there was, *I* decide who talks to me." Her smile flattened between clamped lips. "I'm offering you a drink, medicine for your cuts, and amicable conversation." She narrowed her eyes. "Kindness is rare around here. I wouldn't pass it up if I were you."

"Why do you have medical supplies in your cell?" Ricky crossed his arms.

"Since Garra is determined to block every challenge aimed at me, the least I can do is keep supplies on hand whenever he eats a fist."

"That happens often?" Ricky asked.

She shrugged.

Every item acquired in Jaulaso was earned, traded, or bought with prison currency, such as cigarettes or food. It would've taken her months, if not years, to collect alcohol and medicine. And she was offering her invaluable stash to two strangers.

Why? He trusted her about as much as he trusted everyone else in Jaulaso, but she might be their only access to Hector La Rocha.

The cartel boss didn't let women into his dirty fraternity. But he made an exception for Tula Gomez. She must've been important to him.

Ricky entered her cell with a tingle of apprehension between his shoulder blades. Martin followed, and she shut the door behind them.

"What about you?" She stepped toward the small sink and rummaged through the supplies on the floor. "Any spouses or committed relationships waiting at home?"

"Nope." He stood beside the cot, scrutinizing the claustrophobic space.

Several crates of books, cartons of cigarettes, a portable cooking stove, and an old cell phone summed up her belongings. She'd definitely been here a while.

He and Martin only had the clothes they were wearing and the cash in their pockets. Everything else had been confiscated during their arrest, as expected.

"Tequila?" Crouched beneath the sink, she held out a bottle behind her.

"Thanks." Martin lifted it from her hand and removed the cap, glaring at the gold contents as if hesitant to drink.

"I don't have cups. Are you not used to slumming it?" She snatched the tequila and sipped straight from the bottle. "Where did you say you were from?"

"We didn't." Ricky grabbed the bottle and swallowed a long pull, savoring the smooth burn of agave before handing it to Martin. "Where did you learn to speak English so well?"

"College. I'm a Spanish high schoolteacher in the States." She paused, and her eyes lost focus as if she were rearranging her thoughts. "I *was*." She blinked. "Never dreamed I'd end my career with a prison sentence, but here I am." Her fist gave an unenthusiastic pump in the air. "Killin' it."

"What are you in for?" Martin lowered onto the mattress and rested his elbows on his knees, watching her from beneath the bloody gashes on his brow.

"Drug smuggling."

Why did you do it? Did you do it? The silence exhaled the questions so loudly they didn't need to be voiced.

"I'm innocent." She grabbed some gauze and a bottle of antiseptic solution. "Same thing every prisoner says." She held up the supplies. "Who's first?"

He nodded at Martin. "This guy needs all the Band-aids you got. He's been holding back tears since we left the yard."

With a swollen-lipped scowl, Martin flipped him off.

"Take off your shirt." She peered at Martin from beneath her lashes. "I'll soak it in the sink and try to get the blood out."

This would be interesting. Martin wasn't exactly the touchy-feely type, especially around strangers.

"Don't bother. It's ripped to hell." Martin reached behind his head with a pained grimace and pulled off the shirt.

Ricky lowered onto the bed beside Martin and examined the defined cuts of muscle he'd been drooling over for seven years.

Martin had always been fit, but the past six months of training had turned his body into a chiseled work of art.

He and Ricky had spent several grueling hours a day together, rolling around on a mat, boxing in a ring, and lifting weights. The torture hadn't just been physical.

His hands knew every inch of Martin's body, and it wasn't enough. The urge to reach for Martin plagued him constantly, to feel all that strength against him, the press of hot skin, and the gust of frantic breaths as their bodies moved as one.

"How do you know each other?" She poured the antiseptic solution onto a swath of gauze and inspected Martin's swollen eyes. "I assume you were arrested together?"

"It's a long story." Martin angled forward, putting his face within an inch of hers.

"We have nothing but time." She didn't try to reclaim the personal space he penetrated. "Get it? Time?" She sighed. "Prison joke."

"Why are you helping us?" Martin leaned back and pressed his scowl to the lip of the bottle, taking a swig.

"Why are you here?"

"Drug trafficking," Ricky said.

He and Martin could be honest about everything except their alliance with the Restrepo Cartel and the assignment that put them here.

"Let me guess." She touched the medicated gauze against the cut above Martin's eye. "You're innocent."

"We're guilty of many things." Ricky grabbed the tequila and slugged it back.

She glanced between them, and her eyebrows gathered. "Are you lovers?"

The alcohol went down the wrong pipe, and he tried his damnedest to stifle a coughing fit.

"No." Martin glared at him. "Why would you ask that?"

"You seem close. I don't know." She shrugged. "The way you look at each other... It's intimate."

"I'm attracted to him." Ricky calmed his gag reflex and took another drink. "He's attracted to women. At the end of the day, all that matters is our friendship."

"Oh. That..." She moved the gauze to the cut on Martin's lip. "Sounds complicated."

"We don't make it complicated." He winked at Martin, coaxing a soft smile from that handsome face.

"Such a guy thing to say." She gave him a dissecting look, up, down, and through the heart. "Are you only interested in men or do you—?"

"Don't worry, Tula." His direct eye contact made her swallow. "You're definitely my type."

"That's not what I—"

"Then why did you ask?"

"Just making conversation." She gathered more gauze.

"Asking a man his sexual orientation is one way to make conversation." He rubbed his jaw. "Tells me where your mind's at."

Her mouth opened, closed, and opened again. "You brought it up."

"No, *you* did when you asked if we were lovers."

With an annoyed inhale, she rolled her eyes to the ceiling. Then she turned back to Martin. "Your friend's a pain in the ass."

Martin bit back a smile, likely anticipating Ricky's response.

"Darling," Ricky said in a low voice, "if I was in your ass, *pain* would be the last thing you'd feel."

The bottle of antiseptic fell from her hand.

"Shit." As she leaned down to recover it, her gaze found Martin's. "I can't tell if he's a smartass, a badass, or just an ass."

Martin grabbed the bottle before she reached it. "Most people don't know how to take him."

"It's kind of a gift." Ricky devoured the view of her backside as she bent to examine Martin's chest for wounds.

"How long have you known each other?" she asked.

"Seven years." Martin handed her the antiseptic. "I needed a place to live. Ricky and the others had a spare bed."

"The others?" She wiped away a smear of blood on his chest.

"We have a few roommates."

"Is that the long story you mentioned?"

"Everybody has one." He squinted at her. "What's yours?"

"Wrong place. Wrong time." She edged closer, her eyes fixed on his lap as she reached for a splotch of blood on his waistband. "Looks like you got hit—"

Martin sprung from the bed in a blink. His hand seized her throat and slammed her back against the wall before Ricky could process what was happening.

TWELVE

"Martin!" Ricky's heart rate doubled as he jumped to his feet. "What the fuck?"

Tula jerked against Martin's hand at her throat and went for the gun in her waistband. Ricky beat her to it and tossed it out of reach on the bed.

"Hey, man." He put his face into Martin's line of sight without touching him. "Snap out of it."

Martin bared his teeth through a feral grimace. His green eyes glazed over with a faraway look, one he wore whenever he fell into the mysterious black hole of his past.

It could've been his time in Van's attic or something from his childhood. Whatever haunted him had been set off when Tula touched his waist.

"Let go!" She thrashed beneath his grip and shoved uselessly at his chest. Her wide eyes darted to Ricky, the brown depths pooling with fear. "Get him off me!"

"Martin, look at me." He hardened his tone. "Right now."

Slowly, Martin turned his head. His lashes lowered and lifted through a long blink, and he dropped his hand.

She clutched her splotchy neck and gulped for air. Her cheeks went from pale to an angry shade of red, and her eyes zeroed in on the gun.

In the next breath, she launched for it, but Ricky caught her around the waist.

"Hold up." He didn't have to restrain her or use much force to guide her slight weight in the opposite direction. "Martin, how are you doing?"

"Fine." Martin paced away, dragging his hands down his face.

Muscles rippled along either side of his spine, and he rolled his shoulders as if trying to shake off his demons.

The impulse to erase the distance and comfort Martin gripped him hard, but it would only end in rejection.

Breathing heavily, Tula backed away, her eyebrows squished in confusion.

Ricky turned to the mess that had been made during the scuffle and used Martin's ruined shirt to wipe up the spilled antiseptic solution. Thankfully, the bottle of tequila still sat upright on the floor.

"What did I do wrong?" She picked up the scattered gauze and approached Martin cautiously. "Tell me so I don't repeat it."

"Nothing." Martin shifted to the sink and rested his backside on the edge. His hand went to his brow, rubbing restlessly as he blew out a breath. "You did nothing wrong."

"Liar." She stepped right up to him and gazed into his eyes. "I touched your waist. Or was it your hip? Is there a no-touch zone?"

"What?" Irritation vibrated through his tone.

"What?" she snapped back.

They seemed to be feeding off the tension in the air between them, but there was something else going on.

They scrutinized each other, not in a confrontational standoff, but in some kind of intense, wordless conversation.

Whatever Martin read in her eyes started to calm the storm in his. Her expression softened, growing solemn. After a suspended moment of eye contact, she spoke.

"When I was arrested two years ago, the Mexican military tortured me with…" Her chest hitched. "I don't know what it was. They electrocuted me with a rod, vaginally and anally, for eight hours straight."

Ricky's insides turned to cement.

She stared into Martin's stark green eyes. "Then they transported me here, and on the first night, an inmate attacked me." Her hands flexed and released at her sides. "I strangled him. I don't know how, but I killed him."

The rumors were true? Maybe she was lying, but if so, she had a damn good poker face. He'd never seen a woman look as vulnerable as she did now.

With her shoulders curled forward and the dull sheen over her eyes, she appeared to be drowning in a violent ocean of memories.

"I gave a prison guard all my cash to bring me here." Her voice wobbled, and she pressed the heel of her palm against her stomach. "Area Three was supposed to be safer. I didn't know I'd have to pay rent for this cell."

A chill spread across Ricky's scalp. Martin said nothing, but his stony expression spoke volumes. They both knew what sort of payment would be demanded of a beautiful woman in prison.

"That same night," she said quietly, "I had to pay with my body. It felt like rape. Or *worse* because I couldn't say no. I had to just lie there and take it." Her gaze slipped to the bed before jerking back to Martin. "I killed a man for trying to rape me, yet the one who succeeded still lives. He's not a threat to me anymore, but I struggle with...what he did to me. Maybe someday, I'll forgive him, but I doubt it."

He glanced between her and Martin, his chest tight as he processed her words. Not only had she been tortured by electrocution, but within hours, someone had forced himself inside her injured body.

Was it Garra? He seemed to be the property manager around here. If he raped her, that would explain his possessiveness, as well as the standoffish way she interacted with him.

Ricky's pulse elevated, and his blood heated to punish that son of a bitch.

"What about you?" She drifted closer to Martin, leaving a sliver of space without touching him. "Is the source of your pain still alive?"

Ricky leaned forward, holding his breath.

She might've figured out Martin had a tortured past, but she would never be able to draw the details out of him. He wouldn't even talk to Ricky about it.

Seconds filled the silence, each one stirring a disquiet through the room as she watched Martin, waiting for an answer.

Ricky was confident his friend wouldn't respond.

Until Martin reached for her hand.

"I killed the first one." Martin closed his fingers around her tiny, tattooed wrist. "The second one still lives, and like you, I doubt I'll ever forgive him."

Ricky's heart stopped, and pinpricks stabbed the base of his skull. The one who lived was Van Quiso. But who was the first one?

He'd suspected something terrible had happened to Martin before Van captured him, but Martin had never given any indication he'd killed someone.

Someone who had caused him pain.

Was it a relative from his childhood? A stranger on the street? Was the murder premeditated or self-defense? Had he been alone? What happened to the body?

Martin had given Tula—a woman he'd just met—more insight into his past than he'd ever offered Ricky. Why her? Because she'd shared a tragic story? He didn't even know if she was telling the truth.

Ricky tried to rein in the hurt that smoldered in his gut, but it only magnified as he watched them look at each other with mutual understanding.

Unbelievable.

He could actually feel the beginning of something spark and hold between them. Made him feel like a goddamn third wheel, interloping on a private moment.

Jesus, get a grip, you jealous fuck.

He and Martin were here for a job. If the sexy little vixen had a thing for his best friend, they could use that to ply her into spilling secrets about Hector La Rocha.

Screw it. They could eye fuck each other for as long as they wanted.

He reached for the medical supplies and tended to his wounds. But after a few irritating swipes of the gauze, he couldn't stop his gaze from gravitating back to them.

Martin guided her hand to his waist and pressed her palm against his skin, proving he didn't have an issue with touching.

Very few people invaded his personal space because of those fuck-off vibes he exuded. But she'd reached right through that when she touched him the first time.

That must've been what triggered him. He wasn't used to physical contact. Except she'd put her hands on his face to clean his wounds. He hadn't flipped out until she went for his pants.

Now that he'd given her permission to touch, she splayed her fingers against his nude stomach, lingering there for a long moment. Then she explored the mouthwatering grooves that carved a *V* from his hips to the low-waisted dip of his jeans.

Ricky imagined all that honed power flexing against his own hand — the corrugated ridges of abs and the heat of life pumping beneath warm, smooth skin.

A surge of hunger raced through his veins, and his body hardened as he indulged in an unobtainable fantasy where the three of them fell into bed together. In the heat of passion, Tula gave them the locations of the cartel's major players in the sex trafficking ring. Martin realized he wanted Ricky as deeply as Ricky wanted him. They vowed to protect the woman in their arms and fucked one another in every position imaginable for the rest of their lives.

"I was going to check the bleeding here." She glided her palm toward the red splotch on Martin's waistband.

"It's not my blood." Martin watched her from mere inches away.

"Oh. Okay, I might be able to wash it out."

"I'm not taking off my pants."

"No, of course not. I..." Her fingers brushed the flat expanse of his abs as she withdrew her hand. "I'll check your back if you turn around."

Ricky clenched his teeth and twisted away to clean the broken skin on his knuckles.

The bottle of tequila on the floor caught his eye, and he nudged it closer with his foot. As he finished patching up his hands, he poured the potent drink down his throat, hoping to escalate the *D* in drunk. Or the *E* in *ebrio,* if he wanted to be really Mexican about it.

A moment later, the soft sound of her footsteps approached, bringing with it the feminine scent of her shampoo or soap or whatever the hell she used to make her body smell so damn delicious.

"Want me to clean that cut on your face?" She tapped her fingers on her denim-clad thighs.

"Already took care of it." He rose and stepped around her, headed toward the sink.

Martin shifted out of his way. He didn't look at those green eyes as he washed his hands and face, but he felt them burning into the back of his head.

Her cell was too small for the three of them, and ignoring Martin made him feel hot and itchy in his skin.

If he looked at Martin, there would be a confrontation, and this wasn't the time to clear the air between them. Not with Tula cataloging everything. He didn't trust her.

A knock sounded on the door.

She opened it, and lo and behold, her scowling guard stood on the other side.

"Their cell is ready." Garra glared at him and Martin before giving Tula a possessive once-over. "Number 24. Right above you." He flicked a finger toward the ceiling.

When he strode away, she closed the door and turned.

"You got us our own cell?" Ricky dried off his face with the hem of his shirt.

"Yeah." Her attention dipped to his exposed abs, and her lips parted.

He lowered the shirt, his thoughts stuck on why and *how* she arranged a room for them.

"Explain how the rent works." Martin approached her, voicing Ricky's chief concern.

If Garra expected sex from her or them in exchange for a cell, he could eat his own dick. They would continue sleeping on the floor in the common area.

"There's no rent." She raised her chin.

"How?" Ricky asked.

"I have some leeway here."

"How?" He asked again, harder this time.

She drew in a breath and released it. "I work directly for the boss."

"You work for Hector La Rocha?" Martin crossed his arms over his chest. "A little thing like you—"

"Go ahead and misjudge me. That'll be fun."

Martin barked a derisive sound of laughter that immediately cut off as she shoved the barrel of her pistol beneath his jaw.

Ricky froze, and his training kicked in.

Her finger wasn't on the trigger, and most of her weight rested on one leg. He could sweep that foot and redirect the gun before she fired. One miscalculation, however, would put a hole through Martin's head.

How the hell did she even recover the gun without them noticing? She must've grabbed it when she answered the door?

"Tula," Ricky said slowly and captured her eyes. "The rumor that your boss doesn't employ women is clearly incorrect. As for the gossip that you can defend yourself against men twice your size? I can dispel that rumor, too." He looked at the gun and back to her. "You absolutely can."

She searched his face, her huge eyes shining with distrust and perhaps a hint of appeasement.

He held still, letting the moment work itself out as he drank in her incredible beauty.

Black satiny hair tumbled to her elbows. Tawny skin radiated beneath swirls of ink on her toned arms, and rosy lips pursed with suspicion. She reminded him of fire, glowing in warm hues of red, gold, and black against the cold gray cement of her cell.

Finally, she lowered the gun and opened the door. "Use the stairwell on the left. Your cell is on the second floor. Above mine. Number 24."

His chest tightened. She was kicking them out.

With a glance at Martin, he stepped into the hall.

"Thank you for getting the cell." Martin followed him out and turned back. "Why are you helping us?"

"Not for the reasons you think."

"What are—?"

She shut the door in his face.

THIRTEEN

Ricky made a choking sound in the dark, windowless concrete cell, wishing he hadn't just taken that weary breath. The sweltering, roach-infested space reeked of human waste and poor life choices.

The socket above the sink didn't have a bulb, but the door had a lock. Not that he would close it right now and block the only light from the hall.

Two mattresses sat side by side on metal frames, leaving a small walkway to the toilet.

This was where he would be sleeping with Martin for the next three months.

On the bright side, it was a step up from the floor in the common area. The lock on the door would allow them to sleep with both eyes closed.

Martin glanced up and down the empty hallway and stepped into the cell. In two long-legged strides, he reached Ricky's side.

His bruised face closed in, and his green eyes burned for a fight. "What the fuck is your problem?"

"*My* problem?" Ricky whispered harshly. "You're the one who lost your shit. Why did you attack her?"

"It won't happen again. Can you say the same?"

"About what?"

"You know what." Martin scraped a hand over his head. "Jesus, fuck, Ricky. You can't get butthurt whenever I talk to her."

"Why did you tell her about your past?"

"I told her *one* thing. Nothing important."

"It was more than you've ever told me."

"This is exactly what I'm talking about. Your fucking jealousy —"

"Who did you kill?"

Martin's head drew back stiffly, his lips flattening in a stubborn line. Then he narrowed his eyes. "I've killed several men with Camila. You were there."

"Before her. Before the Freedom Fighters. Who did you kill?"

His silence stabbed with refusal.

"Why her?" Ricky slumped against the wall and wiped the pain from his expression. "Why now?"

"There's something... Shit, I don't know. She has this pure sort of openness about her that compels me. Not just her story, but the look in her eyes, the sadness in her voice." Martin bowed his head, causing the shadows to shift across the sharp angles of his features. "She gave me a vulnerable moment."

"I've never given you that?"

"No." Martin braced an arm on the wall beside Ricky's head. "There's nothing vulnerable about you. You're confident in your skin and strong as hell. Look at how you handled Van. You and I endured the same hell in his attic. Yet you overcame it without looking back. Fuck, I admire that and expect nothing less from you." Martin touched Ricky's jaw. "I wouldn't want you any other way."

"You don't want me in *any* way." He turned his neck, jerking away from the extraordinary touch.

"That's not —"

"Forget it. I'm just being a dick."

He'd mastered the art of pretending Martin's rejections didn't hurt, but every interaction hit hard and dug deep. For seven years, he suffered in silence, shouldered the agony of wanting what he couldn't have, and buried the ache whenever Martin rubbed up against his space.

Like now.

He pulled in a breath and focused on the mission. "She's not as vulnerable as you think."

"No, she's not." Martin's mouth hovered an inch away, his voice low. "She survived this place for two years on her own."

"An American high school teacher, and she works for Hector La Rocha. It's too unbelievable to be a lie. I mean, if she's going to feed us bullshit, she'd make it easier to swallow, right?"

"Exactly. She hasn't lied to us." A muscle twitched at the corner of Martin's swollen lips. A smile. Barely. But a smile, nonetheless.

"You're attracted to her."

"That's an understatement. But..." Martin's gaze darted to the hall, and he tipped his head as if listening for footsteps. Then he bent in and put his mouth at Ricky's ear. "*You* are going to fuck her."

Sudden, raw desire spun up his pulse and caught his skin on fire. The gravelly command in Martin's voice, the heat of Martin's body against his, and the thought of fucking Tula Gomez while Martin watched — all of it gripped him between his legs, tightening his balls and lengthening his cock.

He pressed himself against the cold concrete wall, fighting the impulse to kick his hips forward and mindlessly grind against the gorgeous man leaning into him.

Martin seemed to sense his inner battle and started to move away.

"Wait." He gripped Martin's waist, holding tight to hard muscle. "Let me have this. Just… Just let me feel us for a second."

The cost of having feelings for Martin had left him needy and destitute. He had no romantic relationships, no interest in finding someone else. His heart wanted Martin or no one at all.

He braced for the bane of his life to push away, his mind already closing itself off to the possibility of a stolen moment.

Martin shifted and stretched an arm toward the door. His fingers caught the edge, and he swung it closed, blanketing them in darkness.

Every cell in Ricky's body thrummed to acute awareness.

With a long, heavy exhale, Martin slowly eased his weight against the front of Ricky's body. Chest to chest, hip to hip, Martin let him feel the press of hot skin and six feet of carved masculinity.

He fisted a hand in Ricky's hair and rested their foreheads together, breathing softly, comfortably, sinking into the bond.

Goddamn, the divine torture. The blissful hell. It was everything and not nearly enough.

He dug his fingers into Martin's waist, his cock throbbing in his jeans, trapped between the crush of their hips.

Martin didn't rock against him or jerk away in repulsion. Ricky's need was front and center, a bulging rock between them, conspicuous and unrequited.

"I'm sorry I can't give you what you need." Immersed in blackness, Martin tightened his fingers in Ricky's hair and flattened his other hand on the wall. "If I'd met you before… Before my head got all fucked up, I would've made you mine."

Ricky's heartbeat went off the deep end and crashed into a pool of chaotic hope.

"You mean —" He choked on a leaden tongue. "You're open to being with men?"

"I never told you I wasn't. You made assumptions."

"You never told me you *were*." An overload of ecstatic hope consumed him. "If you can be with men…"

"I'm broken, Ricky. Incapable of being with anyone." With a sigh,

Martin removed his touch and stepped away. The mattress squeaked, signaling his distance in the dark.

"Why? Because of the man you killed?"

"Never said it was a man."

"You didn't have to."

Ricky was tempted to open the door so that the hallway would shed light on Martin's expression. But maybe the concealment of darkness would make it easier to expose secrets.

"Tell me what he did to you." A pang gnawed in his chest as he imagined the level of hurt Martin would've endured to push him to kill someone. "How does it connect to Van Quiso?"

"I can't talk about this."

"Why not? I'm your best friend. The person you trust more than anyone else."

"Because everything that happened…" Martin's voice dropped to a raspy whisper. "It was *my* fault. *My* ignorant choices. I'm fucking ashamed of it, and I won't… I refuse to change your perception of me."

"I would never—"

"Drop it. I'm done discussing it."

His heart collapsed. "I need to say one more thing." At Martin's silence, he pushed off the wall and glared into the rancid darkness. "It doesn't matter who you open up to about your past. If it helps you to talk to Tula, I won't get butthurt over it."

When Martin said nothing, he opened the door and surveyed their dismal cell in the light. They needed to eat, but he wasn't in the mood to scrounge up their next unsatisfying meal.

Instead, he tackled the filthy mattresses. Martin helped him drag them into the hall and beat the dust out of them.

Once the beds were put back together, he cursed his sore ribs and surveyed the darkening bruises on Martin's face.

As Martin reclined on one of the mattresses, his movements were slow and stiff. An indication he was in more pain than he let on.

Today's fight in the yard wouldn't be their last physical altercation. The inmates were walking powder kegs, ready to explode and looking for a target. If he and Martin limped into the common area in search of food right now, they would probably be attacked again.

They needed to sleep, give their wounds time to heal, and discuss Tula Gomez.

"Can you wait until tomorrow to eat?" He gave the quiet hall another glance.

"I'll manage."

He closed and locked the door and lay beside Martin in the foulness of their pitch-black cell. His mind churned through everything that had transpired today and stalled on something Martin had said.

"Why did you tell me to fuck her?"

"She's our way in, and women never refuse you."

"I could say the same about you, but your damn self-imposed celibacy—"

"It's not an option."

"Fine, but she might not know anything about the sex trafficking operation."

"She works directly for Hector and has the means to find out. The first step is getting her to trust you."

"In bed."

"Yeah."

His cock twitched, ready to jump on the idea. "Fucking her doesn't guarantee she'll switch sides. Hector probably sent her to us to figure out where our loyalties lie."

"We'll tread carefully." Martin shifted, creaking the mattress springs. "Keep in mind, if we convince her to work against the cartel, it'll no longer be just our lives at stake."

Good point. The cartel thrived on its draconian rules. If she turned her back on them, they would kill her.

He and Martin would be released from Jaulaso in three months, but Matias wouldn't be able to free Tula.

Maybe she was a conniving murderous cunt and planned to gut them while they slept. But deep down, he agreed with Martin.

There was something about her. Like a shyness beneath the tattoos. Uncertainty behind the gun. He'd detected sweet, straight-laced schoolteacher vibes long before she told them her career.

Turning on his side, he strained to see Martin in the blackness. "What will you be doing while I'm with her?"

Matias Restrepo had been adamant about them never being alone in Jaulaso. As long as they stuck together, they had twice the eyes and double the strength.

"I'll try to help," Martin muttered.

"What?" A shocked laugh erupted from his chest, and he sat up, reeling in the dark. "You're going to help me have sex? How would that work?"

"Fuck off, asshole. I'm not fucking impotent."

"Are you sure? You haven't used your dick in seven years."

"My dick works fine. It's my goddamn head that—" Martin grunted. "Doesn't matter. Let me worry about it."

The thought of Martin watching him having sex was a glorious turn on. But if Martin participated? Holy fuck.

"I can hear the direction of your thoughts." Martin whacked him across the head. "Shut that shit down and get some sleep."

Swallowing a groan, Ricky stretched out on his back and closed his eyes.

He should've gotten laid before the arrest. Between the daily training for this mission, the horrifying disappearance of his roommate, Kate, his move to Colombia to work with Camila, and Kate's rescue two weeks ago, his downtime had been nonexistent.

How long had it been since he'd had sex? Six months? Longer?

On that thought, he slipped in and out of restless sleep, his senses piqued for sounds in the hall.

The second floor seemed to be the quietest section of Area Three. Whoever resided in this cellblock didn't spend a lot of time in their rooms. Most inmates kept to the yard and common area, where drugs, whores, and parties coalesced every night.

After an endless hour, maybe two, he lay wide awake, listening to someone's footsteps pause just outside the door.

"Martin," he whispered.

"I hear it."

They stood at the same time as a fist rapped on their door.

Martin rested a hand on his shoulder and squeezed, silently telling him to go ahead.

He shook out his arms and loosened his muscles for whatever waited in the hall. Then he opened the door.

Stark light poured in, and he shielded his eyes.

Tula stared up at him, holding a large box in her arms.

"No light bulb?" She squinted into their dark cell.

"No." He glanced back at Martin and winged up an eyebrow.

Martin slid his hands in his pockets, his face expressionless.

She set the box on the floor and dug through the contents.

"Hopefully, this works." She removed an old dusty bulb and held it out.

Martin took it from her and screwed it into the socket. Rusty metal squeaked with each turn until light flooded the room.

As Martin returned, Ricky leaned a shoulder against the doorframe and gave her a questioning look.

"So..." She pulled in a breath and released it with a rush. "You're from the States, and I miss my life there. You speak English, and I miss that, too. You don't have track marks from drug use or tattoos that celebrate the kills you've made. You don't have *any* visible tattoos. Not that I have anything against ink." She held out her tattooed arms. "Obviously."

He exchanged a look with Martin.

"From what I can tell, you guys don't belong in a place like this.

Neither do I." She bent down and lifted the box, hugging it to her chest. "You seem like... I don't know. Maybe if I'd run into you in a park or at a bar, we would've been friends. Maybe not. But I could really use a friend *here*."

He stared at this inviting woman, with her black hair twisting around her slender arms, and her makeup-free face angled upward, unguarded and staggeringly beautiful. Eyes of molten brown were steeped with susceptibility — an attribute he and Martin would either learn to trust or use against her.

"I guess what I'm trying to say is..." Her gaze drank him in and slid to Martin. "I'm lonely." She lifted a stiff shoulder. "That's why I'm helping you."

FOURTEEN

Tula bit down on the inside of her cheek.

She did it. Against Hector's advice, she'd spoken the truth and put herself at the mercy of two intimidating, potentially dangerous men.

After Ricky Martin—*yeah, she referred to them as one entity*—left her cell, she went straight to Hector and gave him an update.

He wanted her to move forward under the ruse of turning against the cartel. He believed if she pretended to be a traitor, they would be more inclined to confide in her.

But since he left the plan up to her, she decided to do it her way. She was already uneasy about the job. Putting on an act would've turned her into a blubbering nervous wreck.

Coming here alone was the scariest thing she'd ever done. If they worked for another cartel, they would likely kill her before she figured out who they were.

The smart thing would've been to keep her mouth shut and let Luis get rid of them quietly. But her conscience couldn't accept murder as a solution until she knew for sure they were bad men.

So here she was, standing before them on the microscopic chance she was saving their lives, which would only happen if they joined sides with La Rocha Cartel.

Martin folded his arms across his shirtless chest, the valleys between his abs obscenely deep in the glow of the dingy light bulb.

The swollen bruises around his eyes didn't diminish his hotness. His square jaw bore a speckle of darker hairs in an otherwise blond five o'clock shadow.

The golden hair on his head was short enough to maintain order while Ricky's spiky black strands stuck up in every direction.

Ricky took the heavy box from her, and the sight of veins and sinews bulging in his sculpted forearms swept a tingling heat through her.

God, had she ever seen anything sexier?

Arms. She was drooling over forearms.

"Come in," Martin said, making the invitation sound more like a command.

She stepped in and locked the door behind her, scrunching her nose at the putrid stench of sewage.

"There's a scented candle in the box." She coughed against her fist. "It might mask the smell."

They stared at her with blank expressions. Maybe her spiel about needing a friend had been too honest? If they didn't believe her, they might kill her on suspicion alone.

The gun in her waistband felt hot against her tailbone. She wasn't a good shot, and Ricky had already disarmed her once. She was out of her league.

"Smells like you brought food." Ricky turned to the box and removed the candle, followed by plastic containers of pork *pozole* and Mexican rice. "This is for us?"

"Yeah. Everything in there is yours." She rubbed her hands on her jeans. "I gathered what I could."

The box included basic supplies, such as clothing, soap, shaving razors, toothbrushes, towels, blankets, toilet paper, cutoff plastic milk cartons to use as dishes, powdered milk, instant coffee, and her only cooking stove.

Martin removed a stack of shirts and cotton pants. "How did you get all this?"

"I bartered a few things. Some of it I already had."

Home-cooked meals were brought in by families of the inmates, and she knew who to approach to trade for it.

Ricky dug through the box, the muscled column of his neck stretching into sloping shoulders and taut ripples of brawn along his spine.

Her cheeks heated.

"This is incredible, Tula." He lit the candle with a match and located a plastic spoon for the *pozole.*

She glanced at Martin and found him watching her with a glint of suspicion in his emerald eyes.

Her mouth dried. "I promise I didn't poison anything."

His expression hardened.

She returned his glare. "If I wanted to kill you, I would've just let you starve."

"Eat." Ricky smacked the container of rice against Martin's chest and turned to her. "Come here."

Two uncertain steps carried her the short distance. She craned her neck to look at him.

Lord have mercy, he wasn't even touching her, yet she felt him up and down the front of her body. As she swayed into his force field, his dark masculine scent curled around her.

The light press of his knuckle lifted her chin, igniting tiny shocks of electricity across her skin.

"I'm going to thank you now." His rich brown eyes darkened as they dipped to her mouth.

Oh, God. He was going to kiss her. She ached for it as much as she dreaded it. He scared her. This scared her. She didn't know what the hell she was doing.

Her teeth sank into her bottom lip, causing his breathing to accelerate. He angled in and pressed his thumb against her lip, tugging it from her bite.

His cheeks rose with amusement. Or pleasure. Maybe both. Then he grabbed her and crushed that heart-melting smile against her mouth.

Warmth flooded her chest, and her pulse burst into a gallop. It wasn't just the hot glide of his lips. It was him, breaking through the walls she'd erected two years ago.

His hands tingled down her spine and skimmed around the shape of her butt. They rested on the backs of her thighs, his fingers tucked between her jean-clad legs. He used that grip to hold her tight against him.

He didn't open his mouth to deepen the kiss, but a promise breathed past the seam of his lips. *When* he decided to take her, it would be explosive and unstoppable.

"Thank you," he murmured against her mouth.

Her entire face tingled as she stepped back.

Martin's presence felt like a pulsing beacon in the small space. When she peeked at him, she was surprised to see a soft smile in his eyes.

"I brought a bottle of tequila to wash that down." She motioned at the spoonful of rice he lifted to his mouth.

He took a bite and chewed slowly, his throat bouncing as he swallowed. Watching him eat felt strangely suggestive. The flex of his jaw and the groan in his chest conjured images of twisted sheets and whiskers scratching inner thighs.

"It doesn't need to be washed down. It's really good." Martin passed the rice to Ricky.

"Okay, well..." She reached for the door. "If you need anything else—"

"Stay." Ricky gripped her hand.

"Oh, I—" A tremble hijacked her voice. *Damn nerves.* "I thought I woke you."

"We couldn't sleep." He tugged her away from the door and removed the blankets from the box.

Within minutes, they had the beds made and the food devoured.

"You guys were starving." She sat at the end of the mattress, watching Ricky sort and stow the supplies.

"Not anymore, thanks to you." He grabbed the tequila and three plastic cups. "Let's drink."

Ricky projected a smile no woman could refuse. She wanted to feel it against her lips again. And other places. *All* the places.

She squeezed her thighs together.

"Confession." He sat beside her on the bed and poured three shots of alcohol. "Before today, I only consumed tequila using the lick-swallow-suck method."

"How very American of you."

"That's not how you drink it in Mexico?"

"No way. We don't need salt or lime. No licking or sucking. We sip it straight—"

"Say that again." Martin shot her a good hard stare.

"What?"

"Licking and sucking." He curled his lips around the words, drawing out each syllable in his sexy American accent.

Her pulse pounded in her throat, and Ricky fell still beside her.

A palpable hum charged the air, skittering along her arms and rousing the tiny hairs on her nape.

"Sip." She reached for one of the cups and took a deep breath.

Ricky followed suit, holding his up. "One…"

"Two…" She lifted the shot toward her mouth.

"Wait. Martin's not ready."

Martin, who sat on the other mattress looking underwhelmed by the prospect of drinking, picked up the third cup.

"One…" Ricky grinned at him. "Two… Three."

He and Martin threw the tequila down their gullets and gagged.

She sipped hers, and her throat closed in protest. She swallowed the rest and breathed through her nose as the liquid burned all the way to her stomach.

"Shit." She slammed down the cup and wiped the tears from her eyes. "That's horrible."

"What the fuck is this?" Ricky inspected the faded half-torn label on the bottle. "It tastes nothing like what we drank earlier today."

"What you had earlier is almost gone, so I got a new bottle, which is always hit and miss. Sometimes, it's watered down. Other times, it's mixed with something."

"This one's laced with paint thinner." Martin tossed his cup toward Ricky.

As the fiery burn faded from her throat, she breathed a sigh of relief that it was over.

Until Ricky announced, "Another round!"

They repeated the process again and again. With each round, the tequila went down smoother, and their smiles grew bigger.

Innocuous conversation filled the pauses between choking laughter. Embarrassing moments in school, favorite music, theories on dinosaur extinction—they covered a safe and wide range of topics.

As the bottle of turpentine neared its final drop, her memory began to blank, and her skull pounded as if she'd been hit in the back of the head by a shovel.

She remembered tipping into Ricky's lap, laughing hysterically at something he said. Martin had cut them both off from drinking sometime before that, but not soon enough.

She woke hours later.

Lying face down in the running position, her brain wailed, *Why, why, why?*

Oh, God, her stomach, her head, her unfortunate split ends… Everything hurt.

Never again.

She cracked open her eyes, immediately blinded by the light bulb over the sink.

Martin lay on the other bed beside her, his oh-so-pretty features void of the tension he carried when awake.

The weight of Ricky's arm rested across her back. She took up most of his bed, forcing him to squeeze between her and the wall. He pressed so close to her side his soft snores ruffled her hair.

The intimacy of it startled her tequila-addled brain. She did a mental inventory of her body. Still fully clothed. Still armed with the gun in her waistband.

They could've forced themselves on her, beaten her, or killed her. But they didn't.

They still could.

No, they were good people. Except they were convicts. More importantly, they were the sexiest men who ever walked the Earth.

Hang on. What did that have to do with anything? And why was she thinking in English? Wait, that was Spanish.

Shit, she was wasted.

With slow, dizzying movements, she crawled out from between them and swayed on her feet.

The room spun, and saliva rushed over her tongue. She was going to be sick.

Neither man stirred as she opened the door and backed into the dark hallway. No lights. That meant it was sometime before dawn.

Her senses heightened as she stumbled toward the stairway. It wasn't safe to wander around alone.

She always showered around three in the morning while everyone slept, but never when she was hammered. Her clumsy movements and foggy head made her paranoid and jumpy.

As she rounded the corner to the stairwell, the sound of a pained cry hit her ears.

A child's cry.

Her heartbeat banged in her head, and she staggered sideways, catching herself against the wall.

She gulped down the next breath and held it in her lungs, listening, shivering, waiting.

Nothing.

Sometimes, she woke in her cell, convinced she heard a weeping child. The nightmare felt so real she often ran into the corridor, searching for an actual kid, only to realize she was chasing the haunting remnants of memory, the echoes of the little sister she once had.

She heard it again and froze. The cry sounded so small, so scared and sad. She spun, overshooting her steps and crashing to her knees.

Vera, Vera, Vera.

Goddammit, she missed her sister so fucking much.

A sob crawled up, and she pushed herself into the stairwell, teetering, lurching, unable to escape the crushing pain.

Tears spilled free as she wobbled on the top step. The stairs rippled beneath her blurred eyes. Maybe she would fall and break her neck.

Awwwwesome.

Would the eternal darkness welcome her? She was already in hell. What could be worse than this?

Shouldn't she have a legit reason to die, though? She needed a valiant cause with a colorful flag that she could wave as she rode off to face her death.

She had no flags, no causes, no reason.

But hey, if there was nothing worth dying for, there was nothing worth living for, either.

She should just take that final step into the bowels of yonder stairwell and find out what came next. Maybe Vera would stop crying.

A hand gripped her shoulder, and she jumped, releasing a yelp as she whirled.

"Tula." Ricky yanked her away from the stairs and clutched her shoulders, steadying her. "What are you doing?"

"Shhh." She tried to press a finger against his lips. Her hand knew roughly where to aim, but it landed on his jaw. "Do you hear her?"

"Who?"

"My little sister."

Her balance felt off because seriously, two legs weren't sufficient in keeping a person upright in a wave. The thought made her thirsty. Could she get dehydrated while swimming? Why was she swimming?

She wriggled her lips into the shape of a grin. "I'm drunk."

"No shit. You were about to take those stairs face first and..." He gripped her jaw, forcing her to meet his eyes. "Were you crying?"

She touched her cheek, and her fingers poked through a soggy cloud. "I can't feel my face. But..." She leaned in, and her nose collided with his concrete chest. "You should know that if I had a grilled cheese sandwich, I would most definitely, positively, accurately hit my mouth with it."

Laughter shook the warm wall that held up her head. "That so?"

"Mm-hmm. A Ricky Martin sandwich would work, too, but I call the middle." She gasped. "Oh, no. We lost Martin."

His hand guided her face to the hallway. She blinked, focusing hard until three blond Viking gods merged into one.

Oh, dear lord, Martin was magical.

He reclined against the wall a few feet away, fingertips resting in the front pockets of his jeans, looking for all the world like he could strip away her panties with only the intensity of his eyes.

"Don't do it." She pointed at him. "Don't you dare. My panties are *mine.*"

"All right, *querida*. Here we go." Ricky hooked his arms under her and cradled her against his chest.

She floated down the stairs in a haze.

"This is nice." She hugged his neck and breathed in his intoxicating male scent. "Except whoa... My brain is moving slower, I think. By a half-second or so."

Ricky chuckled softly at her ear. "Slow down a little more, and you'll be thinking at Martin's speed."

A glance behind him gave her a direct view of Martin. He trailed at a distance, his gaze sweeping the perimeter.

"Am I the only one who drank too much?" She dropped her hundred-pound head on Ricky's shoulder.

"We all drank the same amount, but Martin and I are a lot bigger." He touched his lips to her brow. "You're going to hurt tomorrow. I'm sorry."

He lowered her onto a bed, and she looked around, recognizing her room.

Martin sat beside her feet and removed her shoes.

"Don't forget the toes." She stared at the rotating ceiling and gagged on the toxins gurgling from her stomach.

"What about the toes?"

"They need polish. It's been too long. I'm a girl, dontcha know?"

"Yes, I'm fully aware you're a girl."

Was that Martin talking?

"The strong, silent type." She waved a heavy hand at the silhouette beside her feet. "You just sit there and look pretty."

She lost Ricky in her periphery, but after a few long blinks, he was there again.

"Drink." He pushed her potable water jug into her hands, forcing her to suck it down.

"My jeans…" Her waistband constricted her stomach, making her restless and itchy. "I can't sleep in this."

"No, wait." Ricky caught her hand on the zipper. "They need to stay on." He cleared his voice. "For protection. Just keep them on."

"Protection is good." She sank into the bed and drifted into a spinning, nauseating half-sleep.

"Tula." Martin's rumbling drawl popped her eyes open. "Why did Hector make you a member of the cartel? How did that happen?"

"I saved his life." She closed her eyes against a hammering headache. "Then I taught him English. If you want to join La Rocha, I'll make it happen. Just tell me you want in."

A hand stroked through her hair, brushing strands away from her face. "How long are you in for?"

"I have three years left in prison. Forever with La Rocha Cartel."

"Are you involved in their human sex trafficking operation?"

"It's drugs," she mumbled. "And guns. That's what they smuggle. I stay out of that stuff."

"Hector abducts women and children, Tula." Ricky's voice penetrated her fuzzy mind. "He sells them as slaves. You know that, right?"

"No, he doesn't." She tried to laugh, but holy hell, she felt severely tired and sick to her stomach. "He's a nice old man and respects women. He respects *me*. Tula Gomez. A high school Spanish teacher from Phoenix. I was just a teacher, you know? I didn't do anything wrong. I tried to help my sister, and she…" Tears burned her scratchy eyes. "I lost her. I lost Vera."

A sob swelled in her throat, but she didn't have the strength or focus to give into it.

"Hey." A strong pair of arms pulled her into a blanket of heat.

"You're not alone. Not anymore."

As it turned out, she had the energy to cry after all.

Bracketed between two hard bodies, she wept until the pain faded into darkness.

FIFTEEN

"We disproved one rumor." Martin lay face down on his cot, his limbs heavy from sleep. "She can't drink the biggest man under the table."

"It's also safe to say…" Ricky rose from his bed and stretched, wearing only a pair of boxers. "She doesn't know Hector's secrets."

"Maybe not, but she knows *him*."

"It's weird how she looks up to him like she's forgotten he's a cartel boss and all-around horrible human being." Grabbing his toothbrush, Ricky lumbered to the sink. "Do you think she's brainwashed?"

"I don't know."

The sight of all that flawless, nude skin made him lose his train of thought. He turned his face into his folded arms beneath his head and tried to concentrate on something other than his best friend's half-naked body.

They'd stayed in Tula's cell until dawn, watching her sleep and keeping her safe in her inebriated state. Before Area Three began to stir, they'd hurried back to their own cell, relieved that none of the supplies she'd given them had been stolen.

Slumber had come quickly and sucked away most of their day.

They should go check on her, make sure she was okay. It was his first thought when he woke, a stabbing instinct in his gut.

Was she still asleep? Did she have pain medication to soothe a hangover? Was she drinking water? Was anyone bothering her?

Imagining her venturing out in her weakened state among two-hundred male inmates made him feel goddamn feral. He needed to be at her side, protecting her the same way he and Ricky watched out for each other.

But she wasn't his responsibility. No one had forced the alcohol down her throat. Even so, they'd deliberately coaxed her into drinking too much.

When she'd told them she brought tequila, the idea had popped into his head. He saw the same plan formulate in Ricky's eyes right before he started pouring shots.

Getting her drunk had been easy. Loosening her tongue had been even easier. But watching her cry herself to sleep? That had been fucking brutal.

Her longing for her sister had bled through his skin. Her hiccuping cries lingered in his bones. Her tears fused her pain with his and messed with his head.

He hated that she was hurting, and there was nothing he could do to stop it.

Ricky spat toothpaste into the sink. "We need to see how she's doing."

"Yep." Instantly on his feet, Martin brushed his teeth and splashed cold water on his face.

They dressed and stepped into the hall. The short walk to the stairwell and down to Tula's cell led them past throngs of glaring inmates.

He didn't look at the floor or aggressively return the menacing scowls. He kept his eyes focused straight ahead, determined to reach Tula's cell without being attacked.

When they arrived at her door, his relief was short-lived. Ricky's knock was met with the violent sounds of retching on the other side.

They stormed into her room. Martin scanned the empty space as Ricky raced to her kneeling position.

Bent over the toilet, she dry-heaved uncontrollably. Tremors shook her shoulders, and her cheeks glistened with tears.

Martin felt that unnerving instinct again. The one that compelled him to protect her from anything that might cause her pain.

It wasn't an unfamiliar urge. He experienced it every day with Ricky — the imperative to shelter, comfort, and take care of his best friend.

Crouched beside her, Ricky slid a hand in her hair, holding the velvet curtain away from her face. His other arm supported her midsection as she continued to gag into the toilet.

There was nothing left in her stomach.

"You need to try to eat something and sleep it off." Martin collected some of her clothes and located her toothbrush. "We're taking you upstairs."

Ricky touched his brow to the back of her head. "You're not alone."

"Okay." She breathed out a ragged sound. "Thank you."

For the rest of the day, she drifted in and out of sleep in Ricky's bed, curled up against his chest.

As Ricky dozed with her, Martin warmed a can of broth on the portable stove and indulged in the pleasure of watching them.

Ricky's long, hard body fit possessively around her petite form. His black hair made hers look brown where it caressed its way down her back, reaching toward her firm ass.

There was a caginess about her, too much hesitation in her movements and caution in her eyes. Even as she slept, she exhaled a whimper and squirmed uncomfortably. She wasn't used to being handled so intimately.

After spending an entire night with her, he'd gained a lot of insight into her personality and circumstances.

Her tattoos gave her a bold, edgy look that stood out against her bronze skin, but she hadn't sleeved her arms to honor a memory or express her individuality. Last night, she said it was her armor, to look the part of a hardened prisoner.

Beneath the artwork lurked a sweet, modest woman, one who shied away from attention and avoided chaos and drama. Hours of unguarded, drunken conversation had revealed a gentle soul. She adored children, teared up when she laughed, and dreamed of a simple, quiet life.

She was in the most violent prison in the nation, right here, only feet away, but it was so easy to see her in a classroom wearing a conservative dress, her hair gathered in a low bun, and pink lipstick on her beautiful, patient smile.

She didn't belong here.

She did, however, look perfect in Ricky's arms.

If she let him, Ricky would treat her like a queen.

Like Martin, Ricky had been sexually trained by Van. Whoever was lucky enough to share Ricky's bed reaped the benefits of that training. And his expertise was only one of his strengths.

Ricky was, quite simply, the most selfless and dependable person Martin had ever met.

He trusted Ricky with his life. Those brown eyes were his home, and whenever they rested on him, he never felt more whole, more peaceful, or more healthy.

But there was something else there, too. A physical attraction that compelled him to stare too long, too hungrily. Seeing Ricky and Tula together only magnified his desire, doubled the temptation.

A deeply buried need pricked at the edges of his awareness, taunting him with what-ifs.

What if he gave in and finally tasted Ricky's lips? What if he put his hands all over Tula's delectable body? What if he buried his damn nightmares and joined them in bed?

It was only a matter of time before Ricky stripped Tula down to her skin and charmed his way between her legs. The thought hardened Martin's cock and made his blood run hot.

When he imagined them in the throes of passion, he was right there with them, commanding their movements, devouring the union of their sinful bodies, and taking himself in hand, stroking, groaning, and coating their flesh with his come.

Ricky's hard lines against her delicate curves, his muscled arms holding her carefully, protectively, and their expressions soft with sleep — they were painfully beautiful and mesmerizing in their stillness, like a sculptured masterpiece of the gods.

His attraction to them was visceral, but his desire went deeper. What he felt was the start of a much-needed inhale that pulled through his senses and sank into his chest. It was a starved breath that turned into a hypnotic hum as it hit his blood and fed his soul.

He could watch them forever — sleeping, talking, and Christ, he ached to watch them fuck.

Damn if that didn't make him feel like a predator.

It made him feel like Jeff.

Jeff and his heavy fists, ruthless demands, and his taking, forcing, breaking...

His stomach hardened, killing the warmth in his groin.

If he had to do it again, he would. He would pick up that hammer and bash the motherfucker's skull over and over and over.

He scrubbed his hands down his face and looked up.

Ricky's gaze met his, catching and holding. He tucked Tula tight against his chest and ran his nose through her hair. Without looking away, he skimmed a hand down the back of her leg and tangled the other in her hair.

His brown eyes glimmered, teasing.

Come here, they said. *I dare you.*

Martin squinted sternly, his voice low. "Hungry?"

"Always."

"Dinner." He held up the warmed can of broth.

A groan vibrated from the beauty in Ricky's arms. "I feel like death."

Ricky grazed his lips along her slender neck. "If death looked as good as you, suicide would be all the rage."

"Oh, God, stop." She pushed against his chest and rolled to her back. "I need a shower."

He and Ricky tensed.

Privacy didn't exist in the communal showers. How did she wash without getting assaulted? Is that where Garra came in? Did he clear out the bathroom while she showered?

"Where's Garra?" Martin shifted down the mattress, erasing the distance to hold out the broth to her.

"I relieved him from his job." She sipped from the can and handed it back.

"Why?"

"I wanted to talk to you, get to know you. I couldn't do that with him breathing down my neck."

He detected truthfulness in her words, but not the whole truth.

"You gave up your protection." He bent toward her, propping his forearm on his leg. "You think that was wise?"

Her face reddened. "I came here last night, hoping for friendship. Showing up with a guard doesn't exactly engender good will. Was I naive to think I don't need protection from you?"

"Yes. Extremely naive." Ricky gripped her arm when she started to pull away. "You know nothing about us. We could've hurt you."

"But you didn't." She yanked her arm free. "I trusted my gut, and it didn't steer me wrong."

He met Ricky's eyes over her head. She preferred their protection over Garra's, and they both knew why.

"How many times did Garra rape you?" The question burned like venom from his throat.

"Just the one time." She struggled to look up, but after a moment, she summoned enough courage to meet his gaze. "I'm tired of being alone."

They were leaving in three months. Where did that leave her?

Here. Alone. For three more years.

"You're safe with us." Ricky touched her chin, guiding her face to his. "But I'll be honest. The prospect of you showering in a bathroom full of hard dicks is horrifying. We can only fend off so many men."

"Oh, I…" She picked at a frayed hole in her jeans. "I always shower between three and four in the morning, when everyone's asleep."

Martin nodded, impressed with her adaptability. "We have a few hours to wait. How do you feel?"

"Better. I haven't been that wasted since college." Her eyes narrowed. "I don't know whether to be mad that you got me drunk or thankful you stuck around to clean up the puke." She slumped back on the bed. "How many secrets did you wheedle out of me?"

"Only your dirtiest, darkest ones." Ricky leaned his back against the wall and lifted her denim-clad legs to rest across his lap.

"I'm serious. What did I tell you?"

He appreciated her directness and couldn't think of a reason to lie to her. "You described your first few weeks in Jaulaso, how your relationship with Hector came to be, and why he made Garra your personal guard. You asked Hector to castrate him? That was a risky move."

"I was desperate." She stared down at her lap and bit her lip.

"We know you have three years left on your sentence." He waited for her to look up. Then he let his eyes convey his sincerity. "You're serving time for a crime we know you didn't commit."

"None of that is a secret." She shrugged.

"You told us you lost your little sister." Ricky traced a finger along her calf.

"Oh." Her shoulders hunched forward. "I vaguely remember her crying last night. I dream about her sometimes and wake up thinking she's here. As a child. It's fucked up."

"What happened to her?"

"Wish I knew. The morning I was arrested, Vera called me. She was in trouble again..."

She talked through the events that led to her arrest, her sister's possible connection to the cartel, the mistaken identity, and how the military tortured and framed her for drug smuggling.

"I've kept in touch with the detectives at the Ciudad Hueca police department." She hooked an arm around her waist. "There have been no leads, no body, nothing. She just...vanished."

Ricky gave him a knowing look.

Yeah, they knew a guy. Cole Hartman had a specialized skill set and a military background that connected him with a lot of unsavory people. He located Camila's missing sister and rescued Kate when she was abducted. If anyone could find Vera Gomez, it was Cole Hartman.

But they couldn't contact him. Not until they were released.

Matias Restrepo had warned them that all cell phones in Jaulaso were strictly controlled by La Rocha Cartel. The inmates tracked transmissions and monitored every phone call.

Cole Hartman was tied in with Restrepo Cartel, a sworn enemy of La Rocha. Calling him from any phone would expose their loyalties.

"Hector's looking for her." She folded her hands on her lap.

"Is that right?" He cocked his head, unable to decipher her stony expression. "What else does Hector do for you?"

"What does that mean?"

"Does he touch you?"

"No!" She gasped. "Never. He's not like that."

Something was off about their relationship. Why would Hector treat her so kindly? What did he gain from it?

"Does he talk to you about his human trafficking operation?"

Ricky asked.

"Oh, my God." She sat ramrod straight, her eyes igniting with fire. "You *did* say that last night. I thought I dreamed it." Her hands balled into fists. "You don't know what you're talking about."

"It's true, Tula." Ricky reached for her.

She jumped back and scrambled off the bed.

"He's kidnapping women and children in the U.S." Martin moved to the edge of the mattress, prepared to grab her if she went for the door. "He smuggles them across the border and sells them as slaves. Thousands of *children.*"

"He wouldn't do that." She snatched the toothbrush he'd brought from her cell and moved to the sink. "I sit in all his meetings. I would've heard them discussing it." She tackled her teeth in a frenzy, scrubbing and spitting. "I was just like you before I met him. His reputation terrified me, but I was wrong about him. He's a good man."

"By *good man*, you mean nine levels of vicious, terror-reigning, mass-murdering tyranny."

"No." She spat into the sink.

"He's a cartel boss."

"That's a job title, not a character trait."

Hard to argue that. Matias Restrepo actively hunted down and decimated slave operations across Latin America, and he was the leader of the biggest cartel in Colombia.

Hector La Rocha, however, did nothing of the sort.

Their vigilante group, the Freedom Fighters, had been collecting evidence against him for years. But he couldn't share that with her without revealing his connections.

"Are you *procesados*?" She leaned a hip against the sink and crossed her arms. "Or *sentenciados*?"

Under the Mexican Constitution, pretrial defendants whose cases were still in process — *procesados* — were to be housed separately from prisoners who were serving sentences — *sentenciados*.

The same Constitution prohibited the blending of male and female prisoners in the same facility.

Jaulaso was one of several cartel-controlled prisons that gave the Constitution the middle finger.

"We're still in process." He glanced at Ricky and returned to her. "Why?"

"You'll be charged within four months. That's the law. And they'll do it without your presence in court, even if you have a good attorney."

"Is that what happened to you?" Ricky stroked his jaw, his attention fully engaged.

"Yeah."

They didn't need an attorney. They had the Mexican government and a resourceful cartel boss on their side.

"How do you want to do your time?" She ran a hand through her hair. "Do you want the welcoming committee to extort a pound of flesh from your bodies every day? Or do you want to be one of the guys in the welcoming committee?"

"I think," Ricky said, "I'll just pass my time making macaroni necklaces for my eight kiddos at home."

Her mouth dropped open.

"Ricky." Martin pinched the bridge of his nose. "Neither of us has kids, nor do we have any desire to be involved in cartel politics and disputes." He met her eyes. "That's what you're suggesting, yeah? You want us to work for La Rocha?"

"You either work for them or against them."

"Did Hector send you to us with that sales pitch?" He glared at her. "Or are you just looking out for us as a *friend*?"

Her spine straightened. "Hector doesn't trust you, and it sounds like that goes both ways. Look…" She lowered onto the bed beside him, her expression open and pleading. "I don't condone the violence, and if I could quietly do my time and stay away from all of it, I would. But that's not an option in Jaulaso. Trust me on this."

He trusted her motivations, but she wasn't telling them everything.

"What does he know about us?" Ricky clenched his teeth.

"Nothing. That's the problem." She rolled her bottom lip between her fingers. "Why were your identities wiped?"

Ah, so Hector La Rocha had them investigated.

He and Ricky didn't have living relatives and were never reported as missing persons. They were, however, responsible for the murders of some very bad people—rapists, slave traders, and over the last two years, they'd taken out several big players in La Rocha Cartel.

It was paramount that Hector didn't discover the latter.

They could've entered the prison system with fake identities, but that wouldn't have stopped a skilled investigator from linking them to their real names. So they took the safest route and had Cole Hartman erase them from existence. Good thing, too.

"We have enemies from a previous life." The rehearsed lie rolled off Ricky's tongue. "That's none of Hector's business."

She blew out a heavy sigh. "I'm trying to protect you."

"From Hector?" Martin's neck stiffened.

"From everyone."

"Tula." Ricky crooked a finger. "Come here."

Her throat bounced with a swallow, and she shook her head. "I don't think that's a good idea."

The subtle squeeze of her thighs contradicted her words.

If he had to guess, she was attracted to Ricky, but she feared that attraction.

Shifting toward her, he rested his fingers on the back of her neck and guided her gaze to his. "Tell me what you're thinking."

She cut her eyes to Ricky and back to him. "He's going to try to kiss me."

"There's no *trying* involved." Ricky stretched his legs across the bed and reclined against the wall, all lean muscle and confident male.

"And?" He ghosted the backs of his fingers down the curve of her neck, making her shiver.

"We just met yesterday. I don't know either of you, and I never kiss on the first date."

Fucking hell, this woman. She was such a precious rarity, so guileless and straightforward. His chest squeezed at the thought of someone as innocent as her being locked up in this hell for five years. It was fucking unfair.

"I held your hair while you puked last night," Ricky said. "Pretty sure that skips like five dates."

She didn't look convinced.

Martin didn't want to force the issue, but the urgency of a three-month timeline pressed down upon him.

If they couldn't seal a kiss with this girl, there was no way they would convince her to do anything else, like steal information from Hector.

They needed her trust because right now, she was the only angle they had.

"Tula." Martin put his face in hers. "Give that man your mouth. Swear to God, it'll be the best kiss you've ever had."

Her breath hitched. "You know that from experience."

"I know *him*." He didn't look at Ricky, but those dark eyes burned a trail of heat across his skin.

Her eyes flashed. "You kiss him. If you do it, I will."

A shifting sensation squeezed a sharp pang near his heart. Nerve endings tingled along his thighs, and the sudden acceleration of his pulse sent a surge of blood to his groin.

As his body revved up, his mind bristled at her words, making his tone sound meaner than he intended. "That's not how I operate."

"I knew it. You're one of those." She studied her fingernails, baiting him.

"Finish that thought, Tula."

If she made a homophobic comment, he would bend her over his knee and redden her ass.

"I've dated guys like you." She pushed back her shoulders. "Bossy. Controlling. Always has the last word."

He laughed in surprise. "Your point?"

"The thought of kissing him doesn't repulse you. What raises your hackles is someone telling you to do it."

The accuracy of her words hit him directly in the stomach.

He didn't take orders from anyone. Never again.

Memories — a year's worth of sick, brutal memories — unfurled from a desolate place in his mind. He was no different than the son of a bitch he'd killed so brutally.

The pitch-black fantasies he'd kept locked down erupted all at once, spilling from his subconscious in ribbons of depravity.

Restraining, choking, whipping, forcing, using, ripping open, bleeding out, hard and ruthless, unsafe and unwilling, no hole left unpunished — everything Jeff had done to him was exactly what he craved to do to Ricky and Tula.

Violent sex was all he knew, and it aroused him so deeply it terrified him.

A hand rested on his shoulder, warm and familiar. He turned toward Ricky, and their eyes met and held.

Despite the disturbing direction of his thoughts, he found peace in Ricky's gaze. It wasn't where Ricky looked that was important. It was where he didn't look.

Those eyes didn't slide down Martin's body, indicating lust. They didn't stare at his lips, demanding a kiss. They didn't lower to his groin, signaling a desire to touch.

Ricky stared right at him, into him, wordlessly confessing this was more than sexual desire. Ricky didn't just want to fuck him. He wanted it all — friendship, love, intimacy, forever.

It was just a look shared between best friends, but it was powerful enough to punch through Martin's memories, sink past heavily guarded walls, and fuse with the longing he couldn't hide from Ricky.

This wouldn't end with a kiss.

He would hurt them beyond repair.

"For fuck's sake." Tula leaned in, infusing the air with her sweet, feminine scent. "If you two don't kiss after staring at each other like that, I'm going to lose all respect for you."

A delicious shiver slid beneath his skin and froze his lungs. His body might've forgotten how to breathe, but it knew exactly how to take what it wanted.

His hand went to Ricky's nape, a merciless grip that yanked Ricky's head where he wanted it.

Then he took what belonged to him and devoured Ricky's mouth.

SIXTEEN

A vicious fire roared inside Martin, unleashing a dormant need to plunder and consume.

After seven years without sex, he didn't have any restraint left to ease into a kiss. He hauled Ricky against him and mauled that perfect mouth with sharp teeth and bruising lips.

Ricky opened for him with a guttural groan, and Martin swept his tongue inside, hunting and licking every hidden wet crevice between teeth and cheek.

He'd denied himself too long, but that wasn't the only reason he felt so reckless and desperate.

Ricky wasn't just an exceptionally trained kisser. He kissed passionately, feverishly, with every breath, every beat of his heart, and every muscle in his body.

"Sweet Jesus." Ricky gasped and slipped greedy fingers beneath Martin's shirt and along his back.

Blood flowed, and muscles trembled beneath the diabolical caress of masculine hands. His hunger rose in a flood of heat, throbbing between his legs and skyrocketing his heart rate.

They pressed closer, chests colliding, arms winding, and bodies entwining as they frantically deepened the kiss. It wasn't enough.

He hauled Ricky against him and took him down to the mattress, falling atop him in a grinding crush of hips and swollen cocks.

Fucking goddamn, his familiar taste. It was the first time they'd ever kissed, but he recognized the dark, crisp flavor of Ricky's mouth as if it were his own.

The scent of Ricky's hot skin seeped into his lungs. The firmness of

Ricky's lips permanently imprinted the moment on his heart. He melted into the sensations, clinging tight to the pleasure as Ricky grunted and thrust beneath him.

"I need you." Ricky gripped his ass and bit his lips. "Please. Fucking touch me. Hurt me. Put me out of my misery."

The intensity of that surrender vibrated the muscles beneath Martin's hands, but the words gave him pause.

Hurt me.

Ricky didn't know what he was asking.

Gutting memories invaded his senses and coiled his insides into a bloody knot of horror.

How was he supposed to separate the damage he endured with Jeff and Van, the pain Ricky craved, and the hurt he desperately needed to inflict? There were levels of right and wrong, willing and unwilling, and gray areas in between. He didn't know how to navigate intimacy with one person, let alone two.

All he knew was he didn't want to stop.

Lashing his tongue wildly against Ricky's, he indulged in Ricky's surrender. With his hands fisted in Ricky's thick black hair, he bit, sucked, and kissed savagely and mindlessly with abandon.

Until nausea hit his stomach.

He pushed away before it became too much, before he lost himself in the past and puked his guts out. Or worse, before he became the monster he feared.

"Tula," he rasped breathlessly.

She was already there, lips parted, nipples pebbling beneath her shirt, and the burnt umber of her gorgeous eyes glittering around dilated pupils.

"He's waiting." He sat beside Ricky, breathing heavily as he tried to reel in the unraveling mess of his thoughts.

He just needed a breather, and she seemed to read that in his expression.

With a nod, she turned to Ricky and said softly, "That was exciting."

"You liked watching us." Ricky sat up and lifted her onto his lap, arranging her legs to straddle him.

She shook her head and blinked.

Ricky kissed her, just a tease of lips, before boldly pinching one of her hard nipples. "These don't lie."

She batted his hand away and touched her brow to his. "You kissed like you've been lovers for years." She feathered her fingers along his whiskered jaw. "You're in love with each other."

The precision of her words zapped every molecule in the air. Ricky felt it, his eyes locking onto Martin's like beams of energy, holding him stationary in time and space. They emitted a thousand words that didn't require voice or explanation.

Lines had been crossed.

Boundaries erased.

Everything had changed.

"Thank you." Ricky touched his lips to hers. Then he did it again. "You opened a door."

"And now she was walking with demons." Her mouth twisted. "A quote from *The Hellbound Heart*."

Must've been one of the books in her cell. Martin wasn't much of a reader, but the sexy, nerdy, schoolteacher persona she hid from the other prisoners turned him on like nothing else.

"I don't know that one, but I can give you this." Ricky cleared his voice and belted out a familiar tune, "Her lips are devil-red, and her skin's the color mocha. She…will…wear…you…out."

"Livin' la Vida Loca." She threaded her fingers through his hair. "That has me thinking…"

"What's up, *querida?*" Ricky trailed his mouth along her jaw.

"There's no Tula in Ricky Martin."

"Wanna bet?" He nipped at her throat and met Martin's eyes. "I've fantasied about this for years. I want to watch him with you. I want him to watch you with me. I want the three of us together, joined in every position, fucking and ravaging without hesitation or caution."

Christ, the way Ricky just threw that out there in his gravelly voice… His confidence was sexy as hell.

"How could you always want that when you just met me?" she asked.

"In my wildest fantasies, the woman between us was faceless." Ricky inclined his head, edging closer to her lips. "Not anymore." He cupped his hands around her neck. "God help me, I never imagined you'd be this beautiful. Every time I look at you, it fucking hurts."

"Ha." She laughed nervously. "Such a charmer. Men and women everywhere must fall at your feet."

"Not the ones who matter." His hands slipped down around her waist, pulling her hips against his.

She leaned back, and her mouth drew into a straight line.

Her reluctance made Martin tense, but he understood it. He wrestled with himself every second he spent with Ricky. Desire battling fear, the present always at war with the past. It was easier to shut down and pull away. It was safer.

Ricky caught his gaze, and in that moment, they shared the same thought.

She didn't need seduction. She needed compassion, connection, and security—everything he had with Ricky.

Martin rose to his knees and moved in behind her, straddling Ricky's legs and loosely sandwiching her between them.

"I will never disregard what you've been through." He swept the heavy length of her hair to one shoulder and rested his lips against her graceful neck. "Nor will I abuse the trust you gave me when you told me about the electrocution and Garra's assault. You haven't been touched by a man in two years?"

"No."

"Any lasting damage from the torture? Anything I need to be concerned about?"

"No, I'm healed."

She eased a shivery sigh as he kissed a winding path to her upper arm and back again, lingering beneath her ear.

"Tonight, your clothes stay on." He ran his nose through her hair, breathing in the soft scent that was uniquely her. "No pressure. No expectations. No venturing into places you're not ready to go."

"Okay." She rested her hands on his thighs, where they bracketed her hips.

"Are you ready to experience the best kiss of your life?"

"Good God." Her fingers dug into the denim on his legs. "How can you top the kiss I just experienced between you two?"

He locked eyes with Ricky over her head. Their gazes hung, tangling and fusing, neither of them moving.

This was just the beginning. Once she got a taste of Ricky, she wouldn't be able to stop.

It would be a long night of clothes-on torment, but he could handle the kissing. In fact, he couldn't wait to feel her soft mouth against his.

He didn't want to fuck this up. If he stayed right here in their space, reaching for Ricky's gaze, breathing the feminine fragrance of Tula's hair, their bodies aligned and mouths sealed together, he could do this without losing his shit.

"Tula." He reached around her and gripped the back of Ricky's neck. "Give him your mouth."

SEVENTEEN

Ricky's body thrummed to life as Tula leaned in and offered her mouth. She did it slowly, with nervous starts and stops, which only made him want her more.

As the sweetness of her breath quivered across his lips, everything inside him went taut with need. But Martin's hand on his nape reminded him to go slow and keep himself in check.

Dear God, desire looked sinful on her, heating her cheeks and stretching her pupils until her brown eyes turned black.

Her lust-soaked expression was exactly what he wanted to see on a woman before he took her mouth.

With Tula, he started with light teasing sips. Then he sucked faster, more assertively, licking and drinking the hesitation off her soft lips.

"Ricky." Her hands found his hair, tugging him closer as greedy little noises escaped her throat. "More."

That was all the invitation he needed. He trapped her in his arms and kissed her harder, opening her hot mouth with his tongue and delving deep.

Martin tightened his grip on Ricky's neck and lowered his lips to her shoulder. The potency of his presence, the weight of his gaze, the collective sounds of their breaths—all of it coursed blood to Ricky's groin.

Christ, he loved being watched. Never in a million years did he think Martin would participate in something like this. And the woman in his arms? They couldn't have found a better match.

She was submissive and fierce, honest yet cautious, and because he was a man, he had the biggest fucking hard-on for her perfect body.

Holding this sexy, exotic creature on his lap, he knew he would never get enough of her.

He savored her with deep-reaching strokes, ravishing her more aggressively, his pulse singing in his veins as flavors exploded in his mouth. Her clean minty taste, the wet warmth of her breaths, and the honeyed essence of her innocence... He gorged himself on everything soft and feminine and sensual about her.

His hands roved over her shirt, memorizing every elusive dip and beautifully toned curve underneath. He wanted to rip away the cotton and bask in the feel of her satiny skin. But she wasn't ready.

Neither was Martin.

He retreated from the wet heaven of her mouth to steal a glance at his friend.

The emerald facets of Martin's eyes flickered amid the shadows of their small cell. There was a war going on inside that head, an inferno of want raging against a torrent of pain. Whatever happened to Martin years ago had severely messed him up.

Ricky would give anything to teleport through time and save that boy from the horrors he'd endured.

Maybe he and Martin shouldn't have kissed, but he didn't detect a trace of regret in Martin's gaze. Their friendship was too solid, their bond too tight. No matter where they went from here or how they fit Tula into their relationship, they would only grow stronger together.

The hot little vixen between them shifted on his lap, peeking at him from beneath heavy lashes before turning to Martin.

She licked swollen lips and touched a finger to the deep grooves between Martin's brows.

Stretching her spine put her mouth a hairsbreadth from his, and she waited there, eyes wide and unblinking, silently offering her vulnerability.

He glanced at Ricky for a fraction of a second before capturing her lips. He pressed in gently, then harder, sliding his wicked tongue through her mouth.

The sight of them melting into each other stole his breath. The weight of their bodies straddling his lap sent feverish tingles across his skin. He hooked an arm around her waist while his other hand traveled over the thick bones and sinewy thews that sculpted Martin's torso.

His possessive hands remembered Martin's body on the training mat. The corrugated terrace of abs, ripped biceps, and muscled legs locked around him, slick with sweat, and flexing with domination as they grappled and rolled across the floor. All testosterone, agility, and infinite power contracting and heaving beneath tanned skin.

Martin's hands had the strength to grab him and pin him to the wrestling mat without mercy. But as he watched Martin with her, he noted the gentleness in every touch, the way those ruthless fingers slipped through her hair and let the tresses fall slowly, strand by strand, as he kissed her at leisure.

They made a tantalizing couple. Martin's hard jaw gliding against the pixie-shape of her face, their tongues rubbing together and sending soft licking sounds through the room. Panting breaths. Rustling clothes. Pleasure-drenched moans. It was the most erotic thing he'd ever witnessed.

Martin held the bulk of his weight off Ricky's thighs while she sat fully on his lap. With her legs straddling Ricky, she had to twist at the waist to kiss Martin behind her. She felt like a feather on his legs, but she couldn't have been comfortable.

"Lie down." Ricky tapped her thigh.

With the beds pushed together, they stretched out across them with Tula in the middle. Martin lay on his side, propped up on his elbow, mirroring Ricky's position.

A long, deep breath nuzzled between them, silent and content, but there was a slow build in it. It started quietly, stirring the energy in the air.

Inhales chased exhales, the cadence of breaths growing faster, louder. Toes curled against the mattress. Chests rose and fell in tandem, and Martin drifted imperceptibly closer as if he wasn't aware he was doing it.

Tula's warm fingers rested against Ricky's chest. He covered her hand with his, holding her to him, but he didn't look at her. His gaze was confined by Martin's stare.

Spiritual closeness lived and breathed through their eye contact. But it was no longer just a platonic connection between friends.

A fire had been kindled, stoked with a brazen kiss. He couldn't brush it off as a smoldering moment of lust. A cold shower wouldn't douse this.

Their hunger for each other was a waking volcano that had been burning too deep and too long beneath the surface. It would never die out, never grow cold. Not without total devastation.

Face to face, gazes locked, they held onto each other the way they always had. With their eyes, their history with Van, and the trust they'd forged over the years.

Except now, Ricky needed more.

He needed to hold Martin in his arms and wrap his mouth around Martin's cock while thrusting deep inside Tula's body. He needed her right here with them, between them, under them.

"I love the way you look at each other," she murmured. "It's like you're having a whole conversation without moving your lips, like you're reading each other's thoughts."

"I read his expressions." Martin traced a finger along the waistband at her hip. "And the way he holds himself. His body language is loud."

"Is that right?" A smirk pulled at his lips. "What am I thinking?"

Martin angled over her and clutched Ricky's neck. "You're choreographing all the positions you would arrange her in while I fuck your ass."

Sharp, penetrating heat shot along the length of his cock.

"Is that true?" she asked.

"Yeah." He felt wired and overheated as he studied the dark prisms of her eyes. "Since I don't know your expressions yet, tell me what you're thinking. What do you want?"

"This." A small smile trembled at the corner of her mouth. "Two nice, gorgeous, experienced men who kiss like…" Her lips pouted out with a pushed-out breath. "I don't even know. I've never experienced anything like it. You *both* have this incredibly magical, mind-numbing way you kiss, like you were born from the same womb or something." She squinted. "You're not brothers, are you?"

"No." Ricky laughed. "That would be awkward."

"Good, because if you're asking me what I want…"

"I am."

"I want to live in your kisses. For the next hour. For the rest of the night. For as long as we're here. Watching your mouths move together…" Her breath stuttered. "It's freeing. Makes me forget I'm in prison."

The electricity in her words fueled the fire inside him. A fire that burned for his best friend.

His gaze lifted, but Martin was already leaning in. Bent over her chest, he grabbed Ricky's neck and slammed their lips together.

Their tongues met and retreated. Then they clashed again in a possessive duel, whipping and licking and cutting with teeth.

Martin went wild, feeding the flames that roared between them. His fist pulled Ricky's hair as his tongue thrust frantically, relentlessly, fucking Ricky's mouth with brutal strokes. Desire rose and swelled, untamed and ravenous.

Then he broke away, his chest heaving, and his face contorted in torment.

His distress was a knife through Ricky's heart.

"Are you okay?" She reached for Martin.

"Yeah." He let her touch his jaw, and the contact seemed to chase his demons back to wherever they came from. The shadows in his eyes receded, and the cords in his neck relaxed.

No wonder he was celibate. He was navigating around a switch inside him. When it flipped on, it went full throttle, barreling him into a vicious sexual rage.

Ricky wanted him rough, ruthless, and out of control, but not if it caused Martin pain. He needed to figure out how to ease Martin forward without taking too many agonizing steps back.

"I know you said you don't have an issue with touching." She leaned up on an elbow, her brows knitted as she searched Martin's face. "But you have a past like mine, don't you? It helps to talk about—"

"No." Martin glared at her.

She drew back, her shoulders hitching toward her ears.

Ricky shot Martin a disapproving look. "It's not you, Tula. He hasn't told me anything about his life before I met him. He keeps that shit locked down."

"Until he's in an intimate situation." Her eyes darted through the room before returning to Martin. "Does it affect *all* your sexual relationships? Or is it just us?"

Martin's nostrils flared, and Ricky held his breath.

"I'm sorry." She cringed. "That was too personal."

"Don't be sorry." Martin softened his expression and tucked a lock of hair behind her ear. "It's not you. But there's definitely something about you. I don't know what it is…" He stared at her as if utterly gobsmacked. "I haven't had sex in seven years, and I can't for the life of me figure out why I just told you that."

Compassion soaked her quiet eyes, her face a portrait of unguarded trust.

"That's why." He trailed a finger along her cheekbone and looked up at Ricky. "You see what I see?"

"Yeah, I see her."

She was too trusting. While it was a trait that made overprotective guys like him and Martin want to throat-punch any man who looked at her, it didn't belong in a place like this.

Trusting the wrong person in Jaulaso would get her killed, and she put a helluva lot of trust in Hector La Rocha.

"See what?" Her voice lowered with suspicion. "What do you see?"

"You're an inherently good person." Ricky stroked her hair. "Because of that, you see goodness in others, even when it doesn't exist."

Her eyes flared. "That's another way of calling me naive."

She sat up and started to scramble out from between them.

Martin gripped her leg and yanked her down to her back as Ricky bent over her.

"Don't overreact." He nipped at her lips.

"I'm not," she growled, twisting her hips in Martin's hold.

"You're overreacting." Ricky curled a hand beneath her jaw. "No one said you're naive. I'll reserve that label for our conversation about Hector's sex trafficking operation."

Anger sparked in her eyes, and her mouth opened. He silenced her with a finger against her lips.

"Not tonight." He slid his hand down her neck and traced the hollow of her throat. "Tonight, we're going to give you what you want."

Her swallow bobbed against his touch. "You think you can subdue me with kisses?"

"Totally."

She flung a questioning look at Martin.

"My money's on Ricky," Martin said.

"Do you even have any money?" She cocked a brow.

They had millions in the bank because of Van, but that was a detail they couldn't share.

Martin answered her with a mysterious smile. He didn't share those smiles often, so when one appeared, it was disarming.

She sighed beneath it. "I don't understand how the two most attractive men on the planet ended up here, in prison, with me. It defies the laws of the universe. Can you explain it to me?"

She would lose her mind if she saw all the Freedom Fighters together.

Van Quiso and Liv Reed had handpicked every single one of them based on the slave buyers' specifications. Physical beauty was always a requirement.

Ricky didn't give a fuck what he looked like, but he appreciated her compliment and showed her as much by stealing a kiss.

The featherlight touch of lips gave way to another, then another, until the flames lit and the slide of their mouths caught fire.

Martin settled in beside them, his face inches away. When Ricky leaned back, Martin moved in and twisted a hand in her hair.

Watching Tula and Martin together was a feast for the eyes. They stared at each other, their lips not quite touching as their tongues reached and slid together in the space between their open mouths. She angled her head to take him deeply, and he dove in, their hands clawing and gripping with equal urgency.

When Martin's breathing lost rhythm, and his biting became too aggressive, Ricky crowded in and took his place.

Back and forth they went. Kissing her. Kissing each other. Three mouths vying for affection. Three pairs of legs tangling together. Hands grasping and wandering over clothes, and the sounds of panting groans rising into a crescendo.

Martin worked them into a feverish frenzy, and Ricky slowed them down, drew it out.

Between stretches of breathless kissing, they talked and laughed about nothing and everything.

When their lips fell still, they curled up in the cozy silences, content with their thoughts.

Hours later, the clock on her phone struck three in the morning. She still wanted that shower.

Ricky led them through the dark, eerily vacant corridors to the communal bathroom on the ground level.

He and Martin took up posts by the door, listening to her clothing fall on the floor followed by the sound of water sluicing over her naked body. He only needed to take two steps into the bathroom, and he would have a direct view of her around the corner.

"Don't even think about it." Martin crossed his arms over his chest and held up the wall with his back.

"Don't act like you're not tempted."

"I've had enough temptations for one night." Martin's gaze dropped to Ricky's mouth and shifted toward the sound of splashing water. "She's…"

Exquisitely sweet. Sharp as a whip. Sexy as fuck.

"The whole package." Ricky dropped his head back against the doorframe.

"Yeah." Martin lowered his voice. "The next three months are going to fly by."

"And she has three years after we leave."

They couldn't lengthen their sentences or shorten hers. It was an impossible situation with a nebulous outcome.

If she changed her plea to guilty, she might be able to transfer to a prison in the States. She would be safer there. But would she be willing to carry a guilty conviction for the rest of her life?

It was too soon to predict how her priorities might change or where the three of them would go from here. He didn't know how deep her cartel loyalties ran or if she would be able to leave those ties behind after prison. What if she couldn't escape Hector's control?

Bottom line, he and Martin were here for one reason, and they needed her help.

Once they convinced her Hector was rotten to the soul, they would have her spy for them, whether it be listening to conversations, digging through documents in Hector's private quarters, or using her sweet personality to coax information directly from Hector's mouth.

She didn't know it yet, but she was going to help them bring down La Rocha's sex trafficking operation.

Involving her, however, put her life at more risk than it already was. In Jaulaso, working against the cartel was more dangerous than working for it.

But that was where he and Martin drew the line. They would never join La Rocha. Sure, it would make their time here easier — fewer bruises and bloodied knuckles. Becoming a member, however, went against everything they fought for.

As cartel soldiers, they would be required to sell drugs, trade guns, collect money, and kill traitors. All of that shit contributed to a despicable machine that sold women and children into slavery.

He and Martin didn't plant themselves in prison to make La Rocha Cartel stronger. They were here to demolish it.

"I needed that." She stepped around the corner, her long black hair dripping down her tattooed arms, dampening her clean yellow shirt. "If you want to take a shower, this is the best time. There's no one around if you drop the soap."

With a nod, Martin breezed past her, yanking off his shirt as he headed toward the showers. "I don't want you out of our sight."

"I'll wait by the door." She combed her fingers through her wet hair.

Ricky shook his head. "You don't have to watch us, but we need to be able to see you." He pointed at the bend in the bathroom. "Stand there. It'll give you a line of sight to us and the door."

"Why do I need to wait around at all?" She glanced at the exit. "It's late."

"You're sleeping with us from now on." He stepped into her space and pressed his lips to hers. A small touch with a significant message. "The moment we kissed you, you became ours. Our girl. Our responsibility. Ours to protect."

Her eyes softened, and she slipped her hands into her back pockets. "That's a nice thing to say." She turned her face away, her voice thready. "It would really suck if you guys are playing me."

"That goes both ways."

The shower sounded around the corner. In a few seconds, he would rest his eyes on Martin's naked body in a way he'd never been able to before.

Focus, Ricardo.

She raised her chin and gave him direct eye contact. "Do you have an alliance with another cartel or gang?"

The Freedom Fighters weren't just aligned with the Restrepo Cartel. They were married to it, literally, by way of their leader, Camila Dias-Restrepo.

A pang of guilt pinched his stomach. He hated keeping secrets from her, but one thing he wouldn't do was fill her head with lies.

"I can feed you reassuring words." He hooked his thumbs under the front of his waistband, deliberately keeping his hands to himself. "I can kiss you until you melt. Touch you until you scream my name. Or God's name. Same thing." He winked. "But I can't force you to trust me. That requires a valiant act of heroism, and I'm fresh out of those at the moment." He shrugged. "So this—you and me and Martin—this trust we need to build between us? It's going to take time. You know what they say in prison?"

"We have nothing but time."

She believed they had at least three years together. It broke his fucking heart.

"Put your ass where I can see you." He smacked a kiss on her mouth. "And don't move."

She tried to shape those fuckable lips into a scowl, but a smile broke through. "What am I going to do with you?"

He pulled off his shirt and stared down at the fly of his jeans. "You can start with—"

"Stop right there." She held up a hand and stepped to the spot he'd directed her.

"I was going to say..." He tossed his shirt at her. "Bury your nose in that and get used to my scent. You're going to be covered in it from now on."

"Overly optimistic, aren't you?"

"Confident, *querida*." He approached the showers, and his breath ran away from him.

Martin stood under the spray of water, his palms flat against the wall in front of him and defined arms bracing his upper body.

Rivers of water followed the carved grooves in his torso and trickled over the flanks of his tight ass.

"I can feel you staring." Martin lifted his head.

Their gazes collided, and he had to remind himself to breathe.

Distractions were out of the question. No flirty eye contact. No thinking about hand jobs in the bathroom. Even at three in the morning, this was a dangerous place for a man to get caught with his pants down.

He glanced back at Tula.

She stood stiffly against the wall, her body angled slightly away. With her eyes on the door, she held his wadded shirt against her chest.

If anything happened to her...

He couldn't let his mind go there.

Stripping his clothes, he joined Martin under the warm spray.

A bar of soap served as shampoo and body wash. He lathered and rinsed quickly, trying his damnedest to ignore the heated glances from the man beside him.

His cock, however, ate up the attention, swelling with blood and rising toward his abs.

"Your timing sucks." He scrubbed his hands over his whiskered face. "You've had years to look, man."

"I did look. I devoured every inch of you when you weren't paying attention."

His dick throbbed. "Why didn't you tell me?"

"I didn't want to lead you on." Martin shifted to stand in front of him, keeping Tula in their periphery. "But now... I don't know. The rules are different here."

The rules changed because of a beautiful woman. Between her and the kiss she dared them to share, there was no turning back.

"Finish up." Martin leaned closer and put his mouth at Ricky's ear. "And keep your hands off your cock."

Martin slammed a palm against Ricky's ass, echoing a *smack* through the room and shooting shockwaves through his body.

"Killing me," he muttered and finished the shower in record time.

Back in their cell, he lit the scented candle to battle the sewage smell and shut off the light.

The flame cast shadows over her and Martin, where they lay diagonally across the two mattresses. She burrowed into the den of Martin's body, her arms around him, and her eyes already closed in sleep.

Crawling in behind her, Ricky folded an arm around her waist and rested his hand against Martin's chest.

Those glittering green eyes found him across the space above her head. Hooded and warm, they looked content, happy even.

"Feels good, doesn't it?" Ricky whispered. "To be held. To be needed."

"Yeah." Martin rested his mouth against her head.

"I've always needed you."

"I know."

The silence that followed churned with their wants, their fears, and everything in between.

They had to earn her trust, navigate Martin's demons, steal Hector's secrets, and try not to get raped or killed in the process.

But right now, they had this. Skin, heartbeats, and breaths aligned in an unbroken moment. A moment to fight for.

EIGHTEEN

The next week dragged Ricky through the nine circles of hell. Between bone-bruising fights with inmates, lusting after the two people in his bed, and his guilt over hiding secrets from Tula, he felt as though he were running backward in a race against time.

Adding to that was the festering misery of prison life. The despair, the restlessness, the destruction of bodies that the inmates never seemed to grow sick of—there was an abundance of self-hatred in Jaulaso.

But for all the violence, guilt, and torment in limbo, there were glimpses of heaven. They dwelled in the slide of soft lips and hungry tongues.

Christ, the kissing. He'd never devoted so much time and attention to another person's mouth, but holy fuck, that was where it was at.

All those years of dating, countless lovers, Van's sexual training… How had he not discovered the sinful pleasure in a kiss?

He was addicted to it now. Good thing, because after a week of sharing a bed with Tula and Martin, kissing was all they'd done.

Martin had intimacy issues. Tula was hellbent on them joining La Rocha Cartel, and Ricky was left with a crumbling plan, two blue balls, and a black eye.

His busted face was a gift from a four-hundred-pound inmate in the common area two days ago. Martin had managed to escape that particular fight unscathed. The other times, however, he hadn't been so lucky.

Since they only ventured out among the prisoners while Tula was in meetings, she hadn't watched them get their asses kicked over and over.

But she was always there to clean them up afterward.

"She's been gone too long." Martin bent over the sink in their cell, scraping a razor against the stubble on his jaw.

She met with Hector a lot. Sometimes it was a meeting with his advisers. Other times, she slipped away, saying she needed to check in with him.

She swore up and down he never touched her, never hurt her in any way. Didn't stop Ricky from chewing a hole in his cheek. He fucking hated every second she wasn't within eyeshot.

The reclusive cartel boss rarely left his private quarters. In the ten days they'd been here, they'd only spotted the old man twice. When they passed him in the hall, he was surrounded by guards and didn't spare them a single glance.

But he knew they were there. Tula didn't spend all that time with him without talking about the men she shared a bed with every night.

Was she talking about them right now?

Ricky lowered onto the mattress. "With any luck, we planted a seed of doubt in her head, enough to make her question every interaction she has with him."

"She's smart. If she's suspicious of him, she'll dig, ask questions, and find her way to the truth."

"That could work against us, too. If Hector doesn't trust us—"

"That's a given." Martin set the razor aside and rinsed his face.

"Then he's putting the doubts about us in her head."

If she discovered their loyalty to Restrepo, she would feel betrayed. Not just because they worked for a sworn enemy, but because they'd kept it from her.

The sooner they got her on their side, the better.

"You need to seal the deal." Martin inspected his face in the mirror, searching for stubble he'd missed.

"Meaning?"

"Fuck her, Ricky." He turned and folded his arms across his chest. "A woman like that doesn't have sex with a man she doesn't trust. If you open her legs, you'll open her heart."

"That sounds like a great plan. Love her then leave her in three months."

"If we succeed here, we'll be saving thousands of women and children. She'll understand that."

"Maybe." He studied Martin's expression, resenting the secrets lurking behind those eyes.

"Whatever's on your mind, just spit it out."

"You want me to fuck her, but she wants both of us. How can I convince her to trust me enough to sleep with me, when I can't even convince my *bisexual* best friend to do that?"

"It's two completely different things."

"It's the same fucking thing." Frustration burned through his veins as he rose from the bed. "It took all *three* of us to start this relationship, and we can't move forward unless all three of us are committed to it. I know you see that. You're just…" He pulled in a breath. "You're too fucking scared."

"Yeah?" A dark shadow passed across Martin's expression.

Then he attacked. Both hands hit Ricky hard enough in the chest to send him flying backward and crashing onto the bed.

"I'm scared, you fucking asshole." Martin followed him down and unleashed a sharp, backhanded blow across his face. "I'm scared *for you*."

"What the fuck?" His jaw stitched with pain as he raised his arms to defend against the next strike.

Martin aimed low, punching him in the ribs. Ricky grunted in shock and dropped his hands against the hurt, realizing too late he'd exposed his neck.

A muscled forearm slammed against his throat and nailed him to the mattress. He gulped for air, pulling nothing into his lungs.

He clung to the arm at his throat, his fingers digging into muscle as he tried to dislodge the choking hold. But beneath the constricting pain stirred a dark desire.

Martin's crushing weight, cruel scowl, and unbending restraint — all of it heated Ricky's blood and tightened his balls.

"You want me to hurt you?" Martin seethed in his face. "I promise you don't want my brand of hurt."

Give it to me.

He tried to choke out the words, but they hit the air without sound or breath.

With a guttural growl, Martin shoved his free hand between them and gripped Ricky's erection through his jeans.

Oh, God. Don't stop.

His pulse roared. Black spots bloomed across his vision, and all the heat in his body rushed to his dick. He'd never been this hard.

Martin's fingers curled around his nuts and squeezed with agonizing pressure. "You'll beg for death before I'm finished with you."

Martin would cut his own arm off before he crossed a line that couldn't be fixed. To prove it, Ricky shoved his neck against the iron bar of Martin's arm, seconds from passing out.

A knock sounded on the door.

Something passed over Martin's expression, and he blinked. His features softened, and his eyes looked brighter, sharper.

He pushed off the bed, and Ricky gulped for air, dragging starved breaths through his bruised throat.

Martin stabbed his hands in his hair. His chest heaved, and his jeans bulged with the long, engorged evidence of his arousal.

A second—more impatient—knock rapped on the door.

"Fuck." Martin reached for the handle and stopped.

Glancing down, he adjusted his erection and straightened his shirt in an attempt to hide what was too large to be concealed.

Ricky moved to the edge of the bed as Martin unlocked the door and opened it.

Garra stood on the other side, holding a paper bag. He glanced between Martin and Ricky before pushing his way inside.

"Come on in," Martin snarled in Spanish.

Ricky jumped to his feet, and the paper bag dropped on the mattress.

Garra pointed at it. "Use those. *Every* time."

Curiosity moved Ricky toward the bag. He dug his hand in and pulled out a fistful of condoms.

Not what he was expecting.

He dropped the rubbers, unable to conceal the contempt in his voice. "Did you use one when you raped her?"

"Yes." Garra shoved his shoulders back.

No cowering with this one. No sense of self-preservation, either.

Ricky sent a fist into the motherfucker's nose. The wet sound of breaking cartilage accompanied a gush of blood.

Red trickled down Garra's lips and splattered the gold chains around his neck. He didn't roar in pain. Didn't throw a counterstrike.

The son of a bitch smiled.

"If you do that out there…" He stabbed a finger at the hallway, his Spanish thick and nasally. "You might keep her alive."

What the fuck was happening?

Garra pivoted and strode out the door. When he reached the corridor, he turned back. "Before you stick your dicks in her, picture this… Her belly round with your child while she sleeps on a filthy cot, scavenges for prison food, and gives birth on the floor surrounded by violent criminals." He spat a glob of blood in the hall and nodded at the paper bag. "Use the condoms."

Then he was gone.

Martin shut the door and leaned against it. "That isn't a man who's *just doing his job.*"

"You don't say."

"Does he love her?"

"He delivered condoms to two men he doesn't know." Ricky cocked his head. "To use with the woman he loves? I don't think so."

"Good point." Martin stepped to the bed and peeked into the bag. "Nice right hook. You broke his nose."

"I should've broken more than his nose."

"He solved the condom issue."

"We didn't have a condom issue." Ricky had intended to hustle prophylactics from one of the prostitutes. He would've used flattery, charm, a couple cans of soup, whatever means necessary to obtain protection for Tula. Except sex. Tula was the only woman he wanted.

Garra saved him the hassle, but he still wanted to kill the guy.

"Where the fuck is she?" Martin shoved a hand in his hair.

"We need to go find her." He moved toward the door.

"Can you avoid a fight?"

His stomach tightened. The fights found him, not the other way around. "No promises."

NINETEEN

Something by The Beatles hummed from Hector's record player and caressed Tula's senses. She danced slowly in place, one hand on Hector's shoulder and the other resting in the loose curl of his fingers.

The warm cadence of the song calmed her heart. Or maybe it was the warm gaze stroking her face.

"There's just something about the sound of vinyl." She stepped when he stepped, letting his expert foot movements guide her through the slow dance. "It's richer, more authentic."

"You get those little scratches and pops in the records, the hum of the turntable motor, the tactile touch of the needle to the vinyl, and physical friction of the two."

"Listen to you. Your English is so elegant it's poetic. I can barely hear an accent."

"I had a good teacher." He spun her around, making her laugh.

"I'm getting better at this, right?" She pivoted on clumsy toes and straightened her slouching posture. "Lie if you have to."

"I've found you're good at everything, Petula. A natural talent."

"Except recruiting." Her heartbeat quickened. She drew in a long breath and released it. "They said they want to spend their time here quietly and stay away from cartel politics."

"Because they don't like cartels? Or because their loyalties lie elsewhere?"

"The first one, I think."

"If that's the case, they can't be here."

Her insides turned to ice. "Don't kill them."

He narrowed his dark eyes. "You like them."

"I don't know them well enough to feel one way or another, but I want the opportunity to see if I *would* like them."

She was hedging. The truth was she liked them too much, and she was afraid to admit that to Hector.

It was that damn accusation they'd planted in her head.

She wanted to ask Hector about the alleged human trafficking, but if it were true, he wouldn't tell her. Not if he'd concealed it from her for two years.

Asking him outright would make her look like she was siding with the enemy, which she would be doing if Ricky Martin were right.

She couldn't afford for Hector to be suspicious of her. He needed to trust her, and she wouldn't give him any reason not to.

But she wouldn't turn a blind eye, either. Hector La Rocha wasn't a benevolent man. He was a cartel boss with a nasty reputation, one he'd probably earned.

Except he wasn't nasty to her. He treated her like she meant something to him, like she was an important part of his world. He'd always kept her safe, and her life depended on that protection.

In return, all she had to do was remain loyal.

As the song ended, he released her and walked the short distance to the record player.

With his back to her, he lifted the needle and powered off the turntable. "Have you had sexual relations with them yet?"

Her face heated. "No. I need more time."

"And they haven't elaborated on why their identities were wiped? Other than the mention of enemies in a past life?"

"No." A nervous twitch skittered down her spine. "I know it doesn't seem like I'm making progress, but I spend every minute with them, feeling them out and earning their trust. They haven't done anything to make me believe they're a threat."

He shifted to look at her. "Except for their refusals to join me."

And their accusations about his business affairs.

"Give me more time." She squared her shoulders. "They're young and athletic, smart and skilled at fighting. They would serve you better alive than dead."

A grin stole over his mouth, and he ran a hand through his silver-black hair. "Take all the time you need, Petula. You have my confidence."

"Thank you." She needed to return to the guys but couldn't leave without asking, "Have you found anything on Vera?"

His face fell, and his head shook imperceptibly.

"I'm so sorry." He stepped forward and rested a warm hand on the side of her face. "One of these days, I'm going to give you a different answer."

A lump swelled in her throat, amassing with a horrible combination of doubt and hope.

Vera had been gone too long to be alive. His news would likely come with the discovery of a body.

But that would be better than not knowing. She needed closure, so she could finally grieve.

"Thank you. Again." She stood taller. "Why are you so kind to me?"

"You saved my life." He sat at the table and lit a cigarette. "You taught me English, and I enjoy your company." His eyes twinkled as tendrils of smoke curled from his nose. "Why are you so kind to me?"

She laughed, relieved by his answer. "You keep me safe. And I enjoy your company, too."

"Very good." He shooed her away with a hand. "Go recruit the gringos before I change my mind and kill them."

His teasing tone made it possible to walk calmly to the door. But as she stepped into the hall, the threat in his words closed a fist around her heart.

She made a beeline for the stairwell and faltered at the bottom step, her senses buzzing at the commotion of a nearby crowd.

The din of shouting and squeaking footsteps drifted down from the second floor. Something was happening in the stairwell directly above her.

"Fuck you!"

Her heart stopped.

She knew that American accent.

She knew it when it was gravelly with desire, sharp with frustration, and now stony with anger.

Her hand went to the pistol in her waistband. She flipped the safety off and took the first set of steps two at a time.

At the landing between the flights of stairs, she whipped around the corner and slammed to a stop.

A dozen men were gathered on the steps above her, and more spilled out of the top floor. At the center of the throng, Ricky lay on his back beneath four inmates, his body pinned to the steps.

On the landing above him, Martin fought four...five...six men and counting. Every time his fist connected with a body, he received three or more punches in return.

Her pulse exploded as she aimed the gun at the crowd and shouted in Spanish, "Get away from them!"

"Don't interfere, little girl." The man closest to her stepped into her space and crossed his arms. "This isn't your business."

Two more prisoners flanked him.

No guns were drawn, but if she fired her weapon, she would be staring down the barrels of a dozen or more guns.

One of the inmates holding Ricky's legs rose to his full height.

Her stomach turned inside out.

It was Trog. The large, hairy man was known for having a huge penis and a harem of unwilling bed partners.

A zipper sounded, and Trog whipped out his two-foot dick.

"Suck on this, bitch." He wrapped his hand around it, guiding it toward Ricky's clamped lips.

Outrage blazed in Ricky's eyes, his entire body flexing with murderous aggression.

He'd been disrespected by Trog *and* his dick. If Trog raped him, it would be the beginning of the end.

Once a bitch, forever a bitch.

"Name your price." She glared at the men in front of her. "And get the fuck out of my way."

Bribing them for their cooperation shouldn't cost more than thirty soups or a couple packs of cigarettes.

On the top floor, Martin grunted and punched his way through a half dozen prisoners. Outnumbered and losing ground, he would never reach Ricky in time.

Ricky renewed his efforts to escape as his captors held his head immobile. They pried their fingers into his mouth and stretched his jaw open to accept the massive erection angling toward him.

Panic chased her heart to her stomach. Her spine slicked with sweat, and the ringing sound of her fear thrashed in her ears.

She jerked her attention to the men blocking her path. "I need an answer."

TWENTY

Ricky bit down on the fingers in his mouth and tried to summon his nonexistent gag reflex. If he could puke on these motherfuckers, it might give him a fleeting moment to escape.

"You have options." The grizzly-bearded bastard with the donkey dick glared down at him. "While you're staring at it, you can hit, kick, whimper, cry, lick, suck, spit, or swallow."

What was funny about this was that the scaly, bulbous organ jutting toward his face was the ugliest goddamn dick he'd ever seen. What wasn't funny was the likelihood of it ramming into the back of his throat.

"Or you can roll to your stomach, and I'll visit China," the grizzly man said. "I'll leave it up to you and your personal survival instinct. But let's be honest. You're getting it one way or another."

His survival instinct had been honed by six months of training.

An outpouring of adrenaline hit his system, boosting his heart rate and blood pressure. A surge of muscle strength made him feel invincible, but he knew he wasn't.

No amount of training would get them out of this. There were too many men, and they were out for blood.

But he sure as hell wouldn't lie here and take it quietly.

He jerked his head to the side, coughing away from the body odor as he said in Spanish, "Someone's deodorant isn't working."

"It's not me," one of the dumbfucks said. "I'm not wearing deodorant."

A round of laughter erupted, and he used the distraction to twist his arms and break free from the restraining hands.

With a hard shove of his feet, he gained some distance, moving his position two stairs closer to Martin. Then more hands fell upon him, holding him against the steps.

Rough fingers opened his fly. Others joined in, yanking his jeans and boxers to his knees. There was even a goddamn one-armed man in the mix, slamming his only fist into Ricky's abdomen.

He tried to fight them off, wrestling and punching for a dominant position, but he was outmuscled and outnumbered.

With his groin exposed, he couldn't stop them from grabbing and smacking his junk.

He trapped a roar behind his sealed lips. His vision clouded. His ears pounded, as the increased blood flow to his extremities energized his strikes, powering his punches harder, faster, with the intent to kill.

He tried to track the sounds of Martin's fight above him. God knew how many men he was fending off. He was going to get himself killed.

Was Tula still standing at the bottom of the stairs? He'd heard her voice amid the shouting but couldn't see her.

He didn't want her anywhere near this shit show. He couldn't protect her. Couldn't breathe. Couldn't do anything but fight for his life.

He fell into a zone, locked in tunnel vision and moving on instinct. Arms, legs, the core of his body — his muscle groups worked together to defend his most vulnerable areas and keep that hairy prick away from his mouth.

Until they flipped him over and shoved his face against a concrete stair.

Multiple bodies dove onto his back and legs, smothering him in the ripe stench of unwashed armpits. The rest of them restrained his arms above his head.

He was fucked, and in a few seconds, he was going to be fucked in the literal sense.

Never mind the diseases he would contract from the grotesque erection jabbing at his ass crack. He would probably survive the rape. He'd endured this before with Van.

It would be an agony that rivaled death, but that wasn't what terrified him the most.

If they won, he would have to endure it again and again. It would earn him a label no prisoner wanted in Jaulaso. For the next three months, he wouldn't be able to freely walk the halls. They would drag him out of his cell and sell his body for a can of soup.

He couldn't let this happen.

Renewing his efforts, he fought with all his strength to escape the thick press of bodies.

The noise from every direction was deafening — inmates yelling, stomping, and slamming fists. The stairwell was as hot as Hades, dampening his skin and making it easier to slide out of sweaty grips.

But there were too many men who outweighed him. He was overpowered.

The moment he felt greasy fingers separate his buttocks and expose his anus, he knew it was over.

Countless hands prevented him from moving. Sweltering breaths pommeled his neck and back.

He closed his eyes and tried to squeeze his glutes together, fighting the vise of fingers between his buttocks.

The stab of hard flesh pressed against his opening.

No, no, no.

He dug deep and summoned another surge of strength. If he could…just…pull…his legs free—

A gunshot rang out, reverberating in his ears and ricocheting through his chest.

Stunned silence gripped the stairwell for a millisecond. Then chaos broke loose.

The men around him flew to their feet, and the weight on his back tumbled off. The grizzly man's head landed next to his, and he came face to face with a bullet hole. Right through the temple.

His heartbeat convulsed, thudding slowly, thickly through his veins before speeding up and losing control.

"Don't fucking move," Tula screamed.

She stood above him, eyes wild as she waved a gun at the crowd.

Oh, God. Oh, fuck. What had she done?

She shot one of them. She fucking killed a cartel soldier in front of his army.

Weapons appeared in every hand, all of them aimed at her.

He yanked up his pants as he rose in front of her, blocking her body from the Uzis trained in her direction.

She hadn't thought this through. There wasn't a man in this stairwell who would let her walk away after interfering in their business and killing one of their own.

He pressed in and circled his arms around her back, unable to shield her from all sides. He didn't obstruct her ability to fire her gun, but she would only get off one round before they were both dead.

His pulse thundered. Then it redoubled as Martin appeared behind her, with his chest against her back.

With a grimace, Martin blinked through the pools of crimson in his eyes. Blood gushed from everywhere, coating his hair, face, mouth, and chest. Fucking hell, he looked horrible.

But he was alive. For now.

The prisoners stood in a stand-off with their fingers all over the fucking triggers. As soon as the first shot fired, every gun would go off. It only took one dumbass to sneeze or twitch, and the entire stairwell would light up like fireworks.

He met Martin's blood-drenched eyes, and his heart sank with dread. They weren't going to survive this.

"Lower your weapons," someone said calmly in Spanish.

Ricky turned his neck toward the unfamiliar voice.

The sea of inmates parted on the stairs, and Hector La Rocha stood at the bottom, staring up at the crowd.

Then one by one, every gun descended, dropping out of view and tucking into waistbands, including Tula's.

Heads bowed in respect, and tense silence crept in.

Garra leaned against the wall behind Hector, his posture deceptively casual. Ricky didn't miss the small gun tucked in the curl of his fingers. Or the bandage taped across his broken nose.

Hector clasped his hands behind his back and swept his gaze over his soldiers.

He reminded Ricky of Fred Rogers from *Mister Rogers' Neighborhood*. It wasn't just the thin cardigan, buttoned-down shirt, silver-streaked black hair, and warm expression. There was a gentle frailness about him, a sense of unruffled patience in his demeanor.

Was it a ruse? Or was the cartel boss just old and tired?

"You." Hector looked at one of the inmates on the stairs as if randomly calling him out. "Tell me why guns were aimed at Petula."

"She shot Trog, boss." The man pointed at the dead body. "This wasn't her business and—"

"It is her business," Hector said softly. "Trog has been stealing cocaine from my supplies, and I told Petula to deal with it."

A wave of exhales rippled through the room.

Was that true? Ricky didn't think so.

Hector La Rocha hadn't interfered to save Martin or Ricky. Hell, he wouldn't even look at them. They refused to join him, and that made them the enemy.

No, Hector had come here for Tula, to protect her and keep her safe.

"Get rid of this and move along." Hector gestured at the dead man.

A whirlwind of motion erupted around him. Within seconds, Trog's body was dragged away, and every prisoner vacated the stairwell.

Garra pushed away from the wall to leave, but Hector didn't move.

Tula gripped Ricky's bicep as she wriggled out from between him and Martin. Her gaze went to Hector, and they stared at each for an eternity.

Whatever passed between them didn't end with a word, an expression, or a nod. Hector simply turned away and vanished around the corner with Garra on his heels.

She spun toward Martin and Ricky and gave them both a quick once-over. Her features looked molded in plastic, unmoving and lifeless, as if she'd sent her emotions far below the surface.

"Can you walk?" she asked Martin.

"Yeah."

"Follow me." She headed down toward the ground floor.

Where was she going? Their cell was upstairs.

Ricky lunged after her and grasped her arm, yanking her around. "Wrong way. We need to get Martin—"

Martin swayed, and his knees started to buckle.

"Shit." Ricky caught him before he fell down the stairs.

Two-hundred pounds of muscle and dead weight strained Ricky's exhausted, battered body as he leaned Martin against the wall.

Her expressionless mask cracked, releasing a well of tears in her eyes. She quickly wiped it away and pushed back her shoulders.

"I need to…" She coughed to clear her trembling in her voice. "I need to get you both into the showers, wash off the blood and the—"

Her gaze slipped to Ricky's backside and darted away.

"Hey." He held Martin against the wall with one hand and used the other to guide her face to his. "He didn't rape me."

Her eyes widened in disbelief. "He didn't?"

"No, baby. You put that bullet in his head just in time."

Her hand dropped to the railing, bracing her upper body as she sucked in gulps of air.

Beside him, Martin let his head fall back against the wall.

"I thought…" She raked her fingers through her hair and composed herself. "God, that's such a relief." Her eyes flitted to Martin. "I need to get you under the water. Really we all need showers since we'll be holed up in your room until you're healed."

"We can't fend off another attack right now."

"No one will bother us in the bathroom."

"You don't know that." Martin slurred past swollen lips.

"After what just happened…" She rubbed her head and whispered under her breath, "Hector *never* gets involved in fights. By defending me the way he did, he just established my position in the cartel."

"What does that mean?" Ricky asked.

"No one will mess with me for a while. Maybe not ever. And lucky for you, whenever you're with me, no one will fuck with you, either."

MANIPULATE

Ricky looked at Martin, and his friend gave a stiff nod.

TWENTY-ONE

Two hours later, Tula trudged to the sink in their private cell and rinsed out a bloody towel. Her neck ached from bending over, and exhaustion weighed down her bones.

She'd done what she could for the gruesome gash on Martin's head. It had bled so damn much—through his shower, during the walk back to his cell, and the entire thirty minutes it took her to stitch it closed.

His skull had been slammed into a concrete wall. At least, that was what he thought had happened. He was struggling to focus. Hell, he was doing well enough to stay conscious.

Given his dilated pupils and staggering gait through the halls, she worried he had a concussion. Didn't that mean he needed to stay awake? Or was that a myth? She wasn't taking any chances.

She'd cleaned and stitched the laceration on his head the best she could. She didn't know what else to do. It would leave a thick scar along his hairline, but at least the bleeding had stopped.

It could've been worse.

Her mind rewound the scene in the stairwell, shoving her in and out of horrifying moments. She'd watched a dozen men beat Martin into a bloody pulp and listened to Ricky's agonized grunts as he fought off violent, raping men. She'd wanted to die right then and there and take every single one of those bastards with her.

A torrent of grief rose through her chest and seared the back of her throat. She gripped the edge of the sink and tried to choke down the emotion, but she couldn't. She'd been holding it in for hours.

What if she hadn't been able to bribe the men on the stairs to let her pass? What if she'd missed and shot Ricky in the head instead?

Her terror had been so all-consuming it had rattled her grip on the gun as she pulled the trigger.

"I could've missed." A sob tore from her throat, and she clapped a hand over her mouth, knowing better than to cry in this unforgiving place.

"Tula." Ricky's arms surrounded her, and his shirtless chest blanketed her in heat. "What's wrong?"

"I could've shot you."

"You didn't." He lifted her, cradling her body against him as he sat on the bed. "You had perfect aim."

Only because she'd been standing three feet away. A blind person would've hit that target.

"I don't cry." She wiped the back of her hand across her damp cheeks and pulled herself together. "Not since I've been here. I hate that I feel so weak right now."

"You cried the night you were drunk, and you're anything but weak. You saved my ass. Literally."

More tears hit her eyes, and she buried her face in the warm, smooth skin on his shoulder. "I can't believe I drunk-cried."

"You were so beautiful that night." He lifted her chin with a knuckle and kissed the wetness on her cheeks. "Just like now."

She melted against him, forehead to forehead, nose to nose. "Thank you."

"Thank you for helping us." Another kiss. "How did you get past the men at the bottom of the stairs?"

"I traded my gun."

"You what?" He jerked back and swept his hands around her waistband, searching in disbelief. "You used it when you shot Trog."

"That was the deal I made. If they let me by with it, they could have it after the fight. They came to the bathroom when you were helping Martin into the shower." She shrugged stiffly. "I passed it off to them when you weren't looking."

"Goddammit, Tula." His nostrils flared. "I wish you hadn't done that."

It wasn't ideal. Weapons were the most valuable commodity in Jaulaso, and a gun was worth a lot more than the price of a toll. Hector had given her that pistol two years ago, and even though he had an arsenal in his cell, she wouldn't ask for another one.

She was already indebted to him up to her eyeballs. After he lied for her in the stairwell, she owed him more than her life. Now she owed him the lives of Martin and Ricky. She would never be able to settle that debt.

"Rumor is you're good with a knife." Ricky squinted at her. "Where is this knife they speak of?"

"I exchanged it a week ago."

"For what?"

He was going to be angry. It was already bubbling in those milk-chocolate eyes as he anticipated her response.

She blew out a breath and patted the cotton pants on his legs beneath her.

"You traded your knife for our clothes?" The cords in his neck went taut, and his jaw turned to granite.

Yep, he was pissed.

She had no weapons left, but after the boon Hector had given her today, maybe she wouldn't need any.

"Yes, your clothes," she said. "And your razor, toothbrush, blankets... It bought all the supplies I didn't already have." She shoved at his chest. "You're welcome."

He pulled her close and ran his nose through her hair. "Thank you."

With a satisfied sigh, she peered over his shoulder to check on Martin.

He lay on his side, breathing evenly, the swollen skin around his closed eyes already darkening with bruises. He always looked so badass after a fight, all banged up on the surface while his intimidating fuck-off demeanor still vibrated underneath. Even with his eyes closed, she would think twice before creeping up on him.

Wait. Was he asleep?

"Martin!"

"I'm awake." He rolled to his back and hissed in pain. "Are you wet?"

"What?" She flinched.

"He's asking about your clothes." Ricky twisted to glance at Martin behind him. "She's soaked."

That sounded so dirty her belly fluttered with heat.

The three of them had showered together. With the guys naked and the bathroom in constant use by other inmates, she'd left on her bra and undies.

The whole ordeal had lasted less than three minutes. There had been nothing tantalizing about scrubbing blood out of Martin's hair while he knelt beneath the spray of water and fought to remain conscious.

She'd kept her eyes above their waists, and as far as she knew, they hadn't stolen glances at her half-naked body. They'd been too busy trying to get through the shower as quickly as possible without an altercation.

The inmates who had passed in and out of the bathroom had stared menacingly and made threatening comments. Nothing unusual about that. But no one had bothered them.

After the shower, she'd hurriedly yanked on her clothes over soggy underwear and had been itchy and wet ever since.

"Take off your clothes and get into bed." Martin's head lolled toward her.

Despite the injuries that crisscrossed his face, his eyes glinted with unbending authority.

She sucked in a breath.

Normally, when she needed to dress or use the toilet, they stepped into the hall and gave her privacy. Asking them to do that now would be ridiculous, and honestly, she should've dropped the timid act days ago.

How many prisoners shared a bed with a woman for seven nights without molesting or attacking her while she slept?

She'd bet her life that Martin and Ricky were the only two in Jaulaso. They respected her modesty and had been nothing but patient with her.

Maybe she didn't trust their accusations against Hector, but she one-hundred-percent trusted them with her body.

"If I lie down with you..." She crawled off Ricky's lap and knelt beside Martin, inspecting his eyes. *Still dilated.* "You can't fall asleep."

"You'll keep me awake." He lifted the blanket beside him in invitation.

What an invitation. Beneath the covers, he wore only a tight pair of black briefs. The sight of his chiseled body and all its divinity drove her insane.

When her gaze returned to his, he used his tongue to trail an unspoken command across his lips.

Come here and taste.

Her body reacted.

Heated.

Throbbed.

Liquefied.

Movement sounded behind her. Then the light bulb went dark, leaving only the dancing flame of the candle.

She turned, and holy shit, if there was ever a time to swoon, this was it.

Her eyes feasted on Ricky's masculinity, indulging in every inch of his sharply honed anatomy.

He'd stripped to his boxers, revealing a body that was sculpted so flawlessly not even Michelangelo could recreate it.

Her brain stopped working as she drank in the shadowscape of his square-cut jawline, the thick column of his neck, and every beckoning ridge and valley that shaped his torso.

Six feet of ripped muscle towered over her. Not a pinch of fat or a single imperfection. She knew those bulging biceps delivered bone-crushing strikes. His powerful legs carried two-hundred pounds of strength.

And the hard outline in his underwear told her how badly he wanted her.

Little tight pulses gathered between her legs. Her thighs quivered, and her inner muscles clenched with empty spasms, aching for penetration, needing him and Martin, both at the same time.

Good God, she had to physically shake herself out of a building orgasm.

"You can close your mouth," Ricky rasped.

She snapped her jaw shut and dropped from her knees to her hip on the bed. "Not fair."

"What's not fair?" He sat beside her and played with the ends of her hair.

"You. Him." She peered at Martin. "You look like models, fight like Gladiators, kiss like porn stars—"

"Porn stars?" Ricky arched a dark eyebrow.

"I don't know. That's what I see when I replay it in my head."

He trapped a smile between his teeth. "Continue. Please."

Why not? She was on a roll.

"You have all the confidence, none of the fat, and you smell like the best sex I've *never* had." She flopped back on the mattress beside Martin and stared at a patch of mildew in the ceiling. "I feel like a whimpering virgin around you guys because I... I've never..."

Ricky stretched out beside her, sandwiching her in between him and Martin. "You've never...?"

"I've never been with someone like you. Either of you. I've certainly never dated more than one man at a time, and the ones I've been with... They were nice, normal, average. Average bodies. Average jobs. Average conversations."

"They sound horribly boring," Ricky said. "Bet they were average in bed, too."

"I was okay with that." She closed her eyes. "I wanted normal and quiet. I loved my average life."

"And now?"

She wanted a life. With them in it. She wanted them so badly it scared her. "You're way out of my league."

Their silence vibrated against her, prompting her to open her eyes.

"Bullshit." Ricky glowered down at her, his dark, beautiful expression twisting in outrage. "Have you looked in the fucking mirror?"

She didn't have a complex about the way she looked. She had a small chest, but it never bothered her. Two years of poor nutrition had eaten away her figure and dulled the shine from her hair, but she was still pretty.

"Look, I'm not insecure. I know I look fine. I'm just not…" She waved a hand over him and Martin. "I'm not insanely, heart-stoppingly, drop-dead gorgeous like you two."

Martin leaned across her and touched Ricky's lips. Then he trailed his fingers down Ricky's neck, defined pecs and abs, and lingered on the strip of dark hair that vanished beneath Ricky's waistband.

"All of this is for you, Tula." He closed his hand over the swollen outline of Ricky's cock.

Ricky made a strangled sound in his throat, rivaling the loud gasps pushing past her lips.

She trembled to slide her hand over Martin's and stroke that thick hardness with him. But he moved his touch, and in a blink, he closed his fingers around her neck.

"Take off your clothes." His green eyes swirled with intensity. "I won't tell you again."

The only aphrodisiac she needed was the command in his voice. Hearing his salacious order and knowing he expected her to obey, she didn't realize until now how much she wanted to be dominated by a man she trusted.

Not just any man.

These two men.

Martin wasn't just telling her what he wanted. He was telling her what *she* wanted because somehow, he knew better than she did what that was.

His hand gave her throat a warning squeeze and slid away.

Lying on her back between them, she toed off her sneakers. As they thumped to the floor, excitement charged the air.

Martin pushed himself into a sitting position and rested back against the wall. His eyes hooded as they honed in on the wetness between her legs. Wet from the shower. Mostly.

She released the fly on her jeans as her other deeper wetness turned into an inferno, throbbing to be extinguished.

Sadly, there would be no sex with them tonight. Not without birth control. It was a frustrating thought, but she wouldn't let it kill her mood.

The denim was the dampest around her butt, making it awkward to slide the material down her legs. Ricky helped her pull it off. Then he tackled her shirt, ripping it over her head before she could stop him. Not that she would have.

"Goddamn." He pried her thighs apart and knelt between them. "Be still. Just let me digest this for a second."

A voracious tremor rippled through her, and her rabbit heart pattered toward certain death.

She peeked over at Martin to see hungry green eyes studying her from beneath golden lashes. He tipped his head in admiration, angling for a view of the fabric between her legs.

A whoosh pulled through her stomach as his searing gaze drifted along her inner thighs. His expression was as predatory as his posture. Casual and confident, patient and threatening, he reminded her of a lazy lion, watching his meal, waiting for it to come a little closer before he played with it.

She ripped her eyes away as a finger traced the tattered strap of her bra.

Ricky followed the edge where the broken lace met the upper curve of her breast.

"This is what I put on…" A stinging memory clogged her voice. "The morning Vera called me. The last time I talked to her. I threw on some clothes and raced out the door. I had no idea the mismatched bra and undies I absently chose would be the only ones I would wear for the next five years."

His brow pulled down over the shadows collecting in his stricken eyes. He gently caressed the off-white bra cups, carefully touching the unraveling holes along the underside.

Lowering his hand, he glided the backs of his fingers down the faded purple triangle that covered her pubic bone.

She closed her eyes, savoring the sensation of his expert touch. "I had this one set that was burgundy satin with lace trim. The flirty panties were low cut, lots of cheek peek with a cage-back. You know, with the crisscross lattice that shows off the top half of the butt crack?"

"No. Jesus." He groaned. "I have no idea what that is, but it sounds sexy as fuck."

"Yeah. It was." Regret pinched her chest. "I wish I would've thrown on that set before I rushed out the door. Now it's gone, along with everything else in my life."

"I'm here." He lowered onto her, chest to chest, and braced his weight on his arms. "Martin's here, and we're going to make you very happy that we are."

"Martin? Are you sure?" She peeked around Ricky to lift a brow at the quiet, watchful man in question. "He's selfish with his body. He lets us look, but no one's allowed to touch."

"I'll work on him, but right now, I'm going to work on you."

He kissed her long and deep, sending languorous curls of fire through her veins. The warm glide of his tongue ignited her pulse. The hard press of his muscles melted her limbs, and the heady buzz of his presence made her want. Oh, God, how she wanted him.

He released her mouth to trail a scorching path of kisses down her neck. His hands slipped beneath her and deftly removed her bra. As he bent over her breasts, his pink tongue slid between his lips. She wanted it between her legs, and the thought made her hot and restless.

He licked her nipples, and she struggled to remain still. He nibbled and bit, torturing her, making her gasp. She tried to squirm away, but not really.

She needed him. Needed every atom in his body. She wanted to fuse with him at a molecular level so that nothing or no one could tear them apart.

Not just him. She craved them both.

Martin raised his heated gaze from Ricky's mouth on her breast and met her eyes. His fingers moved along his thigh, drawing a winding line as if he were tracing her body. It was profoundly seductive, fucking with her breathing and setting her skin afire.

"How's your head?" she panted.

"Fine. How's your pussy?"

She moaned. "Wet. Come here."

"Lie still and shut up."

She gave him the side eye.

"Do as you're told." He gripped her panties and yanked one side down her thigh.

Ricky took over, sliding the threadbare cotton off while being mindful not to rip them.

Then she was bare, totally nude and utterly exposed beneath the weight of their eyes. They took in the dark hair between her legs, their nostrils pulsing and expressions burning with desire.

Her body was completely natural and all her. No creams, perfumes, polishes, powders, dyes, waxes, surgeries, or enhancements of any kind. But they liked what they saw, and she kind of loved them for that.

"Open your legs," Martin said.

She submitted without hesitation, relishing the way he controlled her. Both her and Ricky.

Ricky was domineering in his own right, but when he was with Martin, he let his friend take the reins. She adored the dynamic, loved that they didn't compete against each other for attention or dominance.

Each of their roles in this threesome felt natural, fitting together seamlessly, effortlessly, without alterations or compromises.

Nothing in her life had ever been this easy or felt this right. It was as if some cosmic force had decided she deserved a chance at happiness, and *poof*, here they were, molding her into a woman who would never want anyone else but them.

"She's lost in her head," Martin said. "Rectify that."

Ricky stretched her legs open and fit his wide shoulders between her thighs. Her heart stuttered as he lowered his mouth to her pussy.

The first touch of his lips bowed her back. He did it again, and she gulped uselessly for air, choking and trembling.

"Breathe." Martin crawled in beside her and brushed her hair from her face. "Deep breaths."

She inhaled slowly, unable to stop her thighs from squeezing around Ricky's ears. "It's been so long."

"I know." He dropped a kiss on her mouth.

He did know. Seven years without sex. She needed to understand why, but she wouldn't push him. Not tonight.

"I don't know if I can have an orgasm." She stared down her body to find Ricky's waiting gaze, the depths glimmering with promise. "I can do it on my own, but I haven't tried in two years."

"Give me your eyes," Martin said.

She looked up and fell into a crystal green ocean.

"You've never come with another person?" He stroked a finger across her lips.

"No."

"Lick her, Ricky. Do it slowly and draw it out."

"I love it when you're bossy." Ricky grinned.

Then he buried that smile between her legs.

The firm, wet warmth of his tongue made her gasp. Martin caught her lips between his, kissing her soundly as Ricky brought her body to life with skillful licks and soft sucking pressure.

Her arms encircled Martin's neck, and she kissed him back, hungrily eating at his mouth while pulling him closer, tighter. She wanted him on top of her, inside her, deep and hard and *more.*

His dark, manly scent drugged her inhales. The potency of his hot skin on hers evaporated her brain cells. The taste of his breath pulled her hips up, spurring her to flex and grind against the diabolical swirl of Ricky's tongue.

Two mouths worshiped her, kissing in sync and catching an urgent rhythm. Her entire body throbbed beneath the pure expertise of their tongues, and that was when she knew she would come.

Pleasure rose from dormancy, bursting from her core with a vengeance. There was no slow build or warning tingles. When the orgasm sparked, it blasted across her vision in Technicolor and shot full-body compression waves through her nerve endings, shaking her down to her soul.

She screamed their names, cursed them in four-letter words, and

Martin devoured every syllable with his mouth over hers.

"I just died a thousand deaths." She shivered against the lingering twitches of the best orgasm she'd ever had.

Ricky crawled up her body, his lips swollen and wet and curved in a breathtaking smile.

"You're the reason the gods invented oral sex," she said to him. Then she glanced at Martin, unable to ignore the massive bulge straining his briefs. "You should let Ricky use his mouth on—"

Martin grabbed a fistful of Ricky's hair, and their lips collided. The kiss skipped slow and gentle and plunged straight into ferocious.

She scooted out of the way as they rose to their knees and crashed together. Their mouths moved violently, rabidly, sucking, biting, groaning, panting. Hands pulled at hair. Fingers clawed down backs. Their hips slammed, cocks grinding. They were fucking each other with only the barrier of underwear between them.

It was so beautiful, so utterly staggering it made her heart hurt.

Martin ripped his mouth away and stared at Ricky's lips. Then he dove in again, his hand tangled in Ricky's hair as he licked around Ricky's open mouth, curling his tongue into the corners and the undersides of Ricky's lips.

She stopped breathing as it dawned on her. Martin was lapping her come from Ricky's face.

Martin leaned back, his gaze unfocused. "Fuck, she tastes..."

"Like resurrection."

Her heart fainted. Then it hammered anew as she watched them stare at each other. The penetrating glares, stiff necks, and swollen need between their legs... The passing seconds hardened and condensed between them.

They weren't finished.

She silently willed them to fall into each other and fuck until they passed out. But she didn't say a word, didn't move a muscle, afraid she would break the spell.

"Let me touch you." Ricky looked down at Martin's strained briefs. "Let me send you into ecstasy."

"Tula." Martin held Ricky's gaze as he said to her, "Lie on your back and spread your legs."

TWENTY-TWO

Ricky's pulse thundered in his ears as Tula moved into position.

With her thighs open and tits heaving, she lay like an erotic buffet spread out before him. He was five seconds from blowing a load in his boxers.

"You're fucking gorgeous." His gaze raked over her sensual body, making her shiver. "Can't wait to bury my cock in your cunt."

"Kneel between her legs." Martin smacked Ricky's ass so hard his breath cut off.

His lips pulled back, releasing a groan of pain, and his entire body tensed to spin around and punch Martin in the face. But he didn't.

A sense of peace stole over him as he obeyed. And there was something else. *Hunger.* It raised his body temperature, accelerated his breaths, and blazed more blood to his cock.

His erection strained harder, taller, tenting his boxers and producing a wet spot at the crest.

Martin moved in behind him and curled a hand around his rigid length.

Fuck, he would never get used to the feel of that fist on his cock. He'd dreamed about it for so long it didn't seem real.

Martin swiped his thumb over the crown, rubbing the slippery wet spot as he bit and licked along Ricky's nape.

"Don't stop." Ricky dropped the weight of his head forward and groaned.

The sharp bite of teeth sank into the juncture between his shoulder and neck. Maddening pain gnawed through the muscle there, stabbing so hard and deep he was certain Martin drew blood.

The agony centered him, and his balls tightened in anticipation.

Beneath his bent position, Tula's jaw dropped an inch, her eyes wide and glistening. "You're hurting him."

"Shhh." Ricky slid his palm between her breasts, holding her to the mattress. "I like it. We both do. But Martin would never force you into edge play."

"If you think I'm playing…" Martin grabbed Ricky's nuts. "You don't know me at all."

That fist clenched viciously, squeezing without mercy. Black spots strobed across Ricky's vision, and his stomach twisted with nauseating pain.

"Are you man enough to make me scream?" Ricky choked out.

"I'm mean enough to make sure you can't." Martin released Ricky's testicles and cuffed his throat, instantly cutting off his airway.

Cruel fingers tightened without care, digging into his vulnerable esophagus as if intending to yank it out.

"You're scaring me." Tula's face paled. "Let him go." She jackknifed upward and pulled uselessly at Martin's arm. "He can't breathe!"

"I didn't tell you to move." The chilling calmness in Martin's voice made her freeze.

Martin's other hand imprisoned Ricky's cock, stroking him ruthlessly, vigorously toward orgasm. He tried to shake his head, to tell her he wanted this, but he had no voice, no air, and no power to move.

She clutched her throat, her eyes watering as she looked down at Martin's pumping fist.

The urgency to come had never felt so terrifyingly pleasurable, and she must've seen that in Ricky's expression because she dropped back on the bed, her gaze lasering on his cock.

Martin's fingers loosened on Ricky's neck, allowing him to drag delicious gulps of air into his lungs. The instant he could breathe without choking, the hand cinched again, strangling his next inhale.

Tula watched with lust-filled eyes as Martin jerked Ricky off, stroking him expertly toward release. Right as Ricky reached the pinnacle, Martin stopped. The vise of his hand squeezed beneath the head of Ricky's cock and stifled the orgasm, causing Ricky's body to shake uncontrollably.

And so it went. Martin tortured him for an eternity, bringing him to the edge of climax, asphyxiating him to the brink of unconsciousness. Then he paused, gave Ricky air, and started again.

Each time grew rougher, harder, and more reckless until Martin started to go too far. Ricky felt a real fear of death beneath the hand on his throat. Midway between desire and unconsciousness, self-preservation kicked in, and he started to fight.

Martin released him and tangled that brutal hand in his hair, wrenching his neck at a painful angle.

"I'm going to fuck your ass." The voice at Ricky's ear spoke without emotion or familiarity. "I'll do it dry while you're tensing in fear. Once you're nice and bloody, I'll shove the handle of a hammer into that ruined hole and ram it hard." Martin ground his erection against Ricky's backside. "Every blow will drive so deep you'll feel it in your stomach. The pain will own you, make you so fucking weak you'll try to puke it out. I'll shove your face in the vomit, make you lick up your own filth. When you start crying, because you will, motherfucker. You'll cry like a goddamn faggot, and I'll piss all over those whiny lips."

A sickening feeling punched Ricky in the gut and sank to the pith of his stomach.

Van Quiso hadn't put those images in Martin's head. This was the creation of something much more sinister.

"Oh, no. Martin." She rose to her knees and pressed a trembling hand against her mouth. Tears poured from her eyes as she shook her head in horror. "Who did that to you?"

She stole the words out of Ricky's head. His dick started to shrivel as he yanked his boxers back in place. Then he turned toward his best friend.

Martin's arms lowered to his sides, and he went hauntingly still. His expression froze, vacant and eerie, as his glazed eyes stared off into the distance.

"Martin." She touched his jaw, her voice thick with tears. "How old were you?"

His brows pinched together, and his breathing lunged into a wheezing panic.

He shoved off the bed and pivoted toward the wall, flattening his palms against it.

Heart racing, Ricky moved to comfort him.

"Don't." Martin dropped his head between his braced arms and sucked heavy gulps of air. "Stay there. Please."

The *please* locked Ricky's limbs. The desperation in Martin's voice gutted him. Martin never pleaded. Never asked. Whatever compelled him to do it now held Ricky in place.

A sob sounded beside him, and he hooked an arm around her, pulling her onto his lap.

He clung to her, suffocating in the wake of Martin's pain as he helplessly watched Martin put himself back together.

Agonizing minutes passed before Martin straightened and stepped toward the bed. Stitches and bruises marred his gorgeous features, but none of it detracted from his strength.

He stood tall and powerful, wearing only briefs. He didn't need the armor of clothing or the security of a masked expression. He let Ricky and Tula see all of him — the soft bulge between his legs, the bobbing swallow in his throat, and the indelible memories of abuse in his eyes.

"How badly did I hurt you?" Martin asked.

"It was nothing that I didn't want or couldn't handle." He shifted to one end of the pushed-together mattresses, taking Tula with him. "I know you don't want to talk about why you —"

"I can't."

"Can you tell me about your parents?"

Ricky had asked that question numerous times, and the only answer he'd been given was Martin had a dad, as in *once had* but not anymore.

Had Martin's father molested him? Was that the man he killed?

His silent glare confessed nothing, his lips refusing to answer.

"I never knew my dad." Tula pulled the blanket over her, covering her nude body on Ricky's lap. "And my mom couldn't get rid of me fast enough. I don't know why. I never gave her any trouble and always did well in school. She and Vera were close, but she kept me at an arm's distance. When I turned eighteen, she begged me to leave. To leave the city. The country. To just go away. So I did." She sucked on her quivering bottom lip and released it. "She died seven years ago, and I miss her so much."

Ricky slid a hand into her hair, raking his fingers along her scalp as he pulled her against him.

"I'm sorry, *querida*." He kissed her head, his eyes locked on Martin, waiting.

"My mother left when I was two." Martin lowered onto the far end of the mattress and leaned against the wall at his back. "I grew up on a small farm in Texas with my dad. He was a good man. Hardworking. He died from a stroke when I was fourteen."

Orphaned at fourteen.

His heart caved in.

Based on his own experience, Ricky could draw conclusions about what happened to Martin. "I was given up at birth and spent my entire childhood in foster care. Fortunately, I was always placed with nice families." He softened his voice. "No pedophiles or abusive foster dads."

"I wasn't put into foster care."

"Orphanage?"

"No."

"Then what — ?"

"Fucking drop it, Ricky."

All three of them had been victims of rape, and they coped with it in different ways. Martin's experiences had been the worst by far, and Ricky knew he hadn't heard the half of it.

He could be patient, but he would never stop trying to help Martin.

Tula adjusted her position on his lap. With her back to his chest, they faced Martin with the length of the mattress between them.

"I know you don't want to talk about it." She kept the blanket clutched to her chest. "But what *do* you want? What do you need?"

Martin's eyes flashed. "Lower the blanket."

"Oh." She tensed against Ricky's chest. After a reluctant moment, she tossed aside the cover.

"*That* is what I need."

"You need my...?" She looked down at her breasts.

Ricky knew the answer before her head popped up.

"My obedience," she breathed.

"Yes." Martin inclined his head. "And your trust. Open your legs."

After what she just witnessed, her trust was a helluva lot to ask for. The mood had been decimated, replaced with a stifling gloom in the air, but that didn't stop Ricky's cock from swelling again. The damn thing couldn't ignore the gorgeous, naked woman on his lap.

Martin bent over the edge of the bed and reached for the box of supplies on the floor. The crinkling sound of a paper bag told Ricky what Martin was doing, and his body hardened in anticipation.

Tula gave him a look over her shoulder, one that said, *I know that's not a banana in your pocket.*

"We don't have condoms." She turned back to Martin and stared at the foil packet he set between her legs. "Okay. Where did you get that?"

"Garra." Martin returned to his perch against the wall. "He delivered a bag of them earlier today."

"Garra?" A sound of surprise left her lips. "That's why he has a broken nose. Which one of you punched him?"

"It might've been the one-armed man." Ricky pressed his grin against her neck.

"I don't care that you hurt him. I'm guessing Hector sent him with the condoms. I don't think Garra gives a shit if I get pregnant."

She was wrong. Garra had a lot more interest in her than what she believed, but Ricky didn't want to talk about that bastard right now.

"Who does this belong to?" He cupped a hand between her spread legs and met Martin's eyes.

"Ricky Martin." She dropped her head back on his shoulder and chuckled. "My pussy belongs to Ricky Martin."

Ricky slapped the silky, damp flesh, making her yelp. "You're going to put that condom on me. Then you're going to slide down in this exact position so Martin can watch your pussy lips stretch and suck on my cock."

"Jesus, you're dirty." She melted against him, sighing. "Why does that turn me on so much?"

"Because you're dirty, too." He slid his touch along her slit, slowly working it up and down, teasing her.

Fuck him, she was tight and wet. He sank two fingers into her velvety heat and stroked her clenching muscles. His other hand cupped her breast, kneading the soft weight.

As she grew slick around his fingers, he curled them into a beckoning motion, again and again. She writhed and panted on his lap, and he turned his mouth toward hers, biting and licking and grunting at her sweetness. So fucking sexy.

"Get the condom." He slipped his fingers from her body and caught her tight little clit, rubbing it until she moaned.

She twisted around and delivered a hungry kiss to his lips. Then she climbed off his lap.

He scooted to put his back against the wall that sat perpendicular to the one Martin leaned against. Then he removed his boxers and widened his legs. One foot touched Martin's hip. His other rested on Martin's ankle.

The position would give Martin the best view of her body as Ricky slid in and out of her cunt.

The thought sped up his pulse and pooled warmth in his balls, drawing them closer to his body. He needed her. *Now.*

Then she was there, kneeling beside him with the condom ready. He grew impossibly harder.

As she rolled on the latex with small, warm fingers, he flicked his gaze between her and Martin, reveling in their presence and absorbing the moment.

Martin's blank expression started to gain color and life, the pain he carried inside him retreating from his eyes. He was a ticking time bomb, that guy. He thought he could keep it all locked up, but Ricky had just found the key.

It was probably going to hurt like hell, but Ricky was confident that sex would set Martin free.

"I think I did it right." She peered up at him, her eyes round and dark with desire.

"Straddle me, facing Martin."

She threw a leg over his lap, giving him a brain-scrambling view of her curvy ass. He gripped her hips, holding her over his cock, keyed up and so damn ready to fuck.

The weight of her petite frame in his hands, the feel of her satiny

skin beneath his palms, the deep pulses at the base of his dick...
Everything suspended, waiting on Martin's command.

For a handful of heartbeats, Martin simply watched them. He bent
a leg and draped his arm over his raised knee. His cock lay semi-hard
beneath his briefs. Then it twitched, moving the fabric.

Dark stormy energy rotated around him, his green eyes aglow in
the shadows of the flickering candlelight. Hell only knew what kind of
thoughts were swirling in his head.

"Give me her orgasm, Ricky," he said in a rock-grinding voice. "I
want to see her face as she forgets every man who came before us."

"What other men?"

Ricky heard the smirk in her response right before he pressed the
tip of his cock inside her.

The tight ring of her opening stole his breath. Her hands went to
his wrists as he held her waist, hovering her over him and making her
squirm on that first inch.

He pushed deeper, and they moaned together. He extended the
torture, turning that initial stroke into the slowest and longest in history.
With every inch he worked in, he felt her wrapping around him,
constricting and pulsing and stoking his need into electrifying chaos.

He wanted to see Martin's expression, but it was all he could do
not to drive himself, hard and fast, inside her. When he finally reached the
back of her cunt, he sucked in a breath and began to fuck her deeply,
languidly, savoring the sinful feel of her strangling heat.

"Martin." He groaned. "She's so fucking tight."

A masculine groan rumbled in answer, and the mattress squeaked
as Martin shifted his weight.

Ricky's control only lasted so long. She felt too good, too damn
warm and sweet. He knew her scent, her taste, and now he knew the
depths of her sex. He was in heaven.

She squeezed down on him, grinding her ass each time he buried
himself to the root. Eventually, he released her hips and let her move on
her own.

Reaching between their legs, she cupped his balls and scratched
her nails up and down his scrotum. He grunted at the wicked sensations
and thrust his hips harder, jerking himself off in her slick pussy.

His blood pressure went up, and his heart rate increased as he
rapidly approached the point of no return. He wanted to come inside her
while staring into her eyes.

But first, Martin was going to see the face she made as Ricky made
her explode.

He snaked his hand into her hair and turned her neck, locking her
into a kiss. She undulated on his cock, driving her hips to meet the

slamming force of his thrusts.

Her mouth opened for his lashing tongue, and the kiss morphed into a mauling of lips and teeth. He was too hungry, and his thrusts were bouncing her too fast. They couldn't keep their mouths connected amid the panting, groaning, full-on fucking.

Using his grip in her hair, he angled her face toward Martin and sealed his lips to her neck. She clenched her inner muscles, and his eyes rolled back into his head. He wasn't going to last much longer.

With a hand between her legs, he tortured her clit. She cried out in pleasure, spreading her legs wider. He circled his fingers around and around the little nub, making her thighs tremble and breaths come faster, harder.

"Look at me." Martin's deep voice penetrated his chest.

He knew Martin was talking to her, but he looked anyway, tilting his head to get a direct view of those green eyes in front of her.

Martin stared at him with the force of fire, stirring the embers of a rising heat. Ricky worked his hand harder around her clit, flexing his hips and spinning them into delirium.

Martin balled and released his fist, and a muscle bounced in his jaw. "Give it to me. Now."

"Tula first." Ricky drove deep, desperate to send her over.

Martin leaned forward, giving her the force of his daunting glare. "Now."

She doubled over and gripped Ricky's knees, bearing down on his cock as she met Martin's eyes. Her hips jerked once, twice, and she let out a throaty roar, growling and panting through clenched teeth. She continued to grind, gasping and milking her release to the last drop.

Ricky didn't breathe through the entirety of her full-minute orgasm. Didn't wait for her to find her bearings. Didn't spare Martin a glance. He didn't stop to do anything as he tossed her onto her back and slammed himself into the tight sheath of her body.

Pinning her pretty tattooed arms above her head, he captured her lips and thrust his tongue deep. All control gone, he hammered his hips, dipping in and out of her slick cunt and spurring them into wild madness.

He couldn't let up, couldn't slow down. He gave and took, raw and mindless, kissing and fucking to within an inch of their lives.

"Holy fuck." She moaned against his mouth, her face radiating with the afterglow of her orgasms.

"That's right, baby. What's my name?" He pounded into her.

"Oh, God." She clawed at his back.

"God is good, aren't I?"

"So good."

She made him feel like a god. In her arms, under Martin's heated gaze, he caught fire.

He'd never felt like this—free, wanted, happy, exactly where he belonged. With her. With Martin. Coming his fucking brains out.

"Fuck, fuck, fuuuuuck!" He stared into her eyes as muscular spasms attacked his body, starting at his face and quaking down to his toes. Even his rectum contracted, squeezing in rhythm with the pulsing spurts of his cock. Heat and sweat spread over his skin and penetrated deep, saturating his insides from his balls to his nipples.

On a squeaky rusted cot, in the most violent prison in Latin America, he experienced the best orgasm of his life.

He rolled to his back, taking her with him. As she settled onto his chest, both of their heads turned toward Martin.

The brutal intensity of Martin's eyes raked over them, stroking more than their bodies. He felt Martin reach inside him and curl around his soul.

He depended on that connection. He needed the completeness of all three of them, and he was so close. Tula reciprocated every touch, and Martin no longer felt like an impossible dream.

She lifted her hips, letting his softening cock slip out of her. "You annihilated my orgasm-less existence."

"I would gladly do it again, every day, for the rest of my life." He removed the condom and tossed it at the bag of trash in the corner.

Her gaze drifted back to Martin, and she tilted her head. "Do you…?" She glanced at his semi and returned to his eyes. "Masturbate?"

Martin's lips bounced before surrendering a grin. "Yes, Tula. I'm quite proficient at it."

"Do you want to do it now? Or I can—?"

"If I need to come, I'll come." He pushed off the wall and crawled to her. "You were devastatingly perfect tonight."

He kissed her, nudging her onto her back as he bent over her. Soft and slow, he licked and nibbled and took his time.

Then he turned to Ricky and placed his hands on either side of Ricky's head. His bright eyes filled with equal amounts of apology and affection. Then he pulled Ricky close and slid his tongue in Ricky's mouth.

The languorous kiss curled warmth through Ricky's chest, and by the time it finished, Martin left no doubt in Ricky's mind that they'd only just begun.

They slid in on either side of Tula and twined their limbs with hers. Martin's hand brushed Ricky's bare hip, curled around his buttocks, and stayed there.

Ricky basked in that touch, in the nearness of this man and woman, in the three of them together.

As he drifted into sleep, *forever* sank into the crevices of his soul.

MANIPULATE

TWENTY-THREE

The next month was the happiest month in Tula's memory.

There had been no attacks on her or the guys. Hector's security guard, Luis, had been released from prison. That meant fewer cartel meetings and more time with Martin and Ricky.

Her sex life had gone from nonexistent to nonstop, and the sex…

Sweet mother of Himeros, Ricky had unending stamina and talent. He was inside her every day, multiple times a day, in every position. Slow and fast, hard and gentle, they went at it so frequently she had to ask Garra for more condoms.

She'd never felt such uncontrollable desire for a man, let alone two.

Martin kissed her and Ricky as often as she and Ricky had sex, but he never allowed himself relief. He never let them touch him sexually, and after that first night she and Ricky were together, Martin stopped touching them, too.

She knew he didn't want another violent episode after the one he had with Ricky. So he sat on the sidelines, seemingly content to watch her and Ricky fall apart at his command.

Behind his tightly controlled bearing, however, simmered a bottomless well of pain and frustration. He tried to bury it, but it burned from his eyes and scorched the air around him whenever he was aroused.

Sex was his trigger, and it made him viciously mean. She couldn't fathom the abuse he'd endured.

Pressing him to talk about it only made him coil tighter, and whenever he lashed out, his fury was loaded with accusations.

Accusations directed at her.

MANIPULATE

She left him and Ricky in bed this morning, telling them she had a meeting with Hector. The lie made her chest hurt, but dammit, she knew they weren't being truthful with her, either.

She sat in her own cell, on a mattress she didn't use anymore, and pored over everything they'd said over the past five weeks.

Martin's distrust resided with Hector, steeped with the notion that Hector's cartel snatched children off American streets and sold them into slavery.

Though Martin never admitted it, she knew he'd been a victim of sexual abuse as young as fourteen. His stance against child slavery wasn't just a moral one. It was personal.

That wasn't the case for Ricky. No, he just flat-out hated Hector.

They had no evidence against Hector's involvement in human trafficking. Their claims came from alleged news reports and rumors they'd heard in the circles they ran in. Or so they said.

That was where her suspicions really niggled. What circles? Who were Martin Lockwood and Ricky Saldivar really? Where did they come from? Why had they paid their way into Area Three if it wasn't to join La Rocha Cartel and take advantage of that protection?

She didn't know all their truths or the details about their pasts. They maintained they were innocent of their drug trafficking charges, which she believed. They were too high-minded and honorable to fuck around with narcotics.

So why were they arrested? She didn't buy their bullshit story about a Mexican vacation gone wrong. The military didn't just scoop up American tourists and throw them in prison.

Except that was exactly what happened to her.

With a self-pitying groan, she dropped her head in her hands.

She cared about them deeply, possessively. They'd taken her from feeling nothing to feeling everything, and it wasn't just lust and orgasms. It was more profound and soulful. She thought of them as hers. Hers to hold and support and love.

She didn't know if she loved them. There was so much about them she still hadn't discovered. Not just the secrets they kept from her, but who they were outside of prison. What did they do when they woke every morning? Where did they go? Who were their friends?

All this could be derived from a conversation, but she wanted to experience it herself. She wanted to be with them outside of these claustrophobic walls, and that couldn't happen for at least three years. Maybe longer, pending their sentences.

Even then, when she was released from Jaulaso, she would never be released from Hector.

Hector.

639

Her loyalty to him was all tangled up in her feelings for Ricky Martin.

Whenever she asked Martin what he wanted her to do about the accusations he threw around, he told her to find the truth.

Open your mind. Be skeptical. Investigate your boss.

If she could be suspicious of Martin and Ricky, why couldn't she be suspicious of Hector La Rocha?

Because she was scared.

Terrified.

Fear had kept her from poking around, but here she was, prepared to do just that.

Her hands slicked with sweat, and her pulse tapped neurotically in her throat. She was a nervous fucking wreck.

Another five minutes passed before she heard footsteps in the corridor.

She rose soundlessly and darted behind the partially opened door to her cell. No one would suspect she was in here. Her cell had been empty for a month.

She held her breath as the movement in the hall passed by without stopping.

Tiptoeing around the door, she peeked out to see the backs of Garra and Hector as they made their way around the corner and out of view.

She blew out a quiet breath.

With Luis out of prison now, Hector had become wary about his personal security. Garra had stepped in to do the job until Hector could find someone permanent to trust with his life.

In the meantime, he reduced the number of meetings in his private quarters and kept to himself more than usual. But he still had to shower, and he did it like clockwork, every other day at eight in the morning.

She stepped into the empty hall and silently raced the thirty feet to his cell. The handle turned. Unlocked.

Only someone with a death wish would enter his space without his permission.

Her heart banged so hard in her chest she thought she might pass out.

She didn't know how long he would be gone. Ten minutes tops. She slipped inside and went straight to the filing cabinets. She'd never seen inside the drawers and expected to find paperwork when she opened them.

Nope. Every drawer held nonperishable food. Pork rinds, bread rolls, cereal, rice, tequila, and enough soup to feed an old man for twenty years. No wonder Hector rarely left his cell.

Her nerves tightened as she stepped toward the rear of his quarters. Behind a heavy drape sat a small bed with folded linens and a soft pillow.

This was the first time she'd ever been back here, and she hoped it would be the last as she ran her hands under the mattress and rummaged through every nook and cranny.

She found a knife under his pillow and left it there. There were no documents. No diaries. Nothing that might incriminate him. Where the hell would he hide his secrets?

Something rustled behind her. Her heart rate exploded as she spun around.

A massive cockroach darted across a paper bag and squeezed into a crack in the wall.

"Fuck!" She pressed a hand against her chest, trying to soothe her wailing heart.

He could walk in at any moment, and she didn't even know what she was looking for. She just needed...*something*. Proof that he was or was not trafficking women and children.

Five running steps carried her to the bookshelves. She thumbed through every text and novel, shaking them on their sides to see if anything fell from the pages.

Nothing.

She continued along the shelves, removing and returning the books. How long had Hector been gone? Four minutes? Five? She needed to go.

"What are you doing?" His soft voice drifted from the door, paralyzing her lungs.

She forced herself to breathe. Then she turned slowly, willing the tension from her neck and shoulders.

"Hey." She pinned a timid half-smile on her lips. "Sorry I was digging through your books. I knocked, but you weren't here." She motioned at the shelves behind her. "I was looking for something new to read."

"Have I not given you enough books?" He remained near the door, his face concealed by shadows.

"You've given me too much."

He'd given her more than anyone else had in her life, and she repaid him by snooping through his shit.

"Any updates on the gringos?" He set down his bath towel and toiletries and joined her at the bookshelf.

She grasped desperately at the change of topics. "Not since last week. We've been..."

"Making use of the condoms?" He lifted an eyebrow. "Garra told me you needed more."

Oh, Jesus. Her face heated, and she looked away.

"You're enjoying yourself." His tone lacked judgment or suspicion. "There's very little pleasure in Jaulaso. Take it when and where you can."

"I'm definitely doing that."

Talking about her sex life with Hector La Rocha creeped her out. But she preferred this conversation over a discussion about trespassing in his private quarters.

"Thank you for letting me have this time with them," she said. "They're...nice. I know that's not enough, and I'm still working on —"

"You're distracting them."

"What?"

"If they intend to take action against me or my cartel, their plan is going nowhere as long as you're with them, keeping them preoccupied."

Was that true? She hadn't meant to distract them. She didn't even know if they had a plan.

He swept his gaze over the bookshelves. "What are you looking for?"

"Non-fiction, I think." She studied the Spanish titles on the spines, disinterested in the contents. "Something educational or —"

"You didn't come here for a book, Petula." The musical rhythm in his voice tingled a chill down her spine. "*What* are you looking for?"

This time, she couldn't turn and look at him.

She couldn't hide the perspiration forming on her skin, the tremors in her hands, or her inability to blink or form a coherent answer.

Lying would only dig her grave deeper. He saw straight through her.

Was he capable of hurting her? Definitely. Would he? She didn't know.

"I sit through your meetings and hear you talk about trafficking drugs and weapons and all the wars over the smuggling routes." She pulled in a shuddering breath and met his gentle eyes. "Why haven't you mentioned trafficking humans or sexual slavery? I mean, all the other cartels do it."

"Not all the cartels. In fact, the Restrepo Cartel in Colombia actively fights *against* it." He clasped his hands behind his back and canted his head, scrutinizing her. "Human trafficking isn't a lucrative business. I make more money in narcotics and guns."

Alarmed by his response, she drew her head back. "If human slavery had better profit margins, you would do it?"

"I answered your question. Now answer mine." *What are you looking for?*

Deep down, she'd come here for more than an answer to the human trafficking accusation.

She was looking for validation that he was a good man. A man she could trust not to hurt her. She needed to know she hadn't been wrong about him.

If he was willing to sell women into slavery for the right price, what was his intention with *her*?

"I'm looking for an answer." She stared into his eyes. "Why am I the only female inmate in Area Three?"

"I've waited two years for you to ask that question." He ambled toward the record player.

"I thought it was because I saved your life." Her neck stiffened.

"That came *after*." He lit a cigarette from his pocket and removed an album from the middle of the stack. "Do you know this one?" He held out *Petula Clark's Greatest Hits*.

She shook her head. "She has an unusual first name."

"Yes, she does. She's been my favorite singer for as long as I can remember." He extended the album toward her. "Go ahead."

Tula just happened to share this woman's name? That couldn't have been a coincidence.

Her mind spun as she moved toward him, her steps laden with nerves. She lifted the record from his hand and reached inside the cardboard sleeve. Her fingers slid along the grooved surface of the vinyl and bumped papers.

She glanced at his unreadable expression and removed a handful of documents.

A smaller paper fluttered to the floor, and she reached for it.

And stopped.

Three photographed faces smiled up at her.

Her heart stuttered as she grabbed the photo and brought it closer to her eyes.

It was a snapshot of Hector in his late-thirties or forties with his arm around a beautiful young woman with black hair.

With a baby on her lap.

The woman.

The baby.

She knew those faces, but her brain struggled to process what she was seeing.

"That's my mother." Her voice cracked, and her heart pounded in her ears. "That's me. We're… We're in a photo with you? How are we —?

She glanced up at his affectionate eyes. Brown eyes like hers. A narrow face like hers. Small bones, petite height, bronze skin… He looked like her. She looked like him. How had she not seen it?

"Oh, my God." She swayed as the strength in her legs deserted her.

"Sit." He guided her to a chair, the cigarette dangling from his lips as he examined her expression. "Are you calm?"

"I'm a little freaked out."

She had a father.

Hector La Rocha.

The notorious crime boss her mother warned her against all her life.

Her mother had sex with him?

Holy.

Fucking.

Shit.

He was her father.

He took the seat beside her and stared at the photo in her trembling hand. "When I saw your name booked in Jaulaso, I had a prison guard bring you to Area Three."

That prison guard had watched her kill a man. *Then* he offered to take her to a nicer part of the prison. His timing had been impeccable.

Because Hector had orchestrated it.

"When he brought me here, Garra raped me." Her throat closed. "If you knew I was your daughter, why did you let that happen?"

"I made it happen."

Her heart collapsed, and a surge of anger raised her voice. "Why?"

"My enemies go to great lengths to try to kill me, including sending a woman by the name of Petula Gomez into my territory. I had to confirm your identity. So I sent Garra to collect your DNA."

"I don't understand." Her hands flexed on her lap. "He could've stolen a strand of my hair or taken my saliva from a cup."

"Vaginal fluid has a high DNA content."

The condom.

Garra had taken it with him after he...

What the fucking fuck? It had all been a setup?

She felt sick to her stomach.

Hector tugged on the forgotten paperwork in her hand, drawing her attention to it.

She stared down at a paternity test. It listed her name as the child and Hector La Rocha as the alleged father. Beneath all the columns of numbers and medical explanations, she read, *Probability of Paternity: 99.9998%.*

Her chest squeezed as she flipped to the header page and found the date.

Two years ago.

He'd known for two years.

Her jaw set. "Why didn't you tell me?"

"Just because you're my daughter doesn't mean you're on my side. I didn't trust you." He huffed at her scowl. "Don't give me that look. You didn't trust me, either. Maybe you still don't."

"I feel manipulated."

"Because of the Garra thing?"

"Yes," she hissed. "Because you had Garra rape me." She leaned back in the chair and stared at Hector with new eyes. "I can't believe you were with my mother."

"For only a couple of weeks." His expression turned wistful. "She was extraordinarily beautiful. But she hated me. Hated the cartel life. She forbade me to come around when she discovered who I was. I only saw you once after you were born." He nodded at the photo. "The day that picture was taken."

"What about Vera?"

"She's not mine. You're my only daughter, and I have four sons." He smiled sadly. "I miss them."

She had four brothers she'd never met, a missing sister, and a father, who had felt like a father since the day she'd met him.

Because his name was written in her genetics.

She looked down at the paternity test, and the sight of the record album beside it clicked another clue into place.

"*You* named me." Her eyes snapped to his. "After your favorite singer."

"Yes."

The signs had been there all along.

Her mother had hated Hector La Rocha with a seething passion. It was the hatred of a scorned lover, and over the years, that hatred transferred into resentment of the daughter who shared his DNA.

Hector, on the other hand, had doted on her from day one. He'd opened up his protective circle to her, the only woman in Area Three, and kept her safe.

But he was still Hector La Rocha, a cartel boss who didn't think twice about sending his only daughter to seduce his potential enemies, Martin and Ricky.

That didn't sit right with her. Did he know more about them than he was letting on? Did he want her to spend time with them, not to gather information, but to distract them from something? But from what?

She felt used, deceived, manipulated. At the same time, she felt connected to Hector in a way that finally made sense.

He protected her because she was his blood. He was kind to her because she was his daughter. He cared for her, but did that mean he would never hurt her?

He pulled the Petula Clark album off her lap. "Want to hear it?"

More than anything, she wanted to race back to Martin and Ricky and tell them everything. She felt the safest in their arms, in the cage of their possessive eyes, and in the reassuring words she knew they would give her.

She itched to run, but she owed Hector her life.

So she nodded. "Sure. I'd love that."

TWENTY-FOUR

"We've been here for forty-five days." Martin gripped the edge of the sink in their cell, digging his fingers into the porcelain as he tried to curb his pent-up rage. "Forty-five fucking days, Ricky. We're halfway through our time, and we're no closer to the goal than we were at day one. We need a new plan."

"Give her more time." Ricky raked a hand through his hair.

They'd been arguing since Tula left this morning. Cooped up in this tiny goddamn cell. Sitting on their fucking hands. Wasting precious hours.

Martin's frustration with himself, Tula's inability to see what was right in front of her, and Ricky with his laid-back demeanor and cock-hardening kisses—all of it was coming to a head because Martin couldn't do it anymore.

He couldn't pretend that watching Ricky and Tula fuck each other wasn't killing him.

He couldn't ignore the fact they would be leaving her alone and unprotected in this place in forty-five days.

He couldn't run from his vicious need to restrain, choke, whip, and mark them until they bleed.

He couldn't touch them without spreading his filth all over their perfections. But he *needed* to touch them. And love them. He just didn't know how. When he allowed himself happiness or pleasure, his impulses took over and turned everything into pain.

His pleasure and their pain. One didn't come without the other.

"Did you hear me?" Ricky rose from the bed and approached him.

"Yeah. You want to give her more time, so you can continue

getting your dick wet."

"Banging her was your idea, you fucking prick." Ricky seethed in his face.

"And it's been a real hardship for you." He shoved Ricky away.

Seven years of celibacy was nothing compared to the past month with Tula and Ricky. Looking without touching. Kissing without fucking. The sounds of their groans, the sight of their joined bodies, the scent of their raw, unbridled arousal in his lungs—it was ecstasy and torture, heaven and hell, death and resurrection.

He coughed to mask an unbidden groan as hunger flooded his body, pulsating and shooting flames low in his belly. The physical need he'd denied himself for so long hardened and swelled between his legs.

He didn't have a second of privacy to fuck his own hand, and he refused to do it in front of them. The shame would've been more than he could bear. Not to mention his unraveling control. He didn't trust himself around them. Letting go while they were within reach was too risky.

If he hurt them, he would never forgive himself.

"Your pissy mood has nothing to do with the mission." Ricky closed in, blocking Martin's view of everything except the glaring frustration in his brown eyes. "You know I'm having the best sex of my life, and you would be, too, if you could get it up."

Martin swung.

The punch crashed across Ricky's face, powered with all the torment and desire that was unfurling inside him.

Ricky hit back, landing a jaw-cracking blow that whipped his head to the side. Blood filled his mouth, and he spat it into the sink. Then they lunged at the same time.

He slammed Ricky against the wall and attacked his mouth with tongue and teeth. "I fucking hate you."

Ricky smacked him, ringing his ears. "I love you, you stubborn cunt."

In a practiced sweep, Ricky's leg shot out and hooked Martin's ankle, taking him to the floor. Martin's shoulder rammed into the frame of the bed on the way down, sending a screech of metal through the room.

They grappled in the narrow aisle, punching with elbows and knees, grinding and twisting for the top position. Slick with sweat and grunting in pain, they rolled over supplies and overturned jugs of water, destroying everything within reach.

Martin boiled from the inside out, burning to fight and fuck, ruin and devour, punish and possess. His mouth glanced off Ricky's lips, trying to capture a kiss that turned into smacking teeth and lashing tongues.

"Say it again." He latched a leg around Ricky's thigh and flipped them, putting himself on top. "Say it, you little bitch."

"I love you." With a furious glint in his eyes, Ricky tore a hand through Martin's hair, ripping it at the roots. The other shoved between their hips and fisted Martin's erection through his jeans. "I need you. Fucking Christ, Martin. I need this cock inside me."

An agonized, animalistic sound escaped Martin's throat as he ground against that firm grip, working his hips into a frenzied rhythm.

"Take off my pants." Ricky ravaged Martin's mouth, biting and sucking and demolishing the last thread of Martin's control. "Fuck me. Give it to me, goddammit."

There was a reason he shouldn't, but his mind emptied. Lust and primal instinct consumed his body. The drive to fuck moved his arms and hips as he wrenched Ricky onto his stomach and shoved Ricky's flimsy cotton pants out of the way.

Ricky's rock-hard glutes filled his hands. He wedged his fingers into the crevice, spreading muscle and flesh to expose the tight, dark hole within.

His dick throbbed with its own heartbeat, jerking against the restraint of his jeans. He stabbed a thumb into Ricky's anus, twisting it as deep as it would go, digging past nerves and muscles that were bone-dry and begging to bleed.

Ricky gasped, and his entire body went taut, strung like a bow. "Fucking spit on it."

"Shut the fuck up." He yanked his thumb out and impaled Ricky's ass with two dry fingers. Then he added a third and thrust.

A low, distressed groan strangled in Ricky's throat, but he didn't fight. Martin rammed harder, faster, stretching Ricky's anal cavity with fiery friction and ruthlessness.

Ricky lifted his hips, flexing into the deep penetration as he wedged a hand beneath him and jacked himself off.

With each piercing stab of his fingers, Martin felt the scorching burn in his own rectum. He felt the hot panting breaths on his back and the river rocks grinding beneath his knees as he flailed beneath excruciating pain.

Memories flogged him, pounding his body and contorting the windowless prison cell into the thick woodland of the Texas wilderness.

He found himself lying on a riverbed, his face in ice-cold water. A huge hand forced his head into the stream as a stiff penis tore things inside him, making him bleed from his butt.

It was his first time camping. Two months after his dad died. Jeff lived in an RV and told him that night they needed to go to the river to catch fish.

He'd lied.

Martin lost his virginity with his face submerged underwater.

Before he passed out, he was given air. When he screamed, he was dunked again.

There had been no lubrication or spit to lessen the brutality. Not that day nor the four-hundred-and-twenty-six days that followed.

But there was always blood. All of his underwear was stained with it. Dark brown reminders of the damage inside him.

He felt that damage now as he forced dry muscles to suck his thrusting fingers. Heavy groans penetrated his ears, so very different than soundless screams he'd kept trapped in his throat.

Blinking rapidly, he yanked his hand away and stared at it. No blood. No damage.

"If you want me to bleed, you're going to have to try harder." Ricky glared at him over his shoulder. "My ass is conditioned to take a pounding."

Van Quiso had ensured that. When he'd fucked Martin and Ricky, he taught them how to take it without tensing. Van knew what he was doing. He was merciless and depraved, but when it came to sex, he was a master. He knew how to thrust without tearing skin, how to whip without leaving a scar, and how to ride that delicate line between pleasure and pain.

Martin had been trained by Van, but he didn't have Van's sophistication. His fourteen-year-old mind had been molded by a savage monster, and that was what he became whenever he tried to have sex.

His cock lay swollen and trapped at an uncomfortable angle in his jeans. He only needed to release it, and in the next breath, he could be deep inside Ricky.

He would lose his mind, his inhibitions. He would go fucking crazy, rutting and humping and undulating his hips until he was spent. Like a feral dog.

Just like Jeff.

He pushed to his feet and stumbled to the sink to wash his hands and clear his thoughts.

"So that's it?" Ricky stood and yanked up his pants. "I know you want this. The proof is straining your zipper. Why don't you at least try?"

"I did try, and I made myself sick." He kept his tone tempered as everything inside him buzzed and throbbed for relief.

Ricky's expression fell, and his gaze thickened with disappointment. "I'm going to take a cold shower." He pointed at the bulge in Martin's jeans. "Take care of that before I get back."

He grabbed a towel and soap and didn't give Martin a backward glance before charging into the hall.

The door closed with a resentful smack, and an iron band wrapped around Martin's chest, squeezing tight.

Ricky shouldn't be out there alone, but it was for the best. They hadn't been attacked since that day in the stairwell, and Martin posed more of a danger to him than anyone else.

He glared down at his raging hard-on and unzipped his pants. This was the first time he'd been alone in almost two months, and he wouldn't waste it.

Releasing his cock was a relief in and of itself. He fisted a hand around it and flattened his other on the wall in front of him. Then he stroked. Long hard pulls from base to tip.

Pre-come lubed his grip as he flexed his ass and thrust aggressively. The sounds of smacking flesh distracted him. They were lonely sounds, echoing inside a lonely man.

He adjusted his feet, making his stance sturdier and leaning into each pump. If Tula were here, he would shove her to her knees and make her swallow his entire length. He would hit her throat, trigger her gag reflex, and fuck her face until she couldn't breathe, couldn't scream—

The door creaked open. Fuck, in his lust-drunk haze, he'd forgotten to lock it.

"Sorry." Tula stood in the doorway, her gaze glued to the angry, swollen erection that pulsed in his fist. "I—I can leave?"

Her fingers clenched briefly at her sides, and she parted her lips. Her nipples beaded beneath her shirt. Denim hugged her hips and legs, highlighting the curves he longed to mark with his teeth.

His hand started moving on its own, rubbing hard flesh and mimicking the strokes he ached to give her. She was right here, breathing heavily and silently asking with those huge, guileless eyes.

"Come here," he heard himself rasp.

She stepped in and closed the door. Her hand lingered on the handle, trembling as she locked it. "Where's Ricky?"

"Shower."

A glance around at the scattered supplies on the floor raised her eyebrows. She didn't know what she'd walked into, but she was about to find out.

Her next two steps put her within arm's reach.

He grabbed a handful of her hair and pushed her to her knees. "Suck me."

"Martin—"

He rammed himself into the hot haven of her throat, making her gag on the first drive of his hips. As he pulled back, she yelped, catching him with her teeth.

Tightening his fist in her hair, he angled her head where he needed her and fucked her mouth with vigor. In and out, hard and harder, he slammed into the back of her wet throat, pistoning his hips, grinding against her face, and chasing his release.

Until he looked down and saw her glistening gaze.

Tears rolled from the corners of her eyes. Her hand clutched his thigh, her fingernails buried in the skin. He didn't register the pain until now, but that wasn't what snapped him out of his madness.

Her other hand was between her legs, massaging the denim seam against her clit.

She was turned on. By him.

He shoved into her throat, over and over, savoring the sounds of her choking cries. "You like that shit?"

Her head nodded, and the hand on her pussy moved faster.

"Such a dirty slut." He grunted at the sensation of her tongue, the tight ring of her lips, and the stunning look in her hungry eyes. "Feels so good. Fucking love your mouth."

If her mouth felt this sinful, he couldn't imagine what her pussy would do to him.

He pulled out and hauled her to her feet. "Turn around and hug the wall. I won't be gentle."

"Martin, wait—"

"How badly do you want my dick?"

"I do. Very much. But can we lie on the bed? I want to see your eyes." She placed a warm hand on his cheek. "I want to help you."

"Here's how you help me." Anger spiked through his blood. "Put your fucking face against the wall and lift your ass in the air."

He didn't wait for her to obey. With a grip on her inked arm, he flung her into position.

"I knew if you did this, if you finally took this step, it would be painful." She pressed her palms against the wall and exhaled. "So I'm not going to say no."

"In a few seconds, you won't be able to make an intelligible sound." He crowded in against her back, released her zipper, and shoved down her jeans and panties.

A tremor skated through her, shaking her luscious body against his.

With an arm holding her to the wall, he glided his other hand over her fine ass. As he reached through the apex of her legs, he grabbed her soaked pussy from behind.

"So fucking wet for me." He pushed three fingers into her tight clasp, making her lift on her toes.

Her breathing quickened, fueling his thrusts. As he fingered her cunt, he stretched his thumb back and impaled it into her asshole.

She gulped, and her buttocks tensed spasmodically.

"Have you ever been fucked here?" He pushed his thumb harder inside her anus while holding his fingers in her pussy.

She cried out. "Don't do this. You're not *him*, Martin."

"You don't know who I am. Answer the question."

"Yes, I've had anal sex."

"Because you're a filthy cock-hungry whore."

"Yeah, I'm a whore." She rammed an elbow into his ribs. "Why don't you fuck me bareback and catch a disease? Or you can believe the truth. I had a lover who enjoyed it."

"Is that what you were doing with Hector this morning? Letting him enjoy your tight little asshole?"

"What?" She gasped, straightening her spine. "No! Hector and I aren't like that!"

"I need names and locations of all the high-ranking officers in his human trafficking operation." He removed his hand from her and freed his cock.

"Why are you—?

"Stop bullshitting me, Tula. I want the truth."

"He's not in that business. He says it's not profitable and—" She went still, filling the silence with the sounds of her labored breaths. "Are you undercover? With the military?"

"Hardly." He slid his length between her legs from behind, rubbing the head along her slick folds.

An inferno rose beneath his skin, his reaction to her body instantaneous. Sweating, panting, teasing himself as much as he teased her, he needed her like he needed air.

She shuddered as he pressed the tip against her entrance, barely penetrating. Then he pulled back to give her back hole the same torture. She pushed against him, grinding and tilting up her ass, begging for it. Fuck if that wasn't the hottest thing he'd ever seen.

Her legs opened for more, and he indulged himself in her perfections, sliding through her decadent arousal as she melted around him, dripping down his length. He dipped in and out of her folds, stroking but not breaching, desperate for her, and denying them both.

If he fucked her, he would ruin her with his filth.

He needed to push her away and keep her at the same time.

"Ricky lets you ride his cock for free, but you have to pay for mine." He gripped his shaft and stirred the crown around the opening of her drenched pussy. "I want names and locations. Give me that, and I'll give you the dick."

He stepped back and stuffed himself away, his muscles shaking with the force of his desire.

"What?" Her ragged gasp cut through his chest. She yanked up her jeans and turned around, her eyes glassy with unshed water. "You're using me? You got close to me because you wanted me to leak information to you?"

"Isn't that what you're doing? Crawling in bed with us every night and running to Hector in the morning to tell him our secrets?"

"No." She shook her head, knocking a river of tears free. "I don't even know your secrets!"

"Because we know better than to tell you anything."

Her chin trembled, and she looked away, trying to suck down a choking inhale.

Stabbing pain hit his gut and burned through his throat.

"You're hurting me, Martin. Fucking breaking me. Right here." She clamped a hand over her heart. "Not just because you're destroying us. But because you're destroying yourself."

She turned to the door, and as she opened it, Ricky walked in.

He looked at her face and shot a murderous glare at Martin. "What did you do?"

She breezed by him.

"Tula, wait!" Ricky grabbed her arm. "Whatever this is, I'll fix it."

"You want to fix this?" She jerked free. "Fix *him!* I'm done."

As her footsteps faded down the hall, Ricky stabbed a hand through his wet hair and sneered at Martin. "What the fuck have you done?"

"I warned you." His heart felt cold and dead in his chest. "You don't want my brand of hurt."

TWENTY-FIVE

Martin slumped onto the mattress, listening to the sound of Ricky's footsteps chase Tula down the hall. His stomach hardened as he waited for the sound to return, knowing it would.

One minute.

Five minutes.

Ten minutes.

There it was.

Ricky stormed back into the cell and slammed the door, locking it. "She told me what happened and refuses to see you. As much as I want to drag her back here like a caveman, I think she's been abused enough for one day."

"I fucked up."

"Yeah, you've been doing that a lot lately." Ricky removed his shirt and kicked off his shoes. "Give me a rundown of your sexual history."

Now there was a subject that should be locked in a vault and dropped in the deepest ocean. He held up his middle finger.

"Listen, motherfucker." Ricky bent over him, eyes flaring. "You're going to lose every person you ever cared about. If that matters to you, you'll figure out a way to make that mean mouth form the words *yes* or *no* to every question I ask."

Fuck. This was happening, whether he wanted it to or not.

Ricky straightened and shoved off his pants, leaving the boxers on. "Have you ever had consensual sex?"

"Yes."

"With a woman?"

"Yes." He'd had a handful of one-night stands in the few years between Jeff and Van. None of them were memorable.

"Have you had consensual sex with a man?"

There it was. Sharp and malignant, the pain cleaved through his airway and smothered his senses. "No."

"Then you've only ever been the bottom? Forced to take it?"

"Yes."

"You've never fucked a man in the ass?"

"No."

"Okay." Ricky swiped a hand down his face and sat beside him. "Have you had anal sex with a woman?"

"Yes."

"The sex you've had willingly… Was it always rough and angry?"

"Yes."

"Did you hurt them?"

"No. I was just a teenager." Young and horny. Broken beyond recognition but not as complicated as he was now. Every year he put between Jeff and him added another layer of anger, resentment, and depravity. "If you think I won't hurt her —"

"You already hurt her." Ricky shifted to face him. "You hurt her with words. With rejection. She feels betrayed and manipulated." Ricky's dark eyes connected with his, solidifying their bond instead of cutting it off. "I can't fix this thing that happened to you. I can't tell you how to cope with it. But I can get you past this one obstacle, which is preventing the three of us from moving forward together."

"If you're talking about sex —"

"Shut up and pay attention." He stood and pushed the last of his clothing to his feet.

His cock hung semi-hard between muscular thighs, thick and heavy and growing by the second.

"This is the last time I will offer myself to you." Ricky knelt at his feet, speeding up his pulse. "We'll do it slow and easy, or not at all."

A swallow stuck in the back of his throat. "I don't know how."

"I know, and I've been part of the problem." Ricky sat back on his heels. "I always tell you to hurt me, fuck me hard, and make me bleed." He shook his head. "The thing is I've had every kind of sex imaginable. Soft, rough, sweet, wild… I've experienced the gamut, and I know what I like. But you haven't. You've never had sensual, affectionate, tender sex."

A quiver of grief skittered along Martin's jaw and burned the backs of his eyes. He fisted his hand in the bedding, fighting the longing that swelled inside him.

"Let me give you that." Ricky lowered his head and placed a kiss on Martin's denim-clad thigh.

He tried to imagine what Ricky was offering, but he couldn't picture it. He didn't know what it looked like or how he would handle the intimacy. But he wanted to know. Every nerve ending in his body pulled toward the idea.

"Tell me you'll try." Ricky rose on his knees and gave him an expectant look.

"I'll try." His mouth dried. "But Tula should be here."

She was the gentle one.

He needed to make sure she was safe. She deserved so much better than him, but that wouldn't stop him from groveling, pleading, and fighting for the rest of his life to get her back. He couldn't lose her.

"One problem at a time." Ricky slid his palms up Martin's thighs. "She promised she wouldn't leave her cell tonight."

"I don't want her sleeping—"

"Shut up."

"I can't do this if you intend to top me." He gestured at the soft bulge of his crotch. "Does nothing for me."

"You think I can't make you hard?" Ricky winged up a sexy brow.

"Not if you're bossy."

"Take off your clothes."

With a sigh, Martin stood and stripped. His briefs hit the floor last, and a masculine sound rumbled deep in Ricky's chest.

As Martin lowered back to the bed, Ricky didn't wait for an objection. He knelt between Martin's thighs and slowly sucked the soft length of him between those talented lips.

"Ah, fuck." His hand went to Ricky's hair, clenching hard.

Ricky released him with a *pop* and shook his head. "Soft and easy."

"Fine." He braced his hands behind him.

Returning to his cock, Ricky licked along the shaft from balls to tip, sending languorous ripples of pleasure through his groin. Ricky went at it assertively but not aggressively. Soft unhurried sucks and teasing licks filled him with blood and quickened his breaths.

"I've wanted to do this for years." Ricky swirled his tongue across Martin's scrotum.

"You've done it a million times in my head, and swear to God, it's never felt this incredible."

"And you're not even punching the back of my throat."

"The urge is there, but…"

Ricky sucked on the crown, flicking his tongue along the underside, where all the nerves resided. "Feel that?"

"Fuck yeah, I feel it." The stimulation of his glans spread electricity through his body. Feverish chills. Breathless invigoration. Every sensation was new and different.

"You don't experience that when you're pounding someone's mouth like a jackhammer." Ricky blew a soft breath along his length. "Don't get me wrong. There's freedom in letting go, but there's so much sensuality in a kiss."

He proceeded to kiss Martin's cock with firm lips and an agonizingly talented tongue. The sensuality Ricky mentioned was a slow burn. A fusion of feelings. A different kind of energy, emotion, and artistry.

His legs shook against a building orgasm, and just when he thought he might come, Ricky's glorious mouth abandoned him.

"Lie back." Ricky patted his thigh.

Martin stretched out across the two beds, and Ricky crawled over him, kneeling between his legs.

"You're so goddamn arresting." Ricky caressed a hand down Martin's chest. "Seeing you laid out like this, aroused and bare for me..." The roving caress continued along his hip and down his leg. "Every inch of you makes me hard."

"Show me."

Ricky rose up on his knees and lazily stroked his cock. Tall and stacked with muscle, the man was fucking gorgeous.

Leaning back down, Ricky angled his hips and aligned their dicks side by side. Then he rubbed them together, gliding his hand up and down the lengths, slowly jacking them off.

There were no words after that. No race to a finish line. No mindless, uncontrollable thrusting. Ricky fondled and explored with expert fingers solely for the pleasure of touch and affection.

Martin saw it in Ricky's eyes, felt it in every loving stroke. Ricky intended to make love to him, and the prospect filled him with a need that went beyond physical lust.

Ricky moved up his body and worshiped him with lips and tongue. A kiss on the scar on his head. A nibble on his ear lobe. A lick across his mouth. Then he slid downward, paying homage to skin and muscle. By the time he finished, he'd kissed every part of Martin's anatomy he could reach.

The adoration left Martin panting and twisting on the bed. Blissful heat bloomed around his perineum and disseminated through his balls and anus. He felt Ricky everywhere, around him, against him, inside him, and they hadn't even had sex.

The eternal buildup had produced the deepest, most intense feeling in his body. The fire Ricky had stoked howled into a conflagration. Martin needed to fuck, and he didn't care how. Hard, gentle, fast, fierce—it was going to happen.

He pushed up, wrapped his arms around Ricky, and flipped him face down on the bed.

"Stop." Ricky didn't move or raise his voice. "I'm not going to fight you, but I need you to listen."

"I'm listening." Martin gripped his ass and speared three fingers between his hard cheeks. "You can talk while I'm fucking you."

"Face to face." Craning his neck, Ricky glared back at him. "I'm going to roll over."

His spine tensed as his mind spun to understand the position. He knew it could be done, but why?

"Martin." Ricky shifted to his back and opened his legs. "Come here."

The heat in Martin's groin evaporated, and his body chilled with unease.

"You've never had sex this way?" Ricky widened his eyes. "Not even with a woman?"

He scoured his mind, digging through old memories—quick fucks, stolen moments, up against a wall, bent over a piece of furniture, doggy in the backseat of a car. Sex had always been a means to an end. A hard, fast release.

"No." His answer fell on a choked breath.

"My tortured, beautiful man. I couldn't be more in love with you." Ricky gripped his hand and pulled him down.

Martin lowered on top of him, chest to chest, cock against cock, and let his weight rest in the cradle of Ricky's powerful body.

Their lips met in a soft caress. A nibble here. A sip there. He inched back to see the lust in Ricky's eyes and closed in again, kissing and breathing as one. His hips rocked in a languid motion, swiveling, grinding, and feeding the heat between them.

He stretched his mouth wide, reaching deeper, and Ricky opened for him, angling his head and licking away doubts and reservations. If sex with Ricky was as poignant and passionate as this, Martin wouldn't be the same afterward.

He'd never felt so wanted, so loved, so damn alive.

His heart sputtered beneath the heavy emotion, and he broke away, panting and clinging to Ricky's dependable gaze. Then he dove back for more, his tongue moving in a dreamlike state, a higher level of oneness. Every touch lifted them in harmony. Every lick burned him hotter.

By the time they came up for air, he was ravenous.

He sat back on his knees and stared down at their cocks. Engorged and leaking from the tips, they jutted across Ricky's abs, side by side. They looked so fucking sexy together.

"I need to be inside you." He grabbed Ricky at the root and stroked. "Right now."

"Keep your eyes on mine." Ricky flexed his hips in Martin's grip and groaned. "No rushing to the end. We're going to enjoy this."

Martin gathered spit in his mouth and angled his head over his aching cock. Parting his lips, he let his saliva trickle out and run down his length.

"I'm going to come just from watching you do that." Ricky shifted restlessly beneath him, clawing at the blankets.

Collecting more spit, Martin lathered his fingers and massaged them against Ricky's anus.

"This is happening." Ricky stared up at him in awe. "We're doing this."

"I don't know if *slow and easy* will be good for you." He lined himself up with Ricky's opening. "I don't know what I'm doing."

"You've been kissing me for a month. I don't think you realize how incredibly affectionate you are."

He was?

The sucking of lips, the drugging sweetness of breaths, the whispered words... Ricky and Tula were under his skin, expunging nightmares and replacing them with dreams.

Dreams of a future with the two people he would give anything to keep.

Ricky pulled his knees toward his ribs, opening himself wide. "Eyes on me."

Falling into that heated gaze, Martin pushed his hips and sank into the nirvana of Ricky's body.

His breath cut off, and Ricky moaned deep in his throat. They trembled together, adjusting to the overwhelming sensations.

Ricky's hand flew to his cock, stroking himself. Martin slid out and pressed back in, his eyes rolling back in his head.

"Seven years." He thrust, digging deep, catching a desperate rhythm. "It was a long fucking time to wait for this. But so worth the wait."

"Holy fuck, Martin." Ricky panted, quickening the pump of his hand. "You're huge. I feel you in my stomach. Fucking feel you everywhere."

Martin wrapped a fist around Ricky's grip and quickened the pace of his strokes, sliding their fingers up and down in sync with the frantic drive of his hips.

"Slow down." Ricky gasped, flexing his glutes and using his legs to meet every thrust.

"I own you." He grabbed Ricky's waist and slammed himself deeply, mercilessly, stuffing that ass, making damn sure Ricky felt him. "You're fucking mine. Every touch, every kiss, every drop of your come belongs to me."

"I love you."

Ricky's quiet words breathed into him, resuscitating him from the darkness. The tempo of his hips faltered, and his blood hummed with life.

The solid body beneath him anchored him to the present, providing dependable, stable footing. Ricky had been here all along. Martin's compass in the storm.

"No one's ever said those words to me." Martin assumed his dad had loved him, but it had never been voiced.

"I'll never stop saying it." Ricky grasped his neck and hauled him in for a kiss. "Fucking love you."

His tongue slid against Ricky's, curling and flicking with the depth of his feelings. He was infatuated with the taste of Ricky's mouth, the feel of his magnificent physique moving beneath him, the heat of his skin, and the sexy Latino glow of it.

More than that, he was addicted to Ricky's devotion, his commitment to their friendship, and the effort he put into it.

He loved everything about this man. Always had. Always would. He'd loved Ricky for seven years.

With an arm between them, he took Ricky in hand, stroking him, grinding into him, desperate to give himself entirely to this.

"I need your come." He rubbed Ricky harder, savoring the friction of Ricky's clenching ass as they locked eyes. "Give it to me."

Ricky's mouth opened. His pupils dilated, and his cock pulsed in Martin's hand.

"Martin, oh, fuck. Oh, Jesus, I'm coming!" Ricky ground his hips, bearing down on Martin's thrusts as he ejaculated ropy strings of come across his chest.

Martin followed him over the edge, hammering erratically while staring into his eyes. "Always loved you. With everything I am."

The intensity of his climax stole his breath and exploded stars across his vision. He came and came and came until there was nothing left. All of him was in his best friend—his body, his love, and his life.

"Definitely worth the wait." Ricky rolled them, putting them on their sides, nose to nose, legs entangled, and breaths mingling.

"I don't deserve you." He took Ricky's mouth, their tongues rubbing through a satiated kiss.

"I'll remind you of that the next time you're a dick."

"Don't I know it." He kissed Ricky again, devouring the intimacy. "Thank you."

In the isolation of their prison cell, he sank into Ricky's embrace in a way he never had before. Hands roamed. Lips touched and held. Cocks brushed. Gazes caressed, and Martin fell. Mind, body, and soul. He gave it all to Ricky, and Ricky gave in return.

In that lazy span of an hour, they had more than they could've ever wanted. But they weren't complete.

"I'm going to get our girl." He slid out of bed and grabbed his jeans.

"Our girl isn't going to listen to you." Ricky joined him, pulling on his own clothes.

"She will." He shoved on his shoes. "I'm going to explain everything."

"Everything?"

He turned and looked his best friend in the eye. "We have a decision to make."

TWENTY-SIX

Martin entered Tula's cell without knocking, his pulse steady, his gait determined, and his eyes set on his goal.

Tula sat on the end of the bed, smoking a cigarette. She glared at him, her face a beautiful shade of fury, before turning away and denying him the view of her eyes.

Martin couldn't remember the last time she'd smoked. She kept some cartons around to use as currency to buy meals and supplies, but she'd dropped the nicotine habit when she started hanging out with him and Ricky.

Ricky followed him in, shut the door, and leaned against it.

As Martin approached her, he marked her stiff spine, rigid jaw, and the flex of her fingers. She had every right to be pissed at him, and he would let her have her anger as long as she listened to what he had to say.

He knelt on the floor before her. "I'm sorry."

She took a long drag without looking at him. Then she met his eyes and released the smoke in his face.

In a calm, calculated motion, he gripped her hand and twisted it in an unnatural direction at the wrist. The technique caused her just enough discomfort to release the cigarette from her fingers.

She yanked her hand away. "Why did you—?"

"I can't be fixed. Not overnight. Maybe not ever." He squashed out the cigarette beneath his knee. "But Ricky and I just had sex."

Her glower darted behind him to Ricky. Her eyes softened for a moment then returned to him, reigniting with fire. "You came here to rub that in my face?"

"No." It probably wasn't the best thing to lead with after teasing her and rejecting her just hours earlier. But he was laying it all out on the table, and having sex with Ricky was the easiest part to confess.

Now came the hard part.

He dragged a hand over his head and centered himself on the presence behind him. Ricky didn't know what he was about to say, but Ricky's strength gave him the resolve to continue.

"His name was Jeff. The man I killed." Martin inched closer on his knees and rested his hands on the mattress on either side of her. "He raped me every day for over a year, starting when I was fourteen. He was my dad's brother. My uncle."

Her posture stooped, and the anger in her expression melted into concern.

A reassuring masculine grip landed on his shoulder and squeezed. Then Ricky sat beside her.

"After the shit I said to you, to you *both*, I owe you my story. It's not an excuse for my actions. I should've been more open with you, but I..." Dread curled in his stomach. "The one and only time I ever told someone about Jeff, it ended very badly."

Ricky caught his gaze, studying him intently as if trying to make a connection.

"I'll tell you about it." He met her eyes. "If you still want to hear it."

"I do." She leaned forward but didn't touch him.

"My history doesn't just include Jeff." He rested a hand on Ricky's knee, his heart pumping with purpose.

They'd made a decision before leaving their cell, one that changed their mission, and with any luck, it would change hers, too.

They trusted her with their lives and would choose her over all else. No matter what happened, she was their priority.

"We're vigilantes." He touched her face and pulled her close to whisper at her ear, "We work to punish and eradicate human sex traffickers. It's personal for us. The way Ricky and I met, everything we do, the reason we're here—it's all entangled with our vigilante group and our alliance with the Restrepo Cartel. We strategically arranged our arrest to come here and gather enough intel to take down Hector La Rocha's operation."

"Jesus." She sucked in a breath. Then her expression tightened with indignation. "That's where I come in."

"You were our angle, yes. But not anymore. Now you're our purpose."

"Your purpose?" Her face reddened. She glanced at the closed door and lowered her voice to a furious whisper. "You're aligned with a sworn enemy and working against Hector. He won't just kill you when he finds out. He'll have you tortured and make a spectacle of your deaths. This is *exactly* what he wanted to know about you, and you just handed me a confession."

Martin absorbed the flux of emotion that crossed her face, fascinated by her thought processes. He wasn't concerned about her ratting them out. She loved them. She just didn't know it yet.

Her brows knitted, and her gaze bounced through the room before landing on him. "Why would you trust me with this? You already figured out that he sent me to you to learn your secrets, and you know I tell him everything. You're not just throwing away your mission. You're risking your lives by telling me."

"Yes, we are."

"We choose you, Tula." Ricky tucked a lock of hair behind her ear. "Over the mission. Over everything."

Her lips parted, and she shook her head. "But you don't know if I'll choose you."

"You already have," Martin said, hoping to hell he was right.

"How's that?"

"I told you I wanted the names and locations of high-ranking officers. You had the past several hours to pass that information along to Hector. But you didn't, did you? You didn't even consider it."

"No. I…" She touched her throat, and her gaze turned inward. "I learned something about Hector today, and I'm still trying to process that."

"What is it?" His pulse sped up. "His human trafficking operation?"

"You first. I want to hear your story. About your uncle." Her fingers slid over Ricky's on the bed. "How you and Ricky met. Your vigilante work. All of it."

"Not here." Martin stood and offered his hand. "In our cell."

If he was going to cut himself open and expose his miserable fucking shame, he wanted to do it in a place where he felt more secure. Despite the stink and gloom of Jaulaso, the cell he shared with her and Ricky was where he'd experienced the happiest moments of his life.

Not to mention, their cell had a lock on the door.

"Okay." She gripped his fingers and followed him into the hall.

When they reached their destination, they kicked off their shoes and climbed into bed together. Tula and Ricky sat with their backs against the wall. Martin stretched out in front of them.

With a leg bent and an arm resting on his knee, he braced himself for the pain and let his mind travel back in time.

"When my dad died, the state sent me to live with my only living relatives. Jeff was an estranged uncle I'd never met. My dad never talked about him. Jeff lived out of an RV in Texas, and he had a son two years younger than me. Ford was his name."

A hot ember formed in his throat, and he swallowed past it. Ricky laced his fingers around Tula's, their gazes soft and watchful.

"Jeff had been a schoolteacher, and he taught me how to fish and build fires. He home-schooled Ford and me as we traveled from one campground to another throughout Texas. He waited two months—" His voice broke, and he tried again. "I was with him for two months before he raped me the first time. Then he did it again, every night, for the next four-hundred-and-twenty-six days." A torrent of anguish welled up in his chest. "I couldn't leave. He told me if I did, he would go to Ford to take care of his physical needs. His own fucking son. I believed him."

The nightmare tore through him, shaking his shoulders. Instead of fighting it down, he breathed it out. "Ford was only twelve. He didn't know what his dad did to me every night when he led me into the woods. Jeff kept it from him. I kept it from him. But Jeff got careless. He was drinking the night he sodomized me with the handle of a hammer."

Tula cupped a hand over her mouth, her eyes soaked with tears. Ricky moved toward him.

"If you touch me right now…" He would break down. "Let me get through this."

"Okay." Ricky sat back and wrapped his arms around Tula.

"The hammer…" Martin inhaled, exhaled, and let the pain lance through him. "Ford watched it happen. He found us in the woods, and I'll never forget his face. The damage to his young mind, the horror of seeing his father doing such a despicable thing… He ran off into the trees, and Jeff was too drunk to chase him. So he sent me. But I was injured, bleeding down my legs from what he'd done to me. I could barely walk. It took me all night and into the morning before I…"

His eyes burned, and his throat closed up. He covered his face with his hands and felt the tears dampening his cheeks.

"Martin…" Ricky's voice fell over him, soothing. "You don't have to finish."

He needed to finish it, purge it from his mind. "I saw him on the railroad tracks not far from our campsite. He just laid his neck on the rail and let a train run over it. That's how I found him. Without his head." His guilt over that night cut him to the bone. "If I'd walked faster, searched harder, I could've stopped him."

"It wasn't your fault."

"I returned to the RV that morning. Jeff was passed out drunk in his bed. His leverage over me was gone. Ford was… He was gone. So I searched for that goddamn hammer, and when I found it, I beat Jeff's skull in with it. Then I ran."

Ricky's arms came around him, and Tula crawled onto his lap. He let the tears fall as they held him. Then he forced out the rest.

"I was fifteen, homeless, and on the run. Over the next two years, I stuck to the border towns in Texas. Found odd jobs in the ghettos. I slept with women, but not often. My depraved urges started to scare me. Then I met a man." He drew in a breath, lost in the memory. "He was sitting alone at a club I used to frequent, and he had a gruesome scar on his face."

"Van," Ricky breathed.

Tula shifted on Martin's lap, confusion furrowing her brow as she glanced between them.

"I don't know if it was the scar that got me. It was obvious someone had hurt him, and I thought maybe he'd been hurt by someone like Jeff. He was also the most gorgeous man I'd ever seen. I was instantly captivated. He bought me a drink, and we shot the shit. Then he asked me if I wanted to get out of there. I didn't hesitate. We walked aimlessly along the dark, quiet streets. I felt comfortable with him. He was easy to talk to. I had never told anyone my story, but that night, I told Van. I told him everything, and he listened without judgment or pity. When I finished talking, he kissed me. And kissed me. The son of a bitch kissed me until I couldn't think straight. I had never willingly had sex with a man, but that night, I willingly went home with Van Quiso. Only he didn't take me to his bedroom. He chained me in his attic, beat me, and raped me for ten weeks."

Ricky knew the rest of it, but Tula didn't. So he talked through the series of events that led from Van's sex trafficking operation to the creation of the Freedom Fighters and the mission that planted him and Ricky in Jaulaso.

By the time he finished, his eyes were dry, and his chest seemed lighter. The pain was still there, branded forever in the marrow of his bones. But it felt different. Duller. Softer. Maybe this was the beginning of catharsis. An opening for the poison to slowly escape.

Tula held him tight and gave him comforting words. As they settled on their sides, she prodded him for details about his sexual training, his relationships with his ex-captors, and the evidence the Freedom Fighters had compiled against Hector La Rocha over the years.

He and Ricky answered all her questions, and the three of them talked late into the night, sharing painful moments, happy stories, and everything in between.

Then she told them about the paternity test.

In a monotone voice, she explained what had happened in Hector's room this morning—why she had gone there and everything Hector had told her. She'd learned he was her father moments before she'd walked in on Martin with his dick in his hand.

She'd come to him for comfort, and he'd treated her like a whore.

"I'm so fucking sorry." He shifted her to face him and studied her expression.

Emotional exhaustion weighed down her lashes and fanned lines from the corners of her eyes. Despite the events of the day, she looked devastatingly beautiful in the glow of the candlelight.

"How are you taking this?" Ricky curled around her back and kissed the top of her head.

"I don't know. Hector has always been kind of a father figure to me, but after everything you told me about his disgusting operation..." Her voice cracked. "I'm sickened and confused, and I have no fucking clue what to do about it."

"There's been too much thrown at you today." Martin scooted down, putting them at eye level. "You don't need to do anything right now but sleep. Let us worry about what to do next."

Her expression turned pensive for a handful of heartbeats. Then she tensed.

"You said you arranged your arrest." She popped up on an elbow, her eyes wide and alert. "Does that mean you arranged your release?"

His heart stopped, and he met Ricky's anxious gaze over her head. "Yes."

"How long?" She looked between them, her fear palpable. "When do you leave?"

He clenched his hands. They didn't have a solution for the one thing that mattered most.

Her safety.

Who would protect her after they left? Because they *would* be leaving her. There was no way to stop it.

They would hire the best lawyers, pull every connection they had, and fight like hell to shorten her sentence. But the likelihood of success was terrifyingly low.

Martin reached for her, holding her tight as he choked out the words. "We leave in forty-five days."

TWENTY-SEVEN

For the next two days, Tula sank into an ebb and flow of heartbreaking conversations, heated arguments, and quiet introspection. She had a lot to mentally and emotionally process, and Martin and Ricky were right there with her, holding her in bed, showering with her at night, and putting together meals from the stores of food they kept in their cell.

She only had forty-three days left with them.

Deep down, she'd suspected they would leave Jaulaso before her. She didn't know how or why, but her heart had tried to keep its distance, expecting their departure.

Her heart had failed, though. They'd crashed right into it and woven themselves into the very essence of her existence. When it came time to sever those ties, it was going to hurt like hell.

They finished a dinner of canned chicken soup, and she lay curled up in Ricky's muscular arms, staring at Martin's back where he sat on the edge of the other bed.

Her quiet, tormented man had been more subdued than usual today.

The absolute hell he'd endured in his short twenty-four years had obliterated her anger with him. Her hurt feelings were nothing compared to the hurt he carried inside that powerful frame.

He'd cried several times over the past forty-eight hours, and she and Ricky had cried with him, holding tight to his trembling body. It was progress. He was finally talking about it, letting it out, openly and painfully.

The details of his life were difficult to hear, but she sensed the promise of healing in his voice, saw it in the clarity of his crystal green eyes. It would take time, *years*, to recover from his trauma, but he was moving in the right direction. He was trusting people to hold him through his pain and bear some of the burden.

He would always have Ricky for that, and maybe she would be there, too.

In three years.

Ricky mentioned trying to stay in prison with her by doing something asinine like attacking a prison guard or starting a riot to extend their sentences. She'd laid into him for even thinking it and quickly shut him up.

They wanted to help her shorten her sentence, but they couldn't do that if they were locked up. Nor could they risk getting stuck in Jaulaso for life. She only had three years left. It wasn't forever.

Maybe they would still want her when she was released. Perhaps they would be waiting for her at the gate the day she gained her freedom.

She fantasized about that moment, about starting a life with them outside of prison.

Her debt to Hector, however, was a lifetime sentence. Didn't matter that they shared DNA. He'd told her on several occasions she would be expected to work for the cartel after her release.

Given Martin and Ricky's resources and connections, perhaps they could help her escape Hector's organization. If they let her, she would join their vigilante group and work with them to take down La Rocha Cartel.

Her loyalty to Hector had taken a hard hit. He'd sent Garra to rape her, kept his parentage from her for two years, and looked her right in the eyes and lied to her about his involvement in human trafficking. What else had he been dishonest about?

She didn't trust him, but she still cared about him. Not just because he was her father, but because he'd always been kind to her, always protected her. She found herself clinging to the idea that he'd been dishonest with her because he wanted to protect her from the terrible things he did.

She talked through all of this with Martin and Ricky over the past couple of days. Together, they speculated and plotted, smiled and cried, argued this and agreed on that.

But at the end of the day, she was left with a crushing inevitability.

They were leaving.

"We can still focus on your mission," she murmured into the silence.

"No," they said in unison, firm and unbending.

"He's kidnapping women and children."

Children who would go through the same abuses Martin had suffered. Her stomach turned inside out every time she imagined it.

670

"We should've never involved you." Ricky ran his nose through her hair. "Thinking about you in his room and rummaging through his belongings when he walked in… It makes me want to bend you over my knee and beat your fucking ass. But it's *our* fault. We pushed you to investigate him and put our damn mission over your safety."

"You didn't know me when you arrived here. You couldn't have predicted what would happen between us."

"What's happening between us?" He coasted a finger along her collarbone, teasing the neckline of her shirt.

"Sex. Really good sex."

"It's more than that, Tula. I need to hear you say it."

Love was a landslide of sorrow and dread, swallowing her chest in the ruin of its unavoidable end. "It hurts. My heart knows you're leaving, and it's trying to protect itself. Please don't make me say it."

"Okay." He pulled her close and rested his forehead against hers. "Fuck, I hate this. It's fucking killing me."

She couldn't bear the pain in his voice. So she steered the conversation back on topic. "I was your best option to get those locations from Hector. It was a brilliant plan, really. Seduce the woman he's closest to and win her over with the best orgasms of her life."

"The best in her life?"

"Don't get cocky." She cupped the side of his face, holding his gaze. "I could talk to Garra —"

"No."

"We haven't tried that angle. I wouldn't be obvious about it."

"I said no."

"I could eavesdrop on his conversations with Simone. If they know the details of the operation —"

"Fuck no." Ricky gripped her chin, forcing her to meet his glare. "The mission is forfeit. We're going to lay low, keep our asses in this cell, and let our time go by. Just like this. *Together*. Then, after Martin and I are released, we're going to get you out of here."

Hector ruled over the city and the prison. If he couldn't get himself released, Martin and Ricky wouldn't be able to do shit for her. But she didn't refute him.

It was the best plan they had.

She wanted every second she had left with them to be in this bed. She wanted their kisses, their hungry breaths, their bodies moving inside her and each other, shaking and groaning in pleasure.

Amid the revelations of the past two days, there had been no sex and no discussions about the sex between Martin and Ricky.

They needed to talk about it. Or better yet, they just needed to do it.

As often as possible.

Because in forty-three days, they wouldn't just be taking her broken heart with them. They would be taking away the only pleasure she'd ever had inside these walls.

Her attention drifted to the silent man sitting on the other bed. With his back to her and his feet on the floor, he braced an elbow on his knee and held his face with a hand. He cried that way sometimes.

Two days ago, the dam broke inside him, drowning him in a ten-year flood that needed to run its course.

But right now, his relaxed posture and steady breaths told her he was deep in thought, not grief.

She shared a look with Ricky and pressed a hand against his shirtless chest, silently asking him to stay. Then she crawled across the beds and knelt behind Martin.

He wore only his briefs and didn't move as she rested her mouth on his shoulder and her fingers on his nape.

She remained in that position for a long time, breathing with him and indulging in the potency of his presence.

"Want to talk?" She ghosted her lips along his neck and inhaled deeply, savoring his masculine scent.

"No."

"Want to fight?"

He grunted. "No."

"Want to make love?"

His head slowly lifted and turned in her direction. His mouth parted, and the tip of his tongue wet the corner.

"I want to know what you feel like inside me." She kissed his strong jaw. "I want to see what your face looks like when you're buried inside Ricky."

"You want my filth in your pussy?" His voice was stony, laden with antagonism.

"At least forty-three times."

"And your ass?" He folded his arms around her and dragged her onto his lap to straddle him.

"Yes." She found Ricky's hooded eyes over Martin's shoulder.

Martin gave her a troubled look and touched their foreheads together. "We only have forty-three days."

"Spend them inside me." She brushed her lips against his, drawing a groan from his chest.

When she pulled back, he chased her, capturing her mouth in a starved kiss. His hands went to her hair and slid down her back, pulling her closer as he worked their tongues into a delicious tangle.

"I don't want to hurt you." He trapped her arms behind her and ground her body onto his hard cock. "I'm fucked up."

"Aren't we all? We're fucked-up people living fucked-up lives with no access to medication or therapy. But we have one another."

His soft laughter filled her mouth.

She breathed in the sexy sound and held it in her chest. "I'm keeping that."

"What?" he rumbled against her lips.

"Your laughter. I'm collecting all your happy moments, just so you know."

"They're yours." He glanced back at Ricky. "And his."

"Promise me something."

"Anything."

"When you get out of here, don't push him away. No matter how hard it gets or how many setbacks you have. Let him make you happy."

"Tula." His expression hardened. "We're going to get you—"

"Promise me."

His gaze shifted to Ricky and held. "I promise."

"You love him."

"Yes." He tucked a finger under her chin, lifting it. "And you. I love you."

A heavy pang hit her heart, and oh, God, the wonderful wretchedness of it. This harsh, deliciously damaged man was worried he'd hurt her with his cruelty. But it was his love that would leave the deepest scar.

He wanted her now, but would he love her in three years? Would she even be the same person by the time she walked out of here?

She couldn't predict the future, but the present was directly in front of her. This moment, right now, was within reach, and she grabbed onto it with both hands.

Their mouths came together. Their chests collided, and they fell onto the mattress in a rolling grind of bodies.

His weight pressed down on top of her, and his kisses turned ravenous. He stripped her of her clothing, and she shoved down his briefs. Then they were naked, skin to skin, heart to heart, staring into each other's eyes.

"Ricky," he said gruffly without looking away.

"Here." Ricky pressed a condom into Martin's hand. "Slow and easy. If it gets dark in your head, I'll pull you back."

Martin tore open the condom and rolled it on. With his hips between her legs, he ran his fingers along her slit, spreading her wetness.

She moaned. "Martin."

He shushed her and bit her lips. Then he trailed those soaked fingers over her nipple. "Are you scared?"

"Yeah. I'm scared you won't ever put it in."

He bared his teeth with a growl and drove his hips into hers, filling her up in one long thrust.

Their eyes connected. Their breaths held. Then they burst into movement.

"Goddamn, Tula." He pistoned into her, holding her close and kissing her with a possessive tongue.

She gasped at the wet burn between her legs and flexed upward, chasing his rhythm, desperate to take all of him.

He was magnificently long and thick. Every thrust required effort, working each inch deeper and deeper. Before he buried to the root, he pulled back, slowly dragging all that heaviness away. Then he plunged again.

"You fit this huge thing inside Ricky?" She squeezed her inner muscles, making him groan.

"I didn't hear any complaints." He rubbed his nose along hers and gave her a gorgeous smile. "You're going to take us both."

Her heart rate went wild. "Don't tease me."

He scooped her up into his strong arms and rolled to his back while keeping them joined. With her legs straddling his incredible body, she sat up and ran her hands over the carved grooves of his chest and abs.

He touched her the same way, exploring the rise of her breasts and plucking at her nipples. She twisted her hips, and he looked down to where they connected, his eyes smoldering.

When his gaze lifted, he took in every detail of her shape, his fingers following the path of his eyes.

The intensity of his attention on her sliced up her breaths into little needy gasps. To be desired by such a beautiful, perfectly sculpted man felt surreal.

"What did you look like before six months of training?" She ground down on his cock, delighting in the sound of his groan.

"He looked the same." Ricky ripped open a condom packet with his teeth. "Pretty sure he has endless layers of abs under those abs. If he loses an eight-pack, he has more to spare."

"You should talk." Martin raked his eyes over Ricky's body, lingering on Ricky's cock as he sheathed it in latex.

Now that she knew their history as trained slaves, she understood how these two flawlessly attractive men had ended up together. Evidently, all their vigilante friends were stunningly gorgeous.

"Tula." Martin clasped her neck and pulled her down to his chest. "You've never taken two cocks at once?"

"You know I haven't." Her body caught fire, and her pussy clenched uncontrollably.

"If you keep doing that..." He kicked up his hips, stroking himself inside her. "I'm not going to last."

"I'm not, either."

She stretched toward his sinful mouth, tasting his lips, chasing his tongue, and grinding down on him. He pressed in and out of her, worshiping her with his hands and watching her expression.

He was so damn sexy like this—aroused and attentive and utterly devoted. She lost herself in his passion as they moved in a drugging rhythm.

Their fucking wasn't fast and mindless. Nor was it soft and easy. Every thrust was heavy, intimate, and thrumming with affection. They rocked together, kissing and sucking, driven by an unquenchable thirst for love—to grow it and hold it and never let it go.

She glanced back to look for Ricky, but he was already there, kneeling behind her.

With her chest pressed against Martin's, she arched her spine, lifting her ass for Ricky.

"Jesus." He groaned and bent down, sinking out of her view. "I wish you could see this. The way your pussy wraps around him, gripping him like a glove as he slides in and out."

Spurred by his words and insanely turned on, she undulated her hips and rode Martin's cock with everything she had.

Until she felt a gust of warm breath on her back hole. Then the wet, sliding stroke of a tongue.

"Holy shit." She faltered, tipping on Martin's chest as her breaths sprinted into oblivion.

Ricky's wicked kiss lowered, licking and sucking the place where she and Martin connected. The sensations were maddening, burning across her flesh and revving her pulse.

When the heat of his mouth vanished, she didn't need to look back to see where he went. Martin's fingers bit into her ass, and he released a long, guttural groan.

"He's licking your balls, isn't he?" She grinned.

"Christ, yes. He's—" Martin inhaled sharply, and his body went rigid beneath her. "Ricky, don't."

"What?" She craned her neck, trying to see behind her.

"Okay, I won't touch you there." Ricky leaned over her back to meet Martin's eyes. "I figured it was off limits, but I needed to know."

"Your ass?" she asked quietly. "You don't want that?"

"No." Martin ran a shaky hand down her arm. "I can't be on the receiving end of anal. Never again."

"That's okay." She gave him a soft smile and spoke against his lips. "If he needs a back door, he has mine."

"I'm going to ruin this pretty little pucker." Ricky pushed his thumb against her rectum, making her shudder. "But tonight, I'm going to share your pussy with Martin's massive cock."

"I'm wildly excited and equally terrified about that," she said. "Is it going to hurt?"

"Probably," Martin said.

"Now I'm just terrified."

"It's not going to hurt." Ricky glided a hand down her spine, massaging her back. "I know what I'm doing, and I'll go slow." He reached between her legs from behind, and his fingers found her, delving inside and stretching along the length of Martin's buried cock. "You're more than wet enough. Fucking soaked."

"I feel you touching me." Martin shifted beneath her and gripped the backs of her thighs. "Touching both of us. It feels unbelievable." He widened his legs, taking hers with him.

In the next breath, a stretch of pressure invaded her pussy. Martin held still, adjusting his hips as Ricky leaned onto her back.

The fullness inside her bloomed into a wicked burn. She writhed through it, gasping as her body throbbed and stretched with the addition of Ricky's penetration.

"How are we doing?" His breathing grew shallow, and the cage of his arms around her began to shake.

"I'm good." She focused on Martin's hooded eyes, his locked jaw, and realized he was too overwhelmed to speak. "We're adjusting."

It was a rough start. With every other thrust, one of them popped out. The positioning of legs and hips took time to perfect, resulting in numerous stops and starts. But once they mastered the alignment and pace, they fell into blissful delirium.

Their hands went everywhere, gripping muscle, bruising skin, pulling one another closer, harder, as their bodies rose and fell like a tide.

Martin kissed her until the connection of lips became sloppy and impossible. She clung to his broad shoulders and panted against his neck as she rode the profound sensations of two cocks inside her.

Then they went wild, fucking into her like flesh and blood machines. She couldn't breathe, couldn't move. All she could do was just lay suspended between them and let their hands move her body up and down, jacking themselves off.

Hipbones ground against her, sandwiching her in. They were so deep, so huge. Muscled physiques, burning skin, vibrating groans, intoxicating male scents, stabbing cocks—they were all around her, inside her, owning her with an intensity that shoved her over the cliff.

"Shit, shit, shit." As the orgasm sneaked up on her, she found Martin's eyes and exploded into panting, trembling ecstasy.

Wave after wave of tingling electricity crashed over her. She ground down on their hardness and screamed their names through multiple octaves.

Martin's pupils dilated. His gorgeous mouth hung open, and she was gone, swept away by pleasure and love and complete happiness.

As aftershocks shuddered through her, she collapsed between them, laughing breathlessly through the wet strands of hair stuck to her face.

"Fuck, that was hot." Martin brushed the hair from her eyes.

"A hot mess." She sighed, utterly content yet hungry for more. "Will you finish inside Ricky?"

She didn't have to ask him twice.

Their hands caressed and moved her limbs as they repositioned around her. She ended up on her back with Ricky between her legs. He slid into the drenched clasp of her body, lazily stroking as Martin knelt behind him.

Then Martin drove his hips, driving into Ricky's ass as Ricky sank in and out of her pussy.

What a spectacular view. She watched their expressions contort with pleasure, their exhales escaping sharply with relief, and their bodies flexing in their urgency.

Martin circled his arms around Ricky's sweat-slick chest and fucked into him with purpose. Hammering hips, slapping flesh, masculine moans—they consumed her with their strength and stamina.

Ricky turned his neck toward Martin behind him, and their mouths mashed together—all tongue and teeth and volcanic desire. Martin gripped his jaw, pulling him deeper into the kiss as he set the vigorous pace of their fucking.

"Fucking hell," Ricky moaned into his mouth.

"I know." Martin released him and pushed down on his back, trapping him between her chest and Martin's.

There wasn't a sliver of space between them, their bodies pressed together so tightly they couldn't press any closer. Yet they managed to keep their weight from crushing her, using the strength in their arms and legs.

Together, the three of them become one body, one beating heart. They moved in tandem, grinding and rocking in a tumble of limbs, mouths, cocks, and sweat. Skin heated. Muscles contracted, and groans grew deeper as they reached a crescendo.

"I'm going to come." Martin bore down on Ricky, his face tight with emotion as he seized her gaze. "Both of you with me."

"I'm there." Ricky panted and caught her mouth in a frenzied kiss.

He pulled back as he came, his breath caught in his throat, his mouth open in a silent roar. Martin followed him over, pounding hard and losing rhythm.

The intensity and love burning from their eyes took her with them. She sailed into the searing depths of brown and green, her hands tangling in the contrasting shades of blond and black hair, holding them to her and falling apart.

They crumbled into a sweaty, sated pile. The tension in their bodies slowly fled. Heart rates cooled down, and they snuggled into warm skin and soft hair, relaxed muscles and caressing hands.

"I finally have the answer," she breathed.

"What?" Martin's voice rumbled in his chest.

"Ricky Martin is the answer to every question I've ever had about life and death. I've experienced both in your arms."

Their quiet laughter enveloped her in joy. It was an impenetrable moment.

Nothing could touch them. Not time or distance. Not the prison walls or whatever awaited outside.

They held onto the moment with six hands.

They held on as tightly as possible, in every position, for the next six weeks.

TWENTY-EIGHT

Tula couldn't sleep. The sound of her heartbeat thrashed brokenly in her ears. Pain stabbed in her chest and throat, and if she lay here much longer, she would break down so inconsolably she would ruin the last hours she had with Martin and Ricky.

She'd promised herself she would be strong.

For her.

For them.

Their time in Jaulaso was over, and they'd spent the past few hours making love to her as if every thrust, every kiss, and every breath was their last.

They'd fucked themselves into a coma.

Moving slowly and silently, she slid out from between their hot, heavy bodies.

Martin grunted, reaching for her, and she froze. His hand curled around her hip, clinging to her in his sleep. She waited with tears in her throat.

Eventually, his fingers loosened, and she slipped out of bed.

She dressed in the dark, grabbed a towel and soap, and checked the time on her phone.

Matias Restrepo had told Martin and Ricky that a military guard would arrive on the ninetieth day with court orders to release them from Jaulaso.

Their ninetieth day started three hours ago.

Hector wouldn't learn about their release until they were gone. She would fake her surprise and pretend like she didn't really care. He believed her relationship with them was just sex and manipulation.

That was all it was supposed to be.

She never expected to fall in love.

She'd been very careful to hide her feelings from Hector. He'd sent her to do a job, and it was compromised the moment she learned he'd lied to her.

To survive the next three years in his prison, she would have to fake every interaction she had with him. His organization thrived on loyalty. Traitors and dissenters were killed without mercy.

The lights were off as she crept into the corridor and soundlessly shut the door.

She wanted to be clean for them when they said goodbye. Not just her body. She needed to cleanse her state of mind.

The Mexican government would honor the deal that was made for their release. In fact, the government was the only entity that had the power to reduce her sentence. Maybe Martin and Ricky could've negotiated for her if they had the intel on Hector that the government wanted. But they didn't.

She faced three years of separation from them. She needed to accept that and purge the bitterness that had been gnawing at her for weeks.

She would say goodbye, absorb their promises, and do what she could to survive the rest of her sentence.

Her trudging gait carried her through the empty corridor and into the dark stairwell. When she entered the ground floor, she glared at the closed door across the hall.

Was Hector asleep in there? Was he dreaming about the women and children he extorted for a business he considered unprofitable?

Maybe his involvement in that operation was so hands-off he didn't know his cartel was kidnapping people and selling them into slavery.

She grimaced. That sounded really naive, even in her head.

With a glance up and down the hall, she found it vacant as usual at three in the morning. One thing she could count on in Area Three was that its residents partied hard and crashed even harder.

Thirty steps from the stairwell, she passed her old cell. Garra had given it to another inmate weeks ago. Not that she cared. After Martin and Ricky left, she would stay in their cell, wrap up in the lingering scent of them, and pass the rest of her time replaying the best three months of her life.

A one-minute walk took her out of the cellblock and into the corridor that housed the showers. She stepped into the bathroom and peeked around the corner.

Empty.

The light in there stayed on at all hours, and she used it to find a clean place to store her towel and clothes.

As she reached for the button on her jeans, she heard a terrified squeal.

The squealing cry of a child.

A horrible coldness trickled down her spine, and her senses went on high-alert.

She used to wake to the sound of a crying child when she slept in her old cell. But she hadn't had a nightmare since she started sleeping with her guys.

Was she having some kind of traumatic flashback?

The cry sounded again, farther away, and the echo lingered, hitting her circulation with electric shocks. The hairs raised on her arms. Her blood turned to ice, and a paralyzing chill trailed goosebumps across her skin.

She wasn't half-asleep or drunk on tequila. She was wide awake, totally alert.

This wasn't her imagination.

Where did the cry come from? The vents in the ceiling? The empty corridor?

Her heart banged in her chest as she approached the door and peered out.

Not a soul in sight. No sound. No crying child.

It wasn't uncommon for the families of the inmates to visit Area Three. Sometimes, those families included children.

Did a kid get trapped in here? The prison guards did a head count on every person who came and went in the prison. How in the fuck could a child have been missed?

She stood on the threshold to the hallway, her feet frozen in ratty sneakers as she waited, listened.

Then she heard it.

A faraway, muffled shriek. The horrifying sound hiccuped into a convulsion of sobs before abruptly cutting off.

Terror struck her gut and locked up her joints.

Someone was hurting that kid.

She ran in the direction of the cry, down the hall and around the corner. The next corridor veered into a part of Area Three she rarely ventured.

Doors led to closets and maintenance rooms housing electrical boxes and machinery that kept the prison operational. No one wandered into this area unless something was broken.

At the next turn in the corridor, she stopped.

Up ahead was a door to another maintenance room. Only this one stood slightly ajar. The broken chain on the hinge must have swung, preventing it from closing all the way.

Pain throbbed in her molars from clenching her jaw, and the strength in her legs threatened to abandon her. The instinct to turn back and run straight to Martin and Ricky made her tremble uncontrollably. But she couldn't leave.

One of the inmates was hurting that child.

She didn't make a sound as she approached the door. She had no weapons, no fighting skills, and her muscles were so taut with fear she could barely move one foot in front of the other.

This might've been the stupidest thing she'd ever done, but she didn't intend to enter that room. She was just going to put her ear there and listen.

She reached the opening with a painful knot in her stomach. Her teeth chattered, and her entire body coiled to spring at the smallest sound.

Holding her breath, she leaned in.

Silence.

She strained her hearing, her gaze darting behind her every second, as she tried to listen over her thundering heart.

A distant footstep drifted from behind the door, then another, followed by the heaving of breaths. Grunting. Panting. The sound of metal scraping against concrete.

All the heat in her face rushed to her feet. None of those noises should be associated with a child.

She looked back down the hall, the impulse to run pulling through her with eye-watering force.

Turning back, she touched the door and gave it the smallest push. The hinges didn't squeak. She pushed again, giving her enough room to wriggle in.

A maze of sewer pipes greeted her. Narrow and long, short and wide, they stacked in various sizes and rows and ran the length of the vast dark space. Some connected at joints and elbows. Others vanished into the ceiling and floor. Most of the pipes were the width of her body.

The sounds of grunting drew her toward a large pipe that ran parallel with the ground. Ducking behind it, she followed it around a bend toward the noise.

The beam of a flashlight shone through the plumbing, aimed at something twenty feet away. She couldn't see through all the pipes that separated her from whatever was breathing on the other side.

But there was a gap underneath.

Her hands slicked with sweat as she lowered to her knees. Chills gripped her spine and crawled over her scalp. She was so fucking scared.

Breathing silently through it, she dipped her head beneath the lowest pipe and stared across the floor to the other side.

Her heart stopped, and her mind fractured in horror, refusing to accept what her eyes couldn't look away from.

Long dark hair floated in a puddle of red. A tiny mouth hung open in a soundless scream, and glassy dead eyes stared right at her.

Bile hit her tongue, and her insides filled with blistering poison.

Only the upper half of the little girl was in view. She couldn't have been older than thirteen as she lay dead and nude in the blood that poured from her torn-out throat.

Tula was too late. Devastation reared up in her chest, crushing her heart.

Who had done this? How could someone kill a child?

The body jerked, followed by a grunt.

No, no, no.

The body rocked again, and again, being pushed by something she couldn't see.

Tremors wracked her limbs as she crawled alongside the pipe until the rest of the child came into view.

A man knelt between lifeless legs.

Rutting.

Raping.

Fucking the dead body.

Saliva rushed over her tongue. Vomit rose, and tears hit her eyes in a combustion of horror and fury. She clapped her hands over her mouth to silence the scream clawing in her throat.

She knew that slim, masculine frame. Knew the linen pants he wore. Knew how soft that thin cardigan felt beneath her hands when she danced with him.

Everything her mother had said about Hector La Rocha was true.

Only this was worse. So fucking worse.

He wasn't alone. Someone stood behind him, holding the flashlight. Watching. Allowing this despicable, gut-wrenching thing to happen.

The overpowering and agonizing feeling of terror, shock, dread, and revulsion incapacitated her. The utter fear of being caught by him immobilized her lungs, her legs, and the blood in her veins. She was afraid to breathe, petrified to make a sound.

The girl was gone. Dead. There was nothing she could do. She needed to get out of there. If he saw her...

The godawful groaning sounds of him finishing sent her scrambling backward in a flailing of arms and legs. She landed on her back, her clammy hands pressed to her mouth and nose, held in a frozen state of hell, and praying they hadn't heard her.

"This one was with the batch we smuggled in from Texas," the man with the flashlight said in Spanish.

She would recognize that slimy voice anywhere.

Simone.

"How many?" Hector stood and zipped his pants.

That sound… God, the ghastly sound of his zipper would forever haunt her.

Stiff and sickened with grief, she edged alongside the pipe, heading toward the door.

"Two dozen. It's getting harder to smuggle them through the border towns. We need new routes."

Realization slammed into her, redoubling her heart rate.

All those cries she heard over the past two years, the screams that had woken her from sleep…

They were real.

There had been other children, and she'd ignored them.

She'd let them die.

She would be next if she didn't get the fuck out of there.

Rising on silent feet, she swayed through bouts of dizziness. Nausea threatened. Her nerves stretched, overtaxed to the point of breaking as her bladder quivered to release.

Push through it and go!

Instinct took over. Self-preservation shoved her toward the door. All pain and thought vanished as her mind narrowed to one imperative.

Survival.

She moved on impulse, out the door, down the hall, around the bend. The compulsion to look back tingled between her shoulder blades, but she ignored it, kept going, started running.

As her legs flew into a sprint, everything came flooding back.

The lifeless eyes. The jerking body. The sound of the zipper.

She gagged, and the violent hacking doubled her over.

Keep going. Run!

If she'd stayed in the sewer room, she might've picked up something valuable from their conversation. She might've heard names and locations of the men running the operation.

She might've been killed.

How did he sneak the children into the prison? What did he do with the bodies? Did he bring them in on a schedule? Could she track it and figure out a way to stop him before he did it again?

The questions fell behind her as she ran into the stairwell. But she couldn't outrun the toxicity of what she'd just witnessed. It boiled inside her, bubbling in her stomach. She made it to the second flight of stairs before her guts emptied in a spew of vomit and tears.

Her knees crashed onto the step, and she heaved great sobbing waves of anguish, puking all over the stairs.

When there was nothing left, she pushed away from the mess and wiped her mouth.

What was she going to do?

How would she look Hector in the eyes and pretend she couldn't see the bloody, gruesome wasteland of his soul?

She needed Martin and Ricky. Her heart demanded she run to them, tell them what happened, and let them console her as she fell apart in their arms. She was desperate for them. They would take this burden from her and make it easier to breathe.

Her chest constricted.

They were leaving in a few hours. If she unloaded this on them, they would sabotage their departure. They would find a way to stay and keep her safe.

Her mind spun through the horrid details of Martin's childhood. After everything he'd been through, he would never let a monster like Hector La Rocha live. If she told him about this, he would go on a killing spree and get himself killed.

Even if she could convince him not to retaliate, how could she put this on their shoulders and send them off without a resolution?

They had come to Jaulaso because they already knew Hector was evil. Telling them what she just saw didn't gain anyone anything.

She only had a handful of hours left with them. She didn't want to spend it rehashing the horrors of what she'd just witnessed. She had the next three years to do that.

But if she didn't tell them, she would be tainting their final moments with dishonesty. She would have to slap on a smile, pretend nothing was amiss, and send them off with kisses and hope.

It was an impossible decision.

She forced herself to her feet and returned to their cell. The short walk didn't give her enough time to shake the trembling from her body.

The deepest shivers would never go away. She would never escape what she saw tonight.

But she could do something about it.

The seed of an idea sprouted as she silently opened the door and slipped into their cell.

Darkness slammed into her, pressing in on all sides. She felt it on her skin, the contamination of Hector's depravity infecting her pores.

"Tula?"

Ringing invaded her ears, disorientating her as she stumbled in the blackness.

"Tula? What are you doing?" The distant voice was smothered by a heavy fuzz of violence.

Grisly images flashed behind her eyes. Long black hair. Pools of blood. Tiny fingers. The zipper.

She swayed in the nightmare, drowning in the pain, trying to keep her head above her and her feet beneath her.

"Tula? Tula?" Warm arms came around her, competing with the coldness. "Are you okay?"

Martin held her up, his presence a beacon in the dark. Then Ricky pressed in behind her, his mouth falling to her neck, anchoring her to him.

This was what she needed. What *they* needed. For the next few hours, she couldn't let anything take this from them.

She knew what she had to do.

She'd promised herself she would be strong.

For her.

For them.

"I had a nightmare." She pressed a kiss to Martin's hard chest.

"Come back to bed."

"Just a sec. I want to brush my teeth." She slipped away, fumbling in the dark for her toothbrush.

"Why are you dressed?" Ricky lit a candle, illuminating the room in a soft glow.

"I was going to take a shower."

"Do it tomorrow."

Today was tomorrow.

Their last day together.

"Okay." She turned away before they saw the plastic smile that wasn't working on her face.

They were half-asleep with exhaustion. That was the only reason they hadn't detected her dishonesty.

Lying to them made her feel sick, but it was the only way she could protect them.

As she brushed her teeth and stripped her clothes, her mind picked up and discarded a dozen ways to deal with Hector La Rocha.

Maybe there were smarter, safer solutions to end his depravity, but there was only one outcome she wanted. The seed of her idea bloomed into a plan.

Right now, though, she only wanted to think about the two people who mattered most to her. She was going to savor every second they had left together.

Then, once they were safely out of Jaulaso, she would iron out how, where, and when.

She was going to kill Hector La Rocha.

TWENTY-NINE

Saying goodbye was the most excruciating thing Tula ever had to do.

She stood between Martin and Ricky in the privacy of their cell and peppered desperate, tear-soaked kisses over their faces and hands.

They were already dressed, seconds from walking out the door.

From the moment she'd crawled back in bed with them early that morning, they'd been saying goodbye.

They said goodbye while moving inside her body. They said it with growly, pain-stricken words. They said it with their eyes as they memorized her features and collected her tears with their lips.

Three months with them hadn't been enough.

A lifetime with them wouldn't have been enough.

"You need to go." She pulled them closer, protesting her own command.

"This is fucking bullshit!" Martin wrenched away and tore his hands through his hair. "We haven't thought through every option. There must be a way—"

"We've beaten this to death." Tears slid free, and she swatted at her cheeks. "You can *not* stay here. Giving up your freedoms helps no one. There's no reason—"

"There's one reason." Ricky cupped her face. "And you're the only reason that matters."

"We're sticking to the plan." She dug in deep and shoved back her shoulders. "You're walking out of here today, and that's final."

There would be no communication. No phone calls.

Over the past two years, she'd only used her phone to contact the U.S. consular. She checked in regularly to monitor the status of her sentence and nag him about an early release.

La Rocha Cartel monitored the call logs of all cell phones in Jaulaso. If she veered from her pattern and called a number she'd never dialed, it would raise suspicion. Even if she called an untraceable number or a reception desk at some random business, Hector would know about it.

She couldn't do anything that might cause him to second-guess her. Especially now that she knew how cruel and truly sadistic he was.

Once he discovered Martin and Ricky's charges had been dropped, he would know something nefarious was going on with them. Drug trafficking charges didn't just go away. Not in Jaulaso.

Martin and Ricky wouldn't be safe in Hector's city. The instant they walked out of here, they would have to leave Ciudad Hueca.

There would be no visits from them. No calls. No letters. No packages. Any contact would make Hector suspect she'd taken sides with them.

They would be heading back to the Colombian headquarters of the Restrepo Cartel, where they lived. Only the residents knew the location. It was a secret they couldn't share.

She would never be able to find them.

They promised to come to her when she was released. She wanted to believe them, but her plan made that impossible.

When they left, she would have to forget them. At least, whenever she stepped out of this cell. Her pain would be trapped in this room, hidden from the rest of the world.

Ricky embraced her in a rib-crushing hug. "We're going to get you—"

"No more promises. Just hold me."

He tightened his arms and kissed her deeply. His breaths shook as painfully as hers, but they kept the tears at bay. They'd cried enough.

Martin moved in, tugging her away from Ricky. His kiss was harder, angrier, more punishing. Every lick commanded she stay safe. Every bite confessed how much he hated leaving, and every sucking pull laid claim to her heart.

They owned her. No matter what happened, she would always be theirs.

As they opened the door and stepped into the hallway, her entire world pulled away, and she was left standing outside of it. Alone. They knew it, too, given the way their shoulders tightened, and their faces hardened.

The pain was unwieldy, like a blanket made of boulders had been draped over her shoulders. It weighed her down and pinned her in place, making it physically and emotionally exhausting to stand beneath.

They glanced back with love and fear, hope and grief filling their parting expressions.

No words were needed. Everything had already been said.

Except the one thing she'd held back.

She told them with her eyes.

I love you.

If she ever saw them again, she would tell them with her voice and every part of her being.

She shut the door before they took the steps that would carry them away.

Her forehead dropped against the doorframe. Her breath perished in her chest, and her fingers slid helplessly up and down the wall as she tracked the sounds of their retreating footfalls.

Then she couldn't hear them at all. She couldn't feel the warm glow of their love pulsing through her body. She was too cold. So unbearably frigid. Her heart actually ached. It ached so ruthlessly it felt as though she were suffocating beneath the colossal pain.

They were still in the building. If she ran, she could catch them before they exited the stairwell.

Then what? More kisses? Another goodbye? It would never be enough.

She pressed her feet firmly to the floor and mentally traced the path they would take through Jaulaso. She imagined herself at their sides as they walked out of Area Three.

No one would stop them. They weren't members of La Rocha Cartel.

They would reach the front of the prison and leave with their escort. A prison guard would notify Hector as that happened.

But they would already be gone.

Safe.

Far away from her.

Her grief sat right beneath her sternum, next to her heart. It expanded with ungodly pressure as her body took deep sighing breaths in an attempt to draw more oxygen. Panic rose with swelling agony, and her chest tightened, fighting a looming anxiety attack.

Martin and Ricky had coached her through this. She could hear their voices in her head telling her to relax and stay calm. They knew the next few hours would be the hardest, and they'd reminded her over and over to not break down.

A knock would sound on her door soon. Meetings would follow. Interrogations about where they went and what she knew.

She would endure it with a disappointed expression fixed on her face while she slowly died inside.

But she had a plan.

What Martin and Ricky didn't know was that she wouldn't be finishing her three years in Jaulaso.

Killing Hector La Rocha wouldn't be easy. If she somehow succeeded, she would have to flee Jaulaso before his body was discovered. Timing would be critical.

Pushing down her grief, she grabbed her phone and dialed the U.S. consular. He answered after a few rings.

"This is Petula Gomez." She pulled in a deep breath and released it.

"Petula." He sighed, exasperated. "Nothing has changed with your sentence."

"I'm not calling about that."

In 1977, the United States and Mexico signed a prisoner transfer treaty. Since that time, some American and Mexican prisoners have been transferred to their respective countries. She'd already been sentenced, which made her eligible to transfer to a prison in the United States.

All she had to do was plead guilty and hope to hell Hector didn't discover her intent to desert the cartel.

"Start the process to send me back to the U.S." She strengthened her voice. "I'm ready to plead guilty."

The consular had been advising her to do this since day one. She hadn't listened to him because she always had Hector's protection in Jaulaso.

And she had her pride.

She was innocent, serving a sentence for a crime she didn't commit. A guilty plea would mar her criminal record forever.

After two years in Jaulaso, she didn't give a goddamn fuck about her pride or her record. She just needed to get out and didn't care what it took.

"I'm confident the U.S. Department of Justice will concur with your request," he said. "Once everything is signed off, arrangements will be made for your transfer."

"How long will it take?"

"You'll be in U.S. custody within a month."

PART THREE

THIRTY

The knock on the door came an hour later. An hour that Tula had spent shoving her pain so far down beneath her bones she could no longer feel it.

She moved stiffly to the door, expecting Garra on the other side. But when she opened it, he wasn't alone.

Garra stepped back to make room for Hector to enter.

The air tried to rush out of her lungs, but she held it in and arranged her features into a mask of pleasant surprise.

He stood two feet away, infecting her precious sanctuary with his pedophilic, child-killing pestilence.

His black hair combed back neatly with silver streaks at the temples. The cardigan was gone, but he wore his signature button-down shirt, open at the collar.

She couldn't think about his pants or the things he did when he wasn't wearing them.

Please, leave.

She didn't want him here. Not in the place she'd shared with Martin and Ricky.

His dark eyes took her measure, the depths warm and gentle, camouflaging the sickness that festered within.

What were his true intentions with her? Had any part of the past two years been real? Or was it all manipulation?

He'd sent Garra to collect her DNA in a violent, repulsive way. He required her to sit through his meetings but kept his human trafficking operation concealed from her. Then he tasked her, his only daughter, to seduce his enemies, not knowing if they would kill her or hurt her. All the while, he protected her from the other inmates, learned English through her instruction, and danced with her. Why?

Her mind delivered the sound of a zipper to her ears, but she didn't react, didn't look down. She blocked out the reminder of who he was and assumed her role.

"Have you seen Martin and Ricardo?" She craned her neck around him to glance into the hall. "They said they were going to get food, but they never returned. I was just on my way out to find—"

"They're gone." His eyebrows knitted together as he studied her.

"What?" She squared her shoulders with feigned indignation. "You had them killed? You said I had time to—"

"No," he tsked. "They left Jaulaso. The military dropped their charges and released them."

"Oh." She slumped onto the mattress and blew out a breath. "Shit."

"You don't know anything about that?" He cocked his head, his expression soft and concerned.

"No." Her fingers trembled, and she flexed them. "What does it mean? Are they working with the military? Like undercover or something?"

"That's my assumption."

"Oh, God." She pressed her face into her hands and made a noise she hoped sounded like a self-loathing groan. "I failed you."

"Petula." He lowered onto the bed beside her, sending her nerves into a shrieking fit of horror. "You kept them distracted. Whatever secrets they came to steal from me remain safely guarded. *They* failed. Because of you."

There was so much truth in that it fucking hurt. If they hadn't become entangled with her, if they hadn't chosen her over their mission, they might've succeeded.

They could've taken down Hector's entire human trafficking operation if they'd learned where his officers were hiding. But she'd gotten in their way.

She'd distracted them just like Hector had wanted.

"I don't feel like I was any help at all." She stared down at her hands, playing coy as she worked up the courage to meet his eyes. "They got away."

When she finally lifted her head, she stared at him through a one-way window. She could see his ugliness, his unadulterated evil. But he couldn't see her. The utter fear she felt in his presence, the grief of losing Martin and Ricky, her plan to kill him—all of it was invisible to him.

Because she was his daughter. Their genetic connection made him partial to her. He *wanted* to trust her.

She would manipulate that trust until her transfer went through.

Then she would kill him with it.

He watched her for a moment, his head tipping with curiosity. She held still, her facial muscles slack as she thought about the gooey goodness of grilled cheese, her favorite passage in *The Hellbound Heart*, the tattered stubs of her shoestrings — anything except the images of him with that little girl.

Disgust raged beneath her schooled features, seething under her skin and cooking her from the inside out.

"You liked the gringos," he said.

She loved them.

Losing that love felt like a straitjacket constricting her body. She would never adjust or grow comfortable in it. She would never be able to take it off. It would forever bind her and prevent her from holding anyone and anything. Maybe it would eventually make her insane, and she would welcome the madness because a reality without them hurt too damn much.

"They were attractive." She shrugged. "I mean… I had a good time *distracting* them, I guess." She glanced around the room. "But it'll be nice to have my privacy back. Can I keep this cell?"

"If you'd like." His gaze drifted to Garra, who waited outside the door. Then he returned to her. "I put an alert out. The entire city is on the lookout for the gringos. If they attempt to contact you —"

"I'll castrate them," she deadpanned.

He laughed, just like she knew he would, and the air around him settled into affectionate trust. She felt like she was going to throw up, but at least he hadn't noticed.

"I'll let you know if they contact me," she said. "In the meantime, I'm probably just going to hang out in here for a while, read some books, and enjoy my alone time. Is that okay?"

He inclined his head. "As long as you delight this old man with a dance every now and then."

The shudder that rose up was so powerful she had to clench her core muscles to stifle it.

"Of course." She stood with him and followed him to the door. "I'm sorry they got away. I hope you're not too disappointed in me."

"You never disappoint me, my girl." He touched her chin in a featherlight caress of fingers and filth.

"Thank you."

He entered the corridor and breezed past Garra, vanishing around the corner.

Garra remained, and his eyes moved over her like lie detectors. She gave him the same treatment, questioning every crease in his brow and twitch in his bearded jaw.

Did he know about Hector's depravity? He was the most loyal

man in the cartel. It was safe to assume he knew about and guarded every skeleton in Hector's closet.

"I will watch over you again," he said in Spanish.

"No, you will not. Did Hector tell you to—?"

"No." He glanced down the hall and looked back at her. "I don't want you wandering around alone. I know you feel safe—"

"I've never felt safe. Not in Jaulaso, and definitely not with you."

He inhaled sharply. "Fine."

As he turned away, she shut the door and locked it.

Her hand lifted to her face where Hector had touched her, and all the pain she'd pushed down over the past hour came roaring back.

She clawed at the stabbing burn in her chest and buckled over, gasping for breath. Her knees gave out as she hurled herself toward the sink, landing against it.

With the faucet on, she shoved her face under the spray and frantically scrubbed away the feel of Hector's fingers.

He was so fucking vile and sick, and he was related to her. How could that be? How could she share DNA with something so atrociously inhuman?

She turned off the water and stared at the yellow stains in the sink. She was alone. Martin and Ricky were gone, and she had to continue on without them. She had to carry the weight of Hector's sins without their protection or help.

It was too late to tell them about the things that happened to her last night. She'd made a decision, and she couldn't take it back. She would never be able to curl up between their bodies and cry through the horrors she'd witnessed.

The safe, happy world she'd lived in with them was gone. That place would never return to her. They could never come back here.

They were gone.

Gone.

Gone.

Their absence swallowed all her attention, smothering her entire existence in desolation. She felt it in her face, throbbing through her gums and consuming her sinuses. Tears burned from her swollen eyes. Her throat filled with lava. The pain spread through muscles, arteries, and organs, weakening everything in its path.

She dragged heavy, useless limbs to the bed and buried her nose in the blankets, breathing in their masculine scents and seeking out the indentations of their body prints in the mattresses.

Mattresses that had been clawed by passionate hands. Walls that had been dampened by the press of sweaty bodies. Bedding that had tangled and twisted in the throes of hunger.

Surrounded by remnants of their time together, she rewound their love scenes, remembering them inside her and clinging to the blissful sensations. She knew them inside and out, and she would never forget.

Ricky's panty-melting smile, the commanding rumble in Martin's voice, the way they stared at each other so intimately and possessively, and how that captivating eye contact eventually included her—all of it tattooed across her soul.

She lost herself in the pain.

She grieved them with her whole body.

Once the sobbing began, she couldn't stop. She fell into the black abyss and didn't try to climb out. Curling up in the darkness, she cried through the rest of the day and into the next one.

No one knocked on the door or tried to invade her isolation. She wouldn't have let them in. She was in no position to show her face.

A few cans of soup and early-morning showers got her through that first week. The two times she ventured out at three in the morning, the sounds of a crying child haunted her. But the corridors remained silent and empty.

Over the next few weeks, she pulled herself together long enough to inject her presence into Area Three.

At night, she walked the halls, listening for children and monitoring the vacant sewer room.

During the day, she watched the inmates from her favorite bench in the yard and swallowed her fear during visits with Hector in his cell.

On the surface, she was the woman she'd been for the past two years—aloof and unapproachable, present but not involved. She sat on the outskirts of the common areas with her nose in a book, just like she'd always done.

But on the inside, everything had changed. She couldn't understand how the world could go on around her when her life had completely stopped.

Life had abandoned her the moment Martin and Ricky walked out that door.

She tried not to dwell on it, but it was a splinter under her fingernail that couldn't be removed. Sometimes the pain dulled, but it never went away. She couldn't think of anything else except for that damn splinter, stuck in a place it didn't belong. Her entire body felt it. She couldn't pull it out, couldn't chop it off. She couldn't escape it.

Three weeks later, she received the green light on her transfer to the United States. It didn't ease the agony of her loss, but it gave her some focus.

In six days, the U.S. Bureau of Prisons would begin her transfer to a federal correctional institution near her home. She was going to a satellite

MANIPULATE

prison camp for female offenders in Phoenix, Arizona.
She knew the date and time of her departure.
She knew when Hector was going to die.

THIRTY-ONE

The morning of Tula's transfer, she waited in the stairwell across from Hector's cell. Her heart hammered in her stomach, and her legs burned to run.

She'd managed to keep her scheduled departure a secret. In fact, the whole transfer process had been shockingly easy.

Too easy.

Something felt off, but she couldn't put her finger on it.

A late phone call to the consular last night confirmed everything was in order.

She could just go now. Run straight out of Area Three and head to the front of the prison. Her ride would be here in a few hours. She could find a place to hide and wait it out.

Maybe she could contact the Mexican military and tell them Hector was smuggling children into the prison. But part of her suspected they already knew.

They'd tortured her for information on the cartel, desperate to bring down the whole organization. Then they framed her.

She didn't trust them.

But if she ran now, how many children would be raped and murdered while she served the rest of her time in the States?

This was the only way.

Right on time, Garra appeared at Hector's door to walk his boss to the showers. She slipped out of view in the stairwell, listening to their voices and tracking the retreat of their footsteps.

Then she waited through a minute of nerve-wracking silence before she sneaked into his cell.

MANIPULATE

Over the past few weeks, she'd cataloged the placement of everything in his quarters. It took her five seconds to locate the knife under his pillow. Another five seconds to slide it into the narrow space behind the record player.

In under a minute, she was out of his room and strolling back to her cell with deliberately slow steps.

Then she waited for an hour—hands drenched in sweat, fingers trembling uncontrollably, and pulse pounding in her head.

Once she stepped out of this prison cell, she would never return. If she lived through the next part, she would head straight out of Area Three without looking back.

One more glance around the room filled her with unbearable sorrow. She had to leave it all behind. The signed novel of *The Hellbound Heart*. The candles that illuminated so many nights of pleasure. The box of men's clothing that was scented by them. A distinctive fragrance that would forever haunt her.

It was okay. She could do this. It was just stuff, and this cell was just an empty space they'd left behind.

Time to go.

No amount of detachment or determination could overpower the terror that owned her body as she walked back to Hector's cell. Maybe this would've been a good time to square things up with Jesus, but she didn't think the Lord and Savior would be on board with what she was about to do.

By the time she reached Hector's door, she'd built a sturdy wall around her emotions. But she wore her fear like an invisible cloak. Ice-cold and unshakable, it clung to her skin and drained all her warmth. She felt it with every breath, but she couldn't see it.

If prison life had taught her anything, it was how to keep her weaknesses hidden beneath a veneer of tattoos and cool reserve.

Or maybe it was an inherited skill that had been passed down in her blood. Hector had mastered the art of concealing depravity beneath a soft cardigan and layers of affection.

He answered her knock on the door, wearing a pleased smile. "Petula."

"Are you up for getting your feet stepped on?" By some miracle, she'd evaded all dancing and touching for the past month.

"I thought you'd never ask. Come in."

As they exchanged their usual greetings, she chewed blistering gashes on the insides of her cheeks.

Drawing this out wasn't an option. Her nerves unfurled with every miserable heartbeat. At any second, he would detect her distress.

"Can I select the song today?" she asked.

"Go ahead."

She floated to the record player on numb legs and pulled an album from the stack. Her hands shook as she set up the record, her mind focused on the knife she'd hidden behind the turntable.

Was it still there? Would she be able to grab it before he stopped her? Would she chicken out at the last minute?

"Which song did you choose?" He approached her, staring too closely at her tingling face.

Fuck, she'd forgotten to look at the album.

Her tongue twisted through the saliva pooling in her mouth. "You'll see."

She adjusted the needle but didn't place it on the vinyl. The next few seconds had to be timed flawlessly.

Deep breath.

"Ready?" She positioned her stance beside the record player, turning her body just right as she opened her arms.

He stepped into her space, pervading her senses with the gruesome echoes of a dark sewer room.

His hand clasped her hip. His other reached for her fingers.

"I'll start the song." She angled toward the turntable and twisted her ankle just right to make it look clumsy.

Her tripping step distracted him away from her hand as he caught her fall. In that blur of a moment, she bypassed the needle on the player and wrapped her fingers around the hilt of the knife.

Her pulse exploded as she swung.

She'd sat in the prison yard for two years, listening to inmates talk about the most lethal ways to kill a man. She would've never considered the armpit as a target. Evidently, neither did Hector.

He saw the knife coming and shielded his core. She put all her strength behind the thrust as she stabbed upward into his armpit. With the blade still pointed up, she yanked it back toward her, making sure she severed the main artery there.

Blood spurted instantly, but instead of falling, he attacked.

His hand caught her throat, and she shoved him off with a surge of ferocity. The blood loss made him weaker, and his injured arm didn't work.

As he shuffled to stay upright, she stabbed him again in the same spot. And again. She must've hit cartilage or bone the second time because the knife stuck, slipping from her fingers as he stumbled backward.

He stared at the protruding weapon in his shoulder, his eyes wide with shock. "Why?"

"You're pure evil. You don't belong here. Not in this world. Not among *children.*"

His hip bumped into the table, knocking it aside, and he dropped to the floor.

The vicious pounding in her chest overpowered her relief. She needed answers.

Kneeling beside him, she squeezed his throat and held him immobile. "I know what you do in the middle of the night."

His eyes blinked rapidly, and he slapped an uncoordinated hand at the knife in his shoulder. Half of his shirt was red, and the puddle beneath him was growing. The artery in the armpit supplied blood to his extremities and sat close enough to the heart to drain him quickly. He didn't have much time.

"Give me the locations of the commanders involved in the smuggling of those kids."

"I sent you to the gringos as a test." The cords in his neck strained beneath her hand, and his English grew sloppy with his pain. "I didn't care about them. I needed to know who *you* were." He switched to Spanish. "I challenged your loyalty to see who you would pick. Them or me." His eyes watered with tears. "I thought you chose *me.*"

"You sick son of a bitch," she seethed. "If you wanted to test me, all you had to do was tell me you were raping and killing children. You would've found out real quick where my loyalties lie."

He held still, staring up at her, eyes locked. A twitch skipped along his clenched jaw that had nothing to do with the knife in his shoulder. He was disappointed with her. Furious. Flames roared in his gaze, ready to ignite everything around him.

Well, fuck him, because her rage blazed hotter. The inferno inside her wasn't explosive or out of control, but it burned mighty and strong at the end of a two-year wick.

The acidity of her wrath resided in her stomach, waiting to be spat from her mouth in a string of venomous words. But she wasn't going to say them. She was going to stab all her hurt and disgust into his dying body.

She slapped a hand over his mouth and yanked the blade from his shoulder. His jaw worked beneath her palm, roaring without sound. His back bowed and spasmed, and more blood flowed from his wounds.

With the knife secure in her fist, she let her fury flood out all at once. The blade came down, fast and relentless, over and over into the lower quadrants of his abdomen.

Though he was screaming, her hand trapped the noise as her other jabbed and twisted the blade, gouging countless holes, goring and mangling. To draw out his death, she avoided the liver, spleen, and big veins that were higher up.

He probably only had seconds left, but she wanted to make

fucking sure he felt every single one of them while staring into her eyes.

Her arm moved like a disembodied appendage, separated from her soul. What she felt wasn't human. It wasn't *her*. The mindless need to kill brutally and ruthlessly... It warped her mind and laced her veins in fire. She was intoxicated with it. And terrified.

She dropped the knife and stared down at the mutilated remains of his lower abdomen. The bloodbath sickened her and thrilled her.

"Vera Gomez," he whispered.

Her heart stuttered. "What?"

"Your sister." A macabre smile pushed through his agony-soaked expression. "She smuggles them for me. All the pretty little girls."

Her breath stopped and restarted as her mind tried to separate the information. "You found her? She's alive? Wait... She works for you? She would never—"

His mouth formed words, but no sound came out. His eyes lost focus, blinking slowly as he stared at nothing. Death moved in, stealing the answers she desperately needed.

"Where is she?" She slapped his slack face, knocking his head to the side. "Answer me!"

"With..." His tongue lolled in his vile mouth, dying with his words. "Your brothers."

He fell silent. No breath. No movement. Eyes glazed and unseeing. Dead.

Hector La Rocha was dead, and her sister was alive.

Vera's alive.

A sob of relief burst from her throat. She gulped down the next tearful exhale and pushed to her feet, teetering and stunned to the bottom of her stomach.

Vera was smuggling children? She was the one Martin and Ricky were looking for? And the Mexican military...

They arrested Tula because of mistaken identity.

Vera wasn't mixed up in this. She would never do anything to harm innocent people.

She couldn't think about this right now. Blood was everywhere, trailing a gruesome path from the record player to his prone body. It splattered her black shirt, coated her hands, and clotted in her hair.

She needed to get out of there.

Racing to the sink, she scrubbed off the evidence. Clothes, skin, hair—all of it received a furious rubbing until only a few damp spots remained on her shirt.

She didn't spare a glance at the body as urgency propelled her to the door. The scariest part wasn't over.

She still had to walk out of Area Three without raising suspicion.

With any luck, Hector's death wouldn't be discovered until she was on her way to the United States.

The corridor would be busy at this hour. The moment she stepped out there, she would have to put on her game face. Business as usual.

A few deep breaths helped her steady her hands. Then she opened the door.

Garra and Simone stood a few feet away. Their conversation fell silent, and both heads turned in her direction.

She glared at them—because that was what she would normally do—while reaching behind her, blindly trying to find the handle and close the door.

In two long strides, Garra was in her space. His hand went to her cheek, and he pulled back a red-smeared thumb.

"What did you do?" he whispered angrily.

Her fingers caught the door behind her, pulling it closed as Simone crowded in, pushing it open.

"That's blood." Simone examined her up and down before angling his head to see into Hector's cell.

Her stomach dropped, and her knees wobbled.

The body lay around the corner, but the goddamn evidence was on her face. She couldn't talk her way out of this. She needed to run.

"I got a bloody nose." She tried to squeeze past them, but multiple hands caught her arms and dragged her back inside.

The door shut with finality, closing her in and sucking all the air from her lungs.

"Get your hands off me!" She kicked and thrashed as they hauled her toward the crime scene. "Let me go!"

And there it was. Hector's body lay in a pool of red, eyes open, with a hundred mangled knife wounds in the abdomen.

"Holy Mother of God." Simone stared at the bloody corpse, stunned. Then his tawny face turned red-hot. "You did this."

"Garra." She twisted in his arms, prepared to beg for mercy from the only man in Jaulaso who might actually listen. "Please, let me explain."

His nostrils flared, and his fingers bit into her back.

Desperation drove her hand to his hair. She gripped hard, touching him for the first time as she put her face in his. "Please, don't hurt me again."

Something moved in his eyes, a soft pulse at the centers, that seemed to humanize his entire expression. He opened his mouth to speak, but his attention darted to Simone behind her.

As she turned, Simone drew a large knife from his boot and lunged for her.

She had no time to react before Garra shoved her out of the way.

She landed on her back beside Hector's body, her breath frozen as Garra crashed into Simone.

They went down in a tumble of fists, rolling across the floor with the knife swinging around them. She scrambled back and dug in her feet to run. Until her gaze snagged on the blade beside Hector's leg.

She didn't think beyond the need to kill Simone. He'd held the flashlight, watched the violence. He needed to die.

With a surge of adrenaline, she grabbed the knife and spun toward the fight.

Simone was bigger, stronger, and had the upper hand as he flipped Garra onto his back and fell on top of him. She saw her chance and raced toward them.

Holding the knife with the sharp edge angled down, she stabbed it deeply and firmly into the back of Simone's neck. When his body jerked, she yanked hard on the hilt, dragging the blade toward the spine and severing everything in its path.

Simone collapsed on Garra's chest, covered in blood and instantly dead. She pressed her fingers to the pulse point in his neck, just to be sure.

Fuck.

She'd just killed another cartel member.

Garra didn't move beneath the body as he watched her closely, his eyes stark and unblinking. Then his lips pulled back with a hiss, exposing blood-stained teeth.

"You're hurt?" She couldn't see much of him beneath Simone and all the blood.

"Yes."

"Are you going to kill me?"

"Never." The intensity of his conviction pulled her to her knees.

She shoved the body, and Garra released a roar of agony. As the weight fell away, she saw the knife.

Buried to the hilt in Garra's stomach, the eight-inch blade had gone all the way through him. He would be dead within minutes.

Against all logic, an ache of compassion swelled in her throat.

"Some letters came for you." He heaved a breath, choking on a mouthful of blood. "Forms you needed to sign to complete your transfer."

"What?" A fresh wave of fear crashed over her.

He knew about her desertion? For how long? Had he alerted the cartel? Would they be waiting for her as she tried to leave?

She bent over him. "What did you do?"

"I hid them from everyone. Forged your signatures and sent them back to the consular."

"Why?" Her head jerked back. "Why didn't you tell me?"

"I didn't want you to know I..."

704

"What?"

"I love you."

She blew out a breath. Didn't matter that he was dying. She couldn't pretend to give a fuck about that sentiment. "Do you know what Hector was doing to children in the sewer room?"

He looked away and coughed out a string of blood. "I didn't condone it and never helped him with that."

Disgust burned in her gut. "How did he get them into Jaulaso?"

"They're drugged. Put inside crates. Brought in with shipments of firearms."

Firearms? Hector and his men had conversations about those shipments in every meeting. Had they been talking about trafficking humans right in front of her?

She clenched her hands. "You did nothing to stop it. Makes you just as guilty as the rest of them."

With a slow nod, he closed his eyes and let his head loll.

"You're not dying yet." She gripped his jaw and forced his narrowed gaze to hers. "Where's my sister?"

"With your brothers, but you can't—" A gulping breath rolled his eyes into the back of his head.

"Garra!" She shook him until he refocused on her.

"Can't go after Vera. Hector's sons... They'll know what you did. They'll avenge him."

"They know who I am? They'll recognize me?"

"Yes. Stay away. They'll kill you." His hand fell to his pants and flopped around his hip. "The bag...my pocket. Take it. Show it on your way out."

His eyes closed, and his breathing slowed to a stuttering wisp. She was losing him.

"Where is Vera? Give me a location. A town. Anything."

He parted pale lips but didn't open his eyes. "C-C-Calaaa—" The rest of it died on his last breath.

Calaaa-what? Off the top of her head, she couldn't think of a town in Mexico that began with those syllables, but she would have plenty of time later to research it.

Shoving her hand into his pocket, she removed a plastic baggie of heroin. "Show this on my way out?"

Confusion morphed to understanding. The drugs were her ticket out of Area Three. Unlike Martin and Ricky, she was a cartel member. She would need a reason for leaving the area.

"Thank you for helping me." She patted Garra's lifeless chest and shoved to her feet.

She ran to the sink, cleaned away the blood, and double-checked her face.

Then she left. Out the door, through the corridors, and into the common area. Her body operated on a flood of adrenaline, racing her heart and pushing away the fear.

An armed inmate stopped her at the door to the exit. "Where are you going?"

"Delivering something for the boss." She pulled the baggie from her pocket and held it up.

He gave it a glance and nodded.

Then he opened the door.

Sunlight baked her eyes as she stepped into the outdoor courtyard and hurried to the other side. It'd been two years since she walked this path, naively following the prison guard that Hector had sent for her.

Only one month ago, Martin and Ricky crossed this same yard.

Where were they now? Did they miss her? Would they try to find her? How would they even know where to look?

She had no way to contact them. No way to tell them she was leaving.

None of this was a revelation. When she made the call to process her transfer, she knew it meant she would never see them again.

As she entered the central part of the prison, she dropped the bag of heroin on the floor and made her way through the filthy halls.

She'd killed Hector La Rocha.

Vera was alive.

She was returning to Arizona.

All of this should've lifted her spirits and carried her faster to the door. But it was overshadowed by longing and heartache.

She should've never fallen in love. But she did. Times two.

Nothing would ever compare to the three months she had with them. They were the touchstone of human integrity. A taste of a full and vibrant life. They were the real deal. Her deepest sorrow. Her greatest happiness.

She'd carried two-hundred dollars into Jaulaso.

Two years later, the only thing she carried out was a broken heart.

THIRTY-TWO

It had been there for three months—this exhausting, unstoppable anger that kept Martin awake at night. He lay in bed at the Restrepo headquarters and twined his fingers through Ricky's hair, trying to quiet his raging thoughts.

They'd been in Colombia for three fucking months, and no one could tell them anything about Tula. They didn't know if she was protected by La Rocha Cartel, unharmed, or still alive.

Hector La Rocha was dead. It was all over the news two months ago. The reports claimed he was brutally murdered in his prison cell, along with his closest men, Garra and Simone. As for who had done it? That mystery was still being investigated.

Maybe it was an inside job by one of the inmates in Area Three. It could've been an attack by the González Cartel or one of the enemy gangs.

But deep down, Martin knew.

Tula had found a way to kill the cartel boss. If Martin weren't so fucking angry with her for risking her life, he would've been beaming with pride.

Three dangerous men.

Murdered.

He couldn't begin to imagine how she'd done it or what had prompted her. But whenever the scenario played out in his head, he couldn't see past his blinding rage and fear.

Just because she wasn't listed among the dead didn't mean the cartel hadn't retaliated in the two months that followed. There had been multiple prison riots since Hector's death. Chaos had erupted in fires, gunfights, and prisoner breakouts.

The news didn't report the names of the casualties from the Jaulaso riots, and none of Martin's resources had been able to obtain that information.

Everything was on lockdown. The entire city was up in arms over the death of their leader, and the Mexican government was scrambling to keep the prison contained. There were talks about shutting Jaulaso down.

Where was Tula during all this? He couldn't stop imagining her holed up in that foul cell, alone and unarmed, while the prison burned down around her.

He gritted his teeth to the point of breaking. His shoulders ached with endless tension. Animosity saturated his blood with acid — burning, seething, poisonous.

He was infuriated with the Mexican military for putting an innocent schoolteacher in Jaulaso. He was outraged with the Mexican government for ignoring his pleas to release her. He was pissed at Matias Restrepo for refusing to negotiate another deal that would send Martin back to prison.

And he wanted to strangle Cole Hartman for making promises he had yet to keep.

When he and Ricky left Jaulaso three months ago, they went straight to Cole. The retired military-spy-secret-agent — whatever Cole was — had been able to spring Van and Lucia out of a Venezuelan prison within one week. Yet he couldn't give Martin a single update on Tula after three months.

Cole said the turmoil in Jaulaso had delayed his progress, but he would find her and get her out. He just needed time.

There was fuck all Martin could do about it, and that was the root of his fury. He was enraged with himself more than anything. He shouldn't have left her.

The only thing keeping him from mentally snapping was the man in his arms.

Ricky carried his own anger with a quiet intensity that Martin envied. Even in his devastation over leaving Tula, Ricky had been able to wrap a blanket of calmness around Martin and cool them both down before they lost their shit.

He used that same calmness to control Martin's unhinged aggression during sex.

Martin was nowhere near cured of his PTSD. Hard, rough fucking triggered him every time, but Ricky never gave up on him. He'd figured out how to battle Martin's demons with a soft rumbling voice, sensual caresses, and assertive eye contact. Didn't matter how deep in the past Martin fell, Ricky always pulled him back.

Even now, as his best friend slept beside him, he felt his rage give way to the patience that seemed to radiate from Ricky's presence.

Black hair lay in tousled waves on Ricky's head. His tanned skin glowed white in the spill of moonlight from the balcony door. Dark eyelashes, straight nose, square jaw — all his features formed a breathtaking portrait of masculine symmetry.

The seam of his full lips hid a tongue that could make Martin shoot his load in under ten seconds, and his nude body exuded all the grace, strength, and chiseled perfection of a demigod.

No one could pull off the freshly fucked look like Ricardo Saldivar. Martin had worked him into a hard-earned orgasm only an hour earlier, hoping to fuck them both to sleep.

At least Ricky had found a moment of solace.

But he was awake now, given the irregular pace of his breaths.

Martin shifted closer, touching their foreheads together.

"I miss her." Ricky opened his eyes, locking onto Martin's.

"Yeah." A clamp of renewed anger constricted his chest. "We promised her we'd get her out."

Loving a woman they couldn't see or touch or protect... It was such a goddamn helpless feeling. But breaking a promise to her felt even worse.

"She's fierce as hell." Ricky gripped Martin's neck. "You know as well as I do, she's the reason Jaulaso went up in flames."

"I'm going to redden her fucking ass for it."

Ricky glanced at the clock on the nightstand. It was two in the morning, but he didn't need to ask Martin why he was awake. They hadn't had a full night's sleep since they left her in that hell.

"You know what I miss?" Ricky connected their mouths in a languorous kiss, sweeping his tongue and igniting the heat that burned between them. "I miss her soft hands and lips."

"I miss her sexy little tits." He licked a path down Ricky's throat, nipped at the flex of pecs, and swirled his tongue around Ricky's nipple.

With a shameless moan, Ricky gripped Martin's swelling erection, rubbing in slow teasing strokes. "And the sound of her husky voice when she wants to fuck."

"Especially when she's quoting her favorite books." Warmth spread through his body as he rocked into Ricky's tight fist. "Her nerdy, schoolteacher thing really does it for me."

"Yeah?" Shifting closer, Ricky pumped his hand and stole hungry kisses. "Her smile does it for me. The sweetness in it, the breathy sounds she makes, the wet grip of her pussy..."

Martin captured Ricky's thick cock and touched the hard length the way he used to touch himself. Fast and aggressive, firm and desperate, he jacked Ricky off until their kissing and stroking turned feral.

"Fuck, I miss her tight little cunt." Kicking his hips, Ricky thrust faster into Martin's fist.

"My hand's not as good as her pussy?"

"No." Ricky groaned through a laugh. "But it gets the job done. Really fucking well. Don't stop."

He didn't stop until he took Ricky's cock into his mouth. He sucked ravenously until Ricky undulated and moaned through a body-shaking orgasm. Then he lubed up, flipped Ricky over, and rode Ricky's hot ass into a slow, grinding climax.

They should've been able to sleep after that, but they couldn't. She was a sadness they shared, a pain that laded their thoughts and kept them on edge.

Stretched out on the bed, face to face, they sank into the intimacy of their eye contact.

Martin traced a finger along the carved terrain of Ricky's abs, marveling at the ease in which he could touch his best friend. He'd been so fucking scared he would hurt Ricky irreparably that he'd denied them this pleasure for seven years.

He should've known Ricky had the physical and emotional strength to handle Martin's pain, even when Martin couldn't.

"I love you." He rested a hand on Ricky's face, roaming his thumb along that strong jawline.

"You, too."

They stayed that way for hours, drifting in and out of sleep.

Sometime before dawn, Martin's phone rang on the side table.

His heart rate tripled as he reached for it. But Ricky beat him to it, lunging across his chest and putting the call on speaker.

Martin didn't have to look at the screen to know the call was from Cole Hartman. His knuckles were white from clenching his fists, and his entire body froze in anticipation.

"You better have good news for us." Ricky set the phone on the bed and rubbed his palms on his thighs, his expression taut.

"She's alive," Cole said. "But she's not in Jaulaso."

All the air in the room evaporated. Martin couldn't catch his breath.

"What the fuck?" Ricky jumped off the bed and dragged his hands through his hair. "Where is she?"

"She transferred to a federal prison in the U.S. the day Hector was murdered. That took planning." Cole let that settle in before he asked, "Can you catch a flight to Phoenix, Arizona?"

"Holy fuck." Martin exchanged a startled look with Ricky. "She's in Arizona?"

"Yes. During her transfer hearing, the U.S. Parole Commission reduced her sentence. She's getting released next week, and I'm not the only one who knows this. Someone put out a contract hit on her life."

THIRTY-THREE

"Petula Gomez." The female corrections officer waved her through the final checkpoint. "You're clear to go."

Tula shoved her hands in the front pockets of her jeans and swallowed around a knot of conflicting emotions. Uncertainty and exaltation, terrible fear and utter joy—all of it burned the backs of her eyes as she pushed through the exterior door.

Two years after her arrest, she stepped out of prison as a free woman.

A buzz of electricity exploded inside her. The good kind. The bursting-with-warmth kind that carried more possibilities than she could hold in her chest. Endless paths awaited her feet, but there was only one path she wanted.

The Arizona sun burned into her retinas as she scanned the parking lot of glinting metal.

Were they here?

What if they weren't?

She would have to figure out where to go and how to get there.

She would have to start a life without them. She'd braced herself for that prospect, but the thought still lanced unbearable pain through her insides.

The scent of asphalt and desert heat filled her lungs. There was no wind, but she felt the wide-open air, vast and alive and all around her.

She swayed beneath the petrifying surrealism of standing outside without walls, bars, or shackles. Hell, she'd been reeling since she left Jaulaso.

She hadn't seen a man, an illegal drug, or a weapon of any kind in three months. Everything was different in federal prison — the rules, the meals, the curfew, the women... Good God, when she'd arrived here, she hadn't been around another woman in two years. She still didn't know how to interact with them.

The differences between this prison and Jaulaso were so extreme she'd spent the last three months in a dazed state of shell shock.

But the biggest shock came last week.

Out of nowhere, someone had deposited funds into her prison bank account. The amount had been more than enough to purchase snacks and nicer prison shoes from the prison commissary.

The anonymous donor hadn't left a message, but she hoped.

She hoped with all the hope that remained in her shattered heart that Martin and Ricky had found her.

If they had, she didn't know how. They would've had to search the U.S. prison databases. How would they even know to look for her in the States?

With her eyes on the parking lot, she wandered down the sidewalk, dressed in the same jeans and t-shirt she wore the day she killed Hector La Rocha.

Her clothes had been in storage, never washed. That meant the black cotton of her shirt retained the bloody specks of Hector's death.

The authorities didn't know she had done it. No one had even questioned her. The news stories called it a deadly dispute within the cartel.

She still couldn't believe she'd killed him.

Her father.

The notorious crime boss of La Rocha Cartel.

The same day it happened, she sat through her transfer hearing, accepted her guilt, and learned her transferred sentence of three years in Mexico converted into only three months in the United States. Transferees didn't always get a reduced sentence, but it happened sometimes. She was one of the lucky ones.

She would never be acquitted of the drug smuggling charges, but it didn't matter.

Nothing mattered more than finding the two men she loved with every breath in her body.

The long sidewalk led her to the parking lot. Cars occupied almost every spot in a sea of steel and glass. Beyond that lay endless desert. She shielded her eyes from the sun and raked her gaze back and forth, searching, aching, panicking.

Nothing moved.

No one was coming.

Just as she was about to let go of the dwindling ray of hope that flickered inside her, the rumble of an engine sounded.

On the far side of the lot, a large SUV pulled out of its spot and slowly motored toward her. More vehicles followed suit—a truck, several sports cars, and a luxury sedan—all scattered through the lot and leaving their parked positions at the same time.

Her pulse careened into a gallop.

Garra had warned her that Hector's sons would avenge their father's death. Had they found her? Would they try to abduct her or kill her on federal property?

She spun back toward the entrance, knowing she would never make it up that long path in time. Terror consumed her as she bolted into a sprint.

Car doors opened behind her, and footsteps closed in.

"Tula!" The familiar masculine voice pierced shards of light through her tunnel vision.

She faltered, gulping for air as she whirled back.

Two pairs of arms came around her, enveloping her in the strange scents of cologne, aftershave, and woodsy shampoo. None of the fragrances belonged to Martin and Ricky, but her body recognized every chiseled inch of them.

Her hands identified the carved definition in their chests. Her fingers distinguished the differences in the textures of their hair as she pulled their heads toward her. Her gaze found green eyes, brown eyes, and all the gorgeous features that had occupied her thoughts since the day they walked into Area Three.

She melted instantly into the press of their bodies, caressing and grabbing solid muscle while trying to maintain eye contact.

"You came." She choked on a sob and pushed back just enough to reach for their faces. "You're here."

"Tula." Martin shook his head, his voice cracking. "We should've never left."

"Don't say that." She stroked his rigid jaw. "This is love. It slays and conquers and never looks back." The hot burn of tears blurred her eyes. "It's the reason you're here."

As she absorbed the sculpted details of their fierce expressions, the walls inside her ruptured one by one. It started as a tingle in her fingers and toes, crashed through her limbs, and rolled over her in a warm powerful tide, washing away her doubts and fears.

Life had returned to her. They were here, breathing with her, touching her skin, and watching her with the same intense longing that curled her fingers into their clothes.

The universe had given her another chance at happiness, and she wouldn't squander a second of it.

"I love you." She met each pair of eyes as great rushing waves of felicity soaked into her heart, mending it as quickly as it had been broken.

"I love you, too." Ricky tightened his arms around her and Martin, wrapping them in a protective bubble. "So damn much."

Martin tangled a hand in her hair, angling her face toward his. "Fucking hell, I need to kiss you right now, but—"

"Idiots!" a man shouted from inside the SUV. "Get your asses in the car!"

"We need to go." Ricky swept her up into his arms and took off toward their ride.

The urgency in his gait sent a chill across her scalp. "Are we in danger?"

"Yes."

She held tight to his broad shoulders. "Those other cars—"

"They're with us." He slid across the backseat of the SUV with her body tucked against his chest.

Martin followed him in, and the vehicle lurched into motion as the door swung closed. Two men sat in the front seat, but she didn't get a look at them before Martin and Ricky pulled her back into their orbit.

She sat sideways on Ricky's lap as Martin positioned her legs across his thighs and drifted close, surrounding her with the potency of his full attention.

"I'm so sorry." Ricky ghosted his lips along her temple, his hand resting on her neck. "We couldn't wait for you at the door. We had snipers lined up—"

She inhaled sharply. "In the other cars?"

"Yes."

"Because of Hector's sons? They're coming for me?"

"They have to get through us first." Martin stared into her eyes and slid his fingers across her cheek, touching her with a stunned sort of reverence, like he couldn't believe she was here.

"How did you find me? How do you even know Hector's sons are looking for me?"

His gaze drifted to the driver, sitting directly in front of him.

The man's brown eyes greeted her in the rearview mirror. His profile revealed a straight nose and trimmed beard that failed to hide the dimple in his cheek. He was handsome, like jaw-droppingly stupid handsome, but a dangerous air circulated around him, raising the hairs on her arms.

"That's Cole Hartman," Martin said.

"You're the military guy." She held his gaze in the mirror, recalling everything Martin and Ricky had told her about his specialized skills and connections in the criminal world. "You're the one who found me?"

"Yes, but before last week, we thought you were still in Jaulaso." He glanced at the road, the side mirrors, and returned to her. "The prison's on lockdown, including all information on its inmates. We didn't know if you were alive or dead."

Ricky's body went stiff beneath her, drawing her attention to the pain he couldn't conceal in his eyes. Martin wore a similar expression, his features bearing the exhaustion from months of stress.

Guilt cleaved through her. "I'm so sorry. I should've told you my plan. The night before you left... I slipped out to take a shower and saw something really...heartbreaking." Her chest squeezed, trapping her next breath. "I'll tell you everything, but not here. Not right now. It's going to hurt to relive it, and I..."

Ricky touched his lips to hers. He didn't try to silence her with a kiss. He just held his mouth there and let their breaths coalesce and shudder together.

"Whenever you're ready. We're not going anywhere." He ran his nose along hers. "Never again."

"I won't let you go. Never again." She closed her eyes, exalting in the connection.

When he leaned back, her attention fell on the other man in the front seat. With model-worthy features, red hair, and a tall, muscled frame, he fit the description of the mechanic roommate Martin and Ricky had always talked about.

"You must be Luke," she said to him.

"Good guess." He twisted around to give her a wink. "They must've told you I was the best looking.

"The best-looking redhead." She grinned.

"The *only* redhead." Cole veered onto the interstate, heading toward the city. Then he found her gaze in the mirror. "I have eyes and ears in the cartel underworld. One of the inmates in Jaulaso contacted Hector's sons and told them you transferred to the States. When they put a contract out on your life, my informants notified me. That's how I found you." He tapped his fingers on the steering wheel. "If you have any information on them or La Rocha business—"

"My sister is alive, and she's with them."

She walked them through the day she killed Hector—how she did it, everything that was said, and the clues Garra gave her before he died.

"They smuggle children inside crates with their weapon shipments." She clenched her hands. "I think, all along, they were discussing their human trafficking operation right in front of me. They just always referred to it as *firearms*. So while I was in the women's camp, I wrote down everything I remembered from those meetings."

She pulled a small journal from her back pocket and squeezed her fingers around it. Two years of memories filled the pages—conversations, smuggling routes, towns in North, Central, and South America that began with *Cala*, as well as the details of that haunting night in the sewer room.

"Give it to Luke." Martin nodded at the redheaded vigilante. "He's leading the next phase of the mission."

"Vera's part of that phase." She clutched the notebook to her chest. "Until I have evidence of her guilt, I won't turn against her."

"I won't kill her." Luke held out his hand, waiting for the journal. "I'm going with you."

"No." Martin put his face in hers. "There's a contract out on all three of us. We aren't going anywhere near Hector's sons until the situation is neutralized. We'll be involved in the operation. In the *background*. Understood?"

Her pulse quickened. "There's a contract on you and Ricky?"

"Yes. They connected us to you. How could they not? We lived among La Rocha Cartel members for three months. Everyone saw the three of us together."

She sucked in a breath and turned back to Luke. "What will you do if you find her?"

"I'll shackle her." He lifted a shoulder. "Haul her ass into the Restrepo headquarters for questioning."

The arid landscape of Phoenix, Arizona blurred past the windows. She was only minutes from her old apartment. That was where she'd been, sitting on the couch and looking forward to summer break, when Vera called. It was the last time she'd talked to her sister.

"Please, don't kill her." She relinquished her journal to Luke.

"I promise."

"Aren't you going to ask where we're going?" Ricky caressed a hand through her hair.

"I don't care where, as long as we go there together."

Whatever lay ahead could be her greatest challenge yet. There would be tears and laughter, fighting and fucking, and everything in between. A lasting relationship with one man was hard enough. But with two? It would be twice the work, twice the joy.

She couldn't wait.

Five miles from her old neighborhood, Cole drove through the wealthiest part of Phoenix. Mansions sat on estate lots, boasting their own lagoons, lush green yards, and wrought iron gates.

When Cole pulled up to one of those gates and punched in a passcode, she straightened on Ricky's lap.

"We're going to stay here for a few days." Ricky kissed her shoulder.

"Is it safe? I assumed we would head to Colombia where you live."

"We will." He turned her to face him. "You've been locked up for two years. Taking you to Matias' headquarters might feel like another prison. We thought you would want to experience some of the places and things you loved here before we dragged you away."

"You're right." A watery breath heaved up, clogging her voice. "Thank you."

"But we won't be alone here. Most of the group came with us, along with some of Matias' men. They're here to keep us safe."

As Cole drove through the gate, the cars from the prison followed in behind him. Towering stone walls surrounded the driveway, with security fences and armed men blocking every alcove and path.

Jesus, they weren't fucking around. This place was a fortress.

"Who owns this property?" she asked.

"It belongs to the Restrepo Cartel." Martin gripped her hand, twining their fingers together. "We're safe here."

Sitting between him and Ricky, she'd never felt safer.

The next hour involved a tour through the ten-thousand-square-foot mansion and introductions to the men and women who made up the Freedom Fighters.

Some of them weren't there. Matias, Camila, Tate, and Lucia were working on another mission in Colombia, and Kate lived on the other side of the world. But she met Josh, Liv, Tomas, Amber, Livana, and the most intimidating presence of them all, Van Quiso.

The massive kitchen buzzed with activity. More food than anyone could ever eat covered the counters. Beautiful people filled the doorways and chairs, and the intimate history between them vibrated through their laughter and lit up their eyes.

They engaged her in friendly conversation and teased Martin and Ricky about their seven-year foreplay.

For a group of ex-traffickers, ex-slaves, and vigilante murderers, they were surprisingly affectionate and gentle. But those were traits she no longer trusted. If it weren't so abundantly clear that Martin and Ricky loved these people, she would've been looking for the nearest exit right about now.

Even so, her nerves felt raw and wired. She wasn't used to so many aromas of food, the constant touching from strangers, and the extravagance of her surroundings. It was too much all at once.

The only thing holding her together was the comfort in the possessive hands that never left her lower back and hips. Their eyes never left her, either. Martin and Ricky watched her as if she might vanish right in front of them.

MANIPULATE

"This is the grilled cheese from the bakery near your apartment." Ricky guided her to the bags of takeout on the table. "We tried to remember all the restaurants you talked about and —" He tilted his head, squinting as he studied her. "You're overwhelmed."

"A little."

"A lot," he said.

"Yeah."

He grabbed a bag of grilled cheese, signaled Martin, and led her upstairs.

THIRTY-FOUR

Tula stood beside a king-sized bed in a master bedroom fit for royalty. Tufted fabrics, rich woods, and elegant decor — the opulence of her surroundings overwhelmed her senses and made her uneasy. Hell, a standard bed in an ordinary room would've put her on edge. She wasn't used to any of this.

She'd eaten the grilled cheese with Martin and Ricky. It tasted just as delicious as she remembered, but it sat heavy in her nervous stomach.

After the quiet meal, she'd changed her clothes in the bathroom, slipping on jean shorts and a dark tank top over a burgundy satin bra and panties set, just like the one she'd described to them all those months ago.

Bags of new clothing and beauty products filled one corner of the master suite. Martin and Ricky had shopped for her, brought in all her favorite foods, and set up house in this mansion to help her adjust and keep her safe.

They'd thought of everything, and she was grateful beyond words. But she didn't need any of it.

She just needed *them*.

Most of her anxiety resided in all the things left unsaid. Months of keeping her emotions locked up weighed on her chest.

This luxurious master suite with its over-sized mattress had all the makings for a sinful night of passion. She wanted that desperately, craved a carnal reconnection with them, but more than that, she needed to give them her ugliest memories.

"Tula." Martin lifted her chin with a finger, anchoring her with that simple touch. "Tell me what you need."

"Hold me while I tell you the rest?"

His expression softened, and an approving grunt sounded in his throat. Then he lifted her and settled them into bed.

Ricky slid in on her other side. They kicked off their shoes, tangled their legs with hers, and for the next two hours, listened to her talk through every decision, every emotion, everything she experienced from the moment she heard that little girl cry until now.

They held her tight between their warm bodies, kissed away her tears, and asked questions. By the time she finished, she felt like a different person. Lighter, more relaxed, finally free.

"Thank you for telling us." Ricky pulled her against his chest and played with her hair. "I'm so fucking sorry you went through that alone."

"I'm not alone now. Thank you for listening."

Tension seeped from her muscles, replaced by a drugging sense of peace. His hand continued its caress, his fingers running from roots to ends, over and over in hypnotic strokes.

Within minutes, she dozed off.

She woke sometime later, sprawled on her stomach with Ricky curled up against her side. The sun had set beyond the window, and sitting in a chair a few feet away, Martin watched her with an intensity that made her shiver.

He'd barely spoken a word since she'd started talking hours earlier. She knew he was compartmentalizing everything from the perspective of someone who had suffered at the hands of a pedophile.

Her heart ached for him. "Tell me what you're thinking."

"I'm going to beat your ass."

"Oh." Her neck stiffened, and a tingle of heat flushed her skin. "Because I lied to you about leaving the room that night?"

"You lied to us, risked your life *multiple* times, and executed a dangerous plan that you deliberately prevented Ricky and me from weighing in on."

"I was protecting you. If I told you that night what I witnessed and what I intended to do, what would you have done? Where would the three of us be sitting right now? It wouldn't be *here*."

His jaw flexed. "You could've died."

"I didn't."

"Come here."

Her heart skipped at the unbending tone in his voice, and she obeyed instantly, willfully, desperate to close the distance between them.

The bed shifted behind her with Ricky's movement as she climbed off to stand before Martin. He unfolded his powerful frame from the chair, rising to his full, towering height.

The coils low in her belly thrummed to life. Breath drawn, blood circulating, she lifted on her toes, gripped his shoulders, and rested her brow against his.

"I fucking missed you." The sublime heat in his words heightened the featherlight caress of his fingers as he slid them around her neck.

"Same. So much the same." She savored the brush of his exhale against her lips and the vibration of his nearness humming across her skin.

An undivided moment of calm caught and held. Breaths fused. Promises issued without voice, and hands began to roam.

It was a slow perusal. The finger he trailed along the neckline of her tank top sought out her collarbone beneath. She traced the taut sinews in his neck and the lines of his whiskered jaw. He stroked the rise of her breast, and she raked her hands through his soft blond hair.

Every touch was a sacrament, every caress a solicitation for more. Through it all, they held an impenetrable stare, eating each other with their eyes, wanting, panting, the need in their bodies growing voracious.

Sliding her palms beneath his shirt and up his torso, she adored the twitching of chest muscles and the heart that beat within. He stripped off her top, and his arms folded around her back, drawing her in close and walking his fingers up and down her spine.

Her entire being shook, mourning the months they missed together and aching to release the tension that had built up during the painful separation.

He pulled his head back to regard her, his chin lifted and eyes drawn to her lips. She couldn't formulate a thought beyond her desire for this man and the one closing in around her back.

Ricky's hands slid over her, exploring her flesh where it greeted the satin of her bra. Then he and Martin touched her together, their movements unhurried yet earnest. The skimming of knuckles, the scrape of trimmed nails, the glide of warm palms—every stroke removed a piece of her clothing and sent shimmers of pleasure between her legs.

When she was finally nude, all the heat inside her had knotted into a bundle, her chest barely coping with the heave of her breaths. Her thighs trembled, and her skin burned and shivered. If they didn't kiss her soon, her nerve endings were going to tear themselves apart.

How the floor beneath her feet vanished, she didn't know. One moment she was standing between them, and the next she was on the bed, face down on Ricky's chest with Martin bent over her back.

As Martin angled his face over her shoulder, she held her breath, ready for his kiss. But he bypassed her and slammed his mouth against Ricky's.

Masculine tongues rolled together, the tips of their lips barely touching as they licked and grunted and rocked their hips with hers between.

They were a union of testosterone and passion housed in muscle and bone. Watching them kiss was a privilege. Witnessing the love they shared in their eye contact was a precious honor, and they were giving her this intentionally, wickedly teasing her and making her wait.

Their kissing was explosive yet intimate as they stared into each other's eyes and murmured indiscernible words. Then those eyes turned to her.

Ricky grabbed her first, his tongue plunging past her lips. She was already gone, spinning with lust, and overcome by the protective feeling of them surrounding her. Broad frames, flexing legs, grinding hips, rock-hard strength... They wore their hunger in the tense lines of their perfect bodies.

Ricky took her mouth possessively, expertly as Martin licked a tingling path across her shoulder and along her neck, stripping her of all self-control.

Her nerve endings responded to his tongue, and her body answered his devotion with a rush of wet heat between her legs.

With a hand in her hair, Martin tore her mouth away from Ricky's and joined it with his own. The deep intensity of his kiss detonated into a throbbing fire.

His fingers turned bruising, his lips punishing as he claimed her, destroyed her, and put her back together. He was so wild and consuming she had to tilt her head away to gulp down some air.

Then the heat of his body left her back. His hands grasped her knees, positioning them on either side of Ricky's hips and forcing her ass upward.

With her chest pressed to Ricky's, she swiveled her neck, bringing her gaze to Martin's vibrant green eyes.

There was no warning in his expression before he slammed a hand against her bare backside. The impact drove a yelp from her throat and sweltering sting through her buttocks.

She stared down at Ricky, shocked, wheezing, and insanely turned on.

"So fucking hot." His brown eyes pulsed around dilated pupils.

"Does he spank you like this?"

"Not enough."

Martin struck her again. And again. And again. His searing blows landed on every inch of her quivering, red-hot flesh, from her hips to the backs of her thighs.

Then his mouth was there, licking the hurt and blowing tender breaths on the fire he'd ignited.

His lips moved lower, deeper, invading her soaked pussy and teasing her anus. He kissed her thoroughly while Ricky took her mouth, their tongues curling and laving her at both ends.

She whimpered against the stimulation, wobbling on boneless legs as she tried to maintain her straddled position over Ricky.

Martin reached between her thighs and tackled Ricky's jeans. Ricky lifted just enough to tear off his shirt, his expression dazed with need.

Their movements grew frenzied, stripping clothes and scooting across the bed. The whole time, she stared into Ricky's eyes, hovering over him and stealing kisses between his panting breaths.

"I need you." She gripped the bulges of his biceps, her knees pressed into the mattress on either side of his trim waist. With her butt in the air, her pussy clenched uncontrollably, dripping, aching to take him in.

"Martin. Condom." Ricky tipped his back, his eyes glued to hers as he gripped his cock between the spread of her thighs. "Hurry."

"No condoms." She held out a hand behind her, staying Martin. "Nothing between us. Whatever happens, happens. As long as we're together."

"Inside you bare?" Ricky stroked himself between her legs, pulling hard on his steely length as he moaned against her mouth. "God, yes, Tula. I've never had sex without a rubber."

She glanced back at Martin, finding him gloriously nude and staring at the exposed wetness of her center. "You're not on the pill."

"No."

He took his erection in hand, lazily rubbing from root to tip as he exchanged a look with Ricky.

In the next heartbeat, he was on her, mounting her backside and pushing inside her with a long, throaty growl. She felt him harden and throb against her inner walls, and holy fuck, it was incredible.

Ricky's body began to shake beneath her as Martin fell into a fast, rhythmic thrust of hips. She collapsed against Ricky's chest beneath the force of Martin's storm, her pussy stretching and contracting around the delicious glide of his cock.

Ricky's fist worked beneath her, and she caught it, slowing his strokes, grinding into him, and gasping at the friction of his hardness against her clit.

His neck went taut, straining in his desperation, his eyes never looking away. "Need inside you."

"Not yet." Martin curled a hand in her hair and slammed into her over and over, panting and grunting. "Swear to God, Ricky. You're going to come the instant you're inside her. She feels so fucking good. Hot and tight and creaming all over my dick."

His growly words pushed her toward her tipping point. She shifted her hips, angling them higher to take more of him.

With a moan, he rammed his heaviness harder inside her, driving deeper, faster, hitting a crescendo. Then he leaned in and reached between her legs to join his hand with Ricky's and hers around Ricky's cock.

Together, they stroked him into a gasping furor of curse words. "Fuck, fuck, fuck!"

"Don't come." Martin set the pace of their hands, in sync with the sliding thrusts of his cock inside her.

"Give me your mouth, *querida*," Ricky said.

She pressed her lips to his, willing to give him everything he demanded.

Ricky's guttural sounds of need filled her mouth, and Martin stretched over her to join the kiss.

Their free hands roved her skin. Their bodies rose and fell against her, three tongues connecting, retreating, and uniting again as they lost our breaths together.

They took her heart with every touch, and in return, they gave her theirs. Happiness swelled so fully in her chest she wanted to scream with every ounce of breath that dwelled in her lungs.

The only thing that would make this better was if they were both moving inside her.

"Need you both." She groaned into Ricky's neck.

"Greedy girl." Martin smacked her hard on the ass and pulled out of her pussy.

Before she caught her next breath, Ricky worked himself inside her.

"Oh, God!" He dug his fingers into her hips. "Feel that?"

"I feel you deep." She wrapped her arms around his magnificent body that was so warm and strong as he unleashed his hunger. "So deep in places no one has ever been."

He stared at her blearily, high on the pleasure, and she melted into his molten brown eyes.

Martin already had the lube and rubbed a cool smear of wetness between her ass cheeks.

Ricky's hand slipped down her throat, danced around her collarbone, and settled into a possessive hold on her breast. Martin caressed her other tit as the head of his lubed dick found her rectum, rubbing a slow circle against the ring of muscle.

She gasped and arched into the pressure, and he went inside, gliding in inch by thick inch as her name fell from his mouth.

Sensations vibrated and throbbed through every pleasure point, causing her ass and pussy to clench around their beautiful cocks.

Martin grunted an agonized sound, and Ricky's breath cut off. She sank her nails into Ricky's shoulders and turned her head, shifting her gaze between theirs, holding that contact, her entire world.

Then they moved, pushing and pulling her against them as she pressed into their thrusts.

The warmth of their skin met hers, and three bodies morphed into a single being.

Three hearts without walls.

Fused into a single soul without bars.

Lost and found.

Locked up and freed.

Together, they became an unbroken forever.

THIRTY-FIVE

Bogotá, Colombia
One month later

The clinking of dishes and the scent of grilled meats accentuated the tranquil ambiance in the elegant dining room. Ricky savored the last bite of his syrupy, spicy tri-tip steak, but not as much as he savored the two people at his table.

Tula sat across from him with Martin at her side, their postures distinctively dissimilar as they stared at him.

Tension tightened her shoulders. Her fingers curled into the linen tablecloth, and her pouty lips made him so fucking hard he had to cover his lap with a napkin.

Martin reclined in his seat with imposing confidence, his bright green eyes fixed on Ricky as he subtly worked his hand between her legs.

The dining room hummed with conversations. Servers in black suits glided from table to table. Restaurant patrons whispered and laughed softly among themselves, and around the perimeter stood a discreet security detail, provided by Matias Restrepo.

During their few days in Phoenix, he and Martin had taken her to restaurants, movie theaters, strolls through the park… They fit in as many dating excursions as they could before boarding Matias' private jet. When they arrived in Colombia, they moved her into the suite he and Martin shared at the Restrepo headquarters.

The three of them spent the past month helping Luke and the others follow up on the information Tula had compiled in her journal.

With Cole Hartman's assistance, they *think* they located the main headquarters of Hector's sons and their human trafficking operation.

Tula's sister hadn't been found yet, but one of Cole's informants claimed Vera had been recently spotted with Hector's sons.

Luke, along with a team of Matias' men, were in Mexico now, checking out the alleged headquarters. Ricky, Martin, and Tula had flown there with him to drop him off. On the way back, they stopped in Bogotá to give Tula a proper night on the town.

"Why can't we just sit here and have a nice meal together?" Her gaze darted through the dining room as her cheeks heated with the quickening of her breaths.

From Ricky's angle, it looked like Martin's hand was just resting on her lap beneath the table. But her restless shifting and breathy little noises were dead giveaways. Martin's fingers had found their way beneath her dress and deep inside her cunt.

"If you wanted to just sit here, you should've picked a couple of boring guys." Ricky leaned across the table and arched a brow.

"I didn't pick you. You picked me." Her nipples hardened beneath the burgundy satin of her cocktail dress.

"Is that how you remember it?" He looked at Martin.

"I succinctly recall," Martin said, adjusting his black tie, "Tula coming to us and asking to be our friend."

She made a gulping sound and gripped Martin's arm as he played with her pussy. "I liked your American accents."

"That's not the only thing you like." Ricky turned in his seat at the sound of music.

Across the dining room, a man sat behind a black piano and tapped the keys into a slow, hypnotic song. Couples floated to a small dance floor, swaying to the melody.

He and Martin had coaxed her into dancing a few times in the privacy of their bedroom. She'd been reluctant at first, but they were determined to replace her memories of Hector with new experiences.

Ricky waited until his erection calmed down. Then he stood and offered her his hand.

Martin slid his touch away as she glanced at the dance floor and sucked in a breath. And another. Straightening the front of her dress, she slowly stood and accepted Ricky's hand.

Burgundy satin hugged her body from tits to thighs. Her long black hair fell in sexy waves around her arms, and a touch of smoky color darkened her brown eyes.

She was the most gorgeous creature he'd ever seen, standing beside the man who loved him as deeply as they loved the woman they shared.

MANIPULATE

Ricky didn't know what the future would bring beyond her sister and the Freedom Fighters. But it was their adventure to take. The three of them together. Hand in hand.

So he laced his fingers with hers, met Martin's eyes, and took the next step.

"Let's dance."

The DELIVER series concludes:

OTHER BOOKS

LOVE TRIANGLE ROMANCE
TANGLED LIES TRILOGY
One is a Promise
Two is a Lie
Three is a War

DARK COWBOY ROMANCE
TRAILS OF SIN
Knotted #1
Buckled #2
Booted #3

DARK PARANORMAL ROMANCE
TRILOGY OF EVE
Heart of Eve (novella)
Dead of Eve #1
Blood of Eve #2
Dawn of Eve #3

DARK HISTORICAL PIRATE
King of Libertines (novella)
Sea of Ruin

STUDENT-TEACHER ROMANCE
Dark Notes

ROCK-STAR DARK ROMANCE
Beneath the Burn

ROMANTIC SUSPENSE
Dirty Ties

EROTIC ROMANCE
Incentive

ABOUT

New York Times and USA Today Bestselling author, Pam Godwin, lives in the Midwest with her husband, their two children, and a foulmouthed parrot. When she ran away, she traveled fourteen countries across five continents, attended three universities, and married the vocalist of her favorite rock band.

Java, tobacco, and dark romance novels are her favorite indulgences, and might be considered more unhealthy than her aversion to sleeping, eating meat, and dolls with blinking eyes.

EMAIL: pamgodwinauthor@gmail.com

Made in the USA
Monee, IL
19 November 2023

46915039R00433